VILLA OF DECEIT

VILLA OF DECEIT

BY

RON SINGERTON

www.penmorepress.com

Villa of Deceit by Ron Singerton

Copyright © 2015 Ron Singerton

All rights reserved. No part of this book may be used or reproduced by any means without the written permission of the publisher except in the case of brief quotation embodied in critical articles and reviews.

ISBN-13: 978-1-942756-40-8(Paperback)
ISBN   -978-1-942756-37-8   (e-book)

BISAC Subject Headings:
FIC014000FICTION / Historical
FIC032000FICTION / War & Military
FIC031020FICTION / Thrillers / Historical

Editing: Chris Paige
Cover Illustration by Ron Singerton
Cover by Christine Horner

Address all correspondence to:
Penmore Press LLC
920 N Javelina Pl
Tucson AZ 85748

A Statement of Appreciation

This novel could not have been completed without the unstinting encouragement of my wife, Darla. Her suggestions (mostly positive) as well as her computer and literary input added enormously to the writing of this novel.

I also wish to thank my editor, Heather Bungard-Janney, who guided me through the editing process. And, of course, Michael James, publisher and supporting friend, for placing *Villa of Deceit* on the bookshelf of Penmore Press alongside its many fine literary works.

Chapter 1

"You're limping; it still hurts?" asked Appian Dio, as he and Gaius wove their way through Rome's teeming streets.

Gaius, touching the mottled swelling said, "Of course it hurts. The bastard did it on purpose."

"You shouldn't have interfered," said Appian Dio as if scolding a child, even though he was only a year older than Gaius.

It was the last night of the April festival of Ludi Flores, which brought many prostitutes, mimes and actors in the streets. Appian rearranged the folds of his threadbare toga while Gaius, wearing a simple boy's tunic, hustled to keep up with him. With every step the pain in his hip jolted through his body.

"Your father has the right to punish the kid," Appian Dio shouted over his shoulder, "and it's not the first time you got in his way."

"He bought the boy only two weeks ago, and the kid doesn't speak Latin. He's from Sisalpine Gaul and he's only ten."

"It doesn't matter. A slave is a slave. You want to practice law, right?"

"I know, I know, my father insists that he can beat, sell or kill any of his slaves whenever he wants to." said Gaius.

"You got it. He has that right and, as your father, he can even do the same to you. So the kid got beat," Appian Dio said pushing his way through the inebriated crowd.

"But he didn't understand."

"He does now. I don't think you realize how much power your father wields. He has eight slaves, sells priceless jewelry to very wealthy families, and fears no one."

Not exactly, Gaius thought. *He is powerful, treacherous and scheming but he does fear.* Gaius stopped and the revelers surged past. Appian Dio turned toward him and in exasperation, said, "For the sake of Great Jupiter, forget about it. This is my last night. Either come or go home."

The crowd parted as a squad of eight legionnaires swaggered past, their ribald laughter drowning out all other sounds. Bunched together, they were applauded by citizens who admired the crossed belts fastened about their tunics.

Gaius sat heavily against a stack of amphorae. His father's ceaseless taunts pained more than the purple welt. He took a deep breath and clenched his fists. Pleasure seekers passed, oblivious to the youth's travails. Appian Dio, his pugnacious jaw set, stared at Gaius, who still wore his metal 'bulla', the good-luck charm worn by all Roman boys. That Appian had long since discarded his only made it clear to Gaius that his friend was leagues ahead in the ways of the world. In the eyes of Rome, Appian Dio was a man and Gaius was still a boy. They had grown up together, were inseparable; but Gaius, living in the comfort of his parents' villa on the vaunted Esquiline Hill, walked in the shadow of his impoverished friend.

"The thing with the boy is over," Appian Dio said, leaning over Gaius, with his hand on his shoulder.

"It's not over."

"It is for me." Appian Dio waited as a rowdy bunch passed, then said, "I've taken my oath and will have six months of training and twenty years in the legion. We'll never be doing this again. You told me, you practically begged me, to do this tonight. Don't let Toronius ruin it for you. I know you've never done this before, though I can't understand why. Anyway, it will be the most memorable night of your 'worthless life'."

He loves to use my father's phrase, Gaius thought, as he put his head back, closed his eyes and took a deep breath. His 'worthless life' teetered on a precipice. Suddenly Appian Dio lunged forward, grabbed the youth's tunic, and hauled him to his feet. "Come on, damn you! You told me you want to find women. I sure as hell do. I want every one of them and I don't have all the time in the world. Do you want it or not?"

Eyes open, Gaius swallowed hard and nearly drowned out by the jostling crowd, shouted, "Yes I do, I really do." Then with a renewed burst of enthusiasm, said, "Let's hurry before they're all gone."

Appian Dio laughed and slapped Gaius on the back. "Then follow me, you worthless piece of dung!"

It was but another of Toronius's insults, but from the mouth of his only real friend, it was the sound of joy.

"Do you know where to go?"

"You're asking that of Appian Dio? I've been doing this since I was twelve. I've had more women than the army has cohorts. You, on the other hand, have worshipped them as if they were statues of Venus, all ivory white and placed on altars. That nonsense has cost you a lot of pleasure. Don't worry, Gaius, they won't all be gone. There are thousands and thousands of them, and they all want that coin."

Sure, Appian Dio would know, Gaius thought. *Appian knows everything, especially how to fight and stay alive.* He was what Gaius's father would have wanted for a son. It had been only that morning when Toronius put his arm on Appian Dio's shoulder and said, "You will be a centurion in no time. The army is damn lucky to get you. Do you still have my letter of recommendation? You will need it for the probatio when they ask you all those questions."

"Yes, Dominus, I have the letter, but it's far too flattering."

"Nonsense!" Toronius had bawled, his jowls reeking from sea urchin and tasty dormouse from the morning's breakfast. "When Toronius Septimius Aquila puts his name to papyrus it is honored, even by tribunes and senators." Then, moving his bulk beside Appian Dio, he asked conspiratorially, "How many women will you have tonight?"

"Maybe five or six, Dominus, but after eightcups of wine I won't remember a thing. But I'm nothing compared to you. Your stamina is blessed by the gods, or so I've heard."

Toronius laughed from deep within his gut. "And I've paid

at their temples too!" Then, with his immense form pushing against his starched toga, he glanced back at his son. In Appian Dio's ear, but loud enough for Gaius to hear, he added, "Not like that child. He embarrasses me."

Appian Dio shot a look at his friend, the wound deep, then said, "He's still young, Dominus. That will change, and he'll know as much about women as we do."

"Not in my lifetime."

Livia, Toronius's wife, walked past them and Appian Dio merely inclined his head. She gave him the briefest smile, then turned away.

"I must go now," said Toronius, perfectly arranging the folds of his toga over his left arm. "I have an important meeting with a praetor, a recently appointed officer of the court. Livia wishes to congratulate you, so stay and sample my Campania wine. I expect great things from you, Appian Dio. Show the legions what a Roman soldier should be."

It was much later, at the fifth hour, when Appian Dio finally came out of the villa and found Gaius currying a horse. "If you still want to go tonight, we can spend the money your father gave me as a going-away present: thirty denarii. I'll meet you outside the balneum at dusk. Don't be late."

*****

"I'm surprised you were able to get away," Appian Dio said, when he met Gaius outside the baths. Gaius had been sitting, and he slowly stood with obvious pain. Pointing to a spot of blood on the tunic, Appian Dio said, "You must have been in a rush to get over here. Were you so excited that you fell all over yourself?"

"Not exactly," Gaius replied. "I'll tell you about it later."

"Well, you don't look too good."

"I don't feel too good. My mother demanded that I stay, but I had to get out of there. I wish I didn't have to go back."

"Toronius again?"

Gaius nodded, took a hesitant step, then followed Appian Dio into the city street.

*****

Prior to meeting Gaius, Appian Dio had gone back to the cramped insula, a six-story apartment block where he lived on the fifth floor with his consumptive mother.

"She's dying, you know. We can't afford a doctor, and one wouldn't do any good anyway. Our room is freezing in winter and a furnace in summer. I think it's the charcoal dust that got into her lungs. Everybody uses braziers, and the place is a firetrap. Nobody but the rich on the second floor will get out if the place burns up. She should have died ages ago. I think her one pleasure is to harp on me," Appian Dio said.

"I know what that's like. My mother's the same only worse. I don't know how any man can stand her," said Gaius, but he didn't want to think about that now.

Instead he asked, "Will we be able to see everything?"

"What?" Appian Dio said, his mind distracted by the thought of rats in the insula.

"The women, will they be naked?"

"Of course they'll be naked, or at least the parts that we want to see. You've seen women at the baths and they're mostly naked."

"That's different, and they're never completely naked." Gaius' excitement began to build, but then he was struck by a sudden fear. "How will I know what to do? I mean, they might laugh at me and—"

"Enough! Just shut up and follow me. 'Doesn't know what to do'," Appian Dio said, shaking his head with disgust. "You do what comes natural, that's what you do. Don't worry; she'll help you out. But you won't last three minutes. I didn't when I did it the first time, but I was only twelve," he added, punching Gaius on the arm. Then he said, "I traded some of the coins your father gave me for spintriae. Those are the only ones the women can accept."

They came to one of the enormous red phallic sculptures that abounded in Rome, and as custom dictated, ran their hands over it for good luck. Gaius had done it many times before, but now it had more than usual significance.

"The tokens have different values, I've heard," Gaius said, his words coming unsteadily. "Which ones did you get?"

"Take a look," Appian Dio said, handing one to Gaius.

"These are the real valuable ones. They're the same type my father uses. I've seen them in the tablinum, his old office, when he left them lying around."

"They are worth eight times what the smaller ones will get you. See how the man is behind the woman? We have enough of those to last all night. Maybe three or four women each," Appian Dio said with a toothy grin.

"But that's not the only way it's done, is it?"

"No. By Jupiter, you have a lot to learn; you'll see."

For years, Gaius had heard women and girls moaning in his father's room, and now he wondered what the man did to make them sound like that.

"Appian," Gaius suddenly blurted, "Did you tell my father that I'm doing this?"

"Of course not. He wouldn't want me to share his money with you. Just don't tell him, he won't like it."

"Don't worry about that, he doesn't like anything I do. But I do want to do this; I need to do this. To tell you the truth, Appian, I don't give a damn how much of his money we go through. Let's spend it all!"

There were dozens of pretty girls on the streets, and a desperate, unfulfilled urge welled up once again. Women were selling themselves everywhere, Appian had said. Their bodies were merely hidden by tunics and on occasion, elegant stolae. The very thought of what lay beneath became terribly exciting.

"It's the most wonderful thing you'll ever have," said Appian Dio, "but you must be the one determining everything. To let a woman take control is a sin in Rome. You could be banished beyond the Aurelian Wall and you'll be an outcast," cautioned his friend.

The excitement of what might happen nearly overwhelmed Gaius. Certainly, he thought he would have no problems, but Appian's dire warning stayed in his head.

Gaius pushed his way through the crowds, then heard

Appian Dio say, "There's no need to rush, we're not going to the brothels, and they don't open for another hour anyway. The owners get fined if they start too early. Besides, they're cramped little spaces, and most of them stink. There are better places to find women."

It was the last day of April, the month named after the Etruscan goddess Aphrodite, and for Rome's million inhabitants it was the most erotic holiday of the year. It was also one of the one hundred sacred days when, except for entertainment, no business was conducted.

Aphrodite was celebrated in the Temple of Flores with bundles of flowers, but the real excitement was the display of nudity. It was said that Romans were dour people, but a casual observer on this night would never believe it.

Gaius and Appian Dio passed the splendid Atrium Vestae, the house of the Vestal Virgins near the city center. Gaius glimpsed one of them and said, "She is so beautiful. And they get the best seats in the Coliseum."

To be a Vestal Virgin was a great honor, and the girls came from the best families. They served for thirty years keeping the Eternal Flame alive, but they would die if it were ever allowed to go out.

"That's not much of a trade. If they ever have sex and are discovered, they're sealed in a room with a loaf of bread and a candle until the air runs out," said Appian Dio.

The house of the Vestal Virgins was the most sacred edifice in Rome, and the passing crowds were momentarily subdued.

"This way," Appian Dio said, leading Gaius down a quieter street near Esquiline Hill, one of the wealthiest of the seven hills where the rich lived behind their high-walled villas. The two came to an abrupt halt when they encountered a delicata, a courtesan who entertained only the wealthiest of men, stepping from her palanquin. She was dressed in the most elegant fashion, and rearranged her pure white stola, the folds of which descended to her jeweled sandals. Not five feet away, Gaius, a tall, handsome youth with broadening shoulders, merely stared at her. Upon seeing him, the beauty bestowed a condescending smile, as if to say, "Perhaps someday, that is, if you can ever afford me." Then, escorted by two former gladiators, she glided through a gate whose heavy doors were quickly shut behind her.

Finding his voice Gaius said, "I wonder how many sestertii she would cost?"

"More than you'll have in five lifetimes," replied Appian Dio. "You won't find her in any whorehouse, that's for sure."

The delicata's astonishing beauty spurred Gaius's desire, and he said, "Maybe we can find a Doris like you told me about, the ones who go around naked, or a Lupus who howls in the night like a wolf."

"No, too many of them have the sickness. I know where to go," said Appian Dio, as they ventured into a necropolis. Rome's cities of the dead were favorite haunts for prostitutes.

"You're shaking, aren't you?" asked Appian.

"No I'm not," Gaius retorted. But he was. The anticipation, knowing that it was getting closer, made his heart race, and he felt a trembling in his legs. He had often seen women and girls taken into his father's cubiculum, the sparse bedroom next to his. Toronius would parade them past him and would whisper, "Not for you."

His mother had her own cubiculum, which was common in Rome, since long-married couples rarely slept together. Gaius had never heard his mother's voice in his father's bedroom. Being a ravishingly beautiful woman, he assumed she had lovers, but assumed that they would never come to the villa. She never said a word about it, and he never asked.

The necropolis was fronted by mausoleums of several stories, and was guarded by the imposing statues of Apollo, the Egyptian goddess Isis, and a bevy of consorting satyrs. Behind the crypts stood a temple honoring the gods of the Underworld, and a temple frieze illuminated by torches featuring a pantheon of all the gods.

The cemetery was not just for the dead; it was a place of copulation for the living. Muted sounds of carnal pleasure rose and fell in the cool night air. Gaius, following in Appian Dio's steps, was distracted by the presence of entwined couples between the graves.

"Four ases," said a woman, suddenly emerging from the deepening gloom. Her face and that of her work mate were plastered with creams and perfumed ointments, and reflected the light of torches. Lifting her shift, she sidled up to Gaius, an enticing smile on her lips. With ribbons in her hair and silver bracelets on her arms, she turned to her companion and said, "Sophia, darling, do come here and meet these magnificent Equestrian gentlemen. This one," she said, her hand deftly slipping beneath Gaius's tunic, "is as handsome as Apollo."

The woman pressed up against him, knowing that she had snared a customer. "Sophia, he's so virile. I know how much pleasure I will give him."

Sophia, having heard the line hundreds of times, eyed Appian Dio, a far more discriminating youth.

"Oh, Venicia, I really like this one," said Sophia.

With hand on chin, Appian Dio evaluated her as intently as she did him. But Gaius, shaking with anticipation, saw none of that.

"You do have the spintriae, don't you, my fine lad?" Sophia said, her thin hand already outstretched.

"I will give you two if you spend a long time with me," Gaius said, his voice shaky.

"One is enough," said Appian Dio, his fingers already exploring the other whore.

"Yes, one is just fine, my Equestrian," said the woman, referring to one of the highest classes of society. There was a fleeting but petulant look following Appian Dio's remonstrance.

"You do look very pretty," said Gaius. "I think I would like to do it with you. It's my first—"

"Shush," the woman said. "You needn't reveal anything of the sort to me. That you are so virile is all that matters."

Gaius sucked in his breath, as the woman with the practiced line and the vigilant eye touched him where no girl had before. He looked to Appian Dio for advice, but the harlot said, "Sophia, let's show these young satyrs our special place, and give them the thrill of their lives."

Feeling like an obedient puppy on a leash, Gaius followed the woman past gravestones with bas-relief carvings honoring legionnaires. In the moonlight he saw one that read, "Claudius Musius, standard bearer of Valeria Victrix. Monument erected by his brother." Other gravestones were adorned with frescoes of tragic masks, while some cursed enemies with graphic detail: "May the gods despoil the organs of Flavius Justinius." But in the excitement of the moment Gaius had no interest in reading anything more.

Gaius and Appian Dio were led to secluded niches between the stone crypts. Clouds raced across the sky, portending rain, and the moon's faint light played tricks on the eye as it caressed the uneven ground. Sophia, who enticed Appian Dio, laid her mat on the ground and waited for him to remove his toga.

Gaius was led to the opposite side of the sepulcher. Into his ear Venicia whispered, "For another token I will really do something special for you. It will be more exciting than you can ever imagine."

He did not know what she meant by 'more' but he found the second spintria, which she instantly snatched. "That's a good lad," she said slipping the coin into a pouch hung around her neck. With a quick movement she uncovered her thin breasts, then sank to her knees. She pulled him down and teased him, as if for her own pleasure. In contrast to her expertise, he felt helplessly inept. Fumbling, he had no idea of where to put his hands and he wondered if he was doing anything right. Was he supposed to say anything about how excited the act made him? Not wanting to appear foolish, he said nothing. His breath came in gasps and the sky seemed to spin as if he had consumed far too much wine.

Venicia lay back on her mat and, drawing up the stained cloth of her cheap tunic, said, "Now, my virgin boy, do it quickly so as not to lose your vigor."

In the fleeting moonlight, he could only see a glint of oiled flesh. He tried to touch her, but the woman pulled his hand away and said, "No, boy, I'll show you what you must do."

Disappointed, he was shocked when she suddenly thrust upward. Grasping him by his hips, she tugged on him, deftly controlling his every move.

It all happened too quickly. Gaius expected some sound from her, but there was only a labored grunt. Appian had told him to go slow, that he should be in control, but it was of no use. The woman knew how to finish him. He felt used and manipulated, as the whore played his body and its responses, working him as though he were no more than a puppet. Quite suddenly, it was over.

He gasped with sudden release and collapsed on top of her. Like fetid air from the Tiber, he could smell her breath through rotted teeth. The sensuous female he had desperately craved had transformed into an old hag. Stunned and disgusted, he recoiled from her. As if from a great distance, he heard her say, "Stay here a while, your friend will think you lasted a long time. It was your first time and you'll never forget it. No man forgets his first time."

But he desperately wanted to.

She pulled his tunic over him and cackled. Gaius wondered if it was a sort of victory laugh, as though she had scored another success, this one against a naïve, witless boy. But then she looked down at him and in a whisper, said, "You will do better next time."

The woman tugged her soiled shift back in place and put a finger to her lips as if to stifle any complaint. But he had nothing to say.

He glanced at her and saw that she was at least three times his age, certainly past twenty-nine, the average number of years a woman lived. *But this shriveled creature must be over fifty*, he thought. *No wonder she plies the graveyards in the dark of night.*

The whore was already searching for her next prey. She looked about to see if Sophia had dispatched the other boy. Impatient, she started around the crypt, then, turning back to Gaius, said, "You can call me Venicia when you want me again."

Gaius stared at her, amazed that she would think him so

vulnerable. The hag turned away, knowing she was wasting her breath.

Except for Appian Dio and his trollop, the graveyard was silent. Yes, Gaius thought, Appian surely knew how to do it; he was lasting a long time. He wondered if Appian's whore was just another played-out wretch. He felt unclean, and wanted to rush to the nearest bath.

Appian Dio's exertions culminated with an explosive grunt. Then he laughed and shouted, "Gaius, are you still doing it, you beast?"

Gaius didn't answer, but a terrifying thought came to him, and into the night he shouted, "Woman, Venicia, are you clean? Are you well?"

The woman did not reply but he heard her say, "Sophia, hurry, I see a man near that big crypt. You've spent enough time with that boy. He's not going to pay you anything more."

*****

"So how was it?" Appian Dio asked, as he and Gaius left the necropolis.

Shrugging, Gaius said, "Okay, I guess."

"I thought I heard her moan. Mine was squealing her head off so I couldn't really hear. But at least you did it. That's good."

"It wasn't..." Gaius said, "it wasn't like I thought it would be. I mean..."

"They're all different," Appian cut in.

"No, she was old."

"So what? You had your first woman. It's what you wanted to do." He was silent for a moment, then said, "There are all kinds of women. Some are loud and others hardly make a sound. I've had beautiful girls who are frigid, and homely ones who wake the dead. This one might not have been the best for you, but there are thousands of others, all willing for a few coins."

"Well, she was nothing I care to remember."

"Then forget her. We still have tokens left and the night isn't over. Buck up, Gaius. Let's go hunting. We'll find better ones, I promise."

"You go," Gaius said, his mind envisioning the sickness the whore might carry. *She refused to answer me*, he thought. He felt nauseous recalling that there was no real cure. The pestilence, said Apollodoros, his father's slave, might show itself within days or perhaps not for years. Whatever the case, if contracted, he would die in agony.

"I really don't feel too good," Gaius said, feeling terror where there had been excitement only an hour before.

"Your leg, where your father hit you?"

"Yeah," Gaius lied. "Well, sort of. I think I should go home."

"You're the only friend I've ever had, Gaius, but sometimes you are the most stubborn thing. I've known deaf and dumb men that can be more fun than you. What did you think it would be like, anyway?"

"Different."

"Well, they're whores, and you're only a token to them. They don't know you're Gaius Septimius Aquila, son of Toronius. I've lived on the streets all my life, just like they have, and it's ugly. That's life, Gaius: putrid, brutal, damn short, and ugly. Rome might be the greatest city, but for a poor man it's the most brutal place on earth."

They walked in silence through the emptying streets. There were just enough revelers out to deter thieves and cutthroats. Doors were shuttered and one could hear dogs behind guarded walls.

Gaius felt like he was drowning in a fetid swamp and rarely took his eyes off the ground. Tolerating the silence no longer, Appian Dio said, "You're too damn quiet for someone who just got laid. Are you angry with me?"

"Not with you."

"Toronius? Your father's a hard man, and he's had a hard life. Beaten by his father and all. And he was born poor, a farm boy. He's an angry man, though he tries to hide it with all that joviality. So my advice is to stay out of his way. You two will never make amends."

It wasn't necessary for Appian Dio to say that "In Rome, a

man's worst enemy is his son."

"My mother's little better," Gaius said bitterly. "Her great joy is making me look foolish."

"Mine's the same. You're my only friend," Appian said, peering into shadowed alleys where danger often lurked. "What about Apollodoros? You like him, and he's taught you Greek and elocution."

"He's my father's slave, and must show respect to everyone in the family. No slave would care to be a real friend, and no master can make him one. My father could sell, trade, or kill him in the morning if he cares to. It would be quite legal. As you said, he's the dominus."

"But still, you like Apollodoros, don't you?"

"I guess, but he's damn haughty even though he is a slave. There's days I can't stand him, and what I did tonight would disgust him."

"He probably hasn't had a woman in twenty years, and will never have one again," said Appian Dio.

They came to a crossroads, and Gaius asked, "Are you going to look for more women tonight?"

"Damn right I am. You can come with me, being experienced and all."

Gaius could barely make him out in the darkness but knew the grin on Appian's face. "I think I'll wait a while." Then, after a long moment, "Why are you going away, Appian?"

"Going away?"

"In the army, joining the legions? I mean, we've always had a good time, and now you'll be gone."

"I told you, I'm dirt poor. I live with my mother in a vermin-infested apartment and she bitches at me all day. I have three skills, Gaius. You know that. Humping, fighting and playing a horn, and I can do all three in the army."

"But you'll have to go to war. There's always another war."

"Of course there is, but in the legion I'll have something. I'll belong to the greatest army the world has ever seen. Do you remember those legionnaires earlier tonight? You saw how respected they were, how everyone honored them."

"We honor lots of people, the delicatae, the Vestal Virgins, the consuls."

"That's different; those come from rich and important families. The eight men who marched past are soldiers. They are not rich men, but they are proud. I saw the medals on their belts. They fought in wars with one of the finest legions. They're heroes. I want to be like them, not a pitiful kid at the bottom of the heap. I want people to stand aside for me too. I want them to pat me on the shoulder and say 'May Great Jupiter bless you.' I want the honor that comes with that, and to pay for my women myself and not have to accept tokens from your father."

Gaius had no reply, but had heard of how many young, inexperienced soldiers were slaughtered in the first moments of battle.

Seeing his friend's reluctance to embrace his quest, Appian Dio finally said, "Look, Gaius, I'm seventeen, old enough to join, and your father wrote me a recommendation. I've already signed and taken the oath to defend Rome, and it's a done thing."

"But you could die," Gaius blurted, fearful that it would assuredly happen.

"Of course I can die! I can be murdered tonight on the way home. We all die, Gaius. It's how we die that's important. I've dreamed about being in the army more than being in women, if you can imagine that. I once heard a man say that if you don't follow your dreams, you're condemned to follow someone else's. Well, I damn well want to follow mine."

"You won't be allowed to marry, you know."

"Marry?" Appian Dio laughed. "That's the last thing I want to do, you idiot. When I was fourteen, my father wanted to marry me off to a girl whose family had money. She was twelve. It would have been a financial boon for my father, but a life sentence for me. She hated me, and I couldn't stand her. There would have been damn little sex, that's for sure. In time I could have divorced her if my father approved, but thank Great Jupiter, he died before the contract was signed. I love doing girls, Gaius, but I never want to marry one. From what I've seen, they have only one good thing going for them. And right now, I'm going to find that, and enjoy the rest of this night. Are you coming?"

"No, I'm going home. Come by tomorrow, if you live through tonight."

"Oh, I'll be alive, but I might be walking kind of funny." He was quiet for a moment then said, "Joining the army doesn't frighten me. Maybe you should consider it too."

"Why's that?"

"One word. Toronius."

Gaius took a deep breath, sat on a stone bench and rubbed his hip.

"Pretty damn swollen, huh?" Appian Dio said, looking at his despondent friend. "So he hit you with his stick. What really happened?"

"Just as I said, the boy was from Sisalpine Gaul and didn't speak Latin, and it was the third or fourth time he misunderstood my mother's instructions."

"That's why he was beaten?"

"Sort of. He grew up in a fishing village and didn't know a weed from a vegetable, so when ordered to pull weeds he tore out her entire garden. When Toronius heard my mother's shrieks he said, 'What has that idiot done now?' He took one look at the garden, hit the boy with his fist, and swung him against a pillar."

"And you saw this?"

"Yeah. I had just come into the peristyle, and pleaded with him to stop, but he raised that stave he carries and slammed it down on the boy. The kid tried to dodge, but the stick slammed into his back and he flew across the floor. There was blood everywhere, but you know my father, when he gets started he won't stop."

"I know that he's killed three slaves."

"More than that. Anyway, I got between him and the boy and he swung again. It was as if he was blinded by hatred. He didn't care who he hit. He missed the kid but got me. I felt paralyzed and the boy lay in a heap."

"And your mother, what was she doing when this was going on?"

"At first she wanted to see the boy beaten, but then she started to say, 'Enough, enough!' and grabbed my father's toga. It was splattered with blood, mine and the boy's. She said that if he killed him he would have to buy her another to take his place. The child tried to crawl away, and Toronius said, 'May the gods damn you, woman, he's not dead yet,' and started to go for him, but I grabbed the stave. He punched me real hard, then said, 'You will never interfere with my absolute right!' He was frothing, shaking."

"Then what?"

"Livia was whimpering. I don't know if it was for me, the boy, or her garden. Toronius threw the stave across the peristyle and stormed off. Mother stood over the boy, but was afraid to touch him. He was a bloody mess. She told me to have Apollodoros examine him and then she left."

"Not a good day to be a slave of Toronius," said Appian Dio.

"Nor his son."

"So, what now?"

"I know just one thing, Appian. That man will never hit me again."

"Well, I've said it before. The army is always an option. Your father's friend, Vercipius, will write you a recommendation when you're old enough. Maybe we can get the same posting, or at least the same legion."

"I've been in a few scraps, but you know I don't like to fight. I'm not good at it," said Gaius.

"That's bullshit. I saw Apollodoros teach you how to use a knife and staff. You looked pretty good to me. How did that Greek learn to fight like that, anyway?"

"He said he learned in a prison somewhere, but he never talks about it. I think it was a long time ago, before I was born."

"Well, as I said, the legions are always there. The army sends you to interesting places."

"Yeah, like the end of the earth."

Appian Dio waved dismissively, turned, and walked down

the road. "My mother's dying," he said. "The gods willing, maybe she'll be gone by the time I get home."

"That's what I admire about you, Appian. You are a loving and warm-hearted person."

"Screw you, Gaius. When she finally coughs up her lungs, I'll inherit the insula. Maybe I'll rent it to you the next time your father has an urge to break every bone in your body."

*****

The voices in the streets ebbed away as Gaius walked the narrow pathway toward home. A half-mile on, but for the screech of an owl, the night became silent. "You must be dominant, make her squeal and beg for more," Appian Dio had said. Gaius shook his head. He had been used, but he'd used her too, he thought, as his walking slowed. Still, it was nothing like he had imagined it would be. He vowed that if ever he would do it again, it would have to be very different—something special.

His life had become hollow like a burned-out tree, and for a moment he wondered if Appian Dio was right. The army might not be so bad. He would be eligible in less than a year. Surely things could get no worse.

The ache from his father's blow came again as the wind picked up. A scattering of leaves blew about him, and he resumed his journey home. It was Livia's shrieks that made Gaius abruptly stop. The villa lay a hundred yards ahead, but her shrill screams pierced the night like the demons of Hades. He listened, and again heard his mother's shrieks as he burst through gates thrown open by Apollodoros.

"Where have you been?" said the tall, stooped man in a hoarse whisper. "There's trouble. Be careful."

As late as it was, there should have been only a few torches lit and one or two slaves still awake, but torches were alight in all the sconces. Everywhere was pandemonium, and Apollodoros said, "You'd better attend to your mother, she's in a total rage."

"What happened?" Gaius asked, his eyes taking in the scene of a half dozen slaves thrashing about in the atrium pool while his father shouted orders.

"It's the boy," said Apollodoros, "We just found him."

"You idiot!" Livia hissed seeing Gaius. "You were told to watch him. Now look at this. The pool is ruined."

A pruning knife lay at the bottom of the shallow pool, and the water, red with the child's blood, obscured its mosaic floor. A slave raised and handed the corpse to another, who laid the body on a stone bench. A deep gash had pierced its throat. Gaius looked into open, sightless eyes. The wound had been washed clean, and lay the throat open like a filet.

"He did it to himself," Apollodoros said. Gaius looked up and saw his father, lips pressed together, cudgel in hand.

"I will bury him in the morning and clean the pool, Dominus," said Apollodoros.

"No, you will bury him in that field tonight!" Toronius barked, indicating a barren spot a quarter-mile away.

"You will go with him," Livia said, pointing her finger at Gaius, "and you will clean the pool."

The crescent moon was high as Gaius and Apollodoros trudged across the field. Behind them, a hulking slave lugged a sack containing the balled up corpse. As the last shovel of dirt was tossed onto the unmarked grave, Gaius said, "I should not have gone tonight."

"Wherever you went it would not have mattered," replied Apollodoros. "The boy was going to do it anyway. He lived in terror; I could see it in his eyes. He expected to be beaten to death. It was better this way."

"He was my father's property. I understand why he did it, for a slave to kill himself is considered theft."

"He would have been sold anyway, and your father paid only a few denarii for him: less than he would have spent on a sheep. Except for the stained pool, he's already forgotten about him. To the Dominus the boy is nothing. Slaves are nothing."

"It depends upon the slave. You are too valuable to him; you made him a lot of money."

"Don't kid yourself. Toronius could sell me tomorrow."

Villa of Deceit

*****

It's all gone horribly wrong, Gaius thought, as he lay on his mattress of linen and straw. He closed his eyes and felt the walls of his cramped and Spartan cubiculum close around him like a coffin. *Maybe the boy isn't so bad off*, he thought.

Images floated before him: the beaten child, the burial, the blow of his father's stave and the throbbing pain, he and Appian Dio, as excited youths on a hunt through the streets of Rome, followed by the grinning old hag, and revulsion. Beyond that there was nothing but emptiness, horror and dismay.

The lusty thoughts of women, so long a fantasy, simply vanished. Again, like every night, he heard sounds coming from his father's room, only now he knew what the dominus was doing to some unwilling girl. He moaned, covered his ears, and waited for the dawn.

Chapter 2

"Where is Valdanik?" Aspacia asked as she breathlessly bolted through the orchard, now devoid of fruit in the last week of fall. She raised her hands to stave off bare twigs in the dusky gloom.

"He went into the hills with the rest of them. They're going to do it," Caladria said, fear in her voice. "They had weapons."

"They'll be found out."

"It's supposed to be a surprise; the Romans don't know."

"We know and others will too. We have to tell Father. He can stop it."

"It's too late," Caladria said. She was shaking as they hurried into the thatched cottage.

*****

"Stupid!" Topiatus said, breathing heavily. "He's pig-headed and impetuous. I warned him not to try it. Does he think the garrison is just sleeping?"

A cold sleet began to fall as Aspacia's father threw on his cloak and swung open the heavy door. He looked past the slumbering village, the orchard and fields, toward a line of distant hills where the legionnaire's camp was perched. A deep moat surrounded a palisade, and high guard towers were placed in each of the four corners. Torches illuminated the towers, and blurred forms could be seen within.

Topiatus, the village headman, had remonstrated with the garrison commander and warned him of a possible revolt, but the officer said he had no options: it had all been decided by the consuls in Rome, and as much as he wanted to keep the peace, he was obligated to do as instructed. That, he reminded the village headman, meant the use of force if necessary. Fearing the worst, he had led thirty-six legionnaires toward the estuary to meet his reinforcements. Now only twenty legionnaires manned the walls.

"How many villagers are with Valdanik?" asked Topiatus.

"At least sixty, maybe seventy: all the farmers. They're afraid of losing their—"

"Yes, I know," said her father. *Maybe they wouldn't get to the rock-strewn overlook*, he thought. With this weather, a storm coming, they might even turn back. The whole thing was folly. And Valdanik, promised to Aspacia, how would his inheritance help if the boy were dead? Even if they succeeded, there would be retribution. He had seen it before, not just here in Lusitania, but wherever the Romans planted their standard.

"Valdanik said that he wanted to be as famous as Viriatus, the 'Protector of the Lusitani'," said Aspacia.

"What nonsense! The man died over a hundred years ago. He won some battles against Rome, but he was betrayed. Certainly he became famous in Lusitania, but he's very dead. Valdanik knows that he will be facing a legion raised by Caesar himself. The Legio VII Gemina will come back and slaughter us even if Valdanik survives this stupidity." Through the mist, Topiatus could see indistinct forms pacing the walls of the Roman encampment. He then said to Aspacia, "If I don't return by late morning, you must take your mother and sister and run. Go north as far as you can. " He put his hand on his daughter's shoulders and said, "Spread the word; everybody must get out. Go to each cottage and tell them to prepare. There will be no mercy."

As the warning spread from hut to hut, panicky villagers huddled in compressed knots in the rutted, muddy lane. Many carried torches that illuminated the faces of smiths, wheelwrights and shoemakers: landless souls who bartered their goods to traders who came from distant lands.

Caladria, a plump girl whose face displayed its usual dour expression, trudged behind Aspacia. Slow-witted, she barely grasped the situation, which only accentuated her fear. "The Romans have been here for years. They haven't hurt me or you, Aspacia. Why are the farmers so angry? My father isn't."

"That's because he lives in the village and makes wool socks and sells them to the Romans. They are his customers. It's different with the farmers. They've been taxed to death: the tributum. And now this new thing with the Roman veterans."

Aspacia pounded on the last door of the village and an old woman peered out. "There's going to be trouble," Aspacia said. "My father said you should go into the mountains."

"I can't walk that far. Are they really going to take the farms?" the woman with a pockmarked face asked with dismay.

"I fear that it's already been decided. The Romans said as much."

"But there's land in the west and across the Rhine, why not there?"

"Papa says that the Romans aren't ready to fight the Germanic tribes. They conquered us, so they send their veterans here and pay them off with land. They'll let us keep the village, but they want the farms."

"My husband went to the harbor four days ago. He saw two triremes and four merchant ships. He was told that there are two cohorts on board and they're expecting trouble from our men."

"That's why you have to get out, that's what my father says. Get as far away as you can."

Aspacia hadn't heard of the arrival of the triremes, the three-banked war galleys, nor the cohorts, each numbering four hundred and eighty men plus auxiliaries. There was also cavalry, and the fat merchantmen that followed the galleys served another purpose, and a far more fearful one.

"We should wait for evening," one villager said. "The farmers might change their mind, and Topiatus will talk sense into them. The Roman centurion said that the lands will be paid for, there will be compensation."

"Hardly enough," another argued. "The farms have been in the families for hundreds of years. A few sestertii will satisfy no one."

*****

Topiatus, his arthritic knees throbbing, made his way up the defile toward the promontory. A cold wind blew and wisps of fog interrupted his view, but he heard shouts and screams above the rain. He had expected to see the contingent of farmers at the summit, but no one was there. Panting heavily, he squinted and looked at the hillside below him. Plainly, huge boulders had been levered free and allowed to cascade into others, causing a landslide, which, like fingers in wet clay, had clawed and torn at the rain soaked earth. Shards of splintered rock littered the hillside, but most of the slide had careened into the narrow chasm three hundred feet below.

*****

The centurion had led his men single file into the pass. There was no way around the rock slide, and he and his troops couldn't see the high ridge through the fog. From time to time the column halted and pickets were sent ahead, some even scaling one hundred feet or more of the steep hillside. They had returned to report that there was no sign of danger from the Lusitani: but the danger was well hidden.

It began with the sudden crack of one stone bounding into another. A shower of small rocks splattered into the legionnaire's shields and ricocheted off their lorica segmentata, the overlapping steel armor. In the rain and fog it was impossible to tell the exact direction of the slide, but the centurion ordered the men to turn and run back the way they had come. The heavy boulders came seconds later. Many of the Romans dropped their packs and bolted down the trail. It was all a matter of luck. Some enormous stones flew over the fleeing men while others crushed and flung men into the chasm. Twenty-three were killed by the avalanche; their bodies lay beside a muddy creek at the bottom of the ravine.

*****

The centurion was dead, and when the last stones fell the survivors gazed upward, not knowing whether the slide had been the work of man or nature. Suspecting the worst, many drew their gladii, their lethal short swords. They had but seconds to wait as over sixty men armed with pitchforks, scythes and knives tore down the hill. The legionnaires, separated by boulders, were unable to form a fighting unit, but would not sell their lives cheaply.

No three or even four untrained men were a match for a single legionnaire, and two dozen farmers fell before the gladius and the pugio, the razor-sharp knife carried by the soldiers. Valdanik, leading the assault, was the first to be impaled. His body fell between the littered stones as enraged men swirled around him. But the weight and numbers of the attack had their effect, and within twenty minutes not a legionnaire remained standing.

The surviving farmers took the legionnaire's weapons and ran past the carnage yelling, "Burn the Roman encampment!"

Slowly Topiatus wended his way past the rutted hillside. Many boulders were perched precariously amongst others, and rocks still skittered downward. He was left alone on the road. Appalled by the scene, he went from body to body hoping to find a survivor. A few men expired as he reached them. He recognized the cloak of Valdanik, the youth who was so anxious to marry his daughter. His eyes were still open and his blood had stained his cloak, ripped open by a javelin. Topiatus knelt beside the corpse, closed the boy's eyes and covered his face. There was a sudden downpour and Topiatus pulled his own cloak about him and began a painful trek back to the village.

It was dusk when he spied weary and wounded villagers descending the hill below the Roman fort. Rain had extinguished flames that had consumed a few of the buildings and one of the towers. But the encampment had not been taken. A concentrated flurry of arrows and projectiles from the bolt-firing "scorpions" had decimated men attempting to cross the moat and ascend the walls. Cold and exhausted from their earlier battle, the farmers were easily repelled by vigilant legionnaires behind stout walls.

Fearing the worst, a junior officer sent runners to the

harbor when their centurion and his men failed to return. Having repelled the villagers, the legionnaires waited for the arrival of the cohorts from the ships. In the gloom of night, the villagers could see two dozen torches burning defiantly above the walls. A number of farmers, some wounded, straggled into town.

"You have brought disaster upon us," said Luvipia, Aspacia's mother.

"We did what we had to," one farmer said, shaking his pitchfork. "We bloodied them, we taught them a lesson!"

"And how many of you lived? The dead lost more than their farms, didn't they?" a tanner said reproachfully. Pointing to the fort, another villager said, "Do you see the legionnaires running for their lives and begging for mercy? No, this idiocy has just begun. You will have us all killed."

There was a chorus of accusations against the farmers. Finding no sympathy, they accused the townspeople of cowardice, then straggled out of the village.

"I'm leaving," one sheepherder announced, "and all of you better do the same." The man hurried back to his hut, and shortly reappeared with his wife and child and a satchel of belongings. Seeing this, two dozen other men did the same and began their trek to the deep forest, twelve miles away.

"We'll wait for your father, but pack what you can carry," Luvipia said to Aspacia and Caladria, as she hastened them into their two room hut. "We must be ready to leave as soon as he returns."

"Valdanik did not return," Aspacia said to Caladria as they sat on their bed after they had put their meager possessions into sacks. Caladria held her hand tightly, her speech coming slowly.

"He may still be alive. Maybe he stayed in the hills to help others."

Aspacia shook her head, her loose black curls swaying around her face. "He's dead. When he asked Father for my hand last week, he said that he would prove himself worthy. I thought he was going to buy oxen he was saving for. But Father knew what he meant."

"I don't think any man will marry me, but I wanted to be at your wedding. I wanted to be a bridesmaid, Aspacia. What will happen now?"

There was a feeble knock on the door and Luvipia opened it. "Thank the Goddess you're back," Aspacia said, as her father stumbled in and collapsed into one of their two chairs.

Catching his breath, he said, "You're all packed? Good. I have to rest, then we'll leave at dawn."

"Did you see Valdanik?" asked Aspacia hopefully.

Topiatus nodded, fatigue weighing him down. "I found his body and closed his eyes myself. I'm afraid we won't have time to give him a proper burial. Many of the other farmers died too."

"And the Romans who went to the coast?" asked his wife.

"All dead."

Shocked, Aspacia said, "Father, we should leave now, the morning may be too late."

"Your father must rest," Luvipia said. "It will take time for the Romans to march from their ships. We will be far away by then."

*****

It was the sound of hoof beats that woke them. Aspacia threw off her blanket and ran to the door as the last of the Roman cavalry raced by, their horses splashing through the muddy street.

"Where are they going?" Luvipia asked anxiously, as she threw on a shawl against the cold. Topiatus rubbed his arthritic knees and groggily stood. "How many did you see?" he asked Aspacia.

"Twenty or thirty, maybe. They were riding toward the forest."

"Some went toward the ravine, I think," said Caladria.

"But why the forest?" asked her mother.

"To capture the ones who fled," said Topiatus. "They want us all. No one will escape. Once they get them, they'll be back."

"I should go to the shrine to pray," Luvipia said.

The shrine for the goddess Diana, a woodland deity, had been built by the Greeks hundreds of years before.

"Not now," answered Topiatus. "I want you to be with me. It may be..." and his voice trailed off.

*****

The Legio VII Gemina had marched all night and surrounded the village at dawn. Drawn up in three ranks, the legionnaires waited, their red capes wafting in the morning breeze. Some distance behind them were dozens of unarmored men, a few wearing bleached white togas and others in rough tunics. Some were perched on the seats of heavy wheeled wagons, their horses winded after the long push to the village.

A blast from the horn of the cunicularius brought the men to attention. Topiatus left his wife and daughters in the road and walked stiffly toward the commanding tribune, a young patrician mounted on a nervous horse. He was backed by a centurion, the Primus Pilum or "first spear": the chief centurion of the legion. They watched as the old man limped to where they impassively stood.

"Far enough," warned the centurion.

Topiatus stopped, bowed and extended his arms in supplication. "I am headman of this village and liaison to the Roman commander. I wish to express my sadness over the loss of the legionnaires. We villagers are not guilty, and we have no dispute with Rome. In fact we welcome you here. We are innocent people and willingly serve the Republic and her consuls. I did everything I could to dissuade the violence. You must believe me."

There was a long silence as the wind propelled thick mists through the legionnaire's ranks and the clusters of villagers, who strained to hear the response to Topiatus's plea.

"I don't believe you, and whatever you attempted, you failed miserably. The garrison commander was crushed to death and thirty-six Roman soldiers are dead. Of this you are guilty. All of you are guilty," the centurion said contemptuously.

He suddenly spurred his horse and slammed the side of his sword against Topiatus's head. There was a scream from the crowd, and with a second horn blast, the Primus Pilum ordered, "Forward, take them all!"

Panic-stricken, many villagers turned and tried to flee only to be overwhelmed by legionnaires. Aspacia, her sister and Luvipia tried vainly to reach Topiatus. Dozens of terrified villagers tore past them, their screams intermixed with brusque orders. A few men, in an attempt to defend their families, swung scythes and axes but were quickly cut down. Suddenly, gaps appeared in the legionnaire's lines as bands of tunic-clad men shot through carrying ropes and chains.

"Don't kill them!" they shouted to the soldiers. Swords drawn, the legionnaires stood aside, the fight having gone out of the townsfolk. Tossing ropes around family groups, gangs led by the slavers, directed their men to assemble their cache near the soldiers. The competition between slavers was fierce as whips cracked over the heads of husbands vainly attempting to shelter wives and children.

"This one, get this one," a venalicius shouted as his men lassoed a strong-looking youth. A fight broke out between two gangs as they pushed and shoved an ironsmith's family toward a stump of a tree. Legionnaires separated the angry mass, and the smithy got in a blinding punch before being knocked unconscious by a legionnaire. A cacophony of screams, shouts and appeals resounded through the mass of mud-caked villagers as they became aware of their fate.

"These two!" a slaver shouted as Aspacia and Caladria were torn from their mother's grasp.

"What about the old woman?" one of his gang said, holding Luvipia by the hair.

"No, I don't want her," the venalicius said while fending off another slaver intent on taking the girls. Aspacia reached out to her mother, but Luvipia had already been hauled off by a weaker gang. With a stout rope encircling them, Aspacia and Caladria were dragged to a prefabricated holding pen, spiked into the wet ground and secured by locks and chains.

"Can you see her?" Caladria asked Aspacia as they were pushed into the cage. Nearly forty terrified souls had been stuffed into the confined space. Shoved together, men, women and their children gasped for air as still more were prodded in by spears and swords. Fifty yards away was a similar enclosure with faces pushed against rusted iron bars.

"I think so," Aspacia answered staring about as slavers and soldiers hurried past, gathering up the last of the Lusitani. She heard a chorus of moans as a line of men was whipped forward, horsemen striking them as they rode past.

"Those are the farmers and the others who tried to get to the forest," said a woman huddling beside Caladria. "If the legionnaires have their way, the farmers won't live past sundown."

The shrieks and screams gradually ceased as the legionnaires formed ranks and the slavers corralled the last of the villagers. In its place were moans and lamentations as some realized that they would be slaves to the end of their days.

"I can't see her anymore," Caladria said to Aspacia. "And where is Father? I don't see him either. Do you think they killed him? Where are they going to take us?"

"I don't know, Caladria. I have no idea where we're going."

Night descended upon the cages, which had been covered haphazardly with tarps. Some guards and slavers huddled in tents for the night beside the prisoners, but most ascended the hill for the warmth and comfort of the fort. Soaked and cold, Aspacia and Caladria huddled beside one another and waited for the dawn.

Except for the cries of the injured, a silence fell over the cages. With the rising of a weak sun, the shivering villagers craned their necks to see what was taking place between the tribune and the venalicii. There was an intense discussion, then an order was given, and the cohorts were broken into nine-man squads. Legionnaires were assigned to the caged villagers and stood guard beside the slavers. A second order was given and the enclosures were opened, and as each individual was allowed out, he was chained to the next.

The light rain that had fallen early in the day turned to a deluge by the time the entire assemblage, led by the centurion, began the trek to the estuary. Those who slipped and fell were helped to their feet by those behind them, but a number of the elderly succumbed to the elements and the long march. They were unchained and dispatched beside the road. The procession then moved ahead, the villagers staring numbly at the bodies of those they had known for years. Those who attempted to touch the dead were thrust back into line.

The rain eventually stopped, and the procession reached the harbor late in the day. Merchantmen wallowed close to the shore, while the great oared triremes stood further out to sea. The wagons that had carried the cages rolled onto the beach, and the iron boxes were again erected.

"Names, trades, and ages will be recorded before they're put back in," a venalicius said to a scribe. Placards with the information were hung over each prisoner's neck before being ordered into their cages.

"What do you think it says?" Caladria asked.

"I don't know, maybe how much we're worth," Aspacia said.

"Worth? I don't know what you mean. Worth what?"

"What they'll sell us for."

Caladria looked at her sister with a blank expression.

"You don't understand, do you?" she said in the softest voice she could muster. "We're going to be sold because we are slaves."

"Slaves?"

"For the Romans, or whoever they sell us to. That's what happens when you lose a war. You become a slave, Caladria."

"Will we ever come back to our home?"

"No, I don't think we will."

"What will they have us do?"

A sudden shudder went through Aspacia. She looked down and noticed how her rain-soaked dress clung to her breasts. "I don't know, Caladria."

But she did.

*****

They huddled together for warmth during the night, and at

dawn when the wind rose. A heated argument broke out between the galley captain, the tribune and the slavers. The dozen venalicii pointed to the sky and the lowering clouds and shook their heads, now united in the fear of losing their precious cargoes.

The captain, anxious to get his ship away from the rocky headlands, prevailed. Annoyed at having to argue with civilians, he turned on his heel and was rowed to his trireme. For the slavers, it was a choice between having a military escort to the port of Ostia, and chancing their slow, unarmed vessels in an encounter with pirates.

With growing anxiety mixed with resignation, they began the loading of slaves onto the pitching vessels. Amphorae, the long clay jars filled with wine and olive oil, filled their hulls and acted as ballast but nothing could still the roll of the leaky tubs.

All seemed settled when another argument broke out between the slavers, as an elderly man was led toward Aspacia's cage.

"I want him, I claimed him earlier!" one venalicius shouted, but he was pushed away by another. The argument became so vitriolic that the legionnaires intervened. Numbed by their fate, Aspacia didn't look up until the man was thrust into their cage and Caladria suddenly shouted, "It's Father! It's Father!"

Unable to stand, Topiatus fell to his knees. The girls wormed their way through the packed throng and threw their arms around him. Tears rolled down Caladria's cheeks and Topiatus stroked her hair.

"We thought you might be killed," Aspacia said, helping him to his feet.

"The tribune wanted me dead, but he was bought off by the slaver. He learned that I speak four languages and could be sold for more than anybody else in the village. So they let me live."

"Have you seen Mother?" Aspacia asked.

"I saw her in a cage. Maybe she'll be with us when we get to Rome. Perhaps I can speak to the venalicius and we can all be together."

The girls nodded and Caladria said, "Then maybe it won't be

so bad."

*****

Aspacia and her sister were bound with twenty other women on the prow of the deck while the men were chained aft. There was a single mast, and a sail was unfurled from its yardarm. At the prow there extended upward a simple figurehead curved inward and a smaller one at the stern. One man stood at the tiller and others sat beside their oars. One by one the merchantmen, low in the water with their human cargo, pulled out of the estuary to rendezvous with the triremes.

The captain of the merchantman studied the lowering clouds and berated his crew for their sloppy seamanship. He sent a man below to check on the cargo lest it shift in the rising seas. Amphorae could roll or break, their contents sloshing about in the bilge, heeling the vessel uncontrollably. His seventy-foot vessel was designed for the calmer waters of the Mediterranean; at sea, dark water broke over the gunwales before running out the scuppers.

The merchantmen attempted to form a convoy between the two warships but couldn't keep up with the larger vessels. In the deepening gloom all they could see was the stern lanterns as the triremes rose and fell in the turbulent seas. The intermittent rain started again.

"It's Mother!" Caladria said grabbing Aspacia and pointing to a slaver wallowing from one deep trough to another. With a start, Aspacia glimpsed Luvipia as a sailor passed by her with a torch. Rising with her chains, she screamed and waved but her mother didn't see her, for a great wave raised her mother's boat then dropped it into a valley of the sea. Through the spray the girls saw men frantically pull on their oars but a second wave added its weight to the first, and the vessel pitched prow-down, its stern high in the air. Aspacia heard muffled screams as the craft stood on end before sliding into the roiling sea.

Caladria, Aspacia, and all those who could, rose and stared at the spot where the merchantman was last seen. A deep moan rose from the chained men of Lusitania, for all knew kinsmen on the lost vessel.

Topiatus held tight to the railing as he stared into the sea. The heads of a dozen sailors and slavers bobbed above the waves. Few could swim, and those who could pleaded for a line to be tossed. But the vessels were scattered and none would dare turn back. Topiatus put his hands to his head and wailed into the night.

Clouds blotted out the stars, and there was no way for the captain to find a course. The seas rose, and the merchantman skewed and heeled. For once, Aspacia was thankful that she was chained to the bulwarks, so that she would not slide across the deck. Suddenly, a rogue wave, far larger than the rest, smashed into the old tub, shearing away the sail and flinging all but four of the slavers and crew into the sea. Amphorae below deck smashed into one another, and when the wave passed, the vessel listed dangerously to port.

The captain shouted to one of the remaining slavers to put the chained men to work at the oars. The slaver grabbed Topiatus and dragged him to his feet along with twelve others, all chained together. Quaking with fury, Aspacia's father wrapped his arms around the man, and as the boat again heeled, pulled him toward the low railing. They swayed there for a brief moment until, with a final jerk, Topiatus and his quarry flew into the sea. Their combined weight and the current dragged in man after man.

Pushing the slaver beneath him, Topiatus rose in the water and howled into the wind.

"Father!" Aspacia and Caladria shouted in unison. Their father stared at them for a moment then, with the heavy chain around his neck, slipped beneath the sea. Fearful that the ship might capsize, the captain grabbed an axe, rushed aft, and chopped through the railing into which the chains were bolted. There was a snap, and the chain flew high in the air before sliding into the depths. Relieved of the weight of twenty men, the boat righted, but without a sail the captain and his three remaining crew could barely keep the vessel pointed into the waves.

One of the slavers motioned to the captain, then pointed to

the women and the empty oarlocks, but the captain waved him off, fearful that the women might also fling themselves into the sea.

The masthead had broken off, but there was still enough to support the yardarm, though the sail was in tatters. The women huddled together in the prow as the cold spray burst over them, their soaked shawls and dresses fluttering in the wind. Standing, the captain's eye caught sight of the garments as moonlight broke through the clouds. With a rush he bolted forward toward Aspacia and Caladria, furious that their father had been the cause of his monetary loss. With a few powerful tugs he ripped off their dresses. Another slaver joined in, and half a dozen women cringed naked as the men tied the garments together, fashioning the fabric into a sail. They tied the cloth to the yardarm and the fluttering ends to ropes tied to the deck. A slaver hustled to the tiller as the improvised sail filled with wind. The storm clouds cleared, a bounty of stars filled the sky and the captain ordered a course.

The sea still ran high with spray, drenching the women who huddled to give warmth to those bereft of clothes. For Aspacia and Caladria, the night seemed endless, but a faint glow eventually rose on the horizon and within hours there emerged the full light of day.

They looked about and could see two of the merchantmen and one trireme. The slave boat barely moved ahead with so few men at the oars. Frantically the captain waved a sheet, and the warship angled toward them. A sailor tossed a line, the crew tied it to the slaver's bow, and the old tub lurched forward in the trireme's wake.

*****

"Thank you," Aspacia said as many women tore their garments and handed her, Caladria, and the other women strips of material with which to cover themselves, as they were herded into a containment area at the port of Ostia. Caladria held tightly to her sister among the dozens of slaves. Men, women, and children from a multitude of lands were corralled together and were watched closely by the mangones, the auctioneers. The venalicius who had first enslaved the villagers hastily sold them to an auctioneer, who would sell them to the highest bidder. Having rid himself of the sick and despondent women, he hastily departed.

"Where are they taking us now?" Aspacia asked a woman, who also had a placard around her neck. The whole procession of over five hundred people had begun the forced march down the Via Ostiensis, the paved road from the port to the Rauduculanae Gate, leading into Rome.

"The auction, a place my father told me about near a forum. He once visited here as a free man, a trader. It's a big market for slaves called the Graeco Stadium. That's where we'll be sold."

There was the sound of a lash and a cry as a straggler was hurried on. Several squads of guards patrolled the edges of the procession.

"How far is it to Rome?" Caladria asked the woman.

She looked about at the clusters of slaves, the guards clearing the way over the large black paving stones, and said, "Maybe three days, and then we'll be put up for auction in lots." Glancing at Aspacia she added, "A pretty girl like you may be shown to a buyer in a special place away from everybody else."

"What kind of place?" asked Aspacia.

"It's called the *arcana tabulate catastae*. Men and even women who go there are usually rich, and buy girls for..." The woman stopped and looked at Aspacia with sadness. "You don't know anything about it, do you?"

Aspacia shook her head.

"I don't want to worry you, but it could be worse, especially for your sister."

"Tell me."

"Pretty women taken there are sold for a higher price and the buyers usually live in nice houses, even villas. At least you won't have to toil on a farm. That is the worst, because slaves on farms are treated like animals."

"But what of my sister?"

The woman shrugged. She looked at the placard that hung

from Caladria's neck. "I can read a little of this."

"What does it say?" asked Aspacia. "I can speak Latin but I have difficulty reading it."

In a hushed voice the woman said, "It tells where she comes from, her age and that she is not very bright. They will put a little cap on her head. It's called a pillei and everybody knows what it means. Some Romans look for slow-minded women who can do mindless tasks." Then conspiratorially she said, "The owners can do anything they want to a slave. If you and your sister want to live, you must do everything they ask. You cannot refuse, or they will beat, sell, or even murder you. They are the law unto themselves and no court will intrude. Unfortunately I doubt that you and your sister will be sold to the same person. I'm sorry to tell you this, but I thought you should know."

"So I may not see Caladria ever again?" Aspacia said with a shudder.

"Probably not, but you never know. My husband said that the slave auction is great entertainment for the Romans, and sometimes entire groups are sold to one buyer." The woman glanced at Caladria, shook her head and softly said, "But I don't know who would want her."

*****

"Did you love him?" Caladria asked Aspacia. The entire procession had been shoved into a field for the night. Fires had been built, not so much for the warmth and health of their charges, but rather to insure that none of them escaped. Chained together, there was little chance of that.

"Valdanik? No, but Father said it would be a good match, with him inheriting a farm and some land."

"But he was handsome," Caladria said as they sat by the fire with other chained souls.

"He was a very rough man, a bore, really, and he liked to fight. He's the reason we are here. Father taught me Latin like the Romans speak and offered to teach Valdanik but he refused. He only wanted to kill Romans, not speak to them."

"I never want to be separated from you," Caladria said,

looking down at her hands. "What will become of me?"

"I don't know, sister. But if we please them in some small way we may live. We may even be together."

Caladria looked into Aspacia's eyes and said, "Maybe it would be better to be with Mother and Father. Maybe it's better that we die."

Aspacia put her arms around Caladria and together they cried.

Chapter 3

There was a light tapping and Gaius rolled over on his straw mattress.

"Young master, it's time to rise," said Apollodoros.

His leg throbbed and the bruise had swelled. Gaius stared at a blank wall of his cubiculum and felt exhausted. Pulling on his tunic he cracked open the door. "I don't want to practice oration and I definitely don't want to conjugate Greek today."

"A pity since your Greek is so atrocious, but your father requires your attendance."

"Requires my attendance? You are so damn formal. Can't you just say he wants to beat me again?"

Apollodoros sighed, cocked his bald head and said, "I am a scholar and learned men speak as such. Indeed, under my tutelage you may become one some fine day. But not at the moment. Your father is not pleased and I, a lowly Athenian slave, suggest that you make all haste."

"I can't wait for my daily dose of insults," Gaius mumbled.

"The Dominus has been at the lararium for over an hour. He's worried. In fact I would say terrified. He's lit a month's worth of incense and has been on his knees praying to all the gods, even Isis," said the Greek in a hushed voice.

"Because of the boy? Does he have remorse?"

"Of course not. It's not about the boy. I heard him mutter 'Alexandria'.

Gaius took Apollodoros by the elbow and led him to the empty kitchen.

"What else did he say about Alexandria?"

Apollodoros wrested his elbow away and said, "Nothing.

Maybe he's seen or heard something. He thinks they're hunting for him."

"Here in Rome?"

"Where else?"

"So it has come back to haunt him," said Gaius.

"Perhaps, but I didn't think it would be so soon," Apollodoros said, a concerned look on his face.

"Only the girl would recognize me or my father. It was very dark."

Toronius finished his prayers and rose unsteadily when his son and the slave entered the atrium. Gaius glanced at his father, then the little shrine to which, like every dominus, he prayed each day. But never before had Toronius been on his knees, and never did his voice quake.

"I saw her, the Egyptian girl," he said, rounding on Gaius. "I'm sure it was her, she was wearing the amulet. You told me she was dead!"

"No, Father, I told you she had escaped by the time I got to the room. I couldn't find her and we had to find a ship."

"There's something you're not telling me," Toronius said, waving his finger.

Gaius said nothing as his father glared at him.

"Where did you see her, Dominus?" Apollodoros asked, hoping to avert another confrontation.

"I saw her and four men leave the popina, the one where Vercipius and I always eat. You could tell the men were Egyptian by their clothing, or lack of it. They went to the bathhouse in the Suburra where the old apartments are. They must have seen me at the baths. I know they're looking for me."

"Master, how would they know where to look? Rome has a million people," said Apollodoros deferentially, spreading his hands.

"The Balneum is not an opulent bathhouse but it's close by. This is a wealthy neighborhood and many merchants live on Esquiline Hill. It would be a logical place to look."

"There are hundreds of Egyptian girls in Rome, Father, and she wouldn't look the same as when you first saw her. Not after what you..." Gaius stopped rather than finish the accusation. Then taking a deep breath, he asked, "How can you be sure that it's her?"

"I just told you! I saw the pendant around her neck. The one I bought in Alexandria. The one you were to take back from her."

"Excellency, is it possible that more than one was made?"

"To grace the neck of a cheap Egyptian whore?"

"Yes, that would be most strange," said the slave, not caring to be the object of his master's tirade.

"I want to be sure it's them. I want to know where they're staying and I want the authorities to expel them from Rome," said Toronius, his hand twitching.

"On what grounds?" asked Gaius.

"Theft, intent to murder, something! You know what she looks like. Find her but don't let them see you," Toronius said to Gaius before turning back to the family shrine. "And check the Forum as well as the baths; they may think I'm there. Now go."

The restaurant and baths lay at the bottom of the hill. Working their way down, Gaius said, "Did my mother see him at prayers this morning?"

"No, I saw her but she was in a hurry. She only gave me a glance. But if she had seen your father, she would have been surprised. He's never looked so frightened."

"She knows nothing about it except that you and I went to Alexandria with him," said Gaius. "I'm certain he hasn't told anybody, but I'm surprised they have come for him now."

"Why wouldn't they? It's already been a year. The girl was a beauty and very popular. She might have been the daughter of the innkeeper. She must have regained her health. Perhaps they brought her along to recognize him."

"Would you know her if you saw her?"

"I doubt it. Not after what Father did."

"But you'll recognize the amulet, the one you let her keep?"

"That's hard to forget. It was pure gold."

*****

The popina was crowded and rowdy as dozens of men sat at tables drinking beer and watered wine. It was a two-story, dilapidated structure, but it had all the amenities any man would crave. The proprietor directed his girls to attend one table after another. The girls, all slaves, were accustomed to being patted on the rump or having their tunic raised by an inebriated customer. The owner kept his eye on the most attractive girls who, with his approval, would take a customer upstairs for an assignation as quick as the service of food and drink. The girl would receive a small coin and the proprietor a few more denarii in his purse.

"They may have looked in here for my master but they wouldn't have tarried," Apollodoros said. "I doubt that they'll be at the baths, either, but I do what the Dominus requires."

The bathhouse bell rang signaling that the impatient crowd could enter. It was traditional that Romans should bathe at least once every nine days, but many went far more often.

"It costs a fourth of an *as*. I brought enough with me to pay for that," said Gaius. "The baths are the cheapest thing in Rome and that's the smallest coin. I don't see how the owners make any money," he added.

"Everybody goes to the baths. They make their money," replied Apollodoros.

"I guess so, I saw my mother starting for the baths earlier this morning. But I thought that was kind of strange," said Gaius.

"Why would that be strange? She likes to swim in the big pool; it's a favorite activity of hers since she has little else to do."

"That pool's closed for repairs and she only goes with her sister Junia, who has been sick all week," said Gaius, perplexed.

There was already a line at the balneum entrance. Toronius went to the baths almost daily after meeting in the tablinum with his clients. Besides the mosaic-tiled pools of water of varying temperatures, the balneum featured gymnasiums, libraries, games and public latrines. The palaestra, attached to the bathing areas, was a place of shops, theaters and tree-lined walkways. Toronius and his silk merchant friend, Vercipius, could usually be found at the bar near the workout rooms. There, in the gymnasium, women would have exchanged their stolae for the briefest of clothing and engaged in a game of hoops, tennis, or ball.

"Have you seen Appian Dio today?" Gaius asked Apollodoros as they stayed in the shadows.

"No, were you expecting him?"

"He mentioned that he might come before he reports to the Campus Martius. I wanted to wish him well since I won't be seeing him for at least six months. You know he comes almost every day. He enjoys my father's company and the money he gives him."

"You think that's the reason he comes to the villa?"

"Well, he also talks to me. Why, is there another reason?"

Apollodoros gave Gaius a quick glance, then, looking away, said, "No, no other reason. Nothing at all."

From the archway they saw a squad of guards lead a group of slaves to a narrow unmarked door on the side of the balneum. Tired, unkempt and ill fed, the slaves workday had not yet begun.

"Someday, if I become a legislator, I will propose laws against that," said Gaius.

"You'll be assassinated the moment you do so," replied Apollodoros. "Who would stoke the fires for the baths if there were no slaves? No Roman would work beneath the floor to heat the pipes. Your slave state began when you conquered Greece. One hundred and fifty thousand of my countrymen were sold in a single day. That's why so many Romans don't work. Laziness will destroy you in the end."

Gaius had heard it from Apollodoros before. 'The shortcomings of Rome' was a common litany with him. Although his life was far better than most other slaves, he had long ago given up any hope of being freed, at least as long as Toronius was alive. The dominus had never said a word about manumission, and Apollodoros knew better than to ask.

They passed the hotter baths, the caldarium, and the warm

pools further away from the underground cauldrons, until they came to the tepidarium. Slaves with strigiles, the curved metal body scrapers, attended the patrons and removed dead skin from the surface of their skin. Of course Apollodoros pointed out that the idea originated in Greece, whose culture he regarded as far superior.

The noise was almost ear-shattering as dozens of people in waist-deep pools shouted to one another. Gaius looked at Apollodoros and mouthed the words, "They're not here." Then he pointed to another room and said, "Frigidarium."

The room featured a deep pool where guests could cool off. It was quieter in the frigidarium, and Gaius said, "This isn't the only place they could be. There are other pools of warm water down those corridors. It's more secluded: a good place for people to hide."

"I'll go first," said Apollodoros. "If they're down there, they may recognize you."

A labyrinth of narrow passages snaked throughout the balneum. Great marble pillars separated one intimate body of water from another. Here the prostitutes, both men and women, lurked, waiting for someone seeking an exciting encounter. Apollodoros and Gaius waved off several and moved into the shadows. Torches in wall sconces illuminated the shallow pools where bathers relaxed or were entertained by the whores.

A very small bath lay at the furthest end of the balneum. Muted sounds of rapture floated from the pool. Apollodoros peered from behind a pillar and froze. The entwined couple was not more than a dozen feet away.

"Go back," said the Greek in a whisper.

"They're there?" asked Gaius.

"Just go back," he repeated.

There was a shrill sound, a shriek that sent a shiver through Gaius. Pushing Apollodoros aside, he knelt and studied the figures through a warm mist that rose from the pool. His mother was facing him. Her eyes were closed and her body was tight against a man. Her nails dug into his back and a trickle of blood ran into the pool.

Gaius looked back at Apollodoros, who stood in the shadows behind him. The slave showed no emotion. It was not his place to do so.

His mother's laugh and high-pitched voice were instantly recognizable. When agitated, that shriek knew no bounds, but never had he heard it as insistent as now.

His mother, he knew, was a beautiful woman not yet thirty, who had many admirers, but he had never heard or seen her in her husband's cubiculum during the night. That she might have a secret lover was something he had not contemplated, though he knew it would make perfect sense since she loved to flirt with important men. He thought that he should avert his eyes but he began to have another thought, one more bizarre than he could have ever imagined.

The man laid Livia on the rim of the pool and turned ever so slightly.

Overcome with lust, Appian Dio did not see who was peering at him from behind the pillar. Eyes wide, Gaius stared in disbelief, then turned to Apollodoros who leaned against a shadowed wall. With the sight and sounds of his mother's carnal pleas, Gaius fled from the baths.

"Did you know?" He finally asked Apollodoros, as they neared the villa.

"Slaves know everything, but learn to say nothing."

"Did it give you pleasure to know something so intriguing and say nothing to me about my mother and Appian Dio?"

"No, though it might have been titillating in other circumstances. But with the state I'm in, how could I possibly tell you? What could I say? 'Oh, young master, did I happen to mention that your best friend is having sex with your mother almost every day? What would you have done about it?"

"I would have—"

"Lost your best friend and infuriated your mother with your sense of morality?"

Gaius let the futility of it all sink in, and then he asked, "Does my father know?"

"That's not the question."

"What is?"

"Does he even care?"

"She's his wife, she belongs to him," said Gaius, still in shock and confusion.

"Everything in the villa belongs to him, including you and me. But Toronius would not want your friend to have sex with his wife if he were present in the villa."

"So they do it at the baths," Gaius concluded.

"Of course, doesn't everyone?"

*****

It was later in the day that Appian Dio sauntered up the hill to a low wall surrounding the villa. Gaius sat on the warm stone and watched. When he reached the wall, he looked at Gaius, who studied him but said nothing.

Cocking his head, Appian said, "You still pissed about the other night?"

"No."

There was a lengthy silence, then Gaius asked, "Did you have an enjoyable time this morning?"

"What?"

"At the balneum."

"The baths. Oh yes, it was pleasant. It always is."

Appian Dio was surprised at the speed that Gaius slammed into him, throwing him against the wall. His head rang, but when it finally cleared he demanded, "What would I have said to her? 'You're a beautiful woman but no thank you, I can't have sex with you because it would hurt Gaius's sensitivities?' Do you live in a cave or are you just stupid?"

"I don't live in a cave, I live in the house you come to almost every day. I thought you were coming because you are, or were, my friend, because..."

"Because we just palled around together? I come here hungry and your mother feeds me. In return she insists that I give her pleasure."

"I'm sure you didn't object."

"Of course not. She times it so that there won't be complications: babies, you know. Do you want to know something else? I'm not the only one. Your mother craves men, usually rich men, which I am not. But I do it better than the others." He fumed for a moment then said, "Gaius, you don't know much about women."

"Not as much as I know about friendship. Friends don't do their friend's mother, Appian."

"I'll do any woman that lets me. Especially if they look as good as she does. And I'll tell you, Gaius, if it wasn't me today, it would be someone else. Maybe one of the gladiators, who would tear her apart then toss her away. They do that you know, it's a sport with them: a numbers thing. How would you like that? You better understand that many women like it as much as men, and Livia more than most. I'm sorry I tarnished the image of your mother, but she was quite insistent. The world is a damn harsh place for a poor kid, but I try to make the best of it. She has made it just a little more tolerable."

He started down the hill and said, "I'll see you in six months. Maybe you'll grow up by then."

"You don't have to come back. In six months my mother won't even remember you."

Appian Dio laughed and said, "She sure will, Gaius; she'll pine for me every day.

*****

Gaius stood beside the pool as slaves wiped away the telltale stains that tinted the mosaic tiles. His mother stood on the opposite side as the men with sponges silently scrubbed. Though petulant as ever, she seemed more relaxed, even distant. When the last crimson traces of the boy's suicide were erased, the valves were opened and water spurted into the pool.

Livia caught his eye as he considered her. He looked away, wondering if she knew. Leaving the peristyle, he was about to pass her when she suddenly turned to him, and with a piercing look said, "Don't you dare judge me. And if you say a single word..."

She knows, he thought. *She knows.*

"I'm surprised to see you up," said Apollodoros, rising to his feet beside a fire pit.

"I couldn't sleep," answered Gaius. "It was stifling in my room. I had to get out."

Apollodoros simply nodded. Gaius could guess what the Greek was thinking, and he said, "It wasn't about Appian or my mother."

"It's none of my business," the slave replied.

"But as you said, you and the others know everything."

"It's how I stay alive. Life is a game of balancing what you must know and what you must never say. We wear masks for every occasion.

A flame streaked across the sky. *What kind of omen is that?* Gaius thought. *Which of the gods would flick fire across the heavens?*

"Why are you by the gate instead of Andronius?" he asked.

"Your father wanted me to stay here tonight. Andronius is too old and won't stay awake. He's sleeping outside my master's door as I always do."

"So you're here because of the Egyptians?"

"He expects me to give the alarm if they try to enter."

"But they don't know where he lives."

"Not yet, but terror runs deep. I suspect that they will come looking. But don't tell him, Master Gaius."

"I don't talk to him unless I have to, you know that."

Apollodoros studied the youth, then nodded. "Yes, he's not interested in anything you have to say."

"So what made you think they would come all the way here? The beating?"

"What else? She must have been a beautiful girl before it happened. But it wasn't the first time he beat a girl in Egypt. I had to remind him to be careful. He even grew a beard once so he would not be recognized." said Apollodoros.

"But there are so many women here, why would he always go back to Alexandria?"

"Because it's a mysterious city, full of souks and very strange women; it whetted his carnal appetite. He might beat a girl there and get away with it, whereas here..."

"But this last time things went wrong."

"True. But, as you know, sex wasn't the only thing he was looking for."

Apollodoros again stared into the fire and listened to any sounds that might be on the street beyond the villa's walls. He looked about, then in a very soft voice said, "You do know that the Dominus was once in the cattle business. He actually made some money."

"Raising cattle?" asked Gaius, a surprised look on his face.

"Stealing them. It was just after he bought me; you were still a baby then. We would venture down to the Forum Boarium beside the Tiber late at night. He would have me distract a guard while he led a cow or two away. Then we would butcher them and sell the meat. Once, we were almost caught and he got scared. The penalty is severe. So he went into the silk trade like his friend Vircipius, but that didn't work either."

"So you suggested the antique business, right?"

"I did. He was wary at first, but he wrangled visits to important people's houses and saw that they collected ancient Egyptian pieces from the time of the pyramids. I speak Greek, and that's the language of trade in Alexandria. It's also where the most valuable objects can be found. Your father pretended to enjoy the Great Library there. Did you know, all scrolls brought into Egypt are confiscated and copied before being returned? Then they're put on the library shelves. The first time we passed the lighthouse at Pharos Island, he tried to hide some maps but they caught him.

"It was very embarrassing. We did nine voyages to the city; the final one was last year when you came with us."

"That's when I met Elizar ben Josephus," said Gaius, "the old Jew who sold him the scarabs."

"Yes, in the souks near the Brucheion, the Royal Quarter. Most of the hawkers of antiquities were thieves, and their merchandise fakes. They would watch for wealthy foreigners and say things like, 'Excellency, I have an amazing collection of scarabs, ankh pendants and an Anubis relief. I even possess canopic jars containing the lungs of Royals.' Then from a filthy rag they would extract a poor imitation of a Horus Falcon."

"If you weren't there, my father would have bought those fakes," said Gaius.

"I had to suggest alternatives to your father, but it had to be done delicately. It would not be good to bruise his ego. In Alexandria I had Toronius buy true antiquities, things wealthy Romans would want to show off: ancient sarcophagus pieces from the time of Amenhotep II."

"I'm amazed that we got any of those pieces out on the night that we ran."

"It was close. That mob would have torn us apart if they had caught us. It still makes me shiver. I knew that they wouldn't stop looking; the Dominus wasn't disguised and I think they knew who he was. I suggested that he not go in there, but he had made up his mind. Maybe he had already seen the girl."

"I was surprised that he had you go with him, when he ordered me to stay with his treasures in the upstairs room," said Gaius in a near whisper. "I didn't like the place; it looked like it had seen lots of violence."

"I'm sure it did. There were always fights and a lot of murders beside the docks. But your father liked the sleaziest bars, the ones down by the waterfront where the barmaids were cheap."

"I really didn't know what he had in mind when he went downstairs later that night."

"Of course not," said Apollodoros. "Think back to that night. What he did was his own business, nothing he would tell you about."

"What happened when you went downstairs with him that last night?" asked Gaius.

"The inn we were staying in had a bar downstairs and a phallic symbol over the door meaning that it was also a whorehouse. It stank of that Egyptian beer and they served a wine with blue lotus blossoms. It's supposed to give a real kick. Anyway, the Dominus sees a table in the corner where there's a Roman naval officer and the man points to an empty bench. He tells your father that he commands the war galleys in the harbor, answers only to the Senate, and knows every woman in the tavern. And that included the young thing that your father already wanted."

"Did the officer want her too?" asked Gaius.

"No, he had his eye on another but he said, 'That one you're looking at with the pert little tits, she's the best here and has a loyal following. A distant relative to some Royal, but fell out of favor. I've had her before but you have to be gentle, real gentle.' He called her over and introduced her to your father. Then Toronius told me to go back to our room. You know the rest."

They were silent for a long moment. "This afternoon, did you know about their trysts before?" asked Gaius.

"About Appian Dio and your mother? I'm surprised you didn't see it."

"I wasn't looking for it," Gaius said, looking down at his feet. "Have they been they lovers for a long time?"

"A few years. Sometimes I was afraid that your father would catch them. Your mother hates your father, and he's very possessive. That's why they met at the bath today, because your father was home. Of course if she were entertaining a wealthy man, then..."

"Appian said he's not the only one." Gaius said tersely.

"Is that what he said?" Apollodoros asked. He sighed and said, "There were others before Appian. She wouldn't lower herself to seek them out. No, she would command me to find her gladiators, strong virile men who could exhaust her. I would have to wait until they finished; sometimes it took hours. I was always worried since I had to be loyal to your father but also obey your mother, the Domina."

"How long has it been since she did it with my father?"

"Not since you were a year old."

"I never heard what happened. Neither of them ever told me. Why does she hate him so?"

Apollodoros again stared into the fire and finally said, "In ancient Sparta, when a male child was born, five learned men, including the father, would determine whether the infant was strong enough to survive the rigors of life and war. If the infant appeared fragile, he would be tossed off a cliff. There were no weaklings in Sparta, but they lost many fine minds who might have done other things. We in Athens never acted that way, and we still won our wars."

"What does that have to do with my parents?" asked Gaius with a sigh. He was often subjected to his mentor's lengthy ruminations.

"You Romans are different, and in a way more cruel, when female babies are involved."

"We don't throw them off cliffs," Gaius said defensively.

"No, but in Roman society the midwife lays the infant at the feet of its father. If the child is picked up, it is claimed and becomes part of family. If not, it is put on the street, and either adopted by a passerby or left to die. This is the fate of female babies much more than boys. Here women are considered almost worthless except for sex and having babies. Their opinions are rarely considered."

"So what happened when I was one year old?" asked Gaius.

"Your mother had a daughter."

"I actually have a sister?" Gaius exclaimed, his attention riveted on his father's slave.

"Perhaps. My master refused to pick her up. He told me to take her to the Forum where she would be seen, and I did as I was told. I waited but didn't see anyone claim her."

Gaius stared at Apollodoros. "A sister. Do you think she lived?"

"Who knows? I do know this; your mother lost all affection for Toronius. Her sex with him became cold."

"How did you learn that?"

"A slave sleeps outside the door of the Dominus's bedroom. You know that. When a woman like Livia stops encouraging a man and goes silent, then..." Apollodoros stopped and said, "Perhaps he hoped that in time she would become a lover again, but she never did. He would scream at her in the middle of the night and every slave could hear him, but he didn't care. Eventually, your father grew tired of her frigidity and they never had sex again."

"She hates him."

"And that is why they hate each other, but Toronius would never divorce her even though he can."

"Why doesn't he?"

"It's obvious. She organizes the cena, all those lavish dinners where he gets chummy with the Equestrian class. They invite tribunes and their wives, who listen raptly to his tales of Alexandria and long-dead pharaohs, and buy his treasures. That's why you live here, and not in a squalid suburbia like Appian Dio."

"Are most marriages like that, like my parents?"

"I don't know, I've never been married."

"Not even before you were a slave?"

"No, and it's not something I care to discuss. But it's very rare that married couples love each other. It's all a matter of property, inheritance and social status. All that is based on the determination of the dominus. Every decision must be approved by the father as long as he lives. That involves everything. You know already, you yourself can do nothing without his consent. It's said that a man has as many enemies as he has slaves, but in Rome his greatest enemy is his son."

Yes, thought Gaius, *that's very true indeed.*

*****

The night seemed endless. Gaius stirred on his straw-filled mattress. His mind, like a house of murky rooms, had doors that opened and slammed shut. Behind each was a ghastly image: Appian Dio and his mother, a sister he never knew, the beatings and death of a child slave. He glimpsed fleeting images of Alexandria, and replayed the chase down dark, twisting alleys, and finally the mob, the lies, and the terror. There behind another door was his father, the ever-powerful dominus hunter and hunted. The door opened and specters flitted by, imploring him to follow into a deep abyss.

He closed his eyes and took a deep breath, hoping to shut out the horrors, but it was not to be. A door slammed open, and the toothless face of the old hag, the prostitute, appeared. There was a scream and Gaius, bolting up, thought it was his; the nightmare of the whore was still so vivid. Despite a cold sweat, he rose out of bed and listened. Over the pounding of his heart he again heard a scream, but it was not the harlot from the night before. Then there were footsteps running through the house and into the atrium.

A moment later Gaius's door burst open and his father, waving a torch, shouted, "Is she in here?"

"In here? No, just me. Who's screaming? Who are you looking for?"

"That bitch, your mother! Stay in here," he said, slamming shut the door. The stave was in his hand.

"Have you seen her?" Toronius shouted to every astonished slave he passed. Peering from his door, Gaius saw the slaves cringing and backing off, shaking their heads.

Apollodoros was standing by the gate when Toronius, breathless, put his hands on his knees and said to him, "You bastard, you let her out."

"No, master. She saw me here, but turned back. She has a knife, Excellency."

"I have a club. Tell her she'd better not fail me tomorrow or she will be running for the rest of her life."

Slowly, carefully, Gaius opened his door and edged down the hall toward the kitchen and into the courtyard where they kept caged chickens, ducks and a goat. He carried a blanket, since the predawn was chilly. It was still dark; no torches had been lit behind the villa. Silently he followed the worn footpath until he came to the wall. Years earlier, when Toronius was in Egypt, Livia had ordered the slaves to buy bricks at the Forum, and she'd put Gaius to work digging a secret depression in the earth, large enough for a bed. He had built steps inside, and covered it with hinged boards and vines. It was not the first time she had fled there.

Gaius knocked on the board five times, their code, and she cracked open the door.

"No one followed me. I'm alone," Gaius whispered as he

passed a blanket to an outstretched hand.

She would not thank him, but to his stare she said, "He came in my room and..."

Gaius said nothing, only closed the hatch and checked to see that the air vent had not been plugged. There was water and dried biscuits inside; Livia would remain there until her husband turned his attention to some female slave. Gaius assumed that in Toronius's frustration and anger, rape would happen very soon.

He had no idea why his father would invade Livia's room after all those years. But what did he really know of the Dominus? Gaius slipped back into his cubiculum and stared at the unadorned ceiling. An hour later, the sun would rise over the hills of Rome, and the game of masks would begin all over again. What frightened Gaius was that he didn't know what masks were to be worn that day.

Chapter 4

"Is it going to happen today?" Caladria asked Aspacia as the mangone bustled about with a cloth, wiping smudge marks from faces and positioning groups in the sequence he wanted.

"That's what the old woman said, but it might be another rumor, just like everything else we've heard," answered Aspacia.

But the charged activity of the auctioneers boded otherwise, and Caladria trembled, her shaking becoming uncontrollable. Seven hundred people had been crammed into the stockade just outside the Aurelian Wall that surrounded Rome. From there they would be marched to the slave market at the Forum.

Groups of chained men were herded from one place to another, as were separate bands of women and children. Most were still numbed, since two weeks earlier they had been living as free men and women. A sense of foreboding and fear permeated the stockade. Many were awaiting their fate in silence, but there was also a cacophony of voices as alien languages churned into one another like roiling torrents. Again wails erupted, as siblings were parted and hustled to one chained group or another.

A mangone followed by his Dacian slave appeared before the sisters with two blank plaques and a piece of chalk. "What is your name and what skills have you?" he asked Caladria. Startled by the man's sudden appearance she said, "Caladria, my name is Cal..." and she erupted in tears.

"She's fat and won't bring a good price," the slave said. "I suggest that she be sold as farm stock."

"Please, Master, she can cook. She is a very good cook and

would serve a household well," Aspacia broke in. That she said it in perfect Latin startled the slave and his master.

"You speak only when told to," the Roman said, glaring at Aspacia. "Now what do you do?"

"I'm a healer, and I grow herbs which my sister makes into wonderful dishes. We work very well together, Excellency." Aspacia hoped that she hit the right note as she put her arm around the sobbing Caladria. The mangone put his hand on his chin and looked from one to the other.

"You might get stuck with the ugly one if you try to sell her alone," offered the obsequious slave.

"Perhaps. I certainly don't want to feed her. Yes, we'll sell them as a set," he said to his Dacian. "Put 'good cook' on the fat one's board, and 'speaks Latin and grows herbs' on the pretty," he said. Then lifting Aspacia's chin, he said, "This one will bring a nice price. I almost want to keep her for myself but we'll show her off. I need the money. And put that little cap on the other. I can't guarantee her. She looks like a cow already."

That said, he moved to a woman holding an infant. He took the child from the woman's arms and gave it to his slave. The woman gave the auctioneer a horrified look, then gasped when he ripped open her blouse. His hands went to her breasts and he squeezed a nipple. A droplet of milk emerged which he smeared with his finger. He squeezed the nipple again and touched the droplet to his tongue.

"Not bad. Write 'breast feeder' on her board," he said.

"And the baby, Master?"

"Give it back. It will show that my claim is true. She will nurse it at the sale."

The woman pulled her ripped garments together, but from her expression didn't know whether to be appalled by the indignity, or thankful to be allowed to keep her child.

When the mangone departed, an old woman standing beside Aspacia said, "The mother is a pretty one. She will be giving milk, all right, but to those who haven't been infants for a very long time."

The stockade doors opened and a line of men were ordered

out, their chains clinking as they shuffled forward. From her position, Aspacia could see guards beyond the gate. An order was given and the gates closed. A second group, boys manacled together, was herded to the gate like a flock of ducklings.

"What will become of them?" Aspacia asked the woman.

She shrugged, then said, "I've heard that Romans like boys. Some will sleep in very warm beds, but not alone."

It was late afternoon by the time Aspacia and her sister were led out of the stockade. If one prisoner slowed or stopped, the chains would pull violently on the person ahead, so everybody learned to keep in step. With guards surrounding them, no one gave any thought to escape. There was no more talking; fear and uncertainty had stilled their tongues.

*****

Livia, with Gaius's help, had slipped back into her room a few hours before dawn. She'd considered remaining there until midday, wishing that the heavy bolt still lay on the inside of the door, but Toronius had ordered it removed years before. Instead, just before the sun rose, and when the house seemed completely still, she located a small piece of iron beneath her mattress and silently stole through the villa into the orchard beyond the peristyle. She stood motionless, her heart pounding, a small oil lamp the only illumination, then made her way through the vineyard to the dilapidated barn at the extreme end of the property.

There was the waning flicker of a candle, the sudden bleat of a goat, and the screech of an owl. Livia stared into the ancient structure with its broken roof tiles and splintered boards.

"Arzeka, are you in there?"

There was no sound. Then, standing inches behind her, he said, "Are you hungry for it, Mistress?"

Startled, she pitched forward, only to be caught by the Berber's sinewy arms.

"Let go of me," she hissed. Smelling his fetid breath she recoiled.

"What does the fine Roman lady want with me? Perhaps a

warm bed on a cold night?" Arzeka asked, his narrow face framed in a scraggly beard.

"Take this," Livia said, producing an iron key. "You do what I told you to. Bring me the money from his office. I'll wait here."

The man waved a finger before her, a shadowy thing in a quarter moon's light. "Not tonight. He will be awake and I'll be beaten again."

"No, he sleeps soundly, especially after he's had a slave girl. It gives him release; you know what I mean. The box is under the stone in the tablinum, just like I showed you. It's too heavy for me. I need twenty sestercii, tonight."

The Berber came close and said, "You will reward me as you said?" His hand reached beneath her night tunic and slid up the inside of her thigh. She trembled at his touch, but it was more from excitement than fear.

"Show me them," the man said and Livia saw the lust. He opened his nearly toothless mouth, touched his tongue to his lips.

"Only this now," she said, opening the top of her blouse. A slip of moonlight illuminated the curve of her breasts, her nipples suddenly taut. The slave's hand closed over one breast as he lowered his head and sucked a nipple into his mouth. She closed her eyes and felt the warmth. It was at once repulsive and thrilling. Was this not a fantasy she had played out in her mind countless times: seduction by a slave to whom she would lose all resistance?

She pushed him away as he reached for the other breast.

"Later. I'll come to you soon. You'll get more," she said, placing the key in his hand.

"You come with me to watch if he wakes up," the slave said. "Not even sex is worth a beating. You come or I don't do it."

Livia pulled up her blouse and shivered. Her mind was racing.

"I'll follow you," she said. The sky was growing lighter and soon the slaves would wake.

"Hurry," she said, fearing that it was already too late.

Toronius owed her, she told herself. She would have her

way. She would get what she wanted and would deal with the consequences later. The man still needed her.

*****

Roman tradition required that each morning the dominus invite his clients to a light breakfast, after which they would be invited to the upstairs tablinum. Now, descending the staircase with senatorial dignity and wearing his finest toga, Toronius smiled magnanimously and stretched out his arms, palms up. He glanced with approval at the tables with their cheeses, wines, and sweetmeats, and was pleased to see his seven guests, several from distinguished families. With a great show of affection he greeted each guest and turned to a recent addition to his menagerie, loudly proclaiming, "Antonius Servius Polonius, welcome to my home." Then, gripping the man's shoulders, he said, "And how is your father? Is his arthritis any better?"

Flattered by the attentions of his portly host, who wore silver rings and gold chains, the young man said, "I'm afraid not, but I'm told you're knowledgeable in medical matters."

Toronius led the young man upstairs, while a dozen others awaited their invitation. Gaius, standing beside Apollodoros, watched as Livia anxiously eyed her husband, playing his role as the honored patrician.

She turned away and Gaius saw a little smile on her lips. Petite and devastatingly attractive, with her hair piled high and set with combs in the most current fashion, Livia closely monitored all whom her husband engaged. Shrewdly she chose who would or would not be invited to her dinners, the most congenial form of social climbing. Though not lavish events by senatorial standards, many of the wealthy were pleased to receive her invitation, and reciprocation would open many possibilities. As Gaius watched, he wondered if his mother thought that Antonius Servius Polonius, whose father was quite wealthy, would be invited to enjoy the cena. Then he wondered if she would have another use for Toronius's young client.

"If you want to know what it's like to be a slave, you must watch everything, listen to everything. Be a step ahead of any demand. That's how I stay alive," Apollodoros had said.

Watch everything, Gaius thought, observing the shrewdness of his mother.

"She manipulates your father but it's very subtle, very cunning," the slave confided to Gaius. "Vengeance motivates her. She spends his money in the guise of social necessity. Why do you think she encourages him to take long trips to purchase his goods? Because when he's away, she's the domina and is free to do whatever she pleases, with whom she pleases."

*****

Opening the door of the tablinum, Toronius gestured to a bench against the wall, while he sat behind his raised desk in the traditional throne-like chair. From there, he was able to conduct business with the client gazing up to him. The young man, an owner of fine racehorses with considerable promise, was given an opportunity to marvel at the new fresco: a man and woman in an erotic embrace. The couple was flanked by images of the goddess Diana of the woodlands, and Venus, the goddess of love. After admiring the work for an appropriate time, Antonius said, "You were about to suggest a cure for my father's ailment. He is an admirer of yours and cherishes the ancient scarab he purchased from you."

"Please tell your father that I hold him in great esteem. I hope that he can once again attend the fine cena that my wife puts on." Rearranging his writing instruments, Toronius said, "In regard to your father's misfortune, I haven't actually tried the remedy, but I spoke to a doctor on your father's behalf—an army doctor, in fact. He strongly urged that one consume a mixture of raw cabbage with coriander, scraps of pork, mashed scorpion, snails and mussels mixed with wine from Catalonia. Here," the dominus said, pulling out a slip of papyrus, "I'll write it down so it can be prepared exactly."

The aspiring client took it and with deference said, "I spoke briefly to your son, and I'm very much impressed by his bearing. He's become a man, Dominus."

"But a young man in need of direction, the type only a

determined father can give. I do have plans for him, Antonius."

"Hopefully they will benefit you, Excellency."

"I will have it no other way." Toronius considered his client's popularity as a provider of horses for the Greens, one of the four chariot teams at the Hippodrome, and added, "I'm inviting all my guests to the baths today. Would you care to join us? I have some friends who would like to make your acquaintance. Besides, it's a holiday. There are always pretty girls at the baths on special days. I'm sure you will like that."

The young man smiled and with a wink said, "I would be honored; it's always a pleasure to see the girls."

"Have my slave Apollodoros send in Plinius Apuleius Regulus, if you will," Toronius said as Antonius closed the door behind him.

Toronius stood and rearranged his toga so that the folds hung perfectly over his left arm. Plinius was of the honored Equestrian class, men who aspired to become quaestors, administrators and even tribunes. That the man was related to a famous family was of great importance to Toronius; even better, they had expressed interest in his artifacts. The only nagging concern, he thought, was that he had already sold most of them. Of course he still had the valuable Isis and Seti, as well as a Horus and an Osiris, but when those were sold what would be left to impress his visitors? The trade had been lucrative—Romans loved the Old Kingdom antiquities—but never again could he chance a voyage to Egypt.

He glanced toward the place where his strongbox was hidden beneath the floor, and stopped in mid-thought. A mosaic tile was out of place. Had he replaced it poorly, or...?

Apollodoros deferentially knocked on the door, then ushered Plinius into the room. Toronius tucked away his concern and effusively greeted his client.

"And how is your esteemed uncle, Pliny? When he completes another of his marvelous books I want it in my collection," Toronius said expansively. Of course he would never take the time to read it, since he was barely literate.

"Indeed, Dominus, my uncle is writing another major work

and I shall tender him your request. Now I do have a favor to ask, if it's not too much, Excellency. My wife loves silks, and I know that you were in that business some years ago. Perhaps you might recommend an honorable salesperson who will accept payment in Roman coin."

"Certainly. It is unfortunate that we can only buy silks from the miserable Parthians, and in gold at that!"

"Has anybody ever figured out where silk comes from, or what it's made of?"

"Supposedly it's made by the Seres people, who live far to the east. Of course the Parthian Empire is in the way, so we've never met the Seres, let alone traded with them. And no, we have no idea what the fabric is made of. Some say it's from a vine that grows on a very special tree. If the Parthians know they certainly aren't saying. But anyway, visit my friend Macius near the Forum shops. Tell him I sent you, and he'll give you a most favorable price."

"I owe you my most sincere thanks. Now, what can I do for you, Dominus?"

Toronius drummed his fingers on his desk and pondered the question. Finally he said, "Well, it's not necessary for you to do anything, but since you ask, perhaps you might extend an invitation to the great Pliny to inspect my Egyptian collection. I still have a number of exquisite pieces. A few will go quickly, but I shall save the choicest if the honorable man is interested."

"I will be visiting him in Herculaneum at the end of the month, and will certainly mention it. I'm sure he will be pleased to see you again."

Plinius was about to leave when he said, "Excellency, I almost forgot. I wanted to mention that my cousin Vitonius is the best friend of tribune Julian Graccus, a member of the Senate. He confides everything to my cousin, which is most fortunate, especially when it comes to dispatching military units for wars to expand the power of Rome."

Toronius gazed at him, not quite understanding his client's innuendo.

"Dominus," Plinius continued, "gold and gems gained from

sacking a city go to the army, but there's another commodity just as valuable. And that goes to those who put money in the right hands. I don't mean mine," Plinius hastily added. "Others, men who can make things happen for a mutual benefit." Seeing that Toronius was still trying to form a coherent thought, the man mouthed the word, "Slaves."

Peering intently at Plinius, Toronius said, "I see. Yes, a most profitable investment, if one can get into the business. Almost our entire work force, one third of Rome's million, are slaves. Even I have six."

"And you want more, I suspect."

"Of course. In fact, I was thinking of going to the market today, but the cost of anything worthwhile is getting higher, ridiculously so. Just between us, I was hoping to find a way around the auctioneers."

"Precisely, Dominus. A proper 'investment', as you term it, can persuade a commander to reserve a select quantity for you."

"But there are import taxes and fees that must be paid, and they're high."

"As I mentioned, a gift in the right hands... I know of such things.".

"And, with your contacts, I presume you're aware of a forthcoming war?"

"The Dacians across the Danube have been raiding the farmlands of Pannonia. Several legions have been assigned to deal with them, and there will be captives, as usual. The army will be on the march in a month or less, Dominus."

Toronius pursed his lips and considered the option while Plinius waited, his eyes noticing the misplaced floor tile. Toronius saw the questioning look and resolved to investigate it as soon as his client left.

"What might it cost to become involved in such a transaction?" Toronius finally asked, diverting the man's attention. "I don't keep a lot of capital on hand."

"I think one or two of your artifacts would be a worthy start for our venture."

"A mutual effort then, Plinius? I'm mildly interested,"

Toronius said, not wanting to appear too anxious in front of his young client. The man, Toronius sensed, was hungry to get into an ever-growing trade without investing money of his own. This "investment" would need to be carefully finessed, Toronius thought, if he were to get the lion's share.

"I realize that war is a gamble, but I do trust in our legions," the dominus said archly. Limitless possibilities were forming in his mind; quite unexpectedly, this young man had become quite valuable to him. Surely Plinius knew of a number of potential investors and might approach any one of them if Toronius balked. The possibility of great profit could not be allowed to slip away, so Toronius said, "What is the soonest you could arrange a meeting with your cousin and the tribune?"

Plinius said, "Tonight, in fact. My cousin just returned from Mauritania Tingitana across the straits from Spain. "

"Has he brought slaves, and is he willing to sell them?"

"I don't know the details, Dominus, but I'm certain he'll tell you all about it."

"Including how to get them past the authorities?"

Plinius gave a tight smile and said, "That I must leave to him. Such information is held very close."

"Yes," Toronius said in a quiet but emphatic voice, "It is for him to judge whether I should be privy to such a secret."

"Exactly, but my introduction will work to your advantage. Be so kind as to meet me at the eighth hour by the Aemilian Bridge; you know it, the oldest one, over the Tiber. And, Excellency... do come alone."

An energetic feeling coursed through Toronius. He stood and escorted Plinius out and his eyes brightened. "I greatly look forward to the meeting, and I'm sure that we shall all profit from it," said the dominus.

After closing and locking the door, Toronius turned his attention to the disturbed tile. His meticulous placement of the stones hid his greatest valuables. Perhaps, he thought, his sandal had caught an edge and dislodged a tile; but that seemed implausible, since he never stepped on those particular mosaics, nor would anybody else step into the very corner of the room. He was about to investigate the abnormality, when Apollodoros again knocked on the door.

Toronius was about to send the man away, but opted to finish the morning ritual instead. He seated himself with a scowl and said, "Enter, Apollodoros."

The Greek escorted in a freeman who was new to Toronius. "Master," said Apollodoros, "may I introduce Octavius Brundeschi from Lugdunensis, near Gaul."

Toronius had heard of him, though they had never met. He was rumored to have connections, mysterious sources from which he had acquired wealth beyond what would be reasonable for a non-Roman. Perhaps he should be invited to recline on the couches for the evening cena, where wine and Livia's company might loosen his tongue. It would be good to know just where all that wealth was coming from.

Of course, talk would have to be terribly discreet. Rome was full of spies, and a misplaced word could find its way to a consul with very unpleasant consequences. Still, Toronius mused, Octavius was up to something, with his flamboyant clothing and gold bands on his arms. It would be of value to make the foreigner welcome.

"Octavius, I'm absolutely delighted that you have chosen to grace my villa, considering that there are men in Rome far more influential than I am."

"But Excellency," replied the freeman with an engaging smile, "you are influential, extraordinarily influential according to my contacts. So it is I who am honored by your hospitality. A man of your status has the skills I am looking for."

"My skills interest you? The feeling is mutual; it seems we may have a common purpose," said Toronius, taking in the expensive rings Octavius was wearing on four fingers of each hand. "And coming from such an important province as Lugdunensis, I'm sure that you know much that would be to our mutual benefit."

"Indeed, but I have been entrusted with certain knowledge that I cannot now divulge. After all, we've only just met," the visitor said with a smile.

"Of course, of course, I understand," said Toronius. "We all have our little secrets, my friend, but naturally in Rome one must be circumspect, especially if there is money to be made. I too have valuable contacts, involvements from which we might both profit. Perhaps we should discuss these opportunities when we have more time."

"It would be an honor, Dominus. Indeed there are several possibilities that come to mind that I'm sure you will find most intriguing."

A slimy, silky bastard, Toronius thought, maintaining his own grin. But a truly honest man would be of little use to him. The world, he surely learned, had a thousand shades of grey, some just a little darker than others.

Octavius, with his ear to the ground and skillfully ingratiating himself with the right people, often gleaned little treasures from indiscreet sources, thought the dominus. There might be a senator who could be bought, or a hot tip on a chariot race to be thrown. That was how money was made. Yes, Toronius decided. He would cultivate the Gaul.

With the potential of a lucrative future, he presented Octavius with a fine silk scarf.

"I am flattered with your generosity," said the Gaul. "It is my wife's birthday, and I shall present it to her."

Then, as if they had already conspired on a delicious scheme, Toronius put his arm about the man's shoulder and escorted him to the door. *Of course*, Toronius mused, *everything now was merely conjecture. No plan had yet been concocted, but there were many possibilities.*

It was what Octavius had not revealed that intrigued Toronius, but there would be time for that later. At the moment there was something far more important demanding his attention.

"Apollodoros," he called from the steps, "I will not be seeing any more clients this morning." With a final nod and smile for Octavius, Toronius reentered his office and locked the door from the inside. Now he would have no interruptions; no one would be in the room to observe him.

Toronius opened a desk drawer, removed a false bottom, and extracted an iron key. Kneeling, his fingers picked away the dislodged stone. It hid a crevice in the floor, into which he inserted his hands, heaving aside a heavy stone.

He held his breath, praying that the dozen sticks carefully arranged beside his strongbox were still in place. They would only collapse if the box were displaced. But to his dismay, they lay between the box and the sides of its stone pit. Whoever had removed the covering stone and the strongbox had no idea of how to replace the sticks in their proper order. It was as Toronius had feared; he had been robbed.

Quickly he threw the sticks aside, lifted the heavy box onto his desk, and with a quick turn of the key, swung open its lid. Someone's hands had rifled through it. Of the nine bags of coins, one was missing and another had been ripped open. Its contents were strewn across the bottom of the chest. Worse yet, one of the precious Egyptian gods, the Isis, was missing.

Sitting back in his chair, Toronius stared into the box. Who except Apollodoros, he wondered, was ever allowed into the tablinum? Never was the key or the chest revealed to the slave. As a subterfuge, the door was never locked, giving the impression that whatever valuables Toronius had were kept somewhere else. Yet someone knew; someone strong enough to lift the heavy stone, and desperate enough to suffer greatly if discovered.

Toronius's mind went back to Apollodoros. Only he and his son would know the true value of the Isis. It had been the Greek slave who had assisted in its purchase, having argued the price with the Jewish merchant in Alexandria, a calculating trader who preferred to speak Greek rather than Latin. But Apollodoros was an academic, and to Toronius he appeared too timid to steal the figurine, let alone endure the punishment if found guilty. Moreover, what could he possibly want with it? What would he do with the money even if he could sell the Isis? In comparison to other slaves, Apollodoros had an easy life. Little was asked of him, and he was privy to the choicest dinner scraps following the cena. He was allowed to follow the dominus to the baths, and even ate at the same table when they were in foreign lands.

Of course there was always the matter of escape; even a trusted slave might consider it. But the very thought of Apollodoros stealing the artifact, selling it, and running away seemed ludicrous. The fugitive hunters were plentiful, and a tall, stooped Greek, skulking around the docks at Ostia, would be easy prey. The letter "F" for *Fugitivus* would be branded on his forehead, and no hair would be allowed to cover it; he would be treated as a felon for the rest of his life. And the penalty for the theft itself was unthinkable!

So, if not Apollodoros, then who? wondered Toronius. Perhaps it was a visitor, or even an observant client who had noticed an anomaly in the floor and guessed that a treasure lay beneath. But that, he surmised, hardly made sense. The key would have to be found, and who would possibly know of that? Of course, years ago, before the birth of the girl, the key had been hidden in a niche in his cubiculum, but he'd removed it after his rupture with Livia. A knock on the door startled him.

"Husband, your clients are still here. They said you invited them to the baths and they're waiting in the atrium."

"Give them coins and tell them to go."

"Are you going to join them?"

"Not now. I have work to do. Leave me be."

He fumed at the interruption. Who had robbed him? Was it simply for money or something else? Revenge? Gaius, whom he had struck with the stave, came to mind. A worthless child he was, a disappointment, and not cunning or brave enough to carry out the theft. And besides that, his very character did not fit.

"I can't figure out what's on his mind, worrying about the wellbeing of slaves and all," Toronius had complained to his longtime friend, Vercipius.

Now, about the theft; what would Gaius possibly do with money from the sale of the Egyptian god? Buy a slave for himself? Not without his father's permission, and there would be no slave in the household not owned by the Dominus.

No, it had to be someone else; perhaps somebody who wanted vengeance. It had to be someone who wanted to show how vulnerable he was, even in the inner sanctum of his own home. Whom had he insulted, defrauded, or lately tricked into a bad bargain? Indeed, who was out to destroy him?

He considered the Egyptians; but certainly his slaves would have alerted him if they had breached the walls. Of course there was at least one who might have considered collusion, but that man was never allowed entry to the house.

A theft at the villa had occurred only once before. The accused slave had been taken to the Coliseum and fed to a pack of hyenas. A fitting and righteous end, Toronius considered. He was sickened by the loss of money and his precious artifact, but the thought of finding another culprit began to excite him. Indeed, it would be an interesting turn to play the hunter, and the ending would be exquisite. Toronius drummed his pudgy fingers on the desk and wondered who would be fed to the hyenas this time.

*****

"Are you ready yet, Gaius? We're taking Apollodoros with us," Livia said, her high-pitched voice more shrill than usual. She had spent an unusual amount of time arranging her hair and applying unguents to her face; Toronius had lost her slave in a game of knucklebones, and now she had to purchase another. That he refused to apologize only added to her petulance.

Her idiot son was trying to be discreet, but she still heard him talking with Apollodoros. "I was ready an hour ago," he muttered. "What's taking her so long?"

"I think she's been waiting for your father to leave," the slave answered. "The Domina seems especially upset and has been watching your father. He's quite energetic today; he gave me a very strange look. I thought he was going to accuse me of something, but he just picked up his staff and left. He didn't say where he was going, and he went without his guards."

From a corner of the atrium, Livia watched Toronius leave the villa. The heavy gate was opened and a slave peeked out to reconnoiter. The slave nodded, but Livia waited a few more minutes before saying, "Let's go; we must hurry before they're all gone."

"What's gone?" Gaius asked, but his mother waved dismissively. Her son was of little consequence, and she would not accord him any time or energy unless she could profit from it.

Toronius was nowhere to be seen as Livia, Gaius and Apollodoros hurried through a maze of narrow streets. Five- and six-story insulae pressed in on the crowded lane. Like other pedestrians, the party sidestepped the body of a man murdered the night before. The unfortunate victim had likely departed an inn by himself and was attacked by thugs. Only wealthy men, accompanied by numerous well-armed bodyguards, would attempt the streets after dark.

Deprived of her female slave, Livia had forsaken her morning bath. A long soak always relaxed her and gave her time to think of her next romantic adventure, but the terror of the night before made her feel anything but relaxed. Instead she felt soiled after her ordeal in the dirt pit and her encounter with the Berber, Arzeka. On the other hand, danger aside, the thrill of that encounter still rippled through her.

But what could have possibly motivated Toronius to storm into her room? He had shown no interest in having sex with her for years. Was it sudden and unfulfilled lust for her? Had he tired of the slave girl, or was it jealousy? Did he know about Appian Dio? His behavior was an enigma, and it scared her. No bolt on the door would keep him out, even if she still had one. She was entirely at his mercy; but, she admitted, she always had been.

No, she decided, the reason for his entry must be quite simple, just as he was: she was seductive and available, and he simply wanted to fuck her. With that worry put to rest, she turned her mind to her current quest.

Like other wealthy Roman women, Livia attended the public baths for her trysts, but often bathed at home. Now her personal attendant was gone, gambled away by her husband

and probably just to spite Livia.

"I have no one to give me a massage, pluck my eyebrows, or attend to my hair," she finally said, as they pushed their way through the streets.

*****

Gaius wasn't sure whether she was speaking to him or just venting her anger at anybody who would listen. He hadn't seen her so vexed since the death of the slave boy. He knew that his mother's former slave, the one lost in the knuckle game by his father, was terribly clumsy. Everyone in the household could hear Livia's tirade when the frightened girl singed his mother's hair with the hollow curling irons. Now Livia wore a wig of black Egyptian hair, her own being treated with the newest remedy of rat droppings and pepper.

"Don't waste my time," she scowled when Gaius slowed to watch a street corner mime.

"There is a slave market past the piazza," ventured Apollodoros.

"Of course there is," Livia shot back. "That's where we're going and why you two are with me. What am I to do, buy a strange girl and take her home by myself?"

"Do you really need another slave, Mother?" Gaius asked.

"I certainly do. And I don't want to hear your nonsense about slavery."

Apollodoros looked at Gaius but said nothing.

"I don't know who's selling them today," his mother went on, "but I hope it's not the same mangone as last time. That man is such a liar."

The crowd was larger than usual when they got there, considering that many of the women and girls had already been sold. Yet many buyers still remained, and after listening to the crowd, Gaius learned it was rumored that a special lot was up for sale.

"Oh, by the gods, it's the same fool," Livia lamented. Turning to a wealthy patrician she said, "Be careful of him, he tried to sell me one he said had never tried to escape. But when her hair was parted we saw the 'F' branded on her forehead."

"Fugitive," the man shouted.

"Unscrupulous! If I had pointed it out to the authorities that mangone would be out of business," said Livia with adamant righteousness. Gaius had to stop himself from rolling his eyes.

Tall and gangling, Apollodoros pushed his way to the front of the crowd, making a path for Livia and Gaius. Upon the steps before them were eleven women and girls, some naked. Two of them, teenagers, were chained together and kept separate from the others. One of the pair, a buxom one, was quaking, and without the support of her slender companion would have sunk to her knees.

Several purchasers were slaves themselves, entrusted to buy merchandise for their masters. They viewed the women dispassionately, contemplating the best buy with the coins given them. A quaestor in charge of public funds stood behind the crowd to monitor the number of sales and remind the mangones of the sales tax. It was something Gaius knew each dealer detested, since he had already paid an import fee for every slave.

Livia was not the only domina at the auction. There were other women who needed young girls, sometimes for kitchen help or as hairdressers, and on occasion for the intimacy their husbands refused them.

"My friends," the mangone said, gesturing to his cache, "these fine specimens are mostly from our province in Lusitania and have been closely inspected for any deficiencies in health, of which, I assure you, there are none. Each is strong and obedient to a fault. I offer them at a reasonable price for the greater glory of Rome and your personal comfort."

There was an exasperated sigh from the crowd; they had all heard it before. A few snickered and rolled their eyes.

"What an ass," hissed Livia and the crowd laughed. The mangone looked about mystified, apparently not knowing what had been said or why people were laughing. He smiled sheepishly and squared his shoulders as he regained his composure.

"That one, the one with the big tits and the baby, how

much?" a fat man bellowed.

"Thirty sestercii, Excellency. See how she suckles the girl child. A fine wet nurse for your brood. Come, feel her breasts, they're quite full."

"That's what I hoped to hear. My sons would love to suck on them if they weren't in the legions, but I will do it for them!"

The crowd laughed again as the man pushed the infant away and inspected her breasts. He squeezed a nipple and was rewarded with a droplet on his finger. He tasted it and to the crowd said, "Delicious." Then, to the beaming auctioneer he said, "I'll give you twenty sestercii and four denarii, but I don't want the child."

"Excellency, I have no need of the child. You may have her for another three denarii."

"Yes, take them both, the baby will be ready for you in eleven years!" bellowed a man in the crowd.

The slaver laughed along with the assembled buyers.

"My offer stands," the purchaser said. "Take it or keep them both."

The mangone shrugged, and said, "The woman is sold to you, sir," then he tugged the baby from its mother's arms and thrust it into the hands of an assistant. The child, held by an arm, was taken away. The woman screamed and sank to her knees. When released from the chain that connected her to the others, she was taken down the steps and deposited at her owner's feet. Sobbing, she prostrated herself before him. The new owner motioned to his slaves, who hustled her to a waiting cart. The drama concluded, the crowd turned their attention back to the unsold slaves. Gaius had witnessed slave auctions before, but it still saddened him.

He looked to the pair he'd noticed earlier, chained together apart from the rest. It was common for all slaves to be presented nude so that any abnormalities could be seen. But it was not unusual, Gaius knew, for the slavers to leave a scrap of cloth over a woman's most intimate parts to pique buyers' curiosity and fan the bidding. The plump one was fully naked except for her cap, while her companion, who was very attractive, only had a loose piece of cloth hung about her hips. The naked one seemed to be searching for a compassionate face in the crowd, while the other, prettier girl, stared straight ahead. The girls' feet were covered in white chalk, a sign that they were from a Roman province. The titulus with its information hung from each girl's neck and partially covered one breast.

The sale of the girls and women went quickly. There was a shout of "Turn that one around and have her spread her legs," as one man closely inspected a fourteen-year-old girl. Satisfied that she was still virgin, he bid high, and grasping the girl by the elbow, propelled her through the crowd.

Finally, the two girls chained together were the only slaves left. The mangone led them to the center of the steps and forcefully said, "These two are sisters and will only be sold as a pair. This one," he said pointing to the plump slave, "is a fine cook, and the pretty one grows tasty herbs. An excellent combination for the cena."

"My master doesn't care about the herbs," said a slave. "He's interested in her tits, and he can't see them through that sign."

Obediently, the mangone lifted the titulus, and the master and his slave wormed their way through a knot of men.

"Fifty sestercii," the slave bellowed, holding up a bag of coins.

"For both? This one alone is worth ten times that," the auctioneer retorted while grasping the slender girl's breasts.

"Fifty-five sestercii," another called.

The mangone nodded and answered, "A worthy start. Now let's have a serious bid for this lovely and her yummy sister. Surely the thighs of the plump one will keep you warm on those cold winter nights. And you, sir," he said, singling out a wealthy patrician, "what a delectable pleasure it would be to have them both attend to your requirements at the same time."

Gaius noticed the attractive slave girl raise her head and look at the leering faces before her: faces impatient to see what was hidden.

The girl's eyes settled upon him when the slaver removed

the cloth covering her sex. Certainly he was staring at her. He had heard one hopeful bidder say that she had beauty to make the gods weep with pleasure. But Gaius looked at her and felt only sadness.

*****

There was a murmur as the crowd pressed forward and Livia scowled as she was jostled. A man, his hand outstretched, tried to push past her, but Apollodoros blocked his way. Then the Greek elbowed Gaius, who pried his gaze off the girl and said, "Mother, she understands Latin. You could speak to her."

"Why should I care that she speaks Latin? And I doubt that the fat one with her can speak at all."

"Mistress," Apollodoros offered, "a good cook could be of great value to you."

"And the slender one appears intelligent, Mother," added her son. "You might find her very helpful."

Livia glared at him. "You want me to buy her because she's pretty, don't you? I know what you're thinking. Don't be so stupid. I won't buy a girl because you think she's pretty. She's a slave, not a playmate."

The mangone, seeing the exchange between Apollodoros, Gaius and Livia, said, "Domina, I recognize you from before and I honor your presence. You have an excellent eye for quality. Certainly you were pleased with your last purchase from me. A striking beauty such as yourself can surely use a slave to assist your toilet, and this girl would be invaluable. And since you are a former client, I will give you both for only seventy sestercii: a true bargain."

"Far too much, Mistress," whispered Apollodoros. "If you want them, I would recommend sixty."

Livia searched Apollodoros's face and he nodded emphatically.

"Sixty-two sestercii is what I offer for the pair. If you don't sell them to me for that, I'll buy from someone else. Someone who doesn't cheat."

"Only sixty-two?" the auctioneer said, making a show of disbelief. "Madam, surely you see that they are worth more than that."

"Sixty-five sestercii and five denarii," shouted a man.

Livia watched through narrowed eyes as the slender girl looked toward the high bidder. The slave's resolve crumbled and like her sister, her manacled hands trembled and her knees buckled. Quickly the auctioneer jerked the girl upright. Gaius took a step forward, but Apollodoros put a restraining hand on his shoulder.

"What do you think you're doing? You don't own her," the Greek said, bending to Gaius's ear. Livia sighed in irritation. This was the son the gods had graced her with.

Gaius wrested himself from Apollodoros's grasp and tersely said, "Buy her, Mother."

The girl's look of terror shifted from the high bidder holding aloft his bag of coins back to Livia and her son.

Livia peered at the boy, a cynical look on her face. She tilted her head and sneered, "Oh, I thought you didn't approve of buying slaves. A sudden change of heart?"

He stood a foot taller than she but her scathing look cut like a knife. She pointed a finger at him and said, "If you're wrong about the girls you will pay, and pay dearly. You will pay me back double."

"As you wish, Mother. I will pay you back, I promise."

"And if I buy her it will be for me, not you. I had to sell some of my jewelry to get the money," she added as an afterthought.

"I will buy the jewelry back for you," Gaius said, his attention riveted on the girls.

"You don't have any money," Livia hissed. She took a few steps forward and looked at the two slaves as if she was evaluating them for the first time.

"Seventy sestercii and six denarii," Livia said in her shrill voice.

"A fine offer, madam, and I will—"

"One hundred and ten sestercii!" a man bellowed from the back. There was a gasp, and Livia went rigid with shock and fear. The mangone stopped in mid-sentence and scanned the crowd. In the rear a heavyset patrician held aloft a silk bag of coins. Surrounded by the mob, neither Livia nor the two men could see the bidder, but the voice made all three of them cringe.

*****

"Come forward, good sir," said the mangone as his assistants made an effort to part the crowd. The awestruck observers made way as the obese man slapped the coins into the slaver's hand. The patrician turned his gaze on Livia and Gaius, his face a mask of hatred, while ankle chains were struck. Grasping the wrist manacles, Toronius pulled the girls from the steps. The heavy one collapsed but was roughly pulled to her feet.

"Walk," the dominus commanded, with a slap across her face. As Toronius passed Livia, he rasped, "These are mine. All mine. I will attend to you later."

The girls, clearly terrified by their buyer, were whisked past Gaius and an astonished Livia.

Never had Gaius remembered Livia holding on to him since he had been a child. Now, she clung to his arm, appearing smaller than ever.

Livia, Gaius, and Apollodoros followed Toronius several blocks until he tired of holding the girl's chains.

"Apollodoros," he called, "take them to the house." Then, turning to Livia and Gaius, he said, "You two will stay in your cubiculi, and don't you dare leave the villa." Handing the girls to Apollodoros, he added, "I have questions for you, too."

That said, Toronius turned down a side street filled with popinas, where pretty girls offered a variety of prepared foods as well as themselves.

"He must know someone there. Another crooked bastard," Livia said to Gaius. Her voice was shrill though he could see her fighting for composure.

"I don't know. Perhaps he's going to speak to his old friend Vircipius."

"That old man doesn't know anything except silk. He's not going to see Vircipius. I think he's going to plan a murder."

"Of whom?" said Gaius.

Livia simply looked at him and said nothing. Livia, his mother, who had been so indomitable and forthright on her way to the Forum slave market, now walked as if dragged by invisible ropes. Her whole body quaked, and Gaius was afraid she would actually fall.

"I know you must feel betrayed, having sold your valuables to get the money," Gaius said, trying to comfort her. "I don't know why Father would have done such a thing. Do you?"

She looked at him for a long moment, then slowly shook her head.

"Perhaps because you hid from him last night. That must be it. A sort of revenge," Gaius said.

"Yes, because I hid from him. Surely that's why," she said, vigorously nodding her head. "I shouldn't have hidden from him," she repeated as if reinforcing the thought.

Gaius had seen his mother shaking before but it was always from rage, either against a slave, Toronius, or Gaius himself. But the look in her eyes told him that the trembling was due to something very different. There would always be angry words, but that was common at the villa. But as they pushed their way past the apothecaries, the barbers, the scribes, and the street-corner priests, Gaius saw that his mother was afraid. In fact, she was terrified—more so than he had ever seen.

Because Gaius and his mother had been walking slowly, Apollodoros and the girls had become separated from them. Gaius could only catch glimpses of them until they began to ascend the hill to the villa. The tall, stooped Greek was pulling them along as if they were going to their death. The little cap and the placards had been removed, and Gaius surmised that the heavy girl had little idea of what would happen next. She constantly looked at her sister for reassurance.

At one point, Gaius saw the pretty sister turn around, causing Apollodoros to falter. The thick curls danced around her face, and for just a moment she glanced at Gaius. He stopped and stared back as his mother trudged on. He suddenly realized that with this girl in the household nothing would ever be the same. What had been a difficult existence would now become one of total rage, and this girl, this slave, would be at the center of it all.

Chapter 5

"Have you seen your father this morning?" Livia asked Gaius as they stood in the peristyle.

"Not today, Mother."

"He's been gone three days, ever since he bought the girls. He's never been gone that long unless it's for antiques and he wouldn't go without Apollodoros. It's very strange. He's up to something and doesn't want us to know about it."

"He didn't say anything to me," Gaius said looking toward Caladria and Aspacia, who stood together by the kitchen.

Livia looked down her nose at him. "Why would he say anything to you?"

Gaius shrugged and said, "No reason. He hasn't spoken to me since Alexandria."

"Alexandria again," Livia said with disgust. "He never told me what happened there. I really want to know, especially if we're in danger. I've asked Apollodoros and he won't tell me a thing."

"He feels that he has to be loyal to his master. I was there, but all I'll say is that Father hurt someone."

"A woman?"

"A young woman, yes. That's why he's been acting that way," Gaius volunteered.

"He's afraid of a girl in Egypt? How can she be any threat to him?"

"She has friends."

"So? Egypt is a long way from Rome."

"Not if her friends are here."

"And he thinks they are?" Livia asked with incredulity.

"He had me and Apollodoros look for them. I think he's afraid."

"Is that so? Maybe it would teach him. Maybe he's as afraid as I am."

"Afraid because of the other night?"

She stiffened and stared at her son, but said nothing. Gaius again looked at the girls. They were huddled together watching, not knowing what was expected of them.

Then Gaius said, "Why do you think Father outbid you at the auction? He could have bought any slave girl for half the price."

"Spite. Spite is a terrible weapon. But I will use those girls just as if I bought them."

"Which one did your hair this morning?" Gaius asked, looking at his mother's perfect coiffure.

"The one who calls herself Aspacia. The other is only fit for the kitchen and yard work. Now that I think of it, I want my garden replanted; they could start on that. I want you to show them what fruit to pick in the orchard and what to gather in the field. And make sure that girl knows a vegetable from a weed. She may not know anything, since that mangone lies about everything."

"I'll show them this morning," Gaius said enthusiastically. He thought about it for a moment and said, "Of course, they are Father's slaves, not yours or mine. He'll do whatever he wants with them when he returns."

Livia sniffed, turned away then said, "If he returns."

Unconsciously her hand went to the top of her stola and she felt the bag of coins hidden beneath the cloth. She would not buy anything now, at least nothing that costly. Did Toronius know where she got the money? she wondered. She'd mentioned to Gaius that she had sold her jewels. He could vouch for that if need be. Of course if Toronius didn't know of the theft, she could put the money back and he would be none the wiser. She might return it eventually. No, on second thought, she would have Arzeka put it back. But he would want to be paid. In kind. Although she fantasized about the barbarian, she wasn't sure that she would be safe with him. Who knew how many diseases he might have? And the man hadn't bathed in years.

*****

With wariness the girls followed Gaius into the orchard where the figs and apples had ripened during the long summer days. He wished more than ever that he was four months older, so that he could wear a toga and appear as a grown man, not a youth still wearing the child's good luck charm. He was unsure if he should affect a casual air or an imperious one, being the eventual inheritor of all their surroundings.

He looked at the girls, who stared back at him with uncertainty. Gaius's attention naturally focused on Aspacia; her green eyes were riveting. So riveting, in fact, that he stood there mute and transfixed, wondering how to begin.

Finally, with an exasperated look on her face, she tilted her head and raised her eyebrows at him. Gaius felt his face redden and quickly turned away. Then with sudden resolution, he strode to a tree and snatched its fruit. Turning to the girls he said, "Apple." He repeated it slowly, then handed one to each of them. Caladria, the simple-minded one, studied it, seeming not to know whether she was to eat it or simply examine it.

"Yes, it's an apple, Master Gaius," said Aspacia, in flawless Latin. "I presume it's Gaius. At least that's what I heard your mother call you." Then, pointing she said, "And that's a fig tree, that one's a pomegranate, over there you have some legumes and some peas. They need water if you expect to harvest them." She stared back at him and gave a self-satisfactory smile as if to say, "I may be a slave, but I know as much as you do about such things, and I bet I'm smarter than you, too."

Taken aback by her audacity, Gaius glanced at Caladria and said, "You can eat the apple. You can eat all the apples you want, as long as you don't make a show of it in front of my parents."

Aspacia nodded to her sister and uttered a few words in Andalusian. The girl took a bite but said nothing. Gaius nodded his approval.

"She only knows a few words in Latin. I will teach her more if you wish."

"That would be helpful, since my mother will be having her cook and we don't speak..."

"Andalusian, Master. Andalusia is a part of Spain. We had a nice village—once. The Roman legion burned it to the ground."

Obviously she wasn't accustomed to behaving like a slave, he thought. Not showing proper respect could put her in danger, but all he said was, "I'm sorry for what happened to your village."

"Since you're being so consoling, Master Gaius, you might consider that my parents were also enslaved and now they are dead," Aspacia said vehemently. "And now I assume I must call you 'Master,' since I'm a slave here. Of course you know everything about me from the placard I wore around my neck."

Gaius thought she had good cause to be bitter, but there was nothing he could do about it. As he was a Roman, he doubted that she would ever like him, but he did not want her as an enemy. She stood quite still as if awaiting his reaction. Perhaps she wasn't aware of how savagely a slave could be beaten for such impertinence. Certainly, he thought she couldn't know if he was hiding a vindictive streak, but having suffered so much, maybe she really didn't care. After all, a little more torment wouldn't make much difference now.

"You're my father's slave," said Gaius. "He will insist that you call him 'Master.' I don't enjoy being called that."

"How noble of you," she said, her arms crossed. "I expect that my sister and I will be slaves here for the rest of our lives, so why don't you tell us what we have to do, unless you want to beat us or something."

"I'm not going to beat you!" Damn, Gaius thought, maybe he should just give her instructions and stay away from her. There wasn't going to be any reconciliation here. He knew so little about women and what he did know was discouraging. There was no sense trying to reason with the girl. Vercipius, his father's friend, had told him never to argue with women. He said that "if you win you still lose, and if you lose you will experience nothing but calamity". And now, just looking at the petite girl with the heart-shaped face and black bouncing curls told him that he was already on the cusp of disaster. He swallowed hard and took a deep breath.

"Yes, Aspacia, I know your name," he said, his mind already a gooey morass. Worse yet, she knew that he had fallen all over himself. If only she wasn't so damn bewitching. They must be born that way—able to make men appear like fools.

Maybe he should try again, he thought. "I am quite literate in both Latin and Greek. You do know what Greek is, don't you?" he said, immediately wishing he had phrased it differently.

"Of course I do. My father was a scholar and he taught me quite well, Master Gaius. In fact I can likely speak it better than you," she said, her green eyes flashing.

The girl is so presumptuous, so stubborn, he thought. *"Master Gaius" again.* There would be no prisoners, no mercy and certainly no love. A few more minutes of this and he would be eviscerated.

Gaius stared at the ground for a moment; he no longer wished to spar with the girl, but she should know what he thought. Not that it would make any difference, her parents dead and a life of drudgery before her, but he said, "I do not believe in slavery. I know that such a view in our world is uncommon and perhaps even dangerous. I had nothing to do with your enslavement. In fact I might have liked to know you before all this happened. But unfortunately you are slaves. I will tolerate your audacity because I can imagine what a terrible thing has happened to you. But you must be careful about what you say, for your own sake and that of your sister."

"That's a sweet sentiment, Master Gaius, but you can't begin to imagine what we have been through," she retorted. "Everyone in our village was killed or enslaved. A month ago we were innocent townsfolk. Some farmers made a terrible decision and Roman soldiers were killed. We were all blamed and now our lives are ruined. We are your slaves and I know that we have to adapt. But it's so hard. If all was normal I would like to see the Forum markets and the gardens my father spoke of. I would like to see the plays and hear the music and do all the things any girl would want to do. But now that's impossible. If I walk out that gate and I'm caught, I will be branded or killed. You think about that, Master Gaius, before you try to impress me. I am a slave; don't you dare try to romance me!"

Her terror had suddenly become palpable, and any attempt at congeniality had vanished. Nothing could come of his playful thoughts, Gaius realized, and it was ludicrous to think otherwise. He felt disgusted that he had begun to have any feelings for her. Certainly she would have no regard for him, and she truly hated Romans.

Gaius glanced at her, looked away, and stiffly said, "Until my father returns, my mother will tell you what to do. She will expect you to behave like a slave, and a very subservient one. Do not contradict her. Do not correct her. And never, never speak to my father in the way that you have spoken to me. Do you understand?"

In a subdued voice, she said, "Of course. May I ask when your father is coming? We haven't seen him since the—"

"I don't know," Gaius said abruptly. "Now I will show you where we keep our garden rakes and hoes."

There was nothing more to be said. His pleasantry had been rebuffed. As far as he was concerned, the two girls would be treated like all the others. They would subsist, do the chores, and be considered nothing more than human property. It was the last time he would make a fool of himself, he vowed.

Aspacia looked past the orchard and fields to a distant barn beside the far wall.

"Do you keep animals in that?" she said pointing to the barn.

"No, it's all broken up. But one of our slaves sleeps in there to guard that part of the property. Never, ever go near that barn."

Earlier Gaius had a dozen questions he'd wanted to ask her. Now he wondered what he could have possibly been thinking.

The thought of his father came to mind. He wondered what

had made him so angry and vengeful, to outbid his mother and buy the slaves for himself. That morning the Dominus had appeared gracious to his clients. It was a practiced façade, he'd even seemed affable, but something must have happened in the intervening hours. Of course Toronius would never say anything about what had transpired. But something quite horrible must have happened. And though Gaius had dismissed the girls as simply additional slaves, he wondered what might befall them when the dominus returned.

They walked back to the atrium in silence. Conversationally Gaius had nothing more to say and, irritated, just wanted to get away. Finally he said, "I suggest that you ask my mother what she wants for dinner. Fortunately we aren't expecting any guests tonight so you shouldn't have much work to do." Then despite his determination not to talk he said, "I have to meet with Apollodoros. He's teaching me elocution."

"For what?"

"Law, of course. I intend to be an attorney." Why, he wondered, was he telling her this? She had made it clear that she despised him. Was he trying to impress her again? What stupidity.

"Is Apollodoros the tall, skinny man?" Aspacia asked.

Gaius really did not want to answer but she persisted and said, "Is he a libertus?"

"No, he's a slave." He was about to add, "just like you," but decided that such a hurt was unnecessary. "My father bought him before I was born. He's an honest man and quite intelligent. You can trust him."

"With what?" Aspacia asked. "I have nothing to entrust to anybody, Master Gaius."

He looked at her for a moment and said, "Yeah, I guess you're right." Then he walked away.

*****

"He is nice," Caladria said after Gaius had left. "He gave us apples."

"He's a boy and just another master. He can do nothing for

us Caladria. Nothing at all."

"He's very handsome."

"Handsome, I guess, but it's useless to even think about that."

"He acts just like the boys did in our village," said Caladria. "I mean when they would try to talk to you. Their words turn to mush and their voices get all wobbly. I think it's because you are so pretty."

"I don't care if he thinks I'm pretty," Aspacia replied. But she thought Gaius's warning was not that of an immature youth, and its weight hung around her neck like a great stone.

"Now we better find his mother before she screams in that awful voice."

*****

After a three-day trek, Toronius and his client Plinius arrived at decayed village of Ardea, twenty-three miles south of Rome, and hid their bullock cart in the barn of an abandoned villa. It had been years since the owners had moved away, and weeds grew everywhere. The Via Ardeatina, the road they had taken, meandered to the port of Latium. The town had once been an important trading center until a Samite raid three hundred years earlier. The port town never recovered and was eventually abandoned. On occasion, the military patrols marched along the rugged coast looking for smugglers.

"Stay in the shadows," cautioned Plinius. He pointed toward a citadel on a plateau rising above the village. "It's sometimes manned by a cohort. We wouldn't want them to know we're here."

"I've never been here," Toronius said, sweating more from nervousness than the sweltering heat.

"We'll be meeting my cousin Vitonius tonight when the tide is low," said Plinius, as he gazed at shattered pillars that once supported a thriving market.

They scurried to a deserted fisherman's cottage and Toronius sank onto a rough wooden bench. "You say he's bringing six, all men?"

"Yes, from Antipatras, north of Jerusalem. They were

fugitives, captured and sold several times. Rough men, but we can sell them for the games or farm work. You know what they say on the farms, 'there are two kinds of animals, those that speak and those that don't.'"

"But they're chained, right?"

"Of course they're chained. We'll keep them in here for the night, then leave at dawn. I'm sure that Vitonius knows people who will buy them, and he will write a document showing that taxes and import duties have been paid. We'll make a good profit, Dominus."

From the house, Toronius could see the fort. He could also make out a crumbling temple high on a hill.

The fisherman's house stank of fish, unwashed bodies, and mold. Slaves had been imprisoned here before, Toronius surmised. Embedded in the walls were iron bolts, and the scent of the sea and remains of animal feces could not overcome the stench of chained men and women.

"There will be a new moon tonight, not enough light for anyone to see us down by the cove," said Plinius. "Just be sure you bring the Egyptian piece."

"But it will be too dark for him to see it," Toronius said.

"Vitonius trusts me as I trust you, Dominus. That's all it requires."

Toronius nodded affirmatively, but suddenly wondered how much trust he should put in his eager client.

*****

It was past midnight when they left the house and made their way down a craggy inlet to the beach. Low tide revealed the remains of a pier, and algae-encrusted columns that had once proclaimed the entrance to the harbor. They waited, the salty dampness of the evening air chilling them despite their cloaks. A sail emerged from the mists, the pale sliver of moon barely illuminating it for the briefest moment. The small boat rose with an incoming wave then dipped into a trough. It rose again and with a pull at its oars, slid onto the pebbled beach.

Plinius embraced his cousin and led him to Toronius, who

anxiously joined them. He tried to make out the faces of the slaves, but in the near darkness they appeared indistinct. He then turned his attention to Vitonius, bowed slightly and saw a man hardened by years at sea. It wouldn't surprise him at all if the man had a criminal past, as well.

"This is for you," the dominus said, gently placing the god in Vitonius's hands. "It's a true treasure," Toronius insisted.

"Of course," Vitonius said. "We will talk further in a few months when I get to Rome. I want to see the other pieces in your collection. But now I want to offload the slaves. We'll help you get them to the house, then I must get out to sea."

Vitonius hurried back to the boat and reappeared with two sailors and six shackled men. A heavy length of chain encircled the men's feet, and their hands were bound behind them with rope. The climb up the rocks was steep; when a captive slipped, the sailor guards struck him with a whip that snapped with a loud crack.

"No noise," Vitonius hissed.

They entered the small room, closed the door, and lit an oil lamp. The slaves were chained to the wall's rings bolts and made to sit on the floor, its ancient mosaics weathered and chipped. Vitonius and Plinius made certain that the chains were well secured "I'll be off now," said Vitonius, and scurried down the rocks as he began his descent to the beach. The oars made no sound over the crashing of the waves against the shore, and in a few moments the vessel was gone.

A fog rolled in, and Toronius shivered as he settled onto the remains of a mattress once home to a family of mice.

"I think we should leave at first light," Plinius said. "There is a rarely traveled road we can take to the outskirts of Rome. I know a farmer, a very wealthy one, who might buy these men. His name is Sentillus and he always needs slaves." He gave a little laugh and said, "I hear they don't last very long with him. I guess he works them to death."

Toronius nodded sleepily. Plinius dozed off after seeing that the captives had done the same. One of the men moaned and clutched his stomach.

"Is he sick?" asked Toronius waking from a deep slumber.

"I'll see," answered Plinius, standing and approaching the bearded man. The weak flame of the oil lamp flickered over a half-dozen men, all now awake. Suddenly, he saw an iron bar pulled from inside a slave's tunic. In an instant the chain was parted and the men sprang to their feet, leapt forward, and fell upon Plinius. He screamed as fists and the iron bar found their mark. Shadows played upon the wall in a dance of violence. One man lunged for Toronius but tripped over a long discarded fishing net. Toronius tore himself away from grasping hands, ripped the door open and stumbled outside. In the confusion and the amazement of their sudden freedom, none of the slaves pursued him.

Unarmed as he was, there was nothing that would entice him to go back inside. Toronius gathered his toga about him and ran into the darkness, tumbling over unseen rocks, rising and hurrying on again. Plinius's moans became fainter then ceased all together.

Toronius passed the edge of the village and stumbled into the night. It had become a nightmare, he thought, and surely Plinius was dead. Worse, those who had attacked him were no longer captives. They were desperate, dangerous men who would plunder and vanish into the countryside. They might even search for Toronius, a wealthy Roman whose coinage could carry them far. A cold sweat engulfed him and he berated himself for being so foolish, so naïve to the dangers Plinius had glossed over.

He should have had somebody else take the risk, he thought. The whole venture had been dicey to begin with. That they were engaging in an illegal enterprise did not particularly bother him; most of his endeavors were shady. But this particular one could have gotten him killed and Plinius, had he lived, would have never have said a word. In the end, this was all Plinius's fault. *Yes*, thought the dominus, *Plinius got what he deserved and his body will be devoured by rats.*

For a fleeting moment, Toronius considered alerting the authorities to the presence of escaped slaves, but there would be questions. *Where did you see them*, they would ask, and *why were you in such a deserted place so late at night?* His answers would raise suspicions, and might implicate him in a crime against Rome. Dominus or not, the penalties would be greater than a simple fine. Rome needed to make examples of those who broke the law; a public execution could not be ruled out.

Bruised and exhausted, Toronius huddled in a scraggly copse of trees for the remainder of the night. With dawn, keeping to a cattle trail, he began his walk. At one point a patrol of legionnaires passed, but failed to see him as he hid in an outcrop of weather-beaten stones. He hoped, by dusk, to reach one of the many villages outside the city and bed down for the night in a proper inn. Then he would make his way to Rome, and that would be the end of this ill-fated adventure.

The sun broke through the morning fog and Toronius plodded on. It was a near thing, he told himself, but not every venture was successful. Everything would be all right in the end, despite the loss of the Egyptian idol figure. There were ways to make up the loss; he still had other valuable pieces. He would host a gala event, a cena that would be extolled by everyone.

The sun warmed Toronius, and he began to feel invigorated. He had escaped disaster, and there were things to look forward to. Indeed, he remembered that there were two new girls at his villa for his enjoyment. He felt young again, and he hastened his pace.

And then he abruptly stopped.

Plinius was a braggart who associated with important men. A venture like this was too lucrative to keep secret. Who had he let in on it? Who would suspect him when Plinius failed to return from his latest trip?

The dominus pondered the possible complication, but now he walked a little more slowly and much more afraid.

*****

"Arzeka, are you there?" Livia called, a tremor in her voice.

The man emerged from the depths of the barn like a specter.

He had the odor of long-dead animals, and his matted hair and beard stuck out like wire.

"What does the woman want from me now? Or does she wish to give me something special?" He leaned into her, one white eye pointing into nothingness. He offered her a crooked smile, and there was a hole where teeth should have been.

"These coins must be returned before my husband comes back; it has to be done tonight. You have to do it."

"And what if I refuse?"

"I will—"

"You will tell the Dominus that you had me steal them for you? That would make for an interesting evening."

"You wouldn't do that."

"Really? You still owe me from last time. Have you forgotten?"

"No, of course not," Livia stammered. "I just needed more time. I will give you—"

"Exactly what I desire," he said, finishing her sentence. "And I will have my payment now. The time you needed has run out."

Only inches away, his rancid breath enveloped her, yet she could not run. In the faint moonlight Arzeka grabbed Livia's nightdress with one hand. He shoved the other beneath her and carried her like prey into the deepest recesses of the barn. He ripped off the frail cloth that covered her and hurled her onto his fetid bedding. Livia shrieked but her protestations were decidedly brief.

The Berber wore nothing other than a loincloth and she tore it off, her long nails ripping across his flesh. His tongue and hot breath were between her thighs. She squealed, her pelvis rising and falling as she clutched at him. Her legs wrapped about his waist, and she pulled him forward with a sudden and desperate need. The Berber's heat ravaged her and her scream penetrated the darkness of the night. She was insistent on having her lust satisfied. Her energy seemed boundless as she tore at his flesh, her mouth sucking at his tongue, his stink and their sweat drenching them beyond the cusp of sanity.

She was oblivious to whomever might hear and Arzeka, the wild man banished to the decrepit shack, abandoned himself to her delirious rapture. She felt herself thrown upon the ground and enjoyed the thrill of her trembling flesh until their orgasms left them in exhausted heaps.

Immobile from his exertions, Arzeka lay atop Livia with his mouth hanging open and his legs sticky. Livia's eyes scanned his emaciated, pestilential body and, her lust satiated, she shuddered. He was the foulest thing she had laid eyes on, and when he finally looked down at her with smug satisfaction all over his face, she felt utter revulsion.

Livia had lost all track of time, but saw by the shadows that the moon was high and knew that everyone in the villa would be asleep. She stood and made an effort to wrap her shredded stola about her.

"It's time," she said. "I'll watch like before. We must do it quickly, before anybody wakes."

The man grunted, and it was obvious to Livia that he did not want to leave the barn and the alluring vision of her naked body. Livia, however, was growing anxious and impatient. She finished dressing and peered out the barn's half-open door. There was no motion; no one was yet awake.

Arzeka rose slowly and reached for his loincloth. Lying beside it was a long, smooth object. He picked it up, saw that Livia's back was turned and studied the object in a shaft of moonlight. A hairpin, an elegantly carved ivory pin had fallen from her coiffure. He slipped on a nightshirt and tucked the pin in its folds. He loathed his assignment but a possibility had presented itself.

Passing through the orchard, peristyle, and atrium, they entered the silent villa. As Arzeka surmised, all seemed asleep. Toronius's son slumbered in his narrow room. Only Apollodoros, stationed at the front gate, was up, but he could not see inside the villa. As usual, the door of the tablinum was unlocked, and Livia placed herself beside it.

Lighting an oil lamp, Arzeka slipped inside and lifted the stone covering. Just like the previous break-in, an assembly of sticks fell into the bottom of the pit but this time Arzeka would not worry about it. The woman was not looking at him; her attention was focused elsewhere, on guard against any sounds in the house. He extracted the chest and placed it on the table, then lifted the lid and refilled the pilfered bags. Removing the sticks from the pit, he replaced the chest and spilled the sticks into their slot between the side of the vault and the treasure box. Then he dropped the hairpin amid the fallen sticks.

"Are you done yet? You're taking too long," Livia hissed.

"Almost," he said, but he wasn't. After a moment's hesitation he reopened the lid of the chest. In addition to the coins, there were still four more Egyptian sculptures, each cocooned in silk. He slid one out, unwrapped it, and peered at it in the faint glow of the lamp. Its gold and lapis lazuli inlays glistened and its coal black eyes stared back at him from some ancient past. He already had one of them, a strange looking thing, horrible to look at. He, a Berber of the Maghreb, worshipped nothing like these bestial images. His sacred god was Ifri, the deity of the cave, the home and the sun. To Arzeka the carvings were ghoulish idols, an insult to his one true god, but he knew that others valued them beyond measure. To Arzeka they were wealth. They could buy him anything. Including escape.

He already had the Isis. He would take just one more. Arzeka hurried now as the Roman slut, impatient as always, hissed at him. Let her hiss, he thought, it would be she who would be blamed. He knew all about Toronius; the man would beat or execute her for the theft. But he, the rider of the Maghreb, would escape and have all the women he ever craved.

Hiding the god thing in his nightshirt, he silently closed the lid of the chest. He placed the heavy stone over it, rose, and brushed past the domina. She did not see his smirk as he scurried back to the darkness of his hovel.

Nor did he see Aspacia who, lying beside a stairwell, watched him disappear into the night.

*****

Livia closed the door, replaced the key to the treasure box, and stealthily padded to her room. Surely, it had all worked out. Toronius would never know of the theft. She closed her eyes and felt herself drift into slumber knowing that everything would be just fine.

*****

The first light of dawn had crept over the hills of Rome when there was an insistent knocking on the front gate. Gaius, a light sleeper, wrapped himself in a cloak against the chilly dawn and hastened out. He joined Apollodoros just as the man slid open the gate's heavy bolt.

"Hurry," a voice said from the road.

The gate swung open, and Gaius was stunned to see Appian Dio standing before him. Before Gaius could react Appian said, "Your father is with me."

Gaius looked toward an ox-driven cart and saw his father climb out. With a hollow look, Toronius lumbered past him without speaking.

"I don't understand. Where was he and why is he with you?"

"Give me a minute and let's get the cart inside."

"I thought you were still in training."

"I am. The optio, the assistant to my centurion, called me into his office and showed me a note. It said that my mother had died. I was given a four-day leave to attend to her body. She had been dead for at least a week. The Dominus wrote the note."

"My father took a letter to your camp?"

"No, he had it sent by courier. He wasn't anywhere near Campus Martius. The Dominus was hiding in my mother's house... with her corpse. He's the one who found her."

"How bizarre. What was he doing in the insula?"

"That's not the half of it."

"Come in, you must be thirsty."

"I'm thirsty and I'm starving."

Apollodoros led the ox and cart into the yard and closed the gate. Then he brought Appian Dio a tankard of beer and a thick slice of bread, and returned to the gate.

"Should I wake my mother?" Gaius asked, looking at Appian; his friend seemed older and more resolute than before.

"No, I think only you should know about this, at least for now." He took a gulp of the thick malt and said, "By the way, are you still pissed at me?"

"Not so much now. I've found out a lot in the last few months. My mother's had quite a lineup of men, and you just happened to be one in a very long line."

"Well that's comforting and informative," Appian Dio said. "Actually I haven't had time to think of women, believe it or not. They work us to death. I know the training will be over in five months, if I live through it."

"That bad?"

"You have no idea. It's brutal, Gaius, but I love it. We have the best damn army in the world. I'll tell you about it someday."

"If you survive."

"Yeah."

"Now tell me about my father. Why was he at your mother's house?"

"I'm not sure. He wouldn't say much, but he'd been on the run, and he was a mess when I got to the flat. He hadn't been shaved and his toga was..." Appian Dio looked about then said quietly, "filthy and splattered with blood."

"His blood?"

"No, he wasn't stabbed or anything. It was someone else's blood. And he wasn't the same. You know, loud, the all-important dominus, lord of the villa. He was afraid, cowering, refusing to leave the flat until dark. He even hid under a blanket in the cart. He didn't want to go with me when I buried my mother, although he offered to pay for the professional wailers. I told him it wasn't necessary. She caused me plenty of wailing over the years. You know that."

"I'm sorry about your mother," Gaius said.

"Don't be. Her last years were miserable. She's better off now even if she is in a pauper's grave."

Gaius was silent for a moment, then said, "I told you about Alexandria, and how people may be looking for him. I never thought he was so scared as to hide in your mother's house. Is there some other reason for him to be afraid?"

"I don't know. I could hardly get a word out of him, but on the way here he repeated the name 'Plinius'. 'Oh that miserable Plinius,' he kept saying."

"Plinius Apuleius Regulus, my father's client? The name dropper?"

"It's possible. What other Plinius did he know?"

"None that I'm aware of. Plinius used to brag about all the great deals he had going and all the important people he knew. Do you think it was Plinius's blood?"

Appian Dio shrugged. "Well, Plinius never misses breakfast here and the sharing of a scheme with Toronius. If he doesn't show up..."

Appian Dio chewed on the bread while Gaius drank his beer.

"Beside the possible death of Plinius, what else is new?" Appian Dio asked.

"We have two new girls."

"Slaves or relatives?"

"Slaves. My mother tried to buy them, but my father outbid her. One of them is very pretty. I kind of like her."

"So you are smitten with one of your father's slaves. Obviously you're planning to commit suicide."

"I didn't say I'm in love with her. I just like her, that's all. If you stick around you could see her. Her name is Aspacia. She speaks very good Latin."

"Oh, that's lovely. You're still the idiot I've always known. Write to me just before your father lights you on fire. I wish I could stay, I never tire of yummy girls, but I have to get back. Missing morning formation is a serious thing, my friend. But I get leave when I finish training. We'll talk more then, if you're still alive," he said.

They walked to the gate and in a solemn voice, Appian Dio said, "Be careful with your father. My gut tells me that something's going on, and it may be even worse than Alexandria."

Gaius stopped and said, "Appian, does he still have the toga, the bloody one?"

"No, he gave me money to buy a new one for him. We burned the other."

"No evidence."

Toronius sat in the atrium for three days and spoke to no one. He was given a wide berth, and on the fourth day he was seen walking through the orchard speaking to himself. From the columned peristyle, Gaius and Apollodoros watched. There were no breakfasts with clients, even though most knocked on the gate hoping that the Dominus would entertain them as usual. Several inquired as to his health, but were assured that there was no problem. Few were convinced.

*****

Another week had passed when Apollodoros found Caladria and Aspacia in the kitchen.

"The Dominus wants to see both of you. He's in his cubiculum," said the Greek.

"Do you know why he wants to see us?" asked Aspacia.

"He confides to me only in matters of business, and I presume this is not about business. At least not business I'll be involved with," he added under his breath. "Follow me; he doesn't tolerate tardiness from anyone, especially female slaves."

The word "slaves" struck Aspacia like a slap. She recalled the hatred Toronius had launched against his wife at the auction and how, pointing to Caladria and herself, he had said, "They're mine!" Aspacia shuddered.

It had been two weeks since they had seen him and though Livia had been demanding with the garden, the kitchen, and her daily makeup, Aspacia had experienced no violence. On days when she was told to pick fruit in the garden it seemed not unlike the days in Lusitania when she did similar chores for her parents. On rare occasion she even put aside the thought of bondage.

And then there was the boy, Gaius, whose eyes followed her.

She really didn't know what to think of him, or whether she should think about him at all. He tried hard to appear indifferent. Aspacia could see a sensitive person in Gaius, and in a way she wished that she had not hurt him. She knew that he would have been quite helpful, if things had started out differently. From time to time he caught her eye then turned away. He was certainly handsome, she thought, but it would be useless to include him in her thoughts.

The death of her parents and the thought of being a slave for the rest of her life consumed her. There was no place in her heart for anyone but her sister, she told herself. Beyond that there was no heart at all.

"Dominus, the girls are here," Apollodoros announced, knocking on the door. He ushered them into the cramped bedroom. Aspacia, shut inside Toronius's room, suddenly felt terrified. Caladria, upon seeing the corpulent dominus, grasped Aspacia's hand and hunched inward.

Aspacia knew that Gaius's room was next to his father's. She looked about fearfully when Apollodoros announced her arrival, and saw Gaius poke his head out the door. Ushered into Toronius's room, she stood rooted to the floor. Everything was claustrophobic. She wanted to scream and turned her head as Gaius glanced at Apollodoros. But the Greek said nothing, and waved a finger in front of Gaius as if in warning. Gaius stood rooted to the floor as the tall, stooped slave turned and walked away.

Toronius, still in his nightclothes, sat on his bed with the girls only a few feet from him. His face revealed nothing and he offered no greeting. "Name?" he said in a clipped voice, pointing to Caladria.

"Her name is Caladria," Aspacia offered. "She doesn't speak very much Latin, Excellency."

Toronius said, "Tell her to undress. I want to see her."

Aspacia looked at Toronius but could not form the words.

"I said undress!" he shouted, but without waiting ripped off the top of Caladria's shift. She gasped and reached to pull it up. The slap was instantaneous and Caladria screamed, her hands flying to her face.

"No," Aspacia shouted but Toronius pointed a warning finger silencing her. Then, pulling Caladria close, he tore off the rest of her clothes and studied her. The girl began to quake as he turned her about, his inspection continuing. He placed his thick hands on her and examined the flesh as he would appraise lamb presented for dinner.

Satisfied, he pointed to Aspacia. She took her sister's place before him as Toronius slipped off her clothes. Savoring the exquisiteness of it all, he did it slowly, teasingly, as if it might excite her. She made no movement and uttered no sound as his fingers explored her breasts. He squeezed them and twisted her nipples. She gasped and he raised his eyebrows as if to say, "Does that please you?"

Caladria stood in the corner of the room, her hand to her mouth staring at the fat man. He sat on his bed, his eyes wandering from Caladria to Aspacia and back again. Aspacia looked blankly at the floor, then at the walls with their erotic frescoes. Then she stared at Toronius. It was not done with impudence but rather with curiosity.

He saw the look, again raised his eyebrows, and unconsciously his tongue went to his lips. Aspacia noticed the cloth rise beneath his nightclothes and she took a step backward.

Toronius again gave them an appraising look as if to say, "Yes, you two will do just fine." Then he abruptly stood. "Go!" he barked. "Take your things and go!"

Naked, the sisters grabbed their tunics and bolted, leaving the door ajar. Aspacia held her clothes to her body and glanced at Gaius, who had remained outside the door.

He stared at her as the girls ran down the hall and into the kitchen. Toronius got up to close the door and met Gaius's eyes. Gaius said nothing, but his father, in a hushed voice, said, "They're mine and it's my right. Now don't you have something to do besides putting your ear to my door?"

"Father, I wasn't—"

"Get away from here, go play," Toronius said slamming the

door.

*****

"One of the girls dropped this," Gaius said to his mother, as she sniffed a flower in the atrium.

"They're in the kitchen. You can give it to them. I'm busy."

"I don't think they'd want to speak to anyone just now. They were in father's room. They were..."

"Yes, I know. He owns them; he can do whatever he wants, just as if they were horses or cows."

"But they're people, girls like you were. Don't you have any feelings for them?"

Livia looked from him to the garden and said, "For them, very little. And yes, I had feelings once, but they're all dried up, Gaius. No flame, no light. You don't have the slightest idea. You don't think I know how they're feeling? I'm a woman; I had to learn just like they will."

"But you're not a slave; you're a free Roman lady."

She gave him a crooked smile and said, "I hope you don't believe that. Now give me that cloth. I'll take it to them. You'll make yourself look more stupid than you are."

*****

The fear had begun to abate as time passed and no officials came to ask uncomfortable questions. Nor had the Egyptians appeared who had raided Toronius's dreams with their demonic faces. Surely, having failed to find him, they were gone by now. It was time to put Alexandria behind him. And as for the misadventure with Plinius, well, that he would forget too. Everything would go back to normal, thought Toronius as he drifted in and out of sleep.

Yes, he would recover, perhaps even find a new way to resurrect his fortune. He must think about that. There would be another great cena with all his favorite dishes and the company of wealthy and influential Equestrians who would buy the last of his treasures. He must reevaluate their worth, catalogue them in his mind and perfect the dazzling history of each piece, enhanced of course with a fair amount of hyperbole.

And then there were the girls. He had already begun to fantasize about them. Toronius rose, consigning the thrill of sex to a very special room in his mind. He strode purposefully to the tablinum and locked the door behind him. The floor tiles were as they had been; apparently no one had dared to perpetrate a second theft. Pushing his table aside, he knelt down and reached for the stone. It was not as heavy as he had thought earlier; indeed, a strong child could lift it. He would have to change that. Gingerly he began to raise the strongbox, and to his horror saw that the sticks he had carefully rearranged had once again fallen in. This time the intruder had not even tried to place them as they had been.

With trembling hands Toronius laid the box on his desk and peered back into its receptacle. Something glinted within. He reached into the pit and lifted an ivory pin, a hairpin that he had seen nearly every day for the last seventeen years. In Livia's hair.

He laid it on his desk and opened the chest. The bags of coins were again full, but something else was missing, something more valuable than all the coins put together. Surely he had not sold it, he thought, his mind reeling. The statuette of Toth was far too valuable to leave on display or show to a lowly client. But it was gone, and the one who took it wore the gold pin in her hair.

Slamming down the lid he snatched up the hairpin and bolted down the steps of the tablinum. The scream, "Livia!" could be heard throughout the villa.

Chapter 6

"I didn't do it!" Livia wailed for a third time. "You said there is a heavy rock above the chest. Do you think I can lift that? I told you, I sold my jewels to buy the girls."

Livia, Toronius and Gaius stood immobile in the atrium. Toronius had his wife against a marble pillar, his hand clutching her arm.

"You're lying! You still have jewels; I saw them on you when I came back."

"I only have a few left. I saved them to wear at the cena. I have to have something on me or they'll think we're poor. Who in the Equestrian class will buy from the poor?"

She tried to free herself from his grasp, but he wouldn't let go.

"Father, on the way to the slave auction I heard mother say that she sold her jewels. She's not lying," Gaius said.

Toronius ignored Gaius but gripped Livia's arm even tighter and said, "My Isis is gone and now my Thoth. You took both of them, didn't you?"

"Thoth? What's Thoth? I don't know any Thoth."

"It's an Egyptian god, woman. An extremely valuable sculpture, and you stole it when you returned the coins. Do you know how valuable that piece is?"

"I didn't take it," Livia said, tears streaming down her face. "I wasn't anywhere near the tablinum."

"Really?" Toronius said, his voice becoming strangely calm, almost conversational. He looked her over and said, "My, my. Your hair seems out of place today, Livia. Isn't that unusual? It's never out of place because it's always pinned. It has been since I made the mistake of marrying you. Are you possibly missing the pretty ivory pin today?"

He released his grip on her arm and she felt for the pin.

"It's not there, is it, my domina?" Then he roared, "It's here in my hand and not in your hair because I found it at the bottom of the pit! Yes, the stone pit where I keep the chest. It fell out of your hair when you returned the coins and stole my Thoth. Trickery. Treachery! I've known your schemes for seventeen years!"

The slap came hard and Livia reeled, falling against Gaius, who said, "Why do you hit her? She said she didn't take it!"

Again he ignored his son, and pointing to his wife, he said, "You better find it; you better return it to me or that little slap is just the beginning."

He turned and approached Aspacia who was tending the garden. "Tell your sister to be at my door tonight."

He started to go, but stopped abruptly when Aspacia said, "Why, Master?"

Toronius whirled his heavy body and stared at her. In a venomous voice he said, "You never question me or I will rent you out for sport. Do you understand?"

Aspacia mutely nodded.

"Stay here," Livia said to Gaius, having heard Toronius's words to Aspacia. A deep red bruise appeared on his mother's cheek as she walked to the girl and guided her toward the kitchen. Livia returned a few minutes later and said, "I'm going to bed, and I suggest that you don't leave your room tonight." Then, after a moment's pause, she said, "Gaius, I didn't take that Egyptian god."

"Do you know who did? Was it one of Father's clients?"

"I doubt it," she replied and Gaius thought he saw a slim smile on Livia's face.

*****

It was past moonrise when Toronius heard the sound of footsteps outside his door. He had been waiting; the thought of the plump girl coming to his room excited him. Certainly he could have had Apollodoros bring her. But that would not be the same. No, he wanted her to come without the others knowing, though he knew that sooner or later all the slaves would know. They always knew everything, not that it would make any difference.

Of course, he could have had the pretty one come to him first. She would be more delicious, but she was still too haughty and might not be as pleasurable. There would be time to break her, to make her an obedient thing to fulfill every wish of the Dominus. That would surely be when he tired of the fat one, he mused, as he rose from his bed and opened the door.

Caladria tried to process what Aspacia had told her, translated from what Livia had told Aspacia when she led her into the kitchen hours before.

*****

"It's something that happens to every slave woman in Rome," said Livia. "Your sister must consider sex with my husband as an everyday chore, like washing dishes or emptying a chamber pot. She must not think of it as a gift given to a lover. That's just the way it is. She must be compliant, and do everything Toronius asks, or she will suffer. He has sold girls who failed to please him. And I've never heard of them ever again."

"My sister has never lain with a man," said Aspacia, her eyes reddened. "Caladria won't know what to do. She's afraid and won't be able to please him."

"She will do what Toronius tells her to do," Livia said, handing Aspacia a cloth to wipe her tears.

"Caladria is a fragile, simple girl. She doesn't know what's happening. I will go in her place," Aspacia said.

"No, he wants her, for now at least."

"Mistress, why are you telling me this?"

Taken aback by the girl's question, Livia said, "I needn't tell you anything, but you are new to Rome and you should know what happens..." she paused, "to women. Besides, I need help from both of you, and if you are sold I will not get another—"

"Slave to do what you choose not to?" Aspacia said.

"Don't be impertinent with me! I'm doing you a favor. Just tell your sister to appear willing, and she may survive the night."

*****

Gaius, half asleep, had no intention of leaving his bed. The girl's footsteps halted outside his father's room. He knew what to expect; it had happened so many times before. The door was opened, and Toronius ushered the girl in. There was a shifting of heavy bodies on the bed, silence, and then a shriek followed by the unforgiving slap. The girl began to babble incoherently. Toronius's grunts were followed by threats, and Caladria, most likely pinned to the bed, whimpered.

Gaius closed his eyes and tried to blot out the girl's pleas, but he knew that his father enjoyed the girl's helplessness.

Toronius tossed her out before dawn. Gaius heard her exhausted tread, and the tightness in his body began to fall away. He knew that what had happened would happen again until his father tired of her. It would only take a few weeks at most, and then she would be sold as those before her had been, and Toronius would move on to the next girl.

He didn't want to think about the next girl, because he knew who it would be. Would he remain in his room when Aspacia was called? Legally the power of a dominus could not be questioned, especially with regard to a slave. He tossed in his bed, not knowing how he would react.

It hadn't happened yet and Gaius liked to tell himself it might not happen at all, but he saw his father look at Aspacia as if she were ripened fruit. How long before he would call her to his bed?

The most dangerous of scenarios flitted through Gaius's mind. What perilous thing was he contemplating, and what would the consequences be? If only he hadn't seen the girl at the slave auction. If only his father hadn't bought her. If only...

In reality he hardly knew her and, he reminded himself, she had shown scant interest in him. But how could she possibly encourage his attention? Certainly he saw her glance in his direction when she thought he wasn't looking. But he knew she considered him terribly immature. He imagined how she laughed at his inept attempts to ignore her. Lying in his cramped room, he felt helpless and very small. Gaius feared for her, and then he feared for them both.

Everything might have been easier if she had utterly ignored him. Then he could have ignored her in turn. It would have been that simple. There were other girls his father had bought, and Gaius had thought little about most of them. And surely they hadn't time or opportunity to think of him.

But Aspacia hadn't entirely ignored him. True, he hadn't said anything to her of late. He hardly knew what to say that would please or entertain her. The fact was, he admitted to himself, that he had never had any girl to say anything to. No wonder Appian Dio laughed at him. Now, as the day's stifling heat invaded his room, Gaius wondered what Aspacia really thought of him.

Suddenly the very walls of his room seemed claustrophobic. Two nights before he had dreamed that the walls were pressing in on him. They morphed into the shape and bulk of his father, and crushed him into a thin wafer. He had awakened in a cold sweat and thought of escape from Rome. He would soon be old enough to join the army like Appian Dio. If he did that, he would never have to encounter his father again, never have to face humiliation and the girl would be forever unattainable. But Gaius knew that he would never join the legion. He, like his father's slaves, would suffer what the gods, in their spiteful games, would choose for him.

*****

"She's worthless, ruined," Livia said to her sister, Junia, who had come in from the countryside. Junia had been a widow since her husband was killed. Childless, she had never remarried and, along with a single female slave, lived on land left to her. Now she and Livia sat in the atrium and absently nibbled on cheese and fruit.

"I haven't been able to get any work out of her. She just sits there like an old sow," said Livia. "Toronius has had her for five

108

nights now. The girl is just mute and gives me that sad hollow stare."

"Can you blame her, Livia? I've seen her face. It's swollen. I remember how you looked the first time he hit you. You wanted to kill him, and sometimes..." Junia stopped herself and looked around, "sometimes I think you still do."

"Half the women in Rome want to kill their husbands," Livia muttered.

Junia gave her a sidelong glance then said, "Will Toronius sell her?"

"Eventually. But he'll use her for now. He actually likes them like that. Cowed and fearful, I mean."

"The man's a bully, always has been," said Junia.

"His father used to beat him before he forced him to marry me. I think it's in the blood."

"You feel sorry for the girl, don't you?" Junia said, looking at Caladria, who sat on the ground beside the kitchen door.

Livia shrugged. "She's just another girl passing through, but I don't know how I'll get another one when she's sold."

"Who's that one? I didn't see her earlier," Junia said, watching Aspacia enter the atrium.

"Her sister. She's a lot brighter."

"I'm surprised that Toronius hasn't bedded her instead."

"He will," Livia said as Aspacia approached.

"What is it?" Livia said, looking at the girl's calloused hands.

"We're out of gorum, Mistress, and you might wish to have it for the cena." The tasty fish sauce was a Roman staple, considered essential for nearly every meal.

"Make everything else. You'll come with me tomorrow and we'll buy some."

Aspacia nodded and began to walk to the kitchen when Livia said, "Tell your sister to go into the kitchen, I don't want visitors to see her like that. Besides, she's the one who's supposed to do the cooking. And Aspacia," Livia added in a softer voice, "talk to her. Tell her that she must work, or the Dominus will sell her to a farmer. Women die on farms."

"Mistress," Aspacia said turning back, "I don't think it

would do any good. She speaks to the ghosts of our parents, and thinks that she is already dead."

*****

"He's growing into a man," Junia said, looking at Gaius, who slowed as he glanced into the kitchen. "Has Toronius found a girl for him yet? My husband was married to me when he was fourteen."

"We're inviting the tribune Retenius to the cena tomorrow night. He has a daughter that Toronius has been asking about. I believe Retenius is bringing the girl. I've only met her once."

"What's she like?"

"Mousy, but very anxious to find a man. Toronius is all for it, since Retenius hopes to be elected to the Senate within the year. But if the tribune has reservations about Gaius, Toronius has other plans for the boy."

Livia took a sip of wine and watched Aspacia carry a tray of herbs into the kitchen. "I have to keep Gaius away from that girl," she said.

"Aspacia? Gaius likes her, a slave girl?"

"He tries not to show it, but it's so obvious. And dangerous." Then changing the subject she said, "Junia, you must stay for the cena, it's the first large dinner we've had since Toronius had his depression. You can share my room."

*****

Livia heard Caladria scream and run out of Toronius's cubiculum the night of the cena. Panting and standing nude beside his door, the dominus bellowed, "Get back here, you cow! How dare you leave my room!"

Junia and Livia left their beds and stepped into the hallway to see what the commotion was all about. The girl was gone and Toronius slammed the door. Livia put a finger to her lips to hush her startled sister and they slipped back into Livia's bedroom.

"She actually ran out of Toronius's room, I can't believe it," Junia said, aghast.

"No girl has ever done that before," Livia said.

"Where would she go? She can't leave the villa, Apollodoros is guarding the gate."

"Maybe the orchard or the atrium. Toronius will find her in the morning," replied Livia.

"The girl's in for a good beating. I hope she knows that," Junia said.

"She'll know it soon enough. But I can't allow him to kill her like he did the boy, the one I told you about."

"If he wants to kill her, he will, and you had better stay out of his way," cautioned Junia.

They returned to their beds and, like the rest of the household, waited anxiously for the dawn.

*****

At first Toronius pretended that it was a game. He made a show of checking the atrium, peristyle, tablinum and even the kitchen. Because he wanted to make a point, he required all the slaves to accompany him, along with Livia, Junia and Gaius. The whole group meandered into the orchard when it was determined that Caladria wasn't in the house. Still pretending to play, as if he were a leopard seeking a hare, he peeked from tree to tree. Then, not finding her, looked out across the field to the far wall of the villa. But it was already hot and he tired of the game.

"Gaius, do you know where she's hiding?" Toronius asked, anger beginning to build.

"I was in my room, father. I didn't see anything."

"Arzeka, perhaps you saw her," Toronius said, turning on the man. The Berber raised his hands and shook his head as if not comprehending.

"You know exactly what I'm saying," Toronius replied indignantly.

"What about out there, the old barn?" Junia said, spying the dilapidated structure.

"A possibility," Toronius said, as he and the entourage began to cross the field.

"I told Caladria to stay away from there, Father," Gaius said, while making sure that Arzeka was out of earshot.

Aspacia exchanged a worried glance with Gaius and dutifully walked behind Livia and her sister. Arzeka saw the direction the entourage was headed and hustled forward. Upon reaching the barn he rushed in, made a show of looking about, then exited, arms spread wide and shaking his head.

Aspacia let out a sigh of relief, but Toronius suddenly grabbed her by the arm and shouted, "Where is your sister? Where is that cow?" Then he turned, motioned to Apollodoros, and together they walked to the barn door.

"A thorough check," Toronius said, ordering Apollodoros inside.

Fetid smells of man and animal struck the group, as bright shafts of light entered through slits in broken boards. Two stalls still remained in the rear of the structure, and the earthen floor was littered with ancient cow puddles and a tumble of mice-infested blankets. Apollodoros pushed aside ancient beams, and then Gaius and the assembled crowd heard a startled cry followed by a prolonged whimper.

Apollodoros led Caladria into the sunlight, his hand gently pulling the blinking girl out to stand dumbly in front of the assemblage. She tightly held a small bundle of old rags.

"She was under a blanket, Dominus," he said, releasing her.

"You said no one was in there," Toronius stormed at Arzeka, who stood at the edge of the crowd. Then, brandishing a coiled whip, he motioned to Caladria and said, "No slave, no girl, leaves my room without permission. This will teach you!"

"No!" shouted Aspacia, whose hands flew to her face. Again she looked at Gaius, who said, "Father, if you beat her she will be of no use to you or Mother. See how frightened she is. The girl will obey. There is no need to whip her."

Toronius allowed the whip to uncoil then let it fly, catching Caladria across her arm. The girl screamed and dropped the rags she had been holding. Toronius was about to swing the braided rope again when the cloth dropped to the ground. He lowered the whip and stared at the little bundle, a roll of silk with an object peeking out. Then, rushing forward, he pushed the girl out of the way. Furiously unwinding the material, he gazed at an ancient figurine.

"My Isis!" he shouted. "You stole my Isis!"

Moving quickly, Gaius said, "When was it stolen, Father?"

"A month ago, before the Thoth disappeared. What do you know about this?" Toronius demanded.

"The girls have only been here for three weeks. Your Isis was missing before they arrived. Caladria was not here to take it, Father. She's not guilty of stealing the Isis."

Wild-eyed, the dominus looked about and fixed his gaze on his wife.

"You! Your hairpin fell into my box. You stole it."

"I would never enter that horrid place, husband. Arzeka said the girl wasn't in there, but he was lying. He's always lied. You said your Thoth was stolen. Tear apart that barn and maybe you'll find it. Then you'll know the real thief."

Turning to Gaius and Apollodoros, the dominus said, "Go through everything, tear apart what you have to, but be careful. If you damage it..."

His words came out through clenched teeth and Gaius's hands were shaking. Arzeka sprang forward to help, but Toronius said, "No! You stay here."

Gaius ripped away rotten boards and stood back as cracked roof tiles spilled onto the ground. He entered the nearly roofless barn, pulled away the blankets, and emerged with a stone wrapped in soiled rags.

"This is what we bought in Alexandria, father. It's Toth."

Toronius nodded to Apollodoros and two other slaves, pointed to Arzeka, and said, "Bind him."

"Shouldn't you call the authorities, Toronius?" said Livia. "They are responsible for the quaestio and the supplicium."

"I don't need anybody else to interrogate him, and I will do the punishment myself. And I'll be damned if it's done in a public forum. The public I want is right here, and it will be done right now."

*****

To a crowd of strangers, the punishment and likely death of

a criminal was a popular spectacle, since Rome was a crime-infested city. But for those who stood in front of the barn, there was little joy in watching blood gush from a man's back. Apollodoros and the other two male slaves observed noncommittally as Toronius, panting from the exertion, gleefully applied the whip.

Livia saw how relieved the other slaves were that the true culprit had been found. They had seen such punishments meted out before: a dozen or two lashes, the subject's eyes rolling back, bone exposed and the loss of consciousness.

Livia could hardly believe her luck. She smugly watched the beating, ecstatic, that she was no longer suspect. How sweet was the retribution! for certainly it was Arzeka who had dropped her hairpin into the pit containing the treasure chest. He would have had her blamed and likely beaten.

The savage whipping seemed to be unending as Toronius vented all his frustrations on the slave. At one point, Arzeka turned his head and stared at Livia. He did not scream, but mouthed the words, "You did this to me." Bitterness, hatred and resignation all streamed together, easy to read on his face even through the pain in his expression.

"Dominus, beat him, kill him," she screamed in her shrill voice. She'd been afraid before; that fear would multiply a thousand times if the Berber lived. She could imagine him skulking through the villa in the middle of the night, slipping silently into her bedroom. It would not be for sex. Livia could already feel the knife draw across her throat. It was palpable, and the very thought made her cringe.

She glanced around at the gathered household. Livia saw Apollodoros wince as each strike of the whip ripped away a strip of flesh from Arzeka's back. Toronius's toga was splattered with the man's blood, but he seemed not to care; vengeance was his for the taking.

Caladria, holding her injured arm, whimpered as Junia looked away. Finally the strength faded from Toronius's arm and he turned to Apollodoros and said, "Fetch a bucket of saltwater. We don't want infection to set in, do we, now?"

Other than a moan and a twitch, Arzeka didn't move. Livia watched as Apollodoros and Gaius dragged him into the remains of the barn and laid the limp, bloody body on a pile of rags.

"I suspect we'll be tossing him into the slaves' grave pits by this time tomorrow," said Gaius as they walked back to the house.

"I doubt it," replied Apollodoros. "I think he'll recover."

"He'll be a cripple. He might as well be dead."

"No, he'll have a reason to live," said Apollodoros.

"And what would that be?"

The Greek looked at Gaius and very quietly said, "Revenge."

*****

"Gaius, with the guests coming for the cena I won't have time to shop. I want you to go to the market and buy the gorum and salt, and everything else we will need. You must be back by the third hour, we have important people coming."

"I'm not sure of all the ingredients. Should Apollodoros come with me?"

"What, he's suddenly become a cook? No, take Aspacia, she'll know."

*****

They had walked for half an hour in silence, from the villa along the affluent, tree-lined Palatine Hill through a narrow valley toward the Tiber. Aspacia trod beside Gaius, her depression lying heavily upon her. What words of comfort might he possibly say to her after the rape of her sister? Then there was the beating of the slave Arzeka by his father, the paterfamilias. Aspacia's eyes were downcast, and the day's warmth did nothing to lighten her spirits.

"I am truly sorry about what happened to Caladria," Gaius finally said. "I would never treat anybody like that."

"But you didn't do anything to stop it, did you?"

"No I didn't. I would have if—"

"It had been me?" Aspacia said, raising her eyebrows.

There was nothing Gaius could say and he slipped back into

silence.

"But still, I must thank you," she said.

"For what?"

"You know. For interceding yesterday when your father would have beaten Caladria."

"He was wrong," said Gaius, "and he knew it."

"The slave who lives in the barn, Arzeka, how would he have gotten those Egyptian deities? Who would have let him in the house?"

"I'm not sure. I guess he could have snuck in when nobody was watching, unless my mother..."

"What about your mother?" Aspacia asked.

"Nothing."

"Is he still alive?"

"Apollodoros went into the barn this morning. The man is alive, but he won't be walking around for a very long time."

They were both steeped in their private thoughts when Aspacia asked, "Where are we going?"

"Several places actually. We have to get vegetables at the Forum Holitorium by the river. Then we have to go to the Vicus Tuscus where the Etruscans used to live. A lot of wealthy Romans think it's filled with the lower classes, but they go there anyway because it's the best shopping street in Rome. It's even better than the Forum Romanum."

"What do they sell at the Vicus Tuscus?"

"Almost everything: perfume, salt, furniture and that gorum my mother needs. Romans use the stuff on everything. We practically drown in it."

She nodded and gave a little smile.

"There are flower markets there too," Gaius added, deciding that he might as well talk to her. It was better than the uncomfortable silence that had marked their walk so far.

"This is a holiday so there will be more flower stalls than usual. We'll pass the Forum Romanum. That's where businessmen meet. It was begun by a consul named Cato a hundred years ago. You can even buy a papyrus newssheet there that's written by scribes every day. It's called the *Acta*

Diurna, and it contains all the gossip and political news. I buy it sometimes just to keep up with the wars against Sparta," he said.

She tilted her head and repeated the little smile. Gaius liked seeing it, but, he reasoned, she was probably just being polite.

From the Forum they could see the old Circus Maximus beside the Via Appia, a major artery leading out of Rome. Beyond that was the Forum Boarium beside the Tiber, where cattle were unloaded from ships. Not far from the Tiber sat Aventine Hill and its temple.

From time to time, Gaius pointed out landmarks and said a few words about each. He did not want to appear like the tour guides who showed foreigners the sights of Rome. Aspacia listened, but made few comments. Eventually Gaius decided that she wasn't particularly interested in the world that had made her a slave. So he was surprised when she suddenly said, "Master Gaius, what temple is on that hill?"

He regarded her for a moment and said, "The marble one on the Aventine Hill?"

"Yes, the beautiful building with all those trees around it."

"It's the Temple of Diana, a Greek temple honoring the goddess—"

"Of the woodlands," she said excitedly. "It's a sanctuary for people in need," she quickly added.

"How did you learn that?" he asked, surprised because it was the first time he had seen her show enthusiasm for anything.

"Diana was my mother's goddess, and mine too. We worshipped her in Lusitania. She is a wonderful goddess. My mother wanted to pray to her the day we were taken but there was no time. I think the goddess would have saved us. I really do," she said very quickly.

Gaius wasn't so sure, but said, "Well, it's an important temple. There is a wonderful statue of the goddess inside. I saw it once. Sometimes the Senate meets there because of its shape. The building's important to Rome because the legislature can only transact public matters in a rectangular building and one that has been approved by the augurs. Those are the priests responsible for examining entrails and prophesying the future. I'll take you there someday if you wish."

"I would like that. But why is it so far away, with no other temples nearby?" she asked.

"Many Romans worship the goddess, but she's considered a lesser deity than say, Apollo, Venus or Mars. So the temple is outside the Pomerium."

"What's the Pomerium?" she asked, wrinkling her nose. "It's a funny name."

Her consternation made him smile and he said, "It's the original circle where Rome was built and it was celebrated in an Etruscan ceremony when they and the Greek kings ruled Rome. That was hundreds of years ago. The circle is considered sacred because it surrounded the city."

Thinking that he might have been wrong about her apparent disinterest, he said, "See that wall over there? It's called the Aurelian Wall and it's inside the circle. It was built after the Gauls sacked Rome and it was the defensive line that even Hannibal couldn't get past. Of course, the city has grown far beyond the wall but even today no army, even a Roman one, can pass through it except during a Triumph honoring a victory."

Their steps took them past a small temple where bulls were lowing. A number of priests with red-stained togas entered leading a quarrelsome beast.

"Why are they taking such a big animal into that little building?" Aspacia asked, stopping to watch.

"They're performing a taurobolium. See that other white bull inside?"

She peered into the sepulchral chamber, where a shaft of light illuminated a bull standing chained atop an altar-like grate. Beneath the latticework stood three worshippers. A priest chanted in a monotone voice and raised his arms in supplication before the tethered animal. Then, selecting a jeweled knife, he slipped beneath the bovine's belly, stabbed upward, and sliced the length of the animal's stomach. The beast roared and pulled madly against its chains, but they held, as they always did.

The worshippers who stood beneath the grate opened their mouths and gulped down the steaming red liquid, their faces and togas instantly drenched. The men then knelt and gave thanks to the god Mithras, the deity cherished by the legions of Rome.

Sickened by the sight, Aspacia clutched Gaius's arm and said, "Let's go, please, it's disgusting. There's nothing in there I wish to see. I don't know why people worship such horrible things."

"I'm sorry you saw that. Many religions have sacrifices but I admit it's a strange god. Along with the bull, the Mithrans worship the sun."

The horrid experience left a chill and he assumed that the bestiality with which she regarded Rome had become even more glaring.

They entered the crowded Vicus Tuscus, teeming with flower carts and hawkers. In addition to the salt and gorum, Gaius was also searching for a new pair of sandals, the straps on one of his having torn off. Aspacia dawdled beside the flower carts, sniffing and admiring the cornucopia of color. He grew impatient, having to remove his shoe and stand on one foot, the black paving stones being too hot to stand on.

"We have to hurry," he said, holding a sack filled with all the dinner's ingredients.

"Then go, Master Gaius. I know my way back to your father's villa, unless you think I'm going to run away," she replied, raising her eyebrows in the coquettish and stubborn way he was becoming used to.

"Don't toy with me, and you don't have to call me 'Master' every time you want to make me appear foolish."

"Well, *Gaius*," she said, putting special emphasis on his name, "I'm merely a slave, so I'm required to do whatever you wish. Now, since we're on such familiar terms, I must say you look quite silly wearing only one sandal and hopping about like a bantam rooster. Let's get you some sandals, before that awful fish sauce begins to stink in this heat. And you should know that I'm starving. I do hope, *Gaius*, that you have enough coins to feed a little slave girl. You do have money, don't you?" she said, once more tilting her head, her very un-Roman curls swishing about.

Gaius stopped, took a deep breath, and simply stared at her.

"Come," she said so quietly that he could hardly hear her over the noise of the street. They pressed through the crowds until they came to a libertus selling copper mirrors. Aspacia peered into one, and Gaius asked, "How much?"

"Five denarii, young man, for a splendid piece for the lady. Notice how it's nicely burnished and how it has the image of Venus on the handle."

"Gaius, it would be a fine gift for your mother," said Aspacia, placing the mirror on a table.

He nodded and gave the man the coins, but handed the mirror to Aspacia. She stared at it, then looked at Gaius.

"I couldn't possibly accept this," she said with disbelief. "It's far too expensive, and what would your father say if he finds it? Who buys a present for a slave?"

"I can buy whatever I want. My mother has a mirror, and now you have one too. Besides, you must look your best when guests come. My parents will certainly understand that."

They left the stand with its display and Gaius felt pleased. It was the first time he had ever bought a gift for a girl. The vendor had slipped the mirror into a cloth bag, and as they wended their way through the crowd Aspacia took it out and looked at her image. Gaius smiled; she looked like he had made her happy.

*****

They entered a wider street near the Forum Romanum, where they admired statues brought back from Greece, then passed the Cloaca Maxima, the sewer that served Rome's population. Aspacia held Gaius's gift close and, to his astonishment, prattled on naming all the flowers she recognized. Perhaps he had misjudged her, he thought, but quickly reminded himself that he knew so very little about women. Yet she appeared to truly like him, and he enjoyed it when the sprightly girl was pressed against him by crowds of shoppers. He even dared to think that such casual days could be a normal way of life.

They observed street corner mimes, acrobats, and even orators singing the praises of one senatorial candidate or another. So it did not seem alarming when dozens of people began to crowd both sides of the busy street. Unlike other assemblages, however, this time the people were not applauding but were issuing sounds of disapproval.

Filled with curiosity, Gaius and Aspacia wormed their way to the front of the crowd.

"Did a speaker say something the people didn't like?" Aspacia asked Gaius, as an armed detachment of guards cleared the street ahead of a moving procession. Gaius watched for a moment, then stiffened, as thirty men, women, and children, all chained together, were herded forward. Many of the women cried, while their children looked about with confused and worried faces. Some of the men appeared stoic but others walked with bowed heads or made appeals to those who lined the route.

"Who are they?" Gaius asked a portly man wearing an immaculate toga.

"Slaves, young sir. One of them murdered their master." The man suddenly spat at a chained boy and shouted, "Die, die!"

Others in the crowd reviled the man and prayed for the mass of humanity, shouting that the forthcoming event was not worthy of Rome.

"What will become of them?" Aspacia asked, her eyes searching Gaius's face.

"They will die, Aspacia. It's the law of Rome."

"As it should be," the portly man said vehemently. Then to Aspacia he said, "If any slave, be they man or woman, kills his master, all slaves in the household must die. Surely you know this."

"That's right," another added, "And it's a damn good lesson

for all of them, even the ones we think are trustworthy. After all, there are three hundred thousand of them in Rome, a third of our population. We must never become complacent, and we should never trust them!"

Another in the crowd shouted, "By the great god Jupiter, take them to the Coliseum and kill them all!"

Aspacia, stunned by the man's hatred, stared at a little boy whose heavy chains slapped against the paving stones. A trickle of blood oozed from his ankles, and his father lifted him into his arms. The man turned and stared at Aspacia and shook his head. The boy held tightly to his father, cringing at the raging noise about him.

"No!" Aspacia suddenly cried as she turned away and fell into Gaius's arms.

The procession of wailing people trudged on, and soon the crowds reentered the street. Gaius stood immobile as Aspacia wept. People walked past, some staring, but Gaius ignored them. She eventually dried her eyes, and they walked back to the villa in silence as the sun began to descend over the hills of Rome.

Chapter 7

Gaius, standing beside his father, bowed in reverence to the statuette of Vesta in the lararium. It was a rite practiced every morning, for only Great Jupiter was as important as the goddess of fire. No day could begin without such devotion. When finished, he joined Livia and Apollodoros in the library where Toronius's Egyptian figures had been placed on display.

"We are expecting the tribune Retenius, his daughter Cornelia, and my husband's client Octavius Brundeschi," Livia said to the Greek. "You will announce the entry of each and be sure that the sow Caladria has the wine and preliminary dishes prepared. Aspacia will serve our guests."

Apollodoros nodded and walked through the atrium, where couches had been arranged on three sides of an exquisite table with inlaid lapis lazuli and teak. There the guests, along with Gaius, Toronius, Livia, and her sister, would relax for the cena. It would begin two and a half hours past the midday sun, the ninth hour of the day.

"I saw the mirror you bought for Aspacia," said Livia. "It's a dangerous idea, Gaius. If your father learns of it..."

"What's that?" Toronius boomed, as he and Junia entered the library.

"Just a mirror Gaius bought, a present for my birthday. You used to buy me presents for my birthday, Toronius," Livia said, petulance in her voice.

"Yes, I used to, didn't I?" Toronius replied as he inspected the arrangement of his Egyptian artifacts.

"Gaius," he said after a moment's thought, "I will have you point out these pieces to the tribune, and I expect you to speak of them eloquently, do you understand? I want you to appear authoritative but not pompous. I require you to make a good impression. I want his daughter to think exceptionally well of you. I will nod toward the statues when the time is right."

"Yes, Father. Do you want me to mention the lighthouse at Pharos and the library at Alexandria?"

"Only briefly, just to set the stage. Concentrate on the value of our purchases and their quality. That is all you need say."

Certainly, Gaius thought, but what he must not divulge would be far more interesting. And what was this about impressing the tribune's daughter? Only now had he heard of this girl. He wondered what his father was planning and looked perplexed. Toronius peered at him and asked, "Is something I said bothering you? Surely you're not confused."

"Not on the Egyptian matters, no."

There was a gentle tap on the door. Apollodoros entered and said, "Master, your guests are here. May I introduce His Excellency, the tribune Dometius Scipio Retenius, and his daughter, Cornelia."

Tall, silver haired, and urbane, the tribune swept in and greeted Toronius with a warm hand clasp, then made a deferential bow to Livia and her sister.

"We are honored by your presence, Excellency, and invite you and your daughter to share our humble home and the cena with us," said Toronius in the most gracious tone he could muster.

"It is I who am honored, to be in such a grand home. I have always admired men such as yourself who, through their wits, have gained prominence amongst us."

Toronius was about to protest when Retenius said, "Oh yes, it is one thing to inherit a fortune, another to build it with determination alone. And of course I do wish to see those magnificent Egyptian pieces everyone talks about, but first I must tell you how much I admire your absolutely radiant lady."

Livia offered her hands to Retenius and he went on, "Toronius Septimius, Great Jupiter has truly smiled upon you. Your wife's beauty is legendary. Many a senator has stolen a glance, and I do not say this for mere flattery."

Retenius continued to hold her hands and very delicately slipped his fingers between hers, then said, "Alas, my own wife was also quite lovely, but as you know, she was taken from me."

"I am truly sorry," said Livia.

"I accept your condolences, dear lady. The doctors said that it was malaria, bad air from the Quirinal Swamps on the edge of Rome. When I become senator, I will have that pestilent morass filled in if it takes every slave Rome possesses."

After an imperceptible squeeze the tribune withdrew his hands and, nodding to Cornelia, said, "My sweet and dutiful daughter has been particularly distressed over her mother's death, but we will put together a new life for her. Isn't that right, Cornelia?"

"Yes, Father," she said dutifully. But the tone was a half note off.

"And this young man," said the Equestrian in a sonorous tone, "must be Gaius." Then to Livia, "Your husband told me all about him when we met at the games. Cornered me, actually," Retenius laughed, "and detailed his accomplishments. And I daresay I am not disappointed. What a splendid young man."

Gaius, standing behind Toronius, glanced at Livia, eyes wide.

"Yes indeed, your father had nothing but praise for you," the tribune repeated as he studied Gaius. "And what great deeds should Rome expect from you, my young friend?"

"I wish to practice law, Excellency," Gaius replied. "Apollodoros, my father's servant, has been teaching me Greek and elocution."

"Excellent. Juries can be swayed by a knowledgeable attorney, but only an eloquent one will win the case. As Cato said, a good man skilled in oratory is essential. But beyond elocution and cold logic, one must be familiar with all the laws of Rome, its legal decisions, judicial forms, and learned writings: in effect, all the finer points of law. Once you receive your toga you will be formally presented to the court. It will be a splendid day with much fanfare."

"But to gain the knowledge required he must be guided by someone of stature, an administrator, a praetor practiced in the law," said Toronius. "Someone such as yourself."

Retenius regarded Gaius for a moment, then said, "Yes, someone such as myself." There was a long pause before he asked, "What have you been reading to prepare yourself, Gaius Septimius Aquila?"

Gains blanched at the formality, but replied, "I have studied Cicero and read *The Laws,* and his other work, *The Highest Ends, De Finibus.*"

"That's a fine start. I recommend Sallust as well."

"Yes, I've heard of him. I particularly like his attack on corruption and his attentiveness to virtue," said Gaius. From the corner of his eye he saw his father watching, ready to intervene if he broached the subject of slavery.

"I will have you read Lucretius's *De Rerum Natura, On the Nature of Things*, but for the sake of the gods stay away from the Epicureans!" To Toronius he said, "They have no sense of ambition, no political drive. What would Rome be without its legalists, its government?"

Toronius nodded sagaciously and noticed Cornelia glancing at Gaius.

"Of course we must thank Consul Sulla for bringing us those priceless works when he conquered Athens. Without them I hesitate to think of where we'd be," Retenius said pontifically, pointing to Toronius's wall of scrolls.

The tribune's gaze wandered and then fixed upon a Hathor statuette beside the Isis goddess. Toronius caught his son's eye and nodded toward the artifact. "You know, Excellency, that Gaius accompanied me to Alexandria, where we found these ancient and extremely rare specimens."

"Really?" replied the tribune. "I have traveled extensively, but mostly to Carthage and Gaul. I have never been to Egypt."

"I suspect we have a few minutes before dinner; why don't you tell us about it, Gaius?" Toronius said.

"Indeed, I'm sure Cornelia would be fascinated. She enjoys hearing about exotic places, isn't that right, daughter?"

"Yes, Father," she replied in a diminutive voice.

"Well," said Gaius, glancing at the timid girl and then at the dominus, "We first visited the Great Library, begun by the Pharaoh Ptolemy. It's a magnificent building and very busy, with hundreds of scribes and academics poring over thousands of manuscripts."

Focusing on his descriptions of Egypt, Gaius didn't see Aspacia approach Livia to tell her that dinner was ready. When he finally heard her, he turned about to see her staring at him then Cornelia, who was gazing fixedly at Gaius. Aspacia gave him a quick glance and raised her eyebrows. With a nearly imperceptible movement, Gaius shook his head, his palms miming helplessness. Abruptly Aspacia turned and hurried from the room.

Turning back to Cornelia, he stood speechless as the tribune and his daughter stared at him.

"You were saying," his father prompted, his anger barely hidden.

"Yes," Gaius stammered, "I was about to say that we passed through the Brucheion, the Royal Quarter, and wandered through the souks where you can buy anything: jeweled daggers, myrrh and even canopic jars containing the hearts and lungs of pharaohs. Of course, unscrupulous peddlers tried to sell us scarabs and even fake ankh pendants."

"But you knew where to find the real thing," Retenius said with amusement.

"Yes, Excellency. Apollodoros knew the right shop, a tiny place filled floor to ceiling with true artifacts. It's owned by a Jew named Elezer ben Josephus: an honest fellow who sells objects of ancient dynasties. It's said that there are three groups of people in Alexandria: Egyptians, who rob the tombs; Greeks, who study the artifacts; and the Jews, who sell them."

From the corner of his eye Gaius could see that his mother was becoming impatient with his recitation, but Toronius, seeing Cornelia's rapt attention, gave his wife a quelling look.

"What's that one called," asked Cornelia, seeking Gaius's attention. "It looks like a bird."

"The god Horus, a falcon," replied Gaius. "It's a thousand years old, and he's the one who leads the dead before Osiris, the lord of eternity."

"But this one is the most beautiful," said the tribune, examining a ten-inch-high Egyptian goddess.

"It's very delicate," Cornelia volunteered, standing very close to Gaius. Toronius smiled benignly and nodded to Gaius, who, hoping that his father wouldn't notice, created a distance between himself and the girl. Still giving Gaius rapt attention, Cornelia seemed not to notice the slight.

"She is called Hathor and, like our Venus, she's the goddess of love, fertility and the joy of life. They say that the ancient Egyptians loved life in their homeland so much that they never wanted to die outside of it. Only in Egypt were there priests that could embalm them, and without that, they could not go into the next world and experience Egypt for eternity. Of course one's heart would be put on a scale and weighed against a feather and—"

"That's quite enough!" Toronius said with a laugh of exasperation, pleased nevertheless when Retenius applauded Gaius's recitation. What Toronius failed to notice, however, was the way Retenius glanced at the jagged T-shaped scar beneath his left eye, and a ragged one circling his left ear.

Cornelia smiled, sensing Gaius's embarrassment. She moved close to Gaius again and peered at the Hathor statuette with its close fitting sleeveless dress, its black shoulder-length hair with bands of gold running through it, and said, "It is a bit strange don't you think? Look, she has a crown with a red disc between cow's horns. I have never seen anything like it."

Toronius quickly moved to the display shelf, and placing an artifact in her hand, said, "The ancient Egyptians were strange and mysterious people. But Mistress, this one is an absolute gem and so very rare."

"Of course," she murmured, and handed it back. Then she noticed a small stone depicting a man with a smiling face and a headscarf touching its shoulders. Its arms were crossed and hieroglyphs had been inscribed upon it.

"It's an 'Answerer'," said Toronius. "It's extremely valuable and quite ancient. It's from a royal sarcophagus in the time of..."

"Pharaoh Amenhotep II, a thousand years ago, Father," Gaius said, seeing his father's memory falter. "The Egyptians called them 'shawbtis', and they were put in the coffins."

"We don't have 'Answerers' but we do have plenty of slaves to work for us, and fortunately we don't have to wait till we're dead," Retenius said with a jovial laugh.

"Well I think it's charming," said Cornelia. "Don't you, Gaius?"

"It's very nice," Gaius replied haltingly.

"Then I shall buy it for you, Cornelia. Toronius and I can discuss price over dinner," concluded the tribune with a clap of his hands.

Toronius bowed, seemingly pleased to sell the shawbti, but Gaius saw that his father was dismayed that he had not sufficiently interested his guest in the more expensive Thoth, Hathor, or Isis. Of course, he reflected, there was still an evening ahead and a bit of inebriation could work wonders.

But the tribune's eyes once again lingered upon Livia. Gaius was surprised when Retenius gave a salacious grin and said, "Toronius, my dear man, I have heard that the Egyptians have an exotic wine in which they add blue lotus blossoms to stimulate an erotic effect. I assume it's something to dilute inhibitions during evening hours beside the seductive Nile."

"So I've heard, Excellency. But business being business, I never had time or energy for such indulgences. The day's work, searching for the finest artifacts, was simply too exhausting."

"Of course, and with such an alluring beauty to return to, why on earth would a man consort with any woman less enticing?" The tribune smiled and Gaius thought that the glint in his eye would mesmerize a cobra.

*****

"Master Gaius," Apollodoros said as the dining party approached the stibadium, on which they would recline to enjoy their meal. "There is something that requires your attention."

"Now?" Gaius answered, suppressing a grin at the Greek's deference in front of the tribune.

Apollodoros nodded, and Gaius followed him into the vestibulum, the small passageway that led from the atrium toward the main gate. When they were out of sight, Apollodoros turned to Gaius and said, "There may be a problem and you should know about it. I had to go into the kitchen for a sharp knife. There are always five or six knives in the drawer and I could find only one."

"Five knives are missing?"

"Only three now. I became suspicious and looked around. I found one hidden under stones by the impluvium in the atrium."

"But that pool of water has no stones in it."

"Precisely. Someone laid them in there under a water lily and that's where I found one of the knives."

"And the other?" asked Gaius.

"Behind a loose board in the posticum, the servant's gate."

"That's where Caladria sleeps."

Apollodoros simply nodded.

"Do you think she took them from the kitchen and hid them?" said Gaius.

"Why not?"

"Why would she...?" Gaius stopped and looked at the Greek, who again nodded.

"To kill my father. Doesn't she know the penalty?"

"After what he did to her, why would she care?"

"But murder? She, you, and all the other slaves will be executed."

"I doubt anybody's told her about that."

"Somebody had better. Maybe I should warn my father."

"He would have her killed for simply thinking about it. And Aspacia too, as a probable accomplice," Apollodoros said unflinchingly.

"So what do you think we should do?"

"Search for the other knives. Without them she can do nothing. I suggest that you don't mention it to Aspacia just yet. But it might be wise to keep an eye on Caladria, especially at night, and stop her if she comes anywhere near the Dominus's room."

"That might be an all-night vigil."

"I know. She walks in her sleep."

*****

"Gaius, why don't you take that couch with Cornelia," said Toronius in his most pleasant voice. "My client Octavius and I will have Junia sit between us, and the tribune can recline on the third couch with Livia. I think that will be a pleasant arrangement, don't you, Retenius?"

"Quite," replied the tribune, reclining so that Livia would place herself in front of him. He made a show of admiring the stone columns, the gardens with their bronze bird fountains, and gazed up at the the opening in the ceiling from which rainwater would cascade into the impluvium beneath. Being socially superior he felt at ease in the house of a man of dubious fortune—a man who was doing all in his power to cultivate his friendship. And he felt particular pleasure in being granted the opportunity to share the dining couch with Livia. It was, he mused, an enticement: an unusual gesture with interesting potential.

The tribune leaned close, pressed his body against hers and touched the gold and lapis lazuli bracelet dangling from her wrist. "Exquisite," he whispered. His voice, mellifluent and provocative, was intended only for her.

"I had nicer ones until recently," she said glancing at Toronius, "But I thank you for your complement."

"And what is that sublime scent I detect, Lady Livia?" asked Retenius, as his hand languidly moved across her legs. She glanced at Toronius and saw that he was studiously ignoring the tribune's touch.

Titillated by the flirtation, Livia said, "It is myrrh from Oman." Again glancing at Toronius she said, "I had one of my new slaves, or rather my husband's slaves, anoint me with it along with spikenard and a brush of cinnamon."

"But do I not detect sisymbrian on your arms and the essence of thyme on your lovely neck?"

Livia smiled and said, "How unusual for a man to know of such intimate details."

"I pay close attention to intimate details," Retenius replied seductively. "I was once married, and my wife adorned herself with such delicious scents."

Livia laughed and the tribune could feel a quickening of her pulse. She sighed and into his ear said, "This is all quite nice. Perhaps we should enjoy the cena more often."

"Indeed," he said, "If your husband doesn't mind. And I am terribly hungry."

"Then we should dine on delicacies," Livia murmured, and lifted a tiny bronze bell from the table and shook it. It emitted a soft tinkling sound, and Aspacia peeked out from the kitchen.

Apollodoros arrived a moment later and lit oil cups suspended from a tall bronze lamp stand. Beside it, a charcoal brazier glowed warding off an early evening chill.

Aspacia quietly entered and placed a tray of radishes, mushrooms, and oysters on the table, in addition to cups of Campania wine. Her lithe movement was so subtle that all eyes followed her. Then she walked back to the kitchen, pointedly ignoring Gaius.

"A most sensuous girl, Toronius," said Retenius after a moment of silence.

"A sweet tart, indeed, Tribune. Perhaps a little dessert for after dinner," Toronius replied, his eyes moving from Retenius to Gaius.

"It's a pleasant idea, but it will have to wait for some other evening. Cornelia, being a virtuous maiden, should not be privy to such things yet. And I wouldn't want her to think that her father is more lecherous than she already imagines."

Toronius laughed and said, "Quite right. The longer we can disguise our lusts the better. Honor and virtue are everything."

"Everything, Toronius!" then with a whisper into Livia's ear,

"Virtue and honor, yes. But a touch of lust is hardly disgraceful, is it, my dear?" She raised her eyebrows and gently squeezed his hand.

Togas being too cumbersome for true relaxation, the men had changed into the synthesis, a looser garment that allowed greater movement. To further dismiss inhibitions in the convivial atmosphere, the finest wines were served and everyone's sandals were removed.

Octavius Brundeschi, though privileged enough to be invited to the cena, perhaps feeling that he had been ignored in the presence of Retenius long enough, said, "Excellency, I do not wish to intrude upon the evening's pleasantry, but I'm wondering if there's any truth to the rumor of mayhem perpetrated by a band of escaped slaves. I'm referring to the murders on the coast at Ardea, not twenty miles from Rome."

The tribune regarded the man silently for a moment, and the pleasant conversation was momentarily broken.

"Regretfully, my friend, it's not simply rumor. Not only are we contending with the monster Spartacus, but now we're faced with this horrific event." Touching Livia's arm, Retenius added, "Not to alarm you, but one of the closest friends of my client was murdered by slaves snuck ashore at Ardea. They were contraband and damned dangerous. Smuggling is a travesty that should be punished by the full weight of the law."

"Indeed," responded Toronius, looking up from his wine with pronounced fervor. "And may I ask the name of the poor man in question?"

"His name was Plinius Apuleius Regulus, a Roman citizen with fine aspirations, like yourself, Dominus. Personally, I never met the gentleman, but his death is appalling. This band of thugs has murdered eight more innocent people, and only one of the killers has been apprehended."

A cold chill ran through Gaius as he recalled the blood on his father's clothes, his disheveled appearance and how Toronius, in a stupor, kept repeating the name Plinius. With these implications still murky, Gaius rose from his couch and said, "Father, wasn't Plinius your—"

"Not your affair, boy!" barked Toronius. "This is our concern, not yours."

There was a brittle silence as Toronius looked to the tribune, who slowly twirled his wine goblet and let the comment pass.

Toronius allowed his sudden anger to dissipate, aware of how it had stunned his guests. With studied control and the appearance of public concern, he said, "Now, Excellency, you mentioned that one of the culprits was captured. Did he talk? Do the authorities have any leads regarding how they escaped or where they might be?"

"No. There was a reward for the slaves whether they were dead or alive. Apparently a band of veterans cornered one and beat him to death. All we know for sure, beside the murders, is that Plinius's body was found outside the doorway of a fisherman's house by a patrol. I guess no one saw the murder."

"That village has been deserted for years. What was Plinius doing in Ardea?" Octavius asked.

"The authorities aren't sure. The road isn't traveled as much as it used to be, but there are inns along the way. He may have been murdered in the afternoon and not found till the next day. Perhaps he was doing business and just stopped in the village for the night."

"But not in one of the inns? And no one else was with him?" Octavius persisted.

"Not that we know of."

"Ardea has been used by smugglers for years," volunteered Toronius. "People we think we know often have peculiar or even nefarious involvements, and Plinius..."

"You're not suggesting that he was involved?" asked Retenius, his eyes sharp on Toronius.

"Not directly, of course not. But I ask, how well did any of us know the man?" asked Toronius with a shrug. "True, he was my client, but I only knew him a short time, and I assure you, he would never divulge complicity in something illegal."

"My dear Dominus, I also knew Plinius and it would only be fair to say that he was a fine man," countered Brundeschi. "In my opinion he was an upstanding Roman citizen, and I doubt he had anything to do with it. He was simply in the wrong place at the wrong time."

"Enough about it for now. What's done is done," said Toronius. "We must trust that the murderers are found and promptly executed. And we shall think only good thoughts about Plinius Apuleius Regulus."

Aspacia, accompanied by Apollodoros, reappeared with dinner, consisting of platters of eels, lampreys, ostrich, dormouse, cheese and lentils marinated in seawater and the ever-essential gorum fish sauce. It was accompanied by large bowls of Falernian and Tiburtine wine mixed with honey and saffron and spiced with a hint of peppercorn.

Livia motioned to Aspacia and said, "Wait an hour before serving the honey-sweet cakes I ordered."

Aspacia nodded then stole a glance at Toronius who sternly waved his raised forefinger. She stared at him for a moment, turned and hurried away.

Engrossed in dinner, the diner's conversation subsided and Toronius had time to consider the fate of Plinius. *Surely*, the dominus considered, *the man had to have been dead when his body was found. But he had to have died inside the house, not outside the door. There had been screams and so much blood. But what if Retenius was wrong, and Plinius had lived a while longer? Did he talk, did he implicate anybody? Of course he would not sully his own name by admitting a felony. Certainly he would not mention the name Toronius. Or would he? No,* thought the Dominus, *that would lead to too many questions.* Toronius took a deep breath and felt relieved, until suddenly he thought of the remaining slaves. They would be captured sooner or later, and under torture, whom would they implicate?

Oblivious to the renewed dinner conversation, Toronius considered that none of the slaves knew his name or where he lived. The fisherman's cottage was poorly lit, and there had been only a sliver of moon. None would ever recognize him and even if they could, who would believe the word of a murderous slave against a wealthy Roman? There was, in the end, nothing to worry about. Of course he would attend the funeral with the shock and sorrow expected. And since Plinius was his client, Toronius would pay for the official mourners and the cremation. It would be lauded as a noble gesture by the dominus. And then the whole affair would be over.

"Isn't that wonderful, Toronius?" he heard Junia say, his mind turning back to his guests.

"What? I'm sorry. I was just indulging in this wonderful dormouse. What were you saying, Junia?"

"I was saying how splendid it is that His Excellency Retenius is constructing a grand apartment building."

"That's splendid," said Toronius. "Rome needs new and safer insulae. I would love to see it under construction. Truth be told, I've always wanted to be a builder myself."

"It will be the usual six-floor apartment, but more ornate than most. Of course it's a terribly expensive project and I had to borrow more denarii than I want to think about. And I'm also constructing a new villa for when I'm elected to the Senate. Impressions, you know," the tribune said with an ingratiating smile.

And that's why he's not going to buy my antiquities, thought Toronius

"The building is still in the works but as far as the apartments are concerned, all the rooms for shops on the ground floor are complete as are the finer rooms on the second floor. Crassus comes by every few days to see the progress."

"Marcus Crassus, the Consul?" Gaius said.

"There's only one, my young friend. Not only is he my lender and the wealthiest man in Rome, but it was he who purchased the land after last month's fire."

"It wouldn't be the first time he's purchased land after a fire," said Junia with a little sniff. "And usually for a pittance of what the property was worth. Of course the owner would accept almost anything when his house is burning down," she said ruefully.

"That's a bit harsh, sister," Livia said, concerned that criticism of the consul might get back to him. "I think it's noble that Marcus Crassus would offer the victim any money at all."

"I agree," Octavius chimed in. "I have had the honor of assisting the consul, and I can tell you he's a most honorable fellow."

"And just how did you meet him?" Retenius asked, his hand discreetly slipping under Livia's synthesis.

"Excellency, I'm not a wealthy man, but I do own oxen and four carts. Some time ago I happened to be driving one past a burned-down building, and upon seeing the great man, offered to cart away the debris. He hesitated, thinking that I would overcharge such an august patrician but I surprised him. I said that I would do it for free that day, if he would employ my carts in the future. He agreed, and I have since carted away the remains of dozens of properties. It has become quite lucrative."

"There, Toronius, a man on the make, the embodiment of the entrepreneurial spirit. You are to be congratulated, Octavius Brundeschi," said Retenius.

Octavius bowed and raised his wine cup to the tribune who replied in kind.

Gaius sensed that Cornelia must have become quite bored with the conversation, as she had edged closer to him and placed a hand on his arm. He dared not move away with his father watching, so he said, "Excellency, might I suggest the organization of a firefighting cohort? It would be a metropolitan thing, run by the Senate."

"That's a civic-minded idea. Of course Crassus already has five hundred men doing just that."

"But only for his own ends. And there have been so many fires lately," replied Gaius.

"How dare you criticize the consul? Exactly what are you insinuating?" Toronius said.

"No, Dominus, the observation is quite legitimate. Indeed it shows the logic and quizzical mind of a fine prosecutor. But fires might be due to the weather, or the winds which whip sparks from the charcoal braziers, and everybody has those. But yes, lately there have been more fires than usual," Retenius noted. "However, young Gaius, I would not speculate about such things until proof of malfeasance is at hand. It would be ill-advised to offend the great Consul, a man of punctilious morality, unless you have proof."

"You will not offend him even with proof," interjected Toronius. "In fact, on this matter, you will say nothing at all."

Again there was a moment of strained silence. Gaius said nothing but felt Cornelia squeeze his arm as if to say, "I know he doesn't like you, but I do." Gaius turned toward her and issued a tight smile.

Toronius stuck his utensil into a selection of eel and glanced at Octavius, who seemed to be evaluating him. Toronius raised his eyebrows in question and Octavius mouthed the word "later".

"Now, Dominus," the tribune began, "as I mentioned earlier, I am interested in purchasing that little Egyptian piece Cornelia likes so much, though I will not be able to do it tonight." Seeing Toronius's dismay, he quickly continued, "I know how knowledgeable you are about valuable artifacts from the ancient world. I think that it would strengthen our relationship if your wealth vastly increased. Should you be able to purchase artifacts in great quantity, I would certainly introduce you to suitable buyers."

"That's most gracious of you, Excellency. Of course I'll consider it, and I would give you a handsome commission for your efforts. The traders in Alexandria know our hunger for antiquities. Unfortunately their prices are rising substantially. I may have to look to kingdoms other than Egypt."

Cornelia's hand was firmly attached to Gaius's arm when Aspacia brought the "second tables". Gaius averted his eyes as she placed a silver tray on the table.

"Have you any other requests for the cena?" she asked Livia.

"No, I don't. Do you, husband?"

"Not...tonight," said Toronius, who gazed at Aspacia with a quiet, appraising glance. "But perhaps some other night. Soon."

Retenius gave him a bemused look and, slipping his hand between Livia's thighs, said, "Delicious, simply delicious."

Chapter 8

Livia held a mirror to her face as she evaluated her blonde German wig. Artfully arranged, it completely covered the wire mesh that held it in place. She sat beside the peristyle impluvium, into which trickled the rain of the previous evening. "Do you like this?" she asked her sister.

"It's fashionable, but your own hair is much nicer. I had one of those black Egyptian ones but I don't wear it anymore. I'm just a simple woman and not one for pretense. You know me; I don't pretend I'm somebody I'm not."

"We all pretend, Junia. Last night we pretended that we were terribly literate and oh, so sophisticated. Toronius with his library and those ghastly Egyptian things he peddles. If it wasn't for Apollodoros he would never have known of them, and he still can't remember which is which. It's all about gaining influence, dear sister."

"And that's why he had you lie on the same couch with the tribune? I was astounded by the way Toronius let him play with you. I would have been livid. Weren't you shocked?"

"By Toronius? Absolutely not. For him I'm merely decoration: bait to dangle before men's eyes. He wants to snare the future senator, and I'm the fish on the line."

"But it was so obvious. Even Gaius and that pitiful girl could see it. And you seemed not to mind. It was as if you and the tribune were lovers."

"I only minded that the decision of where to sit and with whom was not my choice. But I had a part to play. As I said, it's all pretend."

"The tribune wasn't pretending."

"Of course not. What man would pass up a chance to explore a married woman's body if her husband lets him? And Retenius did just that. Of course I didn't discourage it. He is a handsome man, and it pleases me to think that I could have him if I wish."

"Is that what you intend to do?"

"Anything's possible, Junia."

"That would be adultery, a high crime in Rome. It's one thing for Toronius to let the tribune play touchy-feely, but letting you have sex with him is something else," Junia replied, sipping her watered wine.

"You know I don't care what he thinks. I'm not like you, Junia. I thoroughly enjoy intimacy with men. Needless to say, I haven't slept with Toronius since he refused to accept my daughter. He'll never touch me again. Our marriage has been a sham for years, but it's a profitable one. As I said, I play my part and I play it very well, thank you."

"And that includes becoming the tribune's mistress?"

"Why not? It's fine with me as long as our family is wedded to his. And I do mean 'wedded'."

"Meaning Gaius and the tribune's daughter."

"Can you think of a better arrangement? Being the mother-in-law to the daughter of a future senator has its attractions. I never forget, Junia, that as children we grew up in a farmer's hut and played with hogs in the pigsty. I shudder when I think of it. I like expensive things, and that includes men with expensive tastes."

"That's just fine for you, but what about your son? He can't stand that girl. I saw him cringe when she touched him."

Livia leaned toward her sister, and in a low voice said, "The new laws allow me to divorce Toronius, but they don't allow Gaius to divorce his father. He will do what the dominus requires. That's also in the law."

"And now you know a tribune who will enforce it, don't you," Junia said just as quietly.

Livia took a sip of her wine and said, "As a matter of fact, I do."

*****

The morning light illuminated Aspacia's face and the sun shone through her tunic, so that her body appeared a silhouette. The girl reached for one last apple to add to the basket at her feet. Gaius stood transfixed, thinking that she appeared like a goddess in a mythical garden.

"Good morning," he said, finally stirring himself.

She looked at him with studied indifference and said, "Good morning, Master Gaius."

"Oh, we're back to that again?"

Ignoring the question, she said, "I presume that you enjoyed the company of your girlfriend last night."

"Is that what you're angry about? She's not my girlfriend. She's a tribune's daughter, and Father required me to sit with her."

"Well she's in awe of you. I think you two would make a fine match, she being an aristocrat and so obviously desperate."

"I have no intention of marrying the girl—and what makes you think she's desperate?"

"Her hand was nailed to you, in case you forgot, and she's one of the homeliest things I've ever seen."

"Do I detect jealousy?"

"Of course not. And may I remind you that slaves don't have the option of being jealous. We just do what we're told," Aspacia replied airily.

She picked up the basket as Livia came into the orchard. "Aspacia, give that to your sister. I really don't want you to be talking to Gaius. You have more important things to do. Now leave us."

Livia watched the girl carry the basket into the villa then turned to Gaius.

"You shouldn't have conversations with that girl. It only encourages her."

"I enjoy talking to her. I think she likes me."

"Don't be stupid. It doesn't matter if she likes you or not."

He grinned and said, "Does she ask you about me? I mean when she's doing your hair and such?"

Livia gave him her usual look of disdain as if he hadn't heard a word she said. "Does she ask about you? She's a sixteen-year-old girl, what do you think? 'Oh Gaius is so handsome, does he ride horses? When will he get his toga virilis and be able to call himself a man? Is he really going to be a lawyer?' I've had to stop her a half dozen times and remind her of her place." Livia shook her head and looked toward the field, wondering why she bothered explaining this to him.

"Yet it does no good. She's as silly as you. But both of you must stop. Your father has plans for you, and they certainly don't involve a slave girl."

"And just what girl do they involve, mother?" Gaius asked, a hint of anger in his voice.

"You know very well what girl. The tribune is an important man. He can teach you law and introduce you to wealthy clients, if that's what father allows you to do. And he surely will. Your future, our future will be secure. We will be very rich and respected by the wealthiest people."

"And all I have to do is marry his simple daughter, right?"

"No one's asking you to love her. Dear boy, who gets married for love? But a marriage to the daughter of such a man will put us all into the Equestrian class and perhaps even higher. In time you may even become a tribune yourself. You have no right to deny us the opportunity of a lifetime."

He was silent until she turned and began to walk away. Then he said, "Mother, I must ask you something."

"About the tribune or Aspacia?"

"No, it's about last night at dinner. Retenius mentioned the murder of Plinius, father's client. I was about to say something when Father stopped me, saying that the matter was none of my business. He must have feared that I would reveal something that might implicate him."

"Why should anything you say implicate Toronius? It only involved Plinius, and some smugglers outside of Rome."

"But think about it; the sequence of events seems so strange. Father was gone for days and was morose when he returned. He didn't speak to anyone, and it was weeks before he invited his clients for the morning salutation. And Appian Dio said that Father kept repeating Plinius's name when he brought him back here."

"Appian Dio was here with Toronius?"

"I wasn't going to mention it to you, but Father was quite shaken. It was as if he had seen something terrible. Perhaps something about Plinius."

"Why was Toronius even with Appian Dio?" said Livia, ignoring the matter of Plinius.

"Because he was hiding at Appian's insula. Appian went to the apartment when he learned that his mother died. Father was there, and Appian brought him back here before going back to Campus Martius."

Livia pondered the matter for a moment then said, "You have no proof that your father was involved in anything. And besides, what could you do even if you knew something about the death of Plinius? Confront him? Report him to the authorities? It would be suicide for all of us. Plinius is dead. Leave it that way."

"Where is Father now?"

"He's in a meeting with Octavius Brundeschi, and I guess they're talking business. I wouldn't interrupt him if I were you."

*****

It was already the seventh hour when Apollodoros found Gaius currying a horse in the field.

"Have you found the other knives yet?" Gaius asked him.

"No, and that worries me. You heard Caladria's screams last night after the cena, didn't you?"

"My father had her longer than usual."

"I told him that she's sick, but he ordered me to bring her to him anyway," said Apollodoros. "She was hiding and it took a while to find her. She begged me not to take her. I couldn't understand her words, and she won't speak Latin to me. The girl collapsed and I had to carry her."

"Did Aspacia see all this?"

"Of course. She told me that she would take her sister's

place, but the Dominus doesn't want her yet. He enjoys Caladria: the way she carries on, I guess."

Gaius was quiet, then said, "You know there's nothing I can do about that except to speak to Aspacia."

"I don't know what good that will do."

"I might be able to learn something about the knives."

"It would be better if I go."

"I doubt she'll reveal anything to you after last night. We'll both go."

*****

"What do you want with us now?" Aspacia hissed when Apollodoros stuck his head into the kitchen.

"I might be a slave but I am also a healer. I am trained. Should I not be concerned?"

"Well, take a good look at her."

Caladria was sobbing as she cut up a leg of boar meat. Aspacia, her arm around her sister's shoulders, turned away from the men and said, "You men are beasts" Then, to Gaius who stood by the door, "Your father has ruined her. What kind of place is this 'Great' Rome? It's you who are barbarians!"

Caladria began to shake and Gaius saw her grip the long, sharp knife so tightly that he doubted that it could be pried from her fingers. He turned to Aspacia and motioned to her to follow him outside. She shook her head, but seeing that he was adamant, reluctantly joined him beside the door. Seeing that her sister was still sawing at the meat, he said, "This is serious, and I'm not accusing anyone, but a number of knives are missing. Apollodoros found a few of them but not all. They have been hidden by someone, and that worries me. It could be dangerous if..."

There was a shriek behind them. Turning, they saw Apollodoros prying the knife from Caladria's right hand, the blade firmly thrust through the left. Blood spurted onto the table as the girl screamed again.

"I tried to stop her but she was too fast," said the Greek, as Aspacia and Gaius rushed in. Aspacia grabbed a rag and wrapped it around the wound, but in seconds the cloth was drenched. Gaius looked about, but the only other fabric was a filthy piece stuck into the boar's mouth.

"Get help, find Livia," Aspacia said as Caladria sank to the floor.

Gaius stared at Aspacia as she ripped away a length of her tunic.

"Don't just stare at me, go!" Aspacia shouted as she bound the cloth around the impaled hand.

Junia and Livia heard the screams from the atrium and heard Gaius say, "Bring cloths and henbane, Caladria stabbed herself."

Livia hurried to the medicine cupboard while Junia rushed into the kitchen. "How bad—"

"She's alive," Apollodoros said as he applied a tourniquet to the girl's wrist, "but I'm afraid her hand is ruined. The knife cut the tendons. Do you have a needle and thread?"

"We need a doctor," Livia said, looking at the ashen-faced girl.

"Apollodoros knows what to do, Mother. His father was a healer," said Gaius.

"The henbane will lessen the pain, but I need clean water and wine to pour on the wound. And make it un-watered wine, Mistress," Apollodoros said.

Livia stared at him, amazed that he would dare give her orders, but he was already carrying the girl from the kitchen.

"Take her to the room I slept in last night," Junia said as Livia hastened to find the pitchers of wine and water.

*****

Gaius held the girl's arm and tried to calm her but she wouldn't take her eyes off the needle and wailed as Apollodoros sutured the wound. Afterwards Aspacia led her sister to Junia's cubicle.

Gaius remained by the kitchen door and watched Apollodoros clean the knife. He was about to put it in a kitchen drawer when Gaius said, "No, put it on that high shelf. Caladria won't look there."

Apollodoros did as Gaius suggested, then with bitterness said, "You haven't seen the degradation of slavery like I have. Most wealthy Romans are removed from it, their overseers doing the whipping while they remain oblivious to the suicides and self-mutilations. Now you see it in your own house. Now you see what it's like to be a slave."

"I would not own a slave and would not wish to see one beaten," replied Gaius.

The Greek merely pursed his lips and shook his head. "Well, Master Gaius, maybe you can see just how ineffective your humanity is. Perhaps you should speak nice things to the girl, though I doubt she would quite understand."

*****

Gaius walked down the hall and knocked softly on the door. When Aspacia opened it he asked, "How is she?"

"See for yourself," Aspacia replied, her face grim.

"I'm sorry this happened," said Gaius.

"It's your father's doing," she said.

Gaius said nothing for a moment. He looked at Caladria who was whimpering uncontrollably. The bleeding had been staunched, but the girl was pale.

"I don't think he'll bother her for a long time, perhaps never again," Gaius finally said.

"So self-mutilation is the cure for nightly rape," Aspacia said angrily. She wiped her sister's face with a damp towel and said, "Master Gaius, there's nothing for you to do here, and I would like to be alone with her. Please go."

"I'm sorry for this," he repeated as he closed the door and walked toward the peristyle.

*****

"Will Father sell her?" Gaius asked Livia when he found her sitting with Junia.

"I don't know what the Dominus will do. She won't bring much of a price, having only one working hand."

"He might have her again just for spite," Junia said lowly.

"No, for spite he would have her sister," replied Livia.

Gaius felt a chill go through him. His mother saw his revulsion, wagged a finger at him and said, "And there's nothing you can do about it."

"Perhaps not, Mother, but I'd be concerned that Caladria might do something about it."

"She would be committing suicide."

"Then maybe you should speak to Father, if that's even possible."

*****

The moon was already high when there was a soft tapping on Gaius's door.

"I was awake," he said as he opened it.

"Someone's in the orchard," Apollodoros whispered as the door closed behind him.

"Is Caladria in Junia's room?" Gaius asked.

"I don't believe so. She might be sleepwalking again."

"The person in the orchard, is it her?"

"I couldn't tell, there's hardly any moon. But I thought I saw a flicker of light. Maybe something metal," said the Greek in a whisper.

"Like a knife? But I'm surprised that she would be up. She's been in that bedroom for three days."

"The girl is stronger than you think, and revenge is a great stimulus."

They walked silently down the hall and tapped lightly on her door but there was no answer. He opened it to see a rumpled bedcover but there was no girl.

Gaius and Apollodoros tore through the corridor toward the peristyle, where they hoped to intercept Caladria. Except for the dripping of a water clock there was no sound. An eerie quiet had fallen over the villa. There were no torches and only a quarter moon. In the dark, Apollodoros was an indistinct shadow following a few steps behind Gaius. From somewhere in the orchard there was an unmistakable cough.

"She must be out there. I wonder what she's waiting for," whispered Gaius.

The scrape of a loose floor tile made both men freeze. The

sound was close by. Gaius knew that Apollodoros was to have cemented the cracked stone back in place but he had put it off. Even in the dark he knew exactly where it was, but whoever had errantly dislodged it had already moved. Someone was in the peristyle thought Gaius. If Caladria had run in from the orchard they would have heard her.

If it wasn't Caladria, then...

There was a sudden rush of footsteps across the stones and a glisten of metal. Gaius turned toward the sound as a blade ripped through his tunic. The assailant charged through the peristyle, but stumbled as Apollodoros fell upon the indistinguishable form. The attacker rose, and the knife reflected moonlight as it plunged downward. Apollodoros grabbed an arm and twisted it violently. The blade spun to the ground and landed by Gaius's feet. He picked it up and rushed forward. The assailant threw him against a pillar and reached for the blade.

"It's not her," Apollodoros managed to blurt as Gaius evaded the grasp. A body was suddenly tight against him and a claw-like hand gripped his throat. Gaius's eyes bulged and air ceased to enter his lungs. Again there was a lunge for the knife, but Gaius, his head swimming, jabbed it viciously into the form that pressed against him. The body was indistinct but he could smell its breath and its foul odor. Terror sliced through him and he thrust the blade in again, deeper this time, then gave it a twist.

The hand released its grip on his throat and the form slid to the ground. The assailant's bony fingers clutched Gaius's blood-soaked tunic. There was a gurgle, then a settling as their attacker expired. Hands shaking, Gaius knelt and dropped the knife. Apollodoros was beside him, his hand feeling for a pulse.

"Dead," he said in a voice of calm.

"I know who it is," said Gaius.

"So do I. I'll get a torch. I think we should bury him at once."

As sinewy as he was, Arzeka was light. While Apollodoros wrapped him in a blanket, Gaius went outside, tied a lead rope to their horse, and led it to the villa. Draping the slave's body across the animal, they began to cross the field with Gaius holding the torch. A copse of trees appeared in the gloom and beside it sat Caladria. Gaius and Apollodoros stopped twenty yards from her immobile form.

"Is she awake?" whispered Gaius.

"Maybe not. I'll hold the horse and the torch," whispered Apollodoros.

Without a sound, Gaius crept toward the girl. He was fifteen feet from her when he stopped. She gazed in his direction but said nothing. He waited for her to speak, but not a sound came from her lips. He waved his hand; her eyes failed to follow the movement.

"She's asleep", he said to Apollodoros.

They took a detour and found themselves beside the grave of the boy who had been buried months before. The ground had sunken over him as his body was consumed by things that lived in the earth.

"It's a desecration, to be sure," said Apollodoros, "but it would be best to lay Arzeka in the depression over the boy. I can scrape away some dirt and pile it over him. No one would suspect that two people are buried here."

"It's our secret. The man simply ran away and vanished," said Gaius.

"Your father will ask."

"There are things he needn't know."

"You probably saved his life, and mine," said Apollodoros.

"Perhaps, and a few others as well," said Gaius as they again approached the trees. The girl was still sitting on the ground but was now awake and sniffling. Gaius took the blanket that had wrapped Arzeka and said. "Don't you wish to come inside?"

Caladria shook her head and said, "I'm with other people, Master Gaius."

"What people?" asked Gaius looking about.

She pointed toward nothing and said, "People, lots of them. Everyone I ever knew."

"Ghosts?" said Gaius.

"Yes, ghosts. All my friends are ghosts, just like I will be."

Gaius wrapped the blanket around her. She merely nodded. He turned to go then saw the moon's glow illuminate branches of the tree. High on one of the limbs there was a metallic glint.

Apollodoros saw it too.

"I'll come back for the knife tomorrow," he said.

Gaius took one last look at Caladria and said, "Yes, if it's still there."

*****

He hadn't slept. The man crumpling to his knees, clutching his tunic with his foul, rasping breath, haunted Gaius. Of course, he'd had to kill Arzeka; there was no choice. Of course; the man would have died for the murder of Toronius, and it would have been a more horrible death. Aspacia, Caladria and the other slaves would never know how close they'd come to their final days, thought Gaius. Nevertheless, by saving them he had ended a life, and now there was another corpse in the villa grounds. Arzeka was the first man he had ever killed—indeed, the first he had ever visited injury upon. Gaius wondered if he would ever have to kill again. A worrisome chill went through him and he knew that he would.

His eyes wandered in the blackness of his narrow room, and Caladria's words came back to him. "I'm with ghosts," she had said, "and I will soon be one of them." What had compelled her to say that? Certainly she was not planning her own death. Was she expecting his father to kill her? Or might it be someone else? It was more than he cared to dwell on. He had hidden his blood-soaked tunic beneath the bed. He would bury it in the field, then scrub the peristyle floor clean before anybody woke. Having but one tunic, he would have to wear the toga praetexta, the boy's toga with the purple trim. Fortunately, Gaius wore it often and nobody would think it unusual.

He drifted off until early dawn and woke remembering the terror of the night. The air was frigid and he threw on his paenula, a round cloak with a hood and a hole in the center, over his tunic. Closing the door silently, he ventured into the andron, the passageway between the atrium and the peristyle, and was surprised to see Caladria sound asleep with the blanket wrapped around her. Noiselessly, he stepped past her shapeless form and hurried into the peristyle.

Blinking in the early morning light, he searched for the exact place of the evening's violence. His eyes focused on a darkly congealed puddle that had spread across the tiled floor and seeped between its stones.

"I think it is blood, Master Gaius," Caladria said, standing directly behind him. Her hand was bandaged but the wrappings were soiled.

Startled, he spun about and nearly collided with the disheveled girl. Her hair was a tangled brown mass and she had a dank smell, a mixture of the wet field and the dung of cattle. She gestured toward the stain on the floor and said, "Yes, I believe it's blood, a man's blood."

"It's not blood. It's only wine. I was drinking wine last night and dropped a flask. I guess I was drunk." What made her insist that the wetness was blood? he wondered. Of course as a cook she saw blood all the time. But she hadn't been in the peristyle when the killing took place. So what made her think the blood was that of a man?

"Do you wish me to clean it?" she asked in a very quiet voice, pulling the soiled blanket about her rotund mass.

"No, it's my mess, I'll wash it up. Why don't you go back to sleep? It's still very early."

"I'll fetch you a bowl of water," she answered and trailed off.

*****

It was far more difficult than he had thought. There was a lingering stain that his mother would surely notice. She would have Apollodoros or another slave scrub the tiles for hours, but now, with its odor and blackness gone, it would appear to be wine. Caladria, who had seemed mesmerized by the cleanup, finally departed. Gaius waited until she waddled through the andron and then vanished into the darkness of the house.

The scent of morning was all about him as he passed through the orchard and tramped through the field toward the copse of trees. He wore a pair of old calcei, a cross between a sandal and a shoe of soft leather, but the dampness penetrated them, leaving his feet wet and cold. There was a screech of a small animal, then an owl sped past with the morsel in its talons before all fell silent again. Gaius stood beneath the trees, his eyes probing from one branch to the next. Surely he had seen something glinting in the moonlight the night before. It could only have been a knife: even Apollodoros saw it as such. The grasses where they had walked were still beaten down and he retraced his steps to see where the knife had been. Perhaps there had been a wind, he thought, and walked around the trees. But he saw no knife, nor anything else that might have reflected the pale light of the crescent moon.

Again Caladria's words came back to him. "It must be blood, a man's blood," she had said, as if it could be nothing else. What did she know and how did she know? What powers had the gods imbued her with? The girl lived in her own world, and perhaps saw things no one else did. He shivered and wondered if she was demonic, infected with vapors from the underworld. No one, perhaps not even Aspacia, really knew anything about the plump, slow-witted thing, who often walked about mumbling to herself or someone unseen.

The girl had been asleep, that was a certainty. The evening had been eerie and terrifying, but suddenly Gaius realized that the most frightening thing was Caladria, the one who hadn't died.

*****

Toronius emerged from the barn, now more dilapidated than ever, and looked around. Arzeka was nowhere about and Toronius hadn't seen him in over a week. Having little use for the slave, he had decided to sell him to a man who owned a villa rustica. Light farm work was all Arzeka was capable of since the beating, reasoned the dominus. In vain he had spent the last hour searching for him, when he spied Caladria plunked down amid the copse of trees in the untilled field. As usual, she appeared to be sleeping.

The screams he usually got from her during the night had

ebbed into a terrorized silence, and now she bored him. He hadn't penetrated her since her self-mutilation. With her hand permanently damaged, she was of less value than a pig or a goat. Toronius ignored her. The witless cow would know nothing about his missing slave, so he continued on. He would sell her too, he decided, even though she would bring almost nothing.

*****

"Where is everybody?" Caladria asked her sister, rubbing the sleep from her eyes.

"It's a holiday, I guess. That's what Apollodoros told me. It's supposed to be an important one, at least for boys, so everybody went to celebrate it."

Caladria sat down heavily and remained silent for a long moment. "They thought I was asleep," she finally said as she examined the scar tissue of her damaged hand.

"Who thought you were asleep?" replied Aspacia absently, while kneading dough into a popular ox head shape. She had been told that there would be guests for the dinner and special dished must be readied.

"Apollodoros and that boy, the one you are in love with."

"I'm not 'in love' with any boy, how many times have I told you that?"

"Yes, you are, I see you watching him all the time. People think I'm stupid, even you do. I hear them call me a fat cow or a sow but I see things. Sometimes I even know things before they happen. Anyway they came right up to me that night with the horse and the man lying over its back. He was wrapped in a blanket. The boy even waved his hand in front of me, but I pretended to be asleep. I wasn't, and later I saw where they buried my friend. I put a flower on his grave. He's out there," she said motioning toward the field.

Aspacia stopped and stared at her. "What in the world are you talking about? And no, I don't think you're stupid. You're just different; even our parents knew that. Now tell me, who was wrapped in the blanket and why was he your friend?"

"It was the man in the barn, the angry man who was beaten.

I was told to take him food every day, remember? I brought him other things too."

"What things, Caladria?" Aspacia said, a concerned look on her face.

"Those things," Caladria answered, a sly smile coming to her lips. She pointed toward the kitchen then made a shape with her fingers.

"Knives? You brought Arzeka knives from the kitchen? Why, what was he going to do with them?" Aspacia stopped, her eyes growing wide when Caladria put a finger to her neck and drew a line across it. She then looked toward the bedrooms.

Aspacia shivered and stared at her sister.

"He said that he didn't kill my friend, but I know he did. He wiped the blood from the stones in the morning. He didn't think I was watching that night when it happened but I was. There was a lot of blood and it was dark and sticky. It took a long time for him to clean it."

Grabbing Caladria's wrist, Aspacia demanded, "Who killed him and wiped up the blood? Sister, this is not real!"

"Yes it is! The boy killed him; didn't I tell you already? I can show you where they buried my friend. It's where nobody would find him because he's in the ground on top of another one, a smaller one, but that one's only bones now. I'll show you if you want me to."

Caladria took her sister's hand and led her through the orchard and across the field.

"Gaius killed Azteca?" Aspacia said in disbelief, but Caladria was already pushing the soil off the face of the corpse.

"See, the bugs ate most of him. But I made him look like he's smiling and I fixed his hair. It was all matted and ugly."

The flesh covering the earth stained head was mostly gone. Caladria gently pushed the skull aside and dug a little deeper. "He's asleep, he won't mind. See now? There's one underneath him." She shook her head as would a very young girl and said, "I don't know who this one is but I think it's a child, don't you?"

"Help me cover them up!" Aspacia demanded as she knelt and pushed dirt over the remains. "You must never uncover them again, and you must never tell anyone you know about them."

"Uh-huh. But Arzeka was my friend. I want to put flowers on him, like we did at home when someone died."

"No, never! You don't understand, do you? He would have gotten us killed. I should have told you about their laws. We all would have died, Caladria. You didn't know that, did you?"

"But my friend was going to kill the bad man, the Dominus and his wife, not us."

"Because of the beating?" said Aspacia.

"He was going to do it because I told him to. He said that I should, but I didn't know if I could do it right."

"And you do now?"

"I think so. Arzeka taught me how to use this," Caladria said, lifting a flat rock beside the grave. A heavy, rusted kitchen knife lay beneath it.

Aspacia took a step back and in a whisper said, "Oh, sister, may the gods have mercy upon us."

Chapter 9

For Gaius and every other young man entering adulthood, the sixteenth of March during the feast of Bacchus was the turning point of his life. It would be the last time that he would wear the bulla, a good luck charm denoting childhood. The family procession, including the tribune Retenius and his daughter, was joined by the families of hundreds of other young men on their way to Capitoline Hill for their formal presentation to the court.

Walking behind Toronius was his client Octavius Brundeschi in a simple tunic and trailing behind Livia, Junia, and the tribune's daughter was Apollodoros. The dominus, playing the part of the proud paterfamilias, carried the toga virilis, a symbol of freedom, virility and purity, which he would present to his son. Wearing it entitled the young man to all the rights accorded a Roman citizen.

The streets were filled with old women wearing ivy wreaths on their heads, hawking cakes of honey that would be placed on altars to celebrate Bacchus and the pleasure of wine. Everybody in the raucous crowd bought them, as joyous processions meandered from the Capitol to the temples and then to the Forum.

Gaius had spent the previous night beneath a saffron colored canopy, wearing a white tunic as was the tradition before the great day. He wondered how differently his father would regard him once the magistrate invoked the words, "*Ante Deos Libera sumpta toga*," while Gaius donned the vestment of manhood he would wear for the rest of his life. He couldn't wait to appear before Aspacia in the flowing, regal garment, and could only imagine how impressed she would be.

For years he had worn the bulla around his neck, the good luck charm worn until the age of sixteen, but it felt more like a millstone and he could not wait to put it aside. Now he would achieve manhood in the Roman Republic and be on a par with all adult citizens. Never again could his parents consider him a mere child. The world was blossoming, and on this fine morning, as he strode past marbled columns, Gaius felt that the gods were in their heavens beaming down upon him.

With the famous words having been spoken, the toga virilis was wrapped about him, and both Toronius and the tribune made a little fuss of arranging the folds and showing him how the right arm could be free, but over the left the folds must fall in perfect balance. Toronius appeared fatherly and stoic, but Dometius Scipio Retenius merely smiled and took it all in stride, as if he had done this many times before.

It was all a harbinger of things to come; Toronius had plans for the lad. But they would not be revealed until the time was right and all the blocks were in place. It would be like a defensive wall, his wall, and Gaius would be just one more stone, concreted, permanent, unassailable until his plans were all in place.

Livia, standing behind her husband, was pleased to see that many in the crowd recognized Retenius. Being a bright, cold day men covered their heads with the material of their togas, but lowered it in respect when they approached the tribune. *He looks so regal*, she thought. Silver haired, tall and strongly built; she fantasized about being in his arms and his bed. The thought wasn't farfetched. On that night of the cena, Retenius had taken the liberty of placing his hand on her thigh. She knew he wanted her; after all, what man would not? But she would not merely be the tribune's plaything, to be used then tossed away. Oh no, he would have to make promises for her favors and promises were to be kept. She pondered how she would ensnare Retenius. Certainly sex would do it; no man could resist that. But she would have to plan for the obvious complications.

To frolic in the highest circles of Rome's elite would require freedom from Toronius. How would she deal with him? Stout and all puffed up, mean, scheming and miserly, making a great show on this day of honoring his son. He cared not a whit for Gaius, she knew. He was a hollow, vain caricature, but venom, not blood, flowed beneath his skin. She would have to be very careful when she made her move, and it would have to be unchallengeable.

No matter how enraged or emboldened she became, Livia knew that Toronius would not divorce her. A beautiful woman charming his clients was too valuable for him to dismiss. She was his property; it was that simple. What, she wondered, would make the Dominus rid himself of her? After all, to Toronius, she was simply an object that would make him money. So money might be the lever allowing Livia to escape from beneath the stone of Toronius. A bribe, then. She required a considerable bribe.

Money. How much money might Retenius offer Toronius to release her from virtual bondage? How much did he really have? He was building a new villa, grander than the one she lived in. If Livia utilized her exquisite and potent assets, Retenius's house could be hers.

The tribune Retenius was a devious man. She knew that. No one who achieved his status did it honestly, at least not in Rome. And certainly he knew that she was no less devious than he. The tribune had to have noticed that she didn't protest in the slightest when his hand proceeded up her thigh. Not protesting was a sign of encouragement, and surely erotic possibilities flooded his mind. But of equal importance to Livia was that Toronius had chosen to ignore Retenius's gesture. In virtually every aspect of his life he was horribly possessive. Envy and jealousy coursed through him, and even though he hadn't had sex with her for nearly twenty years, Toronius would not look favorably on a man pawing his wife. Unless, of course, he had a motive. Did he already have a plan, a scheme? And suddenly, Livia worried that Toronius had some agreement already arranged with Retenius. If that were the case, whatever he had planned would have to be to the dominus's advantage; he would not be short-changed. His deal with Retenius, whatever it included, would be beyond her control. So what exactly was his plan?

Oh, nonsense, she thought. There was no plan, and how difficult would it really be to snare the tribune? she wondered. Certainly it would be worth the effort. Retenius would be her salvation; he represented everything she craved, including the sex. Yes, especially the sex. From this day, she mused, she would spin her web and Retenius, like a moth, would be hopelessly enmeshed.

*****

Toronius was elated to be seen at the tribune's side. He made a great display of showing pride in his son as he walked arm in arm with Gaius to the Forum. At the same time, he bantered with Retenius, mindful of those who envied his association with the man who exuded nobility. But the tribune, several rungs up the social ladder, was in campaign mode, and once the investiture was concluded he quickly turned his attention to potential voters. Toronius hid his disappointment and indulged Retenius, since the tribune's successful bid for the Senate would enhance Toronius's own stature. He could then claim a close friendship with a senator, not an inconsiderable coup.

Toronius glanced back and saw Livia's eyes riveted on Retenius. He smiled to himself and thought, *Yes, my tart, my beautiful trollop, fantasize all you wish, but you are my property, as are my slaves. Scheme all you want, you will do nothing without my consent. You are a pawn, a pretty one, and I will let you play like a mouse on a string.*

As for Retenius, that manicured, cultured and seductive snake, I have his measure. I have spies who frequent the balneae and the bars, asking questions and collecting ugly little snippets. The things I know, my dear tribune. You are poisonous but also infected. A few well-placed words from me...

But you lust for Livia. I will allow that to be, at least for now. I will pretend to ignore your daring sallies. No, in fact I will encourage them. In good time I will pull the strings, and how delicious that will be.

I know you think me a dolt, a semi-imbecile oblivious to your lust for my woman. For the present, I will play that role. As for my son, surely I have made a worthy and fatherly showing on this day. My clients, and those who wish to be, will look kindly on my performance: the paterfamilias behaving in the role of a dutiful Roman father. Of course it's all illusion; theater for Retenius and his daughter. Especially his daughter. After all, she is the prize.

*****

As a candidate for the Senate, Retenius had his slaves chalk his wool toga to a shimmering whiteness. He, an honored candidate, sauntered through the crowd glad-handing men of importance, often leaving Toronius and Gaius behind. The adoring populace sought his counsel, assured him of their votes, and nodded to his pronouncements with earnest agreement. Indeed, Retenius considered himself the soul of Rome, the manifestation of righteousness, power, and above all, virtue. As he ingratiated himself with the surging crowd and heard their adulation, how, he wondered, could he not sit by the side of the Senate's other great men?

His eyes strayed to Livia. None of the elaborate folds of her stola could hide the woman's stunning figure. The thought of her full breasts, narrow waist, and curvaceous hips mesmerized him. He felt a dryness in his mouth and attempted to contain his excitement. He hadn't slept the night of the cena; carnal thoughts enveloped him. It would not be difficult to arrange an assignation, he mused. It could be at the baths or his villa. It would not matter if Cornelia were present or not. Retenius smiled inwardly at the naivety he had projected for her that night.

Certainly Livia would be flattered by his attentions; what woman would not be? But she was a very special gem, and would require more than passing attention. How much more? Retenius could have all the women he craved, and crave them he did, but Livia glowed like shimmering silk. She would be more delicious than any sweetmeat placed on the table; indeed, a most succulent treat. He had to have her, and he would. It was merely a matter of time and place.

And what of Toronius? The man was vulnerable, anybody could see that. He was a sycophant and could be played and it wouldn't take much to do so. According to Retenius's informants, the dominus had failed in virtually every one of his schemes. The man hungered for recognition and wealth. Offer him a tantalizing hint of success, thought Retenius, and that's all it would take to have Livia in his bed.

The informants told him that the dominus hadn't slept with his wife for decades. No wonder she thrilled to the touch. Now Toronius had caught her staring at the tribune as she chatted with her sister. What delicious secrets passed between them as she fixed her gaze upon the tribune? What titillating innuendos were whispered, to be dwelt upon in the darkness of the night? A smile passed over Retenius's lips. The feeling was exquisite and excitement rippled through him.

A group of senators had collected at the steps of the Forum around an imposing figure wearing a toga with a broad purple stripe. To accentuate his regal position the man had donned the paludamentum, a red cloak only he and two other Romans were entitled to wear. Scanning the crowd below, he turned away from his animated conversation and signaled a libertus, who listened, nodded, then bustled toward the entourage milling about Retenius, Toronius, and his client, Brundeschi. Seeing the legislators on the steps, Toronius leaned toward Retenius and said, "Isn't that Consul Marcus Crassus?"

"It is indeed. Yes, co-consul with Julius Caesar and Gnaeus Pompey. He's looking this way, perhaps he wishes to speak to me."

But the libertus ignored the tribune, and finding Octavius Brundeschi, pointed toward the consul and uttered a few words. Octavius excused himself and, escorted by the former slave, joined Crassus. Stepping away from the crowd the consul exchanged a few words with Brundeschi, who gestured toward

Toronius. A moment later the libertus was at Toronius's side.

"His Excellency, the Consul Marcus Lucinius Crassus wishes you and your son Gaius great joy, and asks that you join him for a few moments."

"Of course, it would be my honor," replied Toronius, looking at Retenius with a surprised look.

"And perhaps he would like me to join him?" put in the tribune.

"Not at this time. Just the Dominus, if you don't mind."

Retenius stiffened, then, mindful of the consul's gaze, said, "Well, Toronius, I am duly impressed. I'll wait here with Gaius while you speak with the great man. Do give him my regards." He waved to the consul as the surprised Toronius followed the former slave.

Dismissing the libertus, Crassus, Brundeschi and Toronius slipped into a Forum shop. Gaius, the tribune and the crowd peered toward the store entrance with great curiosity.

"Such an honor," Retenius said to Livia. "To actually be invited to speak with a ruler of Rome."

"Yes, it's truly a great honor, but I can't imagine what he wants with Toronius or Brundeschi," said Junia.

"I can't believe Brundeschi is invited to speak with the consul just because he dumps his trash," added Livia.

In the quietest tone, Junia said, "I think they're up to something."

"What do you mean?" asked Cornelia.

"Oh nothing," laughed Livia. "But it's obviously a secret and that's very intriguing."

Toronius, Brundeschi and the consul emerged from the shop a few minutes later. A few convivial words were exchanged, and Marcus Crassus once again returned to his admirers.

"Well, I'm in exalted company now," the tribune said when Toronius rejoined him. "Of course, I'm terribly curious, if not a bit envious," he added.

"Just a fortuitous introduction and a little business proposal," said Toronius, making light of the impromptu meeting." Looking past Retenius, he went on, "The consul requested that little more be said until everything's finalized, if you don't mind, Excellency."

The tribune smiled indulgently and said, "Of course, I completely understand. But to be in the confidence of the consul! Well, as I said, I'm greatly impressed. Yes, indeed. "He looked at Gaius and said, "Well, young man, the son of a friend of the consul! Not a bad beginning on the day of Bacchus and the assumption of the toga virilis."

As the procession began again, Retenius noted that Livia, Junia and Cornelia attempted to stay close to the men. For the occasion they each wore a short marigold colored cloak, the calthula, and an immaculate stola with a clasp at the shoulder. Roman women were expected to be almost entirely covered, so they all wore the ricinium, a square veil half on the head and partly over the shoulders. And unlike the men, who wore boots, the women were allowed to wear sandals, which were far more comfortable in the heat.

Cornelia, walking beside Livia, said, "Your son already looks like a respected attorney. I just hope I haven't disappointed him." Then in a seemingly concerned voice, she added, "I'm sure the Dominus is considering many young ladies for his bed."

Livia glanced at the girl, surprised at the use of the word "bed".

"Certainly," Livia replied, a little off balance. "He's a fine catch, and many families have approached the paterfamilias about the availability of their daughters, but my husband sees great promise in a marriage of our two families. As a potential mother-in-law, I suggest that you visit us as often as possible. And of course, you must bring your father along." Livia gave Cornelia a little smile. "I think it would be great fun for both of us."

"Oh yes, I'm sure it will," the girl replied, "but father is very protective of me. I doubt that I could be alone with Gaius very often, though I would really like to get to know him better. I hope he comes to like me as much as I like him."

"Liking does not always come at once. But don't worry if Gaius seems a little distant. It takes him time to warm up to people. If Toronius and your father are of one mind, you needn't worry about Gaius. Now, why don't you catch up to him? I'm sure he'd like to impress you in his new toga."

As soon as Cornelia left their side, Junia gave Livia a suspicious look.

"What?" Livia said, arranging her ricinium.

"You are so devious, sister. Have any families approached Toronius about their daughters?"

"Junia, the girl is terribly naïve. I want her to impress upon Retenius how lucky she would be to marry Gaius. That's all she has to know."

Junia sniffed, and gave Livia her disapproving look. "I think the boy will be hopelessly depressed."

"But money, dear sister, is a great antidote to depression."

*****

"So you'll do it; you will assist the consul?" Octavius Brundeschi asked, once he and Toronius had sequestered themselves in the tablinum.

Toronius ran his fingers over his chin and nodded. "Of course, but it could be dangerous."

"He has confidence in you just as he has in me. And as assistant to the consul you will have little to worry about."

"The precepts of power," said Toronius with a tight smile.

"Precisely. Dominus, I see little danger. I have done it for him several times, but he has other assignments for me now. Of course I will show you where and how it must be done. Of course I will be available if it's a major project. And," Octavius added, "It was quite gracious of him to extend you the loan. So you see how important your involvement is. He trusts very few people. You are fortunate that the Co-Consul of Rome places his trust in me."

"And it was gracious of you to mention my name to him," said Toronius. "As you know, and I tell you this in strictest confidence, I'm hoping that the tribune will agree to a marriage between my son and his daughter."

"As a friend of the consul, your prestige will only grow, and Retenius, with his daughter married to Gaius, will profit by the alliance. It's obvious that the tribune thinks highly of you. He applauds men who are aggressive, especially in business. And certainly, he likes your investment in Egyptian artifacts, since they're so lucrative. Will you be going back to Alexandria for more?"

"No, unfortunately I can't rely on my source any longer. I hate to say it but I'm at a disadvantage, considering I must find a way to pay back the loan while finding new sources. And that can be very expensive."

Octavius Brundeschi was silent for a moment, then said, "Dominus, I pride myself in having my fingers in many pies. A little profit here, a little there, you know, but it all adds up. You desire antiquities, but need a good price while avoiding expensive travel. I made the acquaintance of an Egyptian who imported a collection some time ago. He is elderly now—I'd say at least fifty—and wants to liquidate his treasures. He comes from Alexandria and he is quite knowledgeable."

"And reputable?"

"I believe so. If you wish I can introduce you to him. He has lately taken up residence in Rome."

"I'm coming to depend on your introductions, Octavius. My lavish parties have cost so much that my funds, even with Consul Crassus's loan, are limited. I would not want him to think I'm terribly wealthy. Tell him I'll meet with him, but I'll buy only if his pieces are affordable."

*****

It would not do to be too obvious, so Gaius spent several minutes inspecting a chipped fresco in the peristyle. Caladria sat on a stone bench mumbling to herself while her sister snipped herbs for the dinner.

"Sister," Caladria said, pointing at Gaius.

Aspacia stood with the greens in hand and looked at him. He nodded, trying to look dignified; the last thing he wanted to do was to make a fool of himself. She was used to seeing him in the simple tunic he wore around the villa. Now in the gleaming white toga he appeared an entirely different person. As instructed, he balanced the crisp folds over his left arm and, despite himself, stared at her. He was unable to keep the boyish grin from his face and was pleased that his short blond beard was no longer patchy wisps of hair.

"Well?" he finally said indicating the toga.

"It's quite...nice," she said with a nod.

"Nice?"

"I mean you look very grown up in it. Mature, in a way."

"That's sort of kind of you. You really know how to make me feel adult," he said with a little bow. A moment passed and the light shone across Aspacia's face. He gazed at her for a moment and, not wanting the conversation to end, said, "I wished you were there, at the ceremony."

"I'm sure it was quite impressive. A Roman thing, I guess," she said as if distracted.

"Yes, a Roman thing, as you say. But just for your information it's the most important occasion in a young man's life."

"I see," she said tilting her head, her curls dancing about her face. She turned back to her snipping, sighed quite audibly, and said, "I wonder what a girl like me would be honored with? A slave honor, I presume." She turned back to him, smiled sweetly and said, "if such a ceremonial occasion arises you will inform me, won't you, Master Gaius?"

He rolled his eyes, thought for a moment, and said, "My mother told me that you were asking about me. What sports I enjoy and if I had a girlfriend. Things like that."

Aspacia put her hands on her hips. "And why would I ask such silly questions?"

Gaius laughed and said, "And she says you're always looking at me."

"I might have once or twice but I don't anymore. And I want you to stop staring at me."

"You want me to look at you."

"That's not true, and besides, you're wasting your time."

He laughed again. "You know you love me."

"That's the dumbest thing I ever heard!"

Aspacia suddenly tensed and her bantering abruptly ceased.

"What?" Gaius said.

She stared past him. "I have to go. Come, Caladria, come now."

"Aspacia," he said watching her flee from the peristyle.

"Gaius!" His father's voice shot through the building. "You will come with me."

Toronius said nothing to his trailing son until he had closed the door of the tablinum. "Do you really think that piece of cloth you're wearing changes anything?"

"The senator at Capitoline Hill said—"

"The senator reminded you that you are still subservient to your father, the dominus. And I am the dominus!" Toronius shouted. "Need I mention that you are to obey every demand I make? And I demand that you stay away from that girl. She is my slave, and you will not speak with her. You will be married to Cornelia, and I expect you to be most attentive in her presence. Do you understand?"

Gaius said nothing.

"Do you understand?" his father repeated.

"I heard what you said."

"Get out!"

Gaius turned to go when Toronius said, "I will have that slave girl. I will fuck her anytime I wish. Do you hear that, boy?"

Gaius stiffened and, with contempt building, said in a very quiet voice, "Pray to the Lares each morning that the gods are blind to you. There is already talk."

"Talk? How dare you!"

"Plinius, my esteemed father. I've heard people speak of the strange death of Plinius, and they mention your name. Do pray, won't you?"

Taken aback, Toronius glared at him. Gaius glared back and said, "And about Aspacia: don't touch her." Then he closed the door behind him.

Villa of Deceit

*****

Caladria never slept in the same place. If it wasn't raining, she would roll up in an old horse blanket beneath the trees in the field. Often she would find shelter in the remains of the dilapidated barn, now nearly roofless. On this night, she huddled in an open shed a few meters from the locked servant's gate, which was only used during the day. Thus she was quite surprised when she heard footsteps at such a late hour. She knew the sound of every footstep in the villa, and recognized that of Toronius as he tiptoed with his tiny oil lamp. Although deep within the shadows she inched even further back, fearful that he had come to find her.

The dominus wore a simple tunic and guarded against the cold with the heavy paenula pulled over his head. He was in a hurry and it only took a moment for Caladria to realize that he wasn't searching for her, the sound of his heavy breathing diminishing as he reached the gate. Watching him pass before her, she was surprised to see that he was clothed in a stained toga similar to what the extremely poor would wear, something he would never be seen in. Toronius took a final look around, unbolted the gate, and slipped out. Caladria heard the voice of another man say, "It's a long walk to the Caelian Hill. Keep in the shadows, and it's best not to talk, Dominus. There's a slight moon so I suggest we douse the lamp."

Caladria, like all slaves, knew everything that happened under the dominus's roof, including everyone who came and went. She knew the voice of Octavius, and it made her shiver despite the warmth of the horse blanket. She would not wish to be wherever they were going on this cold night.

*****

The ancient insula, hidden behind a copse of trees, occupied a select piece of property. The two men hid amongst the drooping branches and listened. An owl screeched overhead, then all was again silent.

"I'll keep watch. You must learn to do this alone, Dominus," said Octavius, as he gave Toronius the necessary equipment.

168

"Start it in several places, but never anywhere near the door. Once it's done we must leave immediately. Crassus and his people are waiting. We don't speak with him. He will know it's done."

Normally, Toronius would balk at following Octavius Brundeschi's orders, but he had a bad memory of dark streets and alleys at night. He would be careful, he vowed. Wary of lurking criminals, he stayed close to Brundeschi and held tight to a sack containing his best toga.

Toronius pulled his hat down, and in almost total darkness hurried to an empty chicken coop alongside the wooden five-story building. The bottom floor, containing shops, was deserted at this time of night, but he could hear voices on the second and third floors. Toronius struck the flints together and the spark caught in the dry weeds growing along the side of the coop. He knelt and blew into the flame. The henhouse caught and he carefully made his way to the rear of the structure, again setting the flame. This time it was in a bundle of rags beneath a rickety stairway. He heard someone cough and he froze. The coughing ceased. Toronius decided he would dare to start one more blaze, then he would scurry away.

An amphora of oil stored alongside the building had spilled and soaked a nearby pile of rags. A third-story balcony teetered above, part of its railing long since fallen into a pile of scrap beside the cask. Someone was awake in the apartment he heard a man argue with a woman and he told himself that he must hurry. A door slammed just as the oil caught in an instantaneous blaze. Toronius jumped back, the hat tossed from his head, as the angry man stepped onto the balcony.

"By the gods, fire!" the man shouted, as he stared into Toronius's face. Flames from the oil and splintered wood raced up the insula wall, driving the man from the balcony. Toronius, his ragged clothing rank with soot and oil, stumbled back from the raging flames, covered his face and ran.

Startled voices and screams ripped through the night. People in the lowest floors dashed out, but those in the fourth and fifth were forced to jump.

A man was running after him. Toronius had thrown away the flint and gathered up his toga past his knees, running as fast as he could. Octavius was somewhere near the trees. Cold fear shot through Toronius, propelling him on when the exertion began to tire him. He reached the trees and picked up a stout branch.

"Octavius, where are you?" he blurted as his pursuer reached for him. Toronius swung the branch and caught the man in the stomach. With a moan he doubled over and fell to the ground. Brundeschi grabbed Toronius's arm and hauled him away.

The neighborhood began to wake, as flames consumed the apartment building. The fire could be seen racing into the night sky from five blocks away. A battalion of men dashed past, many with buckets of sloshing water, while others carried ladders and axes.

"Crassus's men," Octavius said into Toronius's ear. "If no owner of the insula shows up they'll let the place burn to the ground."

"And if he does?" asked Toronius, still out of breath.

"There will be a hasty negotiation over price, but this one's burning too fast. The consul will buy the property once the building is ashes."

Screams could still be heard as the firefighters were ordered to protect the surrounding buildings.

"Dominus, I suggest that you get home as fast as you can," said Brundeschi.

"That man saw me," Toronius said, his stomach churning.

"Don't worry, just put on the toga. You don't want anybody to think that you're a pyromaniac or some demented drifter. Now hurry."

"You're not coming back with me?"

"No, Dominus, I must organize my wagons for cleanup in the morning. That is *my* arrangement with the consul, remember?"

Toronius absently nodded.

"No light, and Dominus—say nothing about this night."

Making his way home Octavius's words, "simple drifter, pyromaniac, demented," came back to him. It was the same as he had felt in Alexandria, and more recently when he had left Plinius to die in the old house. Toronius halted a half-mile from the flames, which had finally begun to fade. The insula with its ancient wood had been entirely consumed. He sighed and swore to Great Jupiter that he would not do it again; he would find another way to pay Crassus. Yes, he thought, there was another way, and its dangers were far, far, less.

Only when he reentered the slave's gate did Toronius realize that he had not discarded the filthy rags he'd been wearing. In his haste he had stuffed all of it into his bag and carried it with him.

*****

It was the sixth hour of the day when Toronius finally rose and with his old friend, Vercipius, set off for the baths. He had not spoken to anybody except Apollodoros, to whom he'd handed a sack with orders to burn it in the field. The wind was up, and considering the danger, he told the slave that it should be buried instead.

Apollodoros took the sack and watched the men leave. Curious about its strange smell, he extracted a soiled garment as he passed Caladria in the orchard. He knew that she avoided him whenever possible, but there was something about the cloth that apparently caught her attention, because now she followed him. He turned and stared at her and offered a little smile. After all, he thought, there was no sense in her being afraid of him; it was not he who had raped her. Quite the contrary, it was on more than one occasion that Apollodoros had found her in a hiding place, but reported that the girl was nowhere to be seen. Each time, the dominus would explode in fury, demanding to chain her, and Apollodoros would apologize for his ineptness. But it was an atonement, he told himself, and he believed that he had much for which he had to atone.

As usual, Caladria said nothing, though from a distance she watched him dig a hole in the damp earth and bury the sack with its cloth inside. She wandered off to the copse of trees until

Apollodoros had reentered the villa, then dug up the sack. She sniffed its contents, filled in the hole, and stuffed the cloth beneath her tunic before entering the house.

*****

Gaius waited until Toronius left for the baths, then grabbed Aspacia's hand and briskly led her from the kitchen.

"Where are you taking me?" she said nervously.

"Where we can talk."

"What's wrong? Besides the usual," she asked, when they were well away from the house.

"It's about my father. You're in danger. I have to get you out of here."

"He'll find me, Gaius. I know your father, I've seen men like that before, and it will be worse when he brings me back and brands my forehead with an 'F'."

Aspacia was quiet for a moment, gently took his hands in hers and said, "There's nothing that you can do, nothing that we can do. It's the way of things. I just wish it was different."

Gaius had never seen her cry before. Nor had she ever shown real affection for him and, despite the hopelessness, a great warmth flowed through him. There was always an insouciance about her: a taunting, teasing quality that masked the recent horrors of her life. She sniffed and brushed away a tear. Releasing his hands she said, "You are to be married to the tribune's daughter. She's a nice girl, Gaius. She'll make you a good wife. Do what your father asks; it will be better that way."

Gaius shook his head. "I won't marry her. I can't marry her."

"Talking like this only makes our lives more difficult. You can marry no one without your father's permission, and it will be that way as long as he lives."

"As long as he lives," Gaius repeated.

Aspacia shook her head. "No, don't think like that. Don't do anything that you'll regret. Promise me that. It's the only thing you can do for me."

"As you wish; I shall do nothing that I'll regret."

*****

"What are you doing with that dirty toga?" Livia asked Caladria when she saw her sniffing it outside the kitchen.

Apparently baffled by the question, Caladria turned to Aspacia and the two of them said a half-dozen sentences in Andalusian.

"What did she say?" asked Livia impatiently.

"Domina, she said that she dug it up from the field after Apollodoros buried it. She says that it was the one your husband was wearing when he left the villa last night."

"Left the villa? I didn't know he left. Why would he want Apollodoros to bury it?" she asked, taking the clothing from Caladria.

"I don't know, Mistress. But it has a strange smell."

"I never saw the Dominus wear this rag before." Livia put it to her nose then made a look of disgust. "It smells like olive oil and wood smoke." Turning to Aspacia she said, "Your sister must be mistaken; my husband would never wear something like this."

"If you say so, Domina."

"Burn it," ordered Livia as she started toward the pinacotheca, the picture gallery that Toronius had recently installed at the tribune's suggestion.

"I shall do as you require," said Aspacia, "But, Mistress..."

"Yes?" said Livia turning back, a vindictive look on her face.

"My sister sees everything, and she never tells lies."

*****

Toronius had insisted that they start early, since no carts or wagons were to be on the streets once shops began to open. He required Apollodoros's presence as translator, since the ancient Egyptian spoke some Greek but no Latin. Not trusting his son to leave Aspacia alone if he remained at the villa, Toronius had also commanded Gaius to ride with them.

"Is it far, Master?" asked Apollodoros, as the two-wheeled card bumped over Rome's oval black paving stones.

"About five miles, beyond the Viminal Hills and the Servian Wall."

"Just outside of Rome."

"Yes, now make the horse go faster. We must return before dark."

*****

They fell in behind a caravan of empty wagons, having been given permission to be on the road during daylight hours. The roads had been constructed to allow wagons to pass in opposite directions, and Gaius noted that those coming toward them were filled with brick and charred wood. A wisp of smoke rose lazily in the air from smoldering embers as they approached the remains of a recently burned insula. A number of workmen were loading wagons, and many of the former occupants were sifting through the rubble searching for anything of value.

A man who had suffered an injury watched the cleanup, his eyes drifting from the remains of sandals and blackened candelabras to the lumbering wagons. He glanced toward Gaius and Apollodoros and raised his hand, as if saying, "Look at what we're left with." His eyes fixed on Toronius, wearing his white toga with a hat pulled low over his head. The homeless man studied his face for a long moment, and made as if to approach the cart, when he stopped and swept his gaze over the dominus's clothing. Of course, Toronius realized in relief; last night's arsonist was dressed in rags, whereas the man he saw now was likely an Equestrian with his slave. The homeless man gave them a look of disgust and again cast his eyes toward the smoke drifting into the morning sky.

*****

The Egyptian's home was an ancient villa. Gaius thought that it might have been built in the time of the Etruscan kings, long before the Greeks ruled Rome. The stone wall that surrounded it had long since crumbled and the Ionic pillars at its entrance were mere remnants of an elegant past.

"According to Octavius, the man is very cunning," Toronius said to Apollodoros. "You will let him know that I expect a fair price, and am well versed in ancient artifacts."

A large man in a loose Egyptian tunic opened the door and

174

silently ushered Toronius, Gaius, and Apollodoros into an antechamber. The man gave a slight bow and left. Gaius looked about the walls, with their faded murals of Phoenician and Etruscan scenes of oared ships and bustling harbors.

They stood silently for several minutes, and Gaius felt like an intruder who had entered a long-dead world. Eventually an old man emerged. He dragged his left foot as though it had been crippled in a long-ago accident. He gave a respectful bow and silently evaluated his guests. With the slow motion of an arthritic hand he bade them to follow him to a room with a locked and bolted door. The big man who had let them in emerged from a shadow and unlocked the door and lit a number of oil lamps. He then motioned that they should enter.

The claustrophobic room seemed to Gaius like a burial chamber. There was a heady smell of incense, as if the sepulcher had been lifted from the pyramids themselves. The old man, wrinkled and dried by the Egyptian sun, went to a tall cabinet and opened its doors. With a wave of his hand he directed his guests' attention to eleven statuettes. He held a lamp a few feet from them, and in a wheezing voice, named each of the gods.

Toronius peered at them closely and picked up the statue of Hathor, the goddess of love, fertility, and motherhood. He brought it closer to the light and it glowed with a gold sheen, a woman with cow's horns and a solar disc, sacred to Egyptians.

"Tell him it's impressive, but I doubt that it's terribly ancient. Tell him I don't even think it's real."

"Not real?" the old man said in Latin, surprising Toronius. "Certainly it's real. Would I have my friend Octavius Brundeschi tell you to come all this way to see a fake? I am an Egyptian descended from royalty. Do not insult me, Excellency."

Toronius was taken aback but had no intention of apologizing. He replaced the artifact and said, "Why do you wish to sell these?"

"You see me. I am an old man and will die soon, but I cannot die here. Not in Rome. I must die in Great Egypt, where

I will be prepared for the evaluation of the gods, where my heart will be weighed against a feather. Proper preparation by a learned embalmer is a costly thing. Thus I must part with my prized collection, one that took me a lifetime to acquire."

Toronius nodded warily and said, "I would like to see them outside, where I can truly judge their quality."

"Take this one, the others will remain here. If you see one, you will understand the quality of all," the man said, bobbing his skeletal head like a bird. "But I suggest you not dally. I expect a wealthy collector any moment, and he will buy everything."

Accompanied by the big Egyptian, the three entered an overgrown courtyard. Toronius turned to Gaius and said, "Go back in the house. I need to talk to Apollodoros."

"As you wish, Father," Gaius said, assuming that whatever Toronius was scheming was not meant for his ears. Gaius reentered the room and looked about. It was carefully designed to replicate the sanctuary of Egyptian priesthood. The arrangement of the antiquities seemed artificial and it bothered him.

The old man, deep in thought, didn't see Gaius as he walked briskly from an adjoining room. He called to someone else in the house in a strong, authoritative voice.

"Some of these pieces seem recent, like those I have seen in Alexandria," Gaius said, startling the man.

"Oh no, you are mistaken," the Egyptian said, the dry, strained voice suddenly returning.

"Perhaps," said Gaius. Then with a quizzical smile he pointed to the man's leg and said, "I'm pleased to see that your leg has recovered. I guess such ailments come and go, don't they?"

"You should go into medicine, young man, since you seem to know so much about ailments," the man said.

"Maybe I should. I sense that a number of things here are not just so." Then looking hard at the Egyptian, Gaius said, "This place is stifling. I'll leave you to your toys. I'm sure they are as real as you are." He walked out of the room and into the courtyard where Toronius and Apollodoros were deep in conversation.

"Do you think it's actually that ancient?" Toronius asked Apollodoros.

"Only a master of antiquity like the Jew in Alexandria could tell, Master. Is it old? Probably. But an original from a thousand years ago? I am not qualified to say."

"Well, it looks real, and it's original if I say it is. The old man will soon die and only I, Octavius, you, and Gaius need ever know that I didn't purchase it in Alexandria. If anybody asks we'll say that I was keeping the pieces for last because they are so precious."

Apollodoros merely nodded. From a half dozen yards away, their big escort looked on.

Disgusted with his father's chicanery and the Egyptian's duplicity, Gaius interrupted the conversation.

"Father, I must speak with you."

"Not now. I want to do this quickly and leave here. Talk to me later."

"But—"

"Twenty denarii for the lot. I shall pay you right now," Toronius said to the Egyptian, his chin jutting out decisively.

The old Egyptian, having come into the garden, simply glared at him and shook his head. "For five of the pieces, maybe six, but not all eleven. We are talking about ancient treasures. Look," he said, picking up a three inch scarab, "It's decorated with precious stones and inlaid with gold."

"Twenty denarii," Toronius repeated.

"Impossible."

Toronius turned to leave when the man, seeing his potential customer's apparent resolve, said, "Wait."

The dominus stopped; Gaius could see the smug expression on his face, though their host could not.

"I have fifteen more pieces, all excellent quality. Thirty denarii more, and they are yours as well."

After carefully wrapping them in a wooden box, Apollodoros carried the treasures. The old man had excused himself, but the big Egyptian escorted them to the front door. Within moments Toronius and Apollodoros were climbing onto the wagon. Toronius looked back to the house and shouted, "Gaius, let's go. Why are you still in there?"

"I'll be along in a moment, Father. I just want a peek at the murals."

The Egyptian was watching him impatiently when Gaius heard light footsteps behind him. He turned and saw a young woman who had stopped to stare at him. Her hair was long and black and, if it were not for one half-shut eye and a crooked nose, she would have been pretty. The woman said nothing, but her hand went to her chest and touched a gold amulet supported by a heavy gold chain. A chill coursed through Gaius. The big man looked to the girl and back to him, not comprehending anything.

Gaius turned and hurried to the waiting cart.

Chapter 10

"When I am elected to the senate, I will insist on reforms, Dominus. I know that so many in the Senate just nod their heads and say, 'oh yes, things must be cleaned up,' then they worry that I will do just that. Everything requires a bribe, a payoff. My cousin is a centurion in the army—not a very high paying job," said Retenius pontifically. "You may ask how he makes his money. If a legionnaire wants to get out of an onerous detail he pays him a bribe. What does that say to a soldier who can't afford to pay? This has to stop. A corrupt society faces a premature death. I want Rome to live a long life. I value honest men."

"With good reason. It's an attribute I wholeheartedly support," Toronius said, nodding his head emphatically.

"Trust, honesty and morality are everything. Without that the jug is empty," said the tribune as the two toga-clad men edged their way through the crowded Forum. They stopped at a shop with wares from a town near the Pillars of Hercules. Retenius passed a display of fibulae, clasps that fastened women's stolae at the shoulder, and to a saleswoman said, "I wish to see this one."

"It's better to view it in the light, Excellency," she said, taking the jeweled clasp outside the shop and holding it to the sunlight.

"It's a beautiful piece for your daughter," Toronius said.

"My daughter has several. To show my esteem for your family I wish to present it to Livia, with your permission of course."

"I would consider it an honor, but certainly it's far too

expensive."

"She's worth every bit of it, Dominus."

"Then you must make it a special occasion, and I have a gift for you as well."

They halted at an outdoor fast-food popina for cheese and beer, and Retenius said, "I might not have mentioned it, but I'm having a pool built at my country villa. It will be heated by pipes and fires underground just like those at the balneae. I'll have to purchase additional slaves to keep it going, and it cost far more than I expected, but it's worth every As. You and Livia must come and enjoy it. That's when I will present the broach to her."

"She will be delighted. And since my villa is on your route home, you must stop for some refreshment. Livia would love to see you again."

"And I would love to see her."

*****

It was impossible to avoid vats of burning sulfur and carbonate of soda in which the fullers stomped on clothing with their bleached feet. Throughout the day the slaves drowned togas in the tubs all the while coughing and inhaling the acrid fumes.

"They can never remember whose toga belongs to whom," Toronius complained as they tried to avoid the stench. "I've lost at least three."

Like the rest of the bustling shoppers, they skirted the half-naked slaves and stopped in the Argiletum, a neighborhood beyond the Forum. There books were sold and many liberti, mostly Greek, were employed as copyists.

"I believe that a citizen should be well informed, Toronius," said the tribune, giving a coin to a boy holding a clutch of scrolls. "That's why I buy the *Acta Diurna*. It's published every day. Look here," he said, guiding Toronius toward a bench and away from the jostling crowd. "The authorities actually caught that monster."

"Who, Spartacus?" Toronius said, looking over the tribune's shoulder at the cramped writing.

"No, that will require an entire army, perhaps two or three. Spartacus has ninety thousand men. No, Toronius, one of the smuggled slaves has been caught, the ones who broke away and killed Plinius near that deserted town."

"Ardea?" volunteered Toronius.

"That's the place. There were four or five of them. They massacred entire families, Dominus, and as you know, they killed Plinius," the tribune said bitterly.

"And Plinius was an innocent man. But a savage that kills Roman citizens must be strangled immediately. That would be justice; the families deserve nothing less."

"Oh, he'll get justice, but the God of Justice wants him to talk in a court of law. The captured slave claims that Plinius was a smuggler and had an accomplice: someone he could identify. He hopes his assistance will be rewarded with clemency. As a tribune I would love to get him in my court, as well as the one he identifies."

"Personally I don't think the slave is worthy of Roman jurisprudence. In my humble opinion, I think he should be put to death immediately. After all, the man is desperate. He'll accuse anyone. There are a million people to pick from in Rome. I wouldn't put much credibility in his statement if I were a judge," said Toronius, vigorously shaking his massive head. "So what else is in that tattle sheet?"

"It's the vex populi, the voice of the people, Toronius," the tribune said with a deprecating smile. "I'm surprised that a man of your stature doesn't subscribe to it. Now this," said Retenius, pointing to a sentence on the unpunctuated page, "is really a travesty."

"I'm all ears," said Toronius with a playful grin. "But there's another popina over there and I'm still thirsty. I'll buy you the best beer in Rome, better than the last place. Then you can read it to me."

They found a bench in the crowded tavern and were served by a nubile slave girl. Toronius gave her five denarii and thanked her.

"You're a generous man, Toronius," said the tribune,

sipping his beer and watching the girl sashay between tables, aware that all eyes followed her.

"She had an eye for you," Toronius said.

"I still see my late wife in my dreams each night, Dominus. But if I were to take another woman for a lifetime, she would have to be a very special one: beautiful, elegant, and very seductive."

"And you have one in mind?"

Retenius glanced at Toronius, then down at the papyrus, and said, "I was about to read you this, Dominus."

"Oh yes, 'the travesty' you called it. Is it about the rising cost of grain? That's a travesty for sure."

"For the poor, yes. But this is worse. A fire, presumably arson, a few nights ago."

"What fire? I didn't hear anything about it. Of course I had my dick inside Livia most of the night, and she's a real screamer."

"Really?" said Retenius. "I assumed she was passionate, but more of the silent type." He took a long swig of beer and said, "But despite the affection I had for my late wife, finding out how a woman is in bed still interests me. I guess one has to screw them to really know," he laughed.

"It's the only way," said Toronius, nodding his head authoritatively. "Now, what about that fire? What makes them think it was arson?"

Retenius peered at the print then said, "It was on the outskirts of Rome. A survivor, an occupant saw a man lighting a fire that night beneath his balcony and the place went up quickly. He was the only one who got out. His wife and seven-year-old daughter were burned to death. The husband said that he gave chase but he was struck by the culprit and collapsed. According to this, the arsonist, heavy and middle-aged, ran away."

"Then what?" Toronius said, peering over his drink.

"The firefighters, those hired by Marcus Crassus, arrived but could do nothing. The consul came the next morning and bought the property from the owner."

"Most owners of a wretched insula won't mind if it burns down as long as Crassus offers a good price."

"How do you know it's an insula? It doesn't say that here," the tribune said.

"It's just an assumption. Who would burn down anything other than an old apartment?"

"True, but a horrible thing nonetheless."

"Come," Toronius said, "I have something for you at the house: a gift, something you'll like."

The two men entered the street and passed the Forum when a libertus broke through the crowd and, bowing before Retenius, said, "Tribune, praise Great Jupiter that I have found you. The court requires your immediate presence."

"Now? It's already the fifth hour, what can I possibly accomplish before dusk?"

"Excellency, I only bring the message. They have caught someone important and they require your attendance."

"Just how important could that be? Very well, tell them I'll be there." Turning to Toronius he said, "I'll come tomorrow morning for the salutation, if that is all right, Dominus."

"Of course, and please bring your daughter. I think she and Gaius should get better acquainted. And perhaps we might discuss the dowry."

"The dowry? Yes, that is something I wish to speak with you about, but at another time."

"Where have you been?" Aspacia asked petulantly, as she snipped herbs in the garden. Caladria ambled toward her while wiping the sleep from her eyes.

"Out there," she said, pointing toward the field. Her hair was matted, and stains splotched her long tunic.

"You were sleepwalking again last night. I saw you leave the house. Where did you bed down?"

"In that old barn. I like it there."

"There are rats in there, Caladria, and that place is filthy."

"My friend Arzeka used to live there."

"That man is dead."

"Not really. We talk at night. He doesn't mind being dead,

Aspacia. He says he can go everywhere and he sees things like I do. But he can see more things, things that haven't even happened yet."

Aspacia knew it was useless to dispute her visions; it always had been. Caladria, she recalled, had claimed to see ghosts since she was three. After a moment, Aspacia said, "You can help me in the kitchen this morning. The Domina is planning a party."

Caladria swayed back and forth and gazed at her muddy feet. "Arzeka showed me something last night," she said.

"What did he show you, Caladria, a chariot to take us away?" Aspacia said, peeved that Caladria prattled on offering not a bit of help.

"No, I saw something in here," the girl said pointing to her head. "I saw a dolly, a funny looking one too."

"You mean a doll, like a rag doll?"

Caladria nodded. "It was a little skinny one with a head like a puppy dog and eyes of glass beads, not gems or anything like that."

Exasperated Aspacia said, "Are you going to help me or not, Caladria? At least hold this basket."

"And do you know what else? The doll became many dolls and they are all cursed. Someone is going to die in a house like this."

"Who is going to die?" Aspacia put down her trowel, a worried look coming to her face. She stood and took her sister's hand, peering at her as if she were a little child, and said, "Caladria, I ask you again, who is going to die?"

"I'm not sure. Arzeka only laughed when I asked him. He knows everything, Aspacia."

"Is it Gaius?" she said, her hand beginning to shake.

"Gaius? I don't think so. You and Gaius will..."

"Will what?"

"Arzeka told me not to say. I will help you now."

"Caladria!"

"I have to wash my feet. See how muddy they are?"

Aspacia watched as her sister trod to a bucket, poured water over her feet, then walked toward the kitchen with the basket of herbs.

"*Ius vitae necisque*, I have the power of life and death," Toronius kept repeating to himself, wondering how worried he should be. He hadn't slept all night, knowing that the man who had escaped the house fire could identify him. Now the clients were arriving for the light morning meal. He hoped that Retenius would arrive later. It would be uncomfortable if there were any discussion about the fire.

"Octavius, I need to speak with you," Toronius said when the man arrived for the breakfast. Quickly, the dominus led him into the tablinum. "Everybody is reading about the fire. Retenius read it to me yesterday. The man whose house I burned down can identify me. I'm sure of it."

"Dominus, the man doesn't know where you live even if he could identify you. And remember, it was dark and you were wearing those rags. There is nothing that can be brought before the court."

"I'm not so sure. What if he sees me on the street? He will surely accuse me."

"He won't if he values his life. To accuse you might involve Marcus Crassus, and that's a very dangerous thing. You have nothing to worry about. Be yourself, Dominus. Relax. Show only the concern of an alarmed citizen."

Toronius paced the tablinum, his worry not assuaged. "I will raise the money I owe the consul, but I will set no more fires, Octavius. Of that I assure you."

"Fine, set no more fires, but that's between you and the consul. It's his money you borrowed. I'm just a simple drover, but I'll say this: do not play with Crassus."

"Of course, of course," said Toronius, nodding and rubbing his hands together.

There was a knock on the door and Apollodoros stuck his head in. "Dominus, his Excellency Tribune Retenius and his daughter have arrived."

"Tell him that I'll be right down. And Apollodoros, if any other clients arrive, tell them that I'm indisposed and won't be able to speak with them today."

"Dometius Scipio Retenius, and the beautiful Cornelia, welcome again to my humble house," Toronius said generously, arms outstretched. "I hope I haven't kept you waiting. Have you sampled the Falernian wine I just received? It's from Campania vineyards, fifteen years old."

"We have, and it's the finest I've had in a very long time, Dominus. And your son, that remarkable young man, is he here? Perhaps Cornelia and Gaius could share a few moments together while you and I talk business."

"That's an excellent idea. I believe he's in the orchard giving instructions to the slaves."

"I trust that we don't have to chaperone the two of you," the tribune said to his daughter with a grin.

"Father!" said Cornelia placing her hands on her hips. "I am a perfect lady, and Gaius is a most respectable gentleman."

The tribune laughed and wagged a finger at Cornelia. "Then go!" Turning to Toronius, he sighed and said, "Dominus, what do I know about a daughter who is growing up so fast? I only wish my wife was here to tell her all the things I can't. Maybe that's one reason I'm counting on Livia."

"No woman can take the place of a mother, but Livia would love to give her counsel. She always wished for a daughter but regretfully we never had one."

"Well, many men regard daughters as a curse but without them we would have damn few men. I personally deplore a man who refuses to pick up his newborn, regardless of whether it's a boy or girl."

"A worthy point, Retenius. After all, the army needs men and they don't grow on trees."

Then, wiping away his disgust, the tribune said, "You should know, my dear man, that Cornelia speaks of nothing but your son. At least," he chortled, "when she deigns to share her thoughts with me."

"Ah, love. What a wondrous and rare thing. A loving and willing wife is a treasure. Gaius will be a very lucky man. Perhaps we should plan a wedding date. Livia could work out the details with Cornelia."

"It's a fine idea and deserves serious thought."

*****

Toronius led the tribune past the pinacotheca with its newly painted frescoes and into the exedra, a spacious west-facing room with rows of shelves. Oriental rugs hung on the walls as pieces of art, since no Roman would defile such works by laying them on the floor. Retenius gazed at the intricate tapestries before his attention was diverted by Toronius indicating the two dozen artifacts neatly arranged for him.

"Take the ones you like, Tribune," Toronius said expansively, "I just purchased them from an impeccable source. I mentioned a gift for you, so please honor me with your choices."

"They're magnificent!" said Retenius, his eyes scanning the foreign objects. "But I refuse to deplete your collection by taking one."

"What were the poet's words?" opined Toronius sagaciously, "*Quas dederis solas semper habebis opes*, 'the only wealth you keep forever is that which you give away.' I want you to realize how much I value your friendship."

"As I value yours," said, Retenius, again attending to the artifacts. "This may surprise you, Dominus, but I believe I know the names and importance of each of these."

"And I thought my son was being so instructive when you were here last," Toronius laughed. "Ah, you were testing him!"

The tribune smiled broadly and said, "Exactly, but not to learn of the Egyptian gods. No, I wanted to give Gaius a chance to impress me and my daughter. And I must say he did so admirably. Now, let's see if I can remember. This one with the red double crown and the erection is Min, god of fertility, this with the bird beak and staff is Thoth, god of wisdom and, yes, the sitting jackal with the crook is Anubis, guardian of the dead."

The tribune lifted one from the shelf, examined it, and said, "Toronius, I especially like this lady with the scepter and crown.

She is Ma'at, you know, the goddess of justice and order. I think it's an appropriate symbol for one who administers the law. And in the interest of justice I will pay you thirty denarii."

"Excellency, that is far too much! Besides, it's a gift."

"Future father-in-law or not, I insist. There's another gift you might present me if you wish, and that's worth even more."

"Just ask."

"If I feel bold enough I just might do that."

Dometius Scipio Retenius laughed and slapped Toronius on the back, a familiarity the dominus did not expect. Toronius chuckled a little nervously and said, "Of course, consider it yours."

*****

"Oh Gaius, I'm sorry to intrude, I didn't know you were speaking with your father's little slave girl," Cornelia said when she saw Gaius and Aspacia alone in the orchard.

"We can talk later. I have work to do," Aspacia said, quickly dropping Gaius's hand.

Cornelia watched her go. "You allow her to call you 'Gaius'. How democratic. My father and I never allow our slaves to address us that way. But then we have many more slaves, and I guess some houses are more formal than others."

"Aspacia and I are friends."

"So it appears." Cornelia said stiffly, observing Aspacia as she slipped into the villa. Then, dismissing the slave from her mind she said, "Gaius, my father has given me permission to speak with you, so please, come sit and let us talk."

"Of course, Cornelia, we should talk," said Gaius.

Sensing his chill she followed him as he said, "I'll show you our new art chamber. My father hired several fine artists, but I think he did it to impress your father. There's a bench over there. That's where we shall talk."

The pinacotheca was a long, narrow room where, in most villas, private discussions took place. Cornelia could feel the tension between them as they entered the cool chamber.

"I hope the images don't offend you," said Gaius sitting across from the girl. "The artist offered the dominus a choice of paintings like hunts, games, races, and such, but he chose erotica."

Cornelia rose from her chair and walked to the frescoes to study them.

"On the contrary, they don't offend me. I have seen paintings like these before. We don't have any like them in my house; my father might feel embarrassed for me, and he's very proper, being a tribune and all. He has actually sheltered me a great deal." She didn't say anything for a long moment. Then, looking back at Gaius, she continued, "I didn't realize there were so many ways of doing it, but being chaste, how would I know?"

"I guess you wouldn't," Gaius replied.

Cornelia returned and sat on a chair beside him. "Father likes you, Gaius, and your father and mine want us to marry."

"Is that what you want, Cornelia?"

The girl nodded and said, "I like you too, Gaius. Oh, I know that you don't love me, your heart is with the slave girl. Don't deny it, I can see it. But you know you can't marry her; your father will never permit it." She turned in her chair and pointed to the erotic frescoes.

"You can do all of those things to me when we marry. You can teach me and perhaps it will be enjoyable for you. I will be a good wife to you, Gaius, and will give you many sons."

"I have no doubt that you would be a good wife, Cornelia, but..."

"But you don't want me, do you?"

"I want to make any wife of mine happy, and would not want to make you unhappy."

"I think you can make me happy," she said, looking down at her hands in her lap.

In a very quiet voice, Gaius said, "If our fathers have us marry I will try."

"I should not have to convince you to like me; I should not have to say any of this," Cornelia said, rising from her chair, her eyes tearing. She brushed her hand over her face and hurried from the gallery.

*****

An unusually cold wind arose later that afternoon, and Apollodoros ventured into the field to place a blanket over a sleek horse that Toronius had bought but a week before. It struck Apollodoros strange that his master would desire to have one, since he had made no mention of wanting to ride. Certainly it was not purchased for Gaius even though he could ride quite well, but perhaps Toronius wanted to race and bet on it. And who would be better to ride it than Gaius? But his ruminations did not make sense. After the Greek tied the blanket on the skittish horse, he began to walk toward the copse of trees around which swirled thick fog.

"Do not too quickly give away the treasured piece," a voice said above the swishing of wind-blown leaves.

Apollodoros stopped and looked about. Caladria was plopped in her usual spot, head covered with an old horse blanket so that she appeared like the stump of a tree. Coming closer, he peered down at her and asked, "What treasured piece? Give it away to whom?"

Caladria ignored the question, and as if speaking to herself, muttered, "In the black dust after the rain. It will be there. Hide it till later."

"You're not making any sense, child. I have no idea what you're talking about."

"That's okay. It hasn't happened yet, but now you know."

The girl turned her head away and began to hum a child's lullaby. Apollodoros simply stared at the rotund lump on the cold ground, shook his balding head, and walked away.

*****

"I want each wrapped carefully and put into these boxes," Toronius said to Apollodoros and Aspacia after the tribune and his daughter had departed. A silk pouch with a pulled drawstring containing the tribune's coins sat on a table. Gaius watched from the doorway as the artifacts were taken from the shelf to the table for wrapping.

"Gaius, come here; I must speak with you. Tribune Retenius

and I have been discussing your marriage to Cornelia. We are considering a date."

Aspacia gave Gaius a furtive glance. Toronius saw it and said, "Why are you looking at him, girl? You have a job to do. Now do it!"

"Father, I spoke with Cornelia and I don't think—"

"That's right boy, you don't think. You don't think because I think for you. Now I'll tell you what's going to happen," the dominus said angrily.

Caladria, hearing Toronius's raised voice, came in from the kitchen and stood beside her sister as she wrapped the artifacts and placed them in a wooden box.

"What are you doing in here? Get out!" Toronius shouted when he saw Caladria. Startled, the girl jumped back; her leg tripped Aspacia, flinging an Anubis from her hand. They watched in horror as the artifact flew upward before crashing onto the tile floor. Its head broke off and its eyes split into minute pieces.

"You cow! What have you done?" roared Toronius as he stared at the shattered god. He raised his hand to strike Caladria, who cowered by the door.

"Don't!" shouted Gaius.

The dominus turned, his face twisted in fury, when Gaius knelt and picked up the god's eye where it had landed at his feet. Standing, he examined it closely before glancing up. "Father, I tried to tell you something in the courtyard of the old Etruscan house. The Egyptian you bought these from said that these pieces had precious stones and inlaid gold."

"Of course they do. So what?"

"The eyes in this 'artifact' are not garnets or rubies, they're glazed plaster. See, it crushes between my fingers. I tried to tell you about him, but you wouldn't let me."

"Tell me what?" Toronius said, his face tight, fearing the worst.

"Now would you care to know, Father?"

Toronius said nothing but merely nodded his head.

"The old man, the Egyptian, was not a cripple. I saw him

walk perfectly well, and he did not wheeze when he talked to his help. He was a total fake. And I suspect that everything you purchased from him is fake as well."

"The dolly," said Caladria in a voice barely heard.

"What was that?" Toronius barked.

"The doll in your dreams, Caladria? The cursed one you told me about?" said Aspacia, turning to her sister.

Caladria nodded and pointed to the god that lay headless on the floor. "I talked to my friend again," she said in halting Latin. "He told me that the curse is inside."

"What's this prattle about a curse?" said Toronius, his eyes boring into Caladria.

Apollodoros knelt and picked up the shattered deity. A slim piece of papyrus poked from its severed neck. He drew it out and offered it to Toronius. "It's in Greek, Dominus."

"Then read it!"

"Yes," Gaius repeated, "Read it to us, Apollodoros."

The slave stared at the tight script then looked at Toronius. "Master, perhaps it's best if I speak to you alone. It is rather ominous."

"Read it," Toronius said, "I don't believe in curses and superstitions."

Apollodoros again perused the script making sure that he had it right. He cleared his throat and said, "It proclaims that 'All must know that there will be death within the house of him who harbors me."

"Give them to me!" Toronius roared, snatching each figure from Aspacia's hand as she hurriedly removed them from the crate. Infuriated, he tore off their wrappings and mindlessly snapped them in half. Each contained an omen. When only five remained, he raised the heavy box with its bronze fittings and hurled it across the floor.

"Get out! Every one of you!" he shouted. All headed for the door when Toronius said to Apollodoros, "Octavius is in the atrium. Get him in here now!"

Octavius Brundeschi stood by the door as Toronius's eyes bored into him. "You son of a barbarian whore! What have you done to me? All those 'artifacts' I spent my money on are fakes. Not just fakes, they are all cursed. Do you hear me Octavius? Cursed! And I sold one for a goodly sum and not just to anyone. I sold it to the tribune Retenius: the man whose daughter my son is to marry."

Brundeschi raised his palms and appearing shocked said, "Dominus, I had no idea that they were fakes. I knew that you did not want to go back to Alexandria but needed precious pieces. I went all around, asking if anybody had contacts in Egypt, and eventually found the people you went to see. I thought it was so fortunate because the man was highly recommended."

"The fakes were made for me and me alone. It was a trap."

"Then you must have enemies from Alexandria, Dominus. I wonder why? But what if the piece hadn't broken? Then neither you nor Retenius would have known it was a fake. As for the curse, it's a foreign one, and what power could that possibly have?"

"But they were delicate and they could break. If he did find out, what of my reputation?"

"Reputation, Dominus?" Octavius said, displaying his crooked smile.

Toronius sat heavily in his tablinum chair while Octavius Brundeschi sat on the low client bench.

"I dare not sell any more of them. How will I repay Crassus? I was counting on the sale of those pieces."

"I came here today to help you, that's true. I didn't come to your morning salutation for cheap wine, cheese, and a few coins."

"You came to help me? You ruined me."

"The great man you owe has a chore for you, and it will be executed in three days when the moon is down."

"Not a fire! I will not start another fire, Octavius."

"What choice have you? He expects repayment for his loan, plus interest. He is a businessman, and you understand business. But perhaps you have another immediate source of wealth. Of course, you could move out and lease your villa for a year or two, but that might diminish your standing with the tribune. I'm not sure what you could sell besides your slaves; your son, or perhaps your wife. She is quite a beauty. But regardless, my employer is quite insistent."

"You are a swine, Octavius."

Again the crooked smile and Octavius said, "It won't be a big fire, Dominus, but it's an important one. The consul desires property between Palatine Hill and Caelian Hill."

"There's expensive construction being done in that valley, Octavius. Senators own villas there. It's terribly dangerous."

"Crassus will have his people nearby."

"Why me? Why not a slave or a libertus he trusts?"

"Oh, he trusts you, and trusts that you'll do as required."

"I don't know why he's so adamant."

"Of course you do."

Toronius hunched his shoulders and raised his hands in bewilderment.

"You stole his father's cattle. Don't you remember? He does."

"That was years ago! I was only a boy. Sure, I took two or three, but I returned one. I was scared. Our family was poor, and what were one or two cows to him or his father? They were rich."

Octavius ignored the response. "I will come by for you. Wear something nondescript like last time, and speak not a word of this. The consul sees and hears of everything. He has many spies."

"And you are one of them," said a seething Toronius.

"I wish you no harm, Dominus. And as for the consul, it's best to stay on his good side. He's not always a nice man."

Chapter 11

"Livia," Junia said, dangling her feet in the cool water of the atrium's pool, "I heard Vercipius, your husband's old crony, say that Brundeschi and Plinius knew each other quite well. Apparently they trafficked in high end prostitutes here and in Egypt."

"It's hardly illegal. Toronius should have gotten into the business before there was so much competition. Now Rome is flooded with them."

"You're missing the picture. That snake Octavius Brundeschi and the dead Plinius Apuleius Regulus were associates, and Retenius, your future father-in-law, knew Plinius very well."

"Retenius said Plinius was only related to one of his clients."

"Plinius was family, Livia. He was very valuable to the praetor and that's why Retenius was so concerned about his murder. Retenius has hired people to find out who killed Plinius."

"But a slave killed him."

"Because somebody, a Roman or a libertus, made it possible."

"So you think that there's a connection between Retenius, Plinius, and Brundeschi?"

"I'm just connecting the strings, sister. And then there's Consul Crassus," Junia said, as she watched Apollodoros, Aspacia and Caladria standing around the brazier. Beside it was a wooden box.

"I don't see how he fits in," Livia said.

"Octavius Brundeschi works for the consul and he does

more than just pick up trash."

Livia said nothing, her mind focused on what Gaius had told her about Toronius weeks before. Her attention turned to the trio feeding objects into the brazier and she said, "What are they burning? It smells horrible."

"Probably something Toronius wanted them to do," said Junia. She absently picked up a slip of papyrus that had escaped from the coals and flown into the atrium, snagging on her sandal. "What's this?" she mused, holding it up to the light.

Livia glanced over, squinted and said, "It's got some kind of writing on it. It's not Latin, I can recognize Latin."

"Greek, maybe," said Junia. "But I can't read either one."

"Apollodoros can, and Gaius can read some."

"It must be from the brazier; the wind's blowing this way," Junia said rising from the stone bench.

The two women passed through the atrium to the far end of the peristyle. They watched for a minute, their curiosity building when Livia said, "Aren't those my husband's Egyptian things?"

"They are, Domina," said Apollodoros as he stirred the charcoal.

"But aren't they valuable?" she continued, sudden concern in her voice.

"He just told us to burn them. It's not for me to question him, Mistress."

"What does this say?" asked Junia, handing him the slip of papyrus.

Apollodoros peered at it for a long moment and Livia became impatient. "Come on, I know you can read it."

He looked at the cryptic ink once again. "It's in Greek. It's an omen of sorts."

Caladria pulled a similar slip of papyrus from a broken deity and spoke to Aspacia in Andalusian.

"What's she saying? I can't understand that gibberish," demanded Livia.

"It's a curse, Mistress," Aspacia said. "Each of these Egyptian statues had a curse inside."

"What kind of curse?" Junia asked, worry in her eyes.

"We want the truth!" Livia demanded.

Aspacia looked at Livia without flinching and said, "The curse damns every household that contains the god, and says that it will bring death."

"Does the Dominus know about this?"

"Yes, Mistress," replied Apollodoros. "That's why we were told to burn them."

Livia snatched the last god figure from the box and stared at it.

"Why would anyone put a curse in a god statue so long ago? They would have no idea who would come to own it," said Junia.

"It's not old, Mistress, and it's a fake. All the pieces were fakes. He bought them from an Egyptian," said Aspacia.

"The Egyptians again?" Livia said with alarm. Leaving her sister at the brazier, Livia turned toward the tablinum shouting "Toronius, what have you done?"

Octavius was about to leave when Livia swept in. "Don't you dare walk out of here," she said to Brundeschi. "Toronius," she said in her high-pitched voice while waving the papyrus, "I want to know about this. I insist on knowing why you bought those fakes, and with whose money. And," she spat, turning to Octavius, her dark eyes flashing, "I demand to know your part in this!"

Toronius snatched the papyrus slip, ripped it to shreds, and said, "It's none of your damned business. You need to know nothing, woman. Get out of my office!

"And you," he said as he turned to Octavius, "will leave my house and never come to my villa again."

Brundeschi bowed and with a hint of a smile said, "When the moon is down, Dominus."

Toronius grabbed his wife's arm and shoved her out the door.

*****

"What happened?" asked Junia, looking at the reddened blotch on Livia's arm.

"The bastard threw me out. He wouldn't tell me anything."

"He expects you to suffer in silence, like a decent Roman woman."

"Silence is hardly my forte, Junia."

"Sister, just be sure that you don't bring the house down on top of you."

"If I do, I will dig myself from the rubble and that will please both me and the gods."

*****

"Where is that worthless kid with his fancy toga virilis?" shouted Appian Dio as he sauntered into the atrium.

Apollodoros, who had opened the gate for him, said, "I suspect he's lurking around the kitchen."

"Why, has he taken a sudden interest in the culinary arts?"

"Not exactly. Whatever he's cooking up has little to do with food. Do you wish that I announce your presence in a sententious voice, since you're now a great warrior?" asked the Greek.

"You have always been a pompous ass, Apollodoros," replied Appian Dio.

"I am merely a humble servant of limited talents."

"You are the craftiest, most enigmatic person I've ever known, and I've known you my entire life."

"Then you have been blessed," said Apollodoros, hiding a smile.

"Six months in the legions would do you good," retorted Appian. "That will teach you humility."

"Being a slave saves me from that misery. And of course I'm Greek. I see how envious you are."

Appian Dio looked at Apollodoros with incredulity. "Great Jupiter, you are insufferable."

"You've returned!" said Gaius, entering the atrium.

"Your Excellency, Master Gaius, or should I call you 'virilis'? Have you found something to satisfy your virility?" asked Appian Dio, landing a punch on his arm.

"Not exactly."

"I should have known. After what I've been through I want

to screw half the women in Rome. But pray," he said looking at Apollodoros, "get me away from this overbearing and obnoxious Greek!"

Apollodoros raised his eyebrows and tendered an expression of intense hurt. "I know when my powers of reason and moderation are not appreciated by Romans. With your gracious permission, my lords, I shall take my leave."

"Leave!" ordered Appian Dio in his most authoritarian voice.

*****

"So, training's over?" asked Gaius, as he walked with the legionnaire into the peristyle.

"Damn right, but the regimen never lets up. We have thirty-mile marches, mock combat, and more training every month. We build roads, bridges, and fortifications, and pack sixty pounds on the march. I never thought I would feel empathy with a mule. And if you're not up to the expectations of a centurion then you're slammed with the vitus stick. They use it quite liberally. It's supposed to improve your morale."

"It's a pretty idiotic way to live, Appian. You get beaten up by your officers and impaled by your enemies."

"But it's still the best army in the world. And besides, I'm now entitled to wear the crossed belts. It's the sign of a legionnaire and it's a prized possession. But if you fuck up they take them away, and that's a disgrace. Of course, if you really fuck up, they do a lot worse."

"So now you're a munifes?"

"I was. A munifes is a raw recruit with no rank or status. But I have a special skill."

"Screwing."

"Besides that. I can play the horn, so now I'm an immunes, not high in the ranks but not the lowest either. A trumpeter is a cornicen. I escape the worst of the details, but I'll be in the thick of the fighting. That's the fun part."

"Right, until the arms and legs fly off."

"Not mine, Gaius. I joined the Mithraic faith, the army's religion. Its god, Mithras, has saved many a soldier."

"Oh yeah, the one that sacrifices the white bull, and you get to drink all the blood you want."

"Not all of it, you'd drown."

"I never thought of you as religious," said Gaius, his eyes trained on Aspacia as she walked past, giving him a beguiling smile.

"Not as long as it doesn't interfere with..." Appian Dio's voice trailed off as Aspacia disappeared around a corner.

"By the gods, she absolutely bewitching. She's—"

"Aspacia. One of my father's slaves."

"Uh-huh," said Appian Dio. "The Dominus is not the sharing kind. I think you're in deep shit. I know about women. She likes you. She likes you a lot."

"And I'm in love with her," Gaius said quietly.

"That's pretty damn serious," said Appian Dio, throwing Gaius a concerned look. "In fact, knowing your father, that can get you killed. But I'm all ears if you want to talk about it."

"I can't talk about her to anybody else. But not here. I'll walk back to the Campus Martius with you, if you're going that way."

*****

The road to the training grounds, the Field of Mars, led beyond the Servian Wall that surrounded the original Rome. As they walked along the Via Triumphalis the crowd began to thin, and nearing the encampment, they encountered more military. A troop of cavalry charged down the road, mud splattering from horses' hooves.

"Damn them!" shouted Appian Dio seeing the splotch on his newly washed tunic. "They think they're so damn invincible."

"They do look impressive," said Gaius.

"Oh, they look pretty, all right, but they're not worth shit until the infantry win the battle. They're almost always held in reserve or attack vulnerable flanks. Then they come in and wipe up a disorganized bunch of barbarians," he fumed. "You know, Gaius, we were shown horses from Parthia. Their mounts are almost twice the size of ours, and they're covered in bronze armor just like their riders. They're called cataphracts and will beat our horsey guys every time. Only a bolt from our scorpions will bring them down. I hope we never have to fight them. Worthless!" he shouted at the long departed cavalry.

They continued in silence until Appian Dio asked, "Does your father know about you and the girl?"

"Of course."

"I know Toronius pretty well. I bet he's jealous as hell," said Appian Dio.

"He forbids me to have anything to do with her. He's fucked her sister Caladria, but that's only for sport. She's nothing to look at."

"And he's saving Aspacia as a special treat," said Appian with finality. "Of course, as his slave he can do anything he wants to her. What do you do then?"

"I don't know. I forgot to mention that he requires me to marry a praetor's daughter next month. Appian, I'm terrified. The girl, Cornelia, wants to marry me. She's seems sweet enough and will do whatever I want, but she's plain as a rag toy. She means no harm, but there's no spark. She doesn't have Aspacia's playfulness or her intelligence. My father expects that her father will become a senator and will help me gain position. And of course our family will too. But..."

Gaius stopped and said, "Appian, I can't marry Cornelia. She's a simpleminded nothing, and being with her every day and every night will kill me. I won't be able to make her happy, and she knows it. It will be a fucking cold bed, a disaster."

"Speaking of simple, I can read your mind. I always could. You're going to run away with your father's slave, aren't you?"

"I haven't gotten that far, Appian."

"It will be the stupidest thing you've ever done. Where will you two go where Toronius won't find you? You have damn little money, probably not even enough for passage to Africa Proconsularis, and that's only across from Sicilia."

"We can change our names, and I speak some Greek."

"And be a stranger in a foreign land? And where can you go that isn't a Roman province with Roman soldiers? They'll find both of you and brand her forehead with the 'F'. There's a big business in finding runaway slaves. Think of that. Your father's been good to me, but he's not a man to fool with. He will take Aspacia, all right, but he'll drop her like all the others he gets bored with. He has always gone from one woman to the next and she may not be the fantasy he expects. In time, you may buy her; then she'll be yours."

"Even if my father agrees to sell her, it will be too late. I will be married to Cornelia."

"Nothing is permanent except change. This Cornelia will have to tolerate you, and you'll be the paterfamilias of your own house. Until then, Toronius has the patria potestas. He has the power of the father until he dies, and that includes life and death over you. Remember the phrase? *Ius vitae necisque.*"

"Of course, but he may not have as much power as he would like, Appian. The scales may be tipped. He's in debt and could be into some very bad things."

"Such as?"

"The murder of a Roman citizen."

"Plinius?"

"That and maybe something else. Remember what I told you about what happened in Alexandria?"

"The way Toronius beat a girl and left her for dead. The one in the brothel?"

"Well, she's very much alive, and she's *here*. I recognized her when my father bought some fake artifacts from an Egyptian. The seller might even have been her father; she looked like him."

"This is recent?"

"Yes, a few weeks ago."

"Do you think the fakes were made just for him? A kind of revenge?"

"Precisely."

"But how did they track your father down? Rome is a big place. Do they know where the villa is?"

"Perhaps. We could have been followed on the way home."

"Toronius must be terrified."

"I'm sure he's terrified, but he didn't see the girl when he bought the fakes. He thinks she's still in Alexandria, or dead. After he raped and beat her that night, he ran downstairs. My father was a bloody mess; she had ripped him pretty badly, and she'd torn off this gold necklace he was wearing. He had bought it that day. Apollodoros stayed with him in the alley, but my father sent me back for the amulet. The girl was still there, alive but barely."

"And what about the necklace? Did she still have it?"

"Yes. I saw how badly she was beaten and I let her keep it. Then I hurried back downstairs. I could already hear people coming from the bar on the ground floor."

"What did Toronius say when you didn't have the necklace?"

"He was furious. I told him that the girl had been taken from the room and the necklace, the amulet, was gone."

"But you said that she's alive and here in Rome."

"The girl I saw when my father bought the fake gods was wearing the same golden necklace. She recognized me, and knew that I recognized her. And that was despite a broken nose and blindness in one eye. And to top that, each of the fakes contained a curse."

"I see why your father's a worried man. It sounds like they're playing with him like a cat does with a mouse. And you know...the cat always kills the mouse when it gets tired of the game."

"I suspect you're right."

"It would be best to stay out of his way. Frightened men do dangerous and impulsive things. Be very careful, Gaius."

"I'll watch him. But it's Aspacia that I worry about."

*****

Toronius, Livia, Gaius, and Apollodoros were riding together in Retenius's petoritum on the way to the praetor's country villa. The elegant open coach, with its carpeted floor and glittering ornaments, was pulled by four sleek horses. It progressed beyond the Servian Wall and the fashionable Caelian Hill on the Via Appia road. The praetor's country villa rested only a quarter mile beyond the Servian Wall, but seemed miles from the bustling city.

The day had been auspiciously planned by the praetor, for it was the festival of Anna Perenna: a jubilant time celebrating the goddess of the New Year. Toronius sat erect and regal in his finest toga, pinned at the shoulder by a silver broach with an engraved "T" in the center. Gaius sat beside him wearing his toga virilis, while Livia and Apollodoros occupied the rear seat.

Toronius, having unexpectedly received the invitation, had to quickly purchase an appropriate gift. His choice was an elegant silver beaker adorned with bas-relief images of the skeletons and faces of Greek poets: a popular art form in aristocratic company.

Gaius, numb with foreboding, held the wrapped gift in his lap. He had known that this day would come: a life sentence, a virtual execution, and it got closer each day. He had hoped that the announcement of his engagement would be a quiet affair, perhaps even postponed by some calamitous event. But no such event was forthcoming. To Gaius's dismay, he was to be the center of a major pronouncement and a banquet hosting dozens, including senators and friends of Retenius. Moreover, he had heard that there was to be a surprise guest, and a very important one at that. This day, he thought, would be the beginning of a lifelong nightmare.

If his father was aware of Gaius's trepidation, he ignored it; this day would mark his true entry into high society. Through his son he would gain financial rewards that as a desperate and impoverished child he had been able only to dream of.

Livia had given Gaius a close inspection before they boarded the carriage. "It is imperative that you appear enthusiastic before the praetor. He must have no doubts, no second thoughts. He sees you, not your father, as capable of achieving great heights. Any lack of deference, any disinclination toward his daughter, will make tongues wag. Rome lives for gossip and scandal. It would be our ruin, and neither I nor your father will ever forgive you."

"No scandal will be due to my actions, Mother."

"Good," Livia said. "Once you're engaged to Cornelia,

everything else will fall in place. The gods will judge everything," she added, looking intently into his eyes.

Gaius pondered a thought then said, "Mother, there's something really puzzling. Retenius is quite willing to join our family through the marriage of Cornelia. But in comparison to him, we're poor. He's not doing this to gain some fortune; and certainly I won't be earning real money for a long time, even under his tutelage. So why is he doing this?"

"Because the praetor lost his wife, and has only one daughter. She is his delight and she wants to marry you. He may be a powerful man, but Cornelia, I suspect, gets anything she wants. And, though she had a choice of so many truly accomplished men, she wants you. Money is not an issue when it comes to his daughter."

*****

Aspacia said nothing as the carriage passed through the front gate. Gaius, under his father's watchfulness, could only steal a glance at her. He looked immobile, his body stiff as if he were going to his own execution.

Standing beside her sister, Caladria stared at her feet. Then as if fatigue had overcome her, she sat heavily upon the ground and lolled her head back and forth. When the gate was closed and the wagon departed, Aspacia took her by the hand and led her back to the atrium. There would be no cena tonight, no need to cook for the dominus. Aspacia sat with Caladria near the impluvium and stared at the frescoed wall.

"It's all over," she said softly.

"No, sister," said Caladria, shaking her head. "It's just beginning. You will see."

*****

A dozen fancy carriages, each pulled by sleek horses, were parked outside the walls of Retenius's sprawling country house. Unlike the villa rustica, an actual farm, the praetor's home contained no animals except for a host of peacocks and his personal horses. A slave porter, the ostiarius, stood guard at the open gate and bowed as the guests entered the spacious gardens. They sat on finely carved benches, while additional

205

slaves removed shoes and boots and replaced them with the sandals brought by each guest.

The festive occasion began with the serving of fine wines and cheeses as a platoon of slaves perfumed women's hair with essence of saffron. Crowns of lilies and roses festooned their heads and the adornments would be worn until the end of the banquet.

Exotic dances by nubile girls from foreign lands would not begin until nightfall, but the music had already begun. One musician plucked upon the fifteen strings of the lyre while another strummed the triangular-boxed trigon. A young libertus blew high notes on an ebony flute, and a fourth musician kept the cadence with taps on her tambourine.

When Toronius and his party arrived, Retenius pushed through the crowd of guests, held out his arms, and greeted them in a stentorian voice.

"When I made my prayers at the lararium this morning, I beseeched Venus to bless this wondrous occasion. I must say, my daughter Cornelia told me that she was so excited last night that she could not sleep. I suspect that it was the same with you, wasn't it, Gaius?"

"It was, Excellency, I tossed and turned all night with anticipation," he replied, suppressing the urge to say "dread". The praetor smiled and looked at the silver bowl Gaius held. Gaius, seeing the huge assemblage of guests, hoped he could mask his dismay. Momentarily stunned, he looked back at the Retenius, then blurted, "Excellency, my father has selected this gift and asked me to present it to you."

Retenius tendered a slightly amused look, and with a gracious nod accepted the silver urn, which he displayed first to Cornelia then the assembled guests. There was a murmur of appreciation, and Retenius said, "We welcome the Dominus Toronius Pretoria Aquila, his lovely wife, and noble son to my house. And I wish to announce that shortly we will have the honor of another guest, Rome's greatest speaker, who will grace this..." he gazed at Gaius and said, "propitious event."

In a particularly bold move, Cornelia took Gaius's hand and

said, "I would love to show you where our summer garden is to be. That is, until our new villa is completed. Will you come with me?"

"Oh my, I guess she knows what she wants," exclaimed Retenius with a look of artful shock. The assembled senators, senior military officers and clients applauded. One primus pilum, a chief centurion, said, "Excellency, I fear that we should chaperone those two."

"It's too late, soldier, she has already positioned her legions for total victory. Caesar could not have done better!"

Gaius laughed along with the others, but thought that the word "victory" should have been "annihilation".

While Livia joined other women in the garden, Retenius touched Toronius's arm and said, "Let's talk in a quiet place."

They slipped away from the already inebriated guests, and the praetor said, "I have been pondering the question you raised, Dominus."

"Are you referring to the dowry?"

"Yes. Under normal circumstances and in a marriage between families of equal financial and social standing a dowry would be expected. After all, the young man is taking a girl off her father's hands, and we both know how much of a burden that could be," Retenius said with a forced grin.

"I hardly expect a fortune, but—"

The praetor held up his hand and said, "Excellency, please hear me out. There will be time enough for a mutual profit from our arrangement, but in a sense, if you follow me, my daughter's dowry is your admittance to my level of society. It will propel your son into a circle of nobles. That in itself is worth more than you can amass in a lifetime."

"Of course," Toronius replied, seeing that Retenius would brook no compromise.

"You know, and I mention this in greatest confidence," the praetor said in a conspiratorial whisper, "I fear that I have overextended myself."

"How so?" said Toronius, already feeling like family, having been taken into the praetor's confidence.

"You can barely see it from here, it's on the Caelian Hill," Retenius said, pointing beyond his country estate. "It's my new villa, the one Cornelia mentioned, and it's costing me a fortune. Oh, it will be one of the finest in Rome, and it's well under construction, but that expense along with my election bid is eating me alive. And of course there are the bribes. I tell you again, Toronius, the bribes and the extortion will bring us down."

There was cheering in the atrium and Retenius said, "Well our esteemed guest must have arrived. Let's join the others; we can't keep the man waiting."

Marcus Tullius Cicero was regarded by many as the greatest statesman and orator in Rome. Moreover, he was a most prolific writer and read by virtually everyone who was literate.

"I cannot say that I have known him long, but he's the most moral person I've ever known," said Retenius, as they reentered the crowded atrium. "He's the personification of what we should all be."

Cicero magnanimously greeted Retenius.

"How gracious of you to attend my humble domus," said the praetor. "I extended the invitation with great hope but little expectation, considering all the matters of state requiring your time."

"I regard marriage as a sacred institution, my august friend. The announcement that you will be making is the cornerstone, indeed the very foundation of our society," the patrician extolled. "So it is I who am humbled to attend this wondrous and propitious event."

There was an appreciative murmur as Retenius's guests crowded about the man who dazzled the court and the Senate.

"Is it true," Toronius asked the praetor, "that once Cicero argued a case before the court and won, then sometime later argued against it and won again?"

"It's legendary," said Retenius. "I had the privilege of meeting him when he defended a client in my own court. He was most impressive."

"And he won?"

"Of course he won! His presentation was brilliant even though his client was not entirely innocent. But ruling against him, well..."

*****

Lamps glowed in the atrium when the praetor invited Toronius and Livia to stand beside him on a raised dais. Retenius held his daughter's hand while Gaius stood nervously beside her.

"It is my honor and supreme joy to announce the forthcoming marriage of my daughter to Gaius Septimius, son of my dearest friends, Toronius and Livia. The wedding will take place on the twenty-eighth of April at the start of the spring festival of Floralia. Of course, everyone here is invited, and the grand event will take place in my new villa, the construction of which you can see on Caelian Hill."

"I hope it's finished in time," a smiling Cornelia said to her father.

"Perhaps we should put your fiancé to work to speed things along," the praetor said, grinning at Gaius.

There was a titter of laughter and Toronius said, "What a splendid thought. It will give him an idea of what real work is."

Few noticed Gaius's stiffness. He smiled for the guests and said, "Yes, Father, I guess it's something I should learn."

Again there was appreciative laughter to which Cicero said, "When he gets done there, Praetor, send him to my villa, I have walls he could build!"

When the laughter died down, Retenius nodded to Toronius and said, "The excellent dominus, father of the groom, will make his remarks, and then will come the banquet and the evening's entertainment."

Toronius cleared his throat and in a commanding voice said, "Indeed I am honored by Praetor Dometius Scipio Retenius, for the magnificent gift to me and my family of Lady Cornelia to my son Gaius. I shall offer prayers for their happiness in the years to come. I know that Gaius will be a fine husband and, perhaps with the encouragement and tutoring by the exalted praetor, he will also become a highly respected jurist."

The praetor nodded his approval and they all descended from the dais accompanied by an ovation.

While slaves brought platters of food into the triclinium, the banquet room, Cornelia said, "Gaius, I would really like us to talk, now that our fathers have made their pronouncements."

"Now?" Gaius replied, wondering what more there was to talk about.

"Yes, if you don't mind. We could talk in the tower; nobody will know. I go there when I have thinking to do. During the day there's a view of the entire countryside, and at night you can see lamps inside the old Servian Wall."

Every country house contained a stone tower, originally intended for defense. Cornelia led the way up the winding staircase and took a position beside the high open window. Gaius, standing beside her, tried to think of something reassuring, something that would make her feel happy. He stammered, and in the fading light made an effort to touch her hand.

"You don't have to try so hard, Gaius. In fact, once we are married I might propose some ideas that you might find strange. I want to tell you that I am very fond of you and might come to love you. I will come to your bed if you want me. Of course, we will be expected to have a child within the year. You might like that."

"Maybe. It will be something we could share," Gaius said, thinking that a child with her was the last thing he wanted.

"I have a little money; I've been saving," he went on, staring out at the flickering lights beyond the Wall. "I only mention that because I don't know where we can live, unless we use the money from your dowry."

"I was hoping that we could stay in your parents' villa for a while."

"Impossible."

"Because of Aspacia?"

Gaius was silent for a moment. "Not just Aspacia. You should know that I detest my father, and he feels the same about me. I thought we might live here, in your father's house.

It's certainly big enough, and perhaps, when it is finished, I could rent a room in his new villa."

Cornelia shook her head. "I would live in the rankest insula before I would remain in my father's house. Do not, Gaius I beg you, do not ask him that."

"Why?"

"I can't tell you why!" she said, her voice rising. "Nothing is as it seems." Her back was to him and she shook her head. Then turning back she said, "After we marry we should go away. I will get money from my father. He will give it to me, because..."

She stopped and Gaius saw that her face was streaked with tears.

"Yes, that may be the best idea," he said, not having the slightest idea of why she would not care to be near her father. "We could go to Gallia Cisalpina, in the mountains north of Italy, or perhaps Hispania Ulterior beside the great sea."

"Or Athens," Cornelia said more brightly, drying her eyes. "I've heard how beautiful Greece is."

Suddenly she took his hands and said, "I know this is not what you want, but we have little choice and it's my salvation. Let's at least try, and failing that, let's show that we are trying."

Gaius took a very deep breath and said, "Yes, Cornelia, I guess that's what we will have to do."

It was a few minutes before Gaius spoke again. "I was quite surprised when you and the praetor came to my father's house the first time. He said that he met Retenius at the games and invited him to the villa."

"Did he now?" said Cornelia, eyebrows raised. "My father receives many invitations from very important men, who either want his support or wish to support him. Do you think that a man of Cicero's reputation would visit just anyone? This may come as a surprise, but your family is of no particular value to him. Do you honestly think that a praetor, a highly respected member of the government, would waste time at a rather modest villa, the aging house of a dubiously successful trader?"

Gaius frowned. He had already had similar thoughts, but hadn't expected Cornelia to know anything about it. "So why did he come?"

"Because I told him he had to."

"You ordered your father to come to our villa?"

"It was an arrangement, and he had little choice."

"He is the dominus of his household. How can his daughter demand that he come to my father's house?"

Cornelia offered a slip of a smile and leaned against the wall of the tower. She was mostly in shadow and her words were so soft he could barely make them out. But they cut right through him.

"I arranged everything: my father meeting yours at the games, the visit to the villa, even the purchase of that horrid Egyptian thing." Gaius could hear her take a deep breath. "I saw you near the Forum when you were with your father's slave girl. I wanted to meet you. No, I wanted you. You see, I had a very particular reason."

"How did you know where to find me?"

"I followed you. I also learned about you and your parents. I know why you hate Toronius, and I know things about Livia too."

"About my mother?"

"At the baths."

"I see. It must have been interesting for you." Gaius said. He thought for a moment then said, "I often thought I was being followed, or should I say stalked?"

"I was curious and I was attracted to you. Have you never followed a girl you thought desirable? Besides, I might not have been the one always following you."

"If not you, then who?"

In the dim light he could see her shrug. "Who knows? Maybe somebody would like to know where the eligible young man lives. Or perhaps where his father lives."

"Do you know any Egyptians, Cornelia?" Gaius said warily.

"I know many people. I may not be a pretty girl, but I'm not simple or stupid. And I'm not as naïve as my father expects me to appear."

"I'm beginning to see that. I think you gave me a very

different first impression. It was more..."

"Submissive?"

"Endearing, if I may use that word."

"And you were trying to make an impression on me," she said coolly.

"Not on you, at least not directly. My father wanted to make a good impression on the praetor with his Egyptian artifacts. He coached me on what to say; he hoped that through his educated son he would look like a wealthy paterfamilias with important contacts."

A sardonic laugh came from the girl. "My father is hardly interested in your father's paltry wealth and contacts. He knows that Toronius is in debt and nearly penniless. In fact he thinks Toronius is a bag of wind, an impostor, and the son of a pig farmer."

"But you required him to come to my father's villa. How?"

"I won't discuss it now and please do me the favor of not asking," she said with a sniff. Then a little smile reappeared and she cooed, "I must say, however, that your recitation of the Egyptian things did impress me. And you seemed so nervously boyish. And that slave girl! How badly you felt for her. It was all quite charming, really. Of course I knew all that hocus-pocus about the vile Egyptian relics, but I made my mind up right then and there."

"To do what"

"To marry you, what else?"

"Just like that?"

"Of course. When I make my mind up I don't change it. It's like a trap door."

"And your father agreed?"

"As I said, he could not refuse, so I simply arranged it all. Fortunately he likes you, Gaius. You may be valuable to him. Be thankful for that."

As they descended the tower staircase, Cornelia stopped and Gaius nearly stumbled into her. "Oh, I should mention that most men demand that their wives please them in sex. Of course I will do my carnal duty. But I can't see myself doing anything beyond what is absolutely required." He thought she was finished but she turned to him and, recovering her sweet voice added, "Mention to your father that it would be best if he no longer deals in those 'artifacts'. My father does not appreciate fakes."

*****

As darkness fell over the villa, a myriad of slaves cleared the plates and refilled the goblets. A bell tinkled, and a half-dozen exotic dancers entered the atrium, followed by musicians and all the guests. A tambourine player and a girl with small, polished cymbals provided a quick beat while a boy on a flute piped a vigorous tune. The dancers started with an energetic dance, clapping hands to the music.

Each wore a revealing dress of transparent silk. Veils covered their faces, leaving only the mouth and chin showing. They danced in a circle, then a line, and finally separated in order to weave among the appreciative audience. Hips, legs, and arms gyrated, accenting the nubile body of each exquisite dancer.

Then quite suddenly the tempo changed; the musicians began a slow haunting tune, in which the girls slid their dresses upward, revealing their legs, then moved their hands to perfumed and oiled breasts. They glistened in the light of the lamps. Several dancers sought out the praetor, then proceeded to the newly engaged couple.

"You must be enjoying that," Cornelia whispered in Gaius's ear.

*****

In order to get a better view, Toronius had positioned himself beside a pillar, and was pleased that one of the dancers had singled him out. She danced toward him sinuously, curvaceously, again raising the garment to reveal her thighs. Her lips formed a kiss meant only for him. He nodded, staring into the veil. His throat had become dry. She had made it evident; she wanted him, he knew it. The dancer slid past him, the nipples of her pert breasts brushing against the cloth of his synthesis.

"Later," he said, just loud enough to be heard. "In the alcove at the rear of the peristyle."

"Yes, meet me there after our dance," said the girl, in a dialect he could not quite place.

The prospect of exploring the body of the young, supple dancer made Toronius's heart beat faster than it had in years. Soon the dancers slipped away, and the banquet concluded. Numerous guests, few of whom he knew, approached to offer congratulations. He tried to reply with humility and grace, all the while peering toward the peristyle. He couldn't see the girl, and he desperately wanted to get away from everyone. As guests departed, he feared that Gaius or Livia would find him and, the day having been long, wish to leave.

Feigning illness and alluding to the vomitorium, he finally escaped the well-wishers and, hugging the shadows, made his way from the atrium to the deserted peristyle. The muted sounds of the departing guests echoed through the building. Then all was silent except for water dripping into the impluvium. Toronius stood stock-still, wishing that he had asked the dancer's name. For a moment there was no sound. Then he heard a girl's voice. "In here, Dominus, in the vestibule."

Hungering for her, Toronius sucked in his breath; he could feel the start of an erection. He could see her form now. Her hair was piled high on her head in the Roman fashion, but now she had added a loose tunic over her dancing costume. She stood before a closed curtain, her arms beckoning, her fingers motioning him closer. He pushed his body against her, and her tongue darted out like a viper. She offered a deep, languid kiss and a jolt of excitement coursed through him.

The dancer took his hand and allowed him to touch a nipple. Toronius pushed harder against her, a fire welling up in him. He tried to reach beneath her silken tunic but she shook her head. He looked at her curiously. Was she not ready, or was she playing a game, toying with him to build his ardor? Maybe she wanted money, he thought. How silly of him, of course she would want to be paid. Quickly, his hands sought the coin purse beneath his synthesis.

"No," the girl said, "I do not want to see your coins. I want to see something else."

"And what would you like to see, my delicious young morsel?" Toronius said, edging closer for another try.

"Fear, Dominus; I want to see fear," the girl said in a whisper, as she pulled at the neckline of her tunic to reveal a gold chain with an ancient amulet. Toronius stared, gasped in recognition, and took a step back. Then she ripped off the veil to expose her broken face and the red eye with the sightless pupil. Toronius shrieked. The curtain behind her parted and three men, all wearing the long Egyptian tunic, stared back.

Toronius's heart pounded and he tore from the peristyle.

*****

Hearing a shrill scream, Gaius glanced up and asked, "What's that?"

"Someone is running toward the gate," Cornelia answered. Looking past her, Gaius could see a shape dash past in the flickering candlelight. The form knocked over a candelabrum, and flaming oil spilled across the tile floor.

"Who was that?" asked Livia, as slaves hurried to extinguish the conflagration.

"I think I recognized the man," said Apollodoros who ceased putting gifts into a box. "It is the Dominus."

"Toronius?" said Livia, her eyes wide. "Why would he be running?" she asked.

"My lady," said Apollodoros, "He is running for his life."

Chapter 12

"Have you searched the peristyle and the tablinum?" Livia asked.

"I have. Father isn't here," said Gaius, "and neither Aspacia nor Caladria have seen him either."

"I checked the orchard and the field," added Apollodoros, who entered from the atrium with an oil lamp.

"Apollodoros, you said that the man who was running from the banquet was Toronius. Why would he be running, and where would he go without us?" Livia said, perplexed. "I expected him to join us on the way home. Do you think he's still at Retenius's villa?"

"I have no idea, Domina, but if you wish I will return to the villa in the morning. Surely the praetor or his daughter must know," said Apollodoros.

"I'm tired. We'll learn more about this tomorrow," Livia said and walked down the hallway to her cubiculum.

*****

For Gaius, sleep was punctuated by terrifying nightmares. He pulled a coarse blanket over himself, but it wasn't the night's chill that sent terrors through him.

Never had he been so frightened, not even when he had killed Arzeka. That was reflexive, and had happened too quickly to think about. But this marriage would be a slow, ghastly execution, a macabre bleeding of his essence until the day he could rid himself of the woman.

Cornelia had stalked him, he told himself, and she was able to manipulate a strong man with hard, unwavering cunning.

What did she have over her father? he asked himself. What threat, what extortion had forced that exalted patrician to ingratiate himself with Toronius?

If Cornelia had really loved him he might have understood it. *But she does not love me,* he thought. *She said that she only "liked" me.* He even doubted that she meant that; her posture toward him in the tower was abrasive at best. And what girl demands to marry for "like" rather than love? And what girl could possibly demand that a dominus do anything?

He had been so wrong about her, he thought. Certainly she was not the diffident and submissive girl who had been introduced to him at his father's villa. But exactly who was she, he wondered, and why did she insist on fleeing the house of her father?

His own cubiculum, small and claustrophobic, reminded him of the tower where, like a cobra, Cornelia had uncurled and displayed her venom. What had she said, "I will do my carnal duty but not beyond what is required." He had no desire to be intimate with her. Nevertheless, this terse and frigid comment on the eve of their engagement was terribly foreboding. Gaius shivered, pulled the blanket closer, and felt his entire body become rigid. It was as if his life force was being sucked out of him and his breath came in short gasps.

Suddenly he bolted upright, threw on his toga and pulled on his boots. Dawn was just approaching but it was still dark; there was no moon and only one oil lamp illuminated the hallway. He didn't care if Apollodoros or Livia or anyone else heard him. He grabbed the lamp and scurried from room to room, finally finding Aspacia beneath the staircase of the tablinum.

"Wake up," he said, his hand on her shoulder. She opened her eyes and strained to see who would disturb her sleep.

"Caladria?" she asked, trying to focus.

"No it's me, Gaius. Get up, we must go."

"Go where? It's cold, do I have to?"

"We must get out of here, and you have to come with me."

"But it's so early," she protested, trying vainly to pull a threadbare blanket over her head.

Gaius took her arm and gently lifted her to her feet. He wrapped the blanket about her and helped her put on her shoes.

"Where are we going?" she said, rubbing the sleep from her eyes.

"Aventine Hill. It's a long walk, and we have to start now."

Caladria, curled up beside the servant's gate, stirred and in a thick whisper said, "Offer a blessing for me, Aspacia."

"What? What's she talking about?" Aspacia asked, as Gaius whisked her out the gate into the empty street.

"She knows," said Gaius.

"Knows what?"

"She knows where we're going."

"Did you tell her?"

"Of course not."

*****

Aspacia was fully awake as dawn crept over the hills of Rome. "What's so important about the Aventine Hill?" she asked as Gaius kept watch for any lingering thugs who might be hoping to assail unwary prey in the first hour of the day.

"It's where Rome's first temple was built by Servius Tullius. It's more than five-hundred years old."

"That's why you woke me up? To see a five-hundred-year-old temple? And who was Servius Tullius anyway?" Aspacia asked, seemingly confused as to why Gaius would drag her from the villa so early in the morning.

"Tullius was a Greek king, when Rome was still ruled by Greeks and Etruscans. He was born as a slave and got two tribes, the Latins and the Romans, to build a great temple like the one at Ephesus in Asia Minor. It's just outside the pomerium, the strip of land beyond the city's wall."

"Why not inside?" she asked, hurrying to keep up with him. Then before he could answer she said, "Is that where we're going: to see a temple?"

"You ask a lot of questions for one who never seemed interested. The answer to the first is that some gods and goddesses are honored by Romans even though they aren't

Roman gods. Some, like Diana, were never made official, so they remain outside the wall."

"Diana? Are we really going to the Temple of Diana?" Aspacia asked, her eyes widening. "That's who we worshipped in our village because she's the goddess of the poor and enslaved. And did you know that she's also the goddess of childbirth?"

"No, but then I've never given birth," said Gaius.

Aspacia gave him a bemused look then said, "She's also the goddess of the hunt and the woodlands. Do you know that?"

"I do, but more important, the temple is a sanctuary."

"For whom?"

"For slaves. No slave hunter is allowed inside. A slave can stay there as long as the priests allow it."

"Is that why we're going there?"

"It may be the only way I can save you, Aspacia."

He held her hand as they climbed toward a meadow and a copse of trees at the hill's summit. She was pensive and quiet for a long moment then said, "Gaius, you are worried."

"Not worried, I'm scared. I'm scared for both of us. But I want this to be our day, a day we'll remember for the rest of our lives."

Gaius refrained from saying that he had no idea of how his father would react. Surely he would be furious. Yet he knew that something terrible would happen to both of them and it might be the last day they would ever spend together. He thought he would mention that but he didn't have to; Aspacia knew it too.

*****

An oak grove, sacred to those who worshipped the deity, surrounded the temple with its Grecian frieze and Ionic pillars. The marble edifice, the oldest in Rome, gleamed in the morning sun. The faithful had begun to arrive, to bask in the calmness of the grove and to admire the female dancers who, with ribbons in their hair, skipped lightly in a circle. A young man played a panpipe to sad songs so popular with the people of Rome.

Gaius led Aspacia up the steps, and they peered inside.

"Please enter, the Goddess welcomes you," said an acolyte in a soft voice. Then Gaius saw the holy man peer beyond the columns toward men partially hidden in the trees. He shook his head and uttered a silent oath.

Gaius glanced at an inscription inscribed on the lintel spanning the length of the temple and read, "*Do Ut Des.*" Aspacia looked at Gaius, and he said, "I give that you might give."

The cleric nodded and said, "It is good to be in the presence of a literate man and a devout lady. My name is Lysippus. I'm a novitiate of the order and this is my home, my temple. I will live here the rest of my life."

"Then may it be a long one," Gaius replied. He gazed inside the bowels of the temple and saw the great marble statue of Diana. As the goddess of the woodlands, she held a bow and arrow and stood beside the statue of a small stag. Gaius turned to the novice and said, "My name is Gaius Tiberius Aquila, and this is Aspacia, a lady of Rome."

The acolyte made a little bow, smiled and said nothing about the fact that she was wearing a slave's tunic and not an elegant stola. Escorting the pair into the temple, he stopped at a table displaying a number of small marble statues of the goddess. When Aspacia gazed at one, Gaius gestured toward it.

"Six denarii, Gaius Tiberius Aquila. It is an excellent replica of our goddess, and will be a fine addition to your family's lararium."

Gaius gave the coins to Lysippus, who wrapped the image in a silk cloth and gingerly handed it to Aspacia. She stared at Gaius and mouthed the words, "Thank you," then held it close as if it were a child.

From a vase the cleric took a stick of incense, its white smoke curling upward, and gave it to Aspacia. "For your devotion. You may place it before the goddess, my lady."

As Gaius accompanied her to the towering statue she leaned toward him and whispered, "Lady Aspacia? Where did you come up with that?"

"It sounded appropriate. You might be my father's slave, but you're a lady when you are with me."

The interior of the ancient temple was cool and hushed, except for what seemed like a whimper from deep within its interior. Gaius listened then turned to the acolyte, eyebrows raised. Lysippus glanced to a shadowed alcove but said nothing.

Aspacia approached the statue and placed the incense in a golden vase. She bowed her head and whispered a prayer. She appeared so delicate, thought Gaius, as a shaft of light illuminated her face. The beam, like a slow moving finger, traced downward and then caressed her. She raised her face to the goddess and was suffused with the glow of the morning sun. Gaius sucked in his breath and he felt his heart miss a beat. He felt as if he was seeing a goddess in the flesh, entrusting her very being to one in sanctified stone.

Aspacia rose to her feet. "Can we stay a while? It's so peaceful here."

Gaius looked toward the acolyte, who nodded but said, "You may stay as long as you wish, but do not venture far; there is danger in the rear of the temple."

"Maybe we shouldn't go back there," Aspacia whispered as they walked on past Lysippus toward the sobbing voice.

"Maybe we should," replied Gaius, looking warily toward the rear of the rectangular interior.

They walked further into the shadows, the candles being fewer in the great hall behind Diana.

"He's afraid of someone back here," said Gaius.

They stopped and Aspacia said, "Someone is in terrible distress."

"A woman," replied Gaius, straining to see a huddled form in a distant corner. "Come," he said, taking Aspacia's hand and leading her slowly toward the woman.

"Stop!" came a sudden shout. "Go back. I have the sickness."

"What sickness?" asked Gaius.

"The spots. I'm covered with the spots."

"Are they red?" asked Aspacia.

"Yes and anyone who gets the spots will die," the woman cried.

"Not all die, I didn't," replied Aspacia. "Let me help you."

Turning to Gaius she whispered, "Stay here. The red spots are very contagious. Many in my village died from the disease, but not everyone contracts it, even when they are near the sick and dying. And some who get a mild form of it, like me and Caladria, survive. Then we can't get it again."

"Can you bring me some water?" the woman asked when Aspacia knelt before her. "The priests are all afraid to come near."

"I will," replied Aspacia. "How long have you been here?" she asked.

"Four days. I'm a slave, and I escaped from my master's house. I was welcomed here until two days ago when the priests saw my sickness. Are the slave catchers still outside?"

"We saw them as we came in," said Aspacia.

"They are there for me. They will take me back."

"Not if they know you're sick."

A cackling laugh came from the woman. "If I'm allowed to stay till dark they won't know. My master wants me back and will pay them well. I am too valuable for him and his girl."

"His girl?" asked Aspacia, rising to get the water.

"His daughter. He made me watch while he played with her between her legs. Sometimes he would have me fondle him when he put his tongue in her. He liked to do that even when she screamed." The woman breathed deeply and scratched the red spots. "Please hurry, I'm terribly thirsty."

*****

"It is time, you must leave. The goddess will give you comfort," intoned the high priest from many yards away.

"I will care for her, Excellency. Please let her stay here," said Aspacia.

Night had descended upon Rome. In the flickering light of an oil lamp the priest sadly shook his head.

"If it was not for the sickness we would allow her to stay in this sanctuary. But if she stays she will infect us and all who come to give devotion. We can't allow that."

"But she will be captured, tortured," said Gaius. "Can't the catchers be paid off so the woman can go free?"

"Regretfully the monies tithed to the goddess cannot be given to every slave catcher, or they would make a business of it. They would be chasing people in here, slave or not, so they could be paid off. When the Senate heard of such a thing, they would strip us of our sanctuary status. Then we would be valueless to any in bondage. The goddess rejoices in your good intentions but the woman, with our blessings, must leave."

Then addressing the woman, the high priest said, "The novitiate Lysippus will distract the catchers while you make your escape. But you must go now."

The woman gathered up her few belongings and, with the priests following at a distance, limped to the portal of the temple. She looked toward the copse of trees hidden in the gloom and was silhouetted by torches flanking the temple. There was a rustle in the distance when the men saw her. Several stood, while others stirred smoldering coals in their campfire. Two others melted into the darkness.

"I will go with you," Gaius said to Lysippus. "They may back off if they see more than one."

"I doubt it but take this," a priest said, handing Gaius a stout club. "Those are desperate and brutal men. They have killed before. Do be careful."

Gaius accepted the heavy staff then went to a pillar and removed a flaming torch, which he handed to Lysippus.

"Go first; they'll think you're alone. Without a torch they may not see me, but I will be there." said Gaius.

The acolyte descended the steps and moved toward the slave catchers, who faded into the gloom. Gaius followed moments later.

Aspacia and the sick woman remained behind, waiting for a safe moment to move. The woman was about to make her escape, when Aspacia touched her wrist and said, "Please tell me your name."

"Cynthia."

"Cynthia, I'm curious, who's your master?"

"My master? My master's name is Retenius: the praetor Retenius. He's a praetor and he's running for the Senate on the grounds of morality." The woman cackled.

"And his daughter?" asked Aspacia, fearing the answer.

"Cornelia? Oh he's toyed with her for years, even before his wife committed suicide. Yes, he loves to play games with me and his daughter."

The woman watched Gaius and the acolyte scurry toward the trees then looked back at Aspacia.

"I am dying, but the catchers don't know it. That's my secret joy: my revenge."

"What is?" asked Aspacia.

"That I will curse them with my sickness. Those men are already dead."

Then she laughed again and ran toward them.

*****

"Over there," whispered Octavius Brundeschi. "That's where the house is, and there's a barn attached to it."

"I can barely make it out," replied Toronius.

"No matter, it's there. I came here at dawn before anyone was around. I left the barn door ajar so you can get in without making any noise. There's a heavy wagon in front of the door. Just go around it. I made a pile of straw and sticks and soaked it with oil. All you have to do is light it and get out."

"You told me you were coming with me," said Toronius, adjusting his engraved clasp and rumpled clothing.

"No, you go in, Dominus, and I'll keep watch from the wagon at the door."

He hated the way Octavius employed the honorific, and swore that the insect would come to know what powers a dominus could truly wield.

Toronius hesitated then said, "Are you certain we weren't followed?"

"I didn't see anyone. You're wasting time."

"Don't rush me. It's dark, but I heard footsteps earlier and there were many."

"There's nobody out there, and dressed like that, no one would recognize you anyway."

Again Toronius hesitated. "He won't need me to do anything after this, will he?"

"Probably not but you never know with Crassus. I will speak to him if it worries you."

"Of course you will," replied Toronius bitterly. He was exhausted and his hands trembled. He had not gone home but had run to his client's flat, saying nothing about his panic at the praetor's villa. All night he had cringed in a corner beneath a moth-holed blanket. He knew that he had been followed and didn't fall asleep until late in the day. Upon waking he had felt rested at first. Then the horror returned, only to be eclipsed by the horror to come.

"It's tonight," Octavius had said when he returned to his insula. "Crassus expects you to do it an hour before dawn."

"Will he have his firemen there?" Toronius asked, his voice anxious.

"No, the owner refuses to sell. Crassus wants the villa and its barn burned to the ground."

"What if I refuse?" said Toronius. There was fear in his voice.

"We already discussed this. He is a consul and commands the Praetorian Guard and twenty-eight legions. How many do you have, Dominus?"

Fearful of being recognized, Toronius wore an old lacerna, a brown cloak open in the front and held by his clasp at the shoulder. An attached hood would cover his head; no one, he prayed, would have the slightest chance of recognizing him.

The old villa with its adjoining barn sat on a gentle slope at the base of Caelian Hill. According to Brundeschi, the consul had attempted negotiation with the owner five months earlier to no avail. The villa had been in the family for generations and not even a generous offer by Crassus could move him. The consul would take his time. There was no need to raise suspicion by moving too quickly but combustion in abandon buildings was commonplace. There were many vandals and squatters who could be terribly careless. Once the structure had burned, an emissary would contact the owner with a much-reduced offer. There would be, after all, no domus on the property to command a higher price.

Brundeschi gave Toronius a flint and nudged him, saying, "Don't leave the barn until you're sure the flames have caught. Unless of course you wish to do this again."

"I'll do it, but I never want to see you again," Toronius said, gathering his cloak about him.

"Just get on with it," Octavius hissed.

The barn was outlined by a myriad of stars, but the ground before him was pitch-black. He would have to feel his way to the wagon. Toronius couldn't see the shallow ditch in the darkness, and he fell and dropped the flint.

"Hurry!" Brundeschi spat.

Groping, Toronius finally located the sharp stone, then sat perfectly still. They were out there. He heard words, but they were not Latin words. What, he wondered, would they do when he was in the barn? Was Octavius in league with them? Unanswered questions swirled through his mind. What if the man was to murder him on Crassus's orders? It would be easy for Brundeschi to slam the barn door shut and block it while he was starting the fire. Was his death in the flaming barn part of Crassus's plan?

Toronius jumped when a hand grasped his shoulder.

"What are you waiting for?" Octavius fairly shouted in his ear.

Terrified, Toronius rose and bolted toward the wagon, a bare outline against the barn. He rounded it and pushed open a door allowing moonlight to filter inside. The fetid stench of feces and the bloated carcass of a pig assaulted his senses. Hair- and sweat-encrusted saddle blankets hung from hooks, along with leather tack and rags. He took a step forward and was met by a netting of spider webs. He swore and stepped back, wiping the fibrous mass from his face. An uncontrollable shaking came over him. He was certain that he felt the dancing legs of venomous spiders crawling on his skin. He slapped the back of his neck and shivered.

Looking about, Toronius could see stars through an opening in the roof where rain had fallen into a stone cistern: a watering trough for horses long gone. A row of rickety pillars, studded with hooks and cleats, pushed upward to a roof that twisted and sagged.

Again Toronius inched forward feeling for the pile of faggots. He touched straw, dried and brittle, then sticks conically arranged. There was a fluff of cotton soaked in oil. He struck the flint and a spark flew into the cotton followed by a wisp of smoke then a flicker. He blew on it and was surprised to see how quickly it rose and illuminated the tinder-dry barn.

Satisfied, he rose and turned to the door, when he heard shouting and a rush of feet followed by the slamming of the heavy barn doors. Brundeschi, thrown in, lay flat on the ground. Stunned, he shouted to Toronius, his voice a hoarse shriek against the roar of flames.

"Put out the fire!" Octavius roared as he struggled to rise.

Toronius, propelled backwards, shielded his face from the inferno while Brundeschi grabbed a saddle blanket and beat at the flames. A lighted beam toppled forward, striking Octavius and knocking him into a pile of burning hay. The rapacious flames found his tunic and he screamed, tearing away swaths of flaming cloth.

Staggering back from the flames, Toronius stumbled, tripping over ancient shovels and rakes that littered the floor of the barn. Beams became torches that ignited the roof and heavy tiles cascaded to the floor. He tripped again, saw a galaxy of stars through the roof, and toppled into the rain filled trough. Freezing water made him bolt to the surface. He raised his head in time to see Octavius stagger toward him, hair aflame, a slowly revolving human torch. The man's mouth opened but no scream came. Bulging eyes, white with terror, stared at Toronius as Brundeschi sank to his knees. He fell forward, his bodily fluids boiling and hissing into a vaporous stench.

The barn doors fell away and Toronius saw a blur of shadowy forms: three burly men and a smaller figure, a woman.

He lowered himself into the water, his eyes just above the level of the trough. A hot wind rushed through the inferno, parting the flames. Toronius could see the quartet peering in, afraid to come closer. Wiping fetid water from his eyes he strained to see them better. There was a glint of metal, a golden sheen around the woman's neck. "Egyptians," he mouthed silently. He was about to sink into the trough when the woman suddenly ripped off the necklace, and with a great shout, tossed it into the flaming barn. Toronius watched it arc then drop. He took a great breath and allowed himself to sink into the frigid water where he remained submerged for what he thought was a very long time.

His chest bursting, Toronius finally summoned the courage to peer above the trough. They were gone. Much of the barn had fallen in, and he marveled that he was still alive. Most of the smoke had dissipated. Toronius began to rise from the trough when he heard the straining sound of beams parting and splintering. He looked up to see the remains of the barn topple toward him. Heavy struts ripped asunder with a cascade of embers. They toppled around him, driving him back into the trough, its slimy water again covering him. With a crack a great beam struck the side of the trough and snapped in two as splinters ripped at Toronius's clothes. The cloak and clasp were ripped from his shoulders. A flaming shower of embers fell into the water and sputtered out.

Toronius, bruised and bleeding, closed his eyes and remained still, willing the holocaust to cease. It seemed to take forever, but finally, except for the final collapse of floorboards, what remained of the barn disintegrated into a smoking pile of ash. The intense heat that had surrounded him had passed and the water's chill penetrated his body. Rising, he dragged himself from the trough and looked about. He took a few cautious steps but stopped when his foot dislodged an object. He thought he had kicked an ash-encrusted pot. An ember glowed inside, and he bent over to inspect it. He was about to touch it when he looked more closely. He emitted a shriek and bolted from the glowing tissue in the severed skull of Octavius Brundeschi.

The barn was completely gone and so was the villa. He was amazed that no one had come to see its destruction. For a long moment he thought that all was quiet, but he realized that the silence was an illusion. In fact there was a great deal of noise, but it was no longer close. He took in a whiff of smoke and coughed. Turning, Toronius raised his eyes to the Caelian Hill, expecting it to be clothed in darkness, and stared in disbelief as flames raced up the hill, devouring a half completed structure. He could see dozens of people, water buckets in hand, racing to douse the flames before they could spread. Shouts from the inferno assaulted him and again a terrible shiver ran down his spine.

"Retenius, Retenius. Oh the gods save me," were the only words that came from Toronius's mouth.

Gathering up his torn vestments, Toronius trod across the littered floor, glancing once again at the skull, now barely illuminated in the glow of the distant fire. Wracked with pain, he limped through the backstreets of Rome as night morphed into an unwelcome dawn.

<h1 style="text-align:center">Chapter 13</h1>

Gaius thought the throbbing in his head would never cease. Intermittent clouds broken by shafts of sunlight raced over him, and he held a hand over his eyes to blot out the play of intense light and shadow. Voices seemed distant, then far too close. He touched the side of his head and withdrew his hand. The pain was intense and the lump felt the size of a goose egg. There was a cloth bandage, which felt damp; he assumed that it was blood. Gaius dropped his hand and willed the pain to stop and the voices to fade away.

"He is awake now, Holiness," a young man said.

"The Goddess has manifested her kindness. He'll rest here in my study. His slave girl and the Greek can remain with him," he said imperiously to a neophyte.

Apollodoros must have arrived while Gaius was unconscious. The high priest turned to him and said, "It was a serious blow; I wouldn't encourage him to move about too soon. It will be days before the swelling goes down."

That said, the holy man and his acolytes slipped out of the room and closed the door.

A hand gently circled Gaius's wrist and he felt a kiss on his cheek.

"I trust that's not you, Apollodoros," he said, wincing from another jolt of pain.

"I have not kissed anyone in over twenty five years, but being a humble slave, if you insist..."

"I don't. 'Humble slave'," Gaius said, slowly shaking his head. Gaius pried open his eyes, smiled at Aspacia and said, "Just to be sure, you can kiss me again."

"This is terribly melodramatic," Apollodoros said as Aspacia's lips caressed those of Gaius. He stared impatiently at the ceiling. "I didn't think Romans engaged in daytime intimacies."

"I'm not a Roman," replied Aspacia with an impish smile.

"I don't remember what happened," Gaius said after a moment.

"Apollodoros was just in time. He saved your life," Aspacia said quietly.

"Then I am indebted," Gaius said. "But all I can remember is following Lysippus onto the field."

"It was an ambush," said Apollodoros. They knew you and the priest were coming. They ignored him but three of them went after you. You're pretty good with that staff, thanks to me, and one won't be feeling good for a very long time. I managed to do damage to another, but not before you were clubbed."

"Then what?" asked Gaius.

"They caught the woman, but she was all over them before they branded her."

"Then they all left," added Aspacia.

"Where did they take her?" Gaius asked.

"I'll tell you about it later. Just rest for now."

Gaius lay back and closed his eyes. Then he said, "Apollodoros, how did you know?"

"About you being in trouble? I was told."

"By whom?"

"Caladria, of course."

*****

An evening rain soaked through the ashes of the praetor's uncompleted villa on Caelian Hill.

"Thank you for coming at such short notice," Retenius said to Livia, as they surveyed the charred beams that had fallen and shattered onto the buckled mosaic floor.

"I was about to come here anyway. Toronius didn't come back last night or the night before. I thought he might have returned here. I didn't know about the fire until I had Apollodoros read your message."

"I haven't seen him since he left my villa the night of the banquet," said the praetor. Turning to Apollodoros he said, "Have you seen him?"

"I have not, Excellency."

"It's very strange. I heard that he ran from here that night. Some say he was terrified. Have you any idea of what that was about?" Retenius asked Livia.

"I presume he was frightened by someone at the banquet. Did you see anybody who was uninvited?" she replied, her eyes straying down the hill to the remains of a burned farm and villa.

"I, or I should say Cornelia, hired several troupes of performers. Perhaps there were individuals whom she might not have been familiar with, but certainly nobody who was dangerous. No weapons were allowed in, not even the dinner knives that guests always carry. I supplied everything, Livia."

Cornelia came down the hill from the remains of another burned villa and joined the group. Livia embraced her and said, "I'm so sorry. It would have been a beautiful home."

"Yes, it would have. I hope the arsonist is caught and shredded by lions."

"Arson? How do you know that the fire was set?" Livia asked.

Cornelia shrugged and said, "Whoever started the fire might not have intended to burn this house. See that charred building out there? I bet that's where it started,"

"There was a high wind last night," her father added. "Cornelia might be right. The fire likely started out there and spread."

A stiff breeze still blew and Apollodoros picked up a handful of dried ash and released it.

"See," Cornelia said with satisfaction. "The wind blows this way."

"But why would anyone want to burn down that place?" Livia said, looking toward the burned barn and ancient villa.

"There's only one person who makes money burning down properties," said Retenius, "and no one in Rome dares to charge him with arson. Of course he doesn't start the fires himself; he has underlings do it for him."

"If you're speaking of Marcus Crassus, he should be hanged by his thumbs," Cornelia said.

"I have told you before, be careful of what you say," the praetor scolded.

"Then what am I to speak of, Father?"

"Woman's things. Clothing, marriage, babies. Even your forthcoming marriage."

"What about sex?"

Retenius's face stiffened, and Livia thought he was going to strike the girl. Then leaning toward her, and to Livia's surprise, he smiled and in a very quiet voice said, "I think it's something we both enjoy, am I right, daughter?"

"Perhaps you more than me," Cornelia said, brushing past him.

"Come with me, dear," Livia said, intervening but still wishing to hear more. "I want to go to that burned-down villa. We can talk on the way as daughter and mother-in-law." She gave Retenius a curious glance, then said, "Apollodoros, you will join us."

They left the praetor to tread through the remains of his charred dwelling. "I'll tell you a secret," Cornelia said ignoring the presence of Apollodoros who trailed a few feet behind.

"I love secrets. In fact, I have a few of my own. So tell me yours and I'll tell you mine."

"My father likes you very much."

"And I like him."

"I mean he wants you."

"He told you that?"

"He doesn't have to. I can see it."

Livia gave her a little smile and said, "I can see it too."

"And what is your secret?"

"I want him, too."

*****

Except for a few twisted iron implements there was nothing left in the ancient villa. The evening's rain had washed the fallen tiles and settled the ash. They carefully picked their way through it and ventured to where the barn had been. A stone horse trough stood near what had been the rear of the structure. Bits of charred wood and a thick scum floated on its surface. Old nails, melted buckles, handless shovels and rakes stuck up from the ash. There was a smell of charred wood and decay.

"This is where it must have started," Cornelia said, bending to examine a patch of ash that had burned hotter than the rest.

"How do you know that?" Livia asked.

"It's like in the brazier, the remains of the hottest coals are always white ash. So someone had to have started it and I suspect he started it right here." Livia nodded, and noted the girl's perceptiveness. She turned, walked several yards, then let out a gasp.

"What?" Cornelia said.

Livia stepped back and pointed to a jumble of ash-covered bones, many splintered by falling timbers.

"Are they animal bones?" asked Cornelia. Joining the women, Apollodoros knelt and raised one from the ash.

"This is a fibula," he said to Livia. "And it is human." He pushed away a small mound of ash and another piece of bone appeared. He knew what it was. He placed his hands beneath and lifted it.

Upon seeing the skull Livia shrieked and cupped her hands to her mouth.

"He must have died in the fire," said Cornelia, peering at the burned out eye sockets.

"How could that be?"

"That's how," said Apollodoros pointing to the remains of a wagon pushed against what had been the barn doors. "He must have been trapped inside, or he would have escaped."

"So the arsonist died in his own fire," said Cornelia. "How fitting. What justice. We should just leave the skull here as a home for rats."

"Mistress," said Apollodoros, inspecting a fallen beam. "Perhaps you should see this."

Livia grasped Cornelia's hand and apprehensively

approached the slave.

"There's more? What is it?" she asked fearfully. Leaning forward, she studied a piece of blackened metal that Apollodoros freed from a nail. "Oh, by the gods," she said, turning away.

"A brooch," Cornelia said, examining the piece. "I saw this at the banquet. I saw it on—"

"Toronius's cloak," Apollodoros said, completing her statement. "My master."

He stared at Livia, who was struck numb with disbelief. Hands on her head, she let out a howl and ran from the charnel house.

"Toronius. This is indeed a shock," Cornelia said to a stunned Apollodoros. "You must put his bones in a box and take them to his villa."

"What of my mistress?"

"She will stay with us until we arrange the interment. Now do what I say."

With a sudden spurt, the girl ran to catch up with Livia. Apollodoros saw her put her arm around the woman and say something comforting as they walked up Caelian Hill.

He found a weathered crate in front of where the barn had stood. He added sticks to the bottom so nothing would fall through, and went back to where he had placed the skull. There were still a few patches of hair on it, frizzled by the fire. It had an odd color that Apollodoros attributed to the heat of the inferno. He lifted the skull, thinking of how many years had passed since he had first seen the man. Toronius was not then imperious and rotund, playing the part of a landed patrician. He could barely afford a slave, and had haggled over the price. But he'd had Livia, a great beauty, and that had made up for what Toronius didn't have.

At the time I was only sixteen, thought Apollodoros. The same age as Gaius, but he had gone through so much more. There was the atrocity Apollodoros was required to perform, the pirates, and the contempt he had for everything Roman. That was all so long ago. Now, with the death of Toronius, he wondered who his master really was.

The Dominus's remains would have to be cleaned, he reasoned. A jumble of ash-encrusted bones would reflect badly upon him, and he would have to please his new master, whoever that might be. He could clean them at the villa, but it would not do to be seen carrying a box of human bones through Rome.

Apollodoros stood after he had placed the bones in the box. Looking about for something to clean them with, he spied a singed piece of leather, but as he stepped toward it he failed to see an empty posthole filtered over with ash. Quite suddenly he was on the ground, his ankle sprained. He sat there for a long moment, wondering how much longer it would take to arrive at the villa. Disgusted, he leaned forward to push himself up and his hand touched something small and hard.

Apollodoros lifted it, blowing off the ash. It was a necklace, a gold necklace with an Egyptian pendant. He squinted at it. A few pieces of gold had misshapen in the inferno, but most of it had suffered little damage.

He closed his eyes and tried to think. Of course, he remembered, it was the pendant Toronius had bought from Ben Josephus at the Jew's antique shop in Alexandria. Was it really the precious piece that his master had lost in the inn, when he and Gaius were assigned to guard the other purchases? Recalling the night, it was only after Toronius had raped and beaten the girl that Toronius realized that it had been ripped from his neck. It was then that he sent Gaius back to retrieve it from the prostitute. But Gaius hadn't, instead, he had told his father that the woman was gone along with the pendant. And now, Apollodoros realized, it was here in his hand.

The Greek put two fingers to his forehead as he always did when in deep thought. He knew all about the fake Egyptian god statues that Toronius had recently bought and had him burn in the brazier. Yet that hardly connected the Egyptian girl and the statues to the necklace in the burned out barn. She must have been there when it went up in flames, but how did she know that Toronius would be there and why, for Great Zeus's sake, would anyone toss such a valuable necklace into the fire? Of course, he assumed that Toronius had started the conflagration. But what if he hadn't?

There were so many questions and no viable answers. Why, for instance would his master travel to this decrepit place? Was he lured here? And if the Egyptian girl had followed him or laid in wait, was it she who had started the blaze to kill Toronius?

Apollodoros's ankle was still painful, but he managed to hobble to the stump of a tree. He sat and evaluated the necklace once again.

It had belonged to Toronius for less than a day. Then, through Gaius's sympathy it had become the property of the harlot from Alexandria. But who did it belong to now? If it was once owned by Toronius, should it be given to Livia, his rightful heir? That would only be expected, he thought.

He rubbed away a smudge of black soot and dust. He said aloud the word, "Black," and the words "black dust" came to mind. He had heard that phrase before, but where? His brain seemed to open and close rooms of memory. Then a door opened in his mind. There appeared a dense fog within which Caladria, little more than a lump, was sitting upon the ground.

She had spoken to him, or at least it had appeared so. The words, so out of context, had been impossible to comprehend. There was nothing real about them. But that was before. *"Do not too quickly give away the treasured piece."* That, Apollodoros recalled, was what Caladria said. Yes, *"in the black dust after the rain. It will be there."* Then there was the final sentence: *"Hide it till later."*

Hide it till later, he said to himself. It was indeed a treasured piece, it was in "black dust" and it did rain. How did she know? he wondered. But then, how did she know that Gaius would need his help at the Temple of Diana? *What else did she know?* he asked himself. And finally he wondered, *Who else knows that she can see what has not yet happened?*

Apollodoros suddenly realized that he knew nothing about the girl, and had not even made an effort to learn about her or her sister. There had been so many slaves that had appeared and as quickly disappeared from the villa when either Toronius or Livia tired of them. But none had ever been as influential as Aspacia and Caladria. And certainly no female slave had captured Gaius's affections like Aspacia, the consequences of which might have been terribly ominous. But with Toronius's death all that that would surely change.

The Greek slave had regarded Caladria as a cow, a fat old woman in a girl's skin, but what if she were actually a seer?

"Do not too quickly give away the treasured piece," she had said. To know the future, was there any greater power? But who owned her now? And... just as important to Apollodoros... who owned him?

There were two things he'd do, he decided. He would hold onto the necklace until later, and would say nothing about it until he thought the time was right. That resolved, he retrieved the makeshift ossuary and, in the fading light, hobbled to his master's villa.

*****

"Is he any better?" Apollodoros asked Aspacia.

"He's had convulsions, but they've become fewer. He's asleep now."

"Have you said anything to him about his father?"

Aspacia shook her head. "It would only add to the shock. Besides, I think Livia should be the one to tell him. I'm sure she will when she returns."

"If she returns," said the Greek.

"You don't think she will?"

Apollodoros shrugged. "Why should she? Her husband's dead, there's nothing here for her, and she has everything to gain with the praetor."

"What will happen with the marriage of Gaius to Cornelia? Is that still going to happen?"

"It was announced to some of the most important people in Rome. I'm sure Retenius and his daughter expect it to take place."

"But what value would the marriage be to the praetor without Toronius?"

"What value would he have been be if alive? My master had little money and few prospects for making any more. Unless of course he sold us, but that wouldn't have brought him much. Besides, what would a patrician be without slaves?"

Aspacia sat on the peristyle's stone bench beside Apollodoros and watched the sun sink below the building's walls. The crate of bones, covered for modesty's sake, lay on the floor beside him as it had for the last three days.

"I cannot imagine why Toronius would have started the fire that caused his death," Aspacia said after a long moment had passed.

"I'm not sure he did start it. He had enemies and may have been murdered."

"Gaius told me that Toronius feared some Egyptians."

"Egyptians and others. I wouldn't say this if he was still alive, but he was little more than a petty thief, a street thug, when he bought me. He inherited a small dowry when he married Livia and, at least in the beginning, she had a civilizing effect on him. I did, too, since he realized that to rise in society he would have to acquire some culture. I taught him a bit of Greek so he could throw around classical allusions at the cena."

Aspacia watched Apollodoros stir coals in the brazier. "What do you think is going to happen to us now? Do we become Livia's slaves?"

"Does it really matter?" Apollodoros said. "We're still slaves even if she does inherit us."

"Is there any way we can buy our freedom?" Aspacia asked, as a night breeze filtered into the atrium.

"Livia would never allow that, but if Gaius inherited us there might be a possibility."

"Gaius said that he doesn't believe in slavery."

"He never has, but Livia will demand that we belong to her and that may mean we also belong to the praetor, Retenius."

Aspacia looked at him but said nothing. She rose and walked back to the cubiculum where Gaius roamed in and out of consciousness. Apollodoros remained on the bench until the evening's gloom settled upon the hills of Rome. Then, carrying the box, he walked toward the copse of trees where he knew Caladria would be.

"I found the precious thing in the black dust, like you said I would."

Caladria stared into the gloom and said nothing. Apollodoros began to wonder if she had heard him at all. How could this unkempt lump know so much? But maybe that was part of the mystery. No one would ever guess her powers.

Finally she looked at him, or, he thought ruefully, through him.

"It is well that he left the pendant for the harlot, the one in Alexandria," she said.

"The boy? You mean Gaius?"

"Yes, Gaius."

"But that was before—almost two years ago. You weren't here, how could you know of that?"

She merely stared into the distance, her silence saying what she didn't have to.

"I mean, I know that you can see things that have not yet happened, but things in the past?"

She allowed herself a fragment of a smile, the first he had ever seen upon her.

"Past, future, they are on the same road." Her finger made a slow pointing motion. "We travel the road forever and pause here for a little while."

"Perhaps it's as you say. But I know the past; what I want to know is the future. What will happen now that my master is dead?"

"Dead?" She looked away, her face in darkness.

"What do I do, where do I go?" Apollodoros said, ignoring the question in her voice. He appeared quite anxious, tired of riddles and strange pronouncements.

"You will go on a great journey, but not now. What is, is. What will be cannot be changed."

"And what do I do with this?" Apollodoros said, tugging the gold chain and pendant from a sack.

"You give it to Gaius when he comes to you tomorrow."

"What do I tell him about his father?"

"Nothing, if you wish."

"What I wish is that you never came here. Now give me an answer!"

The girl tilted her head and in just above a whisper said, "I told you. What is, is. What will be has already been decided."

He abruptly turned away from her when she said, "Nothing is as it seems. Not even the bones in the box you brought here."

*****

Gaius sat on the stone bench in the atrium and stared at the ossuary. "What did my mother say when she saw them?" he asked Apollodoros.

"She screamed, startled by the sight of them. Then she ran from the remains of the barn. Cornelia had me bring them here."

"There must be a proper funeral," Gaius said. "I should call upon his friend, Vercipius. He knows more about such things."

The Greek hesitated then said, "My master of almost twenty years is dead. Whose slave am I now?"

"I don't know if you belong to anyone. Certainly you aren't mine. Of course, you can stay here if you wish. There is nothing I expect you to do."

"But your mother will insist that I belong to her, and she may wish to sell everything: the villa, me, Caladria and Aspacia, too."

"She won't. Not if I'm head of the household. I'm of age and by law she must do as I say."

"Then you can even free me?" Apollodoros said.

"I guess I can."

Apollodoros nodded and decided not to ask anything more. He waited a moment while Gaius put his head back and sighed deeply.

"I have something else for you," the Greek finally said.

"Isn't this enough?" Gaius said, nodding to the crate of bones.

"I understand how difficult and perplexing all this is for you.

I know you put little value on the relationship you had with my master. You may value this more." He reached in the sack and lifted out the chain and pendant. "Recognize it?"

Gaius bolted upright and stared at it. "This is the one my father bought in Alexandria and I left for the girl before we fled to the docks. And then I saw it on the Egyptian girl the day my father bought the fakes. How did you get it?"

"It was in the ash at the barn. That's where Caladria told me I would find it."

"Before the fire?"

"Weeks before. She told me about finding something precious in black dust, but at the time I didn't know what she meant. It was a mystery to me; I thought it was just the prattle of a demented girl."

"Does my mother know it's here?"

"No, she doesn't even know it ever existed. Caladria told me to give it to you. All your mother has is his fibula, the one that fastened his toga."

"Why would Caladria tell you to give me the necklace?"

"I have no idea, but I'm sure she does. She's the strangest person I've ever known; she scares me more than your father ever did."

*****

"It was a brave thing you did, Gaius, going to the aid of that infected woman. I was more worried than you can imagine. The slave catchers might have killed you," said Aspacia.

"For a while I thought they did. Did they attack Lysippus, too?"

"Yes, but he had the torch and that kept them at bay." She was silent for a while then said, "I should say that I'm sorry about your father."

"It would be a worthy sentiment, had he not been a rapist and a murderer."

"But he was your father sand I think in time you will miss him. I miss my father very much."

"From what you told me, your father was a kind and wise man. You have every right to miss him. The only lasting things my father left me are bruises and a feeling of unworthiness."

"No, he allowed Apollodoros to tutor you. That, from a man who had no education and despised real learning."

"He only allowed it so he could use me. For him everything was for an ulterior motive. But now he's gone."

"Your whole world will change."

"Maybe our whole world," he said, taking her hand.

She looked at the sack on the stone bench and said, "What's in that?"

"A treasure my father bought in Alexandria. It was torn from him by an Egyptian prostitute. He ran after beating her and told me to get it back, but I left it with the girl instead. Apollodoros found it in the barn where my father burned to death."

"Did the girl die in the barn? Surely she must have been wearing it?"

"Apollodoros didn't see any other remains. Apparently she wasn't in there."

Gaius lifted the ancient necklace from the sack and handed it to Aspacia. "It's still awfully valuable, even though some of the gold melted in the flames."

"If he didn't take it from her, then it must have been thrown in. Why would anybody toss away such a valuable piece?" Aspacia frowned in thought, then said, "I think the girl wore it to remind her of the beating. It was an albatross, not a talisman. Throwing it into the fire where your father burned was the completion of a circle. It was a way of ridding her of the pain and the memory, Gaius. For her, it meant that all that was over."

"Should I give it away, sell it?"

"I think you should keep it for now. You may need it someday." Then she said, "Gaius, with your father gone, I was wondering..." Her voice trailed off.

"Cornelia?" he said, reading her thoughts.

"Forgive me. It's not a time for me to ask."

"I hope to never see her again, but only your sister knows what the future holds."

"I pray you don't ask her."
"I fear to ask her anything."

*****

Livia's eyes had not yet adjusted to the cubiculum's dim light. The bedroom of Retenius's country villa was far larger than any she had seen before. Like those in most homes of wealthy Romans, its furnishings were Spartan but of exquisite quality. Besides the bed with its silken coverings, there were two couches and a small table with gold and mosaic inlays.

Retenius ushered her in, but instead of sitting on a couch he motioned to the bed. She sat down and he reclined beside her.

"You're sure that it's his, Livia?" the silver-haired praetor said, turning the partially blackened fibula over in his hand.

"The bronze 'T' is for Toronius. It was his favorite broach, he always wore it."

"And his Greek slave found it in the ashes," he said, handing it back to her. "A keepsake, perhaps?"

She held it for a moment then said, "It's nothing that I would want to keep."

"Then I need not say anything about your loss."

"My loss?" she said. Then she laughed. "No, my dear, not a loss: a gain. I would have divorced him if the court had allowed me."

"That would have been unnecessary if proven that he was an arsonist. He did burn down my house. Had he lived, I would have brought him up on charges myself."

"He might have lost the villa."

"Oh he would have lost far more than that."

"His life?"

"Perhaps, but he would have lost you. That's the only way he would have escaped my wrath. Either you or his life," the praetor said wrapping his arms around her. He kissed her very gently and placed a hand on a breast. She closed her eyes and let the warmth flow through her. He kissed her again, his hand lifting her stola and sliding up the inside of her thigh. He touched a thin garment that was already damp. She moaned softly and he laid her back onto a pillow. She smiled and her hands traced the tight muscles of his torso and moved downward. Kneeling she pulled aside his toga and put out her tongue.

Her eyes had fully adjusted to the half-light and she raised her head when she heard a creak. She suddenly gasped and bolted upright.

"Cornelia?"

The girl languidly reclined on a couch across the room. "Hello Livia. Don't mind me. Pretend that I'm not even here," she said in a half-whisper.

"My sweet daughter has her own peculiarities," said Retenius. Then in Livia's ear, he whispered, "Of course, I had to teach her everything; she is much better than any of my slave girls. She likes to watch now. I know it's a bit unusual, I hope you don't mind."

There was the briefest moment of silence, a quick evaluation of her circumstances. "No, I don't mind. But we shall be discreet, shan't we?" Then, conspiratorially, Livia said, "It will be our own special secret."

"Yes," said Cornelia with a hint of disdain, "Our own special secret, isn't that right, Father? Not even my future husband shall know."

So the marriage plans are still in place, Livia thought. If all worked as she planned, this bed would become hers and the patrician would come to treasure her. Surely the union would solidify her place in his world. In the meantime she would enjoy the luxury of the villa.

Now she slid out of her stola, and brought him close. She touched her tongue to her lips and stared directly at Cornelia. *If this excites Retenius, all the better,* Livia thought.

"You may come closer," Livia said to the girl. "We can all play if you wish."

Cornelia dispassionately observed their lovemaking and Livia wondered whether the girl truly enjoyed voyeurism or was simply required to watch.

"Yes, daughter mine, we should all play together as I taught you. We have never had a woman as beautiful as Livia. Now let's not waste any more time."

"As you wish, Father," Cornelia said, as she slid onto the bed.

Chapter 14

Every villa rustica had an underground prison, the ergastulum, since farms could be dangerous places. Beatings by the farm overseer, the villicus, prompted acts of violence amongst desperate people. It was often said that there were two kinds of animals on the farm, those that could talk and those that could not, and there was little difference in the treatment of either.

The villicus's master, Retenius, had been informed of Cynthia's capture outside the temple, but he was with his daughter and currently entertaining the woman Livia. No doubt he would attend to the slave later.

There had been several others in the prison for the first two days of the woman's incarceration but they had been released. Nobody saw Cynthia until two burly men were thrown into the same cell five days later. The men appeared fearful of their forthcoming punishment, but that was soon put aside by the presence of a woman inhabiting the one and only cell.

Only moments after the cell door slammed shut, there was a scream. The villicus grinned, thinking that the rape had already begun. But the scream was not from the woman.

It was the word "plague!" that made him abruptly stop. Warily, the villicus, accompanied by four liberti, put his eye to a peephole in the door.

"The woman in here has the sickness, let us out!" bawled the men.

"We should put her in the infirmary," one of the freed slaves said.

"The infirmary is not the place for her," barked the overseer.

"Let us out!" again shouted the terrified men.

The villicus shook his head. Backing away, he turned to the liberti and said, "They stay in there. Let none of them out! Keep everybody away."

"I fear it's too late. The sickness is in the air. Quadraginta," said a libertus, already backing away.

"Yes, that's the only thing we can do. Quarantine them for forty days," said the villicus, fearing that they had already released two others. From experience he knew the incubation period to be ten days.

Amongst the wailing he heard a woman's laughter. It was high-pitched and gleeful, then there was the sound of a blow and the laughing ceased.

How many at the villa had already been exposed? the villicus wondered. He and the others retreated from the wailing, incarcerated men. Running as fast as he could, a libertus shrieked, "It's too late! Oh the gods, we'll all die."

*****

"Caladria," the disembodied voice called as she sat huddled in the copse of trees. She swayed back and forth, her mind envisioning the source of the voice.

"Arzeka, why are you waking me so late?"

"Late? Oh yes, that time thing. It is no longer something I consider, Caladria, though I'm sorry to have woken you from mortal slumber. But I wanted to tell you that I'm tired of being here. I am going away."

"You can't go, Arzeka. You are my friend, and you see things that I can't."

"I'll always be your friend, but I want to go home. Besides, you have the power to see. You've always had that."

"Not like you."

"You will. You'll see everything."

"Will you come back to visit me?"

"I don't know if it's possible. There are things in the beyond that I don't know. I am going now."

"No, not yet!" she said aloud. "I won't be able to see

everything—not like you. You must help me to know."

The plum-shaped girl sat still as stone and listened to the silence. Was it only her mind or a whisper in the wind that said, "You know, Caladria; you already know. You do not have to ask me again."?

*****

"Get up, get up," Cornelia said excitedly as she shook Livia.

"I want to stay right here, I'm too tired," Livia replied, feeling a spasm of delight as Retenius's hands played upon her.

His daughter had returned to the bed, having washed away the fluids of the evening's sex. "Father, get dressed," she exhorted. The bedding was askew and she could see that Retenius was already aroused. Sleepily he attempted to coax her down, but she resisted.

"Not now. Get up, I want to go shopping."

"Shopping?" the praetor moaned, only half awake. "That's not what I want," he said as he trilled his tongue over Livia's neck.

"For my wedding! Yes, let's all go to the Forum shops."

"Now? This morning?" Livia said unhappily, raising herself on an elbow. "I was looking forward to the morning's play."

"Absolutely. We must shop. Time is short. Father, send a slave to Livia's villa and have him tell Gaius to meet us at the arch. Oh yes, have that slave girl Aspacia come too. She can carry the packages."

*****

Cornelia, her arm entwined with her future mother-in-law, went from shop to shop selecting the finest silks for her wedding stola. Then, quite alone, she slipped into an apothecary and purchased three beautiful glass vials. Further on, she picked out shoes with gilt inlay and jeweled bracelets, paid for by Retenius who, in mock horror, rolled his eyes at the exorbitant costs.

He and Gaius followed the women. Retenius, in his gleaming toga, extolled the importance of marriage as well as the wondrous qualities of his daughter. Gaius said nothing but nodded his head when he felt compelled. A sickening feeling came over him when he turned to see Aspacia toting the trappings his future wife had chosen.

With studied indifference, he watched as Cornelia piled the packages into Aspacia's arms and with an amused smile asked, "That's not too heavy for you, is it, child?"

Retenius looked on and, putting his arm around Gaius's shoulder, said, "Following the marriage, you and my daughter, at my expense, will enjoy a month in Hispania Citerior. I have a friend who owns a villa right on the coast: a warm, lovely place where you two can really get to know each other. You do know what I mean," he said, a lascivious grin on his face. Then, with enthusiasm, he went on, "After that we will start on your career. I will hire the finest legal tutors and you'll be my assistant at court. That will familiarize you with legal proceedings and you'll meet the most influential counselors. We will be a team. You will help me and I shall help you. It will be grand; I only wish your beloved father could have seen it. I shall make a sacrifice on his behalf. It's the least I can do."

"Father, I must show you this," Cornelia said excitedly, dropping Livia's hand and ushering Retenius into a stall.

*****

"Has Gaius said anything about our marriage?" she said, the flippant excitement replaced by steely concern.

"No, he's hardly said a word to me at all. The boy's worried and distracted, and not about his father's death. He can't take his eyes off that slave girl."

"I expect to marry him, Father. That's what we agreed. I will have him get rid of her the day of our wedding. It will be his gift to me."

"That may prove difficult."

"I'll sell her and he'll never see her again."

"That won't help your marriage."

"Then I'll find him a substitute, but it will be one of my choosing."

They had hardly returned to the street when a man ran through the crowded Forum, his elbow striking Retenius. "Slow down!" the praetor shouted. Another scurried past, a terrified look in his eyes. Shoppers in the street turned their heads as others rushed by. Cornelia peered into a fashionable shop, but the owner waved her away and slammed the shop's heavy door. Cornelia looked at Livia and wrinkled her brow. The same thing occurred three shops further on, the proprietor saying, "Go away, go away, we are closed."

"Something's happening," Cornelia said. "I think we should leave here and go home."

"I'll have Gaius and the slave girl return to Livia's," Retenius whispered to his daughter. "I'll carry the packages to our villa."

"Let me guess," Cornelia said, "You want an encore of last night with me and Livia without any prying eyes."

"Retenius smiled and said, "There's no need to shock the lad right away, is there?"

Cornelia gave her father a tight smile but said nothing more.

*****

"Mother, this is insane," Gaius said to Livia, taking her hand and pulling her into the back room of a linen shop.

"We can't stop now; she has to have proper attire. Only the right husband is more important than the wedding dress," Livia postulated.

"I am not the right man for her. I will not marry Cornelia, and neither you nor the praetor can force me to."

"Your father wanted it and you must honor his wishes. Besides, there are things I have learned about Cornelia that will please you."

"There's nothing about Cornelia that will please me, and my father is dead. He was the only one who could force me to marry her."

"You can't seriously consider abrogating the marriage now, not after all the efforts Retenius made. He would look like a fool, and it could ruin his chances for the Senate."

"You would have me marry that girl so Retenius can win an election? Since when were you interested in honoring Toronius? I think you're afraid that it would ruin your chances for bedding the praetor."

The slap came with rage greater than anything he might have expected.

"You vile wretch!" she said, spittle on her lips. The strained whisper came as a screech. "How dare you destroy any happiness I will ever have. You will marry that little bitch or you'll never have a career in law or anything else. And what's more, I intend to marry Retenius, and my gift to him will be everything we have. And that includes that slut Aspacia!"

Later, he might have regretted picking up the woman and heaving her across the room. Livia slammed into a pile of rolled linen, the breath knocked out of her. Stunned by her son's fury, she meekly struggled to her feet, stared at him, and hastened to join Cornelia.

"Gaius," the praetor said, glancing at Livia, her coiffure a bit mussed, "why don't you and the slave girl go back to your villa? Cornelia and your mother would like to talk alone. I'll send a messenger in a day or two. You could join us then for a cena."

With worried looks, several dozen people rushed past. Murmurs turned into frightened shouts as vendor's gates and shutters slammed.

After Gaius and Aspacia departed, Livia heard Cornelia say, "Father, I'm frightened. Hail me a palanquin, I'd rather not walk."

"And one for me," Livia added. "I want to leave here. Something is happening."

She glanced across the road to an apartment when she heard a woman scream. Another door slammed shut and Cornelia said, "We should hurry. I don't like this at all."

*****

"I would have burned everything Cornelia bought," said Gaius when he and Aspacia reached the villa.

"What good would that have done?" Aspacia asked. "You would have made an enemy of Retenius as well as his daughter."

"She already knows I hate her, and her father will have little use for me if he gains the Senate."

"He seems to have a special interest in your mother," Aspacia noted as they sat in the atrium.

"It goes beyond that. She hopes to marry him; she told me her dowry, her gift to him, would include everything here."

"And that would include me, Caladria, and the other slaves," Aspacia said, downcast.

"That might be up to the courts. As an adult male I should be the inheritor."

"Retenius is a praetor and a powerful man. How difficult would it be for him, by an act of marriage, to be the final inheritor?"

"He might consider it, but I will make sure he inherits very little."

They were silent for a minute when Aspacia looked up to see her sister standing mutely in front of her.

"You should prepare, the others will be here soon," said Caladria calmly.

"Who will be here?" Aspacia asked.

"Frightened people," she said, walking away.

"What frightened people?" Gaius said to Aspacia.

"I have no idea. The only thing I know is that what she predicts will most certainly happen.

*****

The villicus, a powerful former slave, was frantic when the praetor, Livia, and Cornelia entered the country villa. None of the estate's three dozen slaves were working, not in the vineyard, the field, or in the house.

"Some are in hiding, Excellency, but others have run away. I used the whip but to no effect. They are terrified and are running for their lives. But I fear it's too late."

"Too late for what?" Retenius said, scanning the nearly deserted villa.

"The sickness—surely you know of it?"

"That's what it was," Livia said, clutching the praetor's arm. "The terrified people at the Forum; it has already spread."

"It is too dangerous for you here, Excellency," the overseer implored. "The woman the catchers found had the sickness. She brought it back with her."

"Cynthia?" Cornelia asked. "Where is she?"

"Dead. I had her body burned this morning. You must not stay here," the villicus repeated, holding his palms up as if warding them away.

Retenius turned to Livia and his daughter and said, "Livia, take Cornelia to your house. I'll join you very soon. Let no one else into the villa, and don't venture out."

"But what of you?" Livia asked.

"There are valuables I must pack. When I leave, there will be no one to guard the place, and there will be looters. Now leave here before it's too late."

Cornelia was already at the gate when she suddenly turned and said, "Father, please bring all my unguent and fragrant vials. They are precious to me and I cannot have any of them stolen. And do make sure they are well sealed."

*****

It was only the fourth hour when Aspacia heard her sister's whimpering. Caladria was half slumped over the kitchen table when she found her. Alarmed, Aspacia wrapped her arms around her.

"Oh, Aspacia, I'm so worried for you. Something terrible is going to happen."

"What's going to happen?"

Caladria buried her face in her hands, and in a pitiful voice wailed, "I don't know, but something in this dreadful place. I just can't see it like I used to, when I could talk to Arzeka—not since he went away."

"Will this terrible thing cause our deaths?" Aspacia asked.

Bleary-eyed, her sister looked up and said, "No, I don't think so. But it will be something that will make you run." She stopped then added, "Yes, you will both run."

*****

"Secure the gate! Only Retenius is to be allowed in," Livia

commanded Apollodoros. The villa had become as still as death. The screams and terror beyond the walls, and the carts filled with dead being hauled to funeral pyres, cast a dark pall over the villa. Lethargy and foreboding seeped into everyone.

There had not been such terror since the Gauls had raped Rome centuries before. Each morning, the inhabitants of the villa minutely inspected their bodies for signs of infection.

"It sometimes starts behind the ears or at the hairline," Livia cautioned Cornelia. "Then it will spread very rapidly. I heard that there will be spots, red but sometimes white, then a runny nose and a fever. Eventually the whole body is covered."

"How long?" Cornelia asked.

"Before it goes away?"

"No, before one dies."

"Maybe a week, sometimes two," Livia replied, holding a copper mirror to her face.

"I don't think we're infected," Cornelia said hopefully. "If it were not so dangerous we could go to the temple of Cybele and make an offering. It's said that she can cure any disease. But I don't think we will catch it; we would know it by now."

*****

"You won't catch it, neither will Apollodoros," Aspacia said to Gaius, who had shunned Cornelia.

"How do you know that?" Gaius said.

"My sister told me."

"What about Retenius, will he become infected?"

"Caladria didn't want to talk about him. There's something strange...I don't know," she said, sounding confused. "Somehow I don't think he'll get the disease."

"And Cornelia?" Gaius asked expressionless.

"All my sister said is what she often does."

"What does she say?"

"What will be, will be."

It was only the next morning that a terrible wailing came from Cornelia's room. "It's a pustule, see," she said to Livia, who was torn between embracing her and running from the stricken girl.

"Are you certain it's not a scratch or an insect bite? I was once bitten by a flea and got a terrible red swelling, Cornelia."

"No, no," the girl moaned. "It's nothing like that. I have the spot. No, now I have two. Oh, the gods!"

Livia was taken aback to see the girl sink to her knees then lay prostrate on the ground. She took a step forward and was suddenly pushed aside by Aspacia.

"Get wet cloths," she said. "We must get her to bed. She will have the fever by dusk."

Livia stood stock-still, not believing that a slave would order her to do anything, but then she remembered the time of Caladria's self-mutilation when she had followed Apollodoros's orders. Not knowing what else to do, Livia hurried to the kitchen. When she got there, Caladria had already prepared the cloths. Livia stared at her.

"You knew all about this, didn't you?"

Caladria said nothing but merely held out a dampened towel.

*****

In the space of three days, pustules cloaked Cornelia's face in a red, burning mass, and she lay virtually unrecognizable. With swollen eyes the color of a setting sun, she lay in her own sweat and seeping fluids. Fatigued beyond fear, she slept a fitful sleep and often woke ranting deliriously. She invoked the gods and called for her mother, then relapsed into a near coma.

"Aspacia," Cornelia said, using her name for the first time. "Please tell Gaius I meant no harm. I know he doesn't want to see me." Cornelia squinted at Aspacia through narrow slits. "I don't know why you want to tend to me. I have been awful to you."

"Wouldn't you do the same for me, Cornelia?"

The girl looked at her and said, "For a slave? What do you think, Aspacia?"

*****

"She is dying, Gaius. I think you should go to her," Aspacia said on the fourth day, as Cornelia plummeted toward death.

"I won't know what to say to her," he replied.

"What you say doesn't matter. She wants to make amends, clear her conscience."

"She would have destroyed both of us. She should die knowing her deceit. The girl is evil."

"She is what she has become: what others made her. If it hadn't been for Retenius, she might have been a very different person. We are what we are, Gaius. You hated your father; I hate the men who destroyed my family, my world. But it's the end of her world; your presence in her last hours will not diminish yours."

Cornelia was asleep when Gaius went in. Unsure what to do with himself, he stood beside her bed and wondered whether he should wake her. No one else was with him. The girl who had nearly plunged his life into a sickening morass lay in a stupor. Gaius had no desire to touch her. The room felt stifling and infected. He turned away, thinking that he had done as Aspacia asked; he had at least come to her. Then he heard a tiny voice say, "I really liked you, Gaius. You are good, but..." she attempted a smile, "but so naïve. You have no idea about me or Livia."

"I may know more than you think," he said defensively.

She was silent for a moment and he thought he should say something more, something comforting. But what caring thing could he say to someone he detested?

"You don't have to say anything, Gaius. I don't care for sweet words. I never received any that were real. It's enough that you have come." She reflected a moment then said, "Is your mother well?"

"She seems to be."

"That's good. I would like to see her. Have Apollodoros ask for her; she won't be in danger."

*****

Retenius had arrived that morning and was sitting with Livia in the atrium when the Greek slave gave the domina Cornelia's message.

"Do you think it's wise to go to her?" asked the praetor nervously.

"I haven't gotten the disease, and I don't think I will," she said, "but I won't stay with her long."

It was only a short time before Livia left Cornelia's room and rejoined Retenius. "Your daughter asks to see you. She wants to say goodbye."

The praetor sat quietly. Then, as if struggling against some great force, he finally rose and walked to the sickroom.

Cornelia had used every ounce of energy to stay awake. "Father, I'm so glad you have come," she said as gaily as possible when he entered the dimly lit chamber.

"Forgive me, I should have been here sooner," said the praetor, obviously dreading the thought of being there at all.

I'll never forgive you, Cornelia thought, but she said, "No, you should not be harsh with yourself. I was not coherent enough before, but now I would like us to share my final moments together. I asked Livia to pour us two goblets of wine, the finest Campania she had. It's a final salutation, you might say, and you know how much I enjoy fine wine."

"It may not be good for you now," Retenius said in his most fatherly way.

Cornelia tried to laugh but was interrupted by a spasm of coughing. "I doubt that anything else can hurt me now," she was finally able to say. She indicated the goblets and he handed her one.

"What should we drink to, daughter?" he asked, seemingly surprised that she was so convivial toward him; he had expected a tirade of accusations instead.

"Let's drink to the good things we have shared, and the ones we should not have."

Retenius laughed. "I guess that's as good as any, Cornelia. Not too gushy, not too maudlin, right? But it is too bad that you and Gaius could not..."

"Hush, Father, just drink."

Their eyes fixed upon one another as they drained the goblets.

"I probably would have eventually poisoned Gaius and his woman," Cornelia said in a half-whisper, letting the glass drop to the floor. "Marriage to him was the fantasy of a desperate girl." She closed her eyes and said, "I enjoyed the wine, Father. I hope you did, too."

The praetor didn't know if she had fallen asleep or was just pretending, as she had so often done when he came to her during those hot silent nights. He had shared a glass of wine and looked upon the girl for the last time. Pity, he thought, he had enjoyed those nights, not that she had been particularly willing, but, he rationalized, the sex did occasionally excite her.

A soft afternoon light filtered in, illuminating her bottles of perfume. They sat in a perfect line, casting a spectrum of color on the wall. All, that was, except one. It had been opened and now lay on its side, empty. The praetor gazed at it before he ventured to pick it up. He sniffed it, let out an agonized howl, then threw the vial against the wall. Cornelia smiled as her hand went limp.

"You bitch!" he shouted, dragging her out of the bed onto the cold stone floor. His hands encircled her neck and he squeezed, shouting and ranting until Livia ran into the room.

"Retenius, what are you doing?" she gasped, taking in the scene before her.

"She poisoned me! The wretched thing poisoned the wine. I am going to die!"

He stood, bolted past Livia, and ran into the sunlit atrium. The warmth did nothing to melt the ice that ran through his veins.

*****

"They're dead! They're both dead," Livia wailed, kneeling on the floor of her cubiculum. "It's all gone, my life is gone," she sobbed. Her perfect coiffure was a shambles from running her hands through her hair, and her deep eye makeup was streaked as tears rolled down her cheeks.

"Retenius may not be dead yet," Gaius said, standing before her with Aspacia at his side. "I saw him a moment ago."

"He said he was poisoned. Cornelia asked me to fill the

glasses and open that horrid vial. I didn't know it was poison. I killed him. I murdered the praetor. They're going to kill me."

"No one's going to kill you, and you didn't murder him. Cornelia put it in his wine."

"Is she...?"

"Dead?" prompted Gaius.

Livia balled her hands and pressed them against her face. Her head bobbed up and down.

"Yes, Mother, she's dead."

"From the sickness. She died from the sickness, didn't she?" Livia asked plaintively.

"It would have killed her, but she was strangled. Her father, your dear praetor, strangled his daughter. She's lying on the floor."

Livia's eyes grew wide and she said, "Where is Retenius? Where's my praetor?"

"He ran away. He's out there in the streets."

"Oh, Gaius," she wailed, "What am I going to do?"

"What are you going to do? You, who would have me marry a fiend, so you could prance around with a man who would strangle his daughter? Do you really think that I should worry about you? You'll find another praetor by the end of the week. Now, Mother, do excuse me. I believe there is someone who has to be buried."

Livia stared at him: the new master of the house and the man who could control her destiny. *Is this the way it will be from now on?* she wondered. Only weeks ago he was the boy she could denigrate at will and now...now what?

She knelt on the hard stone floor, hands clasped before her as Gaius strode away.

"Are you coming, Aspacia?" he said, turning back to her.

"Not now, I don't want to see Cornelia anymore."

Aspacia sat on a bench across from Livia and was quiet. Then she said, "I'll stay with you, Mistress, if you don't mind the company of a slave."

"Livia looked up at her with teary eyes. "Why would you want to help me? I can't free you or make you happy."

"You don't have to make me happy. In fact there's very little that can make me happy, or my sister for that matter. But we are very few and we should try to survive. That's all we can do, Livia: try to survive."

"Livia," the woman repeated the word. Never had a slave addressed her by her name before, indeed none were ever given permission nor had dared to. But now death seemed a great equalizer.

"Yes, Aspacia, we must try to survive." She took the girl's outstretched hand and stood. She looked at the girl thoughtfully before asking, "What is your sister's name?"

"Caladria."

"Then I shall call her Caladria from now on. Can she really see everything the past and the future?"

"Yes, Livia."

"Do we have a future?"

"There's always a future."

"Even for me?"

*****

"I didn't think you wanted to see Cornelia," Gaius said as Aspacia entered the narrow room. He had placed the girl's body on the bed and covered her with a sheet.

"I don't. I want to talk to you," Aspacia said, arms across her chest. Her tone was cool and there was no smile or warmth in her expression.

"Did my mother upset you?" Gaius asked.

"No, but you did."

"Really? Just how did I do that?" Gaius asked, leaning against the wall.

"I saw a different side of you: the one you showed your mother. It was," she hunted for the words, "very harsh. Very cruel. Insensitive."

"Do you think I should have indulged her, comforted her, because she could not chain me to that corpse?" Gaius demanded, nodding to the girl for whom rigor mortis was setting in. "Should I have mourned Livia's loss of Retenius, who would have used you like my father would have?"

"You hate your mother, don't you?" Aspacia asked.

"No more than I hated my father."

Aspacia gave him a long, dispassionate look then turned to go.

"I think we should talk," Gaius said. "But not in here."

Aspacia shrugged her shoulders. "What choice does a slave have?"

"Stop that nonsense. Now come with me."

He reached for her hand but she pulled away. They walked into the orchard, he pointed to a stump, and she sat down.

"I had a fairly good relationship with my mother after my father refused to accept the girl she gave birth to. I don't know what became of the infant—I only found out recently that she even existed—but Apollodoros told me that my mother never had sex with my father again and because of that I'm their only child. Because of her loss she fawned on me. It was embarrassing, and I was teased mercilessly. My father thought she was obsessed, and since she refused him, he began to hate me."

Aspacia had looked away when he began talking, but it didn't matter; he was looking past her, a flood of memories coming back.

"I saw that at the cena she would make sure to hold my father's hand. It was to show others that they had a loving and stable relationship. It was a façade: a lie. She looked at other men and encouraged them to look at her. Even then, when I tried to think otherwise, I am sure that she had sex with them. I was eight years old when it all changed."

He looked directly at Aspacia and said, "I wasn't really spying on her. My father was not expected home and I thought my mother was alone in her cubiculum. I would often go in, sit on the floor, and talk with her when she reclined. One afternoon I simply opened her door and found her bouncing up and down on the penis of a gladiator. I don't know who was more shocked, the gladiator, my mother, or me. The man laughed, finished with her then snatched his toga and left. On his way out he said, 'You'd better tell your boy to knock next time. I'm going; I have other women to screw.' She suddenly looked like a cheap harlot and I felt very bad for her. But from then on, I've never thought of her in the same way as before."

"What did your mother say?" Aspacia asked.

"What do you think? She was furious with me, told me how stupid and useless I was. She warned me to never say anything about her tryst to my father. But he unexpectedly came home just as the gladiator strode out the front gate. My father was a jealous man despite the fact that he hadn't laid with my mother in years. He would have raped her if she hadn't run into the old barn. Rape was always exciting to him."

"Did you tell him about your mother and the gladiator?" Aspasia asked, as her anger seemed to dissipate.

"No. He found the soiled bed sheets and smelled the man's stink. My mother denied everything and my father beat me to reveal the truth. I didn't talk, but she thought I did. She slapped me across the face again and again and said that I was a coward and a little girl. In her mind, she disowned me, and she made a point to denigrate me as often as possible. I didn't speak to her for three years."

"But you had to communicate with her," Aspacia protested.

"Through Apollodoros, yes."

"And your father? Did you speak to him?"

"He didn't care if I did or not; he wouldn't speak to me. In my place Appian Dio was virtually adopted by my father. In his eyes Appian was everything I wasn't. Of course, I didn't know until later, but I never told him that Appian was screwing his wife."

Aspacia's eyes went wide. "Your best friend was having sex with Livia?"

"This is Rome. It's quite acceptable for a woman of a higher class to have sex with a man of a lower class. Of course technically it's adultery and that's a death sentence. But someone has to accuse her, and it wasn't going to be me."

"Why not? You hated her."

"I hated my father more, and I didn't want to see my friend Appian executed."

"So you wound up hating everyone except Appian Dio."

"No, Aspacia, not everybody. The truth is, I'm in love."

"Really? That's amazing. May I ask who you're in love with? Maybe I'll be jealous," she said.

Emotionally drained, he stared at her then said, "I'm in love with you, Aspacia."

She looked at him, shook her head, and began to walk away.

"Where are you going? I said I love you!"

"It won't work, Gaius. I'm still a slave and I just want to be alone."

*****

As evening settled over Rome, a heavily-bundled man in a stained toga slipped from shadow to shadow. Assiduously he avoided the few who still dared to venture out. It had been weeks since he had left the insula, and now he was shaken by the sight of twisted and bloated bodies cast into gutters and alleyways in the poorer districts. The stench made him raise his garments to cover his nose and he hurried on. From the cramped and fetid apartment in which he had found refuge, he had heard the cries of the stricken and their kin. Indeed, four bodies had been rushed from the apartment and thrown into a pit of lye with no ceremony at all. But the fear that kept him hunkered down in the room was not from the disease.

The man had found a place in the wall from which he could look down on the narrow street five stories below. He watched and listened for countless hours, trying to shut out the noise of crying babies and their brawling parents. His muscles grew stiff and hunger and thirst drove him to make quick sorties to the street vendors. Gathering his flask of water, his cheese, bread and meats he would scurry back to his hovel. Few cared to engage him, for he had nothing to offer. No one of any substance lived on the fourth, fifth or sixth floors of an insula, and certainly not in the attic with the rats and pigeons.

The man had no idea of what had transpired during the absence from his villa; he could not even guess. How many died? What would he say upon returning? Would he have to say anything to his wife? Certainly he had no need to explain anything to anybody else. Maybe they were all dead, he thought. Except for one, that would not be all bad. He had been thinking about her during those long hours and it excited him. She belonged to him; he could do whatever he wanted with her and no one could interfere. It was the law, and for once it would be on his side.

The Egyptians had not come. Perhaps they were gone or thought him dead. He prayed that was the case but one could never be certain about them. But the man, Toronius, could stay no longer. It was time to claim what was his. He left his claustrophobic sanctuary and scuttled down the nearly empty street. He moved ever closer until he could see the walls of the villa against the morning sky.

*****

Gaius could not imagine why the girl was so angry with him. Was he supposed to forgive his mother for the atrocity that had loomed over him, one in which she had so cunningly conspired? Had she ever forgiven him for anything? He seethed as he lay in his bed.

His mind went to the necklace placed beneath the mattress. There was nothing to keep Gaius here. He would have money; he could go abroad, take Apollodoros and Aspacia if she would go with him. He would never tell anyone she was a slave. He could buy her a stola and she could pretend to be a liberta or even a Roman lady from a distant province.

He had told her he loved her, he'd said it twice and she had heard him. But she had not replied. He felt foolish. Gaius had bared his soul. It was Aspacia that he thought about night and day. Had he not taken her to the Temple of Diana, had he not treated her with the utmost respect and shown true caring? What other Roman youth wearing the toga virilis would surrender himself before a girl, much less a slave?

But, he thought *what do I know about women anyway?* Damn little, he had to admit, since she was the only girl he had ever really known, much less cared about. Did she think that the way he dealt with his mother, a vile narcissistic woman, would be the way he would treat her? How could she possibly believe that? Aspacia knew from the outset his love for her. He felt totally helpless. Now he would not even know what to say to her, if indeed he should say anything at all. *Maybe I should just pack up and go.*

His mind swirled, but finally he reasoned that things would be better in the morning. Her anger, as usual, would flash then dissipate like a summer storm. He had seen the fire in her eyes before, but its fury was disarmed by the beauty of those eyes, her bouncing curls, and the hands on her hips accentuating her nubile figure. He would grin in amusement, and her vexation would end with her turning saucily about and stomping away. And she wondered why her words never made him angry. He would be entranced and love her all the more.

But this time it was different. Aspacia had not liked what she had seen of him, and what was said was said. He could do nothing to change it. His mother's actions would have left him with a life of misery. He wasn't a cloth one could simply tread upon. So Gaius erected a wall in defense of his heart. It had a gate, but it would only open to the invited. His mother was not one of them. Aspacia was.

Suddenly, Gaius wanted her. He wanted her next to him; he wanted to stroke her hair, to make her laugh, to kiss her lips. But she wasn't there. Undoubtedly she had found her spot beneath the stairs of the tablinum. He could go to her. He could ask her to join him, but he knew her too well. She had said that she wanted to be alone and nothing he could do could change that. She had a stubborn streak and even held onto opinions she already doubted.

And finally, after all the enjoyment Aspacia derived from his company, all the delicious glances and the flirting, he could not imagine that she would not want to be with him. The very thought of her, frustrated as she made him, left him excited and sleep did not come easily.

*****

Aspacia was surprised when Caladria came in from the field and lay down beside her. "You are cold, you should not be out there," Aspacia said as her sister wrapped herself in her stained and tattered blanket.

"Scared, not cold," Caladria whispered, but she was shaking nevertheless.

"You don't have to be scared, you're with me and I won't let anything happen to you."

"I'm not scared for me," Caladria said. "I already told you; I'm scared for you."

Aspacia held her close. "You had a bad dream. Just go to sleep. Everything will be fine in the morning. You can help me in the garden and I will tell you a story."

Caladria sniffled and settled in. A few moments passed before she said, "You should be with your lover Gaius."

"He's not my lover, and I'm fine right here."

"You should be with him," Caladria repeated, before closing her eyes and falling into an uneasy sleep.

*****

Gaius wasn't sure why he dreamt of his father, but he pictured him in the cubiculum beside his, snoring loudly before waking and ripping the nightclothes off a girl. He pictured Toronius obscenely obese, his bloated stomach and testicles swaying over a girl whose face Gaius could not see. It was a macabre scene filled with screams, pummeling, and finally the penetration of the hapless thing.

Gaius woke in a cold sweat. He sat up and willed the nightmare from his mind. He often dreamt of him and Aspacia walking through a field of spring flowers, but like a thin glass vial, those thoughts were often shattered by the entry of Toronius. Gaius wiped his face and lay down, pulling the damp cover over his head. He closed his eyes and envisioned Aspacia.

He didn't know why he had woken; perhaps it was due to his own snoring. But he wasn't sure; the night spirits often played tricks on one. Gaius pulled the cover from his head and listened more intently. Now he heard it distinctly. There was snoring and it was not his, not that of Apollodoros, nor Livia in her cubiculum down the hall.

Gaius knew the sound; he had heard it all his life and he

gasped, feeling as if cold steel had impaled his gut. He bolted upright and nearly screamed. "But he's dead!" he shouted, as the snoring suddenly stopped. There was a great creak in the bed on the other side of the wall. A door flew open and banged loudly. There were heavy steps, followed by a girl's scream.

Chapter 15

Toronius had come in through the slave's gate, avoiding Apollodoros, and silently padded through the villa. He had opened no doors save his own. Exhausted from his ordeal, he had stumbled to his cubiculum and fallen asleep, only to wake some hours later.

Upon waking, it had taken Toronius only a few seconds to remember exactly why he had returned. He knew exactly where Aspacia was sleeping. He did not bother to put on his workday tunic, just got up and moved silently down the hall. He was startled to see Caladria sleeping beside her sister, but he ignored her presence. Reaching down he grabbed Aspacia, jerked her upright, and propelled the stunned girl into his room and closed the door. Jolted awake, she stared at the naked, corpulent man who stood before her. For a moment he merely gawked at her in return, a treasure about which he had fantasized for weeks. Now there was nothing to stop him. She was the one pleasure he had dwelled upon, the exquisite treat he had put off for nearly a year and saved for a moment like this.

His arm shot out and his fist clutched the tunic that fell over her breasts. He jerked the cloth, tearing it. "Yes!" he said, throwing her onto his bed. His hands shoved between her thighs and a piercing scream echoed down the hall. His fist slammed into her face.

Toronius had seen no need to bolt the door; no one would dare interfere. He jolted in shock when it slammed open and Gaius entered with a cry. The boy shot an arm around Toronius's neck and jerked him off the girl. Toronius emitted a strangled shout and tumbled backward. Rising from his knees he threw a punch, clipping Gaius on the jaw. Gaius appeared shaken but was still on his feet.

Aspacia, clutching her tunic, turned to run only to be punched again by Toronius. She screamed and flew back, her face red and swelling.

Toronius looked from her to his son, and in his moment of distraction Gaius's fists punched into his face. Toronius's hands went up as blows landed hard a second, third, and fourth time. Blood ran freely from the dominus's mouth. Roaring in pain, he spit out a tooth and blindly swung. Gaius sidestepped his blow, then spun and kicked Toronius behind the knee. The dominus sank to the stone floor, gasping for breath.

Aspacia bolted from the room as Livia rushed into the hallway. "Oh the gods," she screamed, "no, no, his ghost has come back!"

"No ghost!" Toronius hissed. Gaius had his knee on Toronius's throat and he could feel his eyes bulging as he fought for breath. Toronius tried desperately to shake Gaius off, to swing him around for a lethal punch, but it was no use, and Toronius began to realize that he just might die. The ancient phrase so often repeated in Rome assaulted his mind: "A son is a father's worst enemy."

"Best not to kill him, Gaius," said Apollodoros, coming out of the shadows. He put his arm lightly on Gaius's shoulder and again said, "Don't kill him, he's beaten. Take Aspacia and go."

Gaius's fist connected with Toronius's face one final time before he rose and slammed the door behind him. Toronius lay on his back gasping for air. His breathing was ragged and he choked on his own blood. He spit phlegm and blood, and rasped, "Mine! That slave girl is mine. I own her. And I will get you!"

*****

Gaius rushed into his room and reached under his mattress. Grabbing the golden necklace, he stomped back to his father's cubiculum and dangled it before Toronius, who struggled to his feet. "Do you remember this? It's from when you beat another

271

woman. She might think you're dead. I'll be sure to tell her you're not. She knows you're here and she'll burn you out again. But the necklace is yours, Father. You can decide if it's cursed or not. I give it to you for Aspacia. A trade. You own her no more; she and her sister are paid for in full." With the speed of a slung stone, the necklace flew into Toronius's face.

"Get out!" the dominus screamed. "I disown you. You will get nothing from me. I will call the authorities and have you put in chains."

"Yes, call them—the soldiers are searching for the accomplice of Plinius Apuleius Regulus. That's you. The captured slave still lives and he knows what you look like, scars and all."

Gaius took Aspacia's hand and began to lead her away.

"Where is Caladria?" Aspacia asked, turning to Livia.

"I don't know. She ran away when the fighting started, but I will find her for you."

"I will find her and I will come after you too," said Toronius from behind them.

"Father, I don't think that would be a good idea," Gaius said calmly.

*****

"Gaius, where are we going?" Aspacia asked, once the villa was far behind them. They had stopped beneath a stand of trees and the day was suddenly quiet. Only now did his hands shake as he blinked in the morning sun.

"I'm not sure. I haven't had time to think about it."

"Do we have to go back?" she asked, covering herself with the shawl Livia had placed about her shoulders.

"We'll never go back. You don't belong to him anymore."

"Who do I belong to?" she asked, looking back at the villa.

"Me. You belong to me," said Gaius.

They were quiet for a moment then he looked at her, the welt on her face having reddened into a great stain.

"The bleeding has stopped but I know it hurts," he said.

"It's not so bad now. Would you have killed him, Gaius?"
"Yes."

She touched his hand and said, "Will he send the catchers after us?"

"I doubt it. He's scared, and he knows that I will find the Egyptians or the authorities. No, you won't ever have to fear him again."

"I'm worried about Caladria. What if she's still there? He might hurt her."

"I'll go back for her tonight, but I'll go alone." His hands stilled, but anger still coursed through him. He looked about and wondered where they would go. He thought of the insula Appian Dio had inherited from his mother, but he didn't know if the lease was up. A moment's reflection told him that the apartment wasn't safe for a pretty girl, anyway.

"Do you have any money?" asked Aspacia. "I mean for food."

"Some, but not enough to stay at an inn or take a boat."

"A boat?"

"I was thinking that we might leave Rome, go somewhere far away."

"Without my sister?"

"We'll take her, but right now I want to get away from the villa."

"Where?"

"Not much farther now. An hour's walk."

"Is it safe?"

"It's safe."

*****

"What do you mean he's alive? Livia told me that Toronius died in the fire," Junia said as she led Gaius and Aspacia into the atrium of her modest home.

"He somehow escaped the fire, but we're sure he was there. We have the fibula he wore to fasten his cloak. The bones that were found belonged to someone else—maybe Octavius Brundeschi," said Gaius.

"I always suspected that they were burning down houses for Marcus Crassus. Is that what you think?" asked Junia.

"I'm not sure. But the Dominus was, or should I say is, badly in debt. Maybe Brundeschi made him a deal. He was always looking for a quick denarius."

Junia placed cups of wine and bread on a simple table as her two guard dogs patiently waited for scraps. She sat down, looked at Aspacia, and shook her head. "And he tried to rape you," she said.

"He must have seen me earlier in the night, but I never heard him. Then he grabbed me. Caladria lay down beside me earlier. She said that she was afraid for me but she didn't say why."

"And Caladria is still there with Livia?" Junia asked.

"I imagine she is," said Gaius. "We looked for her when we left, but we didn't see her."

"I'm afraid for her," added Aspacia. "He might take revenge upon her for not getting me."

"It's more likely that he'll take revenge on Livia," said Junia shivering from a sudden chill.

"I last saw my mother when she ran into the kitchen and came out with a knife. I think she'll kill Toronius before she lets him touch her," said Gaius, draining his cup.

"Perhaps, but her situation's untenable. I'm amazed that she didn't come with you," said Junia.

"I think she's in shock," replied Gaius. "Her great hope was Retenius and he's probably dead. Cornelia's dead, and then the Dominus returns."

"Maybe, and maybe she stayed because Toronius is hurt," suggested Junia.

"That's a kind thought, but it would never occur to her. He's the last thing she wants in her life. If he's gone my mother could find another man, a wealthy one at that," observed Gaius.

"I doubt that she would kill him in cold blood," said Aspacia.

"Cold blood is in their veins, just as in poisonous snakes," said Gaius. "But, truth be told, the two are made for each other."

They were silent for a long moment, then Junia asked, "Where do you think your father was all these weeks?"

"He was hiding somewhere," said Gaius. "I'm sure he knew there was a plague. Maybe he hid to keep from catching it."

"And he came back when it ebbed and because he had nowhere else to go?" suggested Junia.

Gaius gave a little snort. "He only came back for one reason, and that was Aspacia. I know that he always wanted her."

Aspacia put down her cup and said, "Mistress, we wish to thank you for letting us come here and giving us bread and wine. We should not trouble you any longer."

"You're not leaving," Junia said, staring at Aspacia. "You two have no place to go, and Gaius, you said that Toronius disinherited you. I'm sure that you have no money, having left the villa so quickly. You two will stay here until things get sorted out. I have to go to see Livia. I can't bear to think she's in that house with that man. I'll also look for Caladria. Aspacia, you may stay in my late husband's room, and Gaius, you can sleep in the guest room."

Gaius was hoping for a different arrangement but said nothing. He looked longingly at Aspacia, but she turned her face away. Junia stood and was about to lead them from the table when she turned to Aspacia and said, quite solemnly, "I harbor no slaves here; you will call me Junia."

It was nearly dark when the dogs rushed to the front door and began to bark.

"Are you expecting someone?" asked Gaius.

"No, maybe it Livia, but it's so late."

There was heavy banging on the door and Gaius opened a hinged peephole. "Junia, get the dogs back. It's Apollodoros."

"I came as quickly as I could, Livia sent me," said the Greek. He was breathing heavily and rested his hands on his knees. "Caladria is gone."

"What do you mean?" said Aspacia.

"She's not at the villa. Livia and I looked everywhere. She must have run out the slave's gate after you and Gaius left."

"Did my father attack her?" Gaius asked.

"No, he's in bed with a dislocated arm. You hurt him pretty badly. Maybe I taught you too well."

"We have to find her," said Aspacia.

"She could be anywhere, and it's dark now," said Apollodoros. "Besides, she might come back by dawn. She knows how to make herself almost invisible."

"He's right," said Junia. "We could all go in the morning. Maybe Toronius knows something. Besides," she said turning to Gaius, "he may come to his senses and ask you to come back."

"Neither I nor Aspacia will ever live there again. I'll try to find Caladria, and Aspacia will stay here. I don't want him anywhere near her."

"Don't expect him to be repentant," said Apollodoros. "I heard him mumble something about his right to sell you into slavery. But I wouldn't worry about that," he added. "He doesn't know where you are and I think he's very scared."

"He has reason to be. He won't sleep well, even in his own house."

*****

Junia's house stood just inside the Aurelian Wall, not far from Rome's main port of Ostia. The old villa, with its high, solid wall, was not nearly as elaborate as her sister's, having no peristyle or library. It did have a vegetable garden and a dozen fruit trees, which Junia tended with Delia, a woman who was legally a slave but never treated as one. Delia rummaged around and found a blanket for Apollodoros who curled up by the front door with the two dogs. It was not long before the house became silent.

Gaius lit an oil lamp and lay on his mattress. A breeze blew in from a high narrow window and the light flickered like phantom ghosts. He was free of the horror of being chained to a woman who would have killed him, or whom he might have murdered, and he was free of his father's oppression. The golden necklace he had thrown at Toronius surely had gained him Aspacia. He should have felt relief but sensed nothing of the kind.

Gaius shivered and pulled a blanket to his chin. *She doesn't care to be with me*, was the one thought that entered his mind.

Perhaps she was quite pleased to have her own cubiculum, never having had one before. With the petulance she had shown him earlier, she might have been relieved about not sharing the same room, much less the same bed.

He wanted to sleep but he couldn't, and wished that the night would end so he could search for Caladria. Now that Aspacia was safe in Junia's house, there was no need for him to stay. Junia, he reasoned, wasn't going to throw her out, and if Aspacia remained indifferent to him, well, she could live here just fine without him.

He was restless and considered getting up and venturing into the dark. What would Aspacia think, he mused, if he wasn't there in the morning? Would she even miss him? Nothing was as it should be. He sighed and closed his eyes; there was nothing he could do and there was no use trying. The girl was a complete enigma and, he mused, all women were probably the same.

The tapping on his door was very soft. Gaius stirred and listened. The tapping came again. Why would Apollodoros knock on his door in the middle of the night? Gaius rose and opened the door.

Aspacia said nothing. She simply stood there in her long dress, black curls framing her face. Whatever fatigue had enveloped Gaius instantly vanished. He sucked in his breath and stared at her. She took a step forward and wrapped her arms about him.

He was a head taller than she, and he could feel the dampness of her tears through his tunic.

"I'm just a silly, stupid little girl," she said. "I didn't even have the courtesy to thank you."

Gaius held her close but didn't know what to say. Everything would sound patronizing or worse. At that moment she felt so helpless, so frail. But she was his, and all the fears and doubts of the previous hours dissipated like morning fog.

He led Aspacia to the bed and motioned for her to climb in, then stood beside it and pulled the cover to her chin. He didn't know if he should join her or find a place on the floor. He looked about helplessly, then felt a tug on his arm.

"Just be with me. Hold me, Gaius; I need you to hold me."

She nuzzled against him and he held her tight. He could feel the warmth of her breath and the beating of her heart. It was the first time he had been in bed with her. He felt protective, but other urges rose within him and he wondered if she noticed the hardness he could not control. *How could she not?* he thought. Gaius kissed her and felt a tear upon her cheek. Her whole being spoke of vulnerability. He had never beheld such warmth. Her breasts were pressed against him and when she moved he could see her taut nipples. Inwardly, he moaned; every instinct urged him to enter her and become one.

Beneath the cover he sensed movement as Aspacia pulled her nightshirt to her waist. One leg was over his. Her woman-scent assaulted him as his hand slid down her back and sought the soft flesh he so desperately wanted.

"You can have me if you wish; I am your slave," she whispered.

"No more than I am yours," he murmured.

Aspacia giggled. "You saved me, you really did. I know that a slave has no choice, but I give you myself."

The sudden thought of his father impaling the girl with his inflamed staff sent shivers through him. Gaius held her even tighter, but the terror of what might have been raged within him and his hatred for the paterfamilias overwhelmed him.

"What happened? Did I say something?" Her voice trailed off.

"No, I just love you too much."

She kissed him again and the joy and the need roared within him.

"I love you, too," she said. "I always did."

"Every day I prayed to the Lares that someday I would hear you say that."

The flame in the lamp flickered out and they were left in darkness. Aspacia sighed and Gaius felt her body mold itself to his. *Oh, Great Jupiter*, he thought, if only his world could be like this forever. She laid her head on his chest then whispered something unintelligible and fell into a fitful slumber. He wished that he could watch her, but in the blackness he could see nothing. He would have watched her all night if he could. Instead, he listened to every breath and sensed every twitch. She uttered her sister's name and her arm tightened around him. He brushed his lips over hers, and her eyes opened for a brief moment.

"Gaius," she said, and fell back to sleep.

He inhaled deeply and made a vow. It was only an hour before dawn when sleep finally overtook him.

*****

Only in the orchestra, the flat space consisting of benches between the stage and the auditorium, could Toronius make out any faces. They belonged to the priests and high officials, who hooted along with the rest of the audience at the farcical play. Each of the characters was expected to wear a toga, but the one Toronius wore came only halfway down his belly. That, like his gelatinous buttocks, bounced with great abandon for all to see. The actors, wearing obscene masks, chased him about the stage yelling obscenities and poking his ass with sharpened sticks.

The audience faded in and out, then whirled about him like specters wearing musty garments stolen from the dead. Obstacles had been placed on the stage, requiring Toronius to jump from one to the other, which caused his flopping parts to swing and thump and the delighted spectators to be overcome with tears of hilarity. Others doubled up with laughter and rolled between the benches.

Toronius could taste sweat running down his face and saw blood running from his buttocks where the sticks had poked him. Exhaustion was taking its toll and everything becoming a blur. He tried to make out the voices behind the masks. One was a high-pitched wail from a child-sized figure. He recognized it but the boy's name, if in fact he had ever known it, escaped him. The image faded, only to be replaced by a Berber slave in a loincloth, his back a reddened mass of welts. The man's body evaporated and was replaced by an open mouth, its scream and ejecting spit cascading over Toronius like a hot rain.

The phantom figures emerged and faded, each a haunting thing. A youth appeared, someone whose voice he knew. Toronius turned and raised his arm to shield himself from an expected blow, but he was too late. A cudgel slammed into his gut and he fell backward. The assailant's mask flew off. Gaius leaped over him, swung again, and disappeared with Aspacia into a mist.

And still another figure came into his vision: this one a woman holding a knife. She peered down at Toronius, raised her head, and waved the curved blade before her, bringing cheers from the audience. There were wild shouts and gestures and the repeated demand, "cut, cut, cut!"

The woman laughed and spun about, anticipating the joy to come. She wore a smiling mask with deep red painted about the lips and her whirling became a blur. Toronius, on his back, stared up at her, and bleated like a sheep upon feeling the first touch of the blade. The woman emitted a cackle, dropped to her knees, and slashed at his hands. They fell away and flopped beside him. Then the knife was raised again, the blade already crimson. Long-nailed fingers grabbed his petard as the knife plunged downward. It was so swift, he felt no pain until the thing was raised before the gleeful crowd.

Livia ripped off her mask, pierced the shriveled flesh, and shoved the knife with its bloody prize back into the place from where it had come. That was followed by a vicious kick, and Toronius was shot like a bolt into unending darkness.

He felt himself falling, the earth swallowing him up until he emerged in a steamy, narrow tunnel. A fire at one end spewed thick smoke and ash. He managed to stand, and blood spurted where the knife had pierced him. Gasping, he stumbled toward an aperture, but it was blocked by a menacing specter. Toronius looked about and wailed, "Oh, the gods, where am I?"

For what seemed an eternity there was no sound. He was about to ask again when a rush of hot air rolled over him, and the specter whispered, "Welcome to the cave of Dis. Make yourself comfortable; you will be here forever." The god's laugh echoed through the cave. Then, with the rattling of ancient bones, Dis said, "Now be silent, and listen to the sounds of death."

Toronius wracked his brain to remember where evil souls spent eternity. Dis, his father once told him, was where priests in lamentation covered their heads, pounded the ground, and looked away. Only black, defiled sheep with rotted entrails could be sacrificed to the god, and salvation was as distant as the moon.

He had heard that the Senate would decree festivals and make offerings to appease Dis Pater, but he was unsure if such things had ever happened. It hardly mattered. He was already dead.

The fire became more intense, and Toronius groped his way toward another opening, only to peer at a dead, bloated face. It shrieked and fingers with sharpened nails lunged toward him.

"Rape!" the face wailed. He stared at the floating image of a fat girl. The name, "Caladria," tumbled from the god's mouth like flaming coals.

Toronius groped his way to another tunnel, but again Caladria's decaying face appeared, this time distended from her body. The wailing specter appeared and faded, but returned with a scream that tore flesh and snapped bones. Venturing any further was useless. The cave went on forever. Toronius could hear the cries of other souls in the smoke-filled corridors. He staggered and fell into a pile of stinking rags, the detritus of those who had come before and had been consumed by crawling things on tiny legs. Darkness came over him and he waited. He knew the ravenous things would come.

*****

The timid light of false dawn filtered through the cubiculum's high, narrow window. Toronius's whole body convulsed as he propelled himself away from the nightmare. His breathing came in gasps, and his eyes flew open. Instinctively he reached between his legs, letting out a deep sigh when he realized that he was still intact. "It was only a nightmare," he said aloud. Then he lay quietly, catching his breath.

A thought came to him; maybe it was time to visit a temple, time to make a sacrifice to the gods. Yes, Toronius mused, he would go to the temple of Fortuna, the goddess of fate, chance and luck. He needed luck, and he needed fortune. Toronius wiped the sweat from his face and stared into the oozing light. Then he detected a soft glow beneath his door. That was strange; Apollodoros often slept outside the door, but not with a lit candle or an oil lamp. He stared at the light beneath the door, wondering why the light was there.

He felt something wet and warm coating his skin. Could it be an ejaculation? A spurt of sexual excitement prompted by the dream? Certainly the screams of women slaves he penetrated made him ejaculate, but this was different. It was more difficult to make his fluid come as he grew older. Nowadays he could rarely summon more than a few tepid drops. With curiosity, Toronius touched the wetness on the sheet. It was not merely a spurt that had soaked into the fabric, it was a pool. He held his hand up to his face and stared at it. It appeared dark in the dim light, then a drop fell onto his head and another plopped heavily onto his bottom lip. He touched it with his tongue and tasted blood.

Toronius sprang up and in panic ran his hands over his body, expecting to find an enormous gash. The nightmare flooded back and he moaned. He searched his body again, only to find that there were no cuts or abrasions. Panic laced its fingers about him. He lit a candle and held it over the sheet. It flickered and revealed a puddle of red. *So much blood*, he thought. How could there possibly be so much blood when he had no cuts?

Toronius took in a deep breath and his eyes unwillingly strayed to the bottom of the door. A sallow light still flickered beneath it. His heart, which had regained its steady beat, began to pound again. His throat constricted, and for a moment he stood rooted to the cold floor.

He took two steps toward the door before finding his voice. "Is someone there? Is that you, Apollodoros?"

There was no reply. "Is that you? Answer me!" he managed to croak again.

"No." The reply came in a whisper.

A chill ran down the dominus's spine and he felt immobile.

"Open the door." The voice whispered.

He knew that he had bolted the door earlier, but now it was unlocked. That had never happened before. Someone must have entered his sanctuary while he slept. Toronius's hand trembled as he reached for the handle. Suddenly, even before he touched it, the heavy door flew open.

There was a long scream. A bucket of hot blood struck him, soaking his nightshirt. Caladria's tortured face was only inches from his. Toronius dropped the candle, the hot wax showering his bare feet. He screamed, threw her out, and slammed the door. Dizzy, hyperventilating, he fell back, his head striking the stone floor. The dominus did not wake until dawn the following day.

*****

There was a lump on the back of his head, but the villa was abandoned when Toronius awoke. It had all been a nightmare, he decided, though where the blood had come from he could not recall. He sat and thought about it for most of a day. Apollodoros would return, of course, and he could buy female slaves for the kitchen and his bed so he would not be completely alone. There was still plenty of life in him; he would cease to fear. Opportunity still abounded and he would seek it through his only true friend.

*****

The two men moved from the warm tepidarium to the caldarium with its hot plunge bath. Toronius pointed to an empty place and Vercipius followed as they strolled down the steps. It was already late and the noisy crowd had departed. The dominus liked the therma with its soothing waters, the available women, and the opportunities for a business deal, legitimate or not.

"I'm surprised that you hadn't divorced her years ago," said Vercipius as he lowered himself into the bath. He glanced about at the marble columns and followed the steam as it rose to the high roof. "After all, you haven't laid her in years. What man would put up with a woman who won't please him?"

Toronius had known Vercipius since boyhood, and had made his money in the silk business. Cunning and manipulative, he was considered devious, but most of his dealings were borderline legal. He claimed to know the rich and famous as well as fifty senators. A vain man, he wanted to believe that women smiled at him for his looks. But at forty-three he knew that if they glanced at him at all it was for his money.

"Of course, I'm not married and I have a dozen slave girls to keep me entertained, so I guess I shouldn't be advising you. But damn, Livia is one beautiful woman. It's just too bad the way things have evolved. You said she had a knife in the dream and cut it off?"

"It was a nightmare, yes. Then she held it up, or what was left of it, for everyone to see. She would do it; it could really happen. She terrifies me. The court will, must, grant me a divorce."

"On what grounds?"

"Infidelity, of course! She's had at least two dozen men. Oh, she doesn't think I know about the gladiators, and my son's friend Appian Dio, not to mention half the men we invited to the cenas. She was always scheming, hunting."

"Mmm," said Vercipius, wondering just how good Livia would be once divorced. He was considered an old man, but he had a fine villa on Palatine Hill and if Toronius didn't want her...

"So you woke up in a pool of blood," Vercipius continued, putting aside the tantalizing thought.

"In the nightmare I saw Caladria, the fat ugly cow. Like a specter, she came into my room. Livia thinks she speaks to ghosts and can see things."

"What things?"

"The future, the past. It's nonsense. In the dream, the nightmare, she doused me with blood, the bitch."

"But you said it was real blood so it wasn't just a fantasy," Vercipius said.

"I don't know, I tell you. Nothing about it makes any sense."

"You used to do her every night, didn't you?"

"Of course I did. Now, when I find her, I'll strangle her. It's my right."

"If it makes you feel better," Vercipius said, eyeing two teenage girls frolicking in a pool set aside for women.

Toronius let the irritation subside and, following his glance, grinned.

"Not those two," said Vercipius. "They're the daughters of Senator Flavius. He just got reelected, has strong ties to the army, and his slaves are skilled metal workers. Armor, swords, chainmail, that sort of thing."

Toronius touched the lump on the back of his head, but did not avert his eyes from the two girls. "Speaking of senators, have you seen Retenius?" he asked.

"No one's seen him. Rumor is that he died in the plague. He certainly isn't in the Senate and the election is long over. Wasn't his daughter supposed to marry Gaius?"

"Cornelia is dead, and so is Gaius for all I care. I've disowned him. He'll never step into my house again, but I will get the girl back: the slave he ran off with. That will teach him to fight with me."

"I've seen them together. He loves her, anybody can see that."

"So what? She's a slave, my slave, damn it all! What's he going to do, marry a slave?"

Vercipius shrugged. "He can't marry a slave, but..."

Toronius gave him a piercing look.

"That necklace you bought in Egypt—he gave it to you for the girl, didn't he?"

"It was mine to begin with, Vercipius. Do you think he was doing me a favor? He nearly killed me! I can damn well sell *him*, that's the right of the paterfamilias too."

"Technically, yes. But you disowned him. Most youths would hardly give a golden amulet to a man they hated, especially if they were running away with a girl. I tell you, Toronius, I like the lad, I always have. He's a lot tougher than you give him credit for. And he's unusual, do you know why?"

"I hope you're not going to spout some great truth."

"The 'truth' is that he can't be corrupted. That's something neither of us can claim. Maybe it's best that he's on his own. If he makes something of himself, it will be his own doing, without anybody paying his way."

"Nobody paid my way," said Toronius tersely.

"No, you learned to steal early on, for which your father rewarded you then nearly beat you to death. I guess that's why you turned out so successful," Vercipius said, looking toward two prostitutes who seductively appeared at the opposite end of the pool.

Toronius also eyed the girls, snorted, and said, "It's too hot in here, let's go into the frigidarium."

"The cold water won't help your dick if you're still thinking about those two," replied Vercipius.

"I'm not thinking about them, at least not right now," grunted Toronius, raising his bulk and wrapping himself in a towel.

"So what are you thinking about, Dominus?"

The two men slipped gingerly into the icy waters of the frigidarium. The girls, wearing the scantiest of clothing, followed them from the caldarium and sidled up to Toronius. When they saw that neither man was tempted, however, they briskly turned and sauntered away.

"I'm thinking of a new venture, something I can start with only a little investment, but will have a fine return. Maybe something, well, sort of legal," Toronius said as he tried to acclimate to the cold water.

"Not fires, smuggling, Egyptian fakes, or cattle theft? You hit your head pretty hard when you fell, didn't you?" Vercipius said with the dubious look he reserved for his long-time friend.

Toronius waved dismissively. "Well maybe not entirely

legal. After all, there is a very thin line between money and very good money. It's not so much a matter of what you say in a deal, it's the little things you don't mention," he pontificated. "A good businessman needn't be garrulous. If something's not asked it need not be said. It's the duty of the buyer to ask the right questions to get the right answers," he said matter-of-factly.

"Now, as I see it, we Romans have one hundred and fifteen festivals and we celebrate dozens of gods. Almost all require a sacrifice of an animal, be it a sheep, goat, boar, or bullock. Those animals have to be bred and raised. It's a business that makes good money since there's a continuous demand. I own land near Viminal Hill, not far from the Servian Wall on the other side of Rome. I can raise sheep for sacred occasions."

Vercipius laughed and said, "You, a sheepherder?"

"Of course not!" said Toronius recoiling. "That's what slaves are for. I will buy sheep, breed them, and sell them at the Forum Boarium."

"To do that you need special dispensation from the high priests. That's costly, more than you have."

"I know someone who may invest with me, or at least give me a loan."

"You're not referring to me!" Vercipius said, giving Toronius a baleful look.

"Of course I am. You know that I will be practical, judicious and earnest. How can I do otherwise with someone else's money?"

"That's hardly a propitious way to put it, knowing your reputation. Anyway, the first animal sacrifice is one you must make. You must please whatever god you choose to insure that the venture is blessed."

"Yes, of course. As you know, I am a religious man. I burn incense and make offerings at the family shrine each morning. I leave the house on the correct foot each day. But this is a different matter. I'm now asking for the god's favor at the temple, something I've never done before." When Vercipius failed to reply, Toronius went on. "What I wanted to ask you, is which god you think I should propitiate. Any ideas?"

"I can't believe you're involving me in this scheme," said Vercipius, beginning to shiver in the cool water. "Well, let me think," he said, rising and sitting on the round tile edge. "There is Fortuna, the goddess of chance, fate and luck: something you will need for sure. You must sacrifice a pure white female animal to her, since she is a goddess and not a god. With the gods it's always a matter of *do ut des*, 'I give that you might give'. I sacrifice this for you, but you must do something for me."

"And that's how it should be. It's a deal: an agreement. Can you think of any others?"

"Well there is Angerona, the goddess of secrecy, who gives relief from various afflictions; pain, for instance. You can identify her because she has a finger over sealed lips, a warning not to talk. There is Apollo, god of prophecies, and Bonus Eventus, who ensures the wellbeing of enterprises. His temple is on Capitoline Hill."

"That one sounds right, since I'm beginning a new venture. Should I purchase a goat or a sheep?" asked Toronius.

"You should buy a bull; that would be better. Any haruspice who has attended the Collegium Pontificum would prefer to examine the entrails of a bull to those of a goat. But a bull, especially a sacred white bull, is very expensive, yet it could be worth the cost."

"How much is that?" Toronius said, knitting his brows.

"Hundreds of denarii, but this is not a trivial matter, Toronius. Your entire future may hang on the priest's determination of those entrails. If the reading goes badly you will face disaster, and I do not invest in calamities."

*****

"I think I'm going to like being your slave, Master Gaius," Aspacia said drowsily.

"Don't call me 'master'," he replied, breathing in her scent and working his fingers through her curls.

Rising on an elbow she kissed him, then, like a child, began chanting, "Master, Master, Master," and poking him in the ribs.

Gaius wrapped an arm about her waist and tickled her until the tears ran and she begged him to stop. "Okay," she said, breathless, "what about 'Owner of the little slave girl'?"

"Definitely not!" he said, tickling her again.

"What, then, great toga virilis?"

"Just Gaius," he said, kissing her forehead. "That will do for now."

"For now?"

"For now."

"Yes, Gaius," she said softly. The word "master" was even softer.

"I heard that," he said, again administering a tight squeeze. She coughed lightly, batted her eyes, and fell back into dreamy sleep.

Aspacia's warmth seeped into him; Gaius felt that he never wanted to part from her again. Then the word "master" wormed through his mind. She used it so playfully, but the weight of it was there. The word conveyed power and ownership. He had never owned anyone, nor had he really considered owning anyone. Most Romans with any money either owned or rented slaves. It was, after all, quite legal and one third of Rome's population was enslaved. An owner could have them do anything he wanted: work, sex, or any kind of drudgery that had to be done. It was a powerful thought, ownership of someone else, he mused. Aspacia was his property, to do anything that pleased him. Gaius looked at her as she slumbered. But all he really owned was the trust she put in him. What kind of slavery was that?

The word "master" assaulted him again. In the blush of young love, she teased him about her condition of servitude. Yet in future years she would despise that status and hate him for retaining her as something to be used or sold at his discretion. She would never have control of anything, not decisions, property, nor even the clothes she wore. Likely her love would turn to bile and bitter resignation that would grow very cold in long winter nights.

He had "bought" Aspacia from his father with a golden

necklace, but she was worth ten times that. And her love? That was priceless, he thought.

His mind pondered the validity of his purchase. He had been at the slave auction when Toronius bought her. His father had been agitated and in a hurry. There had been no legal document exchanged between him and the mangone. Nor was there anything to prove that a sale had even taken place. And now Aspacia was his; the necklace, cursed or not, was payment enough, Gaius reasoned. But despite the necklace, would his father would pursue them and try to retrieve a girl?

Aspacia lay beside him, a subject of circumstances in which she had no complicity. He was struck by how easily one's life could be not just altered, but completely destroyed, by the actions of others. Something, he reasoned, would have to be done about her status, and it would have to be soon.

He couldn't return to sleep, and it was already dawn anyway. Gaius rose, put on his toga, and walked to the atrium where Junia had prepared the jentaculum of bread, cheese, and watered wine.

"I'm surprised you're up so early," his aunt said, a playful smile on her face.

Gaius smiled back and shook his head. "It was more innocent than you might think."

"Gaius, a pretty girl and a handsome young man in the same bed?"

"Really, Aunt Junia. It's not time yet."

She simply stared at him, and he realized how strange that sounded.

"You love her, don't you? Everybody can see that. So what are you going to do?"

"About Aspacia?"

"Yes, silly. About Aspacia and your future together," she said, exasperated.

"I am thinking about it. In fact I have thought about it," he mumbled, stuffing bread into his mouth. She gave him a look of expectation, but he simply nodded and gulped down his watered wine.

An old woman with graying hair entered the atrium carrying a clay pitcher.

"Delia, you shouldn't be carrying anything that heavy," Junia said, rising. "Give it to me and go lie down. Do you still have the pains?"

"Not so bad this morning, Mistress. I thought I would tend to the new shoots, and the garden needs weeding."

"You never take my advice, Delia. Tomorrow you will be back in bed for working on your knees," Junia said with resignation. "And despite how many times I tell her she still calls me 'Mistress'," she added, turning to Gaius.

"And sometimes I call you 'Domina'," replied Delia with a playful smile.

"Only when peeved," Junia said, pouring her frail companion a cup of wine.

Gaius had known the woman from Gaul as long as he could remember. He merely smiled and said, "But Delia adores you, Aunt Junia, just as you do her. You two are made for one another."

How different his aunt was from his mother, he mused. Childless and a widow, she lived in the modest villa with Delia whom her late husband had bought for her fifteen years before. Though never made a liberta, she had been treated by Junia as an equal since she had been brought to the villa. Junia had been horrified to see how her own father beat slaves and, though not refusing to have Delia, she would never consider disciplining the woman.

Rarely did they leave the villa, and they seemed oblivious to the frantic energy of Rome that swirled about their rural dwelling.

Junia was never a beauty to rival Livia and made no attempt to compete. Only rarely did she adorn herself with bracelets and rings, and she favored a simple stola that her sister would scorn.

"You could remarry," Livia would tell her, but Junia would give a wan smile and say, "What man would have an old woman like me? No, I don't need a husband to order me about. I'm quite content not to be a slave to any man. And that's exactly what a Roman woman is, materfamilias or not."

The villa, a whitewashed ancient structure, encompassed a half-dozen acres. Junia kept four cows, six pigs, and three horses which she rented out for a few denarii here and there. There were also a dozen chickens that pecked at grubs in the garden and occasionally ended up in a stew pot.

"So I was saying, young master Gaius," Junia said, slicing more cheese, "exactly what are you going to do with yourself and that sweet child? My guess is that you're so bedazzled that you have no idea."

"No, Aunt Junia, I know exactly what I'm going to do," said Gaius, rising quickly from the bench. "I will see you later in the day, and things will be quite different."

"What things?" asked Junia.

"You'll see," he replied, and strode from the atrium before she could press further.

Chapter 16

The Forum Boarium was already a place of bustling activity amid the lowing of cattle and bleating of sheep when Toronius and Apollodoros arrived shortly after dawn. Herds of animals had been brought in from everywhere—not only shipped up the sluggish and brown-silted Tiber, but also across the Sublicius Bridge, which led from the plains below the Janiculum Hill into the market on the east bank and inside the protective Servian Wall.

Toronius hurried from one sheep vendor to the next, each extolling the purity of their animals and promising that their sacrifice at the altar would be favored by the gods. Toronius had in a rush of excitement considered purchasing a white bull, but since it was so costly he reasoned that any white male animal would do.

"He wants fifty denarii for that one," said Apollodoros, eyeing the largest of the flock. "It looks quite healthy, Dominus."

"I don't want to pay that much," said Toronius, casting about. "That one, over there in the corner, how much is that?" he asked the herder.

"Thirty-five denarii, Excellency," the libertus replied. "But I recommend the other."

"No, that one will do," said Toronius. "They all look alike to me."

"Isn't that loose stool by its feet?" Apollodoros asked.

"They all wander about in the enclosure. It could be from any of them," replied Toronius, fishing out the coins as the seller tied a cord around the animal's neck.

Villa of Deceit

Capitoline Hill was not only the site of the government buildings, but also of the most honored temples of Rome. It was where Jupiter the Thunderer stood, and after the ground had been struck by lightning, he was worshipped as the most sacred god of all. In addition, the hill also housed the temples of the goddesses Juno and Minerva.

The sacrifice of a mere sheep would be considered insignificant at these august shrines, but Toronius and Apollodoros hurried past them to a lesser temple, that of the god Bonus Eventus, situated in the shadow of the great Temple of Jupiter. Toronius had visited the site earlier. He had paid the custodian and hired the services of the victimarius, who would cut the animal's throat and carry out the dissection on the altar that stood before the pillared temple. The enlistment of priests and attendants was not an inexpensive thing, Toronius reflected, having also to pay for the tibicinis, the flute players whose high-pitched notes would deflect any sound of ill omens from penetrating the proceedings.

Each part of the ceremony had to follow exact procedure; any deviation or interruption would require the entire service to be started again, and that in itself would be a troubling omen.

Apollodoros's tunic was wet and stained from the animal's excrement, having had to carry it after it faltered on the dash from the pens to Capitoline Hill. There was a long line of devotees waiting their turn, but finally a temple priest consulted his records, spoke in solemn terms to Toronius, and ushered him forward. A second priest stood the quivering animal on the altar and sprinkled its head with wine and mola salsa, the sacred ground meal mixed with salt.

The day had started out pleasant enough, but the humidity had risen quickly, and now heavy clouds blotted out the sun. A distant rumble was heard, and more than one parishioner looked warily toward the ever-darkening horizon.

The high priest, the haruspex, stood to the side of the altar where incense burned, and gave the unsteady animal a dubious look. Toronius stood stiffly, making no response when the cleric looked at him with a raised eyebrow.

The priest nodded to the flute player, and a high, fluttering note whistled into the air. Toronius intoned the words, "Great and mighty god Bonus Eventus, I offer this sacrifice to you. Please bless my forthcoming venture with your divine benevolence."

The victimarius stepped forward with a poleaxe and swiftly brought it down on the animal's head. Then, brandishing a sacrificial knife, he sliced the throat and belly of the wide-eyed sheep and extracted the entrails. The gush of blood was caught in a bowl and poured over an altar flame. Were the pronouncement of the haruspex one of approval, the animal would be skinned and its entrails roasted and eaten by its donors.

Next he extracted the liver and gall bladder from the animal. Peering closely, he examined each part, turning the flesh over and over to be absolutely certain that his inspection was entirely accurate. He glanced uncertainly at Toronius before turning to another priest, the extispicus, who would render his interpretation of the entrails. The extispicus turned away from the altar, summoned the haruspex, and the two men conferred in quiet but concerned tones.

Thunder that had been distant was closer now, and the dutiful line of supplicants with their lowing animals began to give Toronius anxious glances. He could hear mumbling and suddenly felt uncertain, as if a doctor was examining a mysterious lump that had arisen where none should be.

Turning back to the carcass on the altar, the priest gave one last evaluation of the animal and pronounced the extispicum concluded. He motioned to Toronius, who approached the altar, and in low tones the priest said, "As you can see, the entrails, the bladder, and liver are diseased. The heavens thunder; the god is displeased. No good can come from this fouled sacrifice. It is obvious that you have committed a sinful act. Our god, Bonus Eventus, is a caring one, who often overlooks the frailties of men. But you have done something that he cannot condone. Your mind must dwell upon that, and when you have corrected the deficiency, you may return with, I trust, a healthier offering. Now go, before the very heavens fall upon you!"

*****

It was deathly still. The humidity from the Tibur lay upon Livia like a damp towel, and Livia herself lay in the delicious stupor where her dreams had floated her. She had squirmed out of her nightclothes and felt the tingling flesh between her thighs. Never, she thought, had she been so alone and so much in need.

If only Retenius had lived, she sighed. She would be with him now, and all she would have to do would be to brush him with her lips and he would be fulfilling her needs, her legs wrapped tightly about him. With each movement he would orchestrate her moans and delight in the uncontrollable quivering and the squeals accompanying each climax.

Nor could Livia suppress her excitement at the thought of having his daughter on the same bed, succumbing to the girl's tongue as Cornelia caressed every inch of her. Then Retenius would casually observe as the girl would raise her to unimaginable ecstasy.

Now that was all gone, and in her solitude Livia had nothing but its replay in her mind. She knew each night's dalliance by heart and, like stacks of papyrus scrolls, each was catalogued in her thoughts by the degree of vivid excitement she had enjoyed during the encounters. Many, of course, had been enhanced by her craving but, she mused, that hardly mattered.

Tonight Livia sorted through a number of such scrolls until she finally came to one that always enraptured her, perhaps because it had been her very first. The very thought of it made her breathing erratic.

Her family had moved from the farm to a third-floor flat in a burgeoning insula when she was twelve. The apartment was an older building with thin walls, through which night sounds seeped like river mists. Livia, already blossoming, would listen breathlessly, knowing exactly who was being pleasured and by whom.

*****

Her best friend, Pelia, who lived on the more affluent second floor, was three years her senior. Her parents also owned property in Herculaneum and often went to the luxurious town, taking their three slaves with them. Two others remained in the apartment, but they belonged to Pelia, not her parents. For the celebration of her thirteenth birthday, Pelia's father had given her the choice of a voyage down the Mediterranean coast, or the ownership of two slaves for her very own. Pelia, herself in bondage to her own desires, had chosen the slaves.

"So you went to the slave auction with your father?" Livia said, as she and Pelia lay beside each other on couches. Pelia's parents had gone again to Herculaneum and they had the apartment to themselves.

"No, not with my father. I didn't want him to have the slightest idea of what I had in mind," Pelia said, suppressing a laugh.

"I went with Agrippa, my mother's slave, who liked me to watch her when we went to the baths. Later during the night, I would call her into my room and have her undress for me. It left us excited and breathless, especially when we touched.

"As I said, my father gave me money to buy two slaves, and of course he expected that they would be full-grown adults. Agrippa and I went to the Forum, and the mangone brought out a teenage boy and his sister. They were both from Egypt and had been sold into slavery by their father, since he had too many mouths to feed and needed money."

"A situation like that is not uncommon, even in Rome," Livia remarked.

"They were beautiful, the color of bronze, and I wanted to tear off their clothes right on the spot. I didn't even haggle over price, but I did insist that they be taken into the small building where they had been held.

"When Agrippa, I, and the siblings were inside and away from prying eyes, the mangone opened his hands as if to say, 'What do you want to do with them?' I was more excited than I had ever been in my life, but I was terribly nervous, never having done anything like this before. I feared what my parents might think of me, but the urge was overwhelming and at that moment I didn't care what anybody thought; after all, they were slaves and I had paid for them. They were mine to do with as I pleased."

Pelia placed a dainty hand on hers, and her breathing became short as she said, "I told Agrippa to undress them—the girl first, then the boy. The slaver simply stood back and watched as if he had seen this many times before: purchasers examining the sexual quality of the flesh they wished to buy."

Then in almost a whisper Pelia said, "The girl looked at me with big almond eyes, but hardly blinked, as if she knew her fate was beyond her control. Agrippa may have wondered why I wanted to see her naked first, but as her eyes strayed to the boy it became obvious. She smiled at me as if to say that I was far more cunning than my years.

"The boy might not have seen a naked girl before, but try as he might he could not take his eyes off her. I had her lean back on a bundle of furs and spread her legs.

"The boy wore only a loincloth and I said, 'Agrippa, remove that rag from him, I want to see everything.' She did as I commanded and I gasped, seeing an erection for the very first time."

"But he was staring at his sister's sex. Wouldn't he have protested, even silently?" Livia asked, just as excited by the salacious descriptions.

"Not at all. You must remember that they were raised on stories of great pharaohs marrying their sisters. Nefertiti was a product of such a marriage. Unlike Romans, it was a part of their culture. And besides, they were likely told that to survive they must do exactly what they were told."

"And I wonder if the boy would have really protested," said Livia, as Pelia's hand touched her breasts.

"The slave girl certainly didn't. It was as if she expected it."

"Oh," Livia replied, more from Pelia's touch than the revelation about the girl.

"I was tempted to let the boy proceed, but I didn't want to

share the excitement with the mangone, so I took them to the insula like exotic prey."

*****

There was a rumble of thunder beyond the Esquiline Hills, and then a patter of raindrops on the tile roof. Livia breathed deeply and played her fingers over the nub of flesh that gave her the greatest pleasure. Now she ran through the corridors of her mind, to the room in which she let the image of Pelia manipulate her mind as well as her sex.

*****

Livia and Pelia lay silent, thrilling to each other's touch until Pelia said, "It's getting dark, and I'm awfully hungry."

"We have cheese and meat in my apartment," Livia said.

"Not that kind of hungry!" She turned to Livia and with eyes wide asked, "Have you ever seen two people do it? I mean a boy and a girl actually do it?"

"You mean..."

"Of course, that's exactly what I mean."

"No, I've only heard people do it. Are you thinking...?"

"Stay here. No, go into my father's cubiculum, he has a big bed. I will find the Egyptian boy and his sister. This will be the most exciting thing you will have ever seen."

"Have you made them do it before?"

"Only twice, but I let them sleep together and I know they do it in the dark of the night."

Livia hurried into the designated bedroom and anxiously waited, naked, beside the bed. Would she actually be able to watch? But watch what? She felt herself shaking with anticipation.

Pelia ushered the boy and girl into the room where Livia waited. In the fluttering lamplight they stared at her, just as her eyes consumed them.

"Why don't you take off his clothes," Pelia said to Livia in just over a whisper.

A bulge appeared in the boy's tunic as Livia's fingers loosened the rough cloth. What the tunic hid had become quite large, and she bit her bottom lip as her fingers delicately touched it. She was astounded at the size, and she wondered what she had done to make it so.

Following Pelia's suggestion, she knelt down before the boy, and was surprised to see his sister do the same. Livia's eyes were wide, her mouth slightly open as she examined him. Then, as if demonstrating how to sample a luscious fruit, the sibling opened her mouth and sucked. Livia looked on in amazement as the boy swayed back and forth and issued a helpless moan.

Then without any encouragement, the girl led her brother to the bed. She lay back and pulled him toward her.

"Just watch this time," Pelia said, as the boy became one with his sister. They held each other tightly, as if each was the only thing the other had left in the world. The penetration was deep and the love and lust became obvious to the enraptured girls.

*****

Livia remembered it all: how Pelia had looked at her with unbridled hunger, how the young couple had moaned and caressed each other, how she had knelt beside them transfixed, wanting and hoping for it to be her turn.

The storm grew in intensity and rain spattered heavily on the roof. Livia swallowed hard, the memory left her hot and torpid. "Oh, the gods," she said wallowing between self-pity and unrequited need. "Please!" she uttered into the empty room. She lit a candle and settled back into the sweat-drenched bed. She thought she heard a soft sound in the hall but corrected herself; it was only the swishing of a tree beside the wall.

Then the door flew open and, startled, she sat up.

"Oh yes!" she blurted and threw herself into his arms. "You're back, you're back," she said, tears streaming down her face.

"Yes, I'm back, at least for tonight," the man said, lifting and depositing her on the bed. He kissed her lips, sucked in her breasts, and blew out the candle. Then Appian Dio and Livia lost themselves in the throes of lust for the rest of the night.

*****

Having concluded his conversation with Junia, Gaius strode into the house and gazed at the slumbering Aspacia. He watched her eyelids flutter and knew she was dreaming, but of what he could only guess. Only her head and a mass of black curls poked out of the blanket, and he thought of her in the temple of Diana, more beautiful than the sculpture itself.

He sat on the bed beside her and ran a finger through her curls. "Wake up," he whispered in her ear. She made a sound and a flicker of a smile appeared.

"You're not really sleeping; you're just pretending," Gaius said.

"No, I'm sleeping, see?" she said, closing her eyes and giving a little snort.

"Most people don't talk very much when they're sleeping."

Aspacia opened her eyes and blinked in the early dawn. Then, like a kitten having been assured that its milk bowl was still full, she closed her eyes again.

"No more silliness," Gaius said, slipping an arm beneath her and putting her on her feet.

"Tired," she responded. "Are we going somewhere?"

"Yes, someplace important."

"Can't we go some other time?"

"No, we must go today. It's nice outside. Get dressed; I'll be in the atrium."

*****

The sun had risen over Capitoline Hill, where the resplendent Temple of Jupiter stood guarded by marble pillars and imposing sculptures. Aspacia stared at them as if they had descended from another world.

"Which one is that?" she said, pointing to another building, hardly less stately.

"That's the Treasury with its accounting houses. And over there is Esquiline Hill with its villas and the Aventine district. See that hill? It's the Palatine where the consuls live," said Gaius as he guided her through the teeming streets.

"Do you see that place with the sculpture of the wolf? No

one is allowed to walk there. It's where the she-wolf suckled Romulus and Remus," he said. "They were the brothers who created the city of Rome."

"Is that really true?" Aspacia said with a bemused look.

"That's what they say. It's not to be mocked. It was a very long time ago, and strange things happened back then," he insisted. Turning from the statue, he said, "Come, we have business to attend to."

As they walked up the hill, Gaius asked, "Where do you think your sister went?"

"I have no idea. Nowadays she just goes where she wants without telling anybody," said Aspacia.

"I wanted her to come with us. Do you think she goes to a special place, or is there someone she sees who we don't know about?"

"The people and things she sees are not always real. But she did say that she wanders all about the city. No one sees her or even knows she's there. But I do worry about her, just the same."

"I just wish we could have found her. This is important," Gaius said, "she would have wanted to come. Now I'll have to make special arrangements."

Aspacia gave him a puzzled look and hurried to keep up. "What arrangements?"

"You'll know soon enough," he said.

"You're awfully smug this morning... you're acting like a big brother."

"I like that. It makes me feel protective and—well, quite mature, to be honest."

"Amazingly mature. So terribly mature. I'm in absolute wonder," she said skipping a few steps beside him.

He grabbed her hand and pulled her alongside him. "I am bigger and older than you and I'm wearing my toga virilis and we will not dally."

"I'm bubbling over with awe," she replied, stifling a giggle.

A few minutes later and somewhat more subdued, she asked, "What building is this?"

They had entered a large marble edifice with an aura of officialdom.

"You'll see," he replied, looking for the signs that would show him the way.

Dozens of officials scurried about with papyrus scrolls tucked under their arms. He stopped an ancient libertus, asked for directions, and was pointed toward an office with an inscription above the door. It read, "Vindicatio in Libertatem."

Aspacia glanced at it curiously.

"I would like to speak with a praetor about an important matter," Gaius said to a scribe. The man eyed Gaius with raised eyebrows and a slightly condescending nod. Holding his toga virilis with studied balance, Gaius gave him an unflinching stare. The scribe gestured for him to wait and soon returned with a self-assured official whose gold neck chain and medallion proclaimed his exalted position.

Gaius made a slight bow and handed him a scroll prepared by a solicitor. "This establishes my—"

The official held up his hand. "I can read what it says, young man."

While Gaius waited, Aspacia, appearing confused by the proceedings, looked at the magistrate then at Gaius. He squeezed her hand and the official glanced at him with curiosity.

"This document must be recorded on the census rolls as a "manumission vindicta," the magistrate said to Gaius. "I presume that you have sufficient reason to engage in this proceeding."

"I do, Excellency," Gaius said authoritatively.

"Do you have a witness?"

"No, is there somebody here...?" Gaius said, suddenly uneasy.

"It's unusual not to have one," the official said, his tone suggesting that he was annoyed at his busy day having been interrupted, "but the Republic can provide one. My assistant will witness the legalities," he said while motioning to a young libertus.

"Legalities? What legalities?" Aspacia asked apprehensively.

Gaius squeezed her hand and said, "Don't worry."

The magistrate, now impatient, cleared his throat. "If you are ready, please have the girl kneel as required by law. You must hold her hand, and touch her with this rod," he declared, handing Gaius the festuca with the golden tip.

"Please kneel," Gaius said, barely able to contain his excitement. He placed his hand on Aspacia's head as she looked at him with a perplexed expression.

"You must say the ancient words. I assume you know them," the administrator said to Gaius.

"I do know the words."

"You may say them now."

"*Mulier libera esse volo*. I want this person to be free."

"Now touch her with the rod and remove your hand," the official continued. "By taking your hand from her, you are saying that you no longer own this woman. She is 'out of your hands' and is no longer a slave, but rather a citizen with all the rights and privileges granted by Rome."

Her mouth open, she turned to Gaius. He smiled, returned the staff to the magistrate, and said, "Now you may stand, Citizen Aspacia."

She began to tremble and in a show of emotion, wrapped her arms around Gaius and cried. A scribe approached and the magistrate ordered, "Record the details of the manumission in the census, and give copies to the lady and her former master."

The process complete, the official nodded curtly and walked down the hall to a waiting senator. When the documents were finalized, Gaius said, "Now we must go to the Forum and find a vestiarius who makes quality stolae. You can't be seen on the street in a slave's tunic. And those shoes are too badly worn. We'll go to the Vicus Sandaliarius where I can buy you new ones. They may not be the latest style, but they'll be better than the ones you're wearing."

Aspacia walked beside him in a state of disbelief. "Am I really free?" she asked him again and again.

"As a bird let out of a cage, except of course for the 'vow of fides', which I can excuse if I'm so inclined."

"What's the 'vow of fides'?" she asked, wrinkling her brow as she did when perplexed.

"It means that as a one-time slave and now a liberta, you owe your former master a kind of fidelity. I become your mentor or counselor, but you're not obligated to carry out any particular services. In a sense you're in my debt for my boundless generosity," he quipped.

"So I'm still in your service?"

"Sort of. But as my wife it will be different."

She instantly stopped and stared at him. "Your wife? You want to marry me?"

"Of course I want to marry you. You didn't know that? I just couldn't marry you when you were a slave."

"I didn't know that you wanted to marry me at all."

"Well I did. I mean, I do. Now please come, we have to shop." He took her hand and strode toward the vestiarius where she would be clothed as a lady of Rome.

*****

The horror of the temple disaster descended upon Toronius. Nothing had brought him happiness or promise. He hated himself for having purchased a sick animal just because he wanted to save a few denarii. How stupid, he thought, to offer it as a sacrifice to a god that was supposed to ensure the success of his new venture. Instead he had been driven from the temple with the scorn of dozens of the faithful.

He covered his face with his hands and blindly ran through the streets, knocking into passersby with Apollodoros trailing behind. His toga was askew and flecked with the blood of the butchered animal.

"Dominus, where are we going?" Apollodoros asked, but all he received was a deep moan that caused people to turn and stare. Toronius was oblivious to the parting crowd rent by a squad of soldiers. Chained at the ankles and wrists was a bedraggled and beaten prisoner prodded along by the constabulary.

"Master!" Apollodoros shouted, but it was too late as Toronius slammed into a soldier tumbling both into the condemned man. Toronius lay breathless on the road's hot basalt stones while the infuriated officers looked on in stunned silence.

"He's my master, and he's been hurt. See the blood on his toga," Apollodoros said bending over Toronius.

"I'm not hurt!" Toronius roared, struggling to his feet. The soldier eyed him curiously as their prisoner shuffled toward him. He stared hard at Toronius, pointed to a scar beneath the dominus's ear, and began to shout.

"What's he saying?" the captain of the guards asked.

"He said that this man, this Roman, was one of the men who smuggled him into Rome along with five others," translated a nearby libertus.

The disheveled man continued his accusation so furiously that he was held tight by the guards.

"He also says that this man is the real murderer and it's he who should die."

"That's a lie!" screamed Toronius. "They, the barbarians murdered Roman families. I only—"

Toronius suddenly stopped; the captain eyed him narrowly and growled, "You only what?"

"I only watched. They murdered my client in the middle of the night. It was a brutal murder."

"Our prisoner seems to have identified you. If you were a participant in the smuggling, and if this prisoner is right, you are an accomplice. You already admitted you were there."

"You believe this monster over the word of a Roman?" Toronius bawled.

Toronius, on his feet and flailing his arms, suddenly lurched past a guard. The entire squad bolted after him, hauling their prisoner with them, when they came to an abrupt halt. The raucous crowd that had gathered suddenly hushed and backed against the shops on either side of the street. Four tall Africans walked stately before a golden palanquin borne by eight men, on which reclined a slender girl with an air of infinite self-assurance. She had been resting against a bejeweled cushion and affected the solemn demeanor of her station as people genuflected before her. A whisper spread through the crowd and the words "Vestal Virgin" were passed from one awed spectator to the next.

Upon seeing the commotion before them, the Africans halted; the palanquin drew to a halt behind them.

At the unexpected halt, the Vestal Virgin raised herself on one elbow and viewed Toronius kneeling before her.

"What behavior am I witnessing? What impedes my progress to Rome's most holy shrine?" she said, in the voice of a thirteen-year-old girl.

"We have in custody a murderer, Your Grace," said the captain of the soldiers, "but also one accused of smuggling onto our shores this barbarian, who carried out numerous killings."

The Vestal Virgin glanced at the foreigner, then at Toronius. She pointed toward him and said, "If true, he will be accused of a treasonous crime, will he not?"

"He will and the punishment will be death, Your Grace."

"I believe that everyone one here will attest that I have come upon this disturbance completely by accident, by which I mean that my involvement is totally unplanned, correct?"

"Absolutely," replied the captain.

"And by the laws of Rome, a Vestal Virgin has in such circumstances the right to adjudicate as she sees fit?"

"That is also true," the officer replied.

The crowd held their breath and as one leaned forward to hear the pronouncement of one of the most sacred voices in the Republic.

"Stand before me, Roman," said the slip of a girl.

Released by the guards, Toronius stood before her. No one moved, there was not a sound except the beating of wings as a flock of birds flew overhead. All glanced upward at the sudden intrusion. They were flying west. A good omen, thought Toronius, but perhaps not good enough.

"Are you guilty of the crime?" the Vestal Virgin suddenly asked, her eyes resting upon him once again.

The officer of the guard tilted his head and glared at Toronius, as if to say, "I dare you not to tell the truth."

Toronius glanced at him, meeting his eyes for the briefest moment. Turning back to the Vestal Virgin, he attempted to summon what was left of his courage and, taking a deep breath, said, "Yes, Your Grace. I am guilty. I defied the law and abetted smugglers who brought the barbarian ashore. I am aware of the fact that it was a crime, but I did not intend or expect it to result in the murder of Roman citizens. For that I grieve most deeply."

The look the captain gave Toronius this time was more skeptical, and Toronius was sure that he was thinking, "A fine show and a bit of courage, but you don't grieve for anything but your own stupidity."

"I have heard what you have to say," said the girl. "As a man guilty of a heinous crime you could be executed in the most horrible manner. I, a Vestal Virgin, will let you live, but you shall live in shame until you justly repent."

Toronius sank to his knees again, held his hands as if in prayer before him, and begged, "How shall I repent? What must I do, Your Grace? How shall I cleanse myself?"

"You must listen to the gods. You must sacrifice everything, cover yourself in mortifying ash, and look into your very essence. Only then will you be redeemed. Now be gone from us, and beg the gods for the redemption of your soul."

Toronius bowed so low that his forehead touched the ground. Then, rising, he walked on cat's paws past the Vestal Virgin before turning to run without looking back.

"And the barbarian, Your Grace?" asked the captain.

"He dies," replied the Vestal Virgin, lying back on her pillows. The sentence delivered, the Africans preceded the palanquin, and one of Rome's most honored personages wended her way on toward the Eternal Flame.

*****

The sun was high when Appian Dio and Livia had finally satiated their lust. The legionnaire sat up and listened.

"What's the matter?" Livia asked, her mind still consumed

by the pleasures of the night.

"There are no sounds; where is Toronius? I heard he was hurt," said Appian Dio.

"I haven't any idea where he is. For a while I thought he was dead. I was hoping he was. He terrifies me."

"What if he comes back?"

"I will be leaving here within the hour. I'm going to my sister's house."

"Under the circumstances, that may be the safest thing. When did you last see him?"

Livia shrugged. "When Gaius beat him."

"Gaius beat him? Why?" Appian Dio demanded, astonished.

"Because he tried to rape Aspacia."

"Is Gaius here?"

"No, I believe he's at Junia's house. He doesn't live here anymore, and neither does Aspacia."

"I don't understand."

"He was disinherited. He very nearly killed Toronius. Apollodoros kept him from doing it."

"So you're alone here?"

"The other slave girl, Caladria, might be here, but I never really know. Lately she's seen only when she wants to be seen. She's an enigma. I mean, she can see things other cannot. It's quite frightening."

Appian Dio considered this. "Who does she really belong to, you or Toronius?"

"I tried to buy her and Aspacia at the auction, but he bought them for himself. He bought them for sex and took Caladria every night, but I guess he bragged to you about that. Now she's the last person he would want to see. I'm sure she put a curse on him. He's doomed. As I said, I have no idea where he is."

"I think I do."

*****

Livia stood transfixed as she stared at Aspacia, who was dressed in an ankle-length stola and finely knit veil. "Free?" She asked for the third time.

"A lady of Rome, a liberta," Gaius said, standing beside her.

"We will marry as soon as I can make all the arrangements," he added.

Livia stared at Gaius, opened her mouth, but nothing would come.

"You can congratulate us at any time, Mother. But you don't have to come to the wedding if you don't wish to."

"Of course you're coming," Aspacia said. "I would very much like for you to come."

"This is very unusual," Livia finally said, sitting down on an atrium bench. "I mean, from a slave to a liberta to marriage. I mean..." She stopped, looking at Junia then back to Aspacia.

"Do you actually love Gaius?" she finally asked.

"I've loved him from the first day I saw him. I think you know that, Materfamilia Livia."

She blinked at the use of her first name by the former slave, then, accepting a cup of wine from Junia said, "Yes, of course you did." Livia gave Gaius a sly look and went on, "You are more than I thought you were. And your bride-to-be is more beautiful than any I have seen in a very long time. If you wish, Gaius, I will attend your wedding."

"And I shall think of you as my mother-in-law and hopefully a dear friend," said Aspacia.

Livia smiled for the second time that day. But this time it was for someone's pleasure other than her own.

Chapter 17

Toronius sat hunched on the tattered couch in the corner of the room. Shafts of late afternoon light streaked in like sword blades from cracks in the rotted slat walls. "I told you everything and I left nothing out. I'm ruined. Worse than ruined."

"But you're still walking about," said Appian Dio, sitting backwards on a chair. "The Vestal Virgin could have had you executed. But she let you live. And there's the matter of a sacrifice that didn't go extremely well."

"You don't harbor much sympathy for your old mentor, do you?"

Appian Dio shrugged and gave a wan smile. "I came here, didn't I?"

"You knew I was here, in your mother's insula with the rats and the screaming kids here all night?"

"Where else would you go?"

"I liked you better before you joined the Legion. You were more fun, more..."

"Respectful of a dominus who owns a villa and a couple of slaves?"

"You were like a son to me, a real son, not like that whining, fawning son of a bitch."

"Gaius never whined or fawned over you or anyone else. You're lucky to be alive. Livia told me that he almost killed you."

"You saw her?"

"Of course. Someone had to satisfy her, since you haven't screwed her for years. As for Gaius, he'll never be a soldier now that he has Aspacia, but let me tell you a little secret. I've gone through the toughest training in the world and have been in god-awful fights, but I would think twice about taking on your son. He has a streak of steel in him as hard as my gladius, and I've put that sword through many a barbarian. I suggest that you reevaluate him. And Dominus, never, never cross him again."

"You have become a real asshole, haven't you?" Toronius said.

"The Legion changes people, old man. It gets a man's life down to the bare bones: living and killing with occasional screwing thrown in. Everything else is left to the fat and lazy, the spoiled citizenry of our beloved city. Rome is like a belly bloated on bread and wine. One good lance, and its guts will ooze out like pus. It's the army that keeps Rome alive so it can spawn more vermin."

"You mean vermin like me?"

Appian Dio said nothing for a long moment. "You shouldn't have disowned him, Dominus."

"Why not? He hurt me."

"As I said, you're alive. I know you don't care to go back to the villa, so you can stay here a while longer. The lease for this flea-infested hole will be up in three weeks, then the landlord will find somebody to take it. Do you want it? It seems like you keep coming back."

"I hate this place; it's diseased."

"But a handy hideout when you have to get away from somebody. Or yourself. What you do is your decision, Toronius. But I'm curious. I've never spoken to a Vestal Virgin. Did she really tell you to appeal to the gods, to look into your essence, make a decent sacrifice and ask no favors? Did she tell you to make a vow and do something truly honorable?"

"Like giving money to a temple or sacrificing a prize bull?"

"Well, perhaps something a little more conservative," Appian Dio said. "After all we don't want to do anything rash. Maybe give a sestercius or two to an armless veteran, or free a slave if you feel especially generous."

Toronius gave the legionnaire a disgusted look, then shrugged. "I'm not feeling that generous."

"Do as you wish. I don't think anything will change you, not even the compassion of a Vestal Virgin."

"And just what makes your life so noble? You're given food, shelter, money. Maybe you have a little fight here or there," Toronius said, peeved that Appian Dio no longer showed him respect.

"No fight is a little fight, Toronius. It's all about killing and no enemy dies easily. You have no idea what it's like. You live a fat life. I fight for my mates and my legion. It's a hard life and it could be a damn short one."

"But you chose it."

"Yes, and it's honorable. No one expects you, of all people, to kill for Rome. Just don't kill any more Romans. You thought we didn't know about Plinius? And yes, look into your very essence, as the Virgin said."

"Why are you so angry with me? I treated you like a son!" Toronius shouted. "I gave you money; I even gave you my wife!"

"I am not your son, I never was. You only treated me that way to torment your real son, and I felt as ashamed as he did. That's why I'm angry, Dominus. Gaius is the best friend, the only friend, I ever had."

Appian Dio had risen and stepped to the door when Toronius asked, "What do I do with him, Appian? What do I do with Livia?"

"You go to them on bended knee, Toronius. Kneel before them and ask their forgiveness."

"I can't do that. I won't do that."

The legionnaire looked back at the rumpled, heavy man. "Yes, Dominus, you're right. I misspoke. That's not something you would ever do."

*****

"I am free," Aspacia said. Her legs wrapped so tightly around Gaius. Their bodies and souls had merged like the confluence of two rivers. He'd told her he would have waited but she would have none of it, hauling him into the tiny

313

bedroom, touching and kissing until his body screamed for every part of her. She had pulled off his toga, her hands exploring him, an Adonis that inflamed her every desire.

"You were dreaming about him last night," Caladria used to whisper to her in the early morning hours when all was still. "Yes, I heard you say his name again and again in your sleep, and you even moaned."

"Don't be silly," Aspacia would reply, but she knew it was true. In those days she could only imagine what he would look like beneath the toga, could only fantasize about what it would feel like to have him inside of her. She wondered if it would hurt or if, as girls in her village said, it would be the most intense and wondrous thing she would ever behold.

Now tears dribbled down her cheeks. Gaius looked alarmed but Aspacia shook her head; the blissful smile came, then the soft moans. Warmth flooded through her and soon her body rose and fell with each movement. He kissed her, wrapped his arms about her as if he would never let go.

The soft words of love intermingled with squeals and even peals of laughter. He marveled at her soft breasts and turned her again and again to marvel at the sight of her body.

"Perfection: you are a goddess," he said.

"I'm not a goddess, but you said that I'm a lady of Rome."

"A Roman lady goddess," he countered, his lips pressed against hers.

For the briefest moment, she remembered Gaius telling her about his first time with a woman, the calamitous night with his friend Appian Dio in the graveyard, and the disgust and despair that had settled in his bones afterward. The very idea of being with a woman had repelled Gaius for months, he had whispered to her, and he had felt unclean no matter how many times he took himself to the baths.

Now he was with Aspacia, and their joy was overwhelming. They lost themselves in each other; the world seemed far away, and their soft caresses built into a fire that raged until it took them beyond Olympian heights. The climax made them gasp, their bodies tightened, their senses spinning before collapsing in delirious wonder.

*****

Toronius had consumed the few scraps of food he had hoarded, but his hunger still raged. Dusk was weaving its way across Rome, and had his belly not cried out, he never would have left the insula. The streets were falling silent; the teeming crowds of the day had sought refuge behind stout doors and vigilant dogs.

Out of habit he tied his cudgel to his waist, reminding himself that no street or alley in Rome was safe after dark. Last night's frantic running of feet on the worn stones, the cries of the maimed and the bodies left for scavenging dogs attested to that. At night the insula became a fortress, barred against entry, and its occupants deaf to any misfortune below.

At least the cool night air was refreshing and Toronius was, despite his misgivings, relieved to be out of the claustrophobic room, with its fetid smells, the cacophony of shouts, and the cries of wailing infants.

The popina Toronius sought out, with its hot bread and soup, was one of the few that stayed open late, for it attracted hungry men whose interests were in the proprietor's slave girls as much as they were in the food and drink. It was obvious that several dozen other men had felt the need to get away from wives and bawling children. Thick Egyptian beer was sloshed on the tables and flies buzzed, but nothing save the gods themselves could deter the raucous banter within.

For the briefest moment, the commotion reminded Toronius of the whore's inn at the port of Alexandria, and the terror that had followed. He dismissed the thought from his mind, however, and ordered a bowl of soup from a slave woman, who dipped a worn ladle into a kettle set into a hole in the stone counter. She shot a glance at the proprietor, who jingled a handful of coins and nodded his consent.

The woman, a Gaul with thick blonde hair, reached out with a smile, patted Toronius's protruding stomach, and said, "I like stout, thick men, Excellency. Are you thick or long or both?"

"Both," said Toronius, appraising the woman. "But not

tonight," he added glumly. Improbable as it seemed, he had no immediate desire for a woman.

There was a noisy game of knucklebones in one corner and marble dice being thrown in another, but Toronius, an inveterate gambler, ignored the games, drank his soup, and retreated to an alcove lit by a sputtering lamp.

"You live in my insula, don't you? I live on the second floor," a pinch-faced, narrow-eyed man said, sitting down beside him. Without awaiting an answer he continued, "My name's Jantinius. Antonius Claudius Jantinius. You probably didn't see me, but I was in the line at the temple, just behind you, when the priest handled the rotten entrails of your animal."

Toronius gave the man a withering glance and said nothing.

"I'm not condemning you! Oh no, that's not my business. It's impossible to predict the quality of a sheep or goat, or even a sacred white bull for that matter." Then, rubbing two fingers together, he whispered, "Sometimes slipping them a few denarii helps out. Examining entrails is not an exact science and the priests, well..."

Jantinius scrutinized Toronius for a moment. "I can tell that you are a man of means, though perhaps you have encountered some problems because of the sacrifice and all. You should move to the second floor, where I am. It's much quieter, and safer if there's a fire. Of course, with an abominable curse upon you, I guess you have good reason to hide. If not from the gods," he said while evaluating one of the serving girls, "then from someone else, perhaps a creditor."

"What makes you think I'm hiding?" Toronius said petulantly, finally confronting the meddler.

"A man who can afford to make a sacrifice, a man who owns at least five if not ten slaves, holes up in that upstairs shithouse for weeks? Just like you, I see things; a good businessman has to, doesn't he? I saw you leave the insula and, to be quite honest, I followed you here. I thought we should meet."

The man had a whining voice; Toronius felt as if an insect was crawling up his spine every time he opened his mouth. Instinctively he despised the man, who not only insulted him but was also a little too perceptive. The neighbor, unperturbed by Toronius's scowl, continued, "I travel from time to time. I have to keep my business fresh, you know. I keep my eye out for the very special specimens, since I'll be opening a new establishment," Jantinius said, appraising another girl.

Toronius felt his anger building. He cared nothing about the man's business and was about to storm out, but curiosity got the better of him. "What kind of business?" he finally grunted, between slurps of his soup.

"Ah, now I see that latent interest, the possibility of reestablishing your fortune—if indeed, as I suspect, it's in a diminished state," said Antonius Claudius Jantinius. He gave a fragment of a grin, displaying yellowed protruding teeth in his cadaverous face. "Actually I'm quite secure, money and all. But it's the women I want," he went on conspiratorially. "Sure, I live in the insula and not some fancy villa, but it's not about the bricks on the outside, it's what's on the inside of the house that counts. You should see the inside, Dominus; you'll be quite impressed."

"Answer my question or I'll leave. I don't give a damn about your house, and I know that you're looking for blood to suck. You seem to be a leech, a miserable parasite looking for a quick denarius. Fraud: I think that's your real business. And, by the gods, I've had enough of that."

Jantinius stared at Toronius as if he had been bitten and the venom stung. He leaned back and raised his open hands.

"I'm truly sorry, Dominus. I didn't mean to offend or seem presumptuous. No, not at all. I am a legitimate businessman, and I pay my taxes as well as my women."

"Your women?"

"Excellency, I own three splendid brothels, and have seventeen of the finest-looking whores Great Jupiter ever laid eyes upon. Two establishments are here in the city. The other is in the port of Ostia, but that one's reserved for wealthy clients: captains, politicians, foreign diplomats. No scum enters that house."

"I have no desire to frequent your brothels, so I don't know why you're still here."

Jantinius eyed Toronius, and in a strangely measured voice said, "Of course I don't expect you to visit my pleasure palaces. I tell you this only because I want to establish a new one, in Herculaneum. It's a wealthy resort town, not far from Pompeii, but Pompeii already has too many brothels. There are cock-and-ball carvings on the doors and in the paving stones everywhere you look. Herculaneum has the same hot baths as Pompeii, all fed by Mount Vesuvius, but there's room there for more houses of the night."

"Vesuvius is a smoldering volcano."

"It was smoldering before the Etruscans, before the Greeks. No matter," Jantinius shrugged. "The point is that I'm looking for an investor, a partner. It's a lucrative field and, like the death business, it's one that never runs out of customers. There's only a few things a man really needs," Jantinius said, nodding sagaciously. He leaned toward Toronius, who tried not to cringe. "Food, wine, delicious women, and a bit of protection thrown in."

"Well, I don't have any money to invest," Toronius said, getting up from the rough wooden bench.

"The profits will be substantial, and of course they include your choice of women. You needn't go to Herculaneum," the man hastily said. "It would be free for you, and you can choose from any one of my establishments."

"Any of them?"

"Of course; you'd be part owner. Think about it. You know where I'm at."

Toronius said nothing, only gave Jantinius a dubious look and left the popina.

*****

A half-dozen steps from the tumultuous restaurant, Toronius readjusted his stained toga and untied the stout cudgel from around his waist. The popina's wine was stronger than usual, he realized, and he had to steady himself. A rotund man staggering about in a seedy neighborhood would be an easy target. There was a slice of moon that raced through a clouded sky, but little light beyond that.

He realized that he was starting far too late. A chill ran through him as he took stock of the empty street. Toronius considered returning to the popina and walking back with Jantinius, or perhaps hiring a few toughs. But returning would show weakness, and that was the last thing he wanted to display to such a weasel.

Instead Toronius took a deep breath, straightened, and set off at what he considered a soldier's pace, determination and pugnacity to the fore. But he could feel eyes following him. He dared not turn or glance from side to side, nor did he increase his speed. He would let it be shown that he was ready for a fight, indeed welcomed it if it came to that.

Toronius was nearly six feet tall, big for a Roman, the average height not being more than five foot six. His bulk, he hoped, might give an attacker pause, at least, it would if there was only one. But he knew that assailants signaled one another up and down a street by whistling, or knocking together rocks or pieces of metal. It was not always done discreetly, for the stalking sounds often made their intended victim panic, making him all the more vulnerable. It was well known that if a man was guarded by his slaves, the assailants would slink into the shadows and let him pass, but someone alone would not be so fortunate.

Whoever might have been watching him seemed to have moved away. The sight of the swinging cudgel in Toronius's hand and his size, he thought, may have deterred attack. He continued his pace, knowing that the safety of the insula, one of three dozen placed wall-to-wall, was closer now.

At first the sound seemed muffled. Then there were bursts of laughter and the ribald shouts of a youth, followed by a girl's scream. Toronius stopped and cocked his head to listen. The commotion came from the ruins of an apartment complex scheduled for demolition. He had passed it earlier and peered inside. Nothing but the charred remains of couches remained on the first floor. Only shops occupied the first floor in most insulae, and this one had sold furniture.

Toronius considered crossing the street to avoid the commotion, but a strange emotion came over him. Later he would wonder if his decision to investigate had something to do with what the Vestal Virgin or the priest had said about salvation. Or perhaps his motivation was due to the scathing remarks from Appian Dio, who had changed beyond recognition.

As devious as he had been in his lifetime, Toronius had to admit that he respected order. It was, after all, the Roman way of life. The thought of young toughs inflicting pain on a helpless Roman girl was the antithesis of that, and contradicted his sense of balance. And of course he rationalized that, except for some occasional shortcomings, he himself was an entirely balanced and civilized citizen.

There were five of them, all shouting and tearing at a crouching form whose clothes were already in tatters. With their backs turned toward him and their lustful excitement raging, they neither saw nor heard Toronius approach.

"Do her, do her!" one of the boys chanted as two others pried her legs apart.

"Me first! I saw her first," another one shouted. The girl sobbed as a youth grabbed and squeezed a breast, while another, holding aloft an oil lamp, said, "She stinks, but I'll spear her anyway."

The downward sweep of Toronius's cudgel split open the head of the boy who labored to spread the girl's legs. The force of his swing was so great that there was no scream, and in the uncertain light the others hardly took note. Again holding the club aloft, Toronius brought it down across the spine of another boy. He did scream, and the others turned; their eyes widened at the sight of the corpulent man in his disheveled toga. Before they could react, the club slammed into the face of the tough with the oil lamp. He dropped it and it clattered to the road. His teeth broken and his mouth filled with blood, the young man's legs collapsed beneath him.

One youth had the temerity to swing at the dominus but he missed, giving Toronius a chance to throw him to the ground.

The dominus pressed his knee into the youth's back and his hands around his throat. Suddenly, all the anger and frustration that had assailed Toronius found its way to the slender neck in his grasp. The boy desperately kicked and squirmed, trying to rid himself of the great weight on his back, but the hands would not release. Toronius closed his eyes, tightened his jaw, and squeezed with all his strength. In an instant, his mind replayed the terror of running for his life, the horror and embarrassment of the sacrifice, and the condemnation by the Vestal Virgin. Toronius had groveled in the street, and he hated himself for it.

His mind churning in rage, he saw his own weakness as compared to the strengths of the only honorable person he had ever known: his own son.

There was a final twitch in the assailant's legs, a gurgling sound then utter limpness. The last of the youths had fled. Two were dead and one was dying, his back broken with bones protruding. The fourth, his face smashed, would likely wear a mask for the rest of his life. The only women he would ever bed, Toronius thought grimly, would be the ones he paid for.

Except for the boys' moans and a sob from the girl, the street was eerily quiet. Toronius slowly pushed himself off the body. He stared at it, but felt totally detached from the killing. The horrific power within him that had wielded the cudgel had entirely dissipated. Turning, Toronius saw the girl, a huddled mass in the darkness, attempting to pull a shift over her body. He approached her as she pulled further into the darkness.

"I won't hurt you," said Toronius, as he leaned over her. She peeked out from the cowl that covered her head and abruptly looked away, then, still hidden by the hood, put out her hand. Toronius took it and helped her to her feet. "You shouldn't be out here this late. They would have killed you had I not come by. Now they won't bother you anymore."

His voice had become shaky and she, beaten and scared, slumped to her knees. She was heavy, and again he struggled to help her stand.

That she said nothing did not surprise him. He knew what it

was like to be savagely beaten; his father had inflicted beatings upon him all the time. Holding her hand, he walked very slowly, amazed that she could walk at all. He wondered if she was mentally feeble; why else would she be out here at night? Unless, he thought, she was a prostitute or an escaped slave on the run.

"I live very near here. It's not a pretty place, but you can stay tonight. You have nothing to fear from me," he said in a consoling voice.

The stairs leading to the fifth floor were steep and became narrower as they climbed. Trash and excrement littered the hallway from the third floor up, and for a moment he thought that the young woman would refuse to go any further. Instead, she grasped the rickety bannister and pulled herself upward, emitting only a sound of labored breathing. Toronius felt for the heavy iron key, fitted it into the lock, and shoved the door open.

The girl followed him into the dark room; he heard her slump against the wall before she settled heavily.

"I'll light a lamp," Toronius said, feeling his way to the only table in the room. A moment later the wick caught and, caressed by a breeze through the cracked wall, flickered uncertainly. He turned and looked at the woman, a shapeless lump huddled in the corner. Curious, he leaned forward, trying to see more of her. The hood still covered her face, so he asked, "Would you mind if I saw who you are?"

She looked into his eyes, sighed, and slowly pulled the cowl back. Toronius let out a wail and recoiled.

"No! Not you. I'm cursed!" Grabbing the oil lamp, he started for the door, but Caladria flung herself before him.

"No, Master!" she pleaded. "I mean no harm. Stay, I beg you, stay." Her hands were wrapped about his feet, and he tried to back away, but her grip was stronger than he could ever have imagined.

"I do not curse you, Master. Believe me!"

He froze in place as she released her grip. He shuddered and lay back against the wall in utter disbelief.

"You knew it was me, didn't you?"

"Yes, Master. I know your voice and your... scent."

"You must have known I was here. You stalked me."

"I knew you were here. I didn't have to follow you."

"I don't know how that's possible," Toronius said, shaking his head. "Did you know about the boys too, the ones who tried to rape you?"

She nodded and said, "I was told it had to happen."

"You were told? By whom?"

"A man."

Toronius furrowed his brow, not knowing what to say or what to believe. The girl sniffed and rubbed her eyes with the heavy cloak. In the dim light, he saw that a tear had run down her cheek. He had seen the girl cry before, of course, but now, at the sight of her tears, he felt a sudden weakness.

"But you came here anyway," he finally said. "In spite of what I did to you before, in spite of what you knew would happen with the boys tonight."

"Yes, in spite of all that."

Toronius sat heavily on his couch. A cold sweat seeped from his armpits and he shivered.

"I didn't know you could speak Latin," he said, fidgeting now. "I never heard you speak before. Apollodoros tells me that you can see things: visions, and things that will happen."

"Sometimes I can."

Toronius edged toward her and in a very quiet voice said, "You know where I live. Who told you?"

"A slave. His name was Arzeka. He went away, but sometimes he still talks to me. You killed him a long time ago."

"I had good reason to kill him. But he talks to you?"

"Not like he used to, but I speak to him. He's on the other side. He knows everything."

"Our future, our end?"

"Yes, Master, everything."

"And so do you?"

"Mmm," Caladria said.

Toronius sat back and considered this. "You are a slave: my slave, in fact. You could have been punished for leaving the villa without my permission. This Arzeka, this specter, may have told you to come but you didn't have to. But still, you came at terrible risk. Why?"

"To save you."

"To save me? I saved you!"

"Is that what you think?"

He frowned and uttered a stifled laugh without any humor in it. "I can't be saved, not even from myself."

"I know all about the Vestal Virgin and the terrible sacrifice. I know what the priest and the Virgin expect from you," Caladria said, her voice almost inaudible.

A shudder seeped through Toronius. "You knew about the Vestal Virgin? And the priest?"

"I know what I know," she said drowsily, as she lay upon the rough wooden floor.

"But what do I do now? What do I do with you?"

He stopped. She was asleep, and he dared not wake her, lest he learn more of what he feared to know. Toronius sat on the edge of his cot with the flickering oil lamp. He would not sleep, but neither would he take his eyes off her for the rest of the night.

*****

"She's here!" said Gaius, as he bolted into the cramped cubiculum where Aspacia was lying half-awake.

"Who's here?" she asked drowsily, the pleasures of the previous night still lingering in her mind.

"Caladria. She's in the atrium."

"Here? How did she—"

"I don't know. Just get dressed. Junia and my mother are with her."

"Is she okay? Is she hurt?"

"I don't think she's hurt. She's... well, you'll see."

Gaius took Aspacia's hand and led her into the atrium, where Aspacia halted in midstride. She looked at Gaius in disbelief, then at her sister. Caladria was standing serenely beside a pillar, her plump form masked by an immaculate, full-length tunic. She wore an embroidered veil of shimmering silk and a pair of newly-fashioned shoes. Aspacia tiptoed toward her, staring as if she had seen an apparition.

Caladria smiled and held out her hands. Aspacia hesitated, took them, then embraced her.

"Tell her, Caladria," Junia said, sitting on a stone bench beside Livia.

Caladria glanced down at her shoes, the first ones she had ever worn. She twirled ungainly, then said, "My master bought these clothes for me."

"Toronius?" said Aspacia, her eyes wide with disbelief.

"Yes. He saved me."

Aspacia stared at her, then at Gaius.

"And I saved him," Caladria added.

Not knowing what to say, or even where to begin, Aspacia sat on the bench beside Livia.

"You saved him?" Livia asked.

"It was because of the priest and the Vestal Virgin. I saw it all in here," Caladria replied, pointing to her head. "I had to make it so my master could be saved from himself."

"From himself?" said Junia.

"Yes, because my master made a bad sacrifice at the temple."

"Toronius made a sacrifice?" said Livia.

"Oh yes, but the ugly guts were real smelly. My master ran away."

"You actually call him 'your master'?" Gaius asked.

"He is my master, and now he means well. He will be a good master to me now," Caladria replied blithely.

"This is not making sense," Livia said, disgusted.

Aspacia put her hand over her mouth and looked at Gaius. He appeared as worried as she. Something abhorrent must have happened, Aspacia thought, for her sister to act as though being the possession of a slave owner could be a pleasant thing. "He means well," she had said. When did Toronius ever mean well?

This was not the Caladria she had known all her life. This girl was a stranger. Aspacia had heard stories in Andalusia of people being possessed by devilish entities and spirits that wended their way among the living and bent them to their will. Surely such a thing must have happened, Aspacia thought. The melancholy, downcast girl had become a giddy child playing dress-up. Which, Aspacia wondered, was the more painful? The dour one was better, she decided. At least it was real.

Junia pushed an errant hair from her face. "Caladria, did he really buy you the clothes at the Forum?"

"Hmm? Oh yes, with a piece of the necklace: the Egyptian one Gaius gave him."

All locked eyes, their mouths open, but nothing was said as Caladria twirled about, admiring her new tunic.

"Where is my father now?" Gaius asked.

"At the insula, I think. It's really stinky there. We had to climb up to the fifth floor. I slept a lot because of the beating."

"My father beat you?" Gaius asked with alarm.

"Oh, no. He saved me. But I think he killed some of the boys, the ones who attacked me. They would have killed me if it wasn't for my master," she said, nodding decisively.

Gaius ran his fingers through his short blond beard and grinned. "This is getting more bizarre by the minute."

"It's time to get ready for the cena, and I'm going to cook today," Caladria declared, suddenly leaving them all and starting toward the kitchen. She turned and asked, "Are you coming, Mistress Junia?"

"Why not?" Junia said, standing, a hand on her forehead. "Nothing else seems to make sense. I guess Caladria and I will prepare a cena."

"And find the strongest wine you can," added Livia. "I intend to get terribly drunk."

*****

"I know your father didn't want to go to all the expense, but I guess he felt it was necessary, even though he's never done it before," Apollodoros said. He was sitting with Gaius in the peristyle of Toronius's villa. Except for the two of them, the place was abandoned. "What happened that day was the strangest thing I've ever encountered. Not the worst, but certainly the most bizarre," the Greek said.

Gaius was tempted to ask what the worst might have been, but knew that there was little chance Apollodoros would discuss his life's secrets; those murky things were never revealed.

"Toronius woke me up early so he could go and buy the sacrificial animal," said Apollodoros. "He was in great haste. I was exhausted, but he didn't care. The sheep he purchased had already soiled my clothes by the time we were halfway to the temple, and I had a horrible feeling about the whole thing."

"Did he say why he was going to make a sacrifice?" Gaius asked, as he looked past the orchard to the charred remains of the old barn.

"Certainly not to me. Perhaps Vercipius knows. Anyway, your father finally found the temple of Bonus Eventus, and the victimarius and the flute player were already in attendance. I was embarrassed by the condition of the animal to be sacrificed and the faithful were horrified. It's unseemly to argue in a holy place, but your father was all bluster. He was terribly upset when the priests looked with disapproval at the offering. In any case, we waited in line for our turn at the altar. A storm was coming, and your father was very impatient.

"The Dominus didn't want the animal anywhere near him until it was time for the sacrifice; he actually had me hold it since it could barely stand. Two women berated me for bringing a sick sheep to the temple, but there was nothing I could do."

"And you say it was a disaster?"

"A complete disgrace. Your father became quite nervous as we got closer to the actual sacrifice. He knew that I had been right, that he should have bought a healthy creature, but he just wanted to get it over with and could care less—until he faced the altar. The sudden reality of being in a sanctified Roman temple with state officials and high priests unnerved him. And then there was the thunder and lightning, evil omens. After the business with the rotted entrails and the priest's condemnation, he ran. He kept tripping over his toga. I would help him up only to be pushed aside. People just stared at him. He careened into people in the street until he collided with the soldiers and the condemned criminal."

"You said the barbarian accused him of a crime and the soldiers believed him."

Apollodoros nodded. "You know that your father has that scar behind his ear that he always hides. The criminal knew of it. He said that your father smuggled him and other slaves into Rome, and that Toronius was there when Plinius was murdered."

"I thought it strange that I never saw Plinius again. He was always here for the morning salutatio, but then my father stopped talking about him. I remember how angry he got toward me when I was about to mention Plinius that night during the cena," said Gaius.

"Yes when the praetor and his daughter were here. Anyway, the guards became very suspicious. Toronius protested, but they know guilt when they see it. He was like a captured animal. The Dominus might have argued his way out of it, but he ran instead, this time straight into the procession of a Vestal Virgin. Everyone was watching, almost holding their breath to see what she would do. Personally, I was confused; she was not more than twelve or thirteen, pardoning and condemning him at the same time."

"Roman tradition says that a Vestal Virgin can waive a death sentence as long as she comes upon the condemned accidentally." Gaius shook his head. "What happened after that?"

"Well, I thought I we were going back to the villa. I tried to follow him, but he waved me off and I realized that he wasn't coming back here. I had no idea where he was going, but I did as he required. It was already dusk when I got to the villa, and I immediately smelled smoke. I lit an oil lamp and went into the orchard. Nothing had burned there, so I continued to the field, thinking that the weeds had burned, but they hadn't."

"Did you see anybody?"

"No one, not at first. I thought it quite strange. Then I followed the burnt smell across the field. It was a full moon, and I could see fallen timbers of the old barn. Its remains were still smoking, but the fire was out."

"Somebody had to have started it. Do you think someone was living in it without us knowing?"

"No, but I walked to the barn just to make sure. I found no one and no bodies, but someone had dug a hole in the field where we buried the slaves Toronius killed. One of the corpses, that of the slave Arzeka, was missing."

A chill shot up Gaius's spine and he stared at Apollodoros.

"I was frightened and hurried across the field to the villa," Apollodoros continued. "When I got to the atrium I saw two forms. One was Caladria in that flea-ridden blanket she wears, but I had no idea who the other might be. I made no noise; I stole from one pillar to the next. Caladria was weeping and rocking back and forth. I could see her wringing her hands and pleading with whoever was sitting in front of her."

"Did you know who it was?"

"No, and I couldn't hear the other person utter a single word, not even a sound."

"What was Caladria saying?"

"A lot of it was muffled—her tears, you know. But I could hear her say, 'No, it can't be, not so soon,' and, 'I won't let it happen.' Then she said, 'You're trying to scare me,' and, 'You don't know this'. Then she said the name 'Tacitus'."

"Tacitus? Who's that?"

"I have no idea. But she said, 'And he'll be a soldier?' as if she was questioning her companion. There were some disjointed words about a silk road and a princess. It made absolutely no sense to me."

"That girl scares me. Where is she now?"

"I have no idea. I think she left here that night through the slaves' gate."

"Was that all Caladria said to the other person? Was it the end of the conversation?"

"No, she cried some more and said, 'I'll do what you say. You know how much it will hurt me.' Then she said, 'I don't know if I should believe you; I can't see how it will be all right when it's over.' She sobbed really hard and then screamed, "I hate you!"

"And you still didn't know who she was speaking to?"

"No. Clouds hid the moon and it got very dark. She was angry. She stood, picked up a rock, and threw it at the person sitting across from her. I saw something fly off and the person kind of slumped. Then Caladria must have sensed that I was there, because she suddenly looked around, but I hid behind a wall. She was still sobbing when she got up and ran into the villa. Then the air grew cold, and a fierce wind began to howl through the atrium. It seemed an omen."

"Did the other person also leave?" Gaius asked, his trepidation growing.

"No. I waited to see what would happen, but the form didn't stir. I moved closer and expected him, or her, to say something, or maybe run away. They did neither, so I went closer. A bit of moon came out, but the light was very faint and a hood covered the person's head. Finally, I summoned the remainder of my courage and called out, 'Who are you? Tell me who you are and what you're doing here.' But there was still no answer."

"And no movement?"

"None. So I knelt down, and ripped the hood back. Then I screamed."

"Screamed?"

"Screamed. You would have, too. I was staring at a skull, Gaius. The whole thing was an assemblage of bones, held together by mud and strips of filthy rags. Rib bones stuck out everywhere, but everything was there: skull, spine, arms and legs. It was like a living apparition. The wind came up again and ripped away the cloth strips; then, like a whirlwind, the dried mud turned to dust and blew away. The bones clattered down into a little heap, but the skull began to roll around. Not as if it were pushed by the wind, either, but as if it had a mind of its own, as if it knew where to go."

"Where did it go?" Gaius asked, his voice hushed.

"Where do you think? It came to a stop on that little mound beneath the trees where Caladria sleeps. It was as if it was on an altar. The wind stopped, but the skull did not. It rolled *up* that mound, and when it stopped it stared at me. It's still there; I dare not touch it."

Apollodoros shuddered, and fell silent. They sat without speaking for a long moment.

"So... Caladria dug Arzeka out of his grave, and made him as close to a living thing as she could. But why? And why now?" asked Gaius.

"Because he must have told her to," Apollodoros said. "He spoke to her with his thoughts, not words. She always knew the future, and I think it was because of him. When I was watching them, he must have told her something and it scared her to death."

"So he told her the future, at least as he sees it," said Gaius.

"Yes, and she'll do what he commands."

"But he said it would all turn out fine."

"He didn't say when or for whom. Once we're all dead, it may be 'just fine'. But still, we're dead."

*****

Leaving Apollodoros at the villa, Gaius hurried back to Junia's house. Caladria's jumbled story of being saved, and the new clothes his father had purchased for her, began to make sense, if any part of the tale made sense at all.

Caladria was playing out a contorted drama, a tragedy, and they were all characters in her play. But then he thought, *No, it is not her play at all*. It was one crafted by a dead slave.

Gaius was willing to bare his very soul to Aspacia. He would reveal his deepest thoughts, hopes and desires, but this, he swore, he would never tell her.

The only thing he could do, he realized, was to end the performance before the next act, perhaps the final act, could play out. And that would require the death of its central character, or at least, the one who was not already dead. But how would he explain the sudden death of Caladria, and how could he convince anyone that he'd had absolutely no choice but to kill her?

On the other hand, the girl was terribly disturbed. Who but one with a warped, simple mind would dig up bones and speak to them? How could Gaius even consider believing the whims and superstitions of such a girl? He would murder to save Aspacia and their future. But in so doing, would he destroy the chance of a bright future for them? Regardless of his reason, if Gaius were to kill her sister, Aspacia would never forgive him. No, he decided, he would not kill Caladria, at least, not now. But he would watch her every move and, if he had to, he would kill to protect the girl he loved. He had killed before; it was not so hard. But that murder would be the most horrible thing he would ever have to do.

Gaius's gut churned as he entered Junia's house. Spying Aspacia in the garden, he rushed to her and wrapped his arms about her. She gave him a startled look, then an inquisitive smile.

"Come," he said, leading her to their tiny cubiculum, "I want to hold you, I want to love you. I never want to let go."

Chapter 18

Aspacia, Livia, and Junia spent the day at the Forum shopping for the special veil, gown, and shoes that Aspacia would wear for her wedding. Livia purchased one expensive garment after another and dismissed Aspacia's protestations about cost.

"I only have one daughter-in-law, and this is a very special occasion so I will spend it gladly," Livia had said.

Gaius had volunteered to join them, but Junia patted his shoulder, telling him, "This is women's work. Your mother wants to spend time with Aspacia. It's something they can share, something to remember. Don't tell her I said so, but your mother has a lot of making up to do. Besides, there are things you can do around here. I know the wedding will be at Vercipius's villa, but we'll have the reception here."

"I did see a weed in your garden. Maybe I can get Apollodoros over here."

"Splendid. You and that insufferable Greek can pull it out together," Junia said.

*****

The women returned during the sixth hour, while the sun was still high. Tired from the trek, Aspacia accepted the wine Gaius offered as they ventured into the peristyle, where water squirted into a small pool from the mouth of a bronze swan.

"Livia was extremely generous," Aspacia said, dangling her feet in the water.

"It's all very exciting for her, and I'm pleased that she cares for you. You're a breath of fresh air, now that Toronius is no longer in her life," Gaius said, happy that his mother had warmed to his fiancée. He remembered the trauma he had experienced when Livia had gone shopping with Cornelia. This time, with Aspacia, it was a triumph.

Aspacia seemed to be thinking deeply. Finally, she looked at him with her dark eyes and said, "What are we going to do about your father?"

"Do about him? Nothing. Is there something we should do?"

"He saved Caladria's life."

"So she says."

"You don't believe her?"

Gaius sighed and took Aspacia's hand. "Caladria is very special. She's blessed, in a way, but she's also... afflicted." The word "cursed" came to mind, but he quickly rejected it. "Caladria has said many things. I just can't take everything she says literally, especially about my father."

"But if it's true, if he really saved her," Aspacia said, a strain in her voice, "maybe you should reconsider. I think he will forgive you."

"Forgive me? He's the one who's committed atrocities. He's a murderer, and it was he who tried to rape you. He did rape Caladria! If anything, it's for me to forgive him," Gaius said, his anger rising. "And Aspacia, I won't do it."

They were silent and watched a robin glide onto a sprawling olive tree in the courtyard.

"You love me, and you wanted to protect me that terrible night," Aspacia said softly. "But if he had bought a slave girl you didn't have affection for, would you have interfered? Would you have objected to what you father would have done? Did you protest when he took others to his bed, before Caladria or me?"

"You think I should have?"

Aspacia shrugged. "This is Rome. It has laws and gives privileges to wealthy men. Owning slaves and raping them is an understood right of a dominus. Despite your anguish and my horror, your father felt he had the right to do with me precisely what he intended."

"Are you thinking of forgiving him?" Gaius asked.

"Oh, I don't forgive him, just as I don't forgive Rome for

destroying my village and enslaving everyone in it. But you have made me an honorable lady and have cast away my chains. Now we will be a family, and I think our happiness must include everyone in it. Anything less will fester and hang over us. Except for Caladria, my family is all gone; yours is the only one I shall ever have."

"I can't do it, Aspacia. What happened is a nightmare in my mind. I made a vow to myself, and vows must be kept."

"That was before. Now that I will be your wife, everything has changed. Your father spoke to Apollodoros and told him that he is willing to make amends."

Gaius sat in bitter silence in the shade of the tree, its branches entwined. Aspacia pointed to the branches and said, "Families are like this tree, Gaius. Nothing is straight; everything is entangled and complex. Nothing in our lives is really certain, not today and not tomorrow."

Gaius thought of how Caladria spoke to Arzeka's ghost, and shuddered. Was this dialogue part of the play, the specter's script? he wondered. Was it Caladria's work? If so, he would despise her for it. But he saw what was coming and steeled himself.

Gaius wrapped a comforting arm around Aspacia, and said nothing.

She continued, "I resigned myself to being a slave forever, and then you appeared and spared me. Your father says that he forgives you, but he's really asking you to forgive him, to work with him."

"So I ask you again, do *you* forgive him?" asked Gaius.

"Yes," she said, "but not because I feel generous. It's because he has an affliction, a cruel one. Without our compassion it will only grow worse. He will continue as he is, and someday he will kill a helpless slave girl. She will be as I was, and he will get away with it. This way, forgiving him, allowing him back into our family, we can help him."

"And you think he'll really change?"

"I think he would like to have a family again. He would like to be the paterfamilias in the same way that your mother wants to be the materfamilias. If we forgive him, he will see me as a friend. Then when I speak with him, he will listen."

Or Caladria will scare the hell out of him, Gaius thought.

Gaius sighed and said, "You are the rarest of creatures, Aspacia. Maybe that's why I love you so much." There was still a telltale mark, a bruise from his father's hand that blemished her cheek. Gaius touched it lightly.

"You honor me, Gaius. Now you must honor your father, just as our son will honor you."

"A son? That would be nice. But what if it's a girl?"

She shook her thick black curls and poked him in the ribs. "I think I'm marrying an idiot!" she exclaimed, and he laughed.

The robin swooped down from the olive tree and landed on the bronze swan. It peered at them with its little black eyes, and did not look away.

"Where I come from, they say that birds are messengers of the gods. Some believe that birds are actually gods that simply changed their shape. Perhaps this one is a god," said Aspacia, studying the bird that sat three feet away. It leaned toward Gaius and cocked its head.

Finally Gaius nodded, and said, "All right. If my father comes and is civil, I will be civil too. I won't promise anything beyond that."

She squeezed his hand and kissed him. It was a long, tender kiss and it warmed him as no rays of the summer sun could possibly do. The robin gave him one last look, chirped, and rose into the sky.

*****

"Vercipius will escort her to the altar," Junia said to Livia, the night before the wedding.

"It's kind of him to do that. He's always liked Gaius," Livia replied, as they inspected the crimson netting that would cover Aspacia's hair. In the morning her coiffure would consist of six thick strands of artificial hair, honoring the style of the Vestal Virgins.

"I'm surprised that she wants the wedding completely in the Roman style," Junia said.

"It was her idea. She was laughing when she said that since she's a 'Roman lady', she must have a Roman wedding."

"Stranger things have happened. I was afraid that with all the turmoil, Gaius would take her away from here and we would never see him again," Junia confided.

"It wouldn't have surprised me," Livia concurred. "Of course, Toronius already disowned him, so he would have had nothing to lose. They could have simply taken ship for Sicily or Spain, claimed to be husband and wife, and no one would have been the wiser."

Junia hummed in agreement. "By the way," she asked, "have you seen Caladria today? Aspacia was asking about her."

Livia shook her head. "She comes and goes where and when she pleases. She's an enigma; I have no patience to figure her out."

Junia took her sister's hand, led her into the kitchen, and closed the door. "What do you think Toronius will do when he finds out they're married?" she asked.

"I haven't given it any thought. What can he do? She's a liberta now, and he's of age. Besides, Gaius paid for her with the necklace," Livia shrugged.

"I just hope there's no trouble. Do you know where he is?"

"I have no idea, but he won't come here. He won't want any part of this. I know Toronius only too well; he's a vengeful man and he remembers every slight. And remember, Gaius nearly killed him," Livia said emphatically.

"But what if Caladria was telling the truth? That he really did save her?"

"I don't believe a word she said about him. The girl's mad."

"But the new clothes? How could she possibly have gotten them? She has no money, she's a slave."

"And a possessed one. There are ways a strange girl can get things, Junia. She could have stolen them, or..."

"Strange, yes, sister. But I believe every word she said."

*****

Heady excitement swirled about Vercipius's villa as

preparations were made in the hours before guests were to arrive. Appian Dio and several of his tent mates had been given a day's furlough and were expected any moment. Livia, Junia, and her slave Delia helped Aspacia with her gown and veil. Gaius peeked in, only to be shooed away.

"You're not supposed to see her yet," Delia remonstrated, then stepped out of the room. "Aspacia is asking about her sister again. Is she here yet?"

"I'll look, but I haven't seen her," Gaius replied.

"I can't imagine that Caladria would miss her sister's wedding."

"I'm sure she'll be here." All he knew was that, if she didn't come, her absence would have a chilling effect.

*****

Vercipius's villa was much larger than Junia's home, and grander, but less pretentious than that of Toronius. Under no condition would Gaius allow the wedding to take place at his father's villa, and he had been pleased when Vercipius suggested that the nuptials should take place in his home.

Guests began to arrive within the hour. Appian Dio and his friends, in their military tunics with their prized crossed belts, were first, followed by Junia's friends. A gaggle of boys were ushered in, hired to play their flutes in the procession to Junia's house after the wedding.

The last to arrive was Lysippus, the novitiate of Diana, who would conduct the marriage ceremony. Accompanying him was the haruspex and his assistants responsible for the animal sacrifice. Their sacred positions forbade them from partaking in the bawdy revelry that the bride and groom were expected to endure, so Gaius found Lysippus in the peristyle, while other guests congregated in the atrium.

"Aspacia and I are honored by your presence."

"I'm the one being honored, my son. To bless your matrimony with the harmony and joy of the Goddess Diana is a wondrous thing. Additionally, I didn't have a chance to commend you for the bravery you showed in your attempt to save the slave woman, the one who sought sanctuary with us that night. It was truly a selfless act. I do hope she recovered from her illness."

"Unfortunately she didn't, but she still provided a great service, at least to me and Aspacia."

The priest gave Gaius a quizzical look, but didn't press for an explanation. "Your bride is a fine young lady, and if the haruspex sees health in the entrails, as I'm sure he will, you will have a long and fruitful marriage. Now, if you will excuse me, I must prepare for the ceremony."

"Thank you, Lysippus. Here, a donation for the temple." Gaius handed him a purse of coins. Lysippus gave a slight bow and a gesture of blessing.

He takes himself quite seriously, Gaius thought, as he returned to greet his guests.

*****

Livia had insisted on purchasing a fine sheep for the sacrifice, but with so many guests, she worried that the animal would not provide enough meat for the traditional sampling.

"What am I going to do?" she anxiously asked Junia.

"I don't know, I hope we don't upset the priests; you know how meticulous they are," said Livia.

Gaius, standing near the altar with Appian Dio, stared in amazement when Aspacia appeared. She wore a simple tunic, honoring the traditions of Rome. Her wedding garments included the traditional saffron-colored sandals and a bright orange veil adorned with a sprightly wreath. She was led between a cheering throng by Vercipius, who proudly walked with the radiant girl on his arm.

"I think it's time to call in the priest," Gaius whispered to Appian Dio. The legionnaire nodded, as Gaius scanned the crowd briefly. Despite his joy, he couldn't help but feel concerned; Caladria was nowhere to be seen.

Lysippus looked over the raucous crowd and raised his hands for silence. The assemblage hushed and, turning to Gaius and Aspacia, the priest motioned them forward. He drew himself up regally, smoothed his robes, and took a deep breath. Before he could speak, however, he was suddenly interrupted by a loud, brutish noise from behind the packed guests. Lysippus stared past them, a perturbed expression on his face. The audience, just as startled, turned to peer at the intruders.

As the crowd parted, Gaius saw Toronius approaching with a leash in hand, urging along the fattest hog Gaius had ever seen. Walking beside Toronius, and holding his other hand, was Caladria.

There was an audible gasp from his mother as she stared at Toronius, the slave girl, and the pig. Livia immediately looked to him and Aspacia, then to Lysippus, who stood stock-still. The priest lowered his hands, and in a low voice, asked Gaius, "Who are these people? Are they guests?"

Aspacia turned to the priest and nodded. "Your Holiness, this man will be my father-in-law, and the lady is my sister. Yes, they are honored guests."

Gaius stood stiffly, staring at Toronius, who stood silent at the edge of the crowd. Toronius gave a slight nod to Gaius, then a reverent bow to the priest.

"Come," Caladria said, as she led her master through the awestruck assembly. The pair moved slowly, stiffly, pulling the hog along until they stood in front of Gaius, Aspacia, and the priest, who evaluated him curiously.

"I come to..." Toronius began hesitantly. He paused nervously, cleared his throat, and glanced toward a nodding Caladria. Then, standing straight and with a stentorian voice, he declared, "Your Holiness, I offer this beast for sacrifice, to honor the marriage of my son to the lady Aspacia. May it please the Goddess Diana."

He handed the leash to an acolyte, who looked to Lysippus for approval. The priest glanced at Aspacia and Gaius, then replied, "The Holy Temple of Diana accepts your gracious offer. We shall now proceed."

Toronius and Caladria turned away and took a few steps back. Then Gaius, in a quiet voice, said, "Stay, Father."

Toronius turned toward him, his expression uncertain.

"You may stay here with us," confirmed Gaius. "And Caladria, too."

A hush settled over the assemblage. A table was brought forward, upon which the animal was laid. The legs of the protesting hog were trussed by the acolytes. Gaius and those in the front of the gathering could see it looking about in alarm, its eyes rolling and the whites showing beneath its long lashes. It emitted muffled squeals as its snout was tied, and its legs twitched when it spied the knife in the hands of the victimarius. The guests backed away from the sacrificial table, since all knew what was about to happen.

Toronius looked on with confidence, for he had allowed Caladria to pick the animal. This time he had not disputed the price, but paid with great relief, the burden of choosing having been lifted from him; he had, in fact, offered the seller even more than was necessary.

"It is a good beast, Master," Caladria had said, as they'd led it away.

"Yes, it looks quite healthy. I thank you."

Toronius had never before shown such appreciation for anything she had ever done. He had been touched when, in response, Caladria took the bold step of touching his hand. He had smiled as they walked to the villa. Anxious though he was, he had nevertheless looked forward to the moment of surprise.

Now, in a mellifluous voice, Lysippus delivered a solemn invocation to the deity, before nodding and stepping back. The victimarius came forward and, in a practiced gesture, slit the pig's throat and sliced open its stomach. The terrified animal emitted a final shriek and jerked at its bindings, before its eyes clouded over.

The haruspex thrust his hands into the depths of the animal and extracted a glut of intestines. As blood flowed onto the table, he studied the entrails, allowing the thick ropes of flesh to ooze through his fingers. He peered at them intently, making it apparent that his examination was a matter of grave concern. After the mass had slipped from his fingers, he turned to confer quietly for a moment with Lysippus. The priest remained silent as he turned back to face the anxious crowd.

The gathering held its breath, waiting for Lysippus to speak; Gaius tightened his grip on Aspacia's hand. If the cleric's pronouncement was inauspicious, the nuptials would come to an immediate halt, and the ceremony would be terminated amid groans of regret. Gaius's heart was racing and his knees felt weak. He and Aspacia stared straight ahead, waiting for the pronouncement.

"Great Jupiter, the guardian of Rome, and Goddess Diana of the Woodlands, bless and look with favor upon this union," Lysippus proclaimed with the authority of his sacred office. Then, beaming at the relieved couple, he went on, "Gaius, with your father's permission, you may be joined in matrimony. You shall come forward and speak your vows."

Toronius nodded his permission to Gaius, and he let out a breath he hadn't realized he was holding.

Vercipius smiled, and said to the priest, "I bring the bride to the altar, in honor of the spirit of her departed father."

Lysippus nodded. "The Lady Diana is gratified by your consideration," he intoned. Turning to Gaius, he said, "You will place the ring on the lady's fourth finger, for as it was believed in Egypt of old, the veins of that finger lead directly to the heart." Gaius slipped the ring onto her finger and looked up at Lysippus, who said, "Now you must say the sacred vow for all to hear."

"*Ubi tu Gaius, ego Gaia;* when and where you are Gaius, then and there I am Gaia," Gaius said, the ancient words relating to the auspicious meaning of the name "Gaius". Aspacia repeated the sacred words of love and devotion, and beamed at him as he raised the veil. He kissed her, an act rarely done in public, and a great shout went up from the guests as they besieged the newlyweds with well-wishes. Cries of "*Felicitas!*" rang out, as the party flowed into the atrium for the opening of the gifts.

Gaius left Aspacia with the jubilant guests and found his father, standing alone beside a marble pillar. Stiffly crossing the atrium, he stopped a few feet from Toronius. Their eyes locked, until his father issued a flicker of a smile. "Congratulations," he said. "I mean it most sincerely."

Gaius nodded in reply. "Aspacia and I wish to thank you for the generous contribution."

"It was something I felt I should do. Strange as it may seem to you, I would be pleased if we could repair..." His words were lost in the boisterous laughter of a guest.

Gaius nodded his understanding. "This is not an easy thing, Father, surely not for either of us. I'm told that certain things are preordained. Maybe they're determined by forces over which we have little control. Perhaps your appearance here is such a case."

"Yes, perhaps. You know, I always prided myself on being in total control, but sometimes the gods pull the strings. This may not be the kind of thing I might have done before, but strange as it is, I have... gone through some changes. Changes caused by extraordinary events. I'm not good at being contrite, Gaius, but I do feel different than before. I suppose I've had a bit of help in that regard."

"Caladria?"

"Yes," Toronius said, looking past Gaius. "Caladria. A strange one, isn't she?"

The briefest smile crossed Gaius's face; then, with a raise of eyebrows, he replied, "The strangest person I ever met."

"I've come to trust her," said Toronius, "though I worry that she knows too much about us." In a quiet voice he said, "Our fates, you know."

Gaius nodded, then his father said with enthusiasm, "I am glad for you and Aspacia. I understand that she's now a liberta."

"Yes, and I fear that I'm now the slave."

Toronius let out a bellowing laugh, which drew considerable attention and cheers from the people nearby. Gaius grinned.

"By the way," Toronius said conversationally, "I'm thinking of taking a voyage to Parthia. It's a great empire, as you know, stretching east on the Silk Road further than any Roman has ever gone. There are treasures to be found there that Roman people would value. I mean real valuables, quality antiquities."

"Apollodoros would be helpful in a venture like that," Gaius replied. "He told me that he had been there with his father. He even took the Silk Road through the Arab lands and past Armenia. They still speak Greek there," Gaius volunteered.

"Would you be interested in coming? It would be better this —" He hesitated. "Better than before."

"What, and leave the most beautiful girl in the world? No, Father. I'm actually thinking seriously of taking up law. Vercipius said he'd help me find a practicing litigator."

"Of course. Law is an honorable profession. You will do well." There was a strained pause. "Aspacia and your mother are looking for you. I think they're a little anxious. You know how women get."

"What I don't know about them I'll surely find out." Surprisingly, they both laughed together, and Gaius found himself wondering at this shift in their dealings with one another. "You are coming to Junia's house with all of us, aren't you?"

Toronius shrugged. "If you really want me to."

"It's fine with me, and Aspacia will insist," Gaius replied, attempting to reinforce this new, still-fragile relationship between them.

Toronius held up his hands and Gaius watched as he seemed to fully relax for the first time that day. "In that case, what choice do I have?"

Aspacia had been right, Gaius thought; forgiveness just might heal their family, after all.

*****

"Appian Dio," Gaius called, "you're coming with us, aren't you?"

The legionnaire motioned, and led Gaius across the atrium where no one could listen in.

"I would love to, but I have to get back to Campus Martius. Pompey's legions are assembling. We'll be moving out at the first hour tomorrow. We're going to war."

A chill ran down Gaius's back. "War?"

"You know the revolt has been going on for years," Appian shrugged. "The Senate wants it over, wants Spartacus destroyed."

"He's chewed up a lot of legions. What makes the senators think they'll get him this time?"

"The man's penned in at the bottom of Italia, and the Consuls, Pompey and Marcus Crassus, are both taking their legions. I'm to go with Pompey." He looked down for a second, then said quietly, "It will be my first real war."

"And against gladiators."

"And other escaped slaves, men along with their women and children, but they aren't invincible. We'll have them outnumbered," Appian Dio said more convincingly.

Gaius nodded. "I heard that Spartacus hired a fleet of pirates to ship his men to Sicily. He would have more room to maneuver there."

"That's what he was counting on, but Rome outbid Spartacus and bought off the pirates. Spartacus isn't going anywhere."

"Funny," Gaius said after a moment. "He should have gone to Helvetia in the Alps when he had the chance, after he destroyed our legions. There was nothing to stop him then. Now, he'll be trapped."

"Worse for him is that his Germans deserted. There were thirty thousand of them."

"So how many are left with him?"

"About fifty or sixty thousand. We think they'll split up. Many will run back to the villages where they came from. But they'll be hunted down and they'll die. Spartacus has never faced an army as big as ours."

Like all Romans, Gaius dreaded Spartacus and wanted the revolt ended, but the thought that the rebels would die or be returned to slavery sat poorly with him. Nevertheless, he put his hand on his friend's arm and said, "Just toot your horn, Appian, and don't do anything heroic."

The legionnaire grinned and said, "That's not how it works, Gaius. As I said, we're going to war and everybody gets to play.

Anyway, it'll be over in a month or two."

They were both quiet for a moment, then Appian Dio slapped Gaius on the shoulder cheerily. "Well, congratulations, you mangy dog. She's a beauty. Just think of how I'm defending the Eternal City, while you'll be humping yourself into oblivion. At least I'm with an army of thousands; you're all by yourself. I hope you survive the night. That girl's going to leave you a quivering idiot."

Gaius laughed. "Believe it or not, Appian Dio, I've already had many a night with her, and I still have most of my senses. And yes, I know exactly what you're thinking," he said with a grin. "She's more passionate than any fifty women you've ever known." He accompanied the legionnaire to the gate. "I shall say a prayer for you at the lararium tomorrow."

"You do that. Pray to Mithras, he's my favorite. And ask him to send me those fifty women. I think I'll need them tonight."

Appian Dio whistled a military tune, and Gaius watched as he descended the hill toward Campus Martius. It would be his first major battle and perhaps his last, Gaius feared. The military demanded a lifestyle that he would never choose: privation, orders, continuous labor, and the possibility of death in every battle. Rome seemingly had an inexhaustible supply of battles. Worst of all, he thought, was the absence of love. *If Appian Dio had had a woman as beautiful as Aspacia, he would never have joined the Legion*, thought Gaius. He feared for him, and prayed that he would see his friend again.

His melancholy was interrupted by Junia's approach. "Gaius, we're all waiting for you," she said, laying her hand on his arm and smiling.

The flute players assembled behind the torchbearers and launched into a medley of playful tunes to accompany the bawdy singing of the revelers, as they headed towards Junia's villa in merry procession. Even Toronius chimed in as he walked with Caladria, who uncertainly hummed the melody. Salacious suggestions and lewd lyrics abounded, making Gaius laugh and Aspacia blush in the glow of the torches. The gathering followed the couple to the door of Junia's house, where little boys threw nuts at the entrance as offerings to the gods of fertility.

With a quick heave, Gaius lifted Aspacia and carried her across the threshold, which had been covered with white linen for the occasion. A bridesmaid had prepared two bowls, one filled with water and the other with burning sticks, which symbolized the two elements of creation, harking back to ancient times. Gaius took each bowl and handed it to his bride. Aspacia took them reverently, said a silent prayer, and returned them to the little girl.

To complete the ceremony, Gaius ushered Aspacia to a couch that had been placed in a bedroom as the crowd followed along behind. He stood before her with guests all about, not exactly knowing how to proceed.

"What are you waiting for, you dummy!" his father chortled amid the laughter of the other guests.

Aspacia laughed and said, "Gaius, you're supposed to do something now."

"So I've been told." Then, spurred on by the raucous crowd, he removed her saffron cloak and untied the nodus herculaneus, the elaborately knotted belt that encircled her waist. Knowing what he would remove next, Junia and Livia began to order the mob out of the room, as disappointed revelers shouted, "Don't we get to watch? This is the best part! Have a heart, Gaius."

But like obedient children, they all filed out and, with the torchbearers leading them, finally started for their homes.

*****

Later that evening, Junia and Livia were sipping wine and finally relaxing. "I'm really happy," Junia said. "They can enjoy their first married night as real lovers and young adults. It's so different from when I was married at twelve, ignorant, naïve, and terrified."

"It's almost always that way," Livia replied. "When Toronius and I were married, neither of us even knew what to do the first night. Or the second or third, for that matter. I think he asked his father, because he finally had me on the fourth."

"I once heard that the Spartans sealed the newlyweds in a room until they copulated," said Junia.

"Well, those two won't have any such problems, I'm sure they have been practicing diligently," laughed Livia.

Junia joined her in laughter. "Still," she said, "I think for Gaius and his bride it turned out well. They are blessed."

"At least for now," Livia replied. Then with a question on her face she said, "Junia, I still don't understand the thing with Caladria and Toronius. What he did, I mean the sacrificial hog, his felicity at the wedding. Even his humor is so uncharacteristic for him. What do you think happened?"

Junia slumped back into her couch. "It must have something to do with Caladria. You saw how Toronius clung to her—like a puppy."

"Do you think it's a romantic thing?" Livia asked, her brow furrowed.

"Oh no, it can't be anything like that. After all, he used to rape her every night. But it was almost like... like she was his conscience: someone who is in control of his fate."

"It seems like he's afraid to leave her side. I mean, is she a seer, an oracle? I just wonder if she's using him. She would have every reason to, the way he treated her before."

"Well, I don't think she's a charlatan. Toronius would never tolerate that. But she's obviously had a dramatic effect upon him," Junia theorized.

"Hmm," Livia said. "At the wedding he seemed to exude a presence, once he got into stride. Almost a sense of dignity, if you know what I mean."

Junia glanced curiously at her sister. Livia, seeming to sense where her thoughts were going, threw her hand up to stop her.

"Oh no, don't get any silly ideas! I detest him as much as ever. He regarded me as little more than one of his slaves."

"Of course," Junia replied. "You have every reason to hate him. But still, you're right; he did portray the dignity of a true paterfamilias."

"It was probably just an act; he's good at that, Junia."

Junia took another sip of her wine. "I guess we'll just have to see."

*****

Gaius, meanwhile, reclined on the couch with his bride, while a sense of promise and excitement flowed through him. He held Aspacia tightly, kissing her again and again, as if she were a dream that might vanish with the dawn. They had entwined their bodies together numerous times, but this night was different from any before. Now, they truly belonged to each other as husband and wife, and their pathway together seemed to stretch beyond the furthest horizon.

With the anticipation having built up for hours, he tried to help remove her clothes. His hands were shaking, and finally, sensing his desperation, Aspacia laughed and stood up. "Let me do it, Gaius, before you become a useless wreck."

No Roman woman was totally nude when she coupled with her lover, but Aspacia was a Roman woman only in part, and as she had mentioned to Gaius, the marriage rites of her own people were far less reserved than those of Rome. Within seconds, their clothing lay on the floor in a tangled mess.

Making love in the dark was another Roman custom, but on this night Gaius wanted to see her—wanted to enshrine her image in his mind forever. He lit a candle and gazed at her perfection. In silence they lay side by side, enthralled by blissful quietude and the touch of their bodies.

"You are mine, my lady of Rome," Gaius said, as he kissed her for the twentieth time that night.

"'Lady of Rome'," she giggled. "Yes, my brave husband has made me a 'lady of Rome'. But in my heart, I was your lady long before I was a Roman or a liberta. I was yours from the very first day."

He recalled the way she had turned and looked at him as she was led away from the slave market. How amazing, he thought, that one look could change one's life forever.

She wove her fingers through his hair, kissed him, and played with the short beard he had grown, a new fashion for young men. Gaius brought her even closer and was pleased when she grasped his manhood. The erection was nearly instantaneous. She wrapped herself around him and they became one. Gaius saw the tears as they rolled down her cheeks.

In alarm he asked, "Did I hurt you?"

"No, no, I'm just happy. Don't stop. It has never been this way before."

He marveled at her perfect breasts and let his tongue play over her nipples. His wife sighed and arched into his touch.

They didn't cease their lovemaking until dawn. After finally falling asleep, they woke only to begin again, reveling in their pleasure until they were fully spent. It was late afternoon when they finally emerged, sleepy and a little abashed.

Junia put her hands on her hips, grinned at them knowingly, and simply shook her head. Livia, standing beside her, asked dramatically, "What has Rome come to?" Then she put her arms around Aspacia and said, "I will pray for a boy."

Aspacia smiled shyly. "I pray for one too."

"And I imagine you have already thought of a name, haven't you?" said Junia.

"I have, if my husband agrees. I thought of the name Tacitus. That's a Roman name, isn't it, Gaius?"

"Yes, it certainly is. I like it," he said, knowing that there could be no other name. And Caladria's words, the very ones Apollodoros had repeated, came back to him: *"And he shall be a fine soldier."* A shiver went through him that the summer sun could not warm.

Chapter 19

"Hurry, Aspacia, we're going to be late," Junia implored.

"I'm almost ready. I can't go as fast as I used to," Aspacia replied.

It was the time of the winter festival of Bona Dea, the goddess of healing and fertility in women, and though she was officially celebrated in the temple on Avertine Hill in May, the winter ceremony was always held in the home of the wife of a magistrate. Midwinter was a time of holidays, and Livia and her sister had vowed to treat Aspacia to as many of them as possible.

"Florala Pacuvia invited us, and it's a very exclusive gathering," Livia explained, as they settled themselves in rented sedan chairs. The bearers hustled them through teeming streets toward the opulent houses of senators and other officials.

It was strange, Aspacia thought, to see no men on the streets, but the festival for Bona Dea, "The Good Goddess", was a women's rite throughout Rome; the appearance of any man on the streets was absolutely forbidden for the duration of the festival.

Once all the women were gathered, two Vestal Virgins began the mystical incantations. Myrrh and incense wafted through the atrium; there was a hush of voices as a viper wrapped its coils around the women's arms. Aspacia gasped, but Junia said, "It's the Greek symbol of healing. It won't hurt, the snake's fangs have been removed."

The propitiations to the goddess continued until late in the afternoon and a chill descended upon Rome. It was December, and Aspacia was five months pregnant now, but she still took pleasure in the constant festivals and celebrations that were part of Roman life, often accompanied by Caladria and Livia. She wrapped her cloak tightly about her, and to Livia remarked, "Gaius is already talking about Saturnalia in two weeks."

"That's Apollodoros's favorite holiday," Livia said. "It's a day when the masters wait on their slaves. No slave is made to work, nor can they be punished. One of them is even chosen as the 'Lord of Misrule', and of course, everyone gets drunk."

*****

It was a surprisingly warm winter day when Gaius and his wife joined the revelers on their way to the Temple of Saturnus, where there was to be the midwinter celebration to the god of wealth, agriculture and harvest, liberation, and renewal. After pigs were sacrificed, all the family trekked to Vercipius's villa. There, formal togas were replaced by the simple cloth "synthesis", and the slaves were served a meal by both Toronius and Vercipius in the spirit of fleeting equality. The festivities were marked with feasting, wine, and the presentation of sacred wax candles, and nothing was allowed to interfere.

"Apollodoros, what are your orders?" Toronius bellowed, looking silly in the pointed felt cap worn by freed slaves.

"More pork and pheasant, and that delicious dormouse. And Toronius, your best wine, not that watered-down swill. Do hurry, will you? I am famished."

"Immediately, Excellency. It's an absolute joy to serve you. I can't wait for your next command. *Io Saturnalia!*" Toronius howled in celebration of Rome's most festive day.

"I'm certain your father thanks Saturnus that this lasts just one day," Aspacia whispered to Gaius.

"He's playing his part well, but I'm sure he can't wait for the sun to go down," Gaius replied while grinning at the sight of imperious slaves playing their part. "Too bad for Apollodoros that it's only one day," he added.

"No, dear husband; it's too bad that he's still a slave."

*****

The middle of Februarius saw Gaius and Aspacia

celebrating Parentalia at the cemetery outside the city, in honor of his ancestors. Like Saturnalia, it was a time for drinking and carousing, with flowers, milk, and wine placed beside the tombs, so that the deceased would not go hungry and torment the living in their displeasure.

That was followed by the debauched festival Bacchanalia, originally a women's celebration held in secret but finally opened to men. Because of criminal activity and political unrest, the Senate was now required to approve the popular holiday which, of course, it always did.

Early in Aspacia's ninth month, she ventured out with Livia for one last celebration before her delivery. The event was called Veneralia and honored Venus Verticordia, the "Changer of Hearts". Aspacia couldn't do much more than watch, as others removed the jewelry that adorned the marble goddess and washed away the dust before placing flowers at her feet. Then, wearing myrtle in their hair, the women proceeded to the baths as a happily fulfilled sisterhood.

It was in that same month of Aprilis that Appian Dio, sporting a slight limp, arrived at Junia's house from Campus Martius.

"You're wounded," Gaius said, leading his friend into the peristyle.

"It could have been a lot worse, but the doctors said that it will heal and I can remain in the Legion."

"How did it happen? Was it an arrow?"

"Not an arrow. Not many of Spartacus's people had bows and arrows. We were surrounded and one of them got in a lucky swipe. Cut me pretty bad, but a medic got to it in time."

"But you had a trumpet and they're real big. You could have whacked him with that," Gaius said, slapping his friend on the back.

"Then I'd be required to remove the dent from it, you idiot. Now, get this honored veteran some decent wine and tell me about married life."

With a wince, Appian Dio sat on the stone bench as Gaius handed him a sloshing cup. "Aspacia is the best thing that ever happened to me. And marriage? It's fantastic. We're going to name the boy Tacitus. Aspacia chose it."

"And if it's a girl?"

"We haven't decided. But we're sure it's a boy." There was no reason, he thought, to go into Caladria's predictions. After a moment of quiet, he went on, "Aspacia hasn't been feeling good lately, but we've been told not to worry. They've told us it's probably nerves, since it's her first child."

Appian Dio nodded. "I wouldn't know. I've never been pregnant and I don't have any offspring. At least, I haven't heard of any."

Gaius laughed, then, looking closely at his friend, said eagerly, "Okay, now tell me all about it. What was it like against Spartacus?"

Appian arranged his crossed military belts and shifted in his seat. "We boxed him in between Crassus's legions and those of Pompey. For Spartacus it was a last stand, and he must have known it. Crassus had been fighting a running battle with him, and the discipline of the slaves and gladiators was breaking down. Crassus forced Spartacus toward Rhegium, across from Sicily, then cut off their supplies and their escape. The slaves fought like madmen; we expected that, since we knew many had families with them."

"I heard that Spartacus tried to make a deal with Crassus, but it fell through."

"Crassus had no desire to negotiate—no need, really," Appian replied. "Some of Spartacus's people headed west into the mountains, but they never made it. The remainder attacked our legions and were massacred."

"Did you see him?"

"Who, Spartacus? No, in battle you don't see anything except what's right in front of you. There were thousands of them and thousands of us, everybody shouting, bleeding, dying. I'll tell you, I couldn't sleep for weeks afterward. It's just sheer terror and everything happens so fast, but some images stand still. Every night, I see this man screaming with his arm sliced off by a gladius, and there was this one woman holding her guts in her hand, dead before she hit the ground. Yes, women were there. They followed their menfolk, and brought their children along, too. Afterward, some people were taken as slaves, but most died—maybe forty thousand."

"And Spartacus?"

"We never found his body. Seven thousand prisoners were taken at Apulia, and Crassus crucified them all: a nail through both ankles, and another one going through both wrists so that they hung down with their spine curved. They died from suffocation; your chest is caved in, hanging like that, you can't take a breath." Appian Dio sighed, "That's how we do it in Rome, Gaius. You can still see their bodies falling apart along the Via Appia from Capua to Rome, a lesson to any slave who might think of rebellion."

Appian Dio took a gulp of wine. "It had to be done, Gaius, and it was a bloody thing. But, *damn*, it was exciting! You might try it someday if you have nothing else to do."

"I can think of better ways of having fun, but I admire your courage."

Appian Dio gave a bitter laugh. "Courage? You just do what you're told. You fight for your tent mates and for your life, and you're damn lucky if you come out in one piece afterward."

*****

"She's here," Livia called to Junia; the midwife had arrived in a wagon, bringing along her two beds and a delivery chair. It was late April, and Aspacia was two weeks overdue, but Livia had told her that was a common thing.

The all-important midwife ordered Gaius, Toronius, and Vercipius out of the house; birthing was no place for a man, she said.

"You worry too much," Vercipius chided Gaius, as they found stools in a popina close to Junia's house. Beer, bread, and cheese were ordered, and they watched the bustle of activity in the quick-serving bistro.

"She's a healthy girl," Toronius reminded him.

"But she's very worried," Gaius replied. He had slowly and

reluctantly accepted his father's friendship, but he feared that his own anxiety now was going to put their new camaraderie to the test.

"Well, if it makes you feel any better, you might pray at the Temple of Asklepios. It's Greek of course, but it's said to be a place of healing," Vercipius offered.

"Aspacia would want me to go to the Temple of Diana. That's where Lysippus is, the priest who married us; she trusts him."

"Do you?" Vercipius asked.

Gaius was pondered the question and then said, "I have no reason not to. I'm sure that Lady Diana will protect her."

"You don't sound convinced," said Toronius.

"I have to go," Gaius said quickly. "I'm going back to the house in case I'm needed."

"And exactly why will you be needed?" Toronius asked.

"I might have to get some medication or something."

"I think you're the one needing medication!" Vercipius brayed, as Gaius hurried from the popina.

*****

The midwife had already administered henbane and a mixture of opium poppies to ease the pain. Aspacia lay on the traditional hard bed that the midwife had brought. When the intense pain continued, Junia asked fretfully, "Do you have any stronger medications, anything?"

"I sometimes make a concoction of powdered sow's dung mixed with honeyed wine. I can also use goose semen, mixed with the water of a weasel's uterus. On occasion, earthworms in raisin help, but right now, we had better get her to the birthing chair."

Weak and feverish, Aspacia was placed in the chair sitting upright. Her hands grasped its arms and she pushed against its back, as the midwife sat on a stool before her. There was a crescent-shaped hole in the chair, through which the baby would be delivered. The midwife wrapped papyrus around her hands, to insure that the infant wouldn't slip from her grip and onto the floor.

Aspacia glanced at the table beside the midwife where there was an assemblage of steel forceps, olive oil, warm water, and sea sponges, along with bits of wool and smelling salts in case she fainted. Between contractions, the midwife called Livia aside. "I have closely examined the girl," she said. "She is very small, and the delivery will be difficult. I have seen this before, dozens of times."

"Is she in mortal danger?" Livia asked, worry stalking her face.

The midwife was solemn as she said, "The baby will live; they usually do. But often, too often, the mothers weaken. We shall pray."

*****

An anxious hour passed, and suddenly Gaius heard the wailing of an infant. Toronius and Vercipius had only just returned from the popina when they saw Gaius rush into the house. His father strode in behind him. "Remember the custom and the obligation."

"Yes Father," Gaius replied, excitement coursing through him. The midwife cradled the swaddled child and laid it before Gaius's feet.

"It's a boy, and he's quite healthy," stated the midwife, before retreating a few steps.

"If you pick him up, you claim him as yours," Toronius quietly reminded his son.

So amazed was Gaius at the sight of the little thing, he simply stared at it, frozen in place. "Why don't you pick him up, son?" Toronius gently urged.

"Yes, yes of course," Gaius said reaching down and lifting the bawling infant into his arms. Beaming, he turned to his father and Vercipius. "I have a son! This is Tacitus, my son."

"A prestigious name," Toronius exclaimed. "This calls for more wine; it's a day for celebration!" he bellowed and slapped Gaius on the back.

*****

Aspacia held the baby for as long as she could. Her breasts

swelled, to the point that the midwife decided to apply a treatment of earthworms across them, along with sow's milk, goose grease, and spider web. When the folk medicine failed, the child was handed to a wet nurse, and Gaius wiped the concoction from his wife's breasts.

"It's a beautiful child. It's our son," she whispered, her breathing labored.

"He's magnificent," Gaius answered, holding her hand.

"He was kicking so hard when he was inside of me. It was as if he were a soldier."

"A soldier—a centurion," Gaius said, looking deeply into Aspacia's eyes.

"Gaius, we should get him a pony as soon as he can walk. You can teach him to ride, I would like that."

"I will. I'll get him the finest pony in Rome, I promise."

He adored her spirit, her joyful smile, and her sassiness, and fully expected that her health would quickly revive. But that did not happen; instead, she weakened as the days progressed. A doctor was summoned, and after an examination, he led Gaius into the atrium.

"Your wife is running a very high fever and was weakened by the difficult birth. I cannot offer any help. I suggest you invoke the name of her god. Only a strong deity can perform the miracle that will save your lady."

"Hurry back," Aspacia managed to say, when Gaius told her of what he must do.

"You don't have enough; take this," Toronius said, giving Gaius a handful of denarii.

"Thank you, Father. I will pay you back."

Toronius shook his head. "Go, hurry, she is growing weaker. Bring back a miracle."

It was still early when Gaius, having run most of the way, reached the temple.

"The baby is well," he explained, "it's a fine boy and I claimed him as my own, but Aspacia is doing very poorly. I fear the worst. The doctor said that only a miracle could save her."

"And miracles do. That is why we worship our Lady Diana.

I'm sure she will grant your wish as she has done for so many others." Lysippus led Gaius inside and put a hand on his shoulder in reassurance. "Pray fervently with all your heart, with your very soul. She will hear you. She sees and hears everything. I, too, will pray for your beautiful lady, for she's a loving and worthy child. The goddess will enter the spirit of your wife and raise her into the full glory of day."

Lyssipus looked on approvingly as Gaius placed the coins in a gold offering plate beside the burning incense. A thin wisp of smoke filtered into the bowels of the marble temple. Gaius and Lyssipus knelt before the silent stone carving.

Gaius imagined that Lady Diana was staring into his heart and surely heard his plea. Lyssipus looked toward the heavens and uttered mysterious incantations. Then he grasped Gaius's hand and said, "She has heard us. All will be well."

Gaius ran all the way back, and burst into the house, only to be stopped by Junia.

"Aspacia is getting weaker. Stay with her for a few moments, then there's something you must do."

"I just came back from the Temple. Lyssipus said that everything will be fine: that she'll live," Gaius said, tears streaming down his face.

Junia stroked his cheek, her eyes sad. "I believe in the gods, just as you do. But that priest will say what he thinks you want to hear. There is only one other person who knows."

"I am afraid," he whispered.

"So am I, but there is no other choice."

*****

He found her huddled beneath the same copse of trees where she had usually slept. Wrapped once more in the stained blanket, she rocked back and forth, a low moan issuing from her.

Gaius knelt down and lifted the cowl that covered her face. "Caladria, you must help me. You must help Aspacia. What must I do?"

The girl continued her lamentations, seeming not to have

heard Gaius at all.

"Caladria," Gaius said again, moving to within inches of her. "She is your sister. You love her, *I* love her. Please help me."

The plum-shaped girl appeared oblivious and despite her weight, Gaius, his anger and desperation boiling over, picked her up and shook her as violently as he could. A deep unworldly moan resulted as her feet swayed above the ground.

"Tell me!" Gaius screamed. "What will happen to my Aspacia?"

He felt a hand gently grasp his arm. "Don't hurt her. What she knows, she can do nothing about. She can't alter fate."

Gaius's strength ebbed like the outgoing tide. He put Caladria down and stared at Toronius. "But she knows, doesn't she, Father? She has always known. Why didn't she tell me?"

"Because it would have ruined everything. You had something I never did: something very rare in our world. You both had love, and you now have a son."

"But Aspacia will die," Gaius said, anguish in his voice.

"We all die. But she has lived because of you. Without you, she never would have. Now, go to her before it's too late."

*****

"Thank Great Jupiter that you're back," said Junia, clutching his arm. "She may only have a few hours. Prepare yourself."

Livia stood beside her sister and, grief-stricken, looked at her son.

Stunned, Gaius knelt beside Aspacia's bed. The midwife, who had remained by her side these past few days, placed the baby beside her one last time.

"The priest said that the goddess has heard, and will heal you. Then we'll be as before," Gaius said.

Aspacia smiled weakly. "Hold me, Gaius; just hold me." He did as she asked, and a moment later she whispered, "Take care of our son. Make him into a man just like you."

"You aren't going to die," Gaius said, staring into her large dark eyes. Her hair was damp from the fever and her breathing was labored.

She took his hand and said, "No, Gaius. I am going to die, but I die free. You made me free again, and that's a most wonderful gift."

"You are free and you will always be mine," he said, seeing her begin to fail. She had closed her eyes and all expression vanished. He grasped her hand and gazed at her, as if his pleading could work a miracle. Minutes passed in silence. Then, she opened her eyes and smiled. A sudden blush filled her cheeks and, almost in jest, she said, "And Gaius, I am most certainly a lady of Rome."

"Indeed. You are that, Aspacia: a lady of Rome," he said, hoping that her enthusiasm was a turn for the better. But the smile faded. She sighed, her hand slipped away and she did not move again.

*****

In silent disbelief, Gaius stayed beside her for a very long time. Junia spoke to Toronius, and he and Vercipius went about making the necessary arrangements. Sometime later, they returned with an undertaker. They had also hired a professional troupe of mourners, along with an elaborate litter and eight slaves to bear Aspacia to the crematorium.

"Her ashes won't be in the columbarium, will they?" Livia asked her husband. It was the first time she had spoken to him in months.

Toronius seemed startled by her question and said, "No, I won't have the urn in the catacombs or the public cemetery. I found a newly built shrine along the Via Appia. It's small, but nicely constructed along Greek lines. I think Gaius will like it."

"What's happening with her body now?" asked Livia.

"A coin has been placed in her mouth. You know, to pay Charon when he rows her across the river Styx."

"How's Gaius?" asked Junia, joining their conclave.

"He's in a daze. He doesn't know what to do," Livia said.

"We ought to get him up and have the procession assemble. I'll have them put Aspacia's body on the bier and we should begin. It's a long walk and then there's the oration afterward," said Junia.

The catafalque appeared and Aspacia was laid on it on her side, her head on her arm in as lifelike a position as possible. The flute players led the entourage, followed by Aspacia's bedecked platform. Behind the bier walked Gaius and his parents, followed by the hired mourners, who alternately sang her praises and cried as if they were her closest friends. At the rear of the procession came Vercipius, Caladria, Apollodoros, and friends of the family.

Gaius moved as if in a fog, hearing snatches of song and the commiseration of those around him.

"She looks so alive, so much in repose," Junia said, walking beside him. "We must always remember her this way. She looks absolutely beautiful."

Gaius nodded at his aunt's caring words, but answering her was beyond him.

The cortege arrived at the Forum Romanum. The place was crowded with shoppers, beggars, merchants, and a bewildering variety of gawking foreigners. Upon hearing the flutes and the wailing of the hired mourners, however, the crowds parted and the procession moved onto the Forum steps.

"Vercipius will make a panegyric in her honor," Livia said to Gaius.

Clearing his throat and addressing the mourners, Vercipius said, "Let us in our hearts praise the beautiful Aspacia, wife of Gaius Septimius Aquila. Emancipated from bondage by her husband, she gave him a splendid son. Aspacia will now be with us in memory, and under the loving protection of her goddess, Diana of the Woodlands." He paused, thought a moment, then went on, "A wise man once remarked that 'those who are not afraid to live should not be afraid to die, for life and death are all part of the same great adventure.' Our dear Aspacia will live that timeless adventure, now and for all eternity. May the goddess bless her on her journey toward a wondrous place, beyond the one in which we souls toil."

Anyone watching Gaius would have seen him stiffen at the mention of the deity, but all eyes were on the orator instead.

Vercipius concluded the eulogy as the slaves raised the bier to their shoulders, and the procession continued on to its final destination beyond the Aurelian Wall. There the deceased were consumed in pyres, the smoke and odor staining the azure blue sky.

Wood had been gathered, and Aspacia's body, now covered in a shroud, was placed on a platform above the fuel. Gaius placed flowers upon the body and bowed his head. Several moments passed before he climbed down and struck a spark to the kindling. The wood, coated with pitch, burst into flame. Gaius stepped back and watched as the inferno consumed the body of his beloved wife. Black smoke engulfed the weakening bier until Aspacia descended into the flames.

The professional mourners sobbed softly as the fire ebbed, hours later. Water was tossed onto the lingering embers, and Gaius gathered her ashes and placed them in a bronze urn that his father had purchased. The urn was secreted in the small marble crypt, and Toronius promised Gaius, "Her name will be inscribed in the stone tomorrow."

Gaius said nothing.

On their way back to Junia's house, Toronius reminded him, "It's traditional to prepare a banquet for the guests upon one's passing."

"You may feed the guests if you wish, Father, but I don't want to attend."

"I understand," Toronius said, patting his son on his shoulder. "I know that you want to be alone, but we all share your grief."

It was the first time since childhood that he had received affection from his father. Perhaps he really meant it, Gaius thought.

The professional mourners, the musicians, and the slaves who carried the bier, having fulfilled their obligations, had all departed. Wanting to be alone, Gaius stepped outside. He walked to a tree beside the house and sat on a gnarled branch.

"Gaius!" a man shouted, hurrying toward him. The priest Lyssipus, panting and bathed in sweat said, "By the gods, I just heard what happened. I came as fast as I could."

Gaius stood and pointed at him. "You needn't have come here, priest. She died holding the image of your stone idol."

Lyssipus halted, seeming stunned by the reproach.

"'Stone idol'? You're speaking of your wife's goddess. How could you possibly say something like that? It's an insult to her; it's blasphemy."

"Is it? I prayed at its feet in your temple. I gave every denarius I had and every one my father gave me. Aspacia prayed. She was a believer, and her plea was ignored. What good is your god? What good are any of them? Tell me that, priest!"

Lyssipus regained his composure and stood imperiously before Gaius. "I know you grieve. I know you are angry and confused by the fragility of life. But it's filled with as much calamity as joy. It's precarious and damned short. The gods aren't perfect. We make our gods, and give them attributes beyond what we mortals possess, but on occasion they fail us, as we fail them. Do not impugn the gods; they're all we have."

"*You* have your god and your exalted position. I have a dead wife. You keep your worthless god," Gaius said, leaving the priest in the road.

A late afternoon wind swirled about the priest, carrying away his final words. Gaius looked back over his shoulder as Lyssipus turned and stalked angrily back to his goddess in the Temple of Diana.

Gaius visited Aspacia's crypt the next morning as a stone-carver engraved her name and epitaph in the marble:

Aspacia Aquila,
loving mother and wife of Gaius Septimius Aquila.
Age seventeen.
A true Lady of Rome.

*****

"Do you still want to go into law?" Toronius asked his son later, as they sat in the atrium of his villa.

"I don't think so. One needs to be social for that, and I don't feel social. I don't care to make friends or argue in the courts. I don't know what I'll do. I may not do anything at all."

"You're not the type to sit around and do nothing. I think you'll do something we would never expect."

"Perhaps you're right. I have actually been thinking of pursuing a very different kind of life. Something I would never have considered had Aspacia lived."

Toronius said, "She was a wonderful lady. I'm sorry, I truly am. I'm sorry for the way I treated her and Caladria. You know what I mean."

Gaius nodded.

"And for the way I treated you. Believe it or not, I hated myself; I always hated myself. I took it out on you."

"You don't have to explain."

"It was weighing on me. I wanted to tell you, just in case."

Gaius gave his father a quizzical look, then asked, "What are you going to do?"

"I might leave Rome, go to Spain or the desert lands before I get too old. Or maybe I'll just go into business with Vercipius, raise sheep or something."

"And Mother, what about her?"

"Livia won't have me. She's still a beautiful woman. She'll find some rich man, or a man will find her. Of that I have no doubt."

Toronius rose and walked into the house, leaving his son in the atrium. It was quiet and empty. Gaius leaned back against a pillar and envisioned Aspacia, dangling her feet in the impluvium. He sighed and murmured, "Where are you now? Can you hear me? Can you see me?"

He listened to the silence and hoped to hear her voice. But he heard nothing, and as a cold hardness seeped in, Gaius knew exactly what he would do. It would not be a pleasant thing, but he would do it extremely well. And he would do it for the rest of his life.

Chapter 20

"I would give it a lot more thought, Gaius," said Appian Dio as they sat in Junia's atrium. "I know you're angry. I can see the bitterness. I would probably feel the same, but you've got to think about it. I'm not saying that you wouldn't do well, but you're different than me. I relish a good fight. I don't think of myself as a particularly mean or vengeful person, but if some barbarian comes at me with a sword or lance he's a dead man. I know you can fight, but you can also love, I saw you with Aspacia. I screw women, Gaius; you love them. I know it's too early to say this... but there are other women out there. Give yourself six months, a year; then decide."

"Aspacia's gone and I'll never find another one like her, Appian."

"There are thousands of girls in Rome, and even more in the provinces. And of course there are slaves. You could buy one and free her, as you did Aspacia. As for the Legion, though, once you raise your hand and swear allegiance, it's twenty years of your life, if you live that long. And if you don't like it after a few weeks, that's just too damn bad. There's no turning back—and desertion is a death sentence."

"I'm better than that."

"Yes, of course, but I'm just trying to tell you how it is. You're under somebody's command all the time, you live in a tent with seven others, and there's no privacy. Training is brutal and it never stops. The centurion is there with the vitus stick, a length of stout old vine, and he'll use it if he thinks you're slacking. It leaves a bruise you don't forget."

"Then I'll get one of my own."

Appian Dio smirked and said, "Don't be silly. You get one if you're a centurion, and that's in ten years if you're lucky. And then you're the lowest rank of centurion."

"How many ranks are there?"

"There are nine levels of centurion rank, but only one chief centurion per legion. He's the primus pilum, the 'first spear.' It's a very lucky man who gets that position. He's one who can put a tribune in his place."

"A worthy goal."

"If you say so. In battle he's exposed, out on the side of the cohort with no protection. Centurions have short lives, Gaius. But as I was saying, as a legionnaire you train all the time. Field marches in full kit are thirty or forty miles in a day, and we do that three times a month. When you're not training for war you're building roads, bridges, and fortifications. We even carry the stakes for the encampment walls. We don't use mules, Gaius, we *are* the mules. Then there are the officers and tribunes—we call most of them 'dolori in culi': a pain in the ass."

"How many of those are in a legion?"

"Six tribunes to a legion, usually young patricians heading for politics. Since they're of the Equestrian class, from influential families, they only sign on for a few years. Time in the army looks good if you're running for Senate. Some are good leaders, but others just ride around trying to look important. We've got one right now who's attached himself to recruit training. He's a dangerous ass, but only the legate can stop him, and so far he hasn't."

"I've heard that there's training equipment available at Campus Martius."

"All kinds of stuff: swords, old armor, javelins, shields, and slings. The militia uses them, as well as civilians who want to play soldier. Why?"

"Because I'll need them."

Appian Dio simply shook his head. "You didn't hear a word I said, did you? You're not cut out for the Legion, Gaius. You'll hate it. You're my best friend; I'm telling you the truth. Don't do it. Find a girl, fall in love again, and have a normal life. Enjoy Rome; it's the greatest city in the world."

"Vercipius will write the letter for me."

"I can't change your mind, can I?"

"No."

"You'll regret it."

"I won't," said Gaius. "Now tell me, how is it that you're in the city so often with all the training going on?"

"I'm a trumpeter, and an immunes. In other words I'm *immune* to a lot of drudgery, and I'm in good with my centurion. He sends me to get special things for the officers. The Legion doesn't make everything, so I'm dispatched to Rome every two or three days."

"Do you have a strict schedule?"

"In Rome? Not really. I just have to get back before dark and stand for the morning formation. Why's that important?"

"I'm just thinking."

"Uh-huh." Appian Dio was quiet, looking Gaius over, then, shaking his head, he asked, "When do you intend to join up?"

"In two months, when I'm eighteen. That's when you'll be done training me."

Appian Dio stared at Gaius with incredulity. "Train you? I can't train you in two months! Recruits spend six months marching, swimming, fighting, cleaning armor. You have to know all the commands: voice as well as trumpet. There's a thousand things you must learn—military procedure, rules, building encampments, the use of the gladius and pugio."

"The knife?"

"Yes, we all carry one."

"When will you be in Rome next?"

Appian sighed. "In two days."

"That's when we'll start. I'll get what I can from Campus Martius and bring it here."

"Why not there? Everything's there," Appian Dio said, clearly thinking that the whole idea of Gaius becoming a soldier was ludicrous.

"I have my reasons."

"That doesn't make sense. None of this makes sense!"

Gaius folded his arms. "But that's the way it's going to be."

"I don't want to see you die, Gaius."

"Train me well, Appian. Then I won't die."

*****

The man led her into the most secluded part of the balneum, one of the smaller, older baths rarely frequented by raucous bathers. Naked, they slipped into a warm, deep pool resembling a grotto and ducked under a waterfall that shielded them from prying eyes.

The man pulled her to him, and smugly moved his fingers to where they gave her the greatest pleasure. With her arms tight around him, she moaned and thrilled to the lust that welled up from the depths of their beings.

Afterward, when they were both satiated, they sat on the pool's steps and she ran her fingers over his lips and down his jaw. "Take me away from here," she said, "take me away from Rome. You once said you would. I'm so terribly bored."

"I said that?"

"You did, a year ago, before it all—"

The man toyed with her nipples. He smiled indulgently and gave her a playful look. "You are still beautiful. A treasure, but I can't now. I have a commitment of sorts. Besides, I like what I'm doing. It allows me to," he paused for a moment, contemplated, then said, "to engage my demons."

"I've heard you're brutal."

"Lust and brutality are the true nature of things."

"You're a cruel man, I have always known that. But I still want you. Is that an enigma?"

"Strength, lust, and yes, even cruelty, are things most women desire. And you demand it all, don't you?"

She gave him a hard look. "You have money, position, and me; what more do you need?"

"Power. It's something I've always craved. And to gain power, I must be where events are shaped."

"In Rome, acquiring real power is a dangerous game."

"I know when to make a tactical retreat; let others take the fall. A man of my position has that option."

"I have options, too. I won't wait forever. I know how to hunt."

"Of course you do, but you'll always come back. You hunger for prestige as much as you lust, and I'm the best, indeed your only hope. Power and lust, my sweet; those are two things you can't live without."

She was suddenly livid and rose from the pool's edge. "You're wrong. In fact, I'm tired of you—and yes, there are others, many others."

"But you'll tire of them, too. I'll be right here when you come back. Don't be too long. I have plans, and they may just involve you."

"I won't be back," Livia said. But she knew she would. She would always come back to Retenius.

*****

"We call this shovel a ligo. We carry it with us along with sixty additional pounds. None of the equipment is strapped to you, since you must be able to drop everything and be ready to fight in thirty seconds. So everything except your fighting equipment is tied to a wooden pole and crossbeam called the furca, this thing here," Appian Dio said, sorting through the pile of equipment Gaius had retrieved from the Campus Martius. "Now grab that log and the ligo, and follow me."

"And the wooden swords?"

"I'll carry them. You have a very long day ahead, so let's hurry."

It was only the second hour of the day as the two young men strode to a corner of the field that extended behind Junia's house. Appian Dio pointed to a flat spot and said, "Dig a two-foot-deep hole. We'll stand that log in it and fill in the dirt so it doesn't move. The post should rise five feet above the ground."

"What's it for?" Gaius asked, once it was secure.

Appian Dio hefted the wooden sword. "This is heavier than the gladius, the actual steel sword. You're going to hold your shield, the scutum, and practice two hours daily against the post. I'll demonstrate, then you'll do it."

"It's an awfully short sword," said Gaius.

"That's intentional. It's a close-in blade for cutting and slashing, but you use the point too. It's a damn good stabbing weapon, especially when you're holding the shield."

"What about the armor? Should I put that on?"

"Tomorrow. Today you'll start with a twenty-mile march—and you'll finish in five hours. It's what all recruits do. If you survive the first day's march, you'll do forty miles in twelve hours the next day. After that, you will do a twenty-hour march with the sixty-pound kit. Do you still want to do this, Gaius?"

"When do we march?"

"Now, you idiot!" shot Appian Dio. "Keep up with me, if you can. The army steps are not a leisurely civilian stroll. Put on those hobnail boots, the caligae, and get a flask of water."

The day grew oppressively hot as their march took them beyond the hills of Rome. "We do a long march three times a month with full pack," Appian Dio said. "Tomorrow you'll march with the shield. You saw how it had metal on all four sides, and a round steel piece in the center? It can also be used as a weapon. It's heavy, but you get used to it."

By the third day, the blisters had broken open, and Gaius bound his feet so the bleeding would stop. Every muscle in his body screamed and sleep only came with total exhaustion.

"There are two types of armor," Appian Dio said on the fifth day. "One is lorica hamata, or chainmail. It's lighter and easier to keep clean, but an arrow can still get through the links. Almost all of us wear armor of steel over a leather frame. It's called the lorica segmentata because there are thirty-four plates and each one had better be spotless for inspection. I'll show you how to wear it and clean it, then we'll throw the pilum."

Only by the third week did the pain in his arm, from beating the wooden gladius against the post and hurling the javelin three hours each day, begin to subside.

"I still don't see why the javelin's iron rod bends so easily," Gaius said to Appian Dio, when the legionnaire returned to

Junia's house two days later.

"It's simple. The iron that sticks out of the wooden shaft will penetrate an enemy shield and bend. If the man's still alive, he won't be able to extract it, and he can't throw a bent pilum back at you. He will also have to discard his shield. That means he's vulnerable—in fact, he's as good as dead."

"But he can dodge it, can't he?"

"You try and dodge eighty pila coming at you all at once! That's how many men are in each cohort, and we carry two pila each. Of course the real ones have a point, instead of this sack of sand, but it's safer for practice that way. Now, today you will recite all the commands I taught you, then I'll give the command and you execute the movement on the march. We'll do thirty miles today. Full kit and shield, then you'll practice vaulting over your horse."

"In armor?"

"Of course in armor. Fortunately Roman horses are small, but if you have to jump on or over a horse in combat, you'll be in full armor. Get used to it."

They took a lunch break at midday, and Appian Dio told him, "By now, the average recruit is complaining to Great Jupiter and cursing the day he joined. You should be doing the same."

"Complaining is weakness, Appian. I chose this, I'll be a voluntarius. Sure, it hurts, but it hurts less every day."

"We'll do battle with the wooden gladius tomorrow. If you don't parry fast enough, you'll know what hurt feels like. Then if you can still stand, we'll do hand-to-hand the army way, and I'll show you how to use the pugio. Knife fighting is an art, and very valuable in close quarters, especially if you lose your gladius. Plus I have some special things I'll show you, things I learned on the street. The Legion doesn't always teach you everything."

The purple bruises from the swordplay took three weeks to fade away, just as Appian Dio had warned. The last month consisted of swimming, martial arts, training with rock and sling, and forced marches. Appian Dio brought his trumpet and played command calls, to which Gaius learned to respond, and to move from one position to the next as if he were a member of a full cohort.

The months with their eighteen-hour days passed quickly, and finally one day Appian Dio said, "I think you're ready; you're in better shape than any new recruit. Tomorrow I'll challenge you with the gladius. You should be good with it by now, even though you've never used it against a real opponent. You remember, I told you that recruits are put up against gladiators and veterans toward the end of their training, right? They're brutal, and have left many a recruit maimed or worse. We'll be using the wooden sword, but you must fight for all you're worth. And just like the gladiators, I'll give no quarter, understood?"

Junia, with Tacitus in her arms, had often come to the field when Gaius was taking instruction from Appian Dio. She interrupted them now. "Vercipius said he will come with the letter. I believe that your father will come, too. They want to be present when you take the oath," she said to Gaius.

"I appreciate that."

"They call the swearing-in and the questions the 'probatio'; it's very important," said Appian Dio. "Be sure to say 'sir' and show no hesitation. The centurion is a very hard man."

Finally, Appian Dio returned to Campus Martius for the night, and Gaius and Junia were alone.

"You look tired, Aunt Junia," Gaius said. "Let's go into the atrium; there's something I have to ask you."

The baby began to cry. Junia rocked him back and forth and put a honey-flavored nipple in his mouth. The child sucked and stared at Junia.

"He likes you. I think you'll be good for him," Gaius said.

"But he needs a father," Junia protested. "I do wish you'd reconsider joining. Of course I will take care of him for as long as I can. I've never had a child, and Tacitus is a wonderful baby... but I'm not that young, Gaius."

"My mother will help, I'm sure of it."

Junia gave a wan smile and put her hand on Gaius's arm. "Livia will come around from time to time. She'll make a big fuss over him, and then hurry on her way. She's not the mothering kind; she never was, and you know that. She's my dear sister, but Livia is only interested in Livia and in who would be good for her."

"Looking for another man, you mean."

"Hasn't she always? She and your father have a platonic relationship, at best, and it's doubtful that it will ever change. She's looking for a man, a rich man, and little Tacitus is not in the picture."

Gaius stared at his feet as he thought. "I will send money, and I'll come back as often as I can. I'll even buy him a pony. I promised Aspacia I would. But, like I told Appian Dio, I don't want another wife. I would not be good for any woman, because I wouldn't *see* her; I would only see the face of Aspacia, and that would be tragic for any bride. Besides, I'm not the same anymore. A part of me died with her, Junia. I think you know that."

She nodded and said, "You used to smile and laugh, Gaius. You used to have that impish grin. I haven't seen you laugh or smile once, since..."

"I have nothing to laugh about."

"The baby. You can enjoy your child."

Gaius shook his head, then with a deep sigh said, "In time, Junia. Maybe in time."

It was already late in the afternoon when, over a cup of wine, Junia asked, "So what is it that you really want to do? What makes you want to join the army? Tell me, Gaius. Tell me the truth, for the sake of the gods."

"I don't believe in the gods, not any of them; they are cruel myths. Aspacia and I honored the gods, prostrated ourselves before them, and they left us at the vestibule of death. But if you really want the truth, I'll tell you."

His face hardened and he looked Junia in the eye. "I'm joining the Legion because I want to *kill*. I want to split men open. I want to kill for Rome, and I want to do it for the rest of my life."

"Is that what I should tell your son?" Junia said, horror on her face.

"Tell him that his mother was the most beautiful woman in the world, and that she loved him to her last breath. Tell him that his father fights for Rome and will keep him safe." He touched his son's cheek and added, "I will be forever indebted to you and will love him dearly. He is my son and the son of Aspacia, and I will be proud of him. I just hope he'll be proud of me."

"You are his father, you accepted him into the world. For that he must honor you. But I am sadder than you can ever imagine."

*****

Junia, with Tacitus swaddled in her arms, followed Appian Dio as he walked with Gaius to a place near the battered training log.

"Not too close, Junia. Give us room," Gaius cautioned her.

"You're ready?" Appian Dio asked as he hefted his wooden gladius. Gaius nodded silently and slipped into a defensive stance.

Neither wore armor as they moved about, looking for weaknesses. The sun was high, giving neither an advantage. Holding the sword in their right hands and the shield in the left, the two began to circle one another. Appian Dio made a feint that Gaius easily parried. He saw the legionnaire improve his stance and reevaluate his tactics.

White puffy clouds floated above, and Gaius glanced up. One shifted as he watched until it looked like the face of a girl. Tendrils of mist spiraled from it and he stared. "It's her," he said in a mere whisper.

"*Remember me, Gaius, remember me,*" he thought he heard her say. A sudden listlessness came over him. He tilted his head and, transfixed by the cloud, lowered his shield. Tears welled up, and Gaius brushed his arm across his face. Appian Dio was a blur and all concentration was lost.

"Yes, I will; I will remember you every day," Gaius said, louder now.

"You will what?" Appian Dio shouted as he slammed his

gladius into Gaius's unprotected side. The force caught him off guard, and he sprawled to the ground, the wooden sword flung from his grasp. The pain was intense, far greater than the hard stomach punches Appian Dio had thrown at him week after week.

"What are you thinking?" he bawled at Gaius. "Are you deranged, or can't you fight? Have I wasted my time? Look at you, staring at clouds! What, you see her in a cloud? You think you will bring her back? You are a greater fool than I thought!"

He was standing over Gaius, his sword whacking at him with angry, vicious blows. Gaius covered his face with his hands and lay in a ball.

"Appian, stop!" Junia shouted. "He's down; he's not going to fight you! You're his friend."

Appian Dio kicked the gladius toward Gaius and said, "You can run, you can throw the javelin, but you can't fight, can you? And you can't bring Aspacia back!"

"I can! I will!" Gaius screamed, rising to his feet, sword gripped in his hand. He tossed away the shield and charged the legionnaire, the gladius slamming into the shield and propelling Appian Dio backward.

"No shield? You want to fight without a shield? That suits me fine!" Appian said, tossing his into the dirt. He thrust at Gaius with a fast jab, but the sword was deflected.

Gaius swung his blade with unpitying fury and vengeance against everything unfair in the world.

The blows came with fanatical force, driving the legionnaire back, depriving him of a chance to counterattack. It was the same hatred, the same insane fury, that once drove the slaves who had fought alongside Spartacus. This was not the disciplined, measured attack of a soldier of the Legion; it was madness, manifesting as a willingness to die to save one he loved. Appian Dio was parrying the blows with increasing desperation. Gaius's face was streaked with tears. He screamed at the gods and shouted, "Kill, kill, kill!"

The stout wood of both weapons shivered in their grasp. Gaius felt a crack in his and knew that it would split with the next strike against Appian's weapon. With months of practice against the post, he made a feint, allowing the legionnaire a chance. With desperation, Appian Dio swung his gladius, but again Gaius parried it away, leaving the man exposed.

In an instant, Gaius's weapon slammed into Appian's chest. He buckled and Gaius, whirling about, struck him again, hard behind the knees. As Appian fell, Gaius, blinded by fury, drew back the heavy weapon for a final blow.

Junia bolted forward, a look of horror on her face.

As Appian Dio's were eyes fixed on the gladius, Gaius stepped forward and his weapon began its descent, when Junia screamed "No!" and threw herself into him. The gladius went wide and, distracted, Gaius lost his balance.

Appian Dio recovered, scrambling to his knees. Sprawled on the ground, Gaius saw Appian Dio's weapon descending, and raised his, only to have it shatter when it met the legionnaire's blow.

"Stop it! Stop!" Junia cried, her hands on Appian's chest.

Gaius slowly rose, then, devoid of all force, he slumped back to the ground. Tears of anguish stained the earth.

Appian stumbled forward and leaned against the post. Breathless in the hot sun, he declared, "I don't know what you are anymore: part god, part man—but you are not of this world." Taking in deep breaths, he stared at Gaius, who mutely shook his head.

"You might as well get up. You'll be the end of many a man." He walked to where his friend knelt and laid a hand on Gaius's shoulder. "You cannot bring her back, but she is with you. She must be; her strength is in you, and you nearly killed me."

"I'm sorry. I didn't mean to."

"Yes, you did, but that's what the Legion is all about. But if you don't mind," Appian Dio said with a very tight grin, "I'd rather not fight you again."

*****

The Legion encampment was a large, well-established, fifty-five-acre base. It was an exact copy of every other Roman fort, the idea being that any arriving units would not have to relearn the layout of the granaries, workshops, hospital, and barracks. There were four gates, but one was hidden by breastworks. The other gates, including the Praetorian Gate, stood in front of the compound's two intersecting roads, which in every fort were named the Via Principalis and the Via Praetoria. Placed near the junction of the two was the principia, the headquarters building where prospective recruits were evaluated and sworn in.

Gaius was ushered into a sparse room; the only furnishings were two desks, a few chairs, and shelves containing scrolls of papyrus. A scribe sat at one desk, and the longest-serving centurion in the legion, the praefectus castrorum, occupied the other. Behind him stood two other officers, the primus pilum, and a man of senatorial rank, the tribunus laticlavius.

"Can you see out of your left eye?" asked the praefectus castrorum.

"Sir, I can see, but not quite as well as in my right eye. I am not blind in it, though," said an anxious young man who had preceded Gaius.

Scanning the youth's letter of recommendation, the tribunus laticlavius said, "It's a worthy letter, and under any other circumstances we would be pleased to induct you, but impeded eyesight is a danger to yourself and everyone else. Battle is never a certain thing, and damage to your good eye would leave you helpless." He looked to the primus pilum, who gave a slight shake of his head.

"I regret that we cannot accept you as a prospective legionnaire," said the primus pilum, "but if you still wish to serve Rome, I will suggest the navy. There are positions on and off ships that need men of good character."

"If you are based at Misenum you may help operate the great sunshade over the Amphitheatrum Flavium," added the praefectus castrorum with a touch of kindness. "Then, of course, you can observe all the games. The navy does have some advantages."

The young man, crestfallen, nodded in appreciation and was quickly dismissed.

"Next," called the praefectus castrorum.

Gaius, wearing his toga virilis, stepped forward and smartly came to attention. He presented the letter of recommendation to the officer who opened the scroll and read it aloud. "Very complimentary," he said, studying Gaius. "Please introduce the men who accompany you."

"Sir, this is my father, Toronius Pratoria Aquila, and his associate, Vercipius Sulla Manlius."

"It was my honor to write the letter," Vercipius said deferentially. "I have known the lad since the day he was born, and I will attest that his character is unimpeachable."

"Your eyesight is good, you have both testicles, and are not married?" the officer asked.

"I have all the required parts and good eyesight. I was married, but..."

"But what?"

"My wife died. In childbirth." Gaius said.

"I'm sorry," replied the praefectus castrorum.

"Excellency," said Toronius following a moment of silence, "I can assure you that my son will be an exemplary legionnaire. I came here expressly to vouch for him. As you can see, he's in splendid shape."

"And he's taller than most," Vercipius chimed in.

"Yes, yes. The training is quite rigorous and more demanding than anything you've ever experienced in civilian life," the officer said. "The army will be your life, and the army involves killing. Brutal killing. I want you to think about that. Many young men only consider the novelty of travel or want to get away from an unpleasant household, parents and such then find that what the Legion expects is worse than anything they ever considered. But by then it's too late. I'll give you a moment to think about it."

"Sir, that's not necessary. I don't wish to waste your time. If you regard me as satisfactory, I shall be pleased to take the oath."

The praefectus castrorum glanced at the tribunus laticlavius, then at the primus pilum, who nodded.

"Very well. I consider the probatio concluded. I will render the oath. When finished, you will be in the service of Rome for twenty years. Unless wounded, there will be no honorable discharge until then. Your family will be given a stipend in case of your death. If this is agreeable to you, step forward."

Vercipius took a deep breath and glanced at Toronius, who stared straight ahead.

"Swear by your gods an unbreakable oath that you will follow your commander wherever he may lead. You will not question his authority. You relinquish the rights of civilian law, and recognize that your commander can have you executed for failure to obey orders or for disobedience. This can be done at his discretion without further trial. You promise to serve the full term of your enlistment, to carry out your duty, and not to abandon your unit until formally discharged. You will serve Rome and your fellow legionnaires faithfully, regardless of danger, and will respect all laws regarding civilians and soldiers of the Republic."

"I do so swear my unbreakable oath," said Gaius.

"Congratulations. Rome welcomes you into its ranks. You will now report to the training officer and be assigned to a contubernium. That is—"

"My tent mates, sir."

"Yes, your tent mates," the officer said, wondering how presumptuous or difficult the young man might prove to be.

*****

"He's different. To tell you the truth, I would hardly recognize him. He's changed so much since Aspacia died," said Vercipius as he and Toronius walked back to the city.

"By next year he'll be a total stranger."

"At least you two departed as friends."

"That's so, and I'm as pleased as any dominus can expect," agreed Toronius, arranging his toga and looking forward to seeing Caladria once again. But what would become of his son, he had no idea.

Chapter 21

"I am Lucius Galium Venicia," the lanky recruit said between coughs as he greeted Gaius at the barracks. "Menalus Tractus, the training officer, gave me the day off to get over this. The medicus, a Greek, said it will take at least a week, but I can't miss that much time. I barely made it into the army as it is. One of the recruiting officers didn't think I was up to it, said I was too weak, but my father wanted me in."

"You don't want to be in the army?" asked Gaius, looking at the man, who appeared frail and very worried.

"It wasn't my first choice, to say the least, but you do what your father tells you to. You know how it is. He's got money and wanted to be able to brag about his patriotic son being in the Legion. Anyway, he crooked his finger and he and the primus pilum stepped outside. I don't know how much my father paid him, but I got sworn in. I hope you have money or know someone who does. Everything here requires a bribe. If you don't want guard duty at the third hour, you pay. If you don't want to muck out the pigsty, you pay. Most of your money goes for bribes."

Gaius let the man prattle on, while he took in the eight-man barracks in which the contubernium slept and ate. There was a small second room, but it was mainly used for storage. The living area was cramped, and privacy was out of the question.

"Just joined up, huh?" Lucius went on, "Well, we've been in training for two weeks now. Everybody's a wreck. We had to march twenty miles yesterday with full kit. I nearly died. See these bruises? The training officer doesn't like me, says I talk too much. He practices using the vitus stick on me. I tell him he doesn't need any more practice, but he doesn't believe me. I just hope you can keep up, or he'll use it on you too. He's a mean son of a bitch. Stay out of his way—and same for that damn tribune, too."

"What's wrong with the tribune?" asked Gaius, finding an empty place to lay down his kit.

"He owns two gladiators, big guys. We'll eventually be trained by gladiators, but the tribune likes to sic his bastards on us. They're merciless, and we've only begun training with the weapons! They might as well be stepping on ants. They've already maimed three recruits and nearly killed another."

"What's his name?"

"The gladiator?"

"The tribune."

"Retenius. Tribune Retenius. Word is he failed in his bid for senator, so he's joined the army to gain laurels. Then he'll try again. He's a sneaky bastard. There are only two things he likes: women and power. Watch your back when he's around."

*****

Seven sweaty, exhausted recruits straggled into the barracks and dropped their kits. "Hurry, clean up, wipe that mud off the plates of your segmentata, we'll be assembling on the field," barked the leader of the contubernium. "Lucius, I don't care how sick you are; you're out there with the rest of us. Get your armor on and no complaints."

"What's happening?" asked Lucius, nearly toppling over reaching for his helmet. Gaius caught him by the elbow, and the youth gave him a thankful nod.

"The legate of the Legion VII Claudia will be addressing all the recruits, all five cohorts, and there will be an inspection afterward."

"Oh great Mars, we're in trouble," said another.

"You know what they say, no battle-ready legionnaire can pass inspection, and no parade legionnaire is ready for battle," said Lucius repeating the oft-heard cliché.

The contubernium leader ignored him and turned to Gaius.

"So you're the replacement? I'm Adolphus Septemius Ropenia, and I'm in charge here." The youth, Gaius thought, was powerfully built, arrogant, and specialized in giving orders. "I was told that you'd be coming. You should have been here two weeks ago. Now you're behind and will catch hell, not knowing anything. That's your kit?" Adolphus asked, pointing to the neatly arranged armor. Without waiting for a reply he said, "Lucius, you arranged it for him? He'll do it on his own from now on."

"He did it, I didn't."

"Really? Well," Adolphus said, "let's see if you can put it on. Janitus," he said to a prematurely balding man with a pocked face, "Help him this one time, he'll need it."

"That's not necessary," Gaius said.

Adolphus cocked his head and gave a little smirk. "Very well. Maybe you know a few things; maybe you don't need any help with it. But you better not bring demerits upon this unit, or you'll deal with me. Now get ready. In the formation you stand in the first row, to the left of Lucius. I shouldn't even let you out there, but I have no choice. Just follow everything we do. Say nothing, stare straight ahead, and if an officer speaks to you, address him as 'sir'. Do you understand?"

"I understand," Gaius said staring resolutely at Adolphus.

"Is that a contemptuous look you're giving me? It almost looks like you want to kill me. Do you?"

"Not unless you're an enemy of Rome. I'm sworn to kill all enemies of Rome."

Adolphus gave him a cold, hard look. With fury, he turned to the other recruits and shouted, "I want this squad to shine. Get off your ass, Lucius, before I put my caliga a foot deep inside it!"

*****

Trumpets sounded, and the cohorts, with eighty men apiece, each swung into massed positions before a dais on the training field. A guard of veterans flanked the stage, and the legate, an aging, erect patrician, was escorted to the speaker's stand by the primus pilum. Behind him marched the training centurion and the praefectus castrorum, the senior centurion. At the rear of the ensemble came the tribune Retenius and his two gladiators.

There was a second blast on the horn, and four hundred eighty men snapped to attention. The primus pilum laid a papyrus scroll on the podium, trained a practiced eye on the recruit cohorts, and when satisfied said, "Today I have the honor of presenting to you the esteemed legate, your commanding general, Leptus Agina Domatius. I do wish, however, to say a few words of my own. As Primus Pilum, the 'first spear', I was once a raw recruit like you. I also came to Campus Martius, here between the Tiber River with Quirinal Hill on the east and the majestic Capitoline Hill on the southeast. This field, blessed by Mars, the god of war, is where you will train to be the best and most disciplined soldiers in the world. It is to that end that we worship and give fealty to the goddess Disciplina, whose statue stands beside our headquarters."

The centurion paused for effect, then continued, "It is unity of purpose, along with diligent and ceaseless training and strict compliance to orders, that determines the outcome of battle. It is through that strength that we govern lands as far as we can march. No one except the ancient Spartans has ever had an army like ours. Yes, we battle brave and desperate men who want to kill us so that they can keep their barbaric ways, but few have any professional training. They fight hard and must never be taken lightly, but they're no match for a Roman legion. We have been tested by the best of them. The Macedonians, the same people led so successfully by Alexander, chose to fight us. They lost, and regret their folly each and every morning they wake. One hundred and fifty thousand of them were sold as slaves in a single day. Spain and southern Gaul were humbled by our legions. Training and discipline is the bedrock of the army and that is why it is so strictly enforced. Your personal identity is of no consequence, but your loyalty to your contubernium, cohort, and legion is. Embrace the Legion, and it will serve you well."

The primus pilum moved away from the podium, and the legate unrolled a papyrus, stepped to the podium, and in a surprisingly high voice, began. "The army consists of twenty-eight legions. You will be part of that force. Its purpose is to defend Rome and expand her frontiers. We take an oath to the Senate and people of Rome. That is what the 'SPOR' means on the standards of each legion.

"In the early days of the Republic, we recruited butchers because they were not squeamish at the sight of blood. Seeing battle for the first time is a frightening experience, but you will become accustomed to it. In time, you will embrace it. Many of our enemies, like the Illyrians and the Greeks, saw nearly bloodless wounds caused by spears or arrows, but fled in horror when they encountered Romans wielding the gladius Hispaniola, the sword that you will carry for the next twenty years. That weapon hacks off arms with the shoulder still attached, and severs heads from bodies with one clean swipe. War with Rome is about intestines tumbling out and heads rolling off torsos. War is slaughter, total horror—the stuff of nightmares. It must be that way, so that barbarians will reconsider the alternative to peace. That's what Rome is all about; bringing peace and civilization, Roman civilization, to the world."

A wind whipped up and blew eddies of dust across the cohorts, who strained to hear the strident voice of the legate.

"Yes," the general continued, "There are many great cities in the world. I have seen most of them; Nimes in Gaul, Nauportus in Pannonia, and Pharsalus in Greece. And of course there is Alexandria in Egypt. But Rome is more than just a city of a million people; it is a concept, just as was Greece centuries ago. Alexander and the Hellenes brought language, philosophy, and logic to the world. Rome brings the Pax Romana and civilization itself. That is what you will defend, and that is, if necessary, the cause for which you will die. There is no greater honor, no greater glory." He stopped and gazed at his new recruits. Then, in the strongest voice he could muster, he shouted, "Hail to the consuls. Hail to the Legion. All hail

Rome!"

From five cohorts a shout went up, "Hail to the consuls, hail to the Legion, all hail Rome!"

*****

The legate had no desire to spend any more time on raw recruits, since one out of ten would be eliminated by injury or the severity of the training. He spoke briefly to Menalus Tractus, the training officer, and to the centurion of each cohort, then marched quickly along the front of each unit. Gaius, motionless, overheard the legate make a disdainful comment about the smudges on the recruits' armor as he passed his contubernium.

"Sir, they just returned from a march and there was a lot of dust," said the training officer.

"Maybe so, but when I do an inspection I want them as clean as that man in the first rank, the tall one."

"General, he just joined and wasn't on the march."

"It doesn't matter, that's the way I want them to look."

"I will assign them a special detail tonight. They'll remember that."

*****

The inspection concluded, the general, along with several other worthies, returned to headquarters. Retenius remained behind and signaled to a centurion as the cohorts prepared to return to their barracks.

"That tall man, in the first rank. Have him report to me."

"Is there a problem, sir?"

"No, no problem, but I require his presence."

Gaius did a smart about-face and walked to Retenius who, having motioned an aide to bring his horse, held it loosely by the reins. "I must say, I'm surprised to see you here, Gaius. I didn't think you were the type."

"Things change. I'm just as surprised to see you here, Retenius."

"*Tribune* Retenius, Gaius. You're in the army now," he whispered with a cold grin. Then, taking a deep breath he went on, "It's too bad things didn't work out between you and my daughter. If you had shown a little more caring, perhaps..."

"She died of the plague, Tribune. I had nothing to do with her death." He was about to say a few words about the poison, or perhaps Cornelia's strangulation, but decided not to.

"Perhaps, but bygones are bygones and there's nothing we can do about the past. But you and I in the courts would have made a terrific team."

Gaius didn't reply.

"You don't think so? Well, strangely you chose the military. It's a difficult life, but I can make it easier on you. It's important to have an ally in high places. We can still help each other. Rumors are commonplace; intrigue and machinations float about like clouds in the sky. I need to know things. The common legionnaire hears and sees what people of my position do not. In a word, I need an inside source."

"You want a spy."

"Don't be smug. There are things afoot. These are turbulent times, and you want to be with the forces of success. Those are the ones who live to see the dawn. That's what this is all about: power and survival, both yours and mine. Join with me, and there will be advancement once your training is complete. With my recommendation you may become a centurion—I can even have you appointed to the general staff as my personal assistant. That does sound good, doesn't it? As it is you have no position, no stature, and no way of getting it. Work with me; it's the best thing that could happen to you."

"My allegiance is to Rome, not the career of a tribune."

"You don't want enemies, Gaius. Think about it."

"You have my answer."

"I can also make things difficult for you. Very difficult." When Gaius failed to reply, Retenius said, "There will be a thirty-mile march with full kit tomorrow. I doubt that you can do it, not having done any training yet. You do look very pretty in that polished armor, but that doesn't make you a soldier."

"A friend of mine was with Generals Pompey and Marcus Crassus when they fought Spartacus. I'm sure you saw heroic combat with them, or perhaps in some other battle," Gaius said, eyebrows raised.

"I was involved in other military activities, but never question my leadership or ability as a soldier."

There was a hard moment of silence between them before Retenius said, "No one will ever learn of this discussion. Understood?"

He mounted his charger and turned to Gaius one last time.

"By the way, I saw Livia the other day. Your mother is still very..." he searched for the right word, "very entertaining. Yes, extremely so."

*****

"Get up, get up, you've been assigned a detail," the training officer roared, as he stormed into the barracks. "Everybody assemble outside. Tunics only; no weapons, no armor."

"It's the middle of the night, sir, we just got to sleep," moaned Adolphus Septemius.

"The legate's orders; he has a detail for you. Contubernium leaders don't complain, they show leadership, Adolphus."

"Is this about the inspection?" another recruit asked.

"That's what I hear. You have work to do. Get it done quickly, and you can go back to sleep. You'll have one other contubernium to help you."

The two squads marched by torchlight across the encampment, to a dozen wagons beside a tiled-roof warehouse.

"The amphorae in those wagons contain wine and olive oil for the cohort," said Menalus Tractus. "You will unload and carefully stack every one of them. Break one, and it comes out of your pay. Septemius, you get to unload like everybody else. Now get started."

Sluggishly, three of the recruits hauled themselves onto the first wagon and began to hand the seventy-pound clay jars to those on the ground. Lucius Galium, weak and feverish, was helped onto the wagon.

There had been a brief shower earlier in the evening, soaking the straw cushion in the wagons and turning the ground into muck. The first four wagons were emptied with dull monotonous motions. Adolphus Septemius waited for Lucius to hand him an amphora. Suddenly wracked by a coughing fit, the sick youth fumbled with the three-foot-long jar, which slipped and pitched forward. Adolphus tried to catch it, but Lucius plummeted onto him. A scream rent the night air as the jar, flung into the air, came down and snapped Adolphus's wrist. Rolling Lucius off of him, the contubernium leader grabbed a stick, came to his feet, and with his good hand cracked the stick across Lucius's head.

Menalus Tractus turned toward them as Gaius, seeing the assault, rushed from the warehouse.

"Adolphus, stop, it was an accident!" Gaius called, pulling him off the recruit, who held his bloody head.

"Get away from me!" Septemius shouted, throwing a fist at Gaius.

The punch was easily blocked as Gaius slammed Adolphus into the warehouse wall, his hand around the man's throat. "The boy is sick; leave him alone."

Septemius tried to pull the hand away, but Gaius's grip didn't budge. His eyes bulged as he tried to work his mouth. "Understand?" Gaius asked. Septemius made a faint nod, and Gaius released his hold.

"You, recruit!" said Menalus Tractus to Gaius. "You will unload the next two wagons by yourself. We'll see how tough you think you are."

"Can we help him stack them in the warehouse, sir? It will speed things up," asked Tiberius Granculus, a beefy recruit.

"Absolutely not. No man is allowed to assault his superior. He will do it all himself."

Gaius clambered onto the wagon and silently removed each amphora, hustling it into the building and returning for the next. Septemius, his wrist bound by a cloth, gloated as the hauling went on. The recruits stood about, eyes half open, watching Gaius finish unloading a wagon.

"Go!" he said to the driver, dozing on his seat. The next wagon took its place and without a pause, Gaius began the laborious task of unloading and stacking the amphorae. The chore was completed an hour later. The recruits glanced at

Menalus Tractus, who ordered, "Now get back to barracks, it's getting late."

*****

The sun was already high when the cohort reached the eighteen-mile marker on their thirty-mile march. Adolphus Septemius, his arm in a sling, trudged along in the first row of the contubernium. Gaius, in the second rank of four, marched beside Lucius, who sported bruises from the previous night's beating. Beside him was Tiberius Granculus.

"Sorry I got you in trouble last night," said Lucius, struggling to hold up his four-foot-long shield.

"I doubt that he will hit you again," said Gaius.

"Was your father or brother in the Legion before?" asked Tiberius. "You seem to know a lot, for having just joined."

"No, but I have a friend in the army. We talked."

"I saw you speaking with Tribune Retenius. Do you know him?" asked Lucius.

"I'd rather not talk about it," Gaius said.

"That's him out there, isn't it?" remarked Tiberius. On his bay charger, Retenius galloped through a field bordering the line of march. He wheeled about, then passed the column again. He smirked as he rode past Gaius, and spun his mount so that the recruits had to avoid the splash of his horse's hooves.

"He doesn't particularly favor you, does he?" Tiberius wiped a clump of mud from his segmentata.

"It must be nice to ride when the rest of us have to march," Lucius observed.

"Horses tire, he might have to march yet," speculated Tiberius, as Retenius spurred his horse and charged ahead of the column, his cape fluttering behind him.

"Keep up, keep up," barked Menalus Tractus, as he swung his vitus stick at a lagging recruit. "This is just a walk in the park. Wait until you do this at the quick-march, going into battle. Then you'll have real things to worry about, especially in the front rank where you will be. Enjoy this."

Coming up to the first contubernium, Tractus said, "Galium, hold that scutum up! In another five months that shield will feel

390

as light as a roll of papyrus."

"In another two months I'll be dead," Lucius whispered. Tiberius laughed as they rounded a hillock of flinty shale. Up ahead, a group of officers stood in a tight knot.

"Isn't that the tribune there?" asked Tiberius.

"It looks like something's wrong with his horse, it's limping," offered Lucius. "My father had horses and I've ridden them. This sharp rock all around here, shale, can pierce a hoof like a knife blade. Then the horse is lame and you can't ride it. Sometimes we had horses with a split hoof, too. Horses look strong, but they're delicate in many ways. Believe it or not, a man will last a lot longer than a horse."

"What about donkeys?" asked Tiberius.

"Tough little animals, but damn small. A man looks silly riding one, but they're great for carrying loads. That's why we have a few of them with the cohort," said Lucius authoritatively. "Of course, since the army's been restructured, we've become the mules."

"So you think the tribune's horse is lame? Will he be walking with the rest of us?" asked Tiberius.

"As long as he can. We still have eleven miles to go, and here there are no houses or inns out here. No place for him to hole up," smirked Adolphus Septemius.

Retenius looked up as the cohorts marched by. An aide took the lame horse as the tribune began to march at the head of the column, along with the training officer and the primus pilum. Six miles later, Retenius was seen limping by the side of the road.

"I bet he wishes we had wagons with us," said Tiberius, when they were out of hearing range.

"Tractus said that wagons are only used in baggage trains, and besides, they're too vulnerable," replied Lucius.

"So he waits for another horse, or..."

A brief halt was called at twenty-five miles. Most recruits simply leaned on their shields, since sitting with a sixty-pound kit was impractical, and no order had been given to remove them. The men took a swig of water and chewed on buccellatum, their hardtack.

"Is that him?" Lucius asked, when he spied a tall man on a donkey, a safe distance from the cohorts.

"Sure is," replied Tiberius. "He doesn't want to be seen by us. He probably has open blisters."

"Like we used to have, but maybe he just can't march," said Lucius.

Upon their return, the six cohorts lined up on the parade ground, and the primus pilum sent out a runner. Shortly, a wagon trundled out and disappeared, only to return with the tribune sitting beside the driver. Retenius studiously ignored the massed recruits and made a show of chatting amiably with a legionnaire, who, not knowing the circumstances, was probably flattered that a tribune would consider speaking to a common soldier.

*****

"Adolphus, can I borrow three denarii? I'm a bit short this morning," asked Lucius as they stood in line outside the open door of the headquarters building. Inside, Gaius could see the training officer Menalus Tractus and his aide, peering at a papyrus sheet.

"Why do you even ask, you whining wimp?"

Lucius ignored the remark and turned to Gaius. "Could you lend it to me? I'll pay you back, you know I will."

"No."

"Honestly, I'll pay you back, with interest, too."

"No, I won't lend it to you."

"Why not, Gaius? It's only three stinking denarii."

"Because I don't want you to owe me anything."

"Yeah," said Adolphus, "You'll be dead after the first battle, and he'll never get his money back."

"Here, for Great Jupiter's sake, three denarii," Tiberius Granculus growled, thrusting the coins into Lucius's hand. "I'm tired of your whining. You will pay me back, and not by robbing me in a dice game. I've already lent you six denarii, and I'm keeping track."

"You can't read," shot Adolphus Septemius, "how can you

keep track?"

Tiberius was illiterate like most of the men, but he seemed to fear little from Adolphus. "I'll use my pugio and cut notches in your puny little cock. How's that for record keeping, you pompous asshole!"

Adolphus gave him a withering look, but said nothing. Gaius had a feeling that he suspected Tiberius wouldn't hesitate to do exactly what he said.

"Next!" barked the centurion.

"Recruit Adolphus Septemius Ropenia, contubernium leader, reporting," Adolphus said, standing erect before the training officer.

"Your wrist is healed?"

"Yes, sir, I'm ready for duty."

Menalus Tractus again scanned his list of the day's duties, then said, "You have a choice: helping rebuild the stone wall on the east perimeter, rather strenuous work, or tossing a few bales of hay to the legate's horses." He looked up and gave a rare smile. His aide, a gnarled veteran at the desk, put out his hand and rubbed his fingers together. Very deliberately, Adolphus placed four denarii in the man's hand. The aide glanced at Tractus, who simply stared at the recruit. Quickly, Adolphus reached into the top of his tunic, extracted a small leather bag, and produced two more denarii. The veteran nodded, made a mark in the duty ledger, and dismissed Adolphus.

"Next!"

"Recruit Gaius Septimius Aquila reporting for duty."

"Oh yes, I remember you. You're the one who got to unload the amphorae all by yourself a few weeks ago. Well, you have a choice just like Adolphus. What about some hole-digging for the 'lilies' that have to be replaced?"

"Yes, sir," said Gaius, thinking of the sharp wooden stakes that were placed in holes to deter an attack against the outer walls.

"Fine," said the aide, holding out his hand palm up.

Gaius looked at the hand, then at the veteran, but did

nothing.

"He wants something," said Menalus Tractus in just over a whisper. The veteran gazed at Gaius and raised his brows.

"Don't just stand there. Have you been struck by lightning?" said the aide testily.

"I don't take bribes, and I don't give them," Gaius replied evenly.

"Is that so? Very noble, very noble. It seems that I happen to have another job for you. The toilet block needs cleaning. Looks like there has been a backup in the drain, and crap is just floating all over the place. It's now the second hour; have it finished by the fourth, then report to the baths."

"But not for bathing," said the aide.

"You will stoke the furnaces beneath the floor until the fifth hour, then practice cavalry defense for the rest of the day. Dismissed," Menalus Tractus said airily.

The veteran glanced at the centurion and remarked, "His choice. He's a strange one, isn't he?"

"That's the type you keep an eye on," said Menalus Tractus.

*****

The quiet, elegant gardens of Consul Sallust lay north of central Rome, on Pincian Hill. A thick stand of trees with overhanging boughs concealed three men, all senators.

"Here he comes now," said an irritated Lucius Analius.

"Sorry to be late, the foot still bothers me, gout or something," Retenius said, nodding to Fannius Tryphon and Lutatius Catulus.

"Yes, of course, but a few miles of limping along could do the same. How is the horse?" asked Tryphon, a faint smile on his lips. "When I was in the Legion, we learned to march."

"Stop it. That's not what we're here for," said Lucius Analius. "Is Uticensis coming, Catalus?"

"No, Cato hates Crassus as much as we do, but won't get involved."

"You didn't give him any details, did you? I mean, if we go ahead, he won't know enough to accuse us, will he?"

"No. Marcus Cato is too damn honorable. That's his problem. He's a Stoic. We could have used his influence—he hates Pompey and Marcus Crassus—but he knows nothing."

Lucius Analius rubbed his jaw. "Crassus has to go. Have you ever heard anything like it? We, twenty, thirty of the Senate, have an assembly and Crassus, imperious as he is, decides to divide up the provinces of Rome. I expected to be governor of Andalusia, but he cuts out me and everybody else who's ever upset him. We protest, of course. Oh, there was a real row; our futures were in the balance. Then he motions to his henchmen, and four senators are slaughtered right there. Then Crassus himself rises from his royal chair and assaults me—actually punches me in the face!"

"So much for that charm and temperance he sprinkles about. It's a façade," said Retenius, breaking his silence.

"The bastard started the fire that burned my villa to the ground. He tried to buy the land from me for a pittance afterward, but I refused. He thinks I've forgotten about it," said Fannius Tryphon.

"That's his modus operandi," said Lutatius Catulus, rearranging his toga with the senator's stripe. Then looking up sharply, he said, "Retenius, you said that you were in. You haven't changed your mind, have you?"

"No, but I want to know what I'll get out of it. And what exactly do you mean by 'getting rid' of Crassus? He is, after all a consul, and a vindictive one. Failure on any level could be a death sentence."

"To 'get rid of him' means exactly that, Retenius. And you will be the one to do it."

"Me? He knows me. If things go wrong and I'm caught—"

"You won't fail, and you won't be caught. The plan is very simple and suits Crassus's proclivities. All it will take is a suggestion by Tryphon."

Retenius was pensive for a moment, and Catulus reminded him, "It was your idea originally. You're not worried now, are you?"

"Not about the deed itself. I'm concerned that my efforts

will be quickly forgotten when this is over."

"I keep my word, Retenius. Your ascendance is assured," said Catalus. "You can honorably leave the army, I will elevate you to senatorial status, and you will become my chief advisor. Not bad for one night's work."

"And the Senate will allow you to become co-consul with Pompey?" asked Retenius, wanting reassurance.

"Pompey favors me. We are personal friends and he despises Crassus. I know the senators will back me. They hate Crassus, too."

"Not all of them. He has his toadies, and he's popular with the public: free banquets, games and the like," said Tryphon.

Analius waved his hand dismissively. "The vox populi doesn't make policy, the Senate does."

"So," Retenius said in a near whisper, "we eliminate Crassus. Am I right, Catulus?"

The man who would be consul simply nodded.

"Then we must plan well, and the assassination must be anonymous," said Analius.

"But where, how?" asked Tryphon.

"Masked, and during a play, a licentious, bawdy one that Crassus would like," said Retenius.

"Exactly," said Catulus, "He will be invited to a visual feast: the chance to view sex with a beautiful masked woman. He is a voyeur, after all, and he frequents theaters where prostitutes display their talents. It's a common thing, a business inducement. So we will entice him to come behind the curtain to a dressing room for a very private showing."

"But he will have his Praetorian Guards," Tryphon pointed out.

"They can be distracted," replied Retenius. "And I know a beautiful woman who can entice Crassus."

"Can she be trusted?" asked Catalus.

"Of course."

"Are you paying her?" asked Analius.

"Not exactly, at least, not in coinage. She's a close friend of mine. Very close, in fact."

"A lover?" queried Catulus.

"From time to time. She wants me to be very successful. She'll do her part and slip away."

"We should know her name and a lot more about her," said Tryphon suspiciously. "After all, she will be in the room with Crassus, and if she talks afterward..."

"She won't. Anything she might say will put her at risk. You needn't worry."

Catulus gave Retenius a long, steady look, then said, "Very well, I think we're all in agreement. I'll set the time and place, and we'll deal with the particulars after that. Now depart—and not a word. Crassus has spies everywhere."

"That's for certain," said Analius, "Half of Rome is employed as spies."

*****

"I didn't think we'd last six months," said Lucius.

"I'm surprised you lasted one," shot Tiberius.

"I think Tractus has a little surprise for us, kind of a final-week test," said Antonius Venatus, the oldest man of the contubernium.

"Veterans. We'll be taking on veterans, the same ones who nearly beat us to death the first week," said Lucius.

"That was for effect, to show us what battle is like. We're better prepared for them now," said Adolphus Septemius authoritatively.

The contubernium fell in with the other units and marched to the training field, where they formed a three-quarter circle, two men deep. None wore armor, only tunics, something many thought unusual. Each carried his wooden gladius and a sheathed pugio, but only a few carried shields.

"You have trained for six months," centurion Menalus Tractus said expansively, standing on a covered platform before them. "Today the legate, the tribune Retenius, and I will observe your performance against trained and battle-hardened soldiers. Remember to include everything you've learned. A week from now, you will wear the crossed belts of a proud legionnaire. But today I want you to fight like legionnaires. The trumpets and drums of war will soon have the sound of thunder, and you will be fighting for your lives and your cohort.

"I want you to see your opponents today not as Romans, but rather as Dacians, Scythians, Gauls, and all other barbarians who would love to display your head on a stick and tell stories of how they disemboweled an entire legion. You will not let that happen!" said Menalus Tractus.

One by one the contubernii were called onto the field. Some were formed into defensive groups with other eight-man units. The veterans sallied into them and the crack of wooden swords, shouts, and orders resulted in semi-organized bedlam. Though not as experienced as the veterans, the recruits gave a good accounting of themselves.

Two squads carried the scutum and formed a testudo, or "turtle", in which the front rank held their shields before them while those behind balanced them over their heads. Like a front wall with a roof, the testudo protected against stones, lances, and arrows. Against these, the veterans threw the training pila, their blunt tips bouncing off the shields.

After an hour of combat, only Gaius's contubernium had not been tested. Watching from the front rank, he saw Menalus Tractus in animated conversation with Retenius. The centurion nodded toward the tribune's two battle-dressed gladiators. One, an eques, quickly mounted his horse and raised his lance, its pendant flapping in the light breeze. He trotted his horse about, holding his small shield close, the sun flashing off his scaled armor. While he continued his ostentatious display, Retenius crossed the field, stared at Gaius, walked a pace, then abruptly pointed to Lucius.

"You, onto the field. You will demonstrate how to repel a single cavalryman."

Lucius was given a shield, and stepped forward as Retenius returned to where the eques had finally come to a halt. Holding the horse's bridle, the tribune said a few words to the gladiator, then, to the amazement of the dignitaries, the primus pilum, and the contubernium, the eques exchanged his blunt practice weapon for a steel-tipped spear. The legate turned to Retenius and emphatically shook his head, but the horse was already at the trot. In a gladiatorial match the eques would employ the spear on horseback, then the gladius on foot, but this man clearly had no intention of dismounting against a lowly recruit.

In all earlier contests that day, the men of the cohort boisterously had hooted at the veterans and cheered on their colleagues, but at the sight of the trainee with only his pugio and wooden gladius, they hushed. Lucius, now visibly worried, glanced at the stone-faced legate, then back at his fellows.

The horseman circled the field twice in a fast canter as Lucius also turned, shield held firmly before him, wooden sword by his side. The eques wore a glistening crested helmet sporting a feather on each side, which fluttered in the breeze. Suddenly turning toward Lucius, the gladiator charged. The tip of the lance struck the metal center of the shield, glanced off, and threw Lucius off balance. He stumbled and spilled onto the ground. Frantically he started to pick himself up, when the cavalryman whirled and charged again, this time plunging the spear through Lucius's shoulder.

Dropping his shield and sword, Lucius screamed and fell to his knees, trying to staunch the spurting wound. The medicus started forward, certain that the fight was over, but hesitated when the gladiator, his lance pointed down for the kill, urged his horse forward once more.

There was a sudden yell from the cohorts when Gaius, tossing away his practice gladius, rushed onto the field.

"Come back!" Adolphus hollered, but to no avail.

Fifty yards never seemed so far to Gaius as he rushed toward Lucius, who was propelling himself backward and leaving a trail of blood that stained the hard ground. The gladiator, going for the kill, was amazed to see another recruit charging across the field. The opportunity to score another kill was too tempting. The eques nudged his mount and bore down on Gaius.

Alarmed at the speed of the oncoming horseman, Gaius drew his pugio, his only weapon.

"Remember what I told you!" Appian Dio's words echoed in

his head. "He will expect you to stand, gladius raised, or worse to run. Then he will put the spear through your back and out the other side. Listen to me; do what I tell you!"

Then Gaius heard a second voice, one he knew so well and from so far away: "*Live, Gaius, live for your son.*" Her voice faded as the drumbeat of hoofs came closer. The rider hunched forward, knees pressed to the horse's flanks, as clods of dirt were thrown up in its wake.

Gaius positioned himself to the right of the horse, making the gladiator move the lance across his mount's neck. Then he burst to the left. With growing frustration, the rider swung the lance again. At the last second, Gaius bolted right and dropped to the ground. The lance fell off-target. His arm thrust upward, and Gaius stabbed his pugio into the animal's belly. The horse screamed, reared, and ejected the startled rider. His helmet flew off as he spiraled to the ground. Aware of his perilous condition, he made a grab for his sheathed sword as Gaius, knee first, plummeted upon him. Clutching a handful of the gladiator's hair, he pulled his head back and sliced the blade across the eques's throat. A rush of blood spewed over them as the gladiator's eyes widened, and his horrified scream came to an abrupt halt.

There was dead silence all about. Gaius turned away from the corpse and started toward Lucius, when the wounded recruit shouted, "Behind you!"

Retenius's second gladiator, a retiarius enraged by the death of his colleague, tore onto the field. The man's net was revolving about the gladiator's head when Gaius turned toward him. A three-pronged trident and small shield were held in one of the gladiator's hands, the net held firmly in the other. Gaius backed away, trying to gain time. The net flew forward but he sidestepped and the snare was hastily gathered for a second toss.

"Gaius!" came a shout from behind him. He turned to see the glint of a steel gladius high in the air. Menalus Tractus stood before the contubernium, his arm still raised as he watched the weapon's arc plummet toward Gaius's feet. Gaius grabbed it, but an instant later the net was upon him, sweeping him to the ground.

The gladiator, a veteran and survivor of dozens of combats, seemed confident of victory. For years he had probably been cheered by thousands of delighted spectators as he drove the trident into wriggling, straining victims. Like a fly in a spider web, once snared, the prey could do little but wait for the inevitable.

Gaius had kept his hands together, the gladius held tightly. The retiarius had time, he knew. He would watch his quarry struggle, would bait Gaius as a cat would a mouse. He would calculate exactly where the trident should be aimed for the kill. In the arena, the terrified victim would try to pull away, maybe even tug desperately on the net to throw the gladiator off balance.

Gaius however, grabbed the net with one hand and swiftly cut a swath through it, grinning viciously at the gladiator's surprise when he saw his quarry roll toward him. The gladiator stared into Gaius's eyes, then raised his trident high. It had only begun its downward plunge when he bellowed, dropped the weapon, and reached for his groin, where Gaius's blade had rent a hole in his flesh. With a half-dozen strokes, the net parted and Gaius emerged, bright red, covered with the blood of two men.

He stood over the gladiator, who writhed on the ground. A femoral artery had been sliced, and blood spurted with every beat of the man's heart.

Furious, shaking with rage, Gaius held the blade over the helpless retiarius.

"Enough! He's as good as dead," said Menalus Tractus, hurrying forward and retrieving his sword from Gaius's hand.

The medicus and his assistants had already carried Lucius off the field. The wound would be sutured and henbane given for pain, with bandages to slow the bleeding. Meanwhile recruits were ordered to remove the gladiator's bodies as Gaius rejoined his contubernium. He was ordered to stand in front of the cohort, but behind its centurion.

Not a word was uttered. Blood ran down Gaius's tunic and caked upon his skin. He swayed in the hot sun, and wiped sweat from his eyes. Everything blurred. An image of a girl with dark eyes and black curly hair appeared and smiled. Softly spoken words, her words, floated through his mind. Then the comforting image faded as quickly as it had come.

A murmur in the ranks was quickly silenced by the primus pilum. The legate, standing on a dais, glanced at Retenius, who stared blankly into the distance.

"Centurion," the general said to Menalus Tractus, "you may lead your cohorts to their barracks. These proceedings are concluded."

With a blast on the horn, the order was given; only those closest to the general heard him say, "Great Jupiter, that's enough for one day!" He then turned to an aide and said, "I want to know that man's name: the one who killed the gladiators. And about the tribune—he will stand before my desk at the fifth hour. Not a moment later."

Chapter 22

"Does she say anything more about the woman with the beautiful face and exquisite body, the one she talked about yesterday?"

"Aspacia didn't say she had a beautiful face. She said the woman would have a figure as seductive as Venus or Aphrodite," replied Caladria, leaning back against her tree and staring at a passing cloud.

Toronius gazed at her, hoping that she would disclose another nugget, anything to reveal the appearance of the woman. The very thought of the lady had kept him up the previous night.

"But you, or she, said that this woman will prostrate herself at my feet. That she will hang onto me for the rest of my life, and will share my bed every night. Caladria, where will I meet her—or will she just come to me? Should I be looking for her?"

"I don't know, Master. I asked Aspacia, but she didn't answer."

"It's too important for her to simply ignore. You must ask her again."

"She has a will of her own; she's not a real person anymore, Master. We can't demand anything of her."

"I know, I know," Toronius said impatiently. "Tell her I apologize for any indiscretion, but the anticipation is driving me mad."

Caladria closed her eyes, concentrated, then let out a deep sigh.

"Master, she's talking to my parents and just waved me off. They're all laughing about the time she fell into the bowl of flour and insisted on walking around our village, white as a ghost. She was just a baby then."

"Aspacia, just tell me," Toronius pleaded. But he knew it was useless.

It was already late in the day and the weather had turned foul. They sat beneath Caladria's tree, bundled against the wind. She had decided that the nice clothes Toronius had bought her should not be soiled, and had reverted to her stained and weather-beaten cloaks and shawls.

Caladria's despondency had abated, and now it seemed to Toronius that she enjoyed her conversations with Aspacia, especially when Toronius offered her wine and sweetmeats to prompt for details.

"Are you going to talk with her today?" he would ask, his eyes lighting up. If she said yes he would dutifully follow her to her tree, since it was only there that she would speak to her sister.

"Master, sometimes she tells me naughty things," Caladria would say, suppressing a giggle. "Aspacia just loves to share gossip. She never used to, you know."

"It's getting colder. We should go in if she hasn't anything else to say," complained Toronius.

Caladria had been quiet for some time, but now she slowly raised a hand. "She's telling me something now. It's very strange, Master."

"What's strange?" He said, pulling his cloak tighter around his enormous bulk. He peered closely at Caladria and recognized how her corpulence so much mirrored his.

"My sister says that you will have visitors, a young couple who will stay here for months."

"What? I haven't invited anyone, and I don't want strangers staying here. Who are they, do I even know them?"

"I don't think so, but they will have a little one here, a baby."

Toronius stared at her incredulously. "A child, here?"

Caladria shrugged and said, "Aspacia says a little one will be born here and stay for three or four months. But you won't have to take care of it."

"I should think not! Does Livia know about this? Did she invite them?"

Caladria shook her head and said, "Aspacia is saying something about your wife."

"Better than what she just told us, I hope."

Caladria cupped her mouth and her eyes grew wide. "She's in great danger, Master. We must watch her."

"Watch her? You mean follow her around and spy on her?"

"Maybe not all the time, but especially when she goes to the theater."

"I didn't know she even goes to the theater. I haven't taken her there in years. Who does she see there?"

"Aspacia doesn't want to talk anymore."

"That girl's impossible! Ask her if the visitors are an omen. Tell her we must know."

"Aspacia says she doesn't have time to talk. She's busy."

"Busy? Where she's at? That girl gives us the most alarming news, and then says she doesn't want to talk?"

"She might tell us more later. She's in a different world, Master, one she can see but we can't. But everything she tells us is true."

Toronius sat back and pondered Caladria's words. "We must be vigilant, Caladria. I'll ask Livia about the houseguests and we'll watch her. But say nothing until we learn more."

*****

Their lust satiated, Livia released herself from Retenius, glided across the warm bath, and rested against a pillar. The tribune, spent from his exertion, found a place beside her. He moved to caress her but she slid away, becoming pensive.

"Has Toronius been a problem for you?"

She shrugged. "No more than usual. I can't stand him; he is so fat and gross. But he asked me something strange yesterday."

"About us?"

"Not about us. He asked me if I had invited a couple to live at our house and stay for a long time."

"Did you?"

"Of course not."

"Why would he ask that?" Retenius wondered, perplexed.

"I'm not sure. He spends time with his slave, Caladria. He believes that she communicates with the dead and he hangs on her every word."

"And he believes what she says?"

"Yes."

"Do you?"

"Not particularly."

"So, she's a fortuneteller. Personally I think they're all quacks, but if she's reliable, maybe she could tell us about our little endeavor. Can you ask her? Not that I'll take seriously anything she says."

"Retenius, darling, I won't waste my time. She's really a freak."

"But you're distressed about what she said; a couple moving into your villa."

Livia sighed and put her hand on Retenius's thigh. "I really don't know what to think, but I certainly won't live there if a family moves in. I require my privacy."

"I don't put much stock in omens. But I think you should stay at my villa until everything's settled. Stay with me, and you can have all the privacy in the world." The tribune placed a finger on a nipple and whispered, "We could have our delicious sessions in my own baths, in much greater comfort." Then, quite seriously, he said, "Livia, I can give you anything you desire. Toronius hasn't an uncia to his name. I told you before, he offers you nothing, not wealth, not sex, not even companionship."

He waited, and when she didn't reply, asked, "Okay, when is this couple arriving?"

"I don't know."

"But you can find out, can't you? It is important."

"Caladria doesn't confide in me. I might have Toronius ask her. Now it's you who's anxious."

"We don't know these 'guests' or their motives. Somebody

may have heard something. They could be spies. Livia, neither I nor my colleagues will brook any interference. It would be too dangerous. Almost everything is in place. You and I have to meet once more, and I'll show you where it will take place."

"You know I'm frightened. You haven't told me much and it sounds dangerous. Is it?"

"Not for you. We will all wear masks. You'll act as an entertainer of sorts, an exhibitionist, as if we're advertising the inducements of a brothel. You should like that. And brothels advertise that way all the time."

"I might enjoy the thrill of it under normal circumstances. But about this, I'm not sure. Who am I performing for, anyway?"

"A very wealthy man. The whole thing will be over quickly, then we'll be gone."

"An erotic performance for a special guest? What's in it for me?"

"You will be rewarded with a small fortune."

"Really? I should receive something, but a small fortune? Unless, of course, this person is very important and I'm in great peril. Am I an accomplice to a murder, Retenius?"

"There are things I can't divulge right now. Regardless, what we do will be for the good of Rome."

"I'm not interested in what's good for Rome. I'm interested in a life of comfort and elegance with beautiful people."

"Then think of our adventure as a pathway to all of that. My friends will take care of everything. Now, enough of this. Let's indulge in what we both live for."

His hands went to her breasts and he kissed her deeply. She returned the kiss and laughed, putting aside her concerns. "Are you still going to buy new slave girls? Really yummy ones, like you said?"

"You'd like that, wouldn't you? I'll let you pick them out and we'll watch them play with each other. That would be exciting; the two of us are voyeurs, after all. We could train them to do exactly what we want."

"Delicious, but we could have your gladiators teach them.

That would be fun to watch."

Retenius stiffened and remained silent for a moment. "My gladiators are dead. Killed."

"In the arena?"

"Not in the public arena. They were killed on a training field at Campus Martius. And do you know who killed them, dear Livia?"

She was taken aback. He was angry and appeared suddenly distant. Apprehensively, she shook her head.

"They were killed by your son! Gaius murdered them."

A peal of laughter filled the balneum. She put her hand to her mouth and looked around. "You are joking! Gaius, my boy, killed your two big gladiators? What did he do, tickle them to death?"

"No, he ran a sword through them. I never suspected it; your 'boy' is a savage." *And I am not done with him,* he thought to himself.

*****

A cold wind blew across Campus Martius while Retenius stood before General Domatius's desk. The legate, in his scarlet cape, gave him a disdainful glance and continued his conversation with the legion's chief centurion. After a few minutes of making Retenius wait, the general dismissed the other officer and did not wait an instant before he rounded on Retenius. "What in the name of Great Jupiter did you think you were doing?"

"Sir, I don't know what you're talking about," Retenius said, startled by the legate's fury.

"Don't know what I'm talking about? That was a training activity, not a war. You disobeyed me. You and your gladiators intended to murder unarmed men!"

"Excellency, it was Menalus Tractus who ordered me to make the scenario realistic."

"But he didn't tell you to kill my recruits!"

There was a frigid silence as General Domatius glared at the tribune.

"I will resign my commission at this moment if it pleases

you," Retenius finally said.

"You will be drummed out when I *allow* it. I can have you stripped of all rank, all Equestrian privileges. I can have you banished, even executed."

"I am—"

"Silence! Tomorrow you will be on the dais with me for the review. It will be at the third hour. Be there."

Seething with anger, Retenius stormed from the headquarters, vowing that once he was a senator and a confidant of the next consul, he would see to it that Leptus Agina Domatius would never command a legion again. But why, he wondered, would the general have him on the reviewing stand after this humiliation? The thought bothered him for the rest of the day.

*****

A hot afternoon wind rose up from the Tiber, bringing leaden drops of rain and flashes of lightning. A gust blew open a door, waking Toronius, who had slumbered fitfully in his room. A pan fell in the kitchen and clattered into the hallway.

Where was Caladria when she was needed? It took Toronius a minute to remember that she would be sitting immobile beneath her tree. Livia wasn't here to close the door, either; he hadn't seen her in three days. With a plodding step he opened the door to his cubiculum and trod heavily down the hall.

At first he saw only a blur, a motion that sped past. Something grazed his forehead. There was a high-pitched screech and the flutter of wings, which caused him to spin around, his eyes following the movement.

"Not in my room!" he heard himself shout, as a hawk shot through the doorway and came to rest on a shelf above his bed. Amazed and perplexed, Toronius stared at the bird of prey as it pivoted its head from side to side, examining the little room. Standing at the door, Toronius debated his next move. The hawk opened its beak and stuck out a claw, talons spread wide, defying Toronius to approach.

The dominus simply stared at the bird at first, then ineffectually waved his hand, saying, "Shoo, shoo."

The hawk tilted its head and gazed back at him. Again it opened its beak, emitted a startling screech, and spread its wings. Toronius took a step back as the bird suddenly launched itself past him and sped down the hall toward the atrium.

Relieved but curious, Toronius followed and watched the hawk circle high above, then dive for Caladria's tree, where it alighted on a branch twenty feet above the ground. Crossing the field, Toronius approached the girl and looked upward. The hawk strode up and down, surveying the twisted limbs.

"Did you see that?" said Toronius.

Caladria, wearing her heavy, hooded cape, merely glanced up, the trace of a smile coming to her lips. She nodded, closed her eyes, and languidly pointed upward. A slow glide was made by another bird, barely a speck in the sky. A moment later, the hawk in the tree bounded from its perch, circled the villa, and joined its mate a thousand feet above.

"An omen?" Toronius asked, as distant thunder rolled across the sky.

"An omen," Caladria confirmed.

He was about to leave when she surprised him by saying, "We must speak to your son, and he should come with me four nights hence."

"Go with you? Where? And what do we tell him?"

"What Aspacia has told me."

*****

Wearing nondescript peasant clothes, Caladria wandered about the market stalls, waiting for a glimpse of Retenius and Livia. Undetected, she had followed her mistress each day, usually to the balneum, only to see Livia exit alone and walk to her villa or Junia's house. Expecting much the same today, she was surprised to see her mistress and the former praetor leave the baths together and wander down the crowded street.

The pair skirted piles of refuse and discarded garments being picked over by the poor. They stopped, and Retenius had Livia conceal herself in a darkened alcove while he proceeded to a theater two blocks away. Hidden from view, Caladria waited in the shadows of a tanning shop, its pungent reek staining the air. It was impossible for her to hear everything, the noise of the street clamoring all about her, but her view was not impaired.

"This is the theater where it will take place," she heard a tunic-clad man say to Retenius, without preamble. He was joined by two others, who spoke in hushed voices, while standing before the grand building with its Ionic columns.

"The lady will come here by herself," Retenius said.

"She must come early so no one sees her," added Lucius Analius.

"I'll make sure of that," replied the tribune, calming the man's fears.

"In two days. That's the final night of the performance. I know that Crassus doesn't want to miss it."

"Will the instrument be in place?" asked Retenius.

"It's already there, and I told you where to find it. It's well hidden; no one suspects anything."

A few more words were exchanged and as Caladria watched, the men departed, each taking a different route.

*****

Appian Dio and four other trumpeters sounded the call, as the legionnaires of the cohort marched smartly from one massed formation to the next. The maneuver was watched with approval by the scarlet-cloaked legate, as the sun rose above the hills of Rome.

Behind the general stood an irritated Retenius, wishing he could be anywhere else. Only the fear of punishment for desertion compelled him to attend. He wanted to get on with what was truly important. Exactly why Leptus Agina Domatius insisted that he be on the dais was still a mystery to him, since he fully expected to be expelled from the Legion. Normally he would be pleased to stand before thousands of spectators in the company of a general, but now trepidation assailed him. In the audience he could pick out Toronius and Vercipius, but was reassured by the absence of Livia, whom he'd told to stay away.

When all the cohorts were aligned, the legate rose from his

chair, unrolled a papyrus, and proclaimed, "I congratulate the recruits on the proficiency and determination displayed during your training. At the conclusion of this ceremony, you will take your place as legionnaires and be awarded the double belt. I know that you will serve with distinction and perform your duties in accordance with the expectations of the Republic."

The legate paused as if to gather his thoughts, then continued, "Rome honors its legionnaires when they perform heroically in battle. You have all seen veterans with their lorica segmentata festooned with bronze medals, the phalerae. Each award is given for exceptional bravery in the face of certain death. They must be earned, and are not awarded lightly or as personal favors. Many legionnaires serve their entire enlistments and never receive one.

"There are many ways to earn such an honor. Saving the Aquila, the legion's eagle standard, is one way, as is killing the enemy in desperate battle. But no honor is higher than saving the life of a comrade, be it a munifice or a general. For that, a legionnaire is awarded the highest honor given to a Roman soldier, the Corona Civica."

For effect the legate again paused. "Rarely, if ever, and certainly not during the years of my service, has the Corona Civica been presented to a recruit, one who has not even been promoted to legionnaire. But that will change today, for I and many others witnessed an act of selflessness and bravery that deserves nothing less."

He nodded to the praefectus castrorum, who stood beside him. In a commanding voice, the aged veteran ordered, "Recruit Gaius Septimius Aquila will step to the front of the cohort."

The audience strained to see a tall youth take a position beside Menalus Tractus.

In the crowd, Vercipius turned to Toronius with wide eyes and demanded, "Did you know anything about this?"

Toronius shook his head, just as shocked. "Livia should have been here to see this."

"Where is she?"

"I have no idea," replied Toronius, wondering exactly what Gaius had done.

There was a murmur of approval, after which the legate continued. "This award of common oak leaves elevates a soldier to the highest stature. With this honor, a man becomes a hero of Rome. Today, the crown will be awarded by a ranking officer who," he paused and said, "witnessed the event."

The legate turned and ostentatiously crooked his finger.

"Me?" was the only word that issued from Retenius.

"Yes, you. To whom else would I give this singular honor?" said the legate with an icy look, as he handed the coronet to Retenius.

Turning back to the cohort he announced, "The tribune Dometius Scipio Retenius is given the honor of presenting the award."

Ashen, Retenius stepped off the dais. Aware of the crowd's eyes upon him, he struggled to assume a military manner as he approached the cohort. He halted in front of Menalus Tractus and held out the chaplet of leaves.

The training centurion shook his head and smiled grimly. "Oh no, Tribune, you have been ordered to perform the honor. I'm sure you don't want to forfeit the opportunity."

Retenius stepped a pace, turned, and haltingly set the Corona Civica on Gaius's head.

"It's not over. Not at all," said Retenius, in a voice too soft for Tractus to hear.

"I hope not. Just don't have me wait too long," whispered Gaius.

Retenius smiled. "I won't. By the gods, I solemnly promise."

*****

The play was a Greek comedy, whose masked actors left everybody howling with laughter. The first act had ended, and was followed by a lengthy intermission in which vendors offered wine and sweetmeats to patrons sitting on stone benches. Marcus Crassus, wearing his toga with the broad purple stripe, was surrounded by a half-dozen sycophants. His personal bodyguard was allowed to relax in the festive environment, and their exalted status attracted a dozen young women eager for attention.

Flute players, acrobats, and mimes entertained the crowd as torches illuminated the theater. No one took notice of three men in actor's masks who silently communicated with one another.

"A delectable pleasure has been prepared for you, Excellency," said Lutatius Catalus, wearing his mask and fanciful costume as he wormed his way to the consul's side.

Marcus Crassus studied the presumed actor with amusement. "And what is the nature of this 'delectable pleasure'?"

Bending toward Crassus and cupping a hand over his mouth, Catalus said softly, "A carnal delight, just for you. It is an opportunity to see Rome's most beautiful consort moan and sigh, when your instrument explores the splendor of her sex. I have seen her, Excellency, and can tell you that she is a true beauty and will offer her enticements most willingly, but only for the most select of clients. She is a delicacy sweeter than all the honey in Rome."

"And that honey is for the sampling?" Crassus asked, his eyes sparkling with sudden anticipation.

"Indeed, and she awaits your pleasure. The woman will do anything you want. *Anything*," Catalus repeated.

"Where is she?"

"In a dressing room nearby. It's very private, and secured just for you. I would be honored to escort you there," said Catalus.

"Perhaps a few of us should accompany you, Crassus," said a senator with a smile and a hint of concern.

"I don't think she'll be quite as natural with a crowd about her," Catalus said with a nervous laugh.

"Quite right," said Crassus. "Consulship has its privileges, gentlemen. But I will give you an abbreviated report when I return."

"No, no, a detailed one," guffawed a senator to general

laughter. When the consul had gone, he said to the huddle around him, "Power and money may eventually jade him, but pussy never will. On that I would bet my fortune."

*****

It was already dusk as Gaius, wearing his crossed belts around a military tunic and armed with his pugio, followed Caladria through the emptying streets. She carried a sack and wore an old hooded cloak. After a lengthy walk, they wound up at the entrance to an alley and she said to him, "I will wait nearby. You should stay here."

"Why? What am I waiting for?"

"For what comes," she said, already padding away.

*****

"What's her name?" asked Crassus, as Catalus led him down a flight of stairs to a stone chamber.

"Dalia, Excellency."

"Is she expensive?"

"She's a gift to you, Excellency. Her madam appreciates your proclivities, and only asks that you recommend her fine establishment."

Catalus knocked softly on a door at the end of a dimly lit hallway, behind which he heard an anxious whisper. Catalus knocked again and the consul said impatiently, "Open the door. I don't care to simply wait here."

Marcus Crassus sucked in his breath as the door swung open and Livia, wearing a cloth mask revealing only her eyes, motioned him in. "Honored Consul, please enter and close the door behind you. I am for your eyes only."

Crassus took no notice of Catalus, who quickly departed. Consumed by the sight of the beautiful body, he failed to see the swish of a curtain at the rear of the room. She was alone; that pleased him. The only objects in the chamber were a bed, a table, and a shelf upon which lay a woman's stola.

Livia was adorned in translucent silk, which she tantalizingly raised as she pirouetted before him. She allowed the top to descend, revealing full breasts and taut nipples.

Crassus gazed at them and touched his tongue to his lips in anticipation. Reaching for his hand, she placed his fingers upon one breast so he could feel the perfect contour. Playfully stepping back, she turned and allowed the remainder of her silk garment to glide down. Deftly, and with the most sensuous motion, she directed his eyes to the apex of her slender thighs.

With a sudden lunge, Crassus lifted and tossed her onto the bed. Then he raised his toga and settled on top of her.

"Allow me," she said. "I enjoy fondling."

"Yes, pleasure yourself," he said, his mouth sucking in a nipple. Then, curious, he whispered, "You will show me your face, won't you? I trust it's as stunning as the rest of you."

"Soon, very soon, Excellency; just honor me with your talents," said Livia.

Crassus sensed her apprehension, but chose to ignore it. He was a physically large man and politically powerful; he knew that either could easily intimidate. He also knew that the woman was his for as long as he cared to dally with her. This would be delicious, and for such an unexpected delight, he would willingly forego the final act of the comedy. Indeed, if she was as skillful as she was sensuous, he might include her in his stable of courtesans.

The prostitute's eyes darted about, but rather than ask what she was looking for, Crassus suddenly entered her.

Behind the curtain, Retenius watched as Livia opened her mouth in a gasp, but remained silent. Crassus muttered something about wanting to hear her moan with delight, like every woman he'd had. Retenius waited as the consul intensified his efforts, concentrating on her every response. Crassus's eyes roamed over Livia's body; even the filmy mask she wore seemed intoxicatingly delicious to him. The thrill of having the spectacularly beautiful woman beneath him was all-consuming, and Retenius smiled inwardly.

In the half-light, Crassus failed to see Retenius emerge from behind the curtain until he stood beside the bed.

Retenius tried to plunge his knife deep into the consul's neck, but Crassus saw his shadow, glanced up, and flung out an arm at the last possible instant. The blade was deflected and, sliced into his shoulder. Crassus roared and bounded off of Livia, as Retenius pulled back to thrust again. Pivoting, the consul threw a punch, slamming the tribune against the wall.

Livia screamed, grabbed her stola, and bolted from the room.

"Guards! Praetorians!" Crassus bellowed.

Still clutching the bloody knife, Retenius struggled to gain his balance and jerked away from the consul, who made a grab for him. His mask askew, Retenius bolted through the door and into the audience as they enjoyed the last moments of intermission.

Livia had already vanished, and Retenius knew that Crassus was only steps behind. Shoving and dodging past startled spectators, the tribune darted toward the nearest exit.

Crassus shouted and the guard, along with a dozen dignitaries, rushed to his side.

"He is hurt!" a senator shouted, as blood stained Crassus's toga.

"The consul's been attacked!" cried another, eyes already searching for the assailant.

"They're all wearing masks. Men and women, they're all accomplices. Let none escape!" shouted Crassus.

A tremor swept through the audience as word spread. Many stood on benches to get a better look. Surrounding Crassus, a knot of bodyguards and senators congregated at the entrance of the underground corridor.

"Consider all the performers guilty, kill them!" ordered the captain, as the crowd began to panic. Spectators pushed to and fro like waves in a tempestuous sea, trying to avoid guards who, with drawn weapons, sought out anyone still masked or in costume.

Screams filled the amphitheater as bewildered actors pleaded with the consul's bodyguard before a gladius was thrust into them.

"He ran out the gate!" a man said to the captain of the elite guard. "I saw him just when the consul came out."

"What gate?" the officer said.

Excitedly, the man pointed to an exit now packed with dozens of people, all trying to flee the maelstrom. Alerted, the guards rushed forward, trampling anybody in their way.

*****

Bile rose in Retenius's throat. Where were Lucius Analius and Fannius Tryphon? Lutatius Catalus was supposed to be here if anything went wrong. There was nobody; they had fled at the first hint of failure. He could hear the panic behind him; surely, Crassus's troops would be close behind. Fear assaulted Retenius as he bolted down one alley, then another. His mind churned; with luck he might get away, but what if one of his accomplices were caught? They would blame him for everything to save themselves. Certainly, they had all run at the first sign of disaster. He would be the one identified, and Crassus would have him decapitated.

Retenius, his head pounding with fear, hated them all: Analius, Catalus and Tryphon. If he lived, he would make sure that they paid for their betrayal.

He cursed himself for having become entangled in the coup attempt—for concocting the whole ridiculous thing! Who, after all, did he really think he was? Yet at first, it had seemed so reasonable, so feasible. Wasn't Crassus hated by so many? Weren't there well-placed men who wanted him gone, and who would welcome the collaboration of an ambitious tribune?

The entire plot was all due to a chance conversation with disgruntled men whose ambitions far exceeded their merit. Retenius should have known that they were using him, that his presumed allies would panic and desert him with the first ill wind.

From the start it was folly to think that he, a man not even electable, could rise to prominence in the wake of such vermin. Spittle mixed with the tears of contempt and self-pity that streamed down his face. Retenius was ruined. He had become a tool, expendable debris in a hopelessly bungled coup. His world was rapidly coming apart.

For a fleeting moment Retenius thought about Livia, who was likely running for her life. How long would it be, he wondered, before she would be ripped open by a Praetorian's gladius?

Then there was the galling matter of the Legion. Retenius had inherited a fortune, played at the fringes of society with his father's money, and seduced every woman he could, including his own daughter. He was anything but a soldier, and yet a year or two in a peacetime army, romping about on a fine charger, had suddenly seemed a splendid way to ingratiate himself with the rich and famous. As a tribune and an officer, he would face none of the travail of a legionnaire. He would consort with other officers at drunken parties, and brag of female conquests over Campania wine and fine dinners. Retenius had envisioned himself in the exalted company of legates and fellow tribunes. Yes, they would revel in his tales and give envious looks of admiration.

Let them celebrate the success and boldness of his conquests, he had mused, both monetary and female. Moreover, he would make a show of military smartness on the field, in spotless armor polished by some hapless recruit. And he would ingratiate himself by cagily whispering tidbits of intelligence to important men, who would reward him smartly.

When his service was complete, Retenius had decided he would again run for the Senate, but this time he would flaunt his stint in the Legion. A little hyperbole as he boasted of heroics at arms would hardly be questioned.

But now the Legion had the taste of ash, and playing at soldier seemed laughable. It was all due to one legate's perverted sense of principle and a minor miscalculation on his part. Dozens, indeed hundreds, of recruits died in training; it was an accepted fact which every legate and training officer understood. Until they became legionnaires, they were expendable. Accidents happened routinely; Retenius had seen pathetic blunders and ineptitude on the part of boys attempting to become men. They died, and not a single centurion, much less a tribune, was ever punished.

Yet Retenius would be excoriated and banished before the assembled cohorts. He might even be flogged to death. He had to get away; his life could not possibly be over. There was more for him to enjoy and he desperately wanted to live. There were women and power still to be had. So he ran.

His mind churned through every possible scenario. His pursuers didn't know who he was, they hadn't seen his face. He could be anyone. He was anonymous, and yes, he would outrun them, outfox them. He had money; he would get to the docks at Ostia, find a ship, and sail somewhere, and if Livia still lived he would take her with him. She, too, would have to escape, and being with him would be her only salvation. They would sail for Egypt and live a luxuriant life on the Nile. That would solve everything. He would escape from the army, and the Legion would forget him. Retenius and Livia would make themselves unrecognizable, and who knows, someday in old age they might return to Rome. That too was possible.

Another few blocks must reveal an open door, thought Retenius: an alley, an escape. He had money in a pouch; surely, he could bribe someone to hide him until the hunt was abandoned.

The bloody knife was still in his grasp. How badly he wanted to drive the blade into the first person he would encounter, thrust it to the hilt and gleefully watch blood spurt into the street.

*****

Oil lamps cast deep shadows, while a handful of vendors awaited the theater crowds returning home. The patrons would be boisterous and arrive in large groups, since there was safety in numbers.

Gaius stood beside the alley where Caladria had told him to wait. She did not say why, and he knew better than to ask; he would never get a straight answer from her. With that girl, he realized, everything was a riddle. *That's the way she is,* he told himself. But he would not question her word, because it wasn't she who was really talking. Caladria was only a conduit; that much he knew.

A woman ran past not ten yards from him. She was almost a blur in the darkness; a bundle of cloth had been hastily wrapped about her body, as if she had just come from the baths and not taken time to dress. But the baths had been closed for hours. The woman wore no boots or sandals, and her feet barely touched the ground. She seemed terribly frightened; for a split second she turned, as if to see whether she was being pursued. Gaius watched and wondered if she, in her flight of terror, had even seen him.

*****

Retenius heard voices and the clacking sound of hobnail boots on the hard paving stones. He knew that sound, too well; every legionnaire wore those boots. The Praetorian Guard was coming, like wolves having caught the scent of their prey. He vowed that if cornered he would fight, even were the struggle short. He still had the knife. He saw one more street ahead, then a narrow alley. Something had to open up; he had to hide.

The tribune came to a doorway and pounded on it, but there was no answer and like all doors in Rome, it seemed, it was bolted shut. A dog howled; Retenius could imagine its gnashing teeth, its fetid breath, and he hurried on. A light appeared in a window high up. Again he banged on the door, but an old woman peered out, shook her head, and motioned at him to get away.

Hatred and fear consumed Retenius until he wanted to vomit. He could hear shouting now: an officer barking orders. They were closing in on him. The blisters on his feet had opened, and he felt the squishiness of hot blood in his shoes. Winded, and with a feeling of dread, he stumbled on.

Rounding a corner, he was astonished to see a man standing in the alley as if blocking his escape. In the dim light, Retenius saw that he wore a tunic, not a toga. Perhaps he was a slave or a libertus. Surely the man would make way; there was no reason for him to be waiting there. But the form did not budge. Retenius waved his arm, panting; the knife in his hand glinted in the wavering light. *Move or die*, thought Retenius; there was no time for anything else.

Vengeance overrode everything. Who would dare block the way of a tribune? Retenius summoned the last vestiges of his energy and charged.

The man drew a knife, a pugio, from a sheath and Retenius saw that his tunic was gathered at the waist by crossed belts. A legionnaire, Retenius realized. Why would a legionnaire be in the alley unless a cohort had been alerted? But there wouldn't have been just one man; the streets would be teeming with soldiers. Who was he; what did he want? What arrogance to defy a tribune, a noble patrician of the Equestrian class!

And then the light from the torches flickered across the soldier's face, and Retenius recognized Gaius.

Rage screamed within Retenius, burning in his throat. He raised his knife, bellowed, "You!" and lunged.

Retenius couldn't imagine how Gaius could have been there, in that exact spot, at that precise time, to block his escape. What had Livia said about Toronius's slave, the one who could see things? What had that demonic girl revealed to her? Was this all a plot to destroy him? What if Livia, feeling jilted, had conspired with his presumed allies to orchestrate the failure of his plot against Marcus Crassus? What if they had envisioned this outcome from the very beginning?

It hardly mattered now. All Retenius knew was that he should have murdered Gaius after his daughter's death. He blamed himself for not having made the proper sacrifices, for neglecting to say the proper prayers before the Lares.

No, it certainly didn't matter now, and never would again. Despite his rank and the armor he wore, Retenius was no soldier, and their fight was over almost before it began. Gaius dodged his inept downward thrust and moved in quickly, the pugio slicing deep into Retenius's chest. The tribune stiffened, and ineffectually raised his knife as a second thrust ripped open his stomach. This could not be happening; it was not real, thought the tribune. He felt himself sinking to his knees and saw the knife sliding out, withdrawing from his intestines. He stared at the blood-covered instrument. Disbelief spread across his face as he was assaulted by the sight of his own blood.

Gaius stepped back and observed Retenius dispassionately. There was no expression on his face; it was as if the legionnaire had turned to stone. Retenius did not expect compassion from the boy, but this assault was so cold, like a judgment handed down by the gods themselves. How could he, a tribune, a man hailed by crowds, be condemned by this boy?

The blackness was coming; Retenius had heard stories of what it might be like. The fear, like his blood, was seeping away too. There was nothing more they could do to Retenius, now; they could not hurt him further. He would not face the lions trained to eat human flesh, nor the hyenas that devoured prisoners while they were still alive. And there would be no banishment or whipping before the assembled legions.

Yet he didn't want to be seen like this, spewing his life out onto the filthy ground. Retenius wanted to disappear into the ether, push away the world, and see but remain unseen. How could he do that? he wondered. What if he could be a specter, a haunt—indeed, a ghost? Livia had alluded to the slave Caladria's ghosts, but Retenius had refused to believe in them. But now? As such an entity, he might even return to his own villa, watch for those who would dare to trespass, steal his wealth, or take up residence. He was a voyeur anyway; as a ghost, he might enjoy luscious sights and sounds for all eternity. What an intriguing thought. Yes, he mused faintly, he would return there and cast his spells forever. How delicious; he wanted that now.

The mask was still in one hand and all was fading. Retenius lifted the mask with its macabre grin and covered his face. And then the light went out.

*****

Gaius looked up and saw the approaching guard, turned, and glanced down the street. It was empty except for two bent women in hooded rags, who were picking over discarded clothing. One of them glanced at him. She motioned to her companion, and they slipped away. Gaius faced the oncoming Praetorians. It would be a very long night.

Chapter 23

Cringing in her bed, Livia existed in terror for five days, waiting for soldiers to pound upon the villa's gate. But they did not come, and eventually she found enough courage to venture into the atrium. Sitting on a marble bench, she stared into the pool of water lilies and pondered how it was that Caladria had just happened to be on the street when she made her maddened dash from the theater. How was it that the girl had a sack of ragged cloaks that disguised them from the Praetorians' eyes? She also wondered who the man was that she glimpsed that night. Above all, however, she worried about Retenius. Hopefully he'd lived even though he had bungled the assassination. Even more worrisome was the possibility that he had been captured and tortured and divulged the names of accomplices. Would Retenius, being torn apart by meat hooks, utter her name?

Livia hadn't heard from him, nor had she dared to ask about him at the villa. In fact she had hardly spoken since that night. Caladria put meals at Livia's door, and Livia took the food inside when the slave's footsteps faded away. Often she heard the heavy trod of Toronius and the lighter step of Apollodoros in the hallway, but refused to open her door or speak to either. She assumed they knew nothing about her role in the attempted coup but she could not be certain. If Caladria had any idea, she might have told Toronius. And the horrible thought came to her: what reward might her husband gain if he gave the consul her name?

She remembered what Toronius had said about the unwanted guests, weeks ago. She hadn't heard any new voices.

Finally, one morning a few days later, Livia approached her husband in the peristyle.

"Toronius," she said with a show of mild curiosity, "you once mentioned something about a couple coming here to live. I thought that they would have appeared by now, though I'm sure you ordered them away since we didn't invite anybody. I would cringe at the thought of a baby living here."

"Oh, they are here," he said with a sly grin. "In fact, they have been here for weeks."

"How could that be? I would have heard them; babies cry all night."

"This one's rather quiet and doesn't show himself much, but I rather like the parents. They come and go a lot."

"And you let them trespass on our property whenever they wish?"

"In a sense, yes."

Livia was perplexed and irritated by the bemused look on his face. She tilted her head and gave him an impatient look.

Toronius, meanwhile, was in no hurry to placate her. Her complicity with Retenius had put them both in danger, and had it not been for Caladria they would likely be dead. Of course he would never disclose that, at least, not yet. He was relieved that she had not been found and assumed that she didn't know that he knew.

He had had sleepless nights and even considered fleeing, but Caladria reassured him. Now, more than ever, he owed his wife nothing. Whether she knew it or not, she was deeply indebted to him and Caladria. So a bit of smugness toward her did not bother his conscience at all. In fact he took delight in her consternation. Their marriage had long been a cold relationship in which he had nothing to lose; every shred of caring had dissipated long before.

"What do you mean you like them?" Livia demanded, amazed and petulant. "Exactly what room are they taking over?"

"Room?"

"Yes, room, or do they live in the vomitorium or the ashes of that old barn?"

"They didn't like the barn. I offered them your cubiculum, but they wouldn't have that either," Toronius said with a matter-of-fact tone.

"How dare you offer them my bedroom? Where are they? I have a right to know!"

"A right? Hmm. I'm not so sure about that, my darling wife."

"Where are you going?" Livia shouted, as he walked out of the peristyle.

"I'm going to see how our guests are doing."

Maddened, but even more curious, Livia followed him past the orchard and across the field, wondering exactly where he could possibly be going. He said they weren't in the barn, she thought, but there was no other structure out there. She spied Caladria, but ignored her as usual.

Toronius stopped when he came to the girl sitting beneath her tree with its sweeping branches. "Is the family home?" he asked her.

"Yes, Master. They just came back with dinner. They're enjoying worms and field mouse, I think."

"Indeed," Toronius said, looking up as a feather floated down. "Have you seen the baby today?"

"Only once. I think he's afraid of heights."

"I am, too. I, with my splendid bulk, would not want to be up there, not even if I had wings."

"Master, you would need very big wings," Caladria said shaking her head woefully.

"What are you two idiots talking about?" demanded Livia.

Caladria gave the woman a long, thoughtful look, then pointed upward. A hawk spread its wings and swooped over the villa while its mate perched on a high branch.

"Birds?" said Livia.

"Not simply birds, my dear wife, they are our guests."

Livia stared at the hawks, then asked, "Should I thank you for this little charade?"

"No," said Toronius, turning away. "But you might thank

Caladria for saving your life."

*****

The thought of living happily with Retenius filled Livia's mind. She was safe now; the tumult over the plot must have subsided, although she had not ventured beyond the confines of the villa to find out for certain. Her existence had become claustrophobic. Surely Retenius had escaped, and life with him would be so much better. She would have him resign his military commission and they would travel to exotic places. She had heard of Gallia Cisalpina beside the high mountains and Illyricum across the Mare Hadriaticum, east of Italia. Retenius had even mentioned going to Cyrenaica west of Egypt on the coast of Africa.

Livia had waited long enough, she thought, and Retenius had done nothing to assuage her fears. Concerned for his safety, she considered going to the baths to see if he was there. It was strange that he had made no effort to contact her, not even through one of his slaves. Of course, it was possible that he thought it too dangerous to be seen with her so soon after the incident. Yes, she mused, that must be it; a matter of personal safety, his as well as hers.

Livia wondered if she had become a liability and, as such, a nonperson in his life. But that could only be for a short time; Retenius would not easily forget her. No, she would not go to the balneum, where he might expect to see her. Instead, she would boldly confront him in his own villa.

Retenius would have to explain himself to her, confess the entire scheme that had put her in such jeopardy, something he had merely glossed over before. And of course, he owed her money for her part whether the scheme had succeeded or not. Truly, he had put her life in danger and that would cost him greatly.

Toronius had said nothing about an assassination attempt on the consul, but surely, thought Livia, all of Rome must know by now. She didn't know if it had succeeded—after all, she had bolted during the first moments of the confrontation. She pondered what Caladria knew and what she might have told Toronius. Hadn't he said that Caladria had saved her life? Certainly he was referring to the night of the attempted coup. Did the slave girl possibly know anything? And worse, what if she knew it all?

There was only one way to find out, Livia surmised. She dressed in her finest stola, slipped out the slaves' gate, and hurried through the streets to Esquiline Hill and Retenius's villa.

It was already the seventh hour, and the slanting rays of the sun meant that she had started out far too late. She should not have had insisted on having Caladria fix her hair; the fat girl had make a total mess of it and then cried in her frustration. There would have to be a new slave, Livia told herself. Caladria simply did not have the creativity, the skill, or even the intelligence to perform her toilet. Angry at her own foolishness, Livia would have to come up with an excuse for the condition of her hair.

Such a thing should never happen again, she vowed. If she lived with Retenius as he had suggested, she would be provided with all the slaves she would ever need. That thought mollified her as she hurried up the hill to his front gate. She knew that she would encounter a slave guarding the villa, who would signal the servant inside to open the gate.

But there was no slave, and the gate had been flung wide open. Had the servant forgotten to lock it, she wondered as she peered into the spacious courtyard. She expected to see workers bustling about, attending to tree trimming or cleaning up after the horses. But there was no one, and no sound except that of a pack of scuffling dogs.

Livia's throat went dry as she picked her way past discarded clothing, crockery, and torn rolls of expensive papyrus. The barking grew louder and three dogs ran out of the villa, its doors open to the elements. One mutt gripped a sack in its mouth and vainly struggled to keep it as two others snatched it away. The sack ripped open and spoiled ham tumbled out, followed by silver plate and a pearl necklace. The dogs were strays; none of them belonged to the household. Livia had no idea of how long they had been there or why nobody had kicked them out.

"Is anybody here?" She called from the open door. "Retenius?" There was no answer. With a seeping dread she stepped inside, avoiding feces, broken pottery and a table with a broken leg. Everything was strewn about as if there had been a raid by Thracians, eager for Roman plunder. But so much was still here, she thought. Why would thieves leave so much behind? Had the guards arrived and chased them away? Priceless artifacts, gold jewelry, and silver urns had spilled across the mosaic floors. Why would any thugs simply discard such valuables, when they were right there for the taking? Had somebody stopped them? Was it Retenius? But if he had stopped the thefts, why hadn't his slaves put everything back in place? And where were his slaves, anyway? Where was Retenius? Nothing seemed right. Indeed, it appeared that something had gone terribly wrong.

There was no logic to it. It was cold in the house, even though the day's heat lingered.

"Retenius, are you here?" she called, now in a frightened voice. There was no reply, at least, nothing she could immediately sense. But there had been something, maybe a sigh, or a laugh, or perhaps even a very quiet hiss. It was almost inaudible, but it was there.

Livia looked about and realized that a fortune lay at her feet, a fortune for the taking. She had no idea as to why it would still be here, but with Retenius, the slaves, and the overseer gone, Livia could have anything she wanted.

If he were truly dead, none of what remained in the villa would be of any value to him. And if he would not have it, she would. It was hers; in fact, Retenius owed it to her. Hadn't he said that she would be awarded a small fortune for her involvement?

Livia was alone and there was no one to stop her. She called his name again—another chance for him to see her, to answer, but he was nowhere about. The obvious came to her mind: he was dead. His chance of escaping had been minimal at best. If the Praetorian Guard had not killed him, he had probably been murdered by his accomplices. Assassination was such a common thing. Surely they would not want him to divulge their plot, and a mere tribune would be expendable. How much she would truly miss her former lover was something she would ponder at a later date.

Livia began to rummage through the sacks hastily left behind. She dumped out objects of lesser value, conscious of how much she could actually tote with her. She examined everything and placed the most precious items in one sack, then another. It was getting late and she thought of returning the next day, perhaps with a cart for a greater load. All this would have to be hidden somewhere safe; it certainly could not be stored at her villa. She could never allow Toronius to get wind of this treasure's existence. Not only might he claim it, but he would ask questions, and that would be intolerable.

Livia thought of taking what she could and leaving the rest, but it seemed ludicrous to abandon such treasures to just anyone who might venture in. No, she would stay the night, hide everything in Retenius's dungeon, and leave in the morning. Then she would make as many trips to the Forum Magnum as necessary, selling off the valuables for coinage.

She had spent many nights in the man's bed, and the thought of another night surrounded by her new possessions was terribly exciting.

Livia wandered from one room to the next, evaluating rugs hung on the walls. No Roman would consider laying them upon the floor, to be stained by inebriated diners or their scavenging dogs.

Wafting from the bedroom there was a lingering scent, a perfume she vaguely recognized. She cautiously entered the cubiculum, remembering that the perfume had once graced Retenius's daughter, Cornelia. Tiny, multi-hued bottles were still arranged on shelves here. Obviously the thieves hadn't gotten this far, but she was pleased that they hadn't.

Livia passed each bottle under her nose, selecting those that pleased her most, then on second thought grabbed them all and dumped them in her sack. This room, like several of the others, felt strangely cold. Again she sensed something, a presence of some sort, as if someone was looking over her shoulder. Livia warily turned, but no one was there.

Suddenly she gasped at a light touch upon her breasts. "Oh!" she exclaimed, as fingers slid down to her belly, unseen but effortlessly proceeding between her thighs, touching her sex. There was another intimate touch, then the wetness of a tongue. She knew the technique; he had done it to her time after time. But before this she had delighted in it.

"Retenius, no!" she screamed as hands slid over her buttocks. She backed into a corner, clutching the sack of gems and bottles close, and pleaded with the invisible specter that groped her. She turned to run and felt a heave on the sack. She would not relinquish it. It was hers, not his. It didn't belong to him anymore.

"Mine!" she screamed. "You owe me, you promised."

"No! It all stays. Nothing leaves my house!" The low guttural voice, barely audible, was very real.

A heavy tray filled with denarii lay ten feet from her. The coins glinted in the weak light. Suddenly they rustled, and Livia was stunned to see a clutch of them rise and fly at her. Most clattered against the wall. Livia bolted for the door, but it slammed in her face.

She turned and with fury screamed, "You miserable bastard! I'm glad you're dead!" Then, to her horror, the tray with the remaining coins lifted into the air and flew at her with malevolent force. She stood paralyzed, expecting it to slice into her face, but the tray suddenly veered in its path, as if knocked away by an invisible stick.

The image of Retenius, blood oozing from wounds, appeared and lifted a chair. It hung in midair before it was snatched from his grasp. His image vanished. There was a swishing of frigid air, followed by sounds of a frantic tussle. The hysterical voice of Retenius became ever more distant, and then it was gone. The room had become dark, the sun having dipped beneath Esquiline Hill. Livia jumped when a soft, disembodied hand, white as clay but strangely warm, took her wrist. Fingers tugged at her. It was insistent, and Livia allowed herself to be pulled from the room.

"Throw away the sack," said a voice beside her.

"It's mine, it's mine," wailed Livia. "It's owed to me."

"It's cursed. Leave it, my father will not let it go, not without vengeance." the voice said. The scent that Livia had detected earlier stained the air. Tears streaming down her face, Livia swung the sack and watched it clatter against the wall. The girl's hand disappeared, and Livia found herself running through the gate, bolting down the hill in the enfolding gloom.

*****

Again, Livia found herself huddled and shivering beneath her blankets. Her sleep had been fitful and replete with horrors. She had imagined herself running through corridors, walls, and doors that appeared from nowhere. An incorporeal figure tore past her, trailing shreds of fiber. Livia woke in a sweat and lay motionless in her bed. The terrifying images assailed her like peals of thunder.

Finally she decided that the macabre visions were simply a terrible nightmare. Nothing about it was real, not the hand upon her wrist, nor the ghostly sounds, not even the coins hurled at her. Believing in any of it was madness. Perhaps she had drunk too much wine before retiring; it would not have been the first time, and her dreams were rarely pleasant anyway.

Livia sighed, rose from her bed, and decided to venture out. It was, after all, a new day, and the night's terrors would surely evaporate like morning fog. She selected her favorite stola, the one she had worn the previous day, and slipped it on. Then, taking a copper mirror, she examined herself, her composure having returned.

She was, Livia reminded herself, a Roman lady of worth, an astonishing beauty, and a patrician who resided in a fine villa. An exciting life could still be ahead for her, and all would be well. No one knew of her complicity in the attempted coup. Indeed, she mused, her prospects were bright. She would enjoy the morning sun.

A glint of metal shone in the mirror. Livia looked closely at the image, then at a crease in her stola. Her fingers touched a hard, round object, and a jolt of fear coursed through her. Frantically, she brushed the folds and a half-dozen denarii clattered to the floor. Livia stepped back, the images of the previous night suddenly wrapping her in cold, penetrating horror. She screamed, sank to the floor, and lay there for the remainder of the day.

*****

"Which one of you worthless mud rats is Gaius Septimius Aquila?" the praefectus castrorum shouted.

"Worthless?" muttered Tiberius Granculus under his breath. "Who's that old fart calling 'worthless'? Just two weeks ago they were saying we were Rome's finest. We were spotless, magnificent."

A peal of raucous laughter accompanied by disgruntled banter rose from the trench where the eighty men of the cohort toiled in knee-deep mud and slime. An ancient clay pipe had broken, flooding the latrine and adjacent field. It would take all day to dig out the pipe, muck out the trench, and make the repairs. The onerous task fell to the newest legionnaires. They were fodder for catcalls and snickering from passing veterans.

"Where's Gaius Septimius, come show yourself," barked the most senior veteran of the legion.

"I'm Gaius Septimius," Gaius said, feeling anything but a hero, much less spotless or magnificent.

The praefectus castrorum in his immaculate tunic stared at the mud-encased legionnaire and declared, "Great Jupiter, Mars, and Cloacina, you are the filthiest, worst-stinking piece of shit I've ever seen."

"But he's our hero, sir, Corona Civica and all that," crowed Lucius Galium. The testament was echoed by Adolphus Septemius as they all slung mud and feces in the trench. An avalanche of slop turned the legionnaires into a dung-covered mass of howling youths.

"Barbarians!" the veteran screamed. "Stop this idiocy! Gaius Septimius, clean up and report to the legate. And do it now."

"Oh are you in trouble," said Antony Venatus, wiping the fetid mud from his nostrils.

"Maybe, but at least I can wash this shit off me, Venatus. Another hour in this muck, and you'll stink for the rest of your life."

"Tell the general we're ready for very close inspection," shouted Lucius, who, to universal disbelief, had turned into a healthy if not totally dedicated legionnaire.

Since he had returned from leave, Gaius had found himself watched by officers and visiting senators. He was wary of the scrutiny and surprised that he had not been questioned further about the night he killed Retenius. The Praetorian Guardsmen had cautioned silence, but those in his contubernium gave him strange looks whenever he was observed by high-ranking officials.

"What the hell have you done now, pissed off a consul or something?" said Adolphus Septemius, who apparently had suddenly found it advantageous to be in the company of one who had been awarded Rome's highest honor.

A concern crossed Gaius's mind, as he scrubbed away the mud and donned a fresh tunic. Who were these senators; were they friends of Marcus Crassus, or a potential threat? But the consul was alive, Gaius had seen him that night beside his bodyguard, and surely he would have dealt with his enemies by now. If Gaius had been perceived as one, he would have died long ago. So why the scrutiny?

*****

Gaius was standing over the body of Retenius when the Praetorian Guard arrived, followed by the consul and a few of his retinue a few moments later. The blood was still on his knife. The guard captain, carrying a torch, held it up to Gaius's face, then scanned down to his crossed belts.

"I'll take the pugio," he said, holding out his hand.

Gaius passed the blade to him, and the Praetorian asked, "Why did you kill him?"

"He attacked me. That's his knife," Gaius said, pointing to the blade that had skittered against the wall.

A senator approached and peered at Gaius. "Where do I know you from?"

"You know this legionnaire?" Crassus asked, a bloodstain seeping through his hastily bandaged shoulder.

"I've seen him before, Consul. He's not an accomplice, I'm sure of it. Now I remember," said the senator, still squinting into Gaius's face. "I recognize you. You're the one awarded the Corona Civica at the legionnaire graduation. I was there. Yes, your name is..."

"Gaius Septimius Aquila, sir."

Turning to the consul, the senator said, "He was awarded the coronet by the legate, Leptus Agina Domatius of the VII Claudia."

"Well, that's splendid and I'm grateful, but who is the bastard that tried to kill me?"

The torch was lowered to the prostrate figure, and the captain removed the mask.

"Dometius Scipio Retenius!" exclaimed Crassus quietly, as he leaned over the body.

"Excellency, you know this man?"

"Of course—a scheming, devious rat, and a fool. Exactly what would he have gained by my death? Did he honestly think he or his cronies could replace me?" Crassus winced at the pain in his shoulder and sighed deeply. "Are there any others left?"

"We killed all the actors, sir, anyone we suspected. But there may be accomplices who weren't in the theater," replied the officer.

"There was a woman involved, supposedly from a brothel and wearing a mask," said another senator.

"We killed three or four women in the theater, but I don't know if any of them were specifically implicated," said the captain, who judiciously asked nothing about the prostitute. Not that it would have been a moral stain, but Crassus's easy yielding to temptation might indicate a lack of judgment, something he wouldn't want his detractors to utilize.

"I expect a thorough search," ordered Crassus. "Arrest anybody involved, interrogate them, and bring them to me. I expect to witness their executions. But do it quietly. I must know everything, but I want this incident buried. It will not happen again."

Certainly, word of the wounded consul, the killing of presumed accomplices, and the ensuing panic were already the hottest topics in Rome, and Crassus knew that no amount of obfuscation could stem rumors. But he would try to brush it off as he did with his fires and property schemes.

Redirecting his attention, he turned to Gaius and gave him a long hard stare.

"Exactly why are you here, and what do you know?" demanded the Consul, still shaken by his near assassination.

"I'm on leave, sir; I have a pass," Gaius answered, handing the Praetorian captain a slip of papyrus. "I'm visiting my family and took a shortcut through this alley. It's the fastest way."

Crassus mulled this over. "You knew Retenius. I heard that you killed two of his gladiators." It was neither praise nor condemnation.

"I did, because they were about to murder one of my tent mates."

"So Retenius had it in for you, is that it?"

"Sir, it's possible that he wanted revenge but I was blocking his escape, here. He recognized and tried to kill me. He failed."

"So you killed the man who tried to kill me," said the consul.

"Sir?" said Gaius incredulously.

"The tribune you gutted attacked me less than an hour ago. The mask hid his face so I didn't know who he was. I only wish we had been able to interrogate him," said Crassus. He thought for a moment then went on, "I owe you my gratitude, even though you didn't kill him on my behalf."

"Sir, I'm gratified that you are safe," said Gaius stiffly, as if overwhelmed by the thought that he was speaking to one of the two consuls of Rome, a man with nearly infinite power.

The consul motioned for the guard captain to return the pugio to Gaius.

"You are dismissed. Return to your family," the captain ordered.

"And stay safe, Gaius Septimius Aquila. We may need you again someday," said Consul Marcus Crassus.

"I'll try, Excellency," said Gaius, as he walked down the narrow alley, on his way to Junia's house.

*****

Anger in the city had been building for weeks, and when food riots erupted, the city guardsmen were overwhelmed by the thousands who broke into bakeries and grain warehouses in the port of Ostia. Smoke from dozens of fires clouded the azure sky, and squads of firefighters scrambled from one blaze to the next. Bakers, mobbed and beaten by Rome's citizenry, could only wring their hands and proclaim their innocence.

"It's the Cilicians! They're the ones to blame, not us. We don't raid the shipments, we're not the pirates," they lamented.

"But you raise the prices and no one can afford bread," came the furious response.

Watching from the walls of Junia's modest villa, Gaius shook his head. "Something's got to be done before the whole city burns down. Do you have enough grain for a few months?"

"Perhaps," answered his aunt. "We also have the vegetable garden. Tacitus and I won't starve, like the people in the insulae."

"Unless mobs break into the villas. I'd stay here to guard the house, but my furlough is up today."

"We'll be all right. If things get bad I'll go to your father's villa."

Gaius ran his fingers through his son's curly blond hair, and gave Junia a hug. "Then I'll be going," he said. "It will take an entire legion to end this rioting."

Putting the toddler down, Junia kissed him on the cheek and replied, "Come back soon, this boy's a handful."

*****

Gaius stood at the legate's door in a clean tunic. "The general will see you now," said a veteran legionnaire. Then in an aside he added, "Be damn sharp in there, or it's your ass."

"Ah, you're here," said Leptus Agina Domatius, looking Gaius up and down. "A little mud never hurts a soldier. You'll probably eat a lot of it in the next twenty years." He then held up a sheet of papyrus. "You've certainly ingratiated yourself since receiving the Corona Civica."

"Sir?"

"This letter is from Consul Marcus Crassus, no less, and he wants you promoted, a reward for vivisecting the exalted tribune, Retenius. How the hell you just happened to be in the right place at the right time is something I'd like to know. Unfortunately, there's no time for pleasant discourse."

"I don't expect any favors, sir."

"Doesn't matter what you expect. I was about to promote you to junior centurion, anyway. That's one hell of an honor for a man just out of training. Most legionnaires, even after twenty years, never get beyond immunes rank. But I witnessed you in battle against experienced gladiators. You earned that Corona, and you have a talent for putting sharp things in people."

Domatius turned to the praefectus castrorum and asked, "Is that idiot Tecleatus still in the infirmary?"

"Yes, sir," replied the senior veteran. "And the medicus says he'll never make a full recovery. Word is, we'll have to discharge him with a pension. If you ask me, General, it was his own damn fault. I'd have him banished to the Gates of Hercules."

"Being of congenial mind, I'm sure you would. But it's his word against the navy dolts, and I'll take his," sighed the legate. Then turning to Gaius he said, "Centurion First Class Tecleatus got into a drunken brawl with a bunch of sailors, and has more broken bones than most legions have common sense. He's not coming back, and we can't get any replacements. It's all about this Cilician piracy and Pompey's mobilization. We're throwing together everything we've got, one hundred and twenty thousand men. So I need a starter centurion, and that's you. Get your kit together and report to the junior centurions' barracks.

Dismissed."

Gaius saluted and turned to leave, when the legate stopped him. "By the way, you're entitled to an aide. Do you have a preference?"

"Yes, sir. Legionnaire Appian Dio, the cornicen. We've known each other since childhood."

The legate glanced at the praefectus castrorum, who merely shrugged.

"Fine, but he still sounds the commands when we're on the field. I can't replace him, either. You have eight centurion grades above you, including the primus pilum, so pay attention —because we're going to war."

*****

"I must be fucking blessed!" said an astonished Appian Dio. "I can't believe that you, the kid who couldn't fight or screw two years ago, are now my boss, and a centurion with a transverse crest on his helmet. I almost shit when I heard it."

"It was a complete surprise to me. You'll tent with me, but if you snore you sleep outside," said Gaius as they hurried to their new lodgings.

"Of course. You know how much I love cold, wet, miserable weather. Excellency, I promise—"

"Don't 'Excellency' me. Now tell me, do you know Justinian Septus, Centurion Second Class?"

"Your immediate superior? Yeah, he was best friends with Tecleatus, and won't be throwing you a grand cena with dancing girls."

"So I have another enemy?"

"You're good at collecting them. He's not really a total ass, just a little pompous. Try not to put your gladius through him." Then as an afterthought he added, "If you can help it."

*****

"So you're our newly minted centurion first rank," said Justinian Septus. As usual, he was out of sorts but wary of insulting the man who, rumor now had it, had killed at least a dozen men, maybe more.

439

"I am, by order of the legate," said Gaius. "It was something I had no control over."

"Yes, of course," Septus said testily. "Well, you've got a lot to learn. You know that I would rather have Tecleatus here. He had experience in real war."

"The legate said we're going into one, so I guess I'll get that experience very soon," said Gaius, standing a head taller than his superior.

"Somebody had to take Tecleatus's place," pointed out Appian Dio. "And one thing you won't have to teach this newly-minted centurion is how to fight."

"Well," said Septus, not ready to concede, "it's one thing to take on a man in single combat. Then you only worry only about yourself. It's another to lead a cohort against a bunch of screaming barbarians. I know. I've been there. We'll just have to see how you do. You know that the centurion's place in formation is outside and to the right of the men. It's a nicely exposed position—don't count on a long life."

"You're still alive," said Gaius.

"I don't appreciate smart remarks." Septus scraped his boot into the dirt. After a moment of reflection he said, "You must work with me, or you'll be back in the ranks. You inherit Tecleatus's gear: centurion helmet, armor, cloak, and all. Everything will be moving faster now. You weren't at officer's call this morning, so I'll tell you the agenda. And this is for your ears, not the troops."

*****

Campus Martius was too small for all the arriving legions; as darkness enveloped the field, Gaius could see campfires for miles around.

"You saw the riots, didn't you?" asked the other centurion. Not waiting for a reply, he continued, "They were the tipping point. The Cilician pirates are from Asia Minor. Not only did they cut off the grain shipments, but they raided the port of Ostia and took Romans for ransom. They even captured that young general, Gaius Julius Caesar. He had to be paid for, and getting him back wasn't cheap. The word is, we're going to annihilate them."

"They have over a thousand ships and practically control the Mediterranean. Triremes, biremes, fast riverboats, you name it," said Appian Dio. "And they're the same people who were going to help Spartacus until we bought them off."

"They've been too cozy with Mithridates of Pontus and we've had a few scraps with his boys," added Septus.

"I was a recruit, so I don't know the specifics," said Gaius.

"Well, I do," said Justinian. "The Senate didn't want to give Pompey the power he needs to exterminate the Cilicians; they're afraid of one man having too much control. So the tribune Aulus Gabinus, Pompey's old buddy, bypassed the Senate and went straight to the popular assembly. They have the ear of the commoners, and they want grain, so they've granted Pompey the right to command the army. He's also received five hundred ships and five thousand cavalry from all the provinces. Besides that, Pompey's personal forces have taken control of the entire Mediterranean and all enemy lands within fifty miles of the sea. That's what this mobilization is all about."

"When does it start?" asked Gaius.

"I don't know. It's being kept secret, but the sooner the better," said Septus.

"If Pompey can pull it off, he'll be damn popular," said Appian Dio.

"Popular, hell," said Septus. "He'll have a Triumph through the streets of Rome, right up to the Temple of Jupiter. He'll be proclaimed a god and have statues in his honor."

"So all he has to do is win a war," said Gaius.

"That's it," said his immediate superior. "And we're going to be right in the middle of it."

Chapter 24

The riots persisted, but Livia was frugal and instructed Caladria to supplement their bread with the villa's vegetables and orchard fruit. Though she could see the plumes of smoke near the Tiber it appeared that most grain depots had not been looted due to reinforced constabulary. There was still great anger and frustration in the streets, but the citizenry, though hardly mollified, was aware of Pompey's enlistment of a great army, as well as his determination to defeat the pirates and reclaim the Mare Nostrum.

It was indeed a law that no Roman army could cross the Rubicon River or enter Rome except for during a Triumph, when soldiers would enter unarmed. Nevertheless, the thousands of legionnaires camped just beyond the city's walls gave pause to any organized rampage.

Except for her concern for their dwindling food supplies, Livia felt that she had nothing more to fear. The ghost of Retenius in his ransacked villa had not followed to haunt her nights. The arrival of the unwanted 'houseguests' she loathed turned out to be a harmless pair of hawks and their offspring.

Livia had spoken little to Toronius and had been surprised to see him hunched over with Apollodoros, laboriously reading works in Latin and Greek. It was so unusual for him, she mused. Indeed, he would have derided the thought a year ago. In some ways her husband seemed a different man now, certainly less violent, less devious. Maybe Caladria had influenced him, Livia thought, or maybe he was just getting old and wary of falling prey to those more unscrupulous than he.

Nowadays Toronius sat in the peristyle with his Greek slave, studiously deciphering the hidden meanings and innuendoes of Herodotus, Thucydides, Socrates and Plato. How different her life might have been, she mused, if her husband had been that way in the beginning. But she reflected that living with a scholar steeped in his scrolls would have been a total bore. There was no fortune to be made in ancient texts, and she enjoyed the things that money could buy—even money illicitly acquired. And it was never too late to try to gain it again.

*****

The intellectual pursuits Toronius shared with Apollodoros hardly kept him from thinking about Caladria's prophecy: the woman with the magnificent body who would come to his bed to fulfill his every delight.

Alone, he paced the streets and the gardens of the great city, visited the baths, and studied every beautiful woman that passed. But none gave him more than a curious glance, and he began to think that Caladria had been teasing him. And yet, on the outside chance that she was right, as she was in so many cases, he plodded along, stopping to stare, and received stares in turn. People might think him strange or even demented. Yet daily he set out on his hopeful quest.

*****

Livia lay in her bed until the fifth hour, when the sun was already high. She felt good, secure in the knowledge that she had escaped capture and probable death from the assassination plot. No one had hammered on the gate in the dead of night. The news of the attempted coup was being overshadowed by the food riots. Bit by bit, she learned that everybody involved in the Crassus incident had been slain. Everybody, that was, except her.

Such amazing luck nearly prompted her to make a sacrifice at the Temple of Fortuna, but Livia had never cared to give precious coins to the gods; they had not come to her aid in the past. No, she decided that she would celebrate her fortune by purchasing a new slave. At first she thought of a girl with skills in hairstyling and makeup. But then a more enjoyable thought came to mind, indeed, a deliciously lascivious one. She would buy a handsome young man who would, in a very sexual sense, take the place of Retenius. Toronius might be surprised by her choice, but he wouldn't dare object since they had not sex for so many years.

The sun glinted down through a high window of her cubiculum, illuminating the expensive mosaic table beside her bed. It was cluttered with perfume vials, a copper mirror, and a shallow but finely decorated marble container. The day's light moved like a finger across its contents and touched a cache of coins. It seemed to Livia that the sun's rays were playfully toying with the pieces of metal, as if asking, "What pleasure will these bring you?"

Languidly, Livia reached for the coins and dropped them one by one onto her blanket. They had been hurled at her by the angry specter of Retenius, but that hoary thing was no more and the coins, slipping into a harmless pile, were hers, all hers.

With a sudden burst of energy, she grabbed the denarii, flung off the covers, and with exuberance she had not known in months, prepared to assault the Forum.

*****

It was unusual for Caladria to plop her mass down beside the villa's main gate, and Livia, with Apollodoros in tow, was surprised to find her there.

"Caladria, what are you doing sitting on the ground like that?" she asked.

The girl was slowly lolling back and forth and rather than answering, said only, "Mistress, don't go. You should not go today."

"Whatever are you talking about? Of course I'm going, why shouldn't I?"

"Don't go today. Just don't go, "Caladria repeated, oblivious to Livia's consternation.

"Open the gate for me, Apollodoros," Livia commanded.

"Mistress, if Caladria says—"

"Stop it. I'm already late, and the best ones might have been sold."

If Caladria's apprehension seemed ominous to Livia she ignored it. She would allow nothing to interfere with the excitement she contemplated. Despite the girl's fortuitous intervention on the night of the attempted coup, Livia had no intention of curtailing her most intimate desires because of a simpleminded slave. Yes, she could apparently speak to the dead, but whatever was bothering her now could certainly wait.

Indeed, Caladria was becoming a nuisance with her prophecies. "Houseguests," Livia said to herself with disgust. Why, she wondered, would Toronius even keep the girl? Surely it was not for sex. How bizarre it had become to see him sitting with the nearly mute slave, waiting for another epiphany. The silliness of it would be an embarrassment to any guest. But it had been over a year since any invitations had been extended, and Toronius appeared no longer interested in hosting grand cenas. Certainly, Livia presumed, he had nothing to sell and no one to impress.

The auction wasn't far and Livia, irritated by the hesitant pace of Apollodoros, reprimanded him in her shrill voice. "Hurry up, you're wasting my time."

Catching up to her, he said, "We should take a different route, Mistress, there's a commotion up ahead. I smell smoke."

"It's nothing," replied Livia, "it won't block our way. Now hurry."

What had been a minor disturbance in front of a bakery had quickly grown into a pushing, shoving mob that made the street impassable.

There was a law, considering the hills and the narrowness of the streets, prohibiting wagons from bringing produce into the city during daylight hours. However the rule was often ignored, especially if a wheel was broken or a horse became lame. Uphill from the bakery was parked a large cart, sitting at an angle because of missing wheels and with a load of barrels, its broken axle propped up on bricks. A stone had been placed under the one remaining wheel to keep it from rolling downhill, but its owner and his oxen were nowhere about.

Swept up by the surging crowd, Livia and Apollodoros passed the cart and were, to her immense frustration, prevented from going any further. In the tumult, someone kicked the wedged stone out from beneath the cart's wheel. There was a sudden cry, followed by shouts and screams as the heavy conveyance gained momentum as it rolled down the hilly street. People panicked and threw themselves into shop doorways and behind whatever tables and stonework they could find.

Barrels, piled upon one another, tumbled off the wagon, gathered speed, and mowed down those in their path. Caught in the terrified crowd, Livia turned to see a barrel strike a wall, then spin and shatter into a dozen pieces. Apollodoros rushed to shield her from the flying debris, but the jagged shards flew everywhere. Livia raised her arms, but to no avail as staves bombarded her. Screaming, she fell as more barrels, along with the splintered cart, slammed into the hapless mob.

It was over quickly. Dozens were dead and maimed. The cries of the wounded mixed with laments for the deceased as tangled bodies were separated. Appeals for help were sounded up and down the street. Apollodoros, with a fractured arm, knelt over Livia, who was barely conscious. She was covered with blood, hers as well as that of others around her. He knelt beside her and extracted a jagged piece of wood that had pierced her arm. Ripping his tunic, he staunched the flow and heard her say in a weak voice, "Apollodoros, take me home."

*****

"Who's Aspacia?" asked Justinian Septus as he and four other centurions accosted Appian Dio outside their barracks.

Puzzled, he looked at the unsmiling men. "Sir, it's not for me to discuss the name or the fate of the lady. I suggest that you ask centurion Gaius Septimius Aquila."

"Oh we'll do that for sure, but first we want to get it from you, since you've known him all your life."

"She was his wife. She died after delivering his child. Why do you ask?"

Septus looked at him with astonishment. "Are you deaf? The man kept us up all night with his ravings."

"I guess I'm a sound sleeper. I didn't hear anything. What did he say?"

"By the gods, man, it was 'Dear Aspacia, I will have vengeance!'"

"He kept saying 'Unfair'," another answered. "And 'Don't even try to stop me.'"

"And then he said, 'I'll kill, I'll kill,' dozens of times," added an exasperated Justinian Septus.

"He even drew his knife," said one. "We were awake all night with our pugios drawn. We didn't know who he would try to kill. But we know that he's good at it," said a centurion fourth class.

"He never hurt anyone in his barracks when he was a legionnaire," said Appian Dio. "You have nothing to worry about."

"But we can't get any rest, trying to sleep with one eye open! So we've decided that you two will sleep in a storeroom or a tent."

"Do you want me to tell him that?" he asked.

"No, that's my job," said Septus.

Appian Dio began to walk away when the centurion stopped him, asking, "Is that why he joined, because of a dead wife?"

Appian paused before replying, "Again, sir, you will have to ask him but he had a broken heart. Now, I doubt he has one at all. And yes, he joined the Legion to kill. He'll do that quite efficiently for as long as he lives. I suggest you don't get in his way."

*****

Gaius had never beheld anything like it. Pompey's armada stretched from one horizon to the next. Massive, three-decker quinqueremes, each with banks of oars, three hundred oarsmen, and one hundred and twenty marines, were in the van. The fleet also consisted of transports and supply vessels, as well as the two-deck biremes, which acted as scouts and interceptors.

It was to one of these vessels that Gaius and his cohort had been assigned. He stood at the stern with Appian Dio and the ship's captain, who had introduced himself only as Paranulus. The captain eyed the mainsail, saw it luff in the breeze, and barked an order to the sailor at the tiller whose sideboard steered the warship.

"We only have half as many oars as the heavies, but we're lighter and faster," said the captain. "I expect we'll be engaging the Cilicians near their port of Coracesium. We should be there in two hours."

"I didn't see any ships with ram bows," said Appian Dio.

"And you won't either, at least not on Roman ships. The Greeks did that; we tried it, but as a tactic it's just as dangerous to the rammer as the rammed. A glancing blow is no good; it's got to be straight on. If there's maneuvering room, an enemy ship could easily turn away. Then there's the matter of withdrawing the ram, which means backing all the oars and pulling away in the middle of a battle. It's nothing I would want to do. Besides, even if they're holed, these ships don't easily sink. They'll fill with water, all right, but it sometimes will take days or weeks before they go under. Especially if they're made with dry wood."

"Then what's the best way to fight, if you don't ram?" asked Gaius.

"We come alongside real fast, pull in our oars, and shear off theirs. Then we toss hooks to pull their ship fast to ours, and your boys scramble onto their decks, gladii drawn. Most people we fight are poorly armed, poorly trained, and they have to maneuver between the arms and legs of rebellious slaves."

"But why don't you drop a ramp on them and just have us run across?" asked Appian Dio, as a pod of dolphins leapt before the ship's bow.

"The corvus with the spike? We tried putting those on our ships, and lost an entire fleet during the first Punic War against Hannibal. The damn things work just fine in calm seas, but they're unwieldy. They had to be lashed upright when sailing, which makes a ship top-heavy. You couldn't easily cut them away, and when he hit rough weather, our galleys rolled over and everyone drowned. We do learn from our mistakes.

"Another misconception," said the loquacious captain, "is that we use fire; again, too dangerous, especially in a high sea. But we do fire all those catapults on the deck between the rowers. That's where our marines come in."

"They're different than the scorpions the army uses," said Gaius.

"Yes, they are. Yours throw a bolt in a high arc—and that's fine against massed troops. But ships are too hard to hit that way. Of course, archers can do that when we get close, but each of the ballistae can fire a bolt or chunks of iron and stone, in a flat trajectory, almost three hundred yards. That's real bad for rowers; they get shredded."

"The fleet is closing now," called the mate, and the captain turned, shouting to the drummers, "Racing beat; I want to see a good wake behind us."

With the faster beat on the drums, a great shout went up from the rowers, three men on each oar, as they accepted the challenge. "That's it, lads," shouted Paranulus to the half-naked men.

"You never use slaves, do you?" asked Appian Dio.

"Never. All rowers on Roman ships are navy. They're volunteers, just like you legionnaires. The pirates use slaves, and they have to be chained because they're a liability. No slave will put his heart into rowing; they have nothing to gain. My men are all loyal, there's no need for chains." He bared his teeth in a ferocious grin. "They're also armed, and will join your legionnaires if needed."

The bireme Gaius and his cohort occupied were part of a sixty-ship squadron that Pompey had directed toward pirates who had wintered in Sicily. By launching his assault early, he caught the Cilicians while they were still making preparations for their spring and summer campaign. Pompey's arrival panicked the pirates and, raggedly formed, they were driven from their harbors into the arms of a waiting squadron.

*****

Months earlier, legionnaires had heard the story of the beautiful Aspacia, and many woke in the night to hear their centurion speak her name in his sleep. In their first engagement against the pirates, Gaius shouted her name again and again as they stormed over the gunwales. "*Aspacia!*" became the battle cry of the cohort, as one enemy ship after another was wrested from its crew.

The pirates engaged the Roman vessels, but they were used to raids against poorly armed merchantmen. The ferocity of thousands of trained legionnaires caused most Cilicians to beg for quarter or plunge into the sea.

Pompey recombined his fleet off Spain and swept down the Mediterranean, where their outposts were torched, thereby eliminating the threat to Rome's wheat shipments. To speed the reduction of the pirate menace, Pompey showed clemency by offering the Cilicians land in exchange for their ships. Word spread quickly, and thousands of pirates, who would otherwise be facing certain death or a life of slavery, gratefully accepted his offer, thereby terminating the war in four months' time.

Laurels were awarded for distinguished service, and Gaius's leadership earned him a position of centurion second class, with a bronze phalera attached to his armor and a medallion sewn to his military belts.

"We have a four-day furlough. What are you going to do?" Appian Dio asked Gaius, following the celebrations and outpouring of gratitude as food poured into Rome.

"I'm going to visit Junia and see my son, and then go to my father's villa."

"To see if he found the woman Caladria told him about?"

"You heard about that?"

"Your father mentioned it before we sailed. He was very excited."

"At least it's keeping him from anything nefarious," said Gaius.

"Apollodoros says he's a changed man, reading the classics and such."

"I wouldn't know. I haven't heard from the Greek since we sailed."

*****

"He's adorable, but the most willful and stubborn child I've ever known!" raged Junia as she tried to comb Tacitus's unruly hair. "Can't you take him on campaign with you?" she asked, as the boy broke and ran to his pony.

"Just looking at him I'd say that he's too dangerous for the cohort," laughed Gaius. "I can't afford to lose my legionnaires to a young barbarian like that. Besides, he loves you."

"Gaius, someday I won't be able to control him at all. Think about that," she said with a deep sigh.

Gaius grabbed Tacitus and put him on the pony's back, then took up the animal's reins and led it around the yard. Junia walked beside him and, after a moment's hesitation, said, "You were at sea and I had no way of getting a letter to you. So much has happened since you've been gone. Especially with your mother."

"What devious scheme is she up to now?" Gaius sighed.

"It's not like that at all," Junia replied. "She would like to see you."

"I'll go to the villa after I leave here. Perhaps Caladria will know where she is."

Junia was quiet for a moment then said, "And I'm sure Toronius would like to welcome you home."

*****

"Ah, young Master Centurion," Apollodoros greeted Gaius as he opened the gate. "I trust that you have slain a goodly number of Rome's foes and restored her dubious glory."

"Of course, thousands of them, you pompous ass," Gaius said, embracing his former tutor.

The tall, stooped Greek smiled. "Have mercy upon this humble slave."

"Mercy? When you taught me Greek you never showed me mercy. I still have the welts to prove it! Now I would like you to start teaching my son."

"If your father grants me the time."

Out of curiosity Gaius asked, "Has he found the woman he's been searching for?"

Apollodoros gave a slight nod and said, "She hangs on his every word, and is in his bed every night, but perhaps you should see for yourself. Now I will bring you a cup of wine; you must be thirsty after so many horrendous slayings."

*****

The woman had her back to Gaius, and clung to his father's arm. The pair walked very slowly, and Toronius spoke to her in a muted voice. The woman's hair was covered by a dark veil, but her simple stola showed that she did indeed have the exquisite shape Caladria had predicted. *So he has found the beautiful woman*, Gaius said to himself as he watched the two meander through the atrium in the summer afternoon. From a distance, he could hear his father speak of Socrates as though he had studied the great sage all his life. The woman said nothing, but nodded each time he emphasized one point or another.

There was something strange about the woman, Gaius thought. With a growing sense of trepidation he walked toward them and stopped. They heard his footsteps, and his father turned and held out his arms.

"My son, my honored centurion!" said Toronius.

"Father," replied Gaius. "It's so good to see you."

"You have come back to us, a true hero of Rome. What a pleasure. I trust you will stay a while."

"I have a few days before I return to the Legion."

The words hung in the still air and Gaius waited, not knowing what to say about the woman with her back to him.

"My dear," said Toronius to the woman, "it is Gaius."

She turned slowly as if resisting a fierce wind. The black veil still covered her face. Then she said, "Welcome, Gaius," but the words were slurred and said with difficulty.

"Thank you, lady..."

She held onto Toronius's arm with one hand and pushed aside the veil with the other. Gaius came closer, cocked his head and peered at the face. The voice, though broken, was all too familiar. She looked at him with her one good eye, the other covered by a drooping lid. Her nose had been broken, as well as her jaw. A crooked smile came to her lips, revealing a mouth half devoid of teeth. The woman made an effort to stand straighter, as if she could resurrect the person she once had been, but then let that image fade as if it no longer mattered. All her pretenses, the expectations of great wealth and fame, the arcane deceptions had faded away.

Gazing at Toronius, she said, "Your father, my love and my protector, has cared for me so diligently since the accident. He is truly a gift of the gods."

"Yes, Mother, a true gift."

Livia, still holding tight to her husband, slowly extended her other hand. "Son, I am so glad to see you well."

For the first time since childhood, he put his arms around her. "I'm happy that you and father are together again."

"And both I and Great Jupiter are pleased," said Toronius, holding Livia's hand. Apollodoros brought three cups of wine, and Gaius sat with his parents at the atrium pool. They spoke amicably together, for the first time he could ever remember.

Chapter 25

"See how big he's getting," Junia said to Gaius, as they watched Tacitus spring onto his little horse and trot it before them. "He's a handful. I wish you could come more often," she added, fatigue in her voice.

"So do I, but the Legion has had to put down revolts and we're constantly on the march."

The agile six-year-old would not take his eyes off of Gaius, who proudly viewed his son's horsemanship. Encouraged by his father's applause, the child whispered into the gelding's ear and the animal charged across the field at a dead run. Then, expertly reining his mount, Tacitus trotted it back to Junia and Gaius.

The boy dismounted and stood before him. He gazed into the man's face and tilted his head to ask, "Are you really my father?"

Junia looked at Gaius, then the child. "Of course he is. Don't you remember him from last time?"

The child shook his head. "Why are you away so much?"

"I'm in the army, son. I must go where they send me and often that's very far away."

"Are you a legionnaire?"

"I was, years ago. I've been promoted to centurion of the sixth rank."

"How many ranks are there?"

"Nine. The highest is called primus pilum, but that's very special and each legion has only one." He knelt and ran his fingers through his son's thick blond hair. The child touched a deep scar on his father's chin. "How did that happen?"

"I was fighting pirates a long time ago. I was on one of Pompey's war galleys off Sicily."

"Did you kill the pirate who cut you?"

"I certainly did."

"What happened to the other pirates?"

"Many were killed, and some were made slaves."

"I want a slave. Will you buy me a slave?"

"You don't need a slave," Gaius said reproachfully. "You just do what Aunt Junia tells you."

"But she's a woman and I'm going to be a man."

"You're wearing a child's bulla, and you won't be a man for a long time. I command you to obey her. If you don't, you will answer to me. Do you understand?"

His voice was as harsh as it was when he reprimanded his troops. He looked at Junia and said, "Let me know if he disobeys you."

The boy looked into the man's rugged face and said, "Father, I don't like you anymore. I'm going to ride my horse." Tacitus clambered onto the animal and galloped away, his face downcast.

"Just trot him," Junia said, but the boy was already racing the pony at breakneck speed.

"I see what you mean," said Gaius. "He must be quite angry with me, being away so much."

"He'll get over it," Junia said. "But he needs a lot more discipline than I can offer. I've even had your father speak with him. Toronius used to be all about discipline, but not any longer. He just says that Tacitus is going through a childhood stage and will come around when he gets older."

"Maybe, maybe not. It worries me," Gaius replied. "I know the burden I placed on you. If he's this way now, it will take something quite drastic to change him."

"As I said, I never had a child so it's like raising my own son. We take short walks and we do have good times, but..." She stopped then said, "I hope he doesn't go too far."

"Because he might fall off?"

"Tacitus? That boy can ride a wild bull. He can stay on

anything, but the pony can fall. It's happened more than once."

"What happens then?" asked Gaius.

"He whimpers a bit, then he gets back on. But he's still a little boy and I worry," Junia said, resigned.

"He's coming back," Gaius said.

Tacitus raced his horse to where Junia and his father stood and reined it in. He pointed and said, "It's Apollodoros. Look how funny he runs!"

"Something's wrong," Junia said, "Apollodoros never runs."

Gaius hurried to meet him. The slave stopped and tried to catch his breath. His tunic was ripped and he had a fearful look. Without preamble he gasped out, "They're dead, Gaius, murdered. You must come at once."

"Who's dead?"

The Greek put his arms on Gaius's shoulders. "Your mother and father. I was with them. I saw it happen. They had gone to Ostia to buy silks for Vercipius. It was a favor and he gave them money to purchase them."

"You're certain they're both dead?"

Regaining his breath, Apollodoros nodded. "Robbers attacked them on the road. I tried to defend them, but there were too many, maybe five or six. They stole the silks and ran but I saw where they hid. I brought your parent's bodies back to the villa. Caladria is there; she's with them now. Will you go to the villa?"

"Of course, once I find their killers," said Gaius. He turned to Junia who held her hands to her face. "I left a gladius and a pugio with you some time ago. Do you still have them?"

The woman nodded vigorously and rushed to the house. She returned with the weapons and handed them to Gaius.

"What are you going to do?" Junia asked.

"I'm going to find the people who murdered my parents."

"But it will be dark soon."

"That's how I want it. Stay here. It will be late when I return."

*****

A thick copse of trees clustered on Janiculum Hill, far

beyond the Aurelian Wall.

"Up there," Apollodoros whispered as he and Gaius knelt in a thicket and studied the low rise. "The ones who attacked us knew what they were doing. They look for undefended wagons, then kill, steal, and run. I'm sure they've been doing it for some time."

"Which means they feel safe up there. I doubt that they've posted any guards." Gaius, after a silence, asked, "Were both my parents dead after the attack?"

"Your father was, but your mother died later. I found her body off the road. They raped her then slashed her open. I held her until she died. I'm sorry, I should have done more."

"Against five in a surprise attack? There wasn't much you could have done. And you were unarmed, I presume."

"I only had the mule whip."

Deep shadows crept up the hillside as night enveloped them. A fire flickered on the knoll, and they listened to inebriated voices that drifted on the evening breeze.

"I'll go with you," Apollodoros volunteered.

"No, stay here and watch for whoever gets away. Don't try to engage them."

"But your father was my master. I owe him my fidelis."

"My parents, my obligation. Besides, by law I inherit you so now you will stay here."

For Apollodoros, the whole world had suddenly changed. He looked at the centurion, nearly hidden by darkness, and said, "I hadn't thought of that. I guess you do."

Silently drawing his gladius, Gaius wove his way up the hill. The voices were louder now. He wished that he had his armor rather than the simple military tunic, but it hardly mattered; the assailants were confident that no one knew their location. Nor would the authorities ever make a night assault.

The first to die was a drunk who wandered into the brush to relieve himself. The urine flowed into the damp earth as the man's head bounced down the hill. Not a sound had been uttered and the body crumpled into a lifeless mass.

"What's taking him so long?" a voice complained.

"Granculus, how long does it take to piss? Hurry back before Ustius finishes all the wine," a man guffawed as he walked to where he had last seen his companion. He issued one unintelligible gasp, as the sword pierced his throat. Gaius dragged him into the brush and stole closer to a canvas awning stretched between trees. In the firelight he could see a pile of booty, far more than a single day's heist.

"Venuvius, Granculus, where in Hades are you?" another called out. Then to one standing beside him, "Something's wrong, they should have answered. Get our knives."

"There's no need for that," Gaius said stepping into the firelight. The pugio whipped across the short distance and buried itself into a man's chest. Mouth open, he stared at the knife, made a desperate effort to pull it out, then sank to the ground. The last thug bolted for a weapon but he lost his right arm at the shoulder and simply stared at the gladius, blood spurting, until his knees buckled and he fell at the centurion's feet.

"It's me," Gaius called quietly, as he edged down the trail to where Apollodoros crouched.

"This one wasn't watching where he was going. He sort of tripped and fell on my stick," the Greek said with a grin.

"I thought I heard someone running away," Gaius replied, looking at the crushed skull of Apollodoros's victim. A thick, bloody branch glistened in the moonlight.

"We'll drag him up to where the others are. When we're done nobody will ever hear of them again," said Gaius.

The pyre grew high as the bodies sizzled in the flames. A stench filled the sky. It was an acrid smoke that Gaius had smelled many times before. When the flames were finally extinguished, Gaius and Apollodoros gathered the loot into sacks, threw them over their shoulders, and descended the hill. Gaius turned and looked back once more. How strange, he thought, that his parents' lives had ended at the hands of peasant thugs. He had long thought that his father would have been slain by some vengeful patrician, his mother at the hands of a jealous lover. Neither had. They had both changed, and peace and an amazing harmony had settled upon them. Certainly neither had seen their end coming so violently. What a strange way to die, thought Gaius.

He knocked on Junia's door and told her, "Apollodoros and I will be staying at my parent's villa for the night, but we will return tomorrow."

On their trek, Apollodoros was quiet and pensive.

"Will you sell me?" he finally asked."

"I don't think so. You really don't make a very good slave."

"You don't think I'm worth much?" Apollodoros asked, with a pained expression.

"You know what I mean. You're too damn haughty and know too much. Slaves are supposed to be humble, servile."

"Oh, I wasn't aware of that."

"That's what I mean. No proper Roman would tolerate you."

"So what are you going to do with me?"

"I don't know. I'll have to think about it."

"I'm certain that's an involved process. But if nothing of substance comes to you, I was thinking that I might be your servant in the army."

"You, in the army? Preposterous. Some of the tribunes and high-ranking officers have slaves, but not men in the ranks. You're not cut out for the military, and besides, I have no need for a slave or a servant. And right now all I'm thinking about is seeing my parents," Gaius said as they entered the villa.

Caladria sat on a stool beside the body of Toronius and Livia. She bowed her head and said, "Master, I am so sorry for your loss. Your parents were good to me."

Gaius nodded and said, "Thank you for watching over them. You may sleep in my mother's room if you wish."

"Thank you, Master Gaius, but I would rather sleep beneath my tree. My sister visits me there, and I want to speak with her tonight."

Gaius nodded, and Caladria took a candle, crossing the atrium and disappearing into the evening's mist.

The two men sat on stone benches beside a glowing brazier. Neither spoke for a long time, then Gaius said, "They surprised me, Apollodoros. I would never have guessed that my mother would have shown my father such affection. Nor could I imagine him caring so much. I hardly recognized them when I returned from the Cilician wars."

"It was like pieces being moved around on a game board," said Apollodoros. "Each one followed another as if nothing was preordained. I brought your mother back here after her accident. A medicus came, but there was little he could do. She remained in her cubiculum for six weeks, and only allowed Caladria to attend to her needs. Livia was terribly despondent. Once, she looked into her copper mirror and screamed most of the night.

"That accident was the end of all her hopes; she knew that she would never be beautiful again. No man would want a woman so disfigured." Apollodoros stopped and gazed at a shooting star.

"But that doesn't tell me why she changed toward my father," said Gaius.

"He did a small thing, but I guess it made her think about her prospects in life. One morning Toronius passed by her room and the door was open. My master peered in and saw his wife, whimpering and curled up in a ball. Perhaps he felt sorry for her; he brought her a cup of wine and some sweetmeats. I doubt that they exchanged any words... at least, I couldn't hear any. It was only an hour later that he, in his finest toga, hurried to the Forum, seeking the beautiful woman that Caladria had said would share his every moment."

"How often did he do that?"

"Every day. He feared that if he missed a single day, he would miss that one special woman. He even sacrificed at the temples of Fortuna and Venus."

"He had such faith in Caladria?"

"Yes, but it was waning. He was becoming frustrated and irritable. I accompanied him once, and he gazed at every beautiful woman with expectation. He became angry when they looked at him strangely. Sometimes the prettier ones even laughed, and it wounded him. And then one night he came back quite late. Your father was vexed. He accused Caladria of playing him for a fool, and said that he would try just one last time. Had he failed again, I suspect he might have sold her."

"Did he try once more?"

"He was about to; it was late, and he said that he would look for her near the Temple of Aphrodite, but I heard Caladria say, 'Master, there's no need to go.' He looked at her strangely and asked why."

"What did she say?"

"She said 'because the lady is here.' Toronius became terribly excited and rushed from room to room searching for her. When he couldn't find her in the house, he ran out to the remains of the barn. He returned to Caladria, quite out of breath, and said, 'I can't find her! You must tell me.' He was nearly in tears after all he had gone through. She merely gazed at him and said, 'Master, you are tired and upset. Why don't you go to bed? You will feel much better in the morning.' He must have been drained of energy, because he just nodded and walked to the house. He went into his cubiculum, and there was a woman in his bed."

"My mother."

"It was your mother. I couldn't see what happened next, but I heard her sob. I was concerned, knowing your father's past, but I shouldn't have been. The tears weren't out of fear or anger. He consoled her; they slept together all night, and were inseparable from that moment on."

"So the woman my father sought was my mother, but he didn't know it. Do you think Caladria did?"

"I'm sure of it; she knew exactly what was going to happen. Aspacia told her."

"But Caladria didn't tell either of my parents, months before."

"No, she could not. It wasn't time and events hadn't progressed far enough. Your mother had not yet had her accident. Only afterwards did she realize that there was only one man who would want or care for her. And she did not see that until he had brought her the wine. Any sooner, and she would have thought it ridiculous."

"And my father?"

"Caladria couldn't tell him, either. He would have scoffed at the very idea that the woman of his dreams was your mother. Caladria must have known that he had to exhaust himself looking for some fantasy beyond the villa. Someone he would never find, before he realized that she was right in front of him. But, Master Gaius, I think he was close to giving up and reality was seeping in. Even though he was a patrician, he was aging, possessed only two slaves, and was almost penniless. I think, despite your mother's injuries, he was immensely gratified that his search had come to an end. They were together for the first time in many years. And when they died, Gaius, they died together."

"I've seen a lot of death, and I'm certain that I'll see more, but their death, a sudden death, seems surreal," said Gaius. He softly said, "Apollodoros, it appears that my father changed from when I knew him as a boy. After he was with my mother again, did he ever talk of freeing you or Caladria?"

"No. I doubt that it ever came to his mind. Freeing slaves is not a common thing, even though there are a number of liberti in Rome."

"Well," Gaius said, not yet willing to make any decisions, "we'll bury my parents in the morning. You should go to sleep now. I'll stay here with them. I have a lot of thinking to do."

Apollodoros rose from his bench and Gaius said, "Greek, you did well in the fight on that hill. I owe you my gratitude."

*****

Apollodoros, worried about his future, slumbered on the tiles at the door of Toronius's cubiculum as he always had. Now Gaius had inherited him, but it seemed unlikely that he would keep him. Perhaps, he thought, he would be sold to work as a tutor or a scribe. He shuddered to think that he might be sold to toil in mines, which were flooded when the ore petered out. Slaves were expendable; drowning them was cheaper than feeding them. Just as bad would be to labor beneath the baths

462

of Rome, where slaves tended the fires that heated pipes for the caldarium.

But then he doubted that Gaius, his former pupil, would be so unkind.

Apollodoros reflected on his former master, the paterfamilias, who until now had snored and fornicated in the cubiculum just beyond the door. For years, at least until his dramatic transformation, Toronius had been an imperious, scheming, and gluttonous master. He was forever greedy for wealth and power, as were so many other Romans who had risen from poverty. Never had he extended much compassion to Apollodoros, despite all the years they had been together.

Yet Toronius relied upon the Greek's business acumen, and had showed appreciation in little ways. Sometimes it was merely a nod or the offering of untouched food after a cena. And though Toronius had an abominable temper, he had never struck him, although that could not be said for his other slaves. But that was all in the past.

Apollodoros slept fitfully, waking at the slightest sound, imagining that Toronius had stirred and would want food or a cup of wine, or perhaps a slave girl. Then, with a start he would remember the murder of his master.

As he tossed and turned, Apollodoros also thought of how he had slain one of the assailants, reflecting on the fact that he had never actually killed a man before, though in his youth he had certainly wanted to.

It wasn't the first time Apollodoros had witnessed killing, but the unflinching and savage mutilation Gaius had inflicted upon the assailants surprised him. This was hardly the boy who had gleefully played hide-and-seek in the vineyard with his friend Appian Dio. Certainly he knew what had shattered the young man's life, what had made him a dour, humorless, and vengeful killer who could so easily end a life. But now he wondered how such a man, away at war for six years, would consider the fate of a slave who once regaled him with tales of faraway lands.

"So what will you do with me?" he had asked.

The ambiguous answer frightened Apollodoros like nothing else since his youth so long ago. He remained awake on the cold floor and the night seemed unending.

*****

The news of the death of Toronius and his wife spread quickly. Vercipius and two of his slaves arrived at the villa shortly after dawn.

"Your father was my closest friend, so I will attend to the funeral details. I feel responsible, since they were doing me a favor, and besides, I doubt that you have enough money for a proper burial," said Vercipius.

Gaius pondered the matter. "A soldier doesn't make much. I would have to bury them in the public cemetery."

Vercipius shook his head. "I will pay for a worthy marble crypt."

"I don't want to borrow from you."

"It's not a loan. I want to buy their house. I've always liked this villa and I will take good care of it. It's a way I can cherish your parents' memory."

"For that I am grateful," Gaius replied. "A centurion has no use for a villa. My house is a barracks or a tent."

Vercipius nodded and said, "You mentioned that you have important matters to attend to. I will look after the funeral arrangements. Try to be back by the fourth hour if you can."

*****

Apollodoros and Caladria followed Gaius as he walked past the Forum Romanum and up Capitoline Hill. Caladria had never been to this part of the city, and was awestruck by the enormity and opulence of the great building they entered. She could neither read nor write, and had no idea of the building's purpose. It was Apollodoros who read the sign above the building's entrance and gave Gaius a questioning look.

Though it was early, the building was filled with men in togas and liberti in simple tunics.

"I recognize you, soldier. You were here, what, seven or eight years ago? You were with a pretty girl if I remember correctly," the praetor said, taking in the stern young man. The official looked at the puzzled slaves and said, "But now you are a centurion with medals."

"Much has changed since I was last here."

Gaius glanced at the gold-tipped festuca that lay upon a table. Beside it was a pile of papyrus documents.

"I've returned for the same reason as before," Gaius stated, indicating Caladria and Apollodoros.

The praetor nodded and said, "Then you know the procedure." The officer called to his assistant to witness the proceedings.

"Kneel," Gaius said to the slaves he had inherited the evening before. "This shall be the last order you will ever receive from me."

Apollodoros appeared stunned but knelt, while the praetor placed the traditional felt cap on his head. Caladria, having only the slightest idea of what was happening, timidly followed. She knelt before Gaius with an uncomprehending expression. Then glancing at the rosewood stick, she cringed, believing that she was to be whipped for some unknown offense.

"It's okay," Gaius said, bending toward her. Then in a solemn voice he said, "In the name of Rome, I, Gaius Septimius Aquila, manumit you. I declare that the slave Apollodoros and the slave woman Caladria are now free and legal citizens of the Republic."

Upon hearing those words, Caladria prostrated herself before Gaius, wrapped her arms around his legs, and cried. To complete the ceremony, Gaius touched each of them with the festuca and said, "You may rise, liberti. You are free. I do not want slaves and have no wish to sell you to anyone."

Both Apollodoros and Caladria were given copies of the manumission, and clutched the papyri tighter than they would a bar of gold.

"You freed me, you really freed me?" Apollodoros repeated again on the road back to the villa.

"For old times and your bravery," Gaius said. "Aspacia would have wanted me to do it. Besides, it's the only way I could discharge my debt to you."

"What debt?"

"For being my teacher, for trying to save my mother, and for killing one of her murderers."

Caladria, babbling her thanks, tried to kiss Gaius's hand until Apollodoros saw his former master's embarrassment, and said to her, "Caladria, stop it; people might think it strange."

Gaius knew that Aspacia had told her sister about so many things, and he wondered about today for much of their walk back to the villa. Finally he asked, "Caladria, did you speak with Aspacia last night?"

"I tried to, but she only laughed and put in my head a flight of doves. They flew wherever they wanted to and nothing stopped them. I didn't know what she meant; she likes riddles and games."

"I think she was saying the birds are free, just as we are," said Apollodoros.

*****

For Gaius, the funeral was a blur. Tacitus accompanied Junia and looked at his father. Gaius remained solemn, his gaze wandering to the nearby crypt of his wife.

"Your mother's ashes are here," he finally ventured, guiding his son to the place of her remains. "You must honor her memory. She was a beautiful woman, and would have been the most wonderful mother in the world. She was a lady of Rome."

The boy thought for a moment, biting his lip, then said, "Aunt Junia told me about her. I try to picture her but I can't. Do you see her in your dreams?"

Gaius was surprised by the question, coming from a six-year-old. "Yes, Tacitus, I see her every time I close my eyes." He was about to say more, to tell him how much he missed her laughter, the toss of her shiny black curls and the touch he had lived for but it was not the time. Perhaps later, he thought, much later, when the boy was older and the pain subsided a little more. But he knew the pain never would.

*****

Gaius gave Caladria a handful of coins, enough for her to live on until she could get a new start. "I wish you well," he said. "You are now free."

"Can I go home?" she asked.

"Caladria, you can go anywhere you want. You can even stay in Rome if you wish."

The girl remained pensive in Junia's atrium all afternoon. Like most other newly-freed libertae, Gaius guessed, she hadn't the slightest idea of what to do or where to go.

Junia saw her sitting on a stone bench and approached Gaius. "I doubt that Caladria will go back to Andalusia. Her village was destroyed, and all the survivors are slaves."

Gaius nodded, frowning. "There would be nothing there for her. I would not want to see her begging on the street, and the coins I gave her won't last long."

"Gaius, she's a very strange girl. I don't think anybody will employ her, and surely no man will marry her. She could live here and help me with Tacitus—he seems to like her."

"That's kind of you. I'm sure that Aspacia would be pleased."

"If Caladria agrees, the matter is settled."

*****

While Apollodoros sat alone in the peristyle of his former master, Gaius wandered through his parent's villa, a place he had scarcely visited during the previous six years. Images of his boyhood flooded back, most of them unpleasant. He poked his head into his old cubiculum, where he had dreamed of the fanciful places described by Apollodoros, like Parthia and Babylon. He crossed into the kitchen, so plain in contrast to other rooms with their mosaics of hunts and frescoes of lovers. He walked through the hallway, where he had accosted his father, and the peristyle where he could never take his eyes off the slave girl Aspacia. He recognized the smells of the lived-in house, and in his mind he could picture his parents as they walked from room to room scheming and chatting with prospective clients... or accomplices. He could easily imagine his father showing a wealthy man an object from Egypt, legitimate or not, hoping that his charade would have a magical effect.

And then there was Toronius's tablinum where, on a desperate night, he had written a letter, which if delivered, would have resulted in his father's murder. It all seemed so long ago. The centurion glanced at the family shrine, the lararium, where like all Roman children, he was brought each morning to honor Vesta, the goddess of fire. The Lares were the household gods and he remembered being told that to fight for "Lares et Penates" was to fight for home and country. At the time, he had never thought that he would be doing it for the rest of his life.

Gaius turned away. The gods and goddesses, he thought, were worth no more than the cold stone from which they were carved. None of them had ever saved a man he'd run his gladius through. Then he stopped. The little figurine of Diana stood alone, as if it was special, or maybe it simply did not belong with the others. He thought and then picked it up, wrapped it in a cloth, and placed it in a satchel with the few objects he would take from the villa. He closed the gate behind him and left the villa for the last time.

An hour later, he and Apollodoros arrived at Junia's house and wandered into the peristyle, with its little bronze fountains and flower gardens. Apollodoros sat pensively for a long time, two fingers touching his forehead as was his habit.

"You seem troubled," said Gaius.

"I was thinking about last night and the man I killed. I have never taken a person's life before."

"Does it bother you?"

"Not that man, not in the least, but it's still a strange feeling," said Apollodoros.

"You'll see a lot of that if you are still considering joining the auxiliaries. The army's job is to keep the peace, extend our provinces, and destroy all those who stand in our way. That usually means killing. And we tend to kill a lot of people."

"I heard that Alexander's Macedonians may have killed a million men in their conquests. How do you cope with the deaths of a million men, Gaius?"

"You think of one man."

"Just one man?"

"Yes, just one man. But he dies a million times."

*****

Junia was in her atrium with Caladria when Gaius joined her.

"I visited your parent's villa after your mother's accident, when she and Toronius had rekindled their marriage. They would often be in the garden together, happy after all that had befallen them. Now their lives have been snuffed out, and the villa is an empty shell. I can't imagine it without them."

"Vercipius will live there, so it will not be abandoned. I'm sure he will welcome you if you choose to visit."

"Maybe. I never thought much of your father until the months before he died. My sister was always very different from me, but she also changed after the accident. I think we became closer. She seemed... more real. All the cunning, the manipulation and haughtiness had dissipated. I will miss her. A visit to their villa would be too painful now."

Rejoining Apollodoros, Gaius asked, "So have you decided what you want to do?"

"I have given it a lot of thought this morning. I am a free man now, a libertus, am I not?"

"You are that."

"As I mentioned last night, I am considering the army. You said I'm eligible for the auxiliaries."

Gaius was sill surprised that his mentor, pedantic and academic, would still consider a life involving violence and possible death.

"And just what would you do in the auxiliaries; surely not fight in the ranks?"

"You think me too old?" asked the former slave.

"Not at all. There are many men in the army far older than you. I've seen veterans over fifty. But I certainly can't see you going through that kind of training. Besides, the auxiliaries are considered expendable. They are the first ones committed to battle."

"Oh, I won't be joining as a fighting man, but I know medicine better than most, I speak many languages, and I'm quite literate. I can be a scribe or a translator. The army should be most pleased to have me."

Gaius smiled for the first time that day. "And you'd be the most presumptuous nincompoop in the entire Legion."

"You forget that I'm a Greek, and we taught the Romans everything they know."

"Everything?"

"Well, anything of importance: literature, medicine, art. Yes, Gaius, I think I will enjoy the military, all that pomposity and marching and shouting and such. You're a high-ranking centurion and can have me attached to your cohort. That way I can protect you. After all, I must maintain fidelity to my former master."

Gaius stared at the balding, lanky man with bowed shoulders and a ridiculous grin. Apollodoros was the last person, he thought, who would ever join the military. But at one time Gaius had also thought he would never march with the legions. What had Aspacia once said? "The only thing that is constant is change."

"You are serious, aren't you?" Gaius asked.

"Most assuredly. If you don't object, I think I'll just follow you to Campus Martius and you can sign me up. They needn't give me one of those medals right away."

"I think you've lost your mind, but if you wish, I'll vouch for you. Just remember, the army is a very different life and you can't simply walk away if it displeases you."

"What else might I do, Gaius? Where would I go? With your parents gone there is nothing for me here, and I've known you since birth. I'll take my chances with you and your miserable Roman army."

"Fine, but unless we're alone you must address me as 'centurion'."

"Then 'centurion' it shall be. Lead on, most excellent

warrior. I shall fall in behind, as I guess they say." The libertus assumed a very strange military posture and, in his own fashion, marched to Campus Martius and a life which would, he was sure, prove to be more terrifying than anything he had experienced before.

Chapter 26

"They're coming again!" shouted Appian Dio, looking toward the chariots massing on the plain. Gaius quickly evaluated the placement of his Seventh Legion, in preparation for the assault by Cassivellaunus, leader of the five tribes of Britons arrayed against Julius Caesar's troops.

"Keep tight. Interlock shields," commanded Gaius, pacing the lines. Drawn by two horses apiece, each British chariot mounted a driver and a javelin thrower. The fast-moving chariots made a difficult target for the Romans' bolt-throwing scorpions, but the Britons, once they hurled their last spear, dismounted and fought on foot. Fierce as they were, they could not assemble solid formations, and as individuals and clans they threw themselves against four legions that refused to buckle. Nearly three thousand pila were launched by legionnaires at the lightly armored tribesmen.

"Draw gladii!" Gaius shouted. He glanced at Caesar who, wearing his scarlet cape, simply pointed. Appian Dio, along with a dozen other trumpeters, sounded a blast and the legions moved forward. Thousands of legionnaire swords were thrust between their shields, and any Britons not impaled began to fall back. Another blast by the cornicens sent five thousand cavalry into a blistering charge.

Though savaged by the legions, the tribes regrouped and prepared for an attack to destroy Roman supplies on the coast.

"We're pulling back," an officer informed Gaius. "We have to save the materiel, along with the ships and the crews."

Caesar devoted ten days to building a stockade that protected all five hundred vessels. With the ships safe, the

472

legions prepared for another onslaught, but the Britons decided to negotiate a peace.

"Those were pretty generous terms Caesar offered them," said Appian Dio to Gaius, a few days later.

"There are problems in Gaul, and he wants to return there, but he's sending me back to Rome."

"Why? You'll be needed in Gaul."

"Caesar can handle Gaul, but he's not done with the Britons. He'll invade again, but he'll need a much bigger army. He wants me to evaluate the new troops at Campus Martius. I leave on a trireme tomorrow morning."

"Oh, since you mentioned ships, one came in this morning with mail," said Appian Dio, handing Gaius a tightly rolled papyrus.

"It's from Junia," said the primus pilum. He opened the letter and read:

Dear Gaius,

I pray that Great Jupiter has shown you favor in your endeavors against the barbarians on that faraway shore. Our friend Vercipius kindly wrote this for me and I am much indebted. I know that you are extremely busy and I thought long and hard about troubling you with this letter. But things have become rather difficult for me, so I hope that you will be allowed to return as soon as possible.

Your son Tacitus is now sixteen and is quite tall for his age, just as you were. Even as a young child, as I'm sure you know, he was headstrong and very independent. Years ago I was able to cope with him, but I am no longer able to and quite frankly, I am worried.

He has taken up with a band of undisciplined youth, as well as a girl of questionable moral character. Her father is dead and her mother, a liberta, spends most of her time at the baths; she is likely a prostitute, though the girl will not admit it. Tacitus vies for her attention and keeps late hours with her. I fear that he might even make her pregnant.

Tacitus, being good with horses, spends many hours at the games with the charioteers, but he's only paid a few denarii for his work. I was alarmed to learn that the other youths in his band commit petty theft. As far as I know, Tacitus has never engaged in that, but if his friends are caught he may suffer along with them. Thus it is imperative that you speak with him as soon as possible, since he no longer abides by my wishes or takes my advice.

I pray that you will come soon. Caladria has been helpful in the kitchen and the garden, and has alluded to events that I simply don't understand.

With all my affection,

Your aunt Junia.

*****

Arriving in Rome, Gaius reported to Campus Martius, then hastily made his way to Junia's old villa. He wrapped his arms around the frail woman and when he released her, she smiled and said, "I feel so old! Forgive me, but I must sit down."

"I wish I could have gotten here sooner," said the centurion. "I received your letter and I'm as concerned as you are. I'm ashamed that my son has made life so difficult for you. Somehow I thought he would show consideration for all you've done for him."

"At heart he is a good boy, but he's in with a wild, I might say dangerous, crowd. You see how I am? He pretends to listen to me, but how many Roman boys actually listen to a woman, especially when they tower over them?"

"This gang you wrote about, are they poor kids from the insulae?"

"Not entirely. One of their fathers is of Equestrian rank, but most of the others are orphans and live on the street. One might even be an escaped slave," Junia said as she swept a lock of gray hair from her forehead. She had aged greatly since Gaius had last seen her. Her once comely face was now deeply lined, and she tired easily.

"You wrote that Tacitus hangs around the Hippodrome. Does he actually race?"

"He exercises the horses and takes a chariot around the course as a warm-up. I think he's been in a few races, and he told me he wants to be a charioteer."

"A charioteer?" Gaius said, his brows knitting. "That's a damn short life. Somebody gets killed in those races almost every time they go around the track."

"In truth, he really doesn't know what he wants to do, except romance that girl. He really needs some discipline in his life," Junia said with resignation.

"Tell me more about the girl."

Junia sighed and said, "Her name's Tullia. She's pretty enough and knows how to use her charms and play the game. I'm sure the boys will do anything she wants. I doubt she has any inhibitions; there are no rules to rein her in. Most likely she's having sex with more than one of them."

"So she's hardly a virgin," Gaius said, knowing that he had been away too long.

Junia nodded. "Apparently she's not pregnant yet, but Tacitus hopes that you will give him permission to marry her, since he just turned sixteen."

"Marry her? That's damn unlikely. She has no father, no family background, and her mother is a prostitute."

"He doesn't think that's important. He says that for all intents and purposes he doesn't have a father, either. Of course I've tried to dispel that notion, but he says, 'If I have a father where is he?' And when I mention the girl's lineage, he says that you married a slave and he should be able to marry anybody he wishes."

"I gave Aspacia her freedom, and she was not sleeping with a bunch of worthless kids!"

The door opened and a gaggle of young people, one wearing a toga, burst in. All were talking at the same time, and were led by Tacitus and his girlfriend. They entered the atrium and abruptly stopped.

"Father?" Tacitus said, staring open-mouthed at the unsmiling soldier standing beside Junia.

"Son," Gaius replied, looking coolly at Tacitus and the mob that had entered with him. The boy, startled by his father's presence, said nothing for a long uncertain moment.

"My father's a centurion," Tacitus said haltingly to his confederates.

"Primus pilum, actually," Gaius said tersely. "You know what that is, I presume."

"Yes, of course," they all answered in unison, appearing very uncomfortable.

"And these are your friends," Gaius said, looking directly at the girl.

"Yes, Father, they are. This is Tullia, my girlfriend. I was hoping to talk to you about me and—"

"We certainly will," Gaius interrupted. "In fact, we have some rather serious matters to discuss. Alone."

Sensing a very hostile reunion, all except Tullia scurried away, having blurted one excuse or another. Anxious to defuse the apparent hostility, Tullia said, "Centurion Primus Pilum, Tacitus rode a chariot for the Greens today, and he won. He is a wonderful horseman."

She gave Tacitus a hopeful smile, then hurried to join the fleeing youths.

Junia rose to go into her cubiculum when Gaius said, "Aunt Junia, if you don't mind, I would like you to stay. I think you should hear what I have to tell my son."

Tacitus, at first cowed by his father's sudden presence, drew himself up and scowled. "Yes, Father, exactly what have you to say to me on my sixteenth birthday, considering that you haven't seen me in nearly five years? I hope you have no fatherly advice for me. I really don't need any from someone who hardly knows me."

If Gaius had had the stout vitus stick he applied to recalcitrant legionnaires, he would have left Tacitus bowled over and struggling for breath. Instead he gave his son a steely look and retorted, "Perhaps if you had been where I was during those years in Gaul, you would be more careful with your choice of words."

Tacitus shrugged and said, "It was your decision to join the army. Personally, I wouldn't have any part of it."

"Personally, son, I don't think you're army material. You'd be drummed out with a missio ignominiosa, a dishonorable discharge from the Legion and banishment from Rome. I believe it would take three days, at most."

Tacitus gazed at his father with a smirk. "Well, Father, I'll never have to concern myself with that. From what I've heard, the army's a place where people go who can't do anything else."

"Except save Rome."

Junia sighed once again and said, "This is what I must deal with, Gaius. I was hoping he'd change his behavior. Since he can now wear a man's toga, perhaps he should find somewhere else to live. There's no reason for him to remain here anymore. It saddens me, because he was once a sweet child."

"I'm not a child anymore, but I'll do as Junia wishes. I will find a place and live with Tullia until I marry her. I guess it would be nice to have your consent, but I doubt I'll receive it."

"That's the first thing you've been right about."

"That hardly surprises me. But I really don't need it—just as you didn't when you took my mother to bed."

With lightning speed, Gaius's fist slammed into Tacitus. He stumbled across the atrium and crashed heavily against the wall. Gaius waited, and when the boy's mind finally cleared he looked up at his father with intense hatred. Gaius tossed a toga into his lap and said, "I had hoped to give you that under different conditions. You will leave this house and never come back."

The boy slowly rose to his feet, hand on his face, and stumbled out.

*****

"I hate the bastard," Tacitus said, blood still oozing from his lacerated jaw. His head throbbed and spots danced before his eyes.

"He doesn't really know you or anything about you," Tullia

responded, wiping blood from his face.

Never had he been hit by anyone other than a youth of his own age. He could not believe the force behind the blow, or the sudden fury of his father's rage. Being a centurion fighting alongside Caesar in Gaul must have something to do with his quick temper, he thought. Though exactly what a primus pilum did had never entered his mind.

"The bastard," Tacitus reiterated, a queasy feeling in his stomach. "I think he really wanted to kill me."

"Nah. He would have finished you off in one more blow if he wanted to kill you," said Galba Pontificus, sitting across from Tacitus and four more of the clan. "My uncle was a legionnaire, he told me about army training and war. They're all killers. Your father would have ended you for sure. I know about things like that," the pimple-faced youth said, glancing at Tullia for affirmation.

The sun was already sinking behind the hills of Rome, and the group had retreated to a clump of trees. It was a daily ritual, since the glen was remote and there was nobody to interfere with their drinking and horseplay. Galba, oldest of the group, vied for Tullia's attention, and, with his father belonging to the Equestrian class, tended to act as though he would prevail. Yet all of the other boys knew that Tacitus was Tullia's favorite.

Dismissing Galba's remark, Tacitus said, "Did you know that he's only seen me five times since I was a child? Five times, and he has nothing for me but utter contempt. And look how he treated all of you, as if you were criminals."

Tullia gently touched his face, huddled beside him, and curled up like a kitten. Then she took his hand and placed it gently upon her tunic where it lay over her breast. He blew out a long breath, gazed at her adoringly, and hoped that Galba got the point.

"Why did he hit you?" asked Plotius, a scheming urchin of twelve. "You must have insulted him."

"I don't want to talk about it."

"But you want to get back at him, don't you?" said Capena, an angry boy of fifteen who was anxious to gain Galba's approval.

"Of course he does, wouldn't anybody?" Galba insisted. "Just think about it. Tacitus has been thrown out of his great aunt's house and has no place to sleep except under these trees."

"Or in the stables of the Circus Flaminius after he does the mucking out," Capena said.

"The first thing you need is money," Galba instructed, showing how he'd earned the name "Pontificus".

"I have work, and I will have money," Tacitus replied.

"Bullshit! There's no money in training horses," Galba said. "You think by hanging around charioteers you will become a professional driver? Sure, I've seen you during intermissions entertaining the crowd with the other desultores, leaping from one horse to the next, jumping them over chariots and the like, but let's see the money. There's none, is there?"

"He won a race for the Greens," Tullia said for the second time that day.

"It was a practice race," Capena said derisively. "And he only drove the chariot in one of seven laps because the regular driver was killed."

"But he still won," Tullia replied defensively.

They were all silent for a moment until Galba spoke up, saying, "I know where we can get a lot of money. We've never done anything like it before. In fact, hardly anybody has, but it will be very exciting."

All looked at him expectantly. "I won't say anything more until tonight. That's when we'll do it—when it's real late and everybody's asleep." He hesitated before asking, "Tacitus, is your father religious? I mean, does he have a favorite god or goddess?"

"Junia tells me he despises all of them; something about my mother's death. She worshipped Diana. Why do you want to know?"

"Just curious."

*****

They were hunkered down in a growth of ancient trees a

hundred yards from the temple.

"I think this is really dangerous," Tacitus whispered. His jaw still throbbed and a tooth was loose from the blow his father had given him, hours before. In commiseration they had all begun to drink cheap wine while Galba led them from one temple to the next. To Tacitus, the one they finally stopped at seemed grander and more affluent than the rest.

"There's only one lamp burning," Galba said to his accomplices.

"Galba, are you really going in there?" Tullia asked, her voice tremulous.

"I am, and so is Plotius. Capena, are you coming?"

"Yeah, sure," the youngest replied, quick to please his leader. The bravado, Tacitus noted, was issued in a quivering voice.

"Some temples aren't even guarded," said Galba. "People store their money in them for safekeeping, and the tithing plates are always full."

"You don't mean to take the offerings, do you?" Tullia said, suddenly realizing how risky the invasion might be.

"Of course I do, that's what we're here for. It will be easy; we'll be in and out in no time," Galba said.

"I don't know, most people think the temples are sacred. Stealing from them seems, well, somehow not right," Tacitus said. The light of the half-moon cast eerie shadows across their faces.

"Since when do you believe in the gods and their temples?" Galba sneered.

"I don't really, I've only been to one or two and that was a long time ago," Tacitus said. "But what about the priests? Don't they protect the offerings?"

"They're all asleep so don't be so nervous. You and Tullia, wait here and keep watch. Don't light your candle. We don't want to attract any attention."

"What temple is this?" Tacitus asked, just as the boys hurried toward the barely perceptible Doric columns.

"Diana's," Capena said in a sharp whisper.

"Wait!" Tacitus said, but they were already gone, intent on riches practically in their hands.

The moonlight cast fleeting shadows on the walls, seeming to crawl across the sky at half its usual speed. Many minutes passed before Tullia finally said, "It's taking too long. They should have been out by now."

"Footsteps!" Tacitus whispered, turning toward the soft tread of a half-dozen men.

Tullia stared into the night, trying to get a better look. Then her eyes widened. "They're priests. Get down!"

"Galba must be warned," Tacitus said, jumping up and bolting for the marble steps as screams and shouts erupted from within.

"Hold them!" a man bellowed from inside the temple, as the youths, already bloodied, attempted to flee. Hearing the disturbance, the six clergymen outside charged past Tullia, who hid behind the tree. The men raced back into the temple. From outside, one could hear the sound of cudgels slamming into bodies, followed by another scream, then pleas and angry curses.

*****

"There is a lady who wishes to see you, Primus Pilum," a legionnaire said as he poked his head in Gaius's' tent.

"What lady?" the centurion said groggily, in the false dawn.

"Her name's Junia and she says it's urgent. She's at the Praetorian Gate."

Throwing a cloak over his shoulders, Gaius hurried down the encampment road to the main gate.

"Open it," Gaius barked to the legionnaires standing guard, and found Junia bundled against the early morning chill. She stood with Tullia and held a flickering oil lamp, its sallow light weak upon their faces. Upon seeing the centurion, Tullia dropped to her knees and prayerfully put her hands together.

"Help us, please help us," she pleaded.

Gaius ignored the anguished girl and escorted Junia away from the gate and the stone-faced legionnaires.

"It's Tacitus," his aunt said, anxiety in her voice. "Tullia says that he and his friends entered a temple over an hour ago and were caught by the priests."

"I didn't know my son was so religious," Gaius said with disdain. "I can only guess why they entered a temple so late at night."

"Some of the boys intended to steal from the offering plates," Junia said, confirming her nephew's suspicions.

"Oh sir," pleaded Tullia, "Tacitus didn't go in there to do that. He was outside with me and went in to warn them when priests came. He's innocent. He's not a thief, I swear."

Gaius gave her a scathing look and said, "Tell me girl, did the authorities arrive before you left?"

"No, Primus Pilum, but it's been awhile now, and..." Her voice trailed off and tears streaked down her face.

Gaius looked at her dispassionately.

"I think Tacitus is hurt," she said. "I heard a lot of yelling and screaming. Some of the boys might have been killed."

"What temple?" Gaius asked warily.

"The Temple of Diana. Aspacia's temple," replied Junia, in just above a whisper.

*****

The first light had already crept over the hills of Rome when Gaius strode up the steps of the Temple. It had been sixteen years since he had last laid eyes on the golden goddess, sixteen years since he'd ceased to believe in the gods. Now the immense statue of the woman with the little stag stared down at him. Blood stains still stained the marble floor.

"No weapons are allowed," an acolyte hissed as the centurion marched across the floor, his hobnail caligae making a hard clacking sound on the cold stone.

"Where's my son?" he barked, grabbing the man by his toga. The young priest squirmed and fixed his eyes hopefully on the approach of the high priest.

"So you're an exalted centurion now, a man of the sword, rather than a believer in our goddess," a voice wheezed with repugnance.

Gaius released the novitiate and wheeled toward the aging

Lysippus.

"I see that you've become even more disrespectful of our sacred lady. How dare you storm into my temple! You didn't want my benediction before, but I suspect you want something from me now; am I right, Centurion?"

"Actually there is something you will give me priest, and it's not your pitiful invocations," Gaius said, standing a foot taller than the balding cleric.

"Most Exalted High Priest is my actual title, if you don't mind," Lysippus said in a grating voice. He glanced at the phalerae and torque medals emblazoned on the centurion's armor. "Hmm, I suspect that you have killed many men, but you will do no harm in here. Your son Tacitus—yes, he was able to mumble his name—is in league with a very unsavory mob. These young criminals, these scum," Lysippus said, spittle issuing from his lips, "attempted to steal contributions to the honored goddess and were apprehended, coins still in their filthy hands. Of course they will die, and it shall be an extremely brutal death. You son is one of them, so why should I give you anything?"

A hand clutched Lysippus's neck and lifted him off the ground. "Because you want to live," Gaius growled, his other hand on his gladius.

A gaggle of acolytes took a step forward. Gaius drew the sword and raised it to the priest's throat, and they came to an abrupt halt. Gaius held the man at eye level as the moment stretched. Lysippus's eyes bulged and he worked his mouth.

"In there," he croaked, gasping when Gaius finally released him. His hand massaging his throat, Lysippus followed his nemesis into a barren room where an oil lamp threw off a disturbing light.

Three youths, bound and gagged, managed to raise their heads. The fourth slumped on the floor with a deep gash in his head, a thickening pool of blood having gushed onto the floor. The priest pointed to him and said, "That one won't desecrate my temple ever again. I personally killed him, Centurion. Yes, you might not think me capable, but I bludgeoned him with extreme pleasure."

Welts and bruises had erupted on the faces of the other boys. Tacitus, the laceration on his jaw reopened, stared at his father with unblinking eyes.

"You've seen him, now come with me," the high priest said, directing Gaius to his study in the rear of the temple. "Your son conspired with the others to carry out a theft in a temple sacred to Rome. It's an offense punishable by death!" said the holy man, shaking with rage.

"It's a grievous offense," responded Gaius, "but I'm told that he entered to warn and dissuade the other boys. He did not have coins in his hands, did he?"

"What difference would that make? He was one of them. He's guilty!" the priest screeched. Then, appearing suddenly exhausted, he sat heavily in his chair. "I cared greatly for your wife, though you won't believe that. I heard what happened the day she died, and I ran all the way to the villa. I only wished to extend my sympathy and my blessing for her journey into eternity. And you excoriated me and banished me from the house. I am a priest of your wife's holy temple. Do you forget that I married the two of you? And that day, her final day, I was humiliated by you, an abominable insult, and I've never forgotten it." Then with a snarl, "I have the right to call in soldiers and have your son hauled off to his execution. Indeed, a most brutal extinction at the games. The mob, bestial all, thrill to watch what a bear or pack of hyenas can do to a man."

"But I would kill you and all your toadies before that would happen."

"You would be a murderer and hunted down! Your son has violated my temple. No one does that and lives!" The man's shriek reverberated through the silent basilica, startling the acolytes who still wiped away blood.

The man's rage dissolved into a muted groan, and he continued, "Your threats are hollow. I would gladly perish for my goddess as would all our believers." He stared at the ceiling for a moment, thinking. "Whatever clemency I give is in memory of your late wife. I remember her name: Aspacia. Yes, I recall that when she was still a slave you introduced her to me as a 'lady of Rome'. Of course I knew she was a slave, but in all other respects she was a lady, and her piety moved me.

"If I were to free your son it would be for her. And in exchange you will do something for my temple and maybe even for Rome. Sparing your boy will cost you every sestercius you have. And beyond that, your son will never enter this holy place again. He will be banished!"

*****

Tacitus, free of his bindings, followed his father past seething priests and down the temple's marble steps. Waiting for them was Tullia, who rushed to Tacitus and threw her arms around him. The centurion waited for the briefest of moments, then said, "That's enough. Say your goodbyes; it's time to go."

Neither Tullia nor Tacitus knew exactly what Gaius meant but they did as ordered. Tacitus kissed her and followed his father, leaving her whimpering at the temple steps.

*****

It was late summer, and the air was hot and humid from the muggy vapors that rose from the Tiber River. Tacitus tramped beside his father on the footpath leading away from the city. He was shaken from his near encounter with death, and the sweat that rolled down his face was as much from apprehension as it was from the heat. That Gaius had remained stonily silent frightened him more than a vicious tirade. The man was implacably cold and terrifyingly resolute.

"This is not the way to Junia's house," Tacitus said finally, wary of what fate his father planned for him. He badly wanted to know on what terms he had been released but was too fearful to ask.

"You're very observant. We're not going to Junia's house. We're going to the Campus Martius."

A horrible dread shot down Tacitus's spine. Momentarily he stopped, then hurried to catch up to his father. Maybe, he reasoned, the walk to the military post was to be instructive. Perhaps his father would insist that he take up some kind of work, something he would readily agree to. Yes, he would promise to do something with himself, something to repay his father for interceding when execution would have been inevitable.

"Isn't that where your legion is? In the Campus Martius?" Tacitus reluctantly asked.

"That's right, and it's also where they train recruits."

Again Tacitus stopped. He could feel his heart beating. "Recruits?"

"That's exactly what I said. Recruits. You will be joining the army today."

"No! I don't want to be a soldier."

"But you will be a soldier. At least for the next twenty years. If you live that long."

"You can't, you won't do this to me," Tacitus said beseechingly. He could feel his knees shaking.

"I am your father, of course I can. I have the legal power to do anything I want. I have the right to sell you. I have the right to strangle you, right here."

The sound of heavy rocks tossed one on top of the other sounded a hollow thud in the morning air. Gaius pointed to the sweating slaves nearby. "See those men over there, the ones loading stone onto those carts? They'll do that all their lives until they drop dead. I can sell you to their owner right now. You have a choice—the only one I'll give you. It's the army, or slavery. Which is it? Hurry now, I supervise forty-eight hundred men, and I never waste time."

Tacitus's head was spinning. This stark indifference for his life and the hatefulness of the man in his gleaming armor revolted him, but also terrified him. "Why can't you just let me go? You'll never have to hear from me again," he pleaded, feeling suddenly very small.

"Because I can't trust you, or any criminals you might collect. Those boys, your accomplices, will be tortured before they die. If I let you go, you'll find others of the same kind, worthless, miserable scum, and in time you'll be executed yourself, because I will not save you again. You have embarrassed me and defiled your mother's temple. What would she have said? Were you trying to insult her memory or scandalize me?"

The same look of hatred on his father's face was, Tacitus imagined, the last thing an enemy of Rome would ever see. The centurion grabbed Tacitus by his shift and stared into his eyes.

"Don't you understand? That was your mother's temple. That was her goddess! And I prostrated myself before that idol and gave everything I had to save her. But she died. She died giving life to you. And now you will pay for your violation of her love and her faith. You will pay for the rest of your fucking life!"

"But I didn't go in there to steal anything," Tacitus pleaded.

"Maybe not, but you didn't stop your friends from doing it, did you? Your name will be bandied about, and letting you go would stain my reputation. I will not have that. Now, I've saved your life. You may die in battle, but you will not die as a criminal with the name Aquila."

Despite his determination not to do so, tears streaked down Tacitus's face.

"Yes, cry. Cry like I did when I buried your mother. She was more sacred than all of those stone gods. More sacred to me than anything in this wretched world. Cry now, but never cry in my presence again. A legionnaire does not cry."

Tacitus wiped his tears and what wondered he could possibly do before they reached the Roman encampment.

"I know exactly what you're thinking: that old proverb, the one that says a son is his father's worst enemy. You're thinking that you will kill me at your first opportunity. Very well; keep your knife sharp, but keep it for Rome's enemies. You will need it before the year is over."

The boy trudged behind his father. Every step drew him closer to his end. He could run, but he knew that his father would catch him. His face was still swollen from the last beating, and he would not risk a second.

"One more thing," the centurion said, pointing a finger at him. "I have never lied in the seventeen years I have served the Legion. But I'm going to lie today. I'm going to praise you before the enlisting officer as if you have been honored by the consul himself. You will say 'yes sir' to the recruiting officer on every count, and you will show enthusiasm. Embarrass me, boy, and you will pray for death every day of your miserable life."

*****

Legionnaires saluted his father, the centurion Gaius Septimius Aquila, as he and Tacitus passed through the Praetorian Gate. They walked toward the principia, the legion's headquarters in the fifty-five acre encampment. Despite his apprehension and loathing, Tacitus was awed by the enormity of the fortress. They passed a proliferation of barracks and workshops and the sacellum, the shrine containing the legion's eagle. The praetorium, a luxurious villa near the main cross street, the Via Principalis, came into view.

"Who lives there?" Tacitus ventured, hardly daring to speak to his father.

"The legate: the legion's general. You will rarely see him, but look damn smart when you do."

Every centurion and legionnaire who passed the primus pilum saluted, and even high-ranking officers nodded to his father respectfully. Tacitus could not have imagined this, never having had contact with anything military. He knew nothing of the traditions or requirements of the service. Rarely had he seen anybody given such deference, and it made him even more fearful. Gaius strode to his private room and reread a sheet of papyrus, while Tacitus watched from an open door.

"This is a letter of recommendation from the priest: a total lie in your case, but from this day on you will behave as if no greater truth was ever told. Do you understand?"

Tacitus dumbly nodded.

"Say it!" barked Gaius glaring at him.

"Yes. Yes, Father, I understand," he said, choking on the words.

*****

The tribune unwound the neatly tied scroll and, like all Romans, read it aloud. "I present to you a youth of excellent character and virtue. He has, through his entire life, displayed unstinting piety and devotion to his family and the gods of Rome. I do attest that Tacitus Marius Aquila, son of the esteemed primus pilum, Gaius Septimius Aquila, will prove himself a loyal and devoted soldier of our Republic. Please accept him as a voluntarius to the legion. Signed, M.N. Lysippus, Exalted High Priest of the Holy Temple of Diana of the Woodlands."

"A fine letter of recommendation," said the tribune. "And of course, young man, you also have the testimony of your father, a distinguished centurion who was awarded the ceremonial golden arrow for valor by Consul and General Julius Caesar himself. I assume you have told your son about your exploits, Primus Pilum?"

"No, sir; it's not for me to proclaim any such achievements."

"Few would possess such modesty," the tribune responded. The officer turned from the centurion to Tacitus, who was trying to control his trembling hands. "So," he said, "You want to be a soldier, a legionnaire, and follow in the footsteps of your father?"

"Yes. I mean, yes, sir."

The tribune smiled and glanced at Gaius. "I see he's learning already."

"He will learn quickly. He's a sharp lad, if I may say so. He recently turned sixteen—a little young, I know," Gaius said, "but he's big for his age and quite strong. He's already very good with horses; even won a race as a charioteer. The 'Greens', wasn't it, son?"

"The 'Greens', yes sir, but it didn't take place before a praetor or anything like that."

"A modest young man, I like that." Turning again to Gaius, the tribune remarked, "So often we get self-congratulatory boys who regret their arrogance in the first week of training." Then, his face hardened, and to Tacitus he said, "Civilian life never confronts the prospect of violent death for oneself. Nor might a civilian be expected to kill unflinchingly. As a soldier, you must often end the lives of those you wouldn't harm in other circumstances. So, Tacitus, will you be able to kill when so ordered, and kill without the slightest remorse?"

The shaking in his hands ceased, and he trained his eyes on his father. "Yes sir," he said steadily. "I can kill."

The tribune stared at Tacitus, then at his father, and raised his eyebrows. Gaius returned his son's gaze, but said nothing.

"Very well," the tribune continued, "we refer to our line of questioning as the 'probatio'. We do it to be certain that you are everything you claim to be. It's also to determine that you are physically capable of withstanding the training. It will be exertion beyond anything you can imagine. I am required to ask that you have good eyesight, no physical impediments, all your fingers and genitalia—not that you'll have much need of that, at least for the next six months," the tribune said, winking at the centurion.

"Probably a lot longer than that," Gaius replied dryly.

"That may be," the tribune agreed. "I will now read you the oath and you will swear your allegiance to Rome and the Legion. From the moment you are sworn in, you will be in the service of the Republic. The violation of any command will be subject to punishment. Depending on the severity of the infraction, it could mean losing rank or pay. We call that the militiae mutatio. A man who falls asleep on guard duty during peacetime will be subject to the castigatio, a severe flogging with the centurion's staff, before his entire cohort. Desertion or cowardice results in the fustuarium or decimation. The latter is when every tenth man in your legion is beaten to death by his comrades. That is rare, but it happens. Marcus Crassus brought the practice back, some years ago now. Have you heard of these?"

"No, sir." *This is sheer terror*, thought Tacitus, the image of his father's fist still in his mind.

"It is the ultimate death penalty," the tribune said, his voice assaulting any previous hopes or aspirations. "Everything we do, everything taught, is based on hundreds of years of experience. We learn from our victories as well as our defeats. The training is intentionally brutal, so that you will know enough to stay alive. And you stay alive to protect your comrades, just as they must protect you. Your tent mates become your family for your entire enlistment. You must remember that." The officer was silent for a minute and regarded Tacitus who stared at the ground.

"Straighten up, son, you are in the presence of a tribune," his father said.

"Based on what I have just said, do you still wish to be a legionnaire?" asked the officer. Tacitus felt his father's stare even before he saw it. Slavery was the alternative, but how much worse could that really be? *Undeniably a whole lot worse*, he thought with resignation. At least he would not be beaten by his father or a slave master, and surely that beating would be inevitable.

"Yes," Tacitus said, his voice barely audible.

"Repeat that with proper determination," the primus pilum barked.

Taking a deep breath, Tacitus looked at the tribune and said, "Yes, sir. I wish to become a legionnaire."

He took the oath and thought, *My life is over, I'm dead no matter what.* He stood still afterward, not knowing what else to say. There was an empty moment while the officer spoke with his scribe. Turning back to Tacitus, he said, "Excellent, you have just joined the Legions."

The tribune expected to see a smile or at least an acknowledgment, but from Tacitus there was nothing but the slightest nod. There were those rare occasions when a young man was overwhelmed by his enlistment, but most new recruits seemed pleased by the prospect of adventure and the comradeship of thousands of other men. But this one showed nothing of the kind. Instead, he had the look of terror. Was the lad actually shaking?

The tribune stared at Tacitus, then glanced at Gaius who said, "You may express your appreciation, son. It is not often a recruit is praised by a tribune."

"Yes, of course," stammered Tacitus. "I guess I'm just a bit overwhelmed by it all. Sir."

"Of course," said the tribune wondering what this was really all about. An unwilling recruit could turn into a defective soldier, and that could be very dangerous. He had a mind to question the primus pilum, but it was already too late for that. The boy, now a recruit, would be in the hands of the training officer, and would be washed out if he was a total failure.

"Very well, young man," the tribune said, more for Gaius than his reluctant son, "I congratulate you on your enlistment in the world's most powerful army. You are now in the service of Rome and will be given a signaculum, a pouch carrying your name on a lead disk, to hang around your neck. I will have the optio direct you to the training area, where you will meet the instructor and your contubernium. Those are the other seven men who will be your tent mates."

Gaius and his son left the tribune's office and walked into the scorching sun. "A word with you," the centurion said. Tacitus, still dumbstruck but resigned to his fate, gazed blankly at his father.

"Many in the army pay bribes to get out of onerous details. You will never give or take a bribe. You will do exactly what you are told, and you will do it willingly. Expect no favors or special treatment from me. You will acknowledge my presence only by saluting, and you will not speak to me unless you are invited to. I will not supervise your training, but I will be watching. Do not fail me, or punishment will be swift and brutal. Do you understand?"

"Yes, Father."

"My rank is primus pilum, chief centurion of General Julius Caesar's Tenth Legion. Without my permission, you will never call me 'father' again."

"Yes, Primus Pilum of General Julius Caesar's Tenth Legion."

Gaius glared at his son and tapped his golden arrow against the greaves protecting his lower legs.

"Now you will attempt to become a legionnaire. Do not fail the legion, do not fail yourself. You shall serve Rome for the next twenty years. You may not think so just now, but I have done you a great favor. You will reciprocate by showing your devotion and your loyalty. I expect nothing less."

Tacitus nodded, and licked his lips nervously. Then he asked, "Primus Pilum, will I ever be able to see Tullia again?" It was the question he had dared not ask.

Gaius shook his head. "No. It would be most unwise. A legionnaire is not allowed to marry. When your service is over, who knows? Both of you will have lived different lives by then. Certainly, she will have married or even died. She's still a child and will soon forget what you even look like. Now your allegiance is to Rome. You have married the Legion."

But I will think of her every day and every night, Tacitus thought, even as his father gave him the dreadful advice.

"If you attempt to visit her again, you do so at your own peril," the centurion said in a matter-of-fact voice. The primus pilum became silent and stared at his son as if, Tacitus felt, he were a captive being evaluated for life or death.

Gaius gave his embossed greaves one last tap, then abruptly turned and strode away. The optio, an aide to the training centurion, approached Tacitus and led him across the encampment to the training grounds.

"Your cohort began training two days ago and will be returning soon for the afternoon meal. Wait here. That will be your home," the optio said, pointing to an eight-man tent. "But don't enter until the others arrive."

"What should I do in the meantime, sir?"

The cynical and grizzled veteran looked at him with amusement.

"You wait, lad. That's what you do in the army. We wait until we are told to fight. Then we fight to save our very souls. If indeed we possess them at all."

The officer turned and marched off. Tacitus looked about the empty encampment, starkly silent in the afternoon sun. He didn't know the regulations; should he stand or sit; should he appear to do something constructive?

A horse was tied to a nearby post. He walked to the animal and scratched behind its ears. The horse rubbed its head against Tacitus and gazed at him with deep brown eyes. It was a familiar look, the only familiar thing in his new world. *At least I know about horses.* Tacitus had heard that every soldier must learn to ride. Well, he already knew how to do that. Maybe he would survive this day, he thought, and perhaps the next one too.

A plume of dust rose in the distance and he saw the recruits striding toward the camp. He stood and waited for his life to begin anew.

Chapter 27

"A woman wishes to speak with you, sir. I think she's the one who was here last time," a legionnaire said to the primus pilum, interrupting the briefing.

"Is her name Junia?" Gaius asked.

"Yes, sir. She said that she's your aunt. There's also a girl with her."

Again that girl, Gaius thought, dismissing the men waiting at the table. *Why would Junia bring her to the Campus Martius after dark?* he wondered, as he walked briskly to the gate.

"It's far too dangerous to be out here this late," he said, putting his arms around Junia. She seemed so frail, he was afraid she would break.

"It's okay," she said, pointing to four stalwart men standing behind her. "I hired porters to carry my litter. They'll protect us."

"I assume that this is about Tacitus," said Gaius, while ignoring the distraught Tullia.

Torches held by the litter bearers and legionnaire sentries illuminated the women's faces. As before, tears ran down Tullia's face.

"We went to the Temple of Diana. The priest, Lysippus, told me that you were to bring Tacitus here, to the Campus Martius," said Junia.

"Did he tell you why?"

"He said that as penance, Tacitus would join the army and that he would be forever banished from the temple."

Gaius looked at Tullia as she began to sob. A waif to begin

with, she appeared pathetic now, with scraggly hair and bloodshot eyes. Her shoulders quaked; she looked as if life had seeped out of her. The spry, coquettish attitude had vanished, and for the briefest moment she reminded him of another girl, one he had known many years before.

"Tullia pleaded with me to bring her here," Junia explained. "She didn't think you'd see her if she came alone. She was hoping to speak with him."

The girl just doesn't understand anything, thought Gaius.

"Lysippus and I made an agreement," the primus pilum said. "For invading the temple, the priest could have had the boy executed. Tacitus allowed his friends to defile a temple protected and sanctified by Rome. Had I not intervened, he would be dead."

"Dead?" Tullia covered her mouth with her hands, aghast.

"Yes, dead, ripped apart at the games. But I didn't let that happen. His freedom was expensive, but he was granted clemency. To save him from repeating anything as foolish as what he'd already done, I enlisted him in the army. His life before today is over, and nothing more can be done."

A heaving moan escaped from Tullia. She sank to her knees and clutched the greaves on Gaius's legs. He backed away and nodded to Junia, who lightly put her hand on Tullia's head. The girl looked up, her face a landscape of anguish.

"But he's not meant for the army, he's not that type of person," she wailed. "He's kind, and he loves me, and if you give your permission we will marry. We'll do it properly, before the gods. I'll give him a son and I'll make you proud."

And you may die just as Aspacia did, Gaius thought. "He's taken an oath, Tullia. He's going to be a legionnaire, and his allegiance is to Rome. He cannot marry you or anyone else. It's over," he said with finality.

"No! You can undo it, you must undo it," she howled.

"You should thank me, girl! I saved his life," the centurion said, anger in his voice at the girl's inability to comprehend. "Now, you forget him, and never come here again. As far as you are concerned, he no longer exists."

She wailed again, then begged him, her voice wavering pitifully, "Please, please, may I speak with him one last time?"

"Absolutely not."

"Stand up now," Junia said softly. Like a child, Tullia's whole body shook with spasms and sobs. Gaius was surprised that she showed so much caring toward his son, especially having dallied with other boys, but he couldn't let it go any further.

In as compassionate a voice as he could muster, he said, "You will find somebody else. The army is not an easy life, but he'll grow into it. Tacitus will be a different person in six months. You won't even recognize him, and you will also change."

Gaius's aunt held the girl close and spoke quietly to her in a consoling voice. Gaius turned to her with a sigh. "Junia, you must make it clear to her that if Tacitus leaves here against orders, it's considered desertion. He would be executed for that. And any letters from her will only cause him pain. There is nothing else I can say."

Junia said, "I'll do what I can. Nothing is simple."

He bid his aunt goodnight and watched as she was helped onto her palanquin. Two of the servants carried torches as the litter was borne into the night. Tullia walked beside Junia, and Gaius could hear her sniffles until they had passed out of sight.

*****

The recruit Sempronius was anxious about his first riding lesson before the training officer, Velleius Septus Pareculus. Thus, he failed to thoroughly inspect the girth that circled the horse's belly. Had he checked it more closely, he would have seen minute cuts, deftly made with a very sharp knife.

"Next!" the officer barked, and Lupus Iberica, a hulking man and the biggest in Tacitus's contubernium, nudged his mount into a labored trot. Having attempted the short exercise, he brought the horse back into the waiting line.

"Don't you understand Latin? I said to break into a *fast gallop* by those trees, and trot back to your original position," the centurion said testily. He looked over the assemblage of the eight recruits, none of whom resembled legionnaires in the slightest, and shook his head. His eyes fell on Tacitus, a youth, rumor had it, who'd joined under strange circumstances and whose father was none other than the primus pilum of the Tenth Legion. On more than one occasion, Pareculus had spied Gaius in the distance observing the training. "Regarding recruit Tacitus," the primus pilum had said to the training officer, "don't spare the vitus; show him no favors."

"Yes, sir, I use the stick quite liberally on all."

Tacitus appeared a decidedly unhappy lad to Pareculus. Contrary to the attitude expected, he seemed to hate every minute of his training. Pareculus noted, however, that he had often seen Tacitus beside the corral in the off-duty hours, as if horses were the only things he cared about. But after six weeks of training, Tacitus had finally made a friend of Sempronius, a hesitant, stuttering youth seemingly unfit for the army.

"Tacitus, you ride next," said Pareculus, ready to pounce if the recruit showed the slightest truculence.

Sitting astride his mount, Tacitus glanced at the grapevine staff grasped firmly in the centurion's hand. Leaning over, he whispered into the horse's ear.

"I said ride, damn it! Are you afraid of the horse?" The officer raised the stick as Tacitus touched the animal's flank, and the mount bolted forward, within inches of the centurion. Enraged by the near collision, Pareculus swung the vitus, but Tacitus, grasping the horse's neck, rolled to the side and the vitus swept wide of its mark. Again the youth touched the horse, and it flew into a dead run, reached the trees, spun about, and cantered back. Tacitus halted the mount before the irate centurion.

"I apologize for coming so close to you," Tacitus said a bit too smugly, dropping the reins.

Seething, Pareculus stared at him, pointed his stick, and said, "Get into formation. You're wasting my time. Recruit Sempronius, you're next. Gallop, charge, and return at a trot."

Sempronius, nervous and unaccustomed to horses, bounced

in the saddle. The mount, aware of the untrained rider, broke into a dead run and bolted toward the centurion. Suddenly the cinch strap parted, and the recruit, along with the saddle, careened into Pareculus, who flew several feet before colliding with the ground. Iberica snickered as the horse, freed from the rider, tore across the field.

"You idiot!" the centurion screamed as he struggled to his feet. A moment later, the truncheon slammed down on the stunned Sempronius. "Get that horse!" bawled Pareculus as the recruit, his eyes blurry, cringed away from another blow. Blood ran down his shoulder as he tried to make his legs respond. Pareculus gave him a solid kick and Sempronius lurched forward, fell, and tried to rise again. Iberica laughed, but the other recruits shot worried glances at one another.

"Didn't I tell you to tighten the cinch, walk the horse, and tighten the straps again?" Pareculus yelled once Sempronius returned, still staggering a little but with his horse in tow.

"Sir, I did. I-I-I swear to-to Great Jupiter I did," the youth stuttered.

"Then I ask you, how the fuck did that saddle fly off?"

"I don't know, sir. It-it-it might have been wo-worn out," Sempronius said, staring at the vitus stick the centurion waved about.

Pareculus grabbed the saddle with a scowl. "Nonsense, this one is new—" He looked down at the cinch, stopped, and looked again. "Cut," he said. "This has been cut!" he shouted. Holding up the saddle, he paced before the squad. "Who did this? Someone in this contubernium used a knife on this cinch. I checked these saddles before you used them, and none had been tampered with. So who did it?"

No one answered.

"Failure to reply to a question or a command is a grave offense. One of you is a coward—and in battle cowards are the first to die. I'll find out who did it, and he will pay mightily. Dismissed!"

Leading their mounts, Sempronius and the recruits trudged back to the stable. The fury of the bruised centurion would make the rest of the day particularly ugly.

*****

"So it was cut," Tacitus said to Sempronius. "Do you think it was Iberica?"

"I-I-I'm sure of it." The youth's stutter was worse than ever. "He ti-tripped me the other day, pu-put his pilum out real fa-fast, and I fell in front of Labinius Tessarius, the pi-pi-principate of the watch. Iberica made me look like a fo-fool," he lamented.

Two years older than Tacitus, Sempronius was the smallest man in the cohort. Three days earlier, despite having spent hours cleaning and polishing his lorica segmentata and its thirty-four separate pieces, Sempronius had failed inspection when Pareculus found dark smudges on two of the steel plates. He was given extended guard duty, then required to practice with the gladius against the post for an additional three hours.

"I po-polished that armor. It-it was spotless," he said to Tacitus. "I ha-ha-haven't done anything to Iberica. I do-don't know why he's doing this."

It was hardly the desire to be a loyal recruit that motivated Tacitus. Certainly, the hatred he felt for his father was greater than ever. He had been determined to make no friends, and his tent mates, upon seeing his dour detachment, largely ignored him. So they probably had thought it strange when a nascent friendship developed between the angry recruit and the stutterer.

Sempronius had joined believing that the Legion would instill confidence he had never had. He'd told Tacitus that he didn't mind the thirty-mile marches in full armor, or the hundreds of hours of throwing the heavily weighted pila. It was all fair, he reasoned, since the grueling tribulations were shared equally by the recruits. But the constant bullying by Iberica was taking its toll.

"I ca-can't win in a fight against him," Sempronius said.

"Ignore him," Tacitus suggested. "He'll get tired of it."

"Not soon enough."

Several weeks passed without incident, and Sempronius confided that he was beginning to think that Tacitus was right. It even appeared that Iberica was ignoring him, when much of the cohort was ordered onto the field and stood before the training officer.

"The sling is a very effective weapon," Pareculus said in a commanding voice, as the men each placed a round stone in the leather cup and practiced swinging it above their heads. The first day's training with the sling had involved the timing of the stone's release. The second day was to achieve distance. Now, on the third day, the recruits were placed some distance opposite one another, the hurled missiles to land ten yards to their front. For safety's sake, each man carried his shield, in case a stone was slung too far.

"On my command, sling your stone toward the man across from you," the centurion ordered. "Then prepare a second stone, and launch that immediately after the first."

Tacitus stood in a line beside Lupus Iberica and one of his cronies, named Fortunius, while Sempronius was in the other line, three hundred feet across the pebbled field from him. "I bet I can hit him," he heard Iberica say to Fortunius, despite the other man cupping his hand over his mouth so that others couldn't hear.

"Don't do it with the first stone," his friend cautioned. "Wait until there are many in the air." Tacitus was staring at him when Fortunius looked up. Masking his complicity, he stared back and said nothing, but Tacitus knew what he'd heard.

"Load stone. Sling stone!" Pareculus barked as he walked behind them. A hail of rocks shot skyward and thudded to earth in front of men on both sides of the field. A second volley was launched. There was a scream and Tacitus saw his friend fall to the ground.

"Who was that?" the centurion called, as he ran to the wounded man.

"It's Sempronius, sir—I think he's alive," said another recruit, kneeling beside the stricken youth.

Sempronius lay on his back, his face pale, staring up at the centurion who was immediately beside him. When he was finally able to sit up, he rubbed his temple and said, "I think I'm ok-k-kay, sir. I guess it just g-grazed me."

Pareculus lifted the shield that had been flung from Sempronius's grasp, and stared at a hole that had pierced it.

"The stone's gone right through," the recruit beside Sempronius said, his eyes wide. "I didn't think that could happen."

"It depends on the angle of the shield and the force behind the stone. But it is unusual," said the centurion, looking toward the line of slingers across the field.

"Whoever did it is damn strong. Someone must have misjudged the distance," exclaimed the recruit.

"It was intentional," Pareculus growled, as Sempronius was helped to his feet.

"It mi-might not have been, sir, no one ne-need be p-p-punished," Sempronius said.

"That's not your call, it's mine, and I want to know who did it. This was no accident. Whoever did it disobeyed an order and orders will be obeyed," Pareculus said.

*****

As the horn blast of the cornicen died away, four cohorts halted before the praefectus castrorum, the chief officer of the camp. Standing beside him was the primus pilum and training centurion Pareculus. A stiff afternoon breeze whipped dust across the Campus Martius, and the recruits strained to hear the terrifying words of the praefectus castrorum, the longest-serving officer of the legion.

"The punishment for the offense in question is as severe as the offense itself," he shouted above the wind. It was the first time the men were to witness the penalty for a serious infraction. They stood in battle formation in their massed ranks, shields held off the ground by their left arm and javelins in their right. Sweat rolled down their faces, but it was less from heat than from the terrible display that was about to commence.

Sempronius looked ashen; Tacitus, standing beside him, felt immobile. Menenia Latinus, the appointed leader of their contubernium, stood stiffly at the front of the squad. They were fifteen yards from the officers' platform, where the punishment would be carried out.

A shaking recruit, his wrists tied to a post, closed his eyes and awaited the first blows from the knotted rope.

"This recruit fell asleep during his watch last night. Had it happened before a battle, he would have endangered the lives of every one of you. Today the penalty for this is flogging: the animadversio fustium. Had the offense occurred in a combat environment, he would receive the fustuarium. That would require his tent mates to beat him to death before the entire cohort."

Turning to a solid veteran, who stood shaking out the multi-strand whips, the officer ordered, "Twenty lashes, legionnaire. Lay it on and spare not."

By the fifth stroke, the youth's back streamed with blood and the lacerations began to rip away the flesh. Stoic for the first two lashes, the recruit moaned, then screamed with each succeeding strike. After each blow the legionnaire shook out the ropes, allowing blood to flick and spatter onto the ground. By the eighth stroke, the youth's legs began to shake and by the ninth he was hanging by his wrists, his knees buckled. He lost consciousness at the fifteenth lash, and fell in a heap when the ropes were cut after the twentieth. Saltwater tossed onto his back woke him, and he whimpered as he was put on a litter and taken to the infirmary. Shaken, the cohorts were marched away.

"Will he live?" Latinus asked Pareculus in the hour after dinner, the only time recruits were allowed free time.

"Most likely, as long as infection doesn't set in. The medicus is good at preventing that, but the recruit won't recover for months. If he can't perform his duties, he will be discharged in disgrace. For his offense, he will have no compensation, and he'll be banished somewhere outside of Rome."

*****

"Is he doing any good?" Gaius asked Pareculus as they watched the recruits from a distance away. It was another morning of training in which the men banged away at the post with their heavy wooden gladii.

"He's the least enthusiastic recruit I've ever seen. If he weren't competent I would recommend his discharge, but he performs well. In some cases very well, Primus Pilum. I may be wrong, but I suspect that his efforts are motivated by anger, indeed some deep hatred. Am I wrong?"

"No. He hates me."

"In war that hatred may fall upon our enemies."

"I suspect he'll save it for me. Has he committed any infractions?"

"Sarcasm during the riding exercises, but he's the best horseman I've seen. He stays to himself, but has befriended one recruit, a stutterer who has been bullied. I find that loyalty worthwhile; it's a good sign, if he is to advance in the ranks."

"That requires leadership from him that I haven't seen. If he can't mesh with the others in his contubernium, he'll be a weak link and that's the first to break. I doubt he will survive his first battle, Pareculus."

"That must be a concern for you, primus pilum."

"Not particularly. Not more than the loss of any other munifes."

Yes, thought Pareculus, the lowest ranking men in the army were always the first to die.

*****

"We will be marching to the Tiber this morning," tent leader Latinus announced to the contubernium, when he returned from the morning's briefing. "It will be another swimming lesson. 'Every legionnaire will learn to swim, no one walks on the bottom'," he announced archly in a parody of Pareculus.

"That water's mud. You can't see a damn thing in it," Gallius spoke up.

"Drink it, and you will crap for a week," Vincinias added.

"Complain all you want, we start in an hour, full armor."

"We're swimming in full armor?" Gallius asked with alarm.

"Only you, Gallius. That way you can tell Pareculus how it is to walk with crabs," said Latinus, shaking his head in disgust. "No, you idiot! You take the damn stuff off before you drown."

As the legate had said when Tacitus took the oath of service, the eight tent mates were expected to form an intensely close-knit unit that would last their entire enlistment. Comrades in war and daily work, the brotherly bonds were meant to be unshakeable. In such groups, disagreements might arise, but the necessity of cooperation would limit the severity of their disputes. But Tacitus's tent mates had not yet seen war, and hadn't been tested under desperate conditions. Tension within the squad worsened as the weeks of brutal training continued.

"You've got to stand up to him," Tacitus counseled Sempronius, as they walked to the stables after a day of horsemanship.

"With the help of the gods and a su-spare legion," Sempronius replied. "He's bi-biding his time; he knows that everybody is watching him."

"You could talk to Pareculus. He could put an end to it," Tacitus said.

"I would be branded a coward and no-nobody would ever speak to me again." Dejected, he gazed at the horses, then went on, "By the way, did you s-see Iberica during the flogging? We were all shaken, but he was absolutely te-terrified. He didn't think I was watching, but I saw him vomit after we were dismissed. And you know what? I've see him no-nod off du-during guard duty. It's happened more than once. He ca-ca-can't keep his eyes open."

"So he's scared of getting caught." said Tacitus.

"Maybe we should keep a w-watch on him. On night guard, I mean."

"That's something to think about. He's not as tough as he wants everyone to think. As Pareculus said, bullies are cowards; that's why they beat up on smaller people."

*****

Putting their armor aside and wearing only loincloths, the

men splashed into the Tiber's murky water. "You will swim to the buoy and back three times," Pareculus ordered. "It's important that you learn to swim, since you may have to cross un-bridged rivers, or swim to shore from landing boats."

Sempronius followed Tacitus as they struck out for the buoy. Tacitus had learned to swim in order to impress Tullia, since none of the other boys would venture into the water. But Sempronius, the son of a farmer, had only waded and dog-paddled in shallow streams. "Keep up," Tacitus shouted as his friend flailed through the silted water.

There was a sudden shout, and Sempronius disappeared. Glancing back, Tacitus saw the bulk of Lupus Iberica rise and plunge down again. Where Sempronius had vanished was only five yards away, but locating a swimmer beneath the Tiber was nearly impossible.

Turning back, Tacitus dove twice without success, but the current carried him into Iberica on the third attempt. Bubbles streamed from the terrified Sempronius as the big man held him under. Three months of wielding the gladius had strengthened Tacitus, and his forearm encircled the assailant's neck. Gagging and choking, Iberica tried vainly to break the hold, but Tacitus only tightened his grip. Bubbles streamed upward as he held Iberica in the murky depths. Mouth open, eyes bulging, the giant was held under until the last air belched from his lungs.

Tacitus shot to the surface and waited for Iberica, who got one gulp of air before being plunged down again. After a frantic attempt, Iberica ceased fighting, probably convinced that Tacitus could surely drown him if he wanted to. Rising to the surface, however, Tacitus grabbed the man's hair and towed him ashore before dragging him onto the riverbank.

"He was having a problem," Tacitus said to Pareculus, who had heard Sempronius shout before disappearing.

The centurion looked at the giant, heaving up river water. "He seemed to be doing all right in the beginning. He should be thankful that you came to his aid. I guess when you're that big it's hard to stay afloat." There was a little smirk on the officer's face when he walked away.

"I'll get you, Tacitus," said Iberica, but he choked again when his mouth was filled with a handful of sand.

A glint of steel reflected in the afternoon light and Tacitus glanced toward an overhanging bluff. A centurion with a red transverse crest looked down at him, his golden arrow shaft tapping his greaves. The man made no other motion, and didn't utter a sound. A moment later he turned, walked away from the river, and disappeared into the trees.

*****

"So nu-now Iberica's out to get you," Sempronius said.

"That doesn't bother me. Everybody knows what happened in the Tiber. He was humiliated, and he wants revenge," replied Tacitus.

"You mi-might have to fight him."

"I keep my pugio sharp. He's clumsy, but I know he's dangerous."

"That's for sure. If you hadn't co-come back he could have du-du-drowned me and nobody would have known. It would have been a per-perfect murder in that water," said Sempronius.

*****

Pareculus pulled Menenia Latinus, the tent leader, aside the following day.

"I cannot allow the conflict in your contubernium to continue," he said. "The discipline and strength of a legion depends on the cohesion of each unit. Weakness in one unit endangers the whole. I will take action if you can't. You must assert yourself if you want to keep your position."

"I will do my very best," Latinus said, wondering what he could possibly say to a man bent on revenge.

*****

"It's your watch," Latinus said to the recruits, who stirred in their sleep.

"Already?" Sempronius moaned, as he and Tacitus reached for their armor in the half-light of a waning moon.

"You have to relieve Iberica and Lepidus. I'll show you where they are. Now hurry," the tent leader said.

As they walked toward their positions in a dense fog, Latinus said, "Pareculus ripped me a new hole yesterday."

"About Iberica?" asked Tacitus.

"Yeah, about Iberica."

Silence enveloped them and Latinus went on, "You know, Tacitus, you gained some respect for what you did, saving Sempronius. You might try mixing with the other men, instead of being such a damn recluse. I don't know why you're so fucking bitter. It's sure not doing you any good."

Tacitus said nothing, and a moment later a voice blurted, "Halt! Identify."

"Latinus, with your relief."

"Advance and be recognized," Lepidus replied.

"Where's Iberica? He's supposed to be here," Latinus asked, peering into the gloom.

"Supposed to be, but he's gone on a little further. He said there's a weak place in the line."

"Stay here, Sempronius, this is your position," Latinus said. "And stay alert, the centurion might be along. Tacitus, come with me. We have to find Iberica."

The contubernium leader, followed by Lepidus and Tacitus, moved silently through the damp mist. An owl beat its wings against the thick air and disappeared into the night fog. They walked for several minutes, when Tacitus heard a soft, low sound.

"Do you hear that?" he whispered, putting a finger to his lips.

"Snoring, he's snoring," said Latinus.

"No noise," Tacitus replied, drawing his pugio. The three approached the huge man in breathless silence until they were two feet from Iberica, who leaned heavily on his scutum, his head buried in his arms. With one swift movement, Tacitus kicked the bottom of the shield, spilling the man onto the ground. Instantly Tacitus had his knee in Iberica's back, his knife nicking the other man's throat. Stunned, Iberica tried to rise, but Latinus held him fast.

"Take off his belt and tie him, hands and feet," Latinus said to Lepidus. With bindings tightly secured, Iberica had no choice but to lie on his stomach, his arms bound behind him and wriggling like a trussed pig.

"Asleep on guard duty," Latinus said. "You came way out here where nobody would see you to catch a little sleep, didn't you? Well, Pareculus told me the punishment is up to forty lashes now. You're a big guy, Iberica, I bet you can take forty lashes."

As the prick of the knife dug deeper, a trickle of blood oozed from the wound. Iberica's eyes bulged and he began to shake as Latinus's words sank in.

"No! By the gods, you won't do that to me, you won't tell," he pleaded. Staring into Tacitus's eyes, he said, "Let me go. I'll pay you with all the money I have. I have money, lots of money. I'll pay you anything you want."

"I don't take bribes," Tacitus hissed, two inches from the big man's ear.

"Actually, now that I think about it, I don't think anybody can live through forty lashes," Latinus said in a conversational tone, while disarming Iberica.

"He would be a cripple for life if he did," added Lepidus. "Then there would be a dishonorable discharge and banishment. They would ship his bloody carcass across the Rhine to barbarian Germanica, or maybe to Thrace. That's where the barbarians skin Roman captives alive. That might be a bit painful, don't you think, Tacitus?"

Iberica strained at his bindings, but the knife drew more blood; he whimpered, knowing that the threat was real.

"We are three witnesses, including the leader of our contubernium," said Tacitus, as Iberica's blood dribbled onto the damp earth. "All of us will swear to seeing you asleep on guard duty, Iberica. Maybe you'll black out after ten or fifteen lashes, maybe you won't be conscious to feel the rest, but you'll be as good as dead."

"You're big, but you're a coward," Latinus added. "You

would have drowned Sempronius if it wasn't for Tacitus. We like Sempronius—and we'll enjoy seeing you scream at the whipping post."

Shaking and terrified, Iberica began to wail in utter despair as tears rolled down his face. The three recruits watched with smug satisfaction.

"How loud will you scream when you're dragged in front of the cohorts, Iberica?" Latinus asked, bending down to gaze into the man's eyes. "Pareculus has given me a hard time over you. He even threatened to strip me of my rank. I like being tent leader. I don't want your filthy money, so what's it worth if we let you go? What else can you offer if we forget about the death sentence?"

"Anything! Anything you want from me."

"What about Sempronius?" Tacitus asked.

Iberica hesitated.

"You better hurry, and it better be good," Latinus prompted, as Tacitus's knife nicked him again.

"I'll become his friend. I'll apologize on my knees, right now! I'll be his protector for the rest of my life. By all the gods, I swear!"

"We'll have to discuss it, Iberica. Don't go away, now," Tacitus said, motioning to the others.

"Let him sweat," Latinus said as they moved away, too low for Iberica to overhear.

Twenty minutes passed before the trio returned. Again, Tacitus placed his knife to Iberica's throat. "If you ever renege, if you ever show the slightest antagonism toward Sempronius or any of us, I promise I will slit your throat. We'll dump you in the Tiber, and you'll never be seen again. That's a promise," Tacitus said.

*****

"You seem to have taken care of it," Pareculus said to Latinus, as he watched the huge man lumbering beside an astonished Sempronius. "Look how he babbles on like a blithering idiot."

Iberica glanced at Latinus as he rounded the track, and gave a little wave.

"He's embarrassing—making a damn fool of himself. It's pathetic. I can't watch it any longer," Pareculus said. "Tell your contubernium that they'll engage veterans with the wooden gladius and shield in the afternoon." Then, glancing at the obsequious giant once more, the centurion added, "He's making a mockery of himself, groveling like that to somebody half his size."

"But, sir," said Latinus, "Sempronius doesn't stutter anymore."

Chapter 28

Drenched by a chilling rain, Tacitus ran through the puddles toward the Campus Martius. He was late, and the dire warnings of the optio sent a shiver through him colder than the winter wind.

The graduation into the ranks of the Legion had taken place three days earlier. The recruits who had survived the rigors of training had been awarded the double military belt, while high officials, tribunes, and centurions looked on. Friends and family members had been invited to the ceremony, but the man Tacitus had expected to see was not in attendance.

"You only have one day liberty," the optio said. "Any delay in your return will be met with disciplinary action. Consider this a test, and fail at your own peril. I remind you that although you have completed your training, you are each still a munifes. Any future promotion begins now. Do not disappoint the Legion. Dismissed," he said to the new legionnaires, who were anxious to be seen wearing the honored military belts.

The thought of Tullia had never left Tacitus's mind. He hadn't spoken about her to anybody, even after he had ingratiated himself with his tent mates, so none of his compatriots knew she existed. She was his secret. For months, he had weighed the risk of seeing her. He had received no mail from her, but he thought it inconceivable that she might have taken up with anyone else. No, he told himself, his father must have warned her off, or perhaps her letters had been intercepted.

Tacitus had lain in his bunk each night, wondering how he could see her once again and how dangerous doing so could be if his father found out.

"Do you want company?" Sempronius asked, as they passed through the Praetorian Gate on their only day of furlough as full legionnaires.

"Not right now. I'll try to meet up with all of you later at the Temple of Mars. You, Iberica, and Latinus enjoy yourselves. I have something I have to do."

Avoiding other legionnaires, he hurried to Junia's house.

*****

"I know it sounds harsh, but your father told her to forget you because it would be in your best interests. She knows that you can't marry her, and seeing you would only cause problems. If your father finds out, there will be trouble," Junia said, looking at the young man who had the determination of his father and the eyes of his mother.

"He won't know if you don't tell him," Tacitus pleaded.

"I won't lie to him if he asks."

"No, of course not. That's a chance I'll take, but it will only be this one time. I just want to say goodbye."

Junia hesitated. She looked at Tacitus, now stronger and even taller than she had seen him half a year before. Images of long ago played in her mind, and she saw another young man standing before her: a hard, bitter youth who had lost his wife, the only thing that had mattered to him until he joined the Legion. Now that boy's son stood before her, and she could not deny him his wish. He wore his military belts proudly, and though she knew he had hated the idea of joining the army, he had assumed the proud bearing of a soldier.

Tacitus waited then asked, "She has spoken to you since I left, hasn't she, Aunt Junia?"

She nodded. "Tullia has come here several times. She said she wants to befriend me, but I know that it's because through me she might learn about you. To be honest, I tried not to encourage her."

"Then Tullia hasn't taken up with anyone else?" Tacitus asked hopefully.

"No, certainly not with any of your old friends. They were all executed, except the Equestrian's son. And that boy is under his father's thumb."

"Does Tullia know that I have completed my training? That I'm on furlough today?"

Again Junia nodded and sighed deeply. Tacitus's decision had been made, she realized, and he would find the girl whether she told him or not.

"She knows that you graduated."

"Then she's waiting for me?" It was more a statement than a question. "Where is she, Aunt Junia? Please tell me."

"She said the meeting place would be where it always was. That's all she would tell me."

Tacitus kissed her on the cheek and dashed outside.

*****

It was late in the afternoon when he reached the glen, surrounded by the familiar copse of trees. He halted by the edge of the great oaks, now bare in winter, and hunkered down, scanning for anyone who might see him. A cold drizzle discouraged trespassers, and after a few moments he determined that no one was about.

Droplets splattered upon the ground from a tangle of tree limbs, as he crept along pathways littered with disintegrating leaves. It was fifty yards in the fading light before he could discern a makeshift tent. An oil lamp glowed within. He stopped again and listened for voices, but there were none. There was a shadowed figure inside the shelter. Tacitus silently stepped up to the flap that covered its front. With one swift movement he lifted it, revealing the girl, bundled in a blanket against the cold.

"Oh!" Tullia exclaimed, startled by his sudden appearance. Tearing away the covering she jumped up, pulled him toward her and wrapped her arms about him.

"I didn't know if you would come. I didn't even know if you still wanted to see me, it's been so long," she murmured, burying her face into his wet cloak.

He kissed her and brushed away her tears. "Of course I would come. I thought of you every day and every night. But I can only stay for a few hours."

"Only a few?" she said with dismay. Then she nodded shakily. "I understand. You are a soldier now, and have to obey orders. But you found me."

"Thanks to my aunt Junia."

"I begged her to tell you that I was waiting. I will always be waiting, no matter how long you are gone."

"It could be a very long time, Tullia; I don't know where the army will send me. There have been preparations. I think we will leave Rome soon, so there's something I have to tell you."

"Tell me later. We must make the most of our time together. We must never forget this night. Hurry," she said shivering from excitement more than the cold. "We'll help each other get our clothes off. I want you so badly."

Certainly Tacitus had enjoyed sex with women before. He and the boys had ventured to the graveyards and the baths where, for a few tokens, they could have any whore they wanted. But he had never had Tullia. She took his hand and put it to her breasts. He lowered his head and sucked one taut nipple into his mouth, then the other. Pulling her close, he felt her tight against him. Tacitus kissed her deeply, and she pulled him down to her rumpled blankets. Instinctively, she guided him into her. His breath came fast, and she moaned. The moment was overwhelming, and Tacitus spent himself in minutes.

They lay embraced until his manhood rose again. Tacitus nuzzled against her supple body and pressed into her once more. Tullia gasped and issued a deep, carnal moan. He held her tight and delighted in every sound she made. He hungered for this girl, and wanted the moment to last forever. How could he tell her that he might never see her again?

Tullia wrapped her legs around him and held him tightly. Tears ran down her cheeks and she said, "Don't leave me." Tacitus could almost feel her desperation, coming from deep within.

When they were finally spent, Tacitus slipped his fingers through her hair and said, "Many legions go to the provinces, where they stay for years. Towns often grow up around them, where men can see their women. We're not allowed to marry, but the women are wives in all but name. If I am sent to such a place, you can come, and we can be together."

She kissed him. "Yes! I will do that. I will pray at the shrine of Venus. Write to me. Send the letters to your aunt Junia. I am her friend now, and she will show them to me."

"Yes, yes. I will, I promise," he said as he nuzzled her breasts and their bodies again became one.

They whispered their devotions to one another, while raindrops played a tattoo upon the darkened tent. Later they fell asleep, her warmth and gentle breathing having lulled Tacitus into a weightless, dreamy state.

He awoke with a start, the sun casting anemic rays through brooding tree limbs. Tacitus kissed his love one last time, then frantically dressed and raced toward Campus Martius.

*****

Tullia knelt on the warm blanket where their bodies had been entwined. It had been the most joyous time of her life, and she prayed that it would not be the end. But now, seeing how fearful Tacitus was, a feeling of dread seeped into her. She had no idea of what his tardiness might result in, no concept of what punishment might be administered, but sensed it would be grave.

She had heard snippets of talk about the army's cruelty. Would they beat him? Might he even be executed by some high-ranking officer? She had done a terrible thing to him, Tullia realized. It was she who had tempted the anger of the gods, who had begged Junia, a caring woman, to crumble and reveal her sanctuary to Tacitus.

Tullia's guilt fell upon her as she realized the enormity of what she had done. Copious tears streamed down her face. "Tacitus, Tacitus," she sobbed to herself, before collapsing onto the blanket.

She clenched her fists, held them to her face, and for an hour lay in a fetal position, the fear not abating. Was there anything she could do? she wondered. Tullia finally sat up, the blanket pulled tight about her. What if she went to the Campus Martius and told them it was her fault? Would someone understand? She would go alone this time. Perhaps, just perhaps, the primus pilum would listen. Tullia would take all the blame and tell him that Tacitus was innocent, even drugged. Yes, she would tell him that.

But she knew it would be futile. Perhaps the sentries had been ordered to turn her away. Nobody would see her, and nobody would listen.

Who could she possibly speak to? Who could tell her what would happen to Tacitus? Indeed, who could tell her what the gods had planned for both of them?

Tullia had avoided Caladria, a strange woman who had found a great tree at Junia's house and made the ground beneath it her home. Tullia had glanced at the plump form, often half-asleep and wrapped in a blanket. There always seemed a sense of doom surrounding the woman. Junia had told her that Caladria was a seer, whom Gaius had inherited and freed because she was his late wife Aspacia's sister.

It was Tacitus who had told her that Caladria knew everything. He'd said that she communicated with her dead sister and could foretell the future. Tullia had never spoken to the strange woman, and wasn't sure if the clairvoyant would even speak to her. Maybe not, but asking her about Tacitus's fate was worth a try.

Impetuously, Tullia jumped up and threw on her clothes, shivering in the chill air. Yes, she told herself, Caladria would know. Caladria could speak to the dead, and it was said that the dead knew everything. Aspacia would protect her son from afar, would sanctify his desires and that of the girl he loved. Surely Aspacia would bless their union, no matter where they might live.

Single-minded and hopeful, Tullia raced through the puddles. She ignored the branches, extending like the bones of long dead hands, that tore at her shawl. It was a great distance to Junia's house, and the rain had not slackened. She hurried past farmhouses blurred by rain and fog. Her heart beat faster. Her breath was short, the trek more demanding than anything she had done in years. In fact she had not run so hard since being chased after stealing a valuable urn. But that was before. She was not like that anymore, she told herself.

Now she was the lover of a proud legionnaire, a soldier of Rome. The immature shenanigans of her earlier life were far behind. She would wait for Tacitus's posting and would join him as a good, supportive woman, whether she could marry him or not. But she had to know.

Then Tullia suddenly slowed. She had assumed that Caladria would tell her something uplifting, something that would give her hope. But what if the soothsayer predicted something dreadful? Did she want to hear that? Perhaps it would be best to let the gods do what they willed, and not demand to know more than she had a right to. But she was at the door of Junia's villa now, so she knocked.

"So last night Tacitus just said farewell and left?" Junia asked, looking at the disheveled and breathless girl. She admitted Tullia into the atrium, but Tullia could see that Junia wished that she had not come, that Tullia would forget Tacitus as Gaius had commanded. No doubt the elderly woman could see the hesitation on Tullia's face.

"He told you that he had to get back before dark. He said that, didn't he?" Junia asked again, this time more skeptically.

Tullia wanted to say, "No, well, not exactly," but the old woman would drag out the truth and a lie would end a sympathetic ear.

"We lay together. We love each other, and..."

"And?"

The tears came again. "And we fell asleep. We didn't mean to, it just happened after..." She stopped.

"I guess that was to be expected. So he was late. Is that what you're saying?"

Tullia stared at her feet and nodded her head. "I think so," she said. "But," she brightened, "he is very fast and he might have gotten there in time."

"Not if it was already morning. His father will have no mercy. You know that, don't you?" Junia said with a fury that Tullia had not seen in her before.

The girl shrank into herself, unable to stop herself, she slumped onto a stone bench and wailed. Junia sat opposite her and for a long time said nothing. When she finally did speak, a trace of pity had entered her voice. "Tullia, why have you come here? Do you really think I can help you?"

Tullia shook her head. "No, you've done all you can, and I thank you. I really do. But I was hoping that I could speak with Caladria."

Junia looked at her in surprise. "What good would that do?"

"Tacitus told me that she speaks to his mother, and that Aspacia knows everything. She would know if Tacitus and I will ever be together, whether we can share our love sometime, someplace. Please let me speak with Caladria, she will know."

"It's not as you think. Caladria is not a simple fortune teller. She hardly speaks since Tacitus's grandfather was murdered. She has never revealed anything to me that Aspacia might have said. And if she does speak to you, well, you might not like what she has to say."

"I thought about that, but if she says anything at all, I want to know."

*****

Caladria slowly woke from her slumber, tilted her head, and stared inquisitively at the girl who knelt before her. Then she gazed up at Junia, who stood beside Tullia.

"Dear Caladria, this girl is Tullia, Tacitus's girlfriend."

"And lover," Tullia added, in just above a whisper.

"She is afraid that she will never see him again, and wonders if you might tell her something. Perhaps something that Aspacia might know."

Expressionless, Caladria looked at Tullia. She sat immobile with a threadbare blanket over her head. The woman seemed oblivious to the rain that dropped upon her from the bare tree.

Tullia waited for a long time, but when Caladria said nothing, she got to her feet and turned to go.

"At night, Tullia. I only speak with my sister at night. You must come back tomorrow night, but..."

"But what?" asked Tullia apprehensively.

"She is mercurial and often speaks in riddles. And she can be very contrary and not say anything at all."

"But she knows about me and Tacitus, she knows what will happen," Tullia said hopefully.

"She knows what is and what will be, but what she reveals..."

"Yes, yes, I'll be here," Tullia said. But there was trepidation in her voice.

*****

It was now the third hour and the rain had turned to a deluge. Heedlessly Tacitus splashed through puddles, his heart racing, furious at having fallen asleep. The morning formation would have been assembled at the first hour, he knew, work parties organized, and any absences noted as the ranks were all counted for attendance. The thought of Tullia's supple body fled into the crevices of his mind. Tacitus slipped once; his tunic ran with ooze, and his newly-awarded belts were smeared with mud. Lightning flashes shot like javelins as he tore through past the Praetorian Gate.

Fear and failure coursed through him as he hurried past a tribune and his family. The officer, wearing a rain-streaked cloak, spoke with the camp legate, while his young son waited in a wagon hitched to nervous horses. The tribune and his wife gave Tacitus a curious glance, then resumed their conversation. Thunder rumbled across the sky, as Tacitus hurried past legionnaires toiling at the day's assignments.

*****

"The optio's been looking for you, and he's in a foul mood. You better get in there," Sempronius warned glumly as Tacitus sprinted by.

To his shock and dismay, not only was he suddenly before

the cohort's second-in-command, but his father and the praefectus castrorum, a ranking officer with a menacing disposition, were also there. A blast of cold air blew into the tent and the three men glanced up from their maps.

"Sir, I was delayed," Tacitus blurted, still catching his breath. Muddy water dripped from his tunic and pooled on the floor. He followed the eyes of the praefectus castrorum to the puddle, and a shiver went through him.

"Delayed? Yes, I see," the optio said, glancing at Gaius who stared, tightlipped, at Tacitus. "Inspection took place at the first hour, the hour you were to be in rank with the rest of your tent mates. Did I not say that?"

Tacitus nodded and said, "Yes, sir, you did, sir." He was about to add something, but his father's glare stopped him cold.

"Your belts," the optio said. "You will leave them here and stand in the road."

"Do you want me to do anything, sir?"

"Do anything? What I wanted was for you to be here when ordered!" the officer roared, slamming his fist on the table. "Now get the fuck out of my tent! You will stand out there and pray that I don't have you flogged. No food for the next three days. You are a disgrace!" he shouted.

Tacitus could feel his father's eyes penetrating his skull as he fled the tent. Any feeling of accomplishment, of completing training and entering the legions, was ripped away as if by an avalanche. It was more than a look of disgust his father leveled at him, it was revulsion and contempt.

"*Do not embarrass me,*" the primus pilum had warned on the day of his enlistment. But now Tacitus had done just that, in the presence of the praefectus castrorum, the senior veteran of the legion, a man who stood above even a tribune in rank.

*****

Rarely have I made a serious mistake in the military, thought Gaius, seeing the questioning look on the face of the senior veteran. Tacitus, bitter and filled with hate for him and the Legion, had committed a serious infraction. *What kind of soldier could the boy ever be?* the primus pilum wondered. *What irresponsible conduct, indeed, what cowardly or mutinous behavior should I have expected?* A cold dread seeped through Gaius.

And who would be called upon to determine the punishment if my son fails? And who, in fact, would be called upon to inflict it? The answer to that he knew only too well. Still, for Tacitus, the army had been the only solution. Better that he grievously fail under the watchful eye of his father than in public, on the streets of Rome. A crime committed by Tacitus there—and knowing the boy, that was something certain to occur eventually—would indelibly stain the reputation of the father. Whether or not he wore the Corona Civica, having a criminal for a son would ruin Gaius in the eyes of Rome.

Gaius sighed deeply, shook his head, and to the praefectus castrorum said, "I shall deal with him. He is my responsibility."

The grizzled veteran nodded, then touched Gaius on the shoulder. "What your son did was troubling, but he is not the first to have made such an error. Especially if a girl was involved last night. I suspect that, in time, he will mature and become a respectable legionnaire."

Gaius grimaced and wondered if his son would ever have that much time. *The Legion,* he thought, *rarely accords a second chance.*

*****

Tacitus halted thirty yards from the tent, beside the Via Principia. Drenched, he stood on a slight rise as the cold rain continued to fall. His tunic, stripped of belts, hung limply like a slave woman's knee-length dress. The withdrawal of the belts was a dishonor every legionnaire dreaded. Men passed and looked at him, but said nothing. Tacitus was a pariah, a leper, even to Sempronius who, gaping at his wretched appearance, shook his head and hurried on.

Wearing a red cape and a horsehair crest on his polished helmet, a decurion, a commander of cavalry, rode a black charger through the gate and was saluted by sentries. Approaching Tacitus, the officer dismounted and thrust the reins into his hands.

"Hold these, and don't you dare let the horse get away from you," he said, ignoring the munifes's hesitation.

"Sir, I was told to stand here and do nothing. A punishment."

"I don't give a damn what you were told. Just hold that horse. Let him go and you answer to me."

The charger, skittish from the lightning and thunder, stamped nervously. Instinctively, Tacitus laid his hand on the animal's neck and whispered into its ear. The mount calmed and rubbed its great head against the youth. A lightning bolt struck a pole and was followed by a thunderclap. The horse whinnied and trembled, but again Tacitus calmed it.

From a distance there was shouting, then a rumbling noise of pounding hooves along with the clatter of wagon wheels. Turning, Tacitus saw two panicked horses, eyes bulging, ears flattened back in terror, tearing a careening wagon down the Praetorian road. Their hooves sent sheets of water spraying in all directions as legionnaires leaped from their path.

"Get that wagon, stop those horses!" a voice shouted into the storm. Peering down the road, Tacitus spied the tribune he had seen when he burst into the encampment. The officer, his cloak billowing behind him, was chasing the terrified animals. His wife, hysterical, followed along with startled centurions and legionnaires.

As the wagon and its bolting horses passed, Tacitus saw the tribune's immobilized son in the rear of the wagon. Little hands clutched the sides as the child wailed in terror. Sentries at the open gate waved their shields to slow the beasts, but sprang away when the horses paid no heed, maddened by ear-shattering thunder. The closest pursuers were hundreds of yards behind, and it appeared to Tacitus that they would never catch up to the wagon and the hapless child.

With one fluid movement, Tacitus swung onto the decurion's mount, put his heels to the horse's flanks, and pointed the charger toward the speeding wagon, which slammed into the gate and spun wildly before it was dragged down the rutted, slippery road. The child, losing his grip, was tossed from side to side. Too afraid to jump, he could only stare back at the frantic crowd.

The charger leapt into a dead run, a black specter masked by sheets of rain. The road angled downward before it reached a sharp turn beside a steep ravine. The wagon, nearly hidden by rain and fog, became more distinct as Tacitus gained on it. For a split second, his mount slipped, then regained its footing, its head low, its hooves reaching forward seemingly into thin air.

The team of horses, themselves blinded by torrents of water, raced down the hill. The speeding horses were causing the wagon to swerve wildly, pulling it closer to the side of the waterlogged road and a plummeting abyss. The boy now saw Tacitus and the speeding horse, but was clinging for dear life to the wagon as it lurched one way then the other. The distance closed as the charger raced forward. Tacitus could feel the strain of the mount, his knees tight against the warhorse's flanks. The dash in would have to be precise, he knew, as the weight of the fishtailing wagon and its stout wheels could splinter the charger's legs, leaving horse and rider a bloody mass on the road.

"Reach, reach!" Tacitus shouted to the boy, whose face lit with desperate hope. A little arm was extended, and with a deft yank, the child flew into Tacitus's lap. With a slight tightening of the reins, the horse slowed and veered from the road, eventually taking shelter from the rain in a thick stand of trees, some distance away.

At the same moment Tacitus pulled the boy from the wagon, the terrified team failed to negotiate a turn and flew over the precipice. The wagon twisted and tumbled, momentarily weightless, until it careened into a tumble of massive boulders. The horses' screams were cut off abruptly as wheels and boards flew into the air in an explosion of debris. Hurled skyward, the shattered remains could be seen by the muddied crowd that raced down the road. They stopped and gaped at the splinters of wood and mangled flesh that lay below them.

The sound of the crash died away. The tribune, his wife, and the soldiers huddled in stunned silence. The woman began to wail as a detachment of legionnaires scrambled down to the wreck, knowing exactly what they would find.

Puzzled, the soldiers picked through the rubble in search of the child—or at least, parts of him—fearful of what they might have to deliver to the tribune and his hysterical wife. Several trudged to a great puddle and scoured the muddy water. They shook their heads, and came back up the steep sides of the ravine.

"Nothing? You didn't find him?" asked the tribune.

"No, sir," said a centurion; then, so that the man's wife could not hear, "not even body parts."

"Perhaps he flew out, a long distance," the tribune said hopefully.

"I had the men check for over a hundred yards. Nothing, sir. I'm so sorry. It's just very strange."

The woman would have collapsed if her husband had not held her up, and her body shook as she sobbed uncontrollably.

"Where's my horse?" demanded the decurion, as he caught up to the returning crowd.

"What horse?" asked the tribune, shielding his eyes from the downpour.

"The one I had the legionnaire hold—the kid who had lost his belts. He was to hold the horse. It's a prize animal, for Great Jupiter's sake."

Mutely they all peered into the rain and fog. There was nothing to see, however, and they started back, a sodden and dispirited crowd. The primus pilum, accompanied by the praefectus castrorum, was coming down the road toward them to see what the commotion was about. Behind them, a wagon and horses were led by two soldiers, who were making certain that the skittish animals would not bolt.

A legionnaire turned, taking one last glance down the mist-filled road. He leaned forward and wiped his eyes. "Tribune," he called. "There's something out there, coming this way."

"Where? What is it?" said the officer, turning to where the man pointed. His wife held him tightly and also turned, peering into the distance. The crowd stopped and strained to see a blurred figure emerging from the distant trees. They were all silent, as if holding their breath as one. No one dared say a word.

The rain slackened, then ceased altogether; the only sound was a blustery wind. A glint of sun broke through the clouds, illuminating patches of ground. A beam of light traced a line toward the trees lining the road near the crash site. Mist floated around their trunks, only to be swept away by the breeze. For a brief instant, sunlight fell upon a horseman. The rider, with a small figure sitting in front of him, slowly walked the horse toward the stunned observers.

"He's alive!" shouted a legionnaire, and the mass surged forward, accompanied by a babble of excited voices. Tacitus brought the charger to a halt and handed the boy to his mother, her outstretched arms clasping the child to her chest.

"Your mount, sir. It's a fine animal," Tacitus said to the cavalry officer, who took hold of the reins as he dismounted. Tacitus touched the animal's neck as the decurion led it away.

"Where are your belts, son?" the tribune asked, appraising the lanky youth who stood in silence, surrounded by officers and gawking legionnaires.

"I had to surrender them, sir, as punishment. I was late to assembly," Tacitus said, made painfully uncomfortable by the rapt attention. There had, for a moment, been a feeling of success, even glory, in saving the boy and riding the majestic charger out of the woods toward the astounded gathering. But that moment had quickly vanished.

"A serious offense, missing formation," said the boy's father, as the optio stood beside him.

The child's mother put the boy down, and the child took Tacitus's hand. Embarrassed, Tacitus tried to disengage, but the child would not let go. His mother took a step forward and standing beside Tacitus, gazed first at her husband then the optio.

The tribune looked at his wife, his child, and then Tacitus. "Optio, I won't tell you what to do; it's your call, but this young man saved my son's life. He's shown the kind of bravery we expect from our men."

The optio studied Tacitus, then glanced at the primus pilum, who showed no expression. There was a long moment of brooding silence.

"It was a daring act," the optio said grudgingly. "The belts will be returned, and under the circumstances I'll disregard further punishment."

The sodden crowd broke up and hastened back to their lodgings, as the tribune's wife pulled Tacitus aside. "I thank you with all my heart. These coins are all have with me, but I want you to have them," she said as she pressed a small purse into his hand.

Tacitus stared at the coins and took a step back. "No, my lady. I can't, I'm not allowed. You see what trouble I'm already in."

"You saved my son. These few coins are the only reward you will be given for your heroic act. You have given me back my son, my treasure. I will not take no for an answer. You are a brave lad, perhaps the bravest I have seen. Now do me this favor. I insist."

The woman's resolve was breaking, and Tacitus saw her shiver, either from the cold or the thought of what disaster had nearly befallen her. Reluctantly, he nodded and put out his hand. A dozen coins clinked, then impetuously she wrapped her arms about him. He stood stock-still. After releasing him, the tribune's wife took her son's hand and, shielding herself, from the icy wind, hurried back down the road.

Still holding her child's hand, she and her husband departed in the waiting wagon, along with the praefectus castrorum. Standing alone in the road was the primus pilum. Tacitus remained silent and looked at his father. Gaius stared back, turned, and swiftly strode toward the encampment.

*****

Drenched by the cold rain, Tacitus retrieved his belts and was assigned to help dig out a mud-clogged trench. It was the return of his belts, not the saving of the child, that prompted his tent mates to nod their heads in acknowledgement of him.

The entire event seemed surreal: the night with Tullia, the loss of his belts, the race to save the boy... and then his father, an enigma who refused to say anything about any of it. Perhaps, Tacitus surmised, there was nothing to be said. But what, he wondered, would it take for his father to approve of him, if his death-defying act was not enough on its own?

For certain his enlistment in the army was not of his choosing. So the belts and all that went with it hardly mattered to Tacitus, since he would likely die in his first battle anyway. If his father could say nothing to him concerning the rescue of a tribune's child, surely he would say nothing about the death of his own son. The only thing Tacitus truly wanted was to be with Tullia, but that seemed less likely now than ever before.

"You're a little muddy, don't you think?" the giant, Iberica, said with a grin when Tacitus returned to his barracks.

"Oh, I won't worry about that," Sempronius said, now Iberica's constant companion. "With another deluge like this, we'll all be drowned anyway."

It was meant to be funny, but Tacitus felt that he had drowned long ago.

*****

The night sky was a canopy of stars; Tullia pulled her cloak tightly about her, as she knocked on the gate of the old villa.

"She will see you," Junia said, "but don't expect too much. I am letting you speak with her as a favor. Please don't ask to speak to her again."

"I promise I won't."

"She is under her tree, with an oil lamp. You may stay here tonight, Tullia; it's too dangerous for you to walk home alone."

A soft glow illuminated Caladria. Tullia stopped in front of her and was about to speak when Caladria put a finger to her lips, silencing the girl. Caladria's lips appeared to be moving as if in conversation, but no words were uttered, until she said aloud, "Is that all, sister? Is there anything more I may tell her?"

Then the discussion with Aspacia ceased, and Caladria made a great sigh.

"You told me to come this night," Tullia said with apprehension. "You said that you would speak to your sister. Was that Aspacia you were speaking to?"

Caladria nodded. "I spoke with my dear sister about you and Tacitus."

"Where is Aspacia?" Tullia suddenly asked.

"She is everywhere; she is here, or there, or wherever she wishes to be. The dead are like that, unless they are ghosts. Then they are trapped here, and don't know anything more than you or I. But Aspacia is not a ghost, so she can see everything."

"And she will tell you everything?"

"No. As I said before, she can be playful or secretive, and sometimes she speaks in riddles." Caladria's voice was very low and seemingly distant. "There are things she refuses to divulge, because they are too painful. She told me that we should not always know the future, because we will try to alter events, especially if they're bad. Doing that would violate the will of the gods, and that's not allowed."

She stared into her folded hands, then looked up, expressionless, into Tullia's eyes.

"Please, Caladria, what does she say will happen? Will I ever be with Tacitus again?"

Caladria pulled the old blanket about her, and sighed once again. "My sister said that you will live a long life and will bear a child. He will be a good and strong lad, like his father."

"His father? You mean Tacitus; is he the father of the child I shall have?"

"She didn't say who the father is."

"But what of us? Me and Tacitus?" Tullia pleaded.

Caladria raised a hand, again silencing the girl. "She said that Tacitus will take a very distant journey, not long from now. One day he will walk in circles and think of another girl, but he will dream of you, too."

"Another girl? How could that be? He loves me, he said so."

Caladria began to rock back and forth. She was about to speak but stopped.

"Okay, another girl, if he's away a long time. Yes, he may know others, but we will be together again, won't we?" Tullia said, tears flooding her eyes.

"My sister didn't say yes or no, except that you should live your life and let him live his."

"Ask her again, please ask her," Tullia cried.

"I cannot. She will reveal no more. Now you must go, I've told you all I can. Dream, and look forward to your son. Trust in the gods; all will be well with you."

Later that night, Tullia was about to close the door of the cubiculum that Junia had offered her, when she asked, "Junia, will you let me be your friend? I will be a true friend to you. Other than Tacitus, I have no one."

Junia looked into the girl's saddened eyes. "You may, if you really want to be my friend. Not because you think I can arrange some tryst between you and Tacitus. I will not do that again. If you can abide by that, you are welcome here."

Tullia nodded. "Yes, I have no ulterior motive. You are a kind woman, as I wished my mother had been. All the rest is in the hands of the gods. Caladria said as much."

Junia was silent, considering. "I, too, have few friends. Yes, Tullia, you can be my friend."

*****

Two months had passed, and the sound of trumpets reverberated through the cold morning air. Every cohort had been drawn up in massed formation. Never before had Tacitus beheld such a huge force, and despite everything, he felt a stirring, indeed a comradeship, with the men about him. He had not anticipated or expected such a feeling, but it had evolved, and like it or not, he was now a member of something big. The legion's eagle was held aloft, and forty-eight hundred men plus auxiliaries would defend it with their lives. Tacitus was part of that, and now he stood in the first rank with the newest legionnaires. The sun reflected off thousands of shields.

Tacitus wore his double belts, and his gladius hung by his side.

Another blast from the trumpet signaled the arrival of the great general himself, along with his entourage. Wearing a scarlet cape, Consul Gaius Julius Caesar rode onto the field. All knew of his exploits in Gaul, his invasion of Britain, and his war with the Celts. Rumor had it that Caesar and his famed Tenth Legion would again be on the move. As consul and general, he was a restless man who, according to the stories, lived for fame and glory. Rarely would he stay in one place very long.

Tacitus had no desire to go to war, but war seemed inevitable. It was not by mere chance that Caesar was inspecting the troops.

It was a new day, and everything, he suspected, would be different than before. He could sense it, as could everyone in the legion. He stood beside Sempronius and Iberica, and watched as Caesar spoke with the legion's legate and a few tribunes. Then the man spurred his horse and halted to the right of the first rank. He leaned over and grasped the shoulder of one of his most favored, a taciturn veteran whom he had personally decorated on the field of battle. The two men spoke for several minutes, until Caesar straightened and bade the man farewell.

The primus pilum saluted the general, then turned and faced his men. For just a moment, Tacitus thought that his father had looked at him. The man was resolute and, so it was said, completely fearless. He would expect the same from every legionnaire. Surely, his father had seen his son's valor. Someday he might even acknowledge it. Until then, Tacitus would march with his cohort, and pray that he lived to return to Tullia once again.

"Are you ready to march?" asked the primus pilum, his voice carrying across the Campus Martius.

"Yes!" came the reply from the throats of thousands.

"Are you ready to march?" the question was repeated, as it had been for half a thousand years.

The reply was even stronger this time, as Tacitus's voice joined the others.

"Are you ready to march?" was asked for the third and last time. The resounding answer could be heard far beyond Campus Martius.

The eyes of Gaius Septimius Aquila bore into the ranks of legionnaires, and this time Tacitus was sure his father saw him. Maybe there was a hint of recognition, but Tacitus could not be sure. The primus pilum turned to the legate and said, "Sir, we are ready to march."

Then, with a blast on the buccina, the curved war-horn, six thousand men marched through the Praetorian Gate, past the city of Rome, and onto the ships in the great port of Ostia.

Tacitus glanced back at the temples on the Seven Hills of Rome, and wondered if he would ever see them again. The tramp of iron-studded boots was almost deafening. He marched beside Sempronius and Iberica, and allowed himself a smile. He realized that this would be the greatest adventure of his life —and only the gods and perhaps his mother, Aspacia, knew how it would all play out.

THE END

Watch for the Sequel

In the *The Silk and the Sword*, tension mounts between father and son as they cross the Euphrates River with the legions of Consul and General Marcus L. Crassus and engage the Empire of Parthia in the horrific battle of Carrhae. Gaius, Tacitus and four hundred survivors, unable to reach Rome through Parthian lands take the fabled Silk Road east toward a rumored sea behind a great wall. Treacherous deserts, ice encrusted mountains, battles and treachery hammer Tacitus into a veteran legionnaire. But his greatest challenge is not war, but a princess in a very distant and mysterious land.

ABOUT THE AUTHOR

RON SINGERTON

After graduating from California State University at Long Beach in 1965, Ron Singerton joined the U.S. Army Security Agency and spent his overseas time in Asia.

The following twenty-five years were devoted to teaching history and art in Southern California High schools where he developed a particular love for writing and historical research.

During the early 1980s, he authored a series, "Moments in History", of some thirty mini books on famous legendary people and events ranging from Columbus to the moon landing. The books were adopted as supplementary teaching material for the State of California and approved by the Los Angeles School board as a teaching aid. Published by Santillana Publishing Company, the original ones are considered collectors' items

An avid horseman and saber fencer with a special interest in the American Civil War, he "heard the bugle and the sound of the drums" and became a re-enactor riding with the Union cavalry in dozens of engagements from California to Gettysburg, Pennsylvania.

Always interested in an exciting but obscure story, his historical research meandered from the nineteenth and twentieth Century back to the ancient world. Singerton once said, "Technology of the past often appears elementary to us, the emotions do not." For the writer, the thoughts of peoples long past, as well as civilizations now little more than sand pitted ruins, still evolve into a pageant of love, intrigue and dire conflict. "It is nothing less than a shadowed mirror of our own world."

Through the writings of Plutarch, Pliny and Julius Caesar he uncovered an epic event that would take him from Rome in the last days of Republic to the Great Wall of China. After years of research the tale became the gist of a two volume novel: *The Villa of Deceit* and *The Silk and the Sword*.

Ron is also a professional artist who, with his wife Darla, owns and creates works for their art gallery, Singerton Fine Arts, in Idyllwild, California, where he works in glass, stone, paint and bronze.

ASSASSINS OF ALAMUT
BY
JAMES BOSCHERT

An Epic Novel of Persia and Palestine in the Time of the Crusades

The Assassins of Alamut is a riveting tale, painted on the vast canvas of life in Palestine and Persia during the 12th century.

On one hand, it's a tale of the crusades—as told from the Islamic side—where Shi'a and Sunni are as intent on killing Ismaili Muslims as crusaders. In self-defense, the Ismailis develop an elite band of highly trained killers called Hashshashin whose missions are launched from their mountain fortress of Alamut.

But it's also the story of a French boy, Talon, captured and forced into the alien world of the assassins. Forbidden love for a princess is intertwined with sinister plots and self-sacrifice, as the hero and his two companions discover treachery and then attempt to evade the ruthless assassins of Alamut who are sent to hunt them down.

It's a sweeping saga that takes you over vast snow-covered mountains, through the frozen wastes of the winter plateau, and into the fabulous cites of Hamadan, Isfahan, and the Kingdom of Jerusalem.

"A brilliant first novel, worthy of Bernard Cornwell at his best."—Tom Grundner

PENMORE PRESS
www.penmorepress.com

Historical fiction and nonfiction
Paperback available for order on line
and as Ebook with all major distributers

THE LAUNDRY ROOM

BY

LYNDA LIPPMAN-LOCKHART

The Laundry Room dramatizes a fascinating moment in the history of the founding of Israel as a self-ruling nation. Based on actual events, Lynda Lippmann-Lockhart follows the lives of several young Israelis as they found a kibbutz and run a clandestine ammunition factory, which supplied Israeli troops fighting against Arab forces following the end of British occupation in the late 1940s. Under British rule, it was illegal for Israelis to possess firearms, so it was necessary not only to create and stockpile bullets for the coming war, but to do so in secret.

The ingenuity, courage, and sheer audacity displayed by the members of the code-named "Ayalon Institute", as they operated their factory right under the noses of the British milItary, make for an intriguing tale. Lippmann-Lockhart shows readers what it might have been like to be one of the young pioneers whose work truly impacted the outcome of Israel's fight for independence. The Ayalon Institute remains standing to this day, and the secret hidden under the kibbutz's laundry room was not revealed until the 1970s. It was made a National Historic Site in 1987 and is open to the public every day of the year except Yom Kippur.

PENMORE PRESS
www.penmorepress.com

Historical fiction and nonfiction
Paperback available for order on line
and as Ebook with all major distributers

WILDFIRE IN THE DESERT

BY

BRUNO JAMBOR

Action Adventure, Crime, Mystery,
Southwest History

Highly entertaining, well researched and original:

A Navy veteran returns home to his ancestral land to escape the pace of modern life. His nephew begs him to hide the drugs he is transporting to escape his pursuers.

An astronomer trying to find a replacement for his estranged wife finds solace in his work with the stars.

Police and the drug cartel try to recover the missing shipment, regardless of consequences, ready to sacrifice any opponent.

The antagonists crisscross the desert of Southern Arizona in a chess game where the loser will be eliminated.

Unexpected help comes from a famous missionary who blazed new paths through the same desert three centuries ago.

The climactic resolution will captivate readers of this thriller with deep spiritual undertones.

PENMORE PRESS
www.penmorepress.com

Historical fiction and nonfiction
Paperback available for order on line
and as Ebook with all major distributers

Force 12 in German Bight
by
James Boschert

Considering that oil and gas have been flowing from under the North Sea for the best part of half a century, it is perhaps surprising that more writers have not taken the uncompromising conditions that are experienced in this area – which extends from the north of Scotland to the coasts of Norway and Germany – for the setting of a novel. James Boschert's latest redresses the balance.

The book takes its title from the name of an area regularly referred to in the legendary BBC Shipping Forecast and one which experiences some of the worst weather conditions around the British Isles. It is a fast-paced story which smacks of authenticity in every line. A world of hard men, hard liquor, hard drugs and cold-blooded murder. The reality of the setting and the characters, ex-military men from both sides of the Atlantic, crooked wheeler-dealers, and Danish detectives, male and female, are all in on the action.

This is not story telling akin to a latter day Bulldog Drummond, or even a James Bond, but simply a snortingly good yarn which will jangle the nerve ends, fill your nose with the smell of salt and diesel oil, your ears with the deafening sound of machinery aboard a monster pipe-dredging ship and, above all, make you remember never to underestimate the power of the sea.

'Roger Paine, former Commander, Royal Navy'.

PENMORE PRESS
www.penmorepress.com

Historical fiction and nonfiction
Paperback available for order on line
and as Ebook with all major distributers

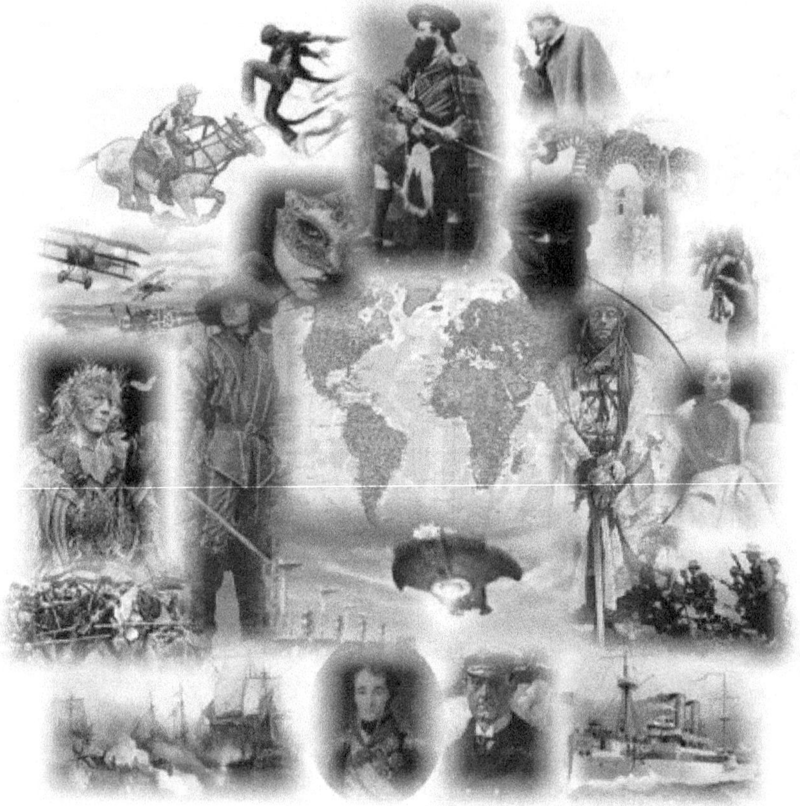

Penmore Press

Challenging, Intriguing, Adventurous, Historical and Imaginative

www.penmorepress.com

www.ingramcontent.com/pod-product-compliance
Lightning Source LLC
Chambersburg PA
CBHW070336170726
48291CB00001B/67